CITY OF GODS AND MONSTERS

BOOKS BY KAYLA EDWARDS:

The *Ice and Iron* series

Dreams of Ice and Iron

The *House of Devils* series

City of Gods and Monsters
City of Souls and Sinners
City of Lies and Legends

CITY OF GODS AND MONSTERS

HOUSE OF DEVILS
BOOK ONE

KAYLA EDWARDS

For Jeff—
My rock, my best friend, my safe harbor.
My everything.

WELCOME TO ANGELTHENE

We hope you enjoy your stay. Please avoid going out after sunset, and keep a form of protection on you at all times. The use of Blood Staves is strictly prohibited. Darkslayers operate in the city, so exercising a high level of caution in all districts is highly recommended for residents and visitors. Avoid unnecessary travel to the Meatpacking District, Hooded Skullcap, Stone's End, Ebonfield, Oldtown, the Narrow Hills, and the Black Alder District. Travel to Angelthene National Forest is recommended only between the hours of seven a.m. and three p.m. All cell phones within city limits are programmed to receive alerts regarding Blood Moons. If a Blood Moon is in the forecast, stay inside the forcefield until dawn. Report any suspicious activity to the Magical Protections Unit immediately.

DARKSLAYING CIRCLES OF ANGELTHENE

THE SEVEN DEVILS
Marked with a horned letter S in the gothic script of an ancient
world, they answer to Darien Cassel, Head of Hell's Gate

THE REAPERS
Marked with the cloaked and masked God of Death, they answer
to Malakai Delaney, Head of the House of Souls

THE HUNTSMEN
Marked with a Hellhound, they answer to Lionel Savage, Head of
the Hunting Grounds and Right Hand of Randal
Slade

THE ANGELS OF DEATH
Marked with overlapping wings in white ink, they answer to
Dominic Valencia, Head of Death's Landing

THE WARGS
Marked with a crescent moon in luminescent ink, they answer to
Channary Graves, Head of the House on the Pier

THE VIPERS
Marked with an animated striking serpent, they answer to Jude
monsoon, Head of the Den of Vipers

All Darkslaying circles in Angelthene answer to Randal Slade, Head of all circles in the city. No one outside of these six circles may operate on Angelthene soil. To do so is punishable by death.

PART ONE

ANGELTHENE ACADEMY FOR MAGIC

Welcome to

ANGELTHENE

WE HOPE YOU SURVIVE

I

"If you so much as *look* at her again, I will break all four of your legs, pup."

If it weren't for Dallas defending her, Loren Calla might've run out the metal doors of the nightclub called Her Infernal Majesty right then and there. The dry-ice smoke choking the dance floor did nothing to hide the hundreds of faces that were watching the scene unfold beneath the blue strobe lights, their eyes hungry with curiosity.

The werewolf standing before Loren—on two very human legs, despite Dallas's insult—had dumped a full glass of beer over her head. Her waist-length golden hair was dripping wet, the white fabric of her short, skin-tight dress soaked and see-through. The beer was fresh off the tap, but regardless of how cold it was, her entire body was heating up from embarrassment.

Witches like Dallas usually got along quite well with wolves. If it weren't for the fact that Loren was human and therefore didn't quite belong in Angelthene—otherwise known as the City of Everlasting Hearts, a sprawling metropolis that catered to and favoured an immortal demographic—the night might've passed without incident. Might've passed without her friend and adoptive sister—a pure-blooded venefica held in far higher regard than Loren—needing to step in and defend her.

When the werewolf had swaggered up to Loren and asked her to dance with him, she had declined as politely as possible. Turned out, he didn't take well to rejection, no matter how polite the rejection may be. But this was girls' night; Dallas had made herself *very* clear about this before dragging Loren and Sabrine Van Arsdell, who was currently fetching another drink across the room, out club-hopping. Dallas would never allow a summer to end without a bang, especially this one—the summer before they would start their freshman year at Angelthene Academy for Magic.

And while most girls Loren's age would've jumped at the chance to paint the city red, Loren had only wished to curl up on the couch. Couches were safe. Couches were ordinary. Exactly how she preferred everything in her life.

The wolf's fire-colored eyes flashed with anger as he looked Loren over, his hands vibrating at his sides as he fought the Shift. Beneath the medley of sweat, puke, and cigarette smoke, the odor of wet dog swept through the room. "Is she your bodyguard or your cock-block?" he said of Dallas.

"She's my sister," Loren bit out in a wavering voice. Her fingers curled into tight fists, nails digging into her palms. "And you've just made an enemy of her."

He glanced between her and Dallas. "A human with a witch for a sister?" He snorted. "What do you think I am—*stupid?*"

"Apparently you are," Dallas said coolly. "Because I literally just warned you that I would break your legs if you looked at her again."

"You want to take this outside, venefica?" he sneered.

A second werewolf wearing an ACU letterman jacket stepped up to his friend's side. There was caution in this one's gaze, and even with the music thumping through the building and shaking the floor beneath Loren's pearlescent leather pumps, she didn't need immortal hearing to make out the words he hissed into his friend's ear. "I'd cool it, Jerome. That's Dallas Bright."

There was nowhere to look without meeting a pair of prying eyes. Loren wrung her fingers before her, looking mostly at the grimy floor than anywhere else. For the hundredth time that evening, she wished she had the power to turn herself invisible. Or, at the very least, teleport herself back to the four walls of her safe and ordinary bedroom at the penthouse.

When she risked a glance up from the floor, she caught sight of half-witch Sabrine heading this way—hand cupped over her glass, elbows shoving clubbers aside with impressive strength for someone her size. Her angular, deep-set eyes narrowed as she took in a soaking wet Loren and an angry Dallas whose expression was utterly murderous.

"What's going on?" Sabrine demanded.

Jerome didn't deign to glance her way. "Stay out of this, half-breed." The ugly insult had Dallas throwing the wolves a cold smile.

Loren's whole body turned rigid at the sight of that smile.

Here we go, she thought.

Dallas stepped forward, her hip-length red hair swaying, an eight-inch ash-wood Focus in a freckled golden hand.

"If you boys knew how to think with the right head, you'd scram before I muzzle your filthy mouths." The chunk of amethyst nestled within the entangle of wood at the point of her magic stave pulsed brightly. Magic sparked, the smell of it—like smoke from blown-out birthday candles—coating Loren's tongue as it swept through her airways.

But Jerome didn't seem to care who any of them were, least of all the pure-blooded venefica standing before him with rage in her silver-green eyes. Dallas's father was general of the Aerial Fleet, the country's organized military force equipped for fighting in the sky. Being threatened by the Red Baron's daughter would've convinced most people to stand down—but apparently, this pup really didn't know how to think with the right head.

Or perhaps he was simply too drunk to realize he'd met his match.

"All right, all right, that's enough," boomed a deep voice. Tension melted away as everyone in the club turned to see a six-foot-seven warlock bouncer pushing his way through the crowd with beefy arms. He pinned their group with a cold stare. "You all know the rules: anyone who starts trouble gets the boot."

Jerome raised his hands in surrender and backed up into the crowd, his friend following suit. "No trouble on my end, sir. I'm not the one threatening someone with a Focus."

Dallas swung around to face Jerome, a strand of her hair catching in her mouth. "You started it by dumping a beer on my friend, *asshole!*" She made to lunge for him, but Loren stepped forward and grabbed hold of her arm.

"Let it go, Dallas!" Her voice was barely a croak, every word trembling harder than her legs. "He's not worth it."

The werewolves disappeared into the throng of people, and after giving Loren and her friends a few stern words, the bouncer returned to his station at the entrance. Now that the excitement was over, the crowds of bystanders returned to their dancing and drinking, releasing Loren from their gazes at last.

Sabrine's mouth curled into a frown as she looked at her cell phone, the screen illuminating her silken black hair and the sharp planes of her honey-brown face. "Girls, it's almost Witching Hour. We should reserve a cab." Oh, crap.

Loren pulled her own phone out of her cross-body purse to check the time—wishful thinking that it might display different numbers than Sabrine's. They'd gone and done the one thing Loren had always promised herself she would never do after sunset: lose track of time. City buses didn't operate this late at night, so cabs were their only option.

Dallas gave a thoughtful hum. She shoved her Focus into her purse, the glowing amethyst reflecting in the black leather of her dress—a strapless number that hugged every curve and dip of her hourglass figure. "What's tonight's forecast?"

Loren felt the blood drain from her face. "Don't even think about it, Dal. That's how people get eaten or attacked by machetes. Did you forget what happened last summer?"

Dallas rolled her eyes. "Relax, Lor," she sighed, snatching up her vodka soda from the sticky linoleum. She took a sip, being careful not to smear her ruby lips—colored not with makeup but with a glamor, though still susceptible to touch. "I was just asking. I hope you realize how long we're going to have to wait for a cab."

Loren hated to admit it, but Dallas made a point. Although nightlife in Angelthene was limited, the few clubs and cabarets dotting the downtown core were packed on weekends, so cabs were a rare commodity. Nobody walked anywhere after sunset, not unless they had a death wish.

Or unless the moon was full, and they decided to take their chances.

Sabrine's stiletto nails clicked against her phone screen. "Skies are mostly clear. Sturgeon moon." She quirked an arched brow and gave Dallas a look heavy with implication.

Dread curled in Loren's stomach. "If you guys want to walk, go ahead. It's not my funeral," she said. "But I for one would rather take my chances with the cabs." She peeled a strand of wet hair off her cheek. As soon as she got home, she would take a shower—but first she would have to worry about making it there in one piece. While most cities had rat infestations, Angelthene's pest problem involved feral demons that crawled on all fours and cared about only one thing: the taste of flesh.

Especially human.

Dallas gave a shrug and drained the last of her vodka soda. The look in her eyes suggested she was itching to argue about the situation further, or perhaps call Loren out on how there was no way in hell she would ever choose to split up from them. But a meaningful glance from Sabrine stilled her tongue.

"Call a cabby, then," Dallas told Sabrine. But Loren was already on it.

She wasn't surprised to find the lines tied up. She got through after making two dozen calls to several different companies, but by that time the clock was inching past Witching Hour.

They waited for the cab out front of the club, beneath the bright, protective glow of the HID lamps that were normally seen at sports stadiums and warehouses. The dry, late-summer heat threatened to bake Loren's very bones, and she found her eyelids drooping shut as she sat at the base of the winged statue of Ignis, Her Infernal

Majesty of the Seven Circles. Only the honk of car horns slicing through the night and the music that dribbled through the metal doors of the club kept her from drifting off.

The full Sturgeon moon shone as brightly as the city's display of billboards that advertised everything from grimoires and magic staves to blood donor clinics for the more civilized vampires of Angelthene. Palm trees lined either side of Gamma Pagasi Street, fronds swaying in a balmy wind that carried the smoky hint of creosote and the cool bite of sage.

If Loren tipped her head at just the right angle, she could make out a faint greenish cast from the protective forcefield that formed a dome over the city, its magic stemming from the Control Tower in the heart of the North End. The forcefield wasn't perfect by any means, but it served as protection for its citizens from outside forces, namely the creatures that awoke during Blood Moons. Of course, it did nothing to shield them from the dangers that were already under the dome, but Loren didn't let herself think about that. Her mind was a dangerous place, especially when she was this tired.

The club began to empty at one in the morning. Werewolves, warlocks, witches, vampires, and humans piled into taxicabs that took off as quickly as they rolled up to the curb at the brightly lit entrance. The odd limousine flitted by, windows half-down, the bass of the sound systems thumping over the asphalt.

Loren sighed. "Our cab driver's sure taking his sweet-ass time."

"School starts in seven hours," Sabrine grumbled. The harsh light of the HID lamp she was leaning against turned her face a sickly shade of gray. "At this rate, I'm not going to get any sleep."

"We *could* start walking," Dallas said. She bent over to rub at her ankles, the skin scraped raw from the straps of her heels. At the sight of her muscled golden legs on full display, a wolf and a warlock staggering by leered and catcalled at her. She rolled her eyes and flipped them off.

The werewolf slowed. His gaze snagged on Loren...and lingered there. He was cute, in a boy-next-door sort of way.

Before he could look away, Loren beat him to it, dropping her eyes to the ground and feigning a sudden interest in the cigarette butts and neon glowsticks littering the sidewalk. Immortals had little interest in humans, and if they did it was only for an hour or a night. Another reason she hadn't cared to dance with Jerome: all she was to guys like him was something pretty to look at. A mere blip in a gloriously immortal lifespan. A *half-life*.

Dallas's voice made Loren jump. "Don't even think about it, fur-face!" Loren looked up in time to see the wolf and his warlock pal scurrying toward their cars.

Loren sighed. "I could've handled that myself, Dal." Maybe she should give Jerome's question—about Dallas being a bodyguard or a cock-block—some more thought. Even though Dal always had Loren's best interests in mind, sometimes she wondered if there were times when the witch simply couldn't handle not being the center of attention.

Dallas snorted and gave her a once-over that was anything but kind. "As if *you* were going to tell him off."

"Maybe I was," Loren snapped.

Every trace of humor vanished from Dallas's face. "You're grumpy tonight."

"I never even wanted to come out."

"Whatever." She waved her away like she would an insect buzzing in her face. Loren tried not to bristle—not to say something she might regret. They were family—and family was in short supply for Loren. "What are you doing sexting over there, Sab?" Dallas peered over Sabrine's shoulder. "Holy burning Ignis, don't tell me you're actually studying right now!"

Sabrine cupped a hand over her screen. "I need to get a head start!"

"Always such a bookworm," Dallas tsked.

Warmth bloomed across the inside of Loren's left forearm. She looked down at the medical tattoo that was visible only when her blood sugar levels dropped dangerously low. The serpent-entwined rod was emitting the same pale blue light as the glowstick she wore around her neck. Blue wasn't as bad as red, at least.

She unzipped her cross-body purse and fumbled through the contents in search of her medication, which was the next best thing when she didn't have access to food. Dread coiled tightly in her stomach as she realized she had forgotten it.

"Lor," Sabrine said, cutting off whatever Dallas was saying to her. "Don't tell me—"

"I'm fine." Loren forced a close-lipped smile that neither of them bought.

"I think we should walk," Dallas said. She looked Loren over with narrowed eyes. "I thought I told you to keep that stupid bottle in your purse."

Loren had just about had it with this night—and Dallas's attitude. "You didn't give me much notice before you dragged me out the door!"

"That has *nothing* to do with it," Dallas hissed.

Loren felt her face turn hot. She squeezed her fingers into fists between her knees, willing herself not to be the first to break eye contact with her sister. "You don't have to be such a bully all the time, Dal—"

"Quit arguing!" Sabrine exclaimed, pushing away from the HID lamp. "You guys are giving me a headache." She blew out a sigh, a strand of dark hair fluttering in her face. She studied Loren, her brows knitting together. "Loren, she has a point. The last thing we need is you fainting on us."

"I said I'm fine." But she wasn't—not really. Her vision was gray and splotchy, and she was starting to feel like she was floating, like she was one of the many palm tree fronds scattered across the sidewalk, stirred about by gusts of wind.

Sabrine sighed. "Do you think your mom would care if I crashed on your couch?"

"Who cares what Taega thinks," Dallas grumbled. "If she doesn't like it, she can kick us all out." While Loren and Dallas lived on the North End, the shack Sabrine called home was in the South. If she were to walk from here, it would take hours, and she would have no choice but to venture through the tangled streets of the Meatpacking District, which simply wasn't an option. People went missing from there all the time, and if they turned up, they were never alive.

"Lor," Dallas beseeched, her face lined with frustration. "We should get you home."

They didn't have much of a choice anymore. Her Infernal Majesty would close at two a.m., and as soon as the doors were locked, the HID lamps would shut off. Which meant the demons that prowled the sewers would no longer have a reason to keep away. No reason but the moon, whose brightness was at constant risk of being stifled by the few fleecy clouds drifting across the sky.

Although ice coursed through her veins at the thought of walking at this hour, Loren kicked off her heels, scooped them into a hand, and heaved herself to her aching feet. "Let's go, then." She raised an index finger. "But no back alleys, or I'm turning around."

They began the trek down Angelthene Boulevard, staying in the light of the streetlamps whenever possible. She joined Dallas and Sabrine in their drunken, bawdy singing as they ambled along, but she soon fell silent. Her aching feet were speckled with blisters, and they were black and sticky with the-Star-knew-what. This had to be the longest walk of her life, and to make matters worse, not a single empty taxicab rolled by.

Traffic lights flicked from red to green to amber and back, without one car passing under them. Rats rummaged in over-turned trashcans, and cats suffering from the mange watched with glowing eyes from dark alleys. While most cities had their share of vagrants huddled beneath awnings or sitting on the benches at transport shelters, Angelthene's level of crime—along with its pest problem—was so severe, only stray shoes and articles of clothing littered the sidewalk. Not one person could be seen for miles.

There was a scuff and a shuffle in a nearby alley.

Loren's lungs tightened. Slowly, she looked over her shoulder, the hairs on the back of her neck prickling. Dead leaves crackled across the asphalt.

She saw something standing at the end of that alley. Something with bony, slumped shoulders and great horns. Loren squinted, blinking hard. Willing it to be a mere trick of the eyes.

But the thing lurched forward and began to scuttle toward her on its hands and knees.

Her breath stopped in a wild gasp as terror stole through her veins. She found herself immobile at the end of the alley as the creature crawled toward her, and when she couldn't hold it back any longer, she blinked.

In the millisecond it took to rewet her eyes, the thing had disappeared.

"Did you guys see that?" Her soft words were nearly drowned out by Dallas and Sabrine's singing. She hurried after them, a chill dripping like a spider down her spine.

"Come on, scaredy-cat!" Dallas called. "Get your butt moving and maybe you won't get eaten." Despite her teasing, she knew Dallas well enough to detect an edge of concern in her words.

"It's not funny," she grumbled. Multicolored chalk runes decorated the sidewalk beneath her filthy feet. "Unlike you two, I don't have a Focus I can use if anything goes wrong." No, as a human, all she had was her nails—painted hot-pink and manicured into long, sharp points—and the useless pepper spray she kept in her bag for a false sense of security. It might protect her against humans, at least. Which she supposed was better than nothing.

Sabrine—bless her—was staring at Loren in concern. "Do you need to stop for a rest?"

"I'm fine." Loren tried not to make it obvious that she was blinking away fog that shouldn't be there. Her tattoo was flaring brighter now, a constant warmth spreading up her arm.

"As long as you're sure," Sab told her. Loren was too distracted by the feeling of her heart in her throat to answer. Too distracted by the misty gloom lurking in every alley.

Loren squinted to make out the letters on the sign above the closest intersection.

It read *Canopus Street*. Which meant they were nearing the Avenue of the Scarlet Star, where Loren worked on weekends at a sentient-plant apothecary called Mordred and Penelope's Mortar and Pestle. She wondered if it might be a good idea to unlock the shop and stay there until sunrise. They would have to sleep on the floor, but...it was better than being outside any longer. And her dog was there—Singer. He would love the company.

Not to mention that her collection of essential oils was *also* there — the peppermint and lavender blends that helped calm her heartrate whenever her panic attacks closed in. Those oils were a godsend; she didn't know how she had ever lived without them.

Dallas fell into step beside her, jolting her back to the here and now. "Relax, Lor!" As if reading her mind, she threw an arm around her stiff shoulders and said, "If it'll make you feel any better, we could go to Mordred and Penny's and call for another cab there. You think they'd mind?"

Loren nibbled on her bottom lip. "I could call them and ask."

"It's going to take us hours to get to the penthouse if we don't," Sabrine chimed in. She was right: they'd underestimated how long it would take to walk to the apartment at Santa Aria Flats. To be fair, they didn't do this walk often. And *often* meant never.

Regardless, Dal's suggestion didn't totally ease her concerns. Several blocks still stood between them and the apothecary, and it wasn't just the demons she was worried about.

In the world of Terra, society was dominated by an array of beings, all more powerful than humans: werewolves, vampires, witches, warlocks, and hellsehers. Loren didn't know which would be worse: running into a vampire who didn't bother with blood donor clinics, or one of the bounty hunting hellsehers called *Dark-slayers* who sometimes killed simply for the sake of killing.

She supposed she had her answer: running into a Darkslayer would be far worse than running into a vampire. Especially one of the Seven Devils, the most feared Darkslaying circle in the city, who'd risen to the top of Angelthene's Darkslaying hierarchy in recent years.

The thought made her shiver, despite that the night was warm and dry. "I think we should go to the apothecary. I'll worry about Mordred and Penny's wrath another day." She only hoped the conjoined witch twins wouldn't kill her for entering their precious shop after hours.

They started walking again. This time, no one bothered to sing. Loren might've blamed it on the alcohol or exhaustion, but she had the sense that Dallas and Sabrine were sobering up the longer they walked. Wind blew hollowly through the streets, sending palm tree fronds scraping across asphalt. For a city of eight million people, it was eerily quiet.

They made it another two blocks before a pair of headlights swept across the road behind them, reflecting in a stop sign up ahead. The harsh, ascending squalls of birds that were huddled in the date palms cut through the quiet, followed by the crunch and pop of gravel under tires as the vehicle rolled toward them.

Loren slowed. *"Please* tell me that's a cab." But she couldn't say; the vehicle's headlights rendered her mortal eyes useless.

The driver lurched to a stop, and Loren found herself stepping off the sidewalk as Dallas and Sabrine continued walking.

It wasn't a cab, Loren realized. Her dragging feet stilled, and her heart skipped two beats. It was a dark sedan.

Everything happened very quickly.

Two men got out—a copper-haired warlock and a blond hellse-her. The latter's eyes—whites and all—were solid black. The color indicated that he was a Darkslayer out on a job—and was calling upon his magical ability known as the *Sight* to track the aura that belonged to his target. Aside from the black that swallowed their eyes while using the Sight, hellsehers looked like mortals, for they, unlike vampires and wolves, had no other characteristics that set them apart. The Sight was an ability exclusive to hellsehers; it allowed them to not only track people by the colors of their auras, but also see through the magical wards on buildings and vehicles that were put in place specifically to *hide* auras.

Dallas sprinted to Loren's side, grabbing her by the wrist and pulling her behind her. The sudden jerk of her arm sent pain rippling up to Loren's shoulder. Her heel caught on the curb, causing her to stumble, her shoes slipping through her fingers and clunking to the sidewalk.

Dallas's Focus sparked a glaring white. *"Exarmaueris!"* she bellowed.

Her spell blasted the warlock into the sedan, the windshield shattering as her magic launched him right through it.

But the hellseher barely budged, absorbing the impact of Dallas's spell as though it were a breeze—as though he *enjoyed* it. He flashed them a wicked smile as he cast his own spell—with hellseher magic that didn't need a Focus, nor fancy incantations to set their powers into motion.

A hellseher's magic was utterly lethal.

The force of his attack slammed into them like a battering ram.

Loren and Dallas flew backward. They hit the asphalt, rolling over top of each other in a tangle of limbs. Loren cried out as her bare arms and legs were shredded open, gravel ripping into her.

Sabrine was shouting hysterically into her cell phone as she ran after Loren and Dallas, begging City Rescue to send officers to Canopus Street immediately.

The hellseher was striding their way, rallying his magic with arms held aloft at his sides, palms facing forward. Gravel hovered above the road, the tendrils of his shoulder-length blond hair drifting above his head as though he were underwater.

There was a symbol tattooed below his right ear. All Darkslaying hellsehers were marked with one, but Loren didn't recognize his. She sorted through the options in her mind, but came up empty; the Seven Devils, the Angels of Death, the Huntsmen, the Wargs, the Reapers, the Vipers... It was *none* of them.

It was the head of a phoenix.

Wincing in pain, Dallas pushed herself to her feet and thrust out her stave. From her shadow sprang her Familiar Spirit, a winged tiger called Ghost. Black and stark as a silhouette, Ghost sank into a protective stance before them, a guttural snarl ripping through his bared teeth.

"Run, Lor." Dallas stepped in front of where Loren was still sprawled on the sidewalk. The witch's body trembled, and blood streamed down her legs.

Behind the hellseher, the warlock was recovering from Dallas's disarming spell. His arms were bloodied up, and he looked more than a little pissed off as he leapt off the crumpled hood and followed the Darkslayer toward them.

"Quit playing!" the warlock snarled at the Darkslayer. "We need her *alive.*"

Loren pushed herself to her feet. "Dallas—"

"*RUN, goddamn it!*" Dallas shouted. "We'll hold them off. They're not after us, Loren. They're after *you!*"

At the same time as Sabrine, Dallas bellowed, *"Exarmaueris!"*

Magic erupted in unison from their staves, and a smattering of lilac sparks floated into the sky. Dust blasted down the street as the spells cleaved the air. The force of the magic shook the trees and buckled the glass of shop windows, the sound like bones breaking.

Loren cried out and covered her face as shards of glass zipped through the air. The magpies huddled within the trees cawed and fled into the night with an explosion of feathers.

Dallas shoved Loren. "Go!" Her voice cracked. "We'll catch up with you—I *promise.*" The sheer terror in Dallas's gaze was the only thing that spurred Loren into action.

She broke into a limping sprint. Her breath tore apart her lungs, the muscles in her calves shrieking in pain as she fled. Every instinct screamed at her to turn back—to help her friends, despite that a human could literally do *nothing* against a warlock and a Darkslayer.

She was helpless. *Pathetic.* Never had she hated being human more than she did in this moment.

She risked a glance over her shoulder.

Dallas and Sabrine were sprinting after her, Ghost bounding at their heels. But the hellseher and the warlock were gaining on them. Had the Darkslayer not been a half-breed—half-warlock, half-hellseher, judging from the silver that glinted in his irises whenever he wasn't using his Sight—he would've already caught up to them.

She wasn't sure what would've happened next if sirens hadn't sounded. They wailed through the night, bouncing over buildings and cutting down alleys.

"Help!" Loren's voice was a high-pitched crackle. *"HELP!* Please —we're over here!" Dallas and Sabrine joined her in shouting, their heels clacking on the road. But two sets of boots were getting louder, gaining on them by the second.

Red and blue lights reflected in the dark windows of buildings up ahead. Loren sobbed in relief at the sight of them—

A familiar scream tore through the panic barking in her head.

Loren staggered to a stop, Dallas doing the same just behind her.

For one terrifying second, time seemed to still. Loren drew in a ragged breath through her teeth, blood roaring in her head, as she took in the scene two blocks behind her.

The Darkslayer had Sabrine in his grip, the muzzle of a pistol pressed against her temple as he towed her toward the car. Toward the back door the warlock was throwing open.

Pavement stretched between Loren and her friend, endless as the ocean.

Loren stumbled forward. "Let her go." Although her voice was a whispered sob, she knew every pair of immortal ears on this street could hear her. *"Please.* What do you want?"

"I want you to get in the car." The Darkslayer's words were aimed at Loren. Not the pure-blooded witch at her side, whose life was worth so much more than hers—than a human's.

Dallas was right: they *were* after her.

Loren gaped at the hellseher, her heart pounding so hard, she thought she might throw up.

Why did they want her? *Why?*

"She's not going anywhere with you," Dallas said, her voice hoarse and trembling. The light of her stave was barely a weak flutter—a mirror of her exhaustion. Even Ghost was spent; Dallas was only a student of magic, so her power reserves were shallow. *"None* of us are."

The hellseher gave a cold smile. Made to say something—

Two squad cars spun around the corner, sirens wailing. The warlock swore at the sight of the peace officers behind the wheels.

Loren saw it coming.

She made to move—to stop the slayer and the warlock from wrestling Sabrine into the back seat as the squad cars came to a screeching halt, lightbars on the roofs flashing.

But they were already in the sedan. They spun around, smashing into the bumper of a squad car before peeling off, tires burning up a reeking black cloud behind them.

Loren took off after the sedan, her heart in her throat, her reflection flitting like a spirit through shop windows. She screamed herself hoarse. Begged them to stop—to let her friend go. She knew it was no use. Her words would make no difference.

But she had to try—for Sabrine.

She had to try for Sabrine.

One of the squad cars raced after the sedan, but they would never make it—and neither would she.

Still, she hurtled along the dark street, dodging piles of trash, feet ripping open on stones and fragments of glass. No matter how fast she ran, the sedan only got farther away.

Loren would never forget the sight of her.

Of Sabrine—thrashing against the hellseher's hold, staring helplessly through the back window as the sedan disappeared around a corner up ahead. Sabrine's gaze was utterly broken and full of anguish.

Just like Loren's heart.

2

The wild cheering that barreled down the damp hallway that led to the Pit was music to Darien Cassel's ears. The excitement of the rowdy audience encircling the sunken fighting ring in the distance told him his opponent tonight would be worthy. If he was lucky, whatever manner of creature he would soon be facing might even make him sweat a little.

Darien kept his eyes shut as he rolled his muscled shoulders and shifted his weight. This idle fidgeting was for the benefit of the half-human bouncers waiting near the latticed grille at the end of the hallway; he had a habit of standing so still, it unsettled anyone in his vicinity, even here in Angelthene—a place where most of its inhabitants could live without sleep and preferred the blood of a freshly killed corpse to the burger joints found on most city blocks.

But as a pure-blooded hellseher and the leader of the Seven Devils, he supposed he could understand their apprehension. If only a little.

Down the hall, the ring announcer was declaring his reputation. As the undefeated champion of the Pit, he was a favorite of the lowlifes and career criminals who clawed out a living making bets on those who entered the ring. Pathetic wastes of life, but it wasn't his business. He came here, sometimes seven nights a week, strictly to take the edge off his temper and combat his Surges—though tonight it wasn't just his temper or his Surges that needed reining in.

Eight years ago, his mother had died. And while fighting served as a useful channel for his rage, it also provided him with a way to forget, even for a few hours.

And tonight, he needed nothing more than to forget.

Darien ran a tattooed hand through his hair, pushing the black strands of his undercut back flat, entirely aware of the bouncers assessing him with caution as they awaited the ring announcer's signal. Even from this distance away, he could smell fear emanating from them like cologne. He supposed he should take it as a compliment that they were still so afraid of him—of the man who'd replaced the heartbroken fifteen-year-old boy who'd stomped in here eight years ago in search of an outlet.

What he could scent more than their fear, however, was the demon—the flesh-hungry beast prowling the Pit on all fours. The oily reek of its hairless, mottled skin snaked down the hallway, burning his airways.

A creature of the storm drains that hated the light. They left their dens only during the darkest hours of the night, which was why the Head of State had recently proposed the idea of a dusk-to-dawn curfew for the city, keeping the citizens safe while giving Pest and Disease Control a chance to scale back the capital's rising numbers of ravenous vermin. No one would face more than a small fine for breaking the said curfew—but might very well pay for their lack of intelligence with their life, and their body dragged into the sewers to be chewed into ribbons.

The thing was agitated, a sign that it had been caught only minutes ago. Judging from the sound of its flesh-shredding claws gouging lines into the cement walls of the Pit, it didn't like being caged. Nor did it like the glaring LED lights mounted above the audience.

One of the bouncers whistled the signal, and Darien opened his eyes. The crowd's cheering rattled the exposed rafters of the vaulted ceiling and set the floor beneath his combat boots rumbling. He let the familiar sounds wash over him, electrifying his blood.

His mouth curved into a lethal smile as he stalked forward, toward the Pit. Toward the creature that had a population of eight million people hiding inside after dark.

It was time. Time to lose himself to blood and gore for a while.

Violence was his drug. His own personal demon.

He only hoped the one waiting in the Pit would put up enough of a fight that he might not feel the need to return here tomorrow.

DARIEN DRAGGED out the fight for longer than he usually cared to. He was beginning to tire of this, but not from exhaustion. He could easily keep going for far longer than the sixteen minutes and thirty-four seconds the timer hanging above the Pit displayed.

He was simply getting bored.

The demon reared back on hind legs, releasing a wet roar that rattled his eardrums and set the crowd foaming at the mouth with excitement.

The feral thing had a maw of serrated teeth, black as obsidian. The curved horns on either side of its near-translucent head were evidence of how long it had been alive. This was one of the stronger ones, yet it bored the hell out of him. He needed to find better opponents — a challenger that was actually worth his precious time.

Sensing that he was being watched by a gaze unclouded by liquor and opioids, Darien tipped his head back to observe the screaming audience. Hundreds of piss-smelling drunkards were packed from the stands to the rafters, shouting out bets and exchanging gestures to communicate as they waved fistfuls of mynet in the smoky air. There were no ropes around the perimeter of the Pit; if anyone fell in, they were fair game. In the years in which Darien had fought in this ring, several people had done exactly that.

Not one of them had lived to tell of it.

As Darien had suspected, far above the walls of the Pit, he spotted a familiar figure. In the sea of sweaty, thrashing bodies, the messenger was the only person standing still. They wore the same white rabbit mask as always, their black clothes nondescript. It was a call all Darkslayers answered: when the mask appeared, it meant a job offer was coming his way.

It was time to end this.

Darien lunged at the same time the demon made a move. It dove for his jugular with a roar, jaws snapping together.

Veering to the left of those gleaming teeth, Darien struck hard, his fingers bursting through the creature's esophagus. The thing gagged and writhed in agony, its beastlike feet fumbling for purchase in the sand behind it.

Darien dug his hand in deeper, twisted —

And ripped out its throat.

The body collapsed to the blood-soaked sand in a heap of quivering flesh.

If he'd thought the crowd was cheering loudly before, it was nothing compared to the noise now thundering through the arena, the racket threatening to shatter the foggy skylight far above.

"Call it," Darien barked at the half-human ring announcer, whose face had blanched.

"Victory is yours," the man choked out.

Wiping his bloody hands on his torn and stained jeans, Darien swept the audience again.

Only to find that the rabbit had already disappeared.

As soon as Darien had finished cleaning up in the shabby change room in the basement of the arena, he made his way to the wrought-iron gates out front of the crumbling building.

His dark hair was still wet from the shower, his long-sleeved white shirt and faded jeans clinging to his damp, suntanned skin. The duffel bag slung over his shoulder was stuffed full of bloody clothes and the kind of weapons only a Darkslayer could get their hands on, along with the Stygian salts that aided his Sight. The salts were a gateway drug—literally. They opened the floodgates of a hellseher's magic and allowed them to see a person's aura—and see through the magical wards on most buildings and vehicles—for extended periods of time, making the act of remotely tracking targets a cinch for people like himself and his Devils.

Wind blew down the dusty street in gusts, setting the palm trees and cypresses lining the sidewalks swaying. Aside from the odd desperate junkie or prostitute straggling through the shadows, the city was mostly deserted at this hour, especially here in the slums, where most of the streetlights had been shot out long ago. The Sturgeon moon was slipping below the horizon, the sky in the distance staining a dull gray as dawn made its approach.

Another night well-spent at his favorite shithole. The no-holds-barred underground fighting ring was in the Meatpacking District, not far from the slaughterhouses that processed every type of flesh a person could name; in a place like this, anything that could breathe was on the menu, and no preference—no matter how foul—was off-limits.

Across the street, where it was parked by the trash-covered curb, his car lurked like a bat in the lingering dark. Unlike any other vehicle whose owner dared to park here, the glass of every window was still in one piece. No keys had scratched the black paint, no graffiti artist had tagged the hood. The people who frequented these parts of town not only knew who he was and to stay away from him —they also knew to stay the fuck away from his car. Some days he enjoyed the infamy that came with ripping apart whoever was stupid enough to walk into that pit with him more than he enjoyed the mynet he received for doing so.

He took his cell phone out of his pocket to find half a dozen unread messages from his sister, along with several from the other Devils and a handful from Valary Sternberg, his most recent fuck-buddy who was starting to get a little too clingy for his liking. This came as no surprise; it was always only a matter of time before women decided they wanted more than rough, no-strings-attached sex from him, but he was never willing to give it.

His mouth twitched into a frown as he skimmed over the messages his sister had sent him, the weight of reality returning as the adrenaline from fighting in the ring vacated his system far too soon.

IVY

Where are you? Don't tell me you went to the Pit...

I thought you meant it this time—that we were going to the cemetery together.

IVY

It wasn't your fault, you know. If Mom was able to talk to you, she would tell you the same thing. You need to stop blaming yourself.

I'll bring extra flowers to Mom's grave for you... Hope to see you there.

The last message was sent two hours after the previous.

IVY

You can't keep running away, Darien. You're not the only one who's hurting.

He shut off the screen so hard, the button jammed.

It didn't matter that he wasn't the only one who was hurting. Ripping apart actual demons was one thing—but confronting his own wasn't something he was ready to do yet.

Blowing out a sigh through his nose, he slid his phone back into his pocket. So much for calming the Surge that had taken over his mind earlier that night; it seemed he would have to return here tomorrow after all.

As he drew closer to the gate, gravel crunching beneath his combat boots, the rabbit stepped into view from where she was waiting for him near the safety of an unshattered mercury-vapor streetlamp. Out of what he knew was respect and more than a hint of fear, she stayed a careful distance away from him—and close enough to the greenish glow of the lamp to feel somewhat of a sense of protection from the demons. Demons like the one whose throat Darien had ripped out with his bare hand minutes ago.

The mask she wore was like something from a horror film. The mouth was pulled into a gaping smile lined with jagged teeth, and the grotesquely large eyes were as white as the rest of it—no pupils. It was no harmless little bunny like those sold at the pet shops on the Avenue of the Scarlet Star—that was for gods-damned certain.

"You're Darien Cassel." *No shit*, he thought. If the ring announcer declaring his reputation had been too subtle for her, the horned letter *S* tattooed below his ear should be an obvious indication of who he was.

Never mind the ever-changing gossip that floated about the streets. People with too much time on their hands enjoyed making up rumors about him, mainly ones that suggested he'd sold his soul to the devil to get to where he was today. He supposed he had sold his soul in a way, but in doing so had more or less become the devil himself.

"That's the rumor." He dug a metal lighter and a pack of cigarettes out of his pocket, placed one of the smokes between his lips, and lit it. "Give me the name and the price and be on your way," he said around a mouthful of smoke. He slid the cigarettes and lighter back into his pocket. "I've had a long night."

"The boss is offering two million gold mynet."

Well, shit. It was a lot of mynet. He couldn't remember the last time a single target had been worth more than a million.

"The name?" he prompted.

"There is no name."

Darien quirked an inky brow. Usually, those who hired him knew the name of who—or *what*—they wanted dead or in captivity. It was rare when he was approached with an offer to find a nameless target, though he could locate them without a problem. He was one

25

of the only people in this city who could. "He would like you to track the target via aura only."

He took another drag on the cigarette as he eyed up that stained and cracked mask.

Tracking auras was not only a lengthier process but a harder one. If he knew the target's name, he could tap into his sixth sense—and the ability to remotely track someone via Sight—a lot sooner. All he would need to do was hack Angelthene's citizen database and pull up a photograph of his target; having a clear mental image of the person he wanted to locate would make remotely tracking them a cinch.

Finding an aura without the aid of a photograph and then trailing it to its current location could take days. Maybe even weeks. And the process often required that he start at the target's origin—either their place of birth or somewhere similar, such as their childhood home, where the aura would be the least diluted—to get a distinct read on who he was looking for. Such methods were also expensive, since he would have to use the Stygian salts for the whole process, and it would require him to tunnel deep into the limitless reserves of his magic, which was no easy feat.

He adjusted the strap on his duffel bag and tapped the ash off the cigarette. "Your boss knows what he wants but he doesn't know *who* he wants," he observed. Pulling up the strap on his duffel had drawn the messenger's attention to the tattoo peeking out from beneath his rolled-up shirtsleeve. Even through the mask, he could tell that she was staring at it—at the tattoo of Elsie Cassel's face.

The rabbit wisely tore her attention from the tattoo and gave a nod. "The target was an orphan. You should be able to pick up on the aura at the Temple of the Scarlet Star. The boss says the target was left there as a baby and adopted soon after."

She retrieved a vial from the pocket of her jacket. Inside the vial was bone powder—the DNA of what was likely one of the target's ancestors. The demineralized bone was the quickest way to help him identify the aura—a field of energy that radiated from every living person or thing, invisible to anyone without a hellseher's Sight—that he was looking for. If the target had indeed spent time at the temple as a baby, then with the help of the bone powder the aura should be easy to pinpoint. And once he became accustomed to the feel of that aura, he would be able to trail it like a wolf trailed its prey, eventually digging up the target's current location.

How the client had retrieved the bone powder—and how they knew who the target's ancestor was but hadn't a clue of their actual target's identity—wasn't his business. He didn't concern himself with the reasons why his elusive clients wanted to track anyone down. Asking questions was not only suspicious and unnecessary, but it was also unprofessional. He was in this line of work only for the cash, and nothing more.

The several minutes he took to consider the offer probably seemed like years to the messenger, because it wasn't long before her pulse was thrumming in her golden neck. There was a scar below her jaw, no more than a pock in her skin. Either from a viral disease or from being held at knifepoint. If this rabbit returned to her employer after failing to negotiate a deal, the cost—if she was lucky—would be her job. If she wasn't lucky, it would be her life.

It was an unjust world he lived in, but nobody got anywhere in life if they gave a shit about the bottom-feeders of this corrupt society.

"Dead or alive?" Darien asked.

"Alive. Preferably unharmed if you can manage it." It went without saying that he could manage it. As leader of the Devils, there was little he couldn't do.

So, Darien said, "I can." He paused. "But I want three million gold mynet."

The rabbit didn't flinch. "Two-point-five." Darien almost laughed. Whoever her boss was, he'd given her clear instructions on haggling.

"Three million, or I'm not playing."

Another beat of silence. And then the rabbit stepped forward and offered him the bone powder. "It's a deal."

Darien's fingers closed around the vial. "I'll need about a week to locate the aura, but it won't be long after that before I can track down the target. Wire me a mil by midnight tomorrow or the deal falls through." He shoved the vial into the pocket of his jeans and then handed her a card that had nothing on it but the number for his wire transfer.

"We'll be in touch with you soon." When the rabbit spoke again, there was a hint of a smile in her voice. "Pleasure doing business with you, Slayer."

His mouth quirked in answer as he tossed the cigarette to the ground and crushed it beneath his boot. "Likewise."

3

Loren stared into the two-way mirror as the peace officer that sat across from her at the dented metal table in the interrogation room shuffled his papers into a stack.

The girl in the reflection was a stranger—a ghost. Hollowed out and drifting through a world she no longer recognized.

She looked like hell. Makeup was smeared across her sticky, tear-stained face, her hair was crusted with beer and road dust, and her dark blue eyes were bloodshot and void of emotion. Even the sunburn on her cheeks did nothing to bring color to the ivory skin that had taken on a sickly pale shade these past two hours.

Sabrine was gone. Sabrine was missing, and it was all her fault.

No one believed her. Not a single person at the Angelthene Law Enforcement holding center had looked at her with anything but disbelief when they'd heard her side of the story. She knew Dallas would be telling the other officers the very same thing—the truth of what happened tonight—in the room adjacent to hers. Maybe they would be more inclined to listen to the Red Baron's biological daughter than the human orphan who had never been—and never would be—anything more than that: *human*.

"Let me get this straight," said the peace officer, in that gruff, no-bullshit tone.

Loren tore her gaze from her reflection—and the people she knew were watching from behind the glass—and turned to face the warlock. The expression he wore was as harsh and unyielding as the room they were in; the frigid concrete beneath her bare and blistered feet, the hard chair she was sitting on that was bolted to the floor, the glaring white lightbulbs stabbing into her eyes from where they were mounted in the corners of the room.

She slid her hands between her scraped knees to stop them from shaking. The tattoo glowing on the inside of her forearm had changed from a pale blue to a glaring red. If she didn't get some medication or food into her soon, she would faint.

The warlock was middle-aged as far as physical appearance went, though the watery cast to his eyes hinted that he was far older than he looked—and had likely abused the reserves of his magic in his years as commissioner to soon come down with the Tricking. In fact, she would be surprised if he hadn't already been diagnosed with it.

The officer laced his fingers on the tabletop and looked her over with a steely gaze. "You believe the Darkslayer was after *you?*"

"I already told you." Loren barely recognized the crackle of her own voice. It was as cold and void of emotion as the expression she could feel herself wearing. "When he held a gun to Sabrine's head, I asked him what he wanted. He said, 'I want you to get in the car.'" This was the third time she'd explained it to this bastard.

He blew out a huff and pretended to look over the paper at the top of the stack. "You are nineteen, Miss Calla. Correct?"

"Yes." Her voice broke.

"And you've lived in Angelthene your whole life?"

"Yes."

"Then I don't think I need to explain to you that hellsehers are a very powerful breed." He set the paper back on the stack. "Their magic is not as restricted as that of veneficae, nor lamiae, and because of this, they know their worth. Hellsehers who hunt for bounties charge hefty prices, Miss Calla. Those prices can run as high as one million gold mynet. Sometimes even higher."

"I understand what you're saying, Commissioner." He was saying no hellseher would bother with someone like her—with a human target whose life had no value worthy enough for them to track down. There was no reason for anyone to want to hunt her, nor pay a Darkslayer's outrageous cost to find her. And yet, she *knew*...

She knew it was supposed to have been her who was taken tonight.

The officer sat back, his chair creaking under his weight. "Can you describe what the phoenix tattoo looked like, Miss Calla?"

She held out a hand in request for a pen. After a moment, he handed his over, along with a piece of ruled paper he tore from his notepad. The scratch of pen on paper was loud in the otherwise silent room as her trembling hand swept across the page. When she was finished, she spun the paper around and slid it his way.

Half a second was all he spared for her drawing. "How's your vision, Miss Calla?"

She stiffened. "What's that supposed to mean?"

"It's a simple question."

"My vision is fine." It wasn't twenty-twenty, but it was clear enough that this jerk shouldn't be doubting her. "I know what I saw. The tattoo was a *phoenix* head, Commissioner." Not the over-lapping wings of the Angels of Death; not the God of Death that was the symbol of the Reapers, nor the striking serpent of the Vipers; not the hellhound of the Huntsmen, nor the crescent moon of the Wargs. And it certainly wasn't the horned letter *S*, the sigil of the Seven Devils, the most feared Darkslaying circle in the city.

The officer stuffed the drawing into his shirt pocket. "Your guardian has been contacted. She will be here shortly to take you home." Loren's head turned featherlight, her fists slackening.

Taega Bright, Dallas's mother, had been contacted. As if this night—she supposed it was technically morning now—could get any worse.

"Is there anything else you would like to say?" the officer asked. The silver ringing his pupils—a peculiar characteristic all veneficae possessed—was as reflective as mirrors under the lights. "Anything worthy of pointing out that we haven't already covered?"

Loren remained silent for so long that he made to stand. But her voice froze him in place.

"You may feel we've covered a great deal, Commissioner. But I don't. Every statement I've made tonight is the truth, yet you've done nothing but dismiss my claims."

He settled back into the chair with another of those heavy sighs that was more of a growl. The badge pinned to his dress-shirt gleamed in the fluorescents. "Can you think of any reason as to why they would've been tracking you?" The tone he used was flat, his disinterest in entertaining what he believed was a cry for attention blatantly obvious. "Is there anything of value on your person that they might've been looking for?"

Loren mirrored his no-bullshit expression. "I have a tube of lip gloss, a half-empty pack of gum, and barely three hundred gold mynet in my bank account, Commissioner. Do you think the Darkslayer might've been after any of these things?"

"Miss Calla—"

"Sabrine was held at gunpoint as a strategy to get *me* in the car." Loren's voice came out as broken as she felt. "They only took her instead of me because they ran out of time when your officers came flying around the corner." Tears burned her eyes, and her lip wobbled. "If you're not going to believe me, then that's not my problem. But I want my friend back, so I beg you to reconsider your opinion after what I just told you."

He assessed her for a moment. "I assure you, Miss Calla, that we will do everything in our power to bring Miss Van Arsdell back home safely. We have a strong team of officers, and our hellsehers are tracking her—"

"Have they figured out where they're keeping Sabrine?" Loren felt a spark of hope in her chest, and she found herself sitting up straighter. It was something the city needed more of: hellsehers working as local law enforcement officials, using their Sight to track down suspects and people who went missing. The process of remotely tracking someone certainly wasn't foolproof, hence why there were so many unsolved crimes, but it couldn't hurt to have more people who were gifted with the Sight looking out for innocent civilians. Most hellsehers either chose not to use their Sight at all due to the Tricking or decided to chase after the fat paycheques that came from illegally tracking down bounties.

The officer merely shifted in his seat. The look on his face told her everything.

"They can't find her," Loren concluded hollowly. She slumped against the backrest of her chair. "Does that mean she's dead?" Her heart was bleeding out in her chest. "She's dead, isn't she? They killed her."

"Loren—"

"It's luh-*ren*," she retorted. He pronounced it like *Lauren*, and it wasn't the first time she'd corrected him. Just as it wasn't the first time that she had explained the night's events to him, only to be received so disrespectfully. "I would like to be excused now."

As finished with her as she was with him, the officer led her out of the interrogation room. Loren limped after him in silence, barely registering the pain that crackled through her cut-up feet with every step. Although he didn't say anything else to her, he no longer looked at her with disdain.

He must've realized that she was standing on a ledge. She was about to break, and not in any way that benefited them as a person of interest in Sabrine's case.

Her friend was gone. And the worst part about it was that it was her fault.

4

Orientation for the first-year students of Angelthene
Academy who were sorted into the House of Salt took
place at seven in the morning.

The rain was drumming a steady rhythm on the umbrella that was
propped up on Dallas's shoulder, shielding mostly Loren from the
downpour than herself. Loren sagged against Dallas's side as they
waited for the last of the Salt freshmen to join the group and
announce their names to the upper-level half-vampire student holding
a clipboard in his milk-white hands. The roster fluttered in the wind,
threatening to break free of the measly spring-clip that held it in place.

Loren hadn't slept a wink last night, and she didn't think Dallas
had either. After Dallas's mother had picked them up from the
holding center, they hadn't said a word to each other. And Taega
hadn't bothered to offer her condolences for their missing friend. In
fact, she hadn't uttered so much as a word to either of them until
they'd entered the penthouse.

"Clean yourselves up in the spare bathroom and sterilize it when
you're done," she'd told them as she swept into her immaculate foyer,
the lean muscles in her golden thighs straining against the white

fabric of her pristine pencil skirt. "The smell of you both is making me sick."

It would've been better if Taega simply hadn't said anything, but nearly nineteen years of living in the Bright penthouse was long enough for Loren to know what to expect from someone like Commander Bright. Loren had let Dallas clean up first, and when she was finished, Loren had locked the door and sat with her arms wrapped around her knees on the marble floor of the shower. For a long time, she had cried in silence, analyzing the events of the evening. She was so lost in trying to remember any details that might help her find Sabrine that she hadn't noticed when the hot water ran out.

Sometime during the hour in which she'd slumped beneath the stream of water, Dallas must've had an argument with Taega. When Loren had gone to bed afterward in the room they shared, Dallas's back was facing her. But when Dallas had reached over to flick off the lamp, Loren had caught sight of the purple mark on her cheekbone. Dallas hadn't been willing to talk about it, which came as no surprise; she never talked about the things that hurt her. She preferred to swallow her pain like a big pill and pretend she couldn't remember how it'd felt going down.

Loren blinked away the recent memory and surveyed the cluster of students talking animatedly as they awaited the tour of the grounds.

All students at every campus in the city were divided into Houses, the process of which was based off their heritage and the most dominant type of magic in their blood, if any. The House of Mercury was for water, the House of Salt was for the earth, and the House of Brimstone was for fire.

As one of the very few humans whose application had been accepted at the academy, Loren had been put into the House most connected to the earth—to the cycle of life and death. Loren tried not to think about that rain-damp roster; the surname *Van Arsdell* at the very bottom of the alphabetical list. The only name with no checkmark beside it. Or perhaps it had already been crossed off, for by now the news channel and the front page of the Daystar would've certainly notified the whole city of Sabrine's abduction.

Loren tried not to think about it. Law enforcement would find Sabrine and bring her home. They *had* to.

The professor who was tasked with directing the orientation meeting for the new students of the House of Salt was Professor Grayson Phipps. A pure-blooded warlock, he was golden-haired and handsome, with the kind of sharp jaw and five o'clock shadow that made heartrates increase and toes curl in shoes.

Professor Phipps joined the group of chattering witches, warlocks, half-breeds, humans, and vampires and gave a brief introduction of himself.

Something sharp struck Loren in the ribs.

She drew in a hiss through her teeth, staggering away from the elbow she was certain had left a nasty bruise. "Ouch, Dal!"

"He's hot," Dallas hissed. "I would ride that broomstick any day." Loren felt her cheeks turn red. She shushed Dallas and ducked back under the umbrella.

The muggy air was frizzing her space buns. Not that she'd spent much time on her hair that morning; the usual things she cared about had taken a back seat. It would be a miracle if she had remembered to bring all her textbooks and grimoires.

Dallas followed Phipps across the lawn, alongside the rest of the students. Loren hurried to keep up with her, the soaking wet grass squeaking against the leather of her uniform shoes. The white button-up blouse—the left chest embroidered with the crest of Angelthene Academy—and mid-thigh-length plaid skirt did nothing to keep her warm. Her teeth were chattering so loudly that Dallas eventually shushed her.

The tour was long and detailed, but Professor Phipps explained the academy's history in a way that held the attention of every student as they made their way from landmark to landmark.

"I wonder if he's married," Dallas went on. Professor Phipps slowed before a statue of a warlock and proceeded to give a brief history of the founder of the academy.

"I'm trying to listen," Loren whispered. It really wasn't true, but she wanted Dallas to shut the heck up before she got them both kicked out.

But the professor heard them. At the head of the group, near a copse of blue jacaranda trees that sheltered the statue, Professor Phipps stopped talking and turned to face them.

"Miss Dallas Bright."

Dallas went rigid as Phipps's eyes found hers in the cluster of umbrellas. One by one, the students turned around to stare.

Loren ducked her head, the weight of all those eyes unbearable.

Phipps was frowning. "Would you care to share with the rest of us what you've found so important as to interrupt my tour?"

Dallas lowered her chin in feigned embarrassment and shook her head. If Loren hadn't known Dal her entire life, she might've fallen for the act. But she could see, clear as day, the smirk playing on the generous curve of Dallas's lips, painted a shade identical to her hair. A glamor, Loren knew—no lipstick could look that perfect. She would give Dallas hell for that later; she shouldn't be using her magic so carelessly, not when the Tricking was running rampant and hospital beds were few and far between.

It was why magic staves had been invented in the first place. The Tricking was a disease that had been around for centuries; if a person abused their power reserves and used their magic for anything and everything—such as makeup glamors—they were more likely to contract the sickness. It plagued immortal people with old age and eventually killed them.

A Focus served as a conduit, the staves a channel for a person's magic to flow through, resulting in a decreased risk of contracting the Tricking. It wasn't a permanent fix, but it worked—for now. Witches and warlocks had been using magic staves for so many years, that few of them could perform magic without one now.

"No thank you, Professor Phipps," Dallas replied in a saccharine voice. "I apologize for interrupting you."

The professor gave a thoughtful hum. "Well, as someone whose job is to answer my students' questions, I would certainly hate to leave yours unanswered, Miss Bright."

"My question?" This time, she wasn't faking the surprise glinting in her gaze.

"I *am* married." Although he wore a poker face, amusement danced in his eyes. "And even if I wasn't, I am two hundred years old. Which is far too old for you."

Students snickered. Girls pressed their hands to their mouths, and grinning boys elbowed each other in the side.

"Now," the professor went on, "can we focus on the tour, Miss Bright?"

Splotches of color bloomed across Dallas's cheeks, but she smiled and replied sweetly, "You have very keen hearing, Professor."

He merely smiled and resumed his tour.

The tour was nearly at a close when Loren slowed to a shuffle before a crumbling building surrounded by a chain-link fence topped with loops of barbed wire.

Oblivious to Loren having stopped, Dallas continued walking, taking the shelter of the umbrella with her, her kohl-lined eyes trained on Phipps's ass. Loren rolled her eyes so hard, she swore she saw her brain.

"What's in that building, Professor?" The storm threatened to swallow Loren's words.

The students slowed as Professor Phipps turned around, holding his clipboard above his head to shield himself from the rain that was increasing in tempo. Suddenly, there was nowhere to look without meeting a pair of curious eyes. Loren felt her shoulders curl in for what seemed like the hundredth time that morning, and she interlocked her fingers to keep from fidgeting.

"That building," he said, "is strictly off-limits." He made to turn away, but Dallas spoke up.

"No, seriously," the witch said as she made her way toward the fence, shaking a strand of hair—frizzed by humidity—out of her face. "What's in it?"

"Seriously, Miss Bright," Professor Phipps said in a mocking tone, "it's off-limits." He started walking again, his pantlegs soaked by the lawn. But he barely made it two feet before his reluctance to talk about the building set the entire group of students to whining.

The professor stopped walking. Turned around. Even with the clipboard he held above his head, his hair was darkened with rain.

Dallas smirked and said of the students, who were belting out their own questions about the building, "It seems we've gained a small army."

The professor surveyed Loren and Dallas for a long time. When the murmuring finally quieted, he relented with a sigh and gave up holding the clipboard as a makeshift umbrella, instead using it to gesture to the building. "This is the Old Hall. It was where classes were held when the academy was established several thousand years ago. When the new academy was built to accommodate the growing number of students, this building was forgotten. It was no longer used for anything except storage."

The vampire who held the roster said, "Is it true there used to be a secret society on campus?" Now *this* was the kind of information Loren was looking for.

"What kind of secret society?" Loren asked.

The vampire's eyes met hers. "A blood magic society. They would sneak into the building at Witching Hour and perform ancient rites to see who was worthy of joining their cult —"

"Not a blood magic society or a *cult*, Stephan," corrected the professor. "It was more a society of outcasts. According to the stories, it was a social club a small number of humans organized to make new friends. They chose the Old Hall as a place to hold their meetings and other activities — a place they could call their own."

Loren stepped up to the fence, gritting her teeth against the magical barrier humming through the air. Interesting how the schoolboard would arrange to give such an old structure an extra layer of protection.

Storage house, my ass.

Squinting her eyes to see better through the rain falling in sheets, she studied the shape etched into the damp threshold.

The next question came from one of the students at the back of the group. "What was the society called?" Loren recognized the familiar shape carved into the wood half a second before the professor spoke.

"The Phoenix Head Society."

THE VAST ARCHWAY of the academy entrance passed over Loren's head, the warmth of the firelit interior wrapping like a blanket around her chilled bones.

Students were packed like sardines in the entrance, chattering about their summer adventures. Wolves, witches, and vampires who'd graduated from the same secondary school as Loren and Dallas greeted the latter with varying smiles, waving their hellos from across the room. No one acknowledged the human friend standing at the witch's elbow, but Loren wasn't fazed—she'd had nineteen years to get used to this kind of treatment.

When they made it to the staircase in the entrance hall, they began their ascent to the House of Salt, consulting the map that was marked with a red X to show where they would find their hall of residence.

Dozens of steps and corridors later, they were greeted by a forked staircase. Each fork led to a different House; the left was for Mercury, the middle was for Salt, and the right was for Brimstone.

They made their way up the middle staircase and down a torch-lit corridor. At the very end of it, an ornamental gilt mirror covered the wall from floor to ceiling. There were no doors—they weren't needed here. The mirror was the entrance into their hall of residence. From what Loren had heard, all three Houses were entered into the same way, though each reflection displayed different alternate realities of the corridor that now lay behind them.

For the House of Salt, it was a corridor of sunshine streaming through tangled green foliage; for Mercury, it was coral walls and white sand that crunched beneath feet; and for Brimstone, it was walls of stone with a floor of magma.

The sight of the forest in the reflection left Loren momentarily stunned. Even though she spent every minute of every day surrounded by the magical and the extraordinary, some things never ceased to amaze her.

"Dal," Loren said, shaking her head to clear it. Dallas had almost made it to the mirror when Loren hurried forward and caught her by the wrist. "Did you hear what Professor Phipps said?"

Dallas whirled around to face her. "About what?" Her eyes were as hard as the spotless glass at her back.

Loren dropped Dallas's wrist like she'd been zapped. "About the Phoenix Head Society."

"What about it?"

Loren blinked. "Didn't you notice that the Darkslayer who took Sabrine had a phoenix tattoo?"

"So?" She crossed her arms and tipped her weight to one muscled leg. "Don't all Darkslayers have the symbol of their circle tattooed on them?"

"That's the thing." Frustration edged Loren's tone. "There *is* no circle of Darkslayers with a phoenix head as their symbol."

Dallas's mouth was set in a thin, bloodless line. "Don't read into it too much, Lor. I wouldn't want to get my hopes up if I were you."

Loren felt like ripping out her hair. They were sisters, yet Dallas had a nasty habit of doubting her. Loren sometimes thought the armor Dallas wore was thicker than her own.

"I'm getting into that building," Loren gritted out, her fingers curling into fists. "Whether you're willing to help me or not."

Dallas's expression revealed nothing. Students began to emerge from the mirror, carrying grimoires and magic staves.

"Come on," Dallas said, her tone as cold and emotionless as her face. "We need to unpack our bags or we're going to be late for our first class."

5

Clear blue skies greeted Loren early Saturday morning. As she walked through the gates of the academy, hugging the stack of posters she'd printed out in the library on campus, the magical barrier shivered over her skin, sending a chill from the crown of her head to the balls of her feet.

Her shift at the Mortar and Pestle was to start in roughly an hour. Located in the northern end of the downtown core, the Avenue of the Scarlet Star was about a thirty-minute walk from the academy. Although taxis were plentiful during the day, they could be quite expensive due to how long they might idle in traffic. Besides that, Loren figured the long walk would do her some good. It was an opportunity to be alone with her thoughts, to not have to force herself to listen if someone were to speak to her. These days, she didn't listen to much at all, including her lessons.

The rest of the week had passed by in a blur. Neither she nor Dallas had mentioned Sabrine since that first day of school. In fact, they'd hardly spoken to each other at all. And despite that Loren had vowed to get into the Old Hall even if it killed her, her reluctance had stopped her from bringing it up to Dallas again. Though it killed her to wonder what it all meant—if the secret society was connected to the Darkslayer who'd taken Sabrine.

With a deep breath, Loren set off, heading for the long road that swept downhill and into the city. Blue jacaranda petals drifted down the sidewalk and spun around her wedge heels.

Near the curb that looped around the cul-de-sac sat a sportscar as fierce in appearance as it was sleek, with glossy paint as black as its rims. A stupidly expensive model seldom seen on the streets, even here in the glitzy North End. It was the kind of vehicle that would make Dallas swoon the same way she did over hot, sweaty boys in hot, sweaty sports gear.

Smiling a little despite herself, Loren dug her cell phone out of the pocket of her jeans and snapped a photo of the car. The shutter clicked...and she froze.

There was a silhouette in the driver's seat. The tinted windows were so dark, she hadn't noticed them before.

Loren ducked her head, hiding behind her curtain of hair. She shoved her phone into her pocket, rolled up the sleeves of her red V-neck shirt, and made her way down the road. The sprawling city was glittering beneath the sun, already lively despite the early hour.

The temperature spiked at an alarming speed as she walked, the sun soon baking the asphalt beneath her heels. She stopped along the way to put up the posters, tacking them to telephone poles and transport shelters, among collages of business cards, lost-pet posters, and advertisements for demon pest-removal services.

Above a black-and-white photo of Sabrine, the posters read MISSING in large block letters, and just below the photo was a question: HAVE YOU SEEN THIS GIRL? With every poster Loren put up, the tighter her throat became. She ran out of posters faster than she thought she would, and as soon as she had tacked the last one to a corkboard near the arched doors of The Blood and Burger Pub, she carried on, walking faster now.

Having grown up on the North End, she knew every shortcut to the Avenue of the Scarlet Star, and although she was in no rush today, she chose to take the twisty, narrow alleys that meandered through residential areas in favour of the main arteries that were packed from bumper to bumper with cars.

It was also likely that the residential neighborhoods dotting the North End were concealed with spells that deterred most Dark-slayers—the same spells that covered the Avenue of the Scarlet Star and Angelthene Academy. There weren't many places in the city that could afford to cloak the locations of their residents and visitors so thoroughly; Loren considered herself blessed for being able to spend most of her days at such places.

But there were some Darkslayers who were advanced in their abilities, and who knew how to utilize illegal Stygian salts to fully open the floodgates of their magic and see past the wards on build-ings and vehicles as though they'd never been there to begin with. But she had to try *something*—and walking down the streets that had zero protection wouldn't make her feel any better.

In the trees above an alley that connected one especially ritzy neighborhood to another, the raspy chatter of birds carried through the branches.

Loren looked up, shielding her eyes with a hand as she scanned the sun-bleached sky and the trees.

It was too bright. Laundry and bunches of herbs hanging from a clothesline in a nearby yard fluttered in a stifling breeze.

The chattering of birds grew in volume. From the sounds of it, there were more than she'd initially thought. And when Loren craned her neck back to look again, she spotted magpies huddled on the branches.

The same birds that had been squawking out a death warning the night Sabrine was taken.

Her footsteps slowed to dragging, her heart stopping dead in her chest as an old nursery rhyme clanged through her head.

> One for sorrow,
> Two for mirth
> Three for a funeral,
> Four for birth
> Five for heaven

Six for hell
Seven for the devil, his own self.

She stopped walking, blood rushing in her head. The birds cawed louder, wings rustling.

One, two, three, four, five, six...

There were seven of them. Seven magpies screeching so loudly that she could no longer hear the cars in the distance. The noise clawed at her eardrums until it felt like they were bleeding.

Clapping her hands over her ears, she ran down the alley, her crossbody bag thumping against her hip. She was nearing the end of the alley and the open road beyond when the sight of a familiar black sportscar had her skidding to a halt.

Sweat beaded on her brow as the engine snarled, and the car disappeared behind the hedges framing the mouth of the alley.

The sound of her heartbeat in her ears was like a hammer on cloth. Her mouth was parched, her lungs pinched to half their size.

Behind her, the birds fell silent. She turned to look at them, and four flew away.

That left three. *Three for a funeral.*

That wasn't any better than seven. Seven for the Devil.

With shaking hands, she dug her phone out of her pocket. The numbers were near-illegible in the glaring sun, but after a moment of fierce blinking, she saw that it was quarter to nine. If she didn't start walking again, she wouldn't have time to buy food before starting her shift, which simply wasn't an option for someone like her. Judging from how light her head felt on her shoulders, and the tattoo that was now pulsing in warning, her blood sugar had dipped dangerously low. Not even her medication would make much of a difference at this point; she *needed* to eat something.

Gritting her teeth as she scanned the now-empty road ahead, she damned it all to Ignis's fiery realm and set off again to the Avenue of the Scarlet Star.

6

Around the corner from the Avenue of the Scarlet Star, Darien Cassel kept the engine idling as he leaned on the steering wheel, watching the girl cross the cobblestone street up ahead. The blonde waves that fell to her narrow waist bobbed from side to side, glinting like gold in the sun, the frozen coffee in her hand dripping condensation with each hurried step.

Boasting some of the city's most prized restaurants and shops, the Avenue of the Scarlet Star was a tourist attraction, so only foot traffic was allowed beyond this point. Which was why he'd had no choice but to park this far away; to wait and see where his target would go next. Another line of salts snorted into his system had revealed the auras queueing in the Terra Caffe, where he'd found the girl tapping her foot at the back of the line while waiting for her turn to order.

Now, as he watched her weave her way through the crowded street, he realized how conveniently this had worked out, since he'd unknowingly chosen a parking stall with full view of the girl's last destination.

The cauldron-shaped sign hanging above the chipped door, where the girl now fumbled through the contents of her bag, read

Mordred and Penelope's Mortar and Pestle. It took her a long moment to locate her keys and then the keyhole—a moment that was extremely painful for Darien to watch, her incompetent hands visibly shaking. Once she finally got the door open, she disappeared inside and locked the deadbolt behind her.

Darien slumped in his seat. How had this turned into such a huge pain in his ass? Not only was a university student his target, but she'd just disappeared into her workplace for what he assumed would be the next six to eight hours. As he considered his options, he remembered the magpies that had squawked so loudly he could hear them through his bulletproof windows. Those Star-damned, fucking magpies.

Because of them, his target had managed to get not one, but *two* very good, very long looks at his vehicle. Not only that, but she'd managed to take a *picture* of it. Never in all his years as a Darkslayer had he encountered something so ludicrous. When the girl had dug her phone out of her pocket—out of jeans so tight they were practically painted on—and snapped a photo of his car, she hadn't the slightest idea that he was there because of *her.*

Because of the Stygian salts that had led him from the Temple of the Scarlet Star, where he'd pinned down her aura with the aid of her ancestor's bone powder mixed into the salts, to Angelthene Academy for Magic, the limitless power he'd tunneled into exposing what was hidden beneath layer upon layer of expensive spellwork. He and the other six Devils were the only people in this city who were skilled enough to see a person's aura consistently through almost any spell; it allowed them to rake in bounties at an unprecedented speed that had earned them not just the right to call themselves the *Seven Devils*, but their individual reputations as well.

Those reputations were the reason why everyone was so afraid of them; why they were able to demand such whopping amounts. When a Devil was hunting you, there was nowhere you could hide.

It was an interesting thing, this girl's aura. When he'd first identified it, it was white. *Solid* white, a sign of innocence, healing, and purity—a color mostly seen in children. Which made sense, considering she was an orphan who was abandoned at the temple as a baby, so the aura he'd located within the walls of the temple would've been in its purest form. But when he'd traced it through the city, to Angelthene Academy, he'd discovered that her current aura was almost *exactly* the same as the trace herself as an infant had left behind at the temple.

In the time he'd spent following her since nailing down her location at Angelthene Academy, the only other glow her aura had displayed was rainbow. Another rare emanation found only in people who were attuned with the fifth dimension and were highly optimistic and full of energy.

The targets he'd tracked down over the years...not a single one had emitted a white or rainbow aura. Most were gray or jet-black, or a mess of muddy, diluted colors that signified a troubled individual. But white and rainbow?

He'd never tracked anybody with a white or rainbow aura before.

He wasn't sure what this meant. Which was why he hadn't acted —why he was still sitting in his vehicle, pissing time away as he watched her go about her morning routine as though nothing were amiss.

Darien watched as the lights flickered to life in the apothecary. Another fifteen minutes passed before the girl flipped the sign in the window, the letters now reading OPEN FOR BUSINESS.

As he settled into his seat, he wondered how in the hell he'd managed to get tangled up in something so ridiculous. Auras didn't reveal a person's breed, but she moved as though she were human. He knew it was impossible; no human life could be worth anyone forking over three million gold mynet to possess.

Half-breed—she had to be a half-breed. Though he wasn't sure if her being a half-breed would make this situation any better. If he gave enough of a shit to find out, he would have to get close enough to catch her scent.

Any other place, and he would've done it already—would've separated her scent from those of the other pedestrians. But with the restaurants, stores, and food trucks pumping fragrances and fumes into the air—not to mention the fresh smell of the misting systems cooling the avenue, the reek of the overflowing trash bins in back alleys, and the heady scent of the grape-flavored blunts the teenaged warlocks were smoking on a nearby corner—his senses were a little overwhelmed.

In all honesty, he shouldn't care what the girl's scent might tell him. Shouldn't give a flying fuck.

He shook his head. "What a load of horseshit," he muttered.

And then he leaned back against the headrest, closed his eyes, and waited.

———

THREE HOURS LATER, the avenue was crowded. Most of the red-brick shops lining either side of it were tailored to pure-blooded witches and warlocks, though vampires, werewolves, and even humans could be seen making their way down the bustling street.

It was half past twelve when the door to Mordred and Penelope's swung open. Since the moment the girl had displayed the OPEN sign in the window, countless customers had entered and left with paper bags stuffed with magical paraphernalia, the odd person carrying out armfuls of potted plants. Considering the apothecary's steady foot traffic, Darien was beginning to wonder if the girl would even bother stopping for lunch, when a familiar head of golden-blonde hair finally poked out the door.

Her eyes scanned the avenue, never once landing on his car that was concealed behind groups of tourists, high school students, and businesspersons.

Once she decided it was safe to venture beyond the threshold, she locked the door behind her and tacked a handwritten sign to its worn surface. The distance did nothing to mar Darien's hellseher eyesight—sharp as an eagle's—as he read the girl's loopy scrawl.

CLOSED FOR LUNCH. WILL RETURN AT HALF PAST.

He watched her disappear down the street, her small stature quickly swallowed up by the throngs of people.

Darien flicked open the glovebox and retrieved a semi-automatic pistol. He ejected the magazine, ripped open a new box of cartridges with his teeth, and loaded it with ammunition.

The pistol would probably be a waste, considering how young and strangely *normal* this girl appeared to be. Usually, he was approached with jobs to hunt down criminals or demons—not girls that had barely entered post-secondary school. There was a reason they were called *Darkslayers*; they didn't hunt or kill good people, innocent people—and they were rarely asked to, most of their targets having done something bad enough to warrant the price stamped on their foreheads.

The simple fact that he was on the Avenue of the Scarlet Star was a joke. This was a place for families; for men with pockets deeper than their minds to take their trophy wives out for stupidly expensive lunches. Even the ground here was cleaner than the floor of his car.

He almost laughed. Almost said 'fuck it' and drove away. Were the other Devils playing some sort of joke on him, and this wasn't a real job?

But he found himself hesitating; found himself looking toward the street, where he could no longer see the girl, nor her aura, but knew she'd be waiting in line for food somewhere.

There had to be an explanation for this. Although everything about her screamed that she was human, it was impossible.

No—there was simply no way. Absolutely *no* way she was just human. And he wasn't about to pass up three million gold mynet over feeling sorry for her. Fuck that.

He slapped the magazine into place with the heel of his hand, tucked the pistol into the concealed holster at the front of his black cargo pants, and set off after her.

LOREN TAPPED her foot as she waited in line at a sandwich cart across the street from Mordred and Penelope's. She hadn't stopped looking over her shoulder all morning, and every time the bells

50

hanging from the apothecary door had chimed, her heart had nearly jumped out of her chest.

She blamed the magpies. The stupid birds had heralded both her death and the devil, and although nothing sinister had come for her yet, she couldn't relax. Some people claimed it was only a silly nursery rhyme, but she'd heard enough stories in her lifetime to suggest the words held some truth.

Dallas probably would've laughed at her for overreacting. But Dallas wasn't here right now, and after Sabrine's disappearance — and the little fact that hadn't slipped Loren's mind, about the Dark-slayer demanding that *she* get in his car, not Sab or Dallas — Loren refused to rule out anything that might alert her to coming dangers.

The line for the sandwich cart moved at a snail's pace, and Loren began to sweat under the glare of the midday sun. The weather had been terribly unpredictable lately, the forecasters even more so. It seemed that jeans and three-quarter-sleeved shirts weren't an option quite yet.

The line shuffled forward, and when she finally made it to the front, she ordered a turkey panini with mustard and extra pickles. She was handing over a crumpled banknote when something compelled her to look over her shoulder.

As she scanned the crowds behind her, her gaze snagged on two figures standing on either side of the apothecary door.

Was it her imagination, or were they watching her?

The sweaty man operating the sandwich cart called her back to attention, shaking her change in her face.

"Keep it," she told him. She turned again to look at the pair standing by the apothecary — a blond middle-aged man and a woman with hair shorn to her scalp.

They were still watching her.

The owner of the sandwich cart began to make her panini, so she stepped out of line. As the seconds ticked by, she kept an eye on those black-clad figures.

Barely two minutes passed before they shrugged away from the brick wall of the apothecary and began making a beeline through the crowd — a beeline that would lead them straight to her.

She considered screaming for help, but she was no stranger to the news channel. She had seen horrifying stories on there that involved innocent civilians slaughtered at the hands of armed robbers and Darkslayers after stepping in to help one another. The immortal leaders of the organized crime groups that ruled from Angelthene's underbelly were so powerful, they often couldn't be stopped — not even by magic.

And unless she wanted to live the rest of her life with blood on her hands for involving innocent passerby, she would have to handle these people on her own.

Loren lowered her gaze, desperately wishing she wasn't wearing these blasted heels, and disappeared into the crowd. The man who'd shaken her change in her face shouted that she forgot her sandwich.

She kept walking, deep into the throng of people. Water from the misting systems lining the restaurant patios cooled her sunburned face. The cooler temperature provided a brief respite from the heat but did nothing to ease the tightness in her chest. The hot air was laden with the scents of sizzling onions, deep-fried pickle spears, and mini doughnuts dusted with icing sugar, all cooked in the restaurants and on the grills in the mobile food trucks that were parked along the avenue.

A glance over her shoulder said she seemed to have lost her trackers. But there were so many people milling about that she couldn't be sure.

When she turned back around to continue, she found two other people — two males old enough to be her father — converging from opposite sides of the avenue. Their eyes never left her face. Their lips were moving, as if they were communicating to each other through wireless headsets. And the tattoos on the sides of their necks...

Phoenix heads.

"Shit." Her heart was in her throat, and her mind spun as she debated what to do.

There was an alley up ahead that cut between the Salted Caramel Ice Cream Parlor and Medea's Magic Tricks, just to the right of the white marble sundial — built hundreds of years ago out of respect for Tempus the Liar, God of Time.

She darted for the shadows between those two crooked build-ings, being careful as she edged around the sundial that spanned nearly the entire width of the Avenue of the Scarlet Star. At the end of the alley, half-starved cats rummaged in an overturned trashcan, the sour odor of fish and spoiled food permeating the air. There was no one down here, and it took her half a second to realize it was a dead end.

With shaking hands, she dug her phone out of her pocket and punched in the emergency number so hard, her nails almost broke. Her legs wobbled as she looked over her shoulder at the bustling avenue, her hair catching in the necklace she always wore.

Her trackers were nowhere to be seen—for a moment, at least. One blessed moment.

A voice picked up after one ring. "Angelthene Rescue—"

"I need help," she croaked.

"I'm going to need your location and what the situation is."

The Avenue of the Scarlet Star, she tried to say.

But an arm wrapped around her throat from behind, and the cold muzzle of a gun pressed against her temple.

The line crackled as her phone slipped through her fingers. It struck the cobbles, screen instantly cracking. "Miss—" But that was all she heard of the officer on the other end.

She stopped breathing. The walls of the businesses on either side of the alley shimmered and lurched as a low and lethal male voice hissed in her ear, "Make one sound and you die."

"YOU'RE COMING WITH ME," said the voice, every word he spoke rich and deep. The male was so close to Loren that her hair fluttered with his steady breathing, the shell of her ear grazed with every exhalation. "You're not going to fight me, and you're not going to make any indication that you are being taken against your will. Do we have an understanding?"

Loren's knees were quivering so badly, she wondered how it was possible that she was still on her feet. Maybe it was because the man

53

holding her hostage had her pinned against his hard chest, his arm wrapped firmly around her throat. The gun at her temple hadn't budged—and Loren still wasn't breathing.

She tried to speak, tried to give him an answer. But she couldn't find her voice.

"Do we or do we not have an understanding?" He gave her a warning shake, the muzzle of the gun digging into her temple hard enough to bruise.

Loren whimpered but managed to dip her head in a single nod.

And then...she thought of something.

"I'll come with you without a fight," she began in a strangled voice. Her lips were shaking, and her heart was punching a hole through her chest. "But only if you promise me that my friend, Sabrine Van Arsdell, will walk free."

A pause. "What are you talking about?"

Loren blinked fiercely against the gray clouding her vision. Just beyond the mouth of the alley—empty apart from herself and the man holding her at gun-point—people milled about the sunlit avenue, laughing, chatting, and sipping on smoothies and frozen coffees, entirely unaware of what was taking place in the cool shadows only steps away.

And within the crowd, she spotted those four black-clad figures —the woman with hair shorn to her scalp and the three men who were all old enough to be her father—scanning the faces of the people they passed. Looking for her. As if this could get any worse than having one gun pointed at her head.

But the arm around her throat stiffened. As if he noticed them, too.

As if he hadn't known they were here.

"You bleed gold or something, girl? Why are those fuckers looking for you?" Loren's mind reeled; she'd assumed that every person who was looking for her today was working as a group, including this one. And if they weren't, then that meant...

What *did* it mean? She couldn't think. Couldn't—

"What the *fuck* are you, girl?" he barked, the volume of his voice hurting her ear. "Answer me."

"I don't know, *I don't know!*" It was the first time she had ever wondered if she was as human as she thought. Her throat burned as a sob clawed its way out. "My friend was taken last week by another Darkslayer who wanted me instead. He tried to get me to go with them, but peace officers showed up—"

"Who was it? The Darkslayer who attacked you—which circle did he belong to?"

She couldn't move her tongue, couldn't bring herself to answer.

He tightened his hold on her throat, his leather gloves hot on her skin. "Which bloody circle, *girl?*"

"I don't know!" she cried, every word a sob.

The four figures in the crowd began pushing their way toward the alley, and Loren felt the blood in her head—what was left of it—drain down to her feet.

The man holding her at gunpoint spun her around to face him so quickly, she teetered in her heels, nearly pitching face-first onto the cobbles.

She lifted her gaze to his face—

Her mouth literally fell open at the sight of him.

He was only a few years her senior—twenty-three or maybe twenty-four by the looks of him, though immortality made it a challenge to accurately determine a person's age. Loren made a point to memorize anything about him that stood out, in case she managed to get away, but she found herself staring at him like an idiot for a much longer length of time than necessary, drinking him in feature by feature, and realizing with each passing second that *everything* about him stood out.

His hair was jet-black and shorter on the sides than the top, the strands slicked back from a face as striking as it was lethal. His mouth was well formed, his jawline strong. He had a straight nose that had clearly never been broken before, which was rare for someone of his...expertise. Loren imagined that if she could see his hands beneath his gloves, there would be enough evidence there to suggest he was the one who got most of the hitting in during a fight.

Perhaps his most striking feature was his eyes. A steel-blue she'd never seen before, made brighter by the way they contrasted with his suntanned skin. Those eyes—whites and all—were swallowed up by the black of the Sight as he swiftly scanned her aura. Towering well over six feet in height, he was all muscle and raw masculinity, his broad shoulders and biceps straining against the worn leather of the black jacket he wore, the material embroidered here and there with patches of symbols and words that belonged to a dead language. The zipper on his jacket was down just far enough to show the three silver pendants he wore around his neck: one a religious symbol, another a protection charm, and the third a wing-shaped locket.

Loren had never picked up a paintbrush in all her life, but for one terrifying second she found herself wanting to capture this moment on paper and trap it under glass.

Had she the chance, she would've called the painting: *Devil—King of the Wicked and the Damned*.

And when she took note of the tattoo below the hellseher's right ear—a tattoo of a horned letter *S* in the gothic script of an ancient world—she realized there would be no escaping this. No escaping *him*.

Because not only was this man a Darkslayer—he was one of the Seven Devils. An elite unit of bounty hunting hellsehers known and feared by all of Terra. They had killed, cheated, and clawed their way to the top of an unjust hierarchy, where humans were no better than fodder, and the Terran Imperator ruled from its peak with an iron fist. Needless to say, the Devils and their kingpin Randal Slade held firmly to their place on the pyramid somewhere just below the imperator himself.

"I don't believe it," the Devil murmured, nostrils flaring wide. "You're human."

Still holding onto her with one hand, the other now pointing the gun below her jaw, the slayer scanned her—the skin-tight clothes that hid nothing—and then went for her crossbody bag.

"I don't have anything." She blinked against the spots of color drifting across her vision. The spots that were making it a challenge to see his face, no matter the fact that he was mere inches away from her. He'd already unzipped her bag and, judging from his unchanging expression as he rifled through the contents, he wasn't

surprised to find that his Sight hadn't lied—she had no magical artifact on her, nothing more valuable than gum and lip-gloss.

Still, she found it necessary to voice the obvious as she went on
to say, her tone one of panic, "There's nothing on me that's valuable
—and I'm *human*. I swear to the gods I'm human. And I don't know
how or why, but *I'm* what you're looking. *I'm* what you want!" It
wasn't the smartest thing to say, and she figured she had just
declared herself to the universe as the next missing person, when he
froze.

He dropped her bag and straightened. Loren didn't dare breathe
as he scanned the alley behind her with the kind of lethal expertise
that only a man ripped from the womb of the underworld would
possess. Footsteps echoed against the brick walls of the businesses
on either side of them.

Four sets of footsteps.

One of the men in the group of four spoke. "Out of the way,
Devil." There was the click of a gun's safety springing free. "Or we'll
have to kill you."

Steel-blue eyes met her own. And somehow, despite the threat
made on his life—and despite that he was outnumbered four to one
—there was no fear in those eyes. And when he spoke, it wasn't to
the four people behind her who were now cocking their guns and
taking aim.

It was to *her*.

"When it starts, get up against the wall and cover your head.
Don't move and don't scream, or I'll kill you." Those eyes flicked
again to the people she knew were only a few steps away—with
more guns pointed at them than the single pistol the Darkslayer
before her held casually at his side, as if it was more a paintbrush
than a killing tool, as if—

As if he didn't need a weapon.

As if he didn't have four pistols aimed at his head.

Loren barely had a chance to process his words before he opened
fire on the figures blocking the mouth of the alley.

7

They didn't stand a chance.

The Devil moved so swiftly, not one of them got in a single shot. And his pistol was so silent, no one in the avenue beyond had a clue what was happening as bullets burrowed into skulls.

Loren didn't heed his advice. As soon as the fourth gunman crumpled to the ground in a pool of blood, she pushed away from where she was huddled against the wall, snatched up her phone, and sprinted for the mouth of the alley—for the safety of the crowd that lay just beyond the cool shade. Somehow, the clack of her heels was louder than any of those gunshots.

She'd almost cleared the alley when she slowed.

The Devil wasn't coming after her.

And she might've been the biggest idiot in all of Terra, but she lurched to a stop, took a deep breath, and slowly...*slowly*...turned around to face him.

He was tucking his pistol into a concealed holster at the front of his black cargo pants, entirely unaffected by the corpses littering the alley at his boots, their lifeblood trickling between the cobblestones.

Four corpses whose necks were marked with matching tattoos of a phoenix head.

Loren waited, hooking her fingers together, as he casually peeled off his black gloves and stuffed them into one of the many pockets in his black jacket. Black upon black upon black.

His intense eyes met hers—and narrowed. "You moved."

"And you didn't kill me." Her voice was so hoarse, she barely recognized it.

"I was waiting for you to start screaming." His expression was serious, but she had a feeling he was making some sick joke.

"Lucky for me that I only moved, then."

A smile teased one side of his sculptured mouth. "Lucky for you," he agreed.

She studied him; the tattooed hands hanging casually at his sides, the mark of the Devils below his ear, the combat boots spattered with blood.

"Why?" She knew he understood what she was asking: why hadn't he killed her yet?

"It seems my client failed to mention one minor detail." She waited, and after a moment he told her, "Nobody said anything to me about a human girl."

Interesting, Loren thought. Was it possible that this soulless killer somehow pitied her? Or was she about to do something extremely reckless?

She blurted, "Did you want to sit down somewhere?" The question had left her mouth before she realized what she was asking him. But he hadn't killed her—*yet.* Instead, he'd killed the people who were after her. And although he, too, had tracked her here, he'd given her a chance to speak—to explain herself. And he hadn't chased her when she ran.

Perhaps she could give him a few minutes of her time. And provided she didn't leave the avenue with him, she supposed it wouldn't hurt.

Hopefully.

The world she'd been born into was a world of wolves, and it didn't take kindly to lambs like her. To survive it, you either had to become a wolf...or make friends with one. She knew she didn't have it in her to become a wolf, so she would have to try for the latter. Though *friend* was the last thing she would expect to call this man.

"You look like you're going to faint," the Devil noted, that intimidating gaze roving over her features. "Know any good restaurants around here?"

What kind of question is that? she wondered. But then she remembered who she was talking to. Someone like him was more likely to frequent the seedier parts of town than a flawless tourist destination. By choice, of course—and certainly not because he couldn't afford it.

"Only all of them," she replied with a careful smile he didn't return. She gestured to the busy street behind her. "We're on the Avenue of the Scarlet Star."

AT A BOOTH in a private corner of Rook and Redding's Restaurant and Bar, Darien leaned back against the button-tufted backrest and studied the girl sitting across from him. She hadn't looked up from her menu for the past five minutes, and not a single word had left her mouth since they'd come to the agreement to sit down at this restaurant.

He wondered if she was regretting this—if she realized how foolish she was for choosing to trust him. Judging from the way her body was angled toward the doors, complete with her toes—her manicured nails painted hot-pink—pointing to the street beyond, he wouldn't be surprised if she ran out of here screaming at any second.

"Are you just going to keep staring at me all day?" the girl said, her soft voice wavering. "Or are you going to decide what you want to eat?" Her hands were clasped in her lap, and her eyes were fixed on the open menu on the table before her, lashes fanning out over her sunburned cheeks.

Darien leaned forward, cupped a hand over his mouth, and pretended to read the lunch options. Out of the corner of his eye, he saw her peek up at him to make sure he wasn't looking at her anymore.

After a moment, he grew tired of pretending to peruse the menu and slapped the cover shut. "Have *you* decided?" he countered.

She closed hers as well, the motion sending a puff of air across the table. Her bouquet—a characteristic scent every person had, fully identifiable only by someone with an immortal's sense of smell—was an intoxicating blend of juicy peaches and just-rained-on honeysuckle, with a faint hint of cedar smoke. "I think so."

A venefica waitress came up to the table with two glasses of ice water and the cherry cola the girl had ordered. The waitress produced a pen and a pad of paper from the pocket of her smock and asked to take their orders.

Darien waved a hand at the human sitting across from him, prompting her to go first.

"I'll have the pumpkin soup." She said it like a question, her voice small and trembling, and then added in a voice that was somehow even smaller, "And the salmon crostini to start."

The waitress faced Darien with reluctance. "And for you?"

"Nothing for me, but thank you," he replied without looking at her.

The waitress gathered up their menus and left.

The girl took a long drink of her cola and shivered, the blonde hairs on her slender arms rising from the icy temperature. "Aren't you hungry?"

He shook his head.

They sat in silence for a while. She tapped her foot beneath the table, making a point not to look at him as her big, ocean-blue eyes thoroughly scanned everything there was to see in the restaurant, no matter how insignificant the item or person. The saltshaker, the hanging light fixtures, a tear in the flecked carpet, the other diners who occasionally snuck concerned and curious glances at their table, the worn bar hugging the east wall, the doors that opened and closed as people left and entered.

The vinyl of the cushioned bench beneath him crackled as Darien leaned forward and folded his arms on the table. "You got a name?"

She finally met his gaze, though she set about fiddling with the hem of the red shirt that hugged her flat stomach. "Loren." Her voice was barely a croak. "Loren Calla."

"Is that a real name or a fake one?"

"Real." She forgot about her shirt and began twirling the straw in her soda, ice cubes tinkling against the glass. "I figured you probably know enough about me that it's pointless to lie."

"Wrong," he said. She quirked an eyebrow. "When my client offered me this job, they didn't give me your name—only the bone powder belonging to one of your ancestors. I was asked to track you via aura. And when I track auras, I don't bother with details such as names. I don't even bother with breed, so when I found you in the alley and saw that you were human, I realized there's more to this than I thought."

"It didn't seem like my being human would've been a problem for those other Darkslayers." She shuddered almost imperceptibly. He wondered what it had felt like for her, coming so close to death. For humans, life was fleeting.

"Mmhmm," he murmured.

"Who do you think those people worked for?" As she twiddled her straw, she kept her focus on the bubbles in her cola as they drifted to the surface, where they gathered to fizz in the warm lamplight before popping. "Their symbol wasn't any I've heard of or seen before."

He made another sound of agreement in his throat, though this one was edged with annoyance. "That's a question I don't have the answer to yet." Being in the dark wasn't something he was used to, nor was it something he cared to admit.

The girl took another sip of her cola, her eyes still downcast. "The Darkslayer who took my friend...he had the same tattoo."

"Did you happen to notice anything else about him?"

"Nothing that really stood out. He was half-hellseher, half-warlock. Blond hair; silver-green eyes..." She looked at him for half a second. "A bit shorter than you."

"Doesn't bring anyone to mind." He frowned. "You're sure it was the same tattoo?"

She surprised him by rolling her eyes. "Don't doubt me so soon. The peace officers gave me enough trouble last week."

That made him crack a smile. "Let me guess. You tried to tell them the Darkslayer was after you and not your friend, and they didn't believe you."

"Bull's eye."

He gave a snort and settled back into the booth. The cushion was hard and uncomfortable as fuck. "Figures."

She shrugged and went back to pushing the ice around with her straw. "I'm human. I suppose I should be used to it by now."

"Ridicule is something no one should tolerate."

"Easy for a six-foot-five bounty hunter to say."

He felt the corners of his mouth twitch upward. "Six-four."

A smile played on her lips. She forgot about her straw and leaned forward, her mass of blonde waves slipping over a shoulder. The motion caused her peaches-and-honeysuckle scent to drift across the table, and Darien found himself breathing it in. "You're one of the Seven Devils." She studied his face for longer than she usually dared. He had to admit, there were men who would give their eyeteeth for someone who looked like her. "The only question is which one."

Darien waited while she thought about it, her eyes searching for hints in his features. It was impressive: the amount of time she managed to look at him without breaking his gaze.

"At first, I thought you were Travis Devlin, but..." She bit her bottom lip, squinting her eyes in thought. Travis was Darien's younger cousin. *The Devlin Devil,* he was called. They'd been mistaken for one another a few times. "Something tells me you're Darien Cassel."

A smile curved his mouth. "What gave it away?"

"Nothing, really." She shrugged, looking a little proud of herself. "Intuition, I suppose."

The waitress returned with a tray bearing food, the dishes rattling from how hard her hands were shaking. Darien was surprised she somehow managed not to spill Loren's soup as she slid the bowl before her, then placed the salmon crostini in the center of the table. After asking if she could bring them anything else, she looked relieved when they said no, and scampered away.

Loren picked up her spoon and tucked into the soup. "Please, help yourself." She gestured to the crostini. "There's no way I can eat all this."

"I'm not hungry." Returning to their former topic of conversation, he said, "When I'm offered a job, I'm usually the only one on it. The fact that other people have been hiring Darkslayers to find you, or are possibly looking for you themselves, means there's something about you that's highly valuable."

"That's news to me." She blew on another spoonful of soup. "How much were you offered to find me?"

He licked his lips as he considered what the truth might cost him. Those eyes—a darker blue under the warm lamplight, like an ocean rippling beneath a setting sun—met his mouth for a fraction of a second before darting away again. Blush dusted her cheeks, and the spoon wobbled in her hand.

"Two million gold mynet," he told her, stamping down the curiosity he felt from seeing her blush. He didn't know why he was even interested; women became all shades of red around him all the time. "But I negotiated three."

She gave a low whistle, eyes flaring wider as she reached for a crostino. She bit off a corner and chewed. "That's a lot of mynet."

"It is. And considering I'm not the only one who was asked to look for you, I think it's safe to assume that more people will come after you now. And those people won't ask questions like I did— they'll either kill you or dump you in the trunk of their car. Plain and simple."

She set the crostino aside but didn't say anything. Her hands were trembling again.

Darien gave her a chance to compose herself, or perhaps ask him any questions of her own. But she remained silent.

"Do you have any means of protection?" he said. "Any way that you can cloak yourself until you figure out why they're after you?"

Loren looked like she was going to hurl. She didn't answer him, nor did she look at him.

When he spoke again, there was an edge of frustration in his voice that he failed to conceal. "Look, I know you're scared. But I'm trying to help you."

She gave him a hard stare. "In case you haven't noticed, I'm *human*. I have no means of protection and no sum of money large enough that I can call my own. So, *no*, Darien Cassel. I don't have any way that I can cloak the target on my ass while I figure this stupid shit out."

For some reason, despite having known her for barely an hour, he'd assumed she didn't have it in her to curse. He had to admit it impressed him, if only a little.

"Then you're going to need help."

She slowly crossed her arms and then her legs before giving him a cheeky look. "And where do you propose I find it?" That attitude darkened his gaze. She used it often enough that he was beginning to understand it was a weapon for her. Armor—the best armor he supposed a human could have in a city like this.

Drumming his fingers on the tabletop, he considered her question for a moment that probably seemed like a lifetime for her—and he might've taken a few extra seconds simply to see if she had another snarky remark up her sleeve. But she didn't break his gaze as he deliberated. Not even when he said, "I'll help you, if you'll let me."

Surprise flickered across her face, but it was quickly replaced with suspicion. "And how can I trust you? For all I know, you might've killed those people in the alley because you want the reward for yourself."

Caligo spare him. He ran a hand through his hair, and when he set that hand back onto the table a little too hard, the steel devil-head rings he always wore on his index and middle fingers clanged against the wood. "Are we going to disagree now?"

"I'm just saying."

He leveled her with a look. "Do you want my help or not?"

She nibbled on that full bottom lip again. He didn't usually allow himself to become distracted in his work, not even by a pretty face. But this one... He couldn't take his eyes off this one. The City of

Everlasting Hearts was overrun with beautiful people, but immortal women often reminded him of a sculpture. Cold and unchanging in a way that was consistent but uninteresting—and so self-absorbed, they often couldn't hold his interest long enough to convince him they had more than half a brain.

And while she looked exactly like the type of girl he would fuck once and then delete her number from his phone without a second thought, there was something different about her, something that made him unable to look away.

Maybe it was that infuriating attitude.

She still wouldn't answer him. So he said, "Do you want to know what would happen if other Darkslayers walked through those doors right now?" He inclined his head toward the entrance of Rook and Redding's, where a young, very normal-looking couple entered the restaurant in search of a table.

Loren waited.

"I would kill them," Darien stated. She paled a little, her mouth parting in surprise. "Want to know what would happen if they walked through those doors and I wasn't here?" He allowed for a heavy pause before saying, *"You* would be killed. Right here on this hideous rug, best cast scenario. Worst case, you would be dragged someplace else to die a much slower death after they got whatever they want from you."

She suddenly started coughing, smacking her chest as if she'd swallowed her spit the wrong way. A few people at other tables turned around in their seats to stare.

Darien pinched the bridge of his nose. *Fucking hell.* This girl was an accident waiting to happen.

She reached for her cola and took a long drink, her eyes glassy.

"Am I going to need to perform first-aid on you, too," Darien said quietly as people continued to stare, "or can I wait until someone is trying to kill you to do the saving?"

She set down her glass and gave him another of those heavy, irritated looks that border-lined eye-rolling. After a moment, she said of his offer to help her, "What's in it for you?"

It was a good question, he had to admit. "What's in it for me?" he repeated. "I guess I haven't figured that out yet."

She wrung her small hands in her lap. No scars covered her ivory skin; no callouses that might indicate she'd ever held anything more dangerous than textbooks and pencils. All mortals were viewed by the likes of him as something that was easily damaged, easily killed. This girl was clearly someone who needed to be held the same way a person might hold a bird, cupping their hands over them out of fear of breaking their bones.

Why would anyone be after someone so delicate, so...*human?*

Darien learned forward, dipping his head to her level. "Trust, Loren Calla." She did that thing where she peeked up at him from under her thick eyelashes. "It's called *trust.* And I'm asking you to trust me."

It took her a minute to reply, and for those entire sixty seconds, she wouldn't look away from him, as if his soul were an open book and she was leafing through the pages of it.

She drew a deep, rattling breath. And then, very quietly, she told him, "Okay."

8

People stayed out of their way as they wove around tables, toward the arched doors of Rook and Redding's and the bright street beyond. Loren knew it had nothing to do with her and everything to do with the six-foot-four deadly bounty hunter at her side. She wondered idly if anyone else noticed the blood on his combat boots, or if it was just her.

The slayer had stared at her the entire Star-damned time. She'd feared she would choke to death on the crostini, and she hadn't stopped sweating for the full forty-five minutes they spent in the restaurant, despite the air conditioning blowing full blast through the vents. And it wasn't just because he was a cold-blooded killer, though that had quite a lot to do with it.

Darien Cassel was stunning. With numerals of an ancient era inked on his knuckles, and the kind of lethal gaze that could make grown men piss their pants in fear, he had trouble written all over him. But these things didn't stop her from noticing that he had the face of a heartbreaker, with a strong jawline, a sculptured mouth, and eyes such a vivid steel-blue, they seemed to glow in certain light.

And his *voice*… Gods. She wasn't even going to get started on his voice.

He was everything the rumors had claimed, and more.

And he scared the absolute bejesus out of her.

A hot gust of dry air threatened to suck out her eyeballs as they left the restaurant. The streets remained crowded, though people gave them a wide berth as they walked. For a moment, Loren wondered where this bounty hunter had been all her life. He would've come in handy all those times she'd wasted nearly her entire lunch hour standing in line at food carts and cafes.

Red and blue lights flashed in the distance, near the shaded alley between the Salted Caramel Ice Cream Parlor and Medea's Magic Tricks. The law enforcement must've arrived sometime while they were in Rook and Redding's—dining as though they had nothing to do with the dead bodies staining the alley red.

The Devil took hold of Loren's elbow and steered her to the right, away from the peace officers that were monitoring the crowds, and the detectives that worked for the Magical Protections Unit analyzing the scene of the crime. Despite that he'd offered to help her, she had to resist the urge to pull away from him. In her defense, he'd pointed a gun at her head not long before that.

"I need to lie low for a while," he said, keeping his head tilted downward as he walked. As if that would help! The man was practically a death god incarnate. Even so, that striking face and body stuck out worse than the tattoo below his ear. "When do you get off?"

Loren ducked under a mister, the droplets of cold water settling in her hair. "Four thirty."

"I'll meet you around the corner up ahead."

They reached the door to the apothecary, and he released his hold on her elbow as she rummaged around in her bag for her keys. No matter how clean she kept the darn thing, she still managed to lose track of them. Maybe it was time she invested in one of those enchanted keychains that would make it impossible for her to ever lose them.

"Four thirty, sharp," Darien added.

And what if I change my mind? she considered asking.

But by the time she looked up, he was already gone.

THE REST of Loren's shift dragged by at a snail's pace, even with the steady foot traffic.

When the clock began ticking down the last thirty minutes, she called Mordred and Penny. The conjoined witch twins picked up on the third ring, greeting her in unison, as did most people who shared everything below the neck. Loren explained to them, for the first time since beginning her internship, that she needed an extra day off. Tomorrow, to be precise.

They immediately jumped to conclusions, talking over one another into the mouthpiece until Loren could no longer tell who was saying what.

"Are you sick, Loren?"

"Is it the flu?"

"Is it a *boy?*"

"Oh, you're right, Mordred! It's *got* to be a boy."

"You have a *date*, Loren?"

Where she was pacing on the second floor of the apothecary, in the large space that served as both a staff room and an office, Loren shrugged, despite that there was no one around to see.

No one except her brown-and-black shepherd dog named Singer, who she adopted when he was an eight-week-old puppy roughly ten months ago, and who stayed here at the apothecary during the school year. Taega had made herself very clear from the moment Loren had brought Singer home that she was to find a place for him to stay by the summer for ten months out of the year. That woman was the very definition of the word *witch.*

"Yeah, sure." Loren knelt to scratch behind Singer's velvety ears. "A date. I have a date." She rolled her eyes at the ridiculous thought, despite the nerves in the pit of her stomach that compelled her to glance out the window overlooking the front of the store—the space overflowing with sentient plants, cages, and crooked bookshelves—every two seconds. As if she would ever date a bounty hunter! She almost laughed.

A few more nosey questions later, and the witches agreed to give her Sunday off. Which was great, she supposed. As long as the slayer was telling the truth and she wouldn't soon find herself gagged and bound to a chair or six feet under cold dirt.

Four thirty arrived far too soon. She flipped the sign in the window, took a steadying breath, and walked out the door.

The torrid heat of the afternoon was like the inside of an oven; it warmed her skin and turned her tongue as dry as the sunbaked ground beneath her feet. She fumbled with her keys, and when she finally twisted the deadbolt and made her way to the end of the avenue, where Darien had agreed to meet her, her pace slowed to a shuffle, and she nearly turned around.

Was she the biggest idiot in all of Terra? Or was she somehow — impossibly — the smartest? If she'd indeed gained a Devil as an ally, perhaps it was the second. But if she was falling for a trick... If the rumors floating about the streets were true, and he was as ruthless and sadistic as people claimed... Well, she supposed she would soon be in for a real treat.

*But...*if he meant her no harm, then maybe he could help her bring Sabrine back home.

The flashy black car — a mean-looking thing with a streamlined body that hinted at the presence of insane horsepower under the hood — was idling just around the corner. The very same car she had desperately tried to avoid only that morning.

How was it possible that so little time had passed since then?

Loren lifted a hand to block the sunlight reflecting off passing cars and the glass of the transport shelter across the street as she approached the passenger's-side door.

Once she opened it, there would be no going back. But if she didn't get the heck off the street and into the car that she knew was cloaked in magical wards designed to conceal auras, she would soon find herself in a different sort of danger.

She decided to take her chances with Darien Cassel, so she mentally kissed her normal life goodbye and swung open the door.

Darien was talking on the phone, an elbow propped up on his open window. He didn't spare Loren a glance as she got in, her legs like jelly as she collapsed onto the air-conditioned seat. It took her a second to gain the courage to close the door behind her, sealing off a gust of wind that carried the hint of creosote and hot asphalt.

The interior of the car had that fresh-off-the-lot, new-leather smell, with faint undertones of candle smoke and tobacco, and the even fainter hint of a mouth-watering cologne that screamed masculinity and sex appeal.

Darien abruptly ended his call and threw his phone onto the dash. Loren watched with wide, unblinking eyes as he pushed the gearshift into drive, flicked on the turn signal, and studied the reflection of the steady traffic in the wing mirror, never once hitting the button that would lock all the doors and trap her in the car. At least...not *yet*.

"How was your shift?" he said, as if he was picking her up for a date. As if she hadn't been in mortal peril four hours ago and he'd somehow decided it would be worth his time to save her neck instead of killing her himself. She wondered how wealthy he was if he could pass up three million gold mynet as though it were pocket change. The thought wasn't comforting, as it only confirmed her fears that she was walking into a trap, so she blocked it from her mind and forced herself to breathe. *Breathe.*

"Fine." She set her purse on the floor of the car. "Where are you planning on taking me?"

"My house." He pulled out into the street before Loren could object, the sudden acceleration flattening her against the seat.

She fumbled for her seatbelt with shaking hands and buckled it. "I'm guessing that means you're taking me to Hell's Gate." Hell's Gate was the name the underworld had given to the dwelling of the Seven Devils.

"Yes."

Sprawling hotels, fast food restaurants, blood donor clinics, and billboards streaked by her window in blurs of color and light. "And this is going to help me in what way exactly?"

"For one, it's the safest place for you in the whole city." He zipped through the streams of traffic, not seeming to notice that she was holding onto her seatbelt with a white-knuckled grip. Maybe he simply didn't care. "No one with half a brain would set foot on my property. And two, Hell's Gate is protected by the most powerful spellwork in the world. And me and my six Devils are the only people in the city who know how to hack the systems as efficiently as we can."

"I'm assuming this car is equipped with those kinds of spells?"

He nodded once, accelerating to clear a yellow light.

"How did those other bounty hunters track me today, if you and the Devils are the only people who know how to hack magical systems?"

"It's not that they don't know how; they just can't do it as quickly or as effectively as we can. New protection spells are always coming available to the highest bidders at the Umbra Forum, so it can be hard for people to keep up."

He accelerated through another light. A box of ammo that was resting on the dash slid off and clattered to the center console. The lid popped open, and several bullets pinged free, flinging into the cracks between the seats and between Loren's thighs. She didn't bother fishing them out, and Darien didn't seem to notice anyway, continuing talking as though nothing had happened.

"To answer your question," he was saying, "I think they started following you sometime after you left campus and appeared again on the streets."

Cripes, she needed to distract herself from how bloody fast he was driving. The vehicle was weaving through six lanes of rush-hour traffic so quickly, she had no idea how he was managing not to hit anyone.

"So, when I walked off the avenue just now," she gritted out, tearing her wide-eyed gaze from the highway, "is there a chance anyone saw me?"

"Maybe." He gave a shrug of his broad shoulders. "If anyone else was looking for you at that immediate second. But they can't track us now; I upgraded the wards on my car last night."

Loren figured it was some peace of mind, at least.

Darien glanced at the clock on the dash. "I'm taking you to your academy first. I figured you'll need to grab a few things if you're staying at my place."

"I don't think we should go to the academy," she said. Darien looked at her in question. "If Dallas… If my friends see me, they'll wonder where I'm going, and I'd rather not be asked a bunch of questions right now."

"Where to, then?"

She gave him the address to the penthouse. He had to change his course, though only slightly, since Taega's apartment wasn't far from the academy. Loren figured this was her safest option, considering it was more than likely that Dallas's mother wasn't home. Taega spent twelve hours a day training new soldiers of the Aerial Fleet at their headquarters near the Control Tower. As for Roark, better known as the Red Baron, he was currently away for work, as he often was. Loren would be in and out of the penthouse in a matter of five minutes; Taega would never even know she had been there.

Hopefully.

They navigated the streets in silence. Loren had lost herself in her own thoughts, twisting her seatbelt in her hands as though she were wringing water from it, when Darien's voice made her jump.

"Relax, Loren." They were idling at a red light. She wondered how long he had been watching her for. "I'm not going to hurt you, I promise."

"I'm fine," she lied. But her voice was a squeak.

He eyed her up. "You're pale, tense as a tightrope, and I'd be willing to bet you're not breathing properly."

"So, what's my diagnosis?" She'd meant for it to come out funnier than it sounded.

Regardless, he smirked a little. "A bad case of fear."

The light turned green, and they carried on.

When they reached the North End, with its pristine streets and fancy apartments, Darien's scar-flecked hand tensed on the steering wheel. Loren had no idea what his problem was, but she instructed him to turn left into the Santa Aria Flats.

"Were your parents born into cash or are they career driven?" His deep, attractive voice was oddly cold.

Not bothering to enlighten him about her tragic past, she said, "Career driven. Nothing they have was handed to them for free."

She gestured up ahead. "You can park by these hedges here, and I'll run inside. Mine is the apartment building on the left."

Darien did as she'd instructed, then circled back to his earlier question as he shifted into park. "Not like you, then."

Loren froze mid-reach of the door handle. "What's that supposed to mean?"

"It means it must be nice to have everything handed to you by wealthy parents." His tone was as scathing as the accusation behind the words.

Loren's hold tightened on the door handle. She wasn't sure why, but she felt wounded, as if he'd slapped her. And she felt...angry— not just at him, but at *herself* as hot tears sprang to her eyes before she could stop them.

On top of the anger and the hurt, she found herself confused. Clearly, he'd known she was an orphan. Was he so bitter about people who were born into cash that he'd forgotten so easily?

When she spoke, she used a tone as cutting as the one he'd used. "Actually, Darien Cassel, despite what you seem to have concluded about me, I have *not* had everything handed to me. I am a foster child whose adoptive mother hates her, and the only *real* family I can say that I have is my adoptive sister, Dallas."

Darien didn't say anything. He only watched her in silence, his face betraying nothing.

"If my guardians were to die, I wouldn't see a copper of their estate, and to be completely frank with you, I wouldn't want it anyway. I would rather Dallas receive all of it as their rightful heir, and after being treated almost as badly as me by her own flesh and blood." A tear escaped the corner of her eye, and she dashed it away as memories of growing up without a mother and a father seared through her mind. "Are you happy now?"

He broke her heated gaze and glared out the windshield. "No, I'm not." His voice was surprisingly gruff. "I shouldn't have said anything." She supposed it was the closest she would get to an apology.

"You're right, you shouldn't have." Her voice cracked on the last word. She opened her door, a balmy breeze sweeping in and ruffling her hair. "Can we get this over with?"

She didn't bother arguing that he didn't need to come with her as he got out of the car and crossed the street to the apartment. A pink sunset had spread across the hills, reducing the palm trees and cacti in the distance to silhouettes. Luckily, no neighbors were around to witness who was escorting her to the doors.

They made their way into the lobby, where Loren keyed in the passcode for access to the elevator and pressed her hand onto the scanner. As the elevator dinged, the chrome doors sliding open, she wondered how much crap she would get in if Taega found out she'd brought a Darkslayer into her apartment.

9

Darien waited in the living room while Loren packed up whatever belongings she deemed necessary for her stay at Hell's Gate.

He had to admit he felt bad for the assumptions he'd made about her, but as he paced back and forth in the spacious living room, with its immaculate wooden floors and ornate furniture that made it look more like a show-home than a place where actual people lived, he felt hostility simmering in his veins again.

In the heat of the moment, while they were in his car, he'd forgotten all about the fact that she was an orphan. It wasn't the first time his fucked-up past had caused him to do things that made him question his own sanity; he was always so quick to verbally stomp a person into the ground if they'd been dealt a hand of cards better than his own. But doing it to a girl like Loren was a new low for him, he had to admit. He blamed it on sitting in the hot car for too long—and this silk-stocking district that had rubbed him the wrong way ever since he'd lived here as a child, back when his mother was still alive. The people here were so rich, they shit gold and wiped their asses with their unending stacks of banknotes.

It wasn't as if he himself didn't have cash; he had plenty. More than he sometimes knew what to do with. But all of it—everything he owned—was paid for with *blood* mynet. With a life he wasn't proud to call his own. Meanwhile, the swanky couple who fostered Loren probably got up every day and drove to their nine-to-five jobs in fancy office buildings, in their fancy suits, in their fancy cars, and came home every day before sundown with more cash than what he received for a night of slitting throats and paying for it with his own soul. After all the shit he'd been through, he would be surprised if he had a single scrap of soul left.

He ran a hand through the straight locks of his undercut, his rings catching in the hair product he'd slapped into it that morning after a long and tiring night.

In the slit where Loren's closed bedroom door met the floorboards, her shadow flitted back and forth as she packed her things.

Darien stepped up to the console table in the hallway that led to her room. His gaze roved over the assortment of framed pictures dotting its surface, his attention snagging on a head of red-gold hair. With a gloved hand, he picked up the photo for a closer look.

Loren's door swung open. She emerged with a small suitcase in hand, her crossbody bag dangling from her shoulder. Instead of the tight red shirt and the painted-on jeans that left little to the imagination, she wore a blue hoodie that was two sizes too big for her, black leggings, and white sneakers. Despite the obvious contrast to what she had been wearing before, she still managed to make him stare at her like some sort of idiot.

"What?" she demanded.

He gestured to the photo in his hand. "You didn't tell me your guardian was Taega Bright."

"I didn't think it mattered." She pulled the bedroom door shut behind her.

"How did the commander of the Angelthene Fleet end up raising a human girl?"

"Taega didn't really choose to. Actually, she had very little say in the matter. The person who made the decision to take me in was her husband."

Darien cocked an eyebrow. "Really." One of Loren's sloped in

78

answer. "You're telling me the general of all Aerial Fleets in this country decided to take in a human orphan." While the general yielded control of the city's Fleet to Taega in his absence, she still answered to him.

"I guess so." She shrugged. "Nineteen years ago, a priest of the Scarlet Star found a baby on the temple steps with nothing but the blanket she was wrapped in...and this."

She pulled up a solar-shaped amulet from beneath the collar of her hoodie—the Scarlet Star, complete with an engraved face and eight rays, each of those rays representing the common gods and goddesses. Caligo, Tempus, Okapi, Ignis, Mortem, Vita, Sapientia, and Sylvan. The religious symbol Darien wore around his neck was another version of the one Loren wore, though his was fashioned after an ancient piece of art known as the Deity of Eight Faces.

Loren continued, "The priest offered the baby to the general, and Roark—being the religious zealot that he is—took it as a sign from a greater power and declared himself my legal guardian."

"I didn't know the man had it in him." Darien wondered if Taega was the reason Loren didn't share her last name. *Calla,* he remembered her saying, like calla lily. Delicate or wimpy-as-fuck, depending on how a person looked at it. From what he'd heard of Taega, she'd likely been aiming for the latter. "Did he play much of a role in your life after that day?"

"No more than Taega has." A flash of sadness entered her gaze and left so quickly he might've imagined it. After how she'd reacted in his car, he supposed he shouldn't have even asked. After a quiet moment she added, "But I know he loves his daughter, Dallas. He just doesn't show it much."

Darien set down the photo and made his way to the front door. Loren followed him, her suitcase banging into the white sectional as she edged around it.

"So," she said, sneakers squeaking, "what's your story?"

"My story," Darien mused as he swung open the door, "is for another day."

NEVER IN HER wildest dreams would Loren have imagined Hell's Gate could be found on the west side of Angelthene, within the red-brick walls of a wealthy community in the heart of the Victoria Amazonica District.

She watched out her window as homes that gave the penthouse a run for its money passed by in a blur. If it hadn't been Darien Cassel himself who'd brought her here, she might've slapped him for being so rude to her about the luxurious neighborhood she'd grown up in. But her irritation fizzled out as he turned onto a gravel driveway that would take them to their destination.

A wall of red bricks enclosed a sprawling property shaded with fern pines and gardens of pink jasmine. The magic protecting the property sensed Darien's approach, the wrought-iron gates swinging open to permit them entrance.

At the end of the driveway sat a vast, red-brick manor house with abundant windows. White pillars framed either side of arched double doors, and twin statues of winged lions rested on either side of the front steps. The house was at least three stories high and was almost as wide as the Bright apartment building was tall.

Now she *really* felt like slapping him.

But she didn't have time to spend feeling angry, because Darien pulled up to the right of the steps that led to the front door and pushed the gearshift into park.

She was at Hell's Gate. And within a matter of what was possibly minutes, she would have to face more slayers than the single one sitting beside her.

She knew all the Devils by name. Maximus Reacher, Jack Steele, Travis Devlin, Tanner Atlas, Ivyana Cassel, Lace Rivera... and Darien Cassel. At least she could check off one from the list of seven—the worst to boot, which was somewhat of a consolation to her.

And the worst Devil was staring at her again, with those eyes she might've called dreamy had his gaze not scared her shitless every time she caught him looking at her.

"You nervous?"

She snorted. "Why in the name of the Star would I be nervous?"

His mouth twitched with the hint of a smile. He didn't strike her as someone who allowed himself to fully smile very often. "You've got quite the sarcastic personality, haven't you?"

Loren ignored him and stared out at the property. At the fern pines swaying gently, and the silent house with its open shutters and bright windows.

"If it'll help," he said, "I'll have you know that none of them are home." At that, she dared to look at him. Those intense eyes were surveying her with what she thought was perhaps sympathy. She wondered if his hellseher sense of hearing was picking up on every erratic thump of her heart.

How utterly embarrassing.

"Promise?" she whispered.

"Promise." He cracked open his door, and the spice of jasmine flooded the vehicle and stirred his hair. "Though what I *can't* promise is that they won't be back any minute, so it's best if we get you inside and find you a room."

THE HOUSE WAS GORGEOUS.

There wasn't a speck of dust from what she could see. No cobwebs hung in the corners. The air was fresh and slightly sweet, fragranced by the collection of lilacs, lilies, and white roses bursting from a crystal vase on the round glass table in the center of the entrance hall. Beside the vase sat a curved wooden bowl, filled nearly to the brim with silver coins and keys. For a building that housed seven bounty hunters, it was far from what she'd expected.

From what Loren could see, as she lingered near the front doors Darien was currently shutting behind her, there was a sitting room to the left, followed by a dining room and a kitchen thrice the size of the one at the penthouse. To the right appeared to be a library, and from what she had observed of the building from the outside, she would wager that the garage lay somewhere beyond that. And directly across from where she stood was a broad, carpeted staircase that swept up to the next levels.

"You'll be staying on the third floor," Darien said, his voice echoing softly. He gestured for Loren to ascend the stairs. "Come with me."

Loren forced herself to cross the distance to the stairs. Was it just her, or did the floor feel like she was walking on a waterbed? She moved up the stairs slowly, Darien at her left, her legs wobbling so hard she nearly fell. She blamed her nerves on how closely he was watching her, as if every miniscule move she made was interesting to him. And she *did* fall when she got halfway up the stairs, her toe snagging on the slightest wrinkle in the carpet.

Darien caught her by the elbow before she could find out what that carpet tasted like.

Loren's heart was flip-flopping; she wasn't sure if it was from the lingering anticipation of pain or because he was still holding onto her. She cleared her throat and straightened, extracting her elbow from his grip.

"You didn't have to do that," she mumbled.

"What was the alternative, exactly?" He was standing so close to her that she had to resist the urge to back up, to look away from the intense gaze she swore she could *feel*, like a caress on her skin. "Watching you smash up your pretty face on my stairs within minutes of entering my house?" His word choice made her flush from head to toe, and she swore the floor tilted again beneath her feet. She wished she was standing closer to the railing, so she could steady herself by grabbing onto it. It suddenly felt very, very hot in here. Darien continued, "I offered to protect you from danger, and I guess that includes wrinkled carpets now, doesn't it?" The corner of his lips tilted up at one edge.

She started walking up the stairs again, ducking her head so he might not see the splotches of color spreading across her cheeks. "If you insist."

Darien was at her side again in no time, and the tone he used was slightly teasing as he said, "I do."

When they reached the brightly lit third-floor landing, Darien led the way to a guest suite that had its own bathroom. A set of glass-paneled doors led out onto a balcony that overlooked the large back-

CITY OF GODS AND MONSTERS

yard. There was a pond in that yard, along with a firepit shaded with palm trees.

"Does it have its own kitchen, too?" Loren joked about the suite. Despite her attempt at humor, her voice was taut.

But Darien cracked a grin, and it was the closest to a real smile she'd seen on his face.

Not really knowing what to do, she shuffled over to the bed and set down her suitcase and purse among the teal and ivory pillows. Darien stayed just inside the door, watching her far too closely, as usual. As if he was trying to figure her out. Too much of a coward to meet his gaze, she busied herself with sifting through her purse in search of anything to occupy herself with.

But then Darien said, "It might be best if you stay in here until I get back."

Loren forgot all about her need to distract herself. Her head snapped up, and she dropped her purse among the pillows. "Where are you going?"

"Out," was all he said. Considering he'd decided to pass up the mynet tacked to her head, Loren supposed he had to make some cash by running other...*errands*.

She swallowed, feeling a little queasy. "Okay."

"I've let the others know you're here in case they get home before I do. They won't hurt you—I promise." A pause, and then he added, "I should probably tell you we've got a house-Hob living with us. He keeps the house clean, the climate comfortable, and the spellwork up to date."

Loren squirmed, wiping her sweaty palms on her pants. "Does he speak?"

"No. But he likes to bite, and he's got nasty little teeth, so it's best not to acknowledge him." He winked at her and then left without a single word more.

Loren sank onto the soft bed, her knees suddenly weak with the realization of exactly where she was—and exactly which six people were aware that she was in their house. The six people who were bound to come home soon.

Not to mention the household spirit Darien just *had* to bring up.

Because of this, she found herself staring into the shadows of the closet and the unlit fireplace as she listened to the front door slam shut downstairs with Darien's departure. She'd never seen a Hob before, but most texts claimed they were small as toddlers and looked like silhouettes, the same as Familiar Spirits.

As the sky faded from a dull orange glow to a black canvas flecked with stars, she had the same feeling a mouse might get if it scurried straight into a den of snakes without stopping to really think it through.

PART TWO

WORLD OF WOLVES

Welcome to
ANGELTHENE
WE HOPE YOU SURVIVE

10

Three hours passed, and Darien had not returned.

When the slamming of car doors had drifted into the house half an hour ago, Loren had left her suite and crept to a window overlooking the front of the grounds, where she'd seen a gray SUV and a red sportscar parked in the driveway. She'd dashed back to her suite before the people who drove those vehicles had made it into the entrance hall.

Two men and a woman with a sheet of white-blonde hair. That was all she saw of them, though she'd spent the past hour listening to the echo of their voices drifting up from the ground floor. She hoped Darien would return soon. She was growing faint with hunger.

But when another forty minutes passed and there was still no sign of Darien, she couldn't take it any longer. Her face had turned clammy, and her hands were shaking. If she didn't get some food in her, there would be nothing left of her for Darien to find.

That is, if he ever came back.

But he'd said the other Devils wouldn't hurt her. And she continued to tell herself this as she crept to the door, cracked it open, and listened.

It sounded like they were in the kitchen.

Great, she thought with a roll of her eyes. Exactly the room she needed. But she damned it all to hell and made her way for the staircase.

When her socked feet landed on the floor of the entrance hall, and she peeked into the kitchen, she supposed there was one good thing about this situation: no other Devils had come in during this time. Only the three she'd seen earlier stood drinking around the kitchen island, entirely unconcerned with her presence...for now.

She shuffled forward, taking them in as she moved.

The white-blonde female was statuesque, the black bodysuit that covered her from shoulders to toes fitting her figure like a glove. She had a gorgeous face with narrow bone structure, and her lips were painted the same vivid red as her claw-like nails. Nails rumor claimed were sharp as knives—and just as deadly.

The man who wore the brown overcoat—the man closest to Loren—was golden-skinned and incredibly handsome. He had short brown hair and a five o'clock shadow that only seemed to serve the purpose of drawing attention to his full mouth.

The last one was ivory in tone, with dark hair cropped short. He was tall and wiry, with full sleeves of blue ink. His eye color was the same as Darien's, and although he had features that were slightly more boyish, she knew the two were somehow related.

All three of them noticed her simultaneously, their laughter from the joke one of them had made fading into heavy silence. The girl with the white-blonde hair—Lace Rivera, Loren knew—gave her a once-over that felt like acid had been thrown in her face.

Loren gave an awkward wave. "Hi, I'm Loren. Darien said he told you I would be here."

None of them said anything.

She started blabbing. Honestly, she had no idea what the heck came out of her mouth for the next minute, and then she said, "So, I thought I would just come down and introduce myself."

Silence. The clock above the gas stove ticked loudly as the seconds dragged by.

Loren was debating throwing herself off the third-floor veranda when the tan one stepped forward and extended a large hand.

"Maximus Reacher," he said.

Loren nearly wet herself at that name, and she wondered if he noticed how sweaty her hand was as he clasped it. She was shaking hands with Maximus freaking Reacher.

Had the look in his eyes not promised death, his sheer size alone would be enough to convince most people not to challenge him to a fight. There were a few idiots who hadn't heeded that warning, she'd heard, but not one had lived to tell of it—or perhaps simply hadn't wanted to.

Maximus gestured to the other male. "This is Travis Devlin." *The Devlin Devil.* A fan of blades, Travis's kills were rumored to be as brutal as they were bloody. Travis merely nodded once in greeting, not bothering to conceal his frown.

Maximus gestured to the blonde, who was sizing Loren up. "And this is Lace Rivera." As she'd suspected.

"It's nice to meet you all," Loren squeaked.

Maximus made to say something else, but Lace interrupted him.

"What's your name again?" she sneered. *"Lauren,* is it?" Loren crinkled her nose but didn't dare correct her pronunciation as Lace went on to say, "How long have you known Darien?"

Loren swallowed, the sound carrying far. "I met him today."

"And yet you're somehow *here.* At Hell's Gate." The room was so silent, no one seemed to be breathing. Or maybe it was just Loren. "That doesn't happen often. In fact, it hasn't happened *ever.* And yet you're in our home. Walking your scrawny ass around like you own the place."

"Lacey," Maximus warned.

But Lace drew a knife from the wooden block on the counter. And suddenly, there was no air in Loren's lungs, no air in the room. No air in the whole world.

Loren began to back away.

Lace took a step toward her, the heel of her stiletto boot clicking on the floor. "You're not welcome here." She flipped the knife in her hand, the sharp edge of the blade gleaming like a wicked smile. "And as soon as Darien realizes whatever trouble you're causing him isn't worth his time, you'll be cast out. And when that moment comes, you'd better hope I'm not around to see you out the door. Because I, for one, will not tolerate half-life *filth* in my house!"

Lace drove the knife into the counter—into the two-foot-wide section of butcher-block Loren had thought added some nice, rustic charm to the space. The wood swallowed the blade with ease, until only the hilt remained.

Loren felt like she was going to pass out as she watched the hilt vibrate with the force of Lace's blow. Her legs were shaking as badly as that blade.

Maximus gave a low whistle, and Travis chuckled under his breath. "Do you have to be so dramatic?" the latter said.

"Okay." Loren withdrew a step. Lace's fingers twitched at her sides, as if restraining from grabbing the knife again and lunging for her throat. "I can see that I'm not welcome here."

Lace gave her a smug smile. "How very observant of you."

"I'll just...go back upstairs." Loren turned on a heel and hurried for the staircase.

She barely made it up two steps—not quite far enough to drown out their voices—before they spoke again.

"Could it have killed you to be a little nicer?" Maximus whispered.

"She doesn't belong here!" Lace hissed.

Silence. And then Travis said, "She's hot though." He chuckled, and Maximus soon joined in, their laughter fading as Loren reached the third-floor landing.

She barricaded herself in her room, dragging an armchair across the floor so she could prop it up under the door handle. She knew it would do nothing to keep people like them out, but it made her feel a little better as she collapsed on the bed, wrapped her arms around her knees, and cried.

IT WAS ALMOST Witching Hour by the time the snarl of Darien's car carried through the house to where Loren was lying on the bed, cradling her cracked phone in her hands.

She couldn't figure out how to reply to the twelve unanswered messages she'd received, all of which were from Dallas. It killed Loren to know her sister was worried about her, especially after Sabrine's abduction. Dallas had started jumping to conclusions after the sixth message had gone through without a reply.

DALLAS

You're a bitch, you know that?

But seriously, I really am worried about you.

Are you working late at Mordred and Penny's? Should I call them?

Helloooooooo?! Anybody there?

I thought you would've answered by now, considering everything that happened with Sab...

If you don't answer me in ten, I'm calling City Rescue.

Nine minutes had passed since that last message. And as Loren heard the front door open three floors below, she typed up a reply.

LOREN

Hey, Dal. Sorry I took so long to answer you. I'm fine, I promise, so don't freak out!... But I'm staying at someone's house this weekend. It isn't safe to tell you everything over the phone, but I PROMISE I'm fine. You don't need to worry. I'll explain everything when I see you on Monday.

A bubble to indicate that she was typing popped up a second after Loren had sent her message.

DALLAS

You swear you're okay?

LOREN

I promise.

Two minutes passed. And then Dallas said,

DALLAS

Okay.

Not knowing what might happen between now and Monday, Loren typed up one more message—just in case.

LOREN

Love you.

The only words that mattered.

She hit send just as the handle on the door to her suite turned. The feet of the armchair she'd propped up against it groaned across the floor as the door swung open.

The hallway light gleamed off Darien's gelled hair as he appeared in the doorframe, looking somewhat amused by her flimsy attempt at barricading herself inside the room. "What's the chair for?" A smile flirted with his mouth.

"You know damn well what it's for." Although she'd willed her voice to come out strong, it sounded as broken and pathetic as she felt. What an awful week she'd had. "And you might want to consider knocking next time. What would you have done if I had no clothes on or something?"

Amusement danced in his eyes, but he thankfully said nothing regarding the question she'd intended to be rhetorical—the question that had her cheeks blazing with embarrassment. She never kept her stupid mouth shut when it mattered.

Darien's gaze swept over her gray cotton pajama set. Screen-printed overtop each of her breasts was a halved avocado, and across the butt in block letters read the phrase *Kiss My Hass*—last year's Yuletide present from the pun-loving Dallas. Before Loren could whip her phone at Darien's face for allowing his gaze to linger too long on her breasts—her *braless* breasts—she realized what he was really staring at was the arm that was slung across her midsection.

And the serpent-entwined rod on the inside of her left forearm— burning the steady vermilion of a medical emergency, the glow reflecting on the screen-printed avocados.

He frowned. "Did you leave this room at all while I was gone?"

"Sort of," she mumbled, shifting her arms to cover her chest anyway. "I mean, if you can count the three minutes it took for your cohorts to let me know I'm not welcome here."

She was surprised to see a glint of anger in his eyes. "What did they do?"

"I got hungry, so I thought I would find something to eat. I introduced myself, and your girlfriend let me know what she thought of me with a few unkind words and a steak knife."

Darien leaned against the doorjamb. "Lace?"

Loren nodded once.

"Lace isn't my girlfriend, but that's beside the point. She threatened you?"

Loren chewed on her pinkie nail. "Doesn't matter. But if you call attacking the kitchen counter *threatening me,* then yeah."

His mouth became a thin line. "I take it you didn't get anything to eat."

"Nope." She made a popping sound on the *p.*

Darien jerked his chin toward the hallway in a gesture for her to follow him. "Come on. You must be starving."

"I'm not hungry anymore," she lied. But the look he gave her was threatening enough that she relented with a sigh and made her way to the door.

II

Maximus, Lace, and Travis were still in the kitchen when Loren trailed Darien into the room. His combat boots thumped on the floor as he strode to the island where the trio stood talking. Empty beer bottles and takeout containers littered the quartz countertop.

As soon as they caught sight of Darien—and the human girl on his heels—they fell silent. None of them made eye contact with him or with each other as he stalked up to the island, shrugged out of his jacket, and tossed it onto a bar stool. He pushed the sleeves of his dark grey shirt partway up his muscled forearms and braced his hands apart on the counter as he looked them over, one by one.

Loren stopped several feet away, near the dining room table that had an extraordinary piece of art burned into its surface—a giant winged devil hovering over the city of Angelthene—and gulped.

"Loren told me she came down and met you guys while I was out." The only one who dared to meet Darien's gaze for more than a fraction of a second was Maximus. "What she also told me is that you were all very welcoming of her. Which is the kind of thing I've come to expect from my Devils, especially after I told you that she would be here this weekend. And *especially* after I made myself perfectly clear that you were not to frighten her. That you were to make her feel welcome for as long as I say." Not even Max met his gaze now.

Darien shoved away from the counter and stalked up to Lace. Her white throat bobbed at his approach. On his way toward her, he took hold of the knife that was still embedded in the cutting block and drew it out with impressive ease, as if it had been stuck in a pat of butter. He didn't stop walking until barely an inch separated him from Lace. The blonde Devil wouldn't meet his eyes as he looked down his nose at her.

"Now, I wish that what I just said was the truth." His voice was lethally quiet. "But instead, you all decided to ignore my orders and treat her however the fuck you wanted."

The ticking of the clock was loud again. Loren felt her shoulders curling inward, despite that she wasn't the one being scolded.

This time, Darien's words were meant for Lace only. "Who brought you here?"

"You." She still wouldn't look at him.

"And who has the power to remove you from Hell's Gate?"

"You," she repeated, her voice like the squeak of a mouse.

"If you so much as consider ignoring my orders again, you'll find your shit on the curb. Do I make myself clear?"

Lace nodded, her pulse thrumming in her neck.

Darien turned to assess Maximus and Travis. "That goes for you two as well. Any questions?"

Travis raised a tattooed hand, and Darien prompted him with a sharp nod. "What does Randal think of this?"

"Randal doesn't have a clue about this and he's not going to. This is *my* business, not his. And if any one of you lets the pussy out of the fucking bag, you will answer to me. Understood?"

They all murmured in affirmation.

"Good." He slid the knife back into the block and waved in dismissal. "Now clear out."

The others were already making their way for the stairs long before Darien had finished speaking.

Loren staggered to the nearest bar stool—the one with Darien's jacket draped over the back of it—and lowered herself onto the seat. Her vision was beginning to cloud over.

"You're shaking," Darien accused.

"I have problems with my blood sugar." The threats he'd made to his slayers hadn't helped with how she was feeling, but he didn't need to know that. Although there was a chance that she might pass out at any second, so maybe it wouldn't be the worst idea if he *did* know... "I've had testing done, but the doctors can't figure out what's wrong with me."

His eyes flashed to the glowing medical symbol on her arm. It was so warm, it nearly burned her. "What will help?"

"Some crackers, if you have any." She swallowed the lump in her throat. "And juice."

Darien rifled through the dark wood cupboards until he found some salted crackers. He set the box before her, along with a glass of fruit juice. She ate in silence for a few minutes, no sound to be heard but the ticking of the clock and the humming of the refrigerator—and her own chewing that she was far too aware of. Her mouth was so dry, the crackers felt like paste on her tongue.

As if noticing how uncomfortable she was with being watched, Darien began opening drawers and cupboards and sifting through the contents. "What do you want for real food?"

"You don't have to make me anything."

But he only repeated, "What do you want for real food?"

The crackers scraped her throat as she swallowed another mouthful. "Surprise me."

Loren finished off one sleeve of crackers and a second glass of juice as Darien went on to cook a full meal in a shorter amount of time than she thought possible. The aroma of garlic and parmesan made her stomach growl, regardless that she'd just scared back two-dozen-or-so crackers.

When he was finished, he set a bowl of pasta with chicken in front of her, stuck a fork in it, and said, "Eat." He watched as she twirled a few noodles around her fork, blew on them, and popped them into her mouth.

Holy *hell*, he could cook. The mix of flavors was out of this world, and she found herself already desiring seconds.

"Bounty hunter and chef," she mused. "I have to admit I'm impressed. Who taught you how to cook like this?"

"I taught myself." He returned to the stove to clean up. "That's what happens when you grow up without a father who gives enough of a shit to show you how to do simple things, like cook." There was zero emotion in his voice. And the reason Loren didn't question him about it was because she knew how it felt to be grilled about her past. And even though he'd done that very thing to her several hours ago, she didn't like the idea of doing it to him.

Darien cleaned up the kitchen in all of five minutes, and then he leaned back against the counter by the stove and continued to watch her. It was unsettling, despite how much of a pleasure it was for *her* to look at *him*.

And then she realized something. "Why aren't you eating?"

He shrugged with one shoulder. "I'm not hungry."

Loren narrowed her eyes. "You didn't eat at Rook and Redding's either." She dropped her fork in the pasta and folded her arms on the counter. "If you're not eating, neither am I."

The smirk he gave her showed the dimple in his cheek. "Is that a fact?"

"Yes, it's a fact. I'm surprised you're not built like a beanpole, considering how little I've seen you eat." No, he certainly wasn't a beanpole. He was perfectly proportioned and strong, and she knew without having to look that he had a washboard for a stomach beneath that shirt. If she let herself be honest about it, he reminded her of the marble statues of flawlessly muscled gods in the Temple of the Scarlet Star.

Loren didn't break his gaze as she waited. Darien relented after a moment and dished himself up from the remaining pot on the stove. And only once he'd picked up his fork and took a bite did Loren resume eating her own food. He was finished with his just as fast as he did everything else, and then loaded his bowl and fork into the dishwasher.

Loren eyed him up. "Did you even chew?"

That broad mouth twitched at the corner. "A little."

A dark blur atop the fridge caught her eye. The Hob moved so quickly she barely saw its fiery black silhouette before it ducked behind the boxes of puffed rice and granola.

A moment later, its shadowy little face peeked out at her, red eyes glowing. She ignored it and reached for her glass of juice.

But Darien noticed where her attention had gone. "Mortifer spends most of his time in the kitchen. He likes to eat the ice chips."

Loren's eyebrows flicked up. "And how does...*Mortifer* feel about having been purchased for your own gain?" Hobs were only available through the Umbra Forum. As incredibly powerful creatures that had the ability to protect a person's home from threats and detection by bounty hunters and other dangerous people, they were very expensive — and very rare.

"I didn't purchase him," Darien said. "He's a rescue. Some piece-of-shit mob boss had him at his house when I was sent for his bounty. After I bagged the mob boss's severed head, I offered Mortifer a way out. He's here by choice, not coercion." Darien gave her a little smile. "Kind of like someone else I know."

"Sorry," Loren mumbled.

"I would appreciate if you wouldn't make assumptions about me, Calla."

"I guess that makes two of us."

He quirked an inky brow, but said, "Fair enough."

She was almost finished eating when Darien's phone buzzed with an incoming call. He excused himself, answered with a muffled, "Hey," and disappeared into the library.

Resisting the urge to lick her bowl clean, Loren scraped the dish until there was nothing left, hopped off the stool, and loaded the fork and bowl into the dishwasher.

Just as Loren was closing the dishwasher, the front door swung open, and she looked up to see Ivyana Cassel strutting in, the stiletto heels of her knee-high black boots clicking on the floor. She tossed her keys into the wooden bowl that sat on the glass table in the entrance hall, spun around, and froze, her dark shoulder-length hair swaying as she caught sight of Loren lingering by the kitchen island.

Loren opened her mouth to say something, but no sound came out. She likely looked like a fish washed up on land, and certainly not for the first time that evening.

"Oh." Ivyana blinked, her thick lashes made darker by the irises that were the same steel-blue as her brother's. "You must be Loren."

Ivyana walked into the kitchen, her movements sure and graceful. Loren had heard plenty about this Devil, as she had the six others, most of those rumors hair-raisingly gruesome. The fact that she was Darien's twin sister wasn't the only reason creeps kept away from her. You couldn't be a Darkslayer, let alone a Devil, without having bloodied your hands enough to deserve the title. But Ivyana was so beautiful and willowy that Loren had a hard time picturing her doing any of the things the rumors had illustrated.

When Ivyana reached her, she offered her a hand. "It's a pleasure to meet you."

Loren took Ivyana's hand, the slayer's skin slightly cold from being outside. She had a grip that was surprisingly firm. "You must be Ivyana," Loren said. "Pleasure to meet you, too."

"Have you had a chance to meet the others yet?"

Loren nodded. "Yes." She cleared her throat; there seemed to be a very consistent frog in it tonight. "They were all very…kind."

Ivyana gave her a smile that suggested she knew exactly how kind they had been. "It'll take some adjusting, but I'm sure you'll fit in here just fine." She gave Loren a once-over that was different than the one Lace had given her. More…curious. As if she saw something in her that the others didn't. "Anyone my brother brings to Hell's Gate is more than welcome here."

"Thank you," Loren said.

Ivyana smiled. "I know this is rather abrupt of me, but I am exhausted, so I'm going to excuse myself."

Loren cleared her throat again. "Okay."

Ivyana smiled and made for the stairs. "Sweet dreams, Loren. You're safe here." She pranced up the stairs before Loren had a chance to reply.

As Loren waited for Darien to return, she wandered about the kitchen, taking in the photos—animated with magic—that were pinned to the fridge. The photos showed the seven slayers who lived here, doing *normal* things. Riding motorcycles, playing poker in their dining room, posing in front of monuments.

Loren carried on to the framed photographs that hung near the front doors. A picture of Maximus in the kitchen with his mouth full; Darien and Ivyana wearing aviation headsets inside a helicopter; Lace, Darien, Travis, and two guys Loren assumed were Tanner Atlas and Jack Steele posing on a white mountaintop in snowboarding gear.

As she studied the countless others, she found herself returning to the one of Darien and Ivyana. And it wasn't until Darien returned from the library after finishing his call that Loren realized why she couldn't look away from that photo: it was because Darien wore a *real* smile in it. Not the half-smiles he'd given her today. As he strode into the kitchen, she saw the contrast there, and it was like night and day.

It wasn't her business, but she wondered what secrets he harbored that had turned him into the person standing before her now.

12

When Loren awoke the following morning, she discovered that Darien was gone.

In fact, there wasn't a single vehicle out front. And although she knew there was a chance the Devils might've parked in the garage, as she ate a bowl of puffed rice cereal in the kitchen (no sign of the Hob, thank the Star), she had the nagging feeling that she was entirely alone in this big, beautiful house. And since Darien hadn't bothered to tell her that he would be ditching her bright and early, she figured she would do the same to him.

As soon as she was finished eating, she washed her bowl and spoon and sprinted back up the stairs to her suite.

Not bothering to fold her clothes, she stuffed them back into the suitcase, wondering how it was possible that the same number of items she'd packed only yesterday somehow had trouble fitting today. Birds warbled outside the windows as she crammed her bag of toiletries into the suitcase and zipped it shut.

If one thing was certain about this whole mess, it was that she didn't belong here. And despite his offer, it seemed Darien had no interest in helping her. She refused to sit here and do nothing while Sabrine was held hostage by a couple of psychopaths.

The day had started out sunny but was now overcast and muggy. Dressed in gray leggings, a white tank, and a denim jacket, Loren swung open the front door and left Hell's Gate.

She'd almost made it to the wrought-iron gates, its magical barrier vibrating invisibly through the air, when those gates swung open to allow Darien's vehicle to pass through.

Loren kept walking, even as he slowed beside her and lowered the tinted window, taking her in over the top of his sunglasses.

"Where do you think you're going." It wasn't exactly a question, but more of an accusation that she was making the wrong move.

"I'm leaving."

He backed up, engine snarling. "And what do you think you'll accomplish by leaving? Other than getting yourself killed."

"I guess I'll deal with it when the time comes." Despite the cheeky tone she managed to muster, she found her footsteps slowing. Bits of gravel clacked against her sneakers.

Darien accelerated backward, snaking the vehicle around to block her path.

"You know as soon as you walk out those gates, the people who are tracking you will see where you are," he said. "And you'll not only be endangering yourself, but you'll also reveal *my* location. Everyone will know I'm helping you."

Loren tossed her hair over a shoulder and edged around the car. But before she could make it beyond the barrier, she stopped, wondering how big an idiot she would be if she actually left.

Where he sat in the vehicle watching her, Darien said, "Get in the car, Loren. I think I know where we can begin our search."

Loren stood there for a long time as she deliberated. The clouds began spitting rain, the cooler temperature slicing through the muggy heat.

What *was* she doing? She wanted to help her friend more than she wanted to breathe, but she couldn't do it without this bounty hunter. The city was simply too big, and without that Sight of his, there was no way she could rescue Sabrine. Maybe he was right: maybe their best chance at finding her lay in figuring out why that blond Darkslayer and the warlock had wanted Loren to begin with.

Loren breathed in deeply, the heady fragrance of jasmine and rain filling her lungs. And then she spun on a heel, marched up to the back door, and swung it open. She tossed in her suitcase and purse, slammed the door shut, and then got into the passenger's side. The rain picked up as she closed her door; it drummed a steady rhythm on the roof and dripped in through the driver's window.

Darien was glaring at her overtop his sunglasses, elbow braced on that open window, the sleeve of his black leather jacket sparkling with rain.

"What's your problem?" she bit out.

Dark brows lowered over eyes that were grayer today than they were blue. "Don't do that again," he warned. The Devil flicked open the center console and rummaged noisily through the mess inside. Metal lighters, matches, mint tins, brass knuckles, knives, boxes of cigarettes, and sealable plastic bags of Stygian salts, the latter of which he threw around as if they had the same value as potato chips.

Loren gave a low whistle. "The only thing you seem to be missing is condoms." The jest had floated from her lips before she could stop it—before she remembered who she was speaking to. She was so used to joking around with Dallas and Sab—the only two friends she'd ever had—that speaking to Darien was an entirely new thing for her. In fact, speaking to *men* in general was pretty new to her, especially one like Darien. The guys at her school tended to fall more under the category of boys than they did men.

"They're in the glovebox," he said with a poker-face. Irritation glinted in his eyes as they flicked up to meet hers for a millisecond.

Loren couldn't tell if he was joking. Regardless, her cheeks reddened. Once again, she should've kept her wise mouth shut.

Finally, he produced a gold chain. Attached to it was a small pendant covered in ancient runes, a closed eye in its center. "Put this on," he said.

Loren crossed her arms. "Umm, thanks but no thanks." Darien looked like he wanted to throttle her, so she added, "Not until you explain to me what it is."

He shoved his sunglasses onto his head, the motion pushing the few locks of his undercut that had fallen astray back flat. "It's an

Avertera talisman. It's one of the only known artifacts that can block the Sight. It'll hide your location and the trails of your aura from Darkslayers for as long as you're wearing it, or until the magic runs out."

Which meant it would stop any new slayers from discovering where she lived, where she worked, what school she attended. It made her feel a tiny bit better about this mess, though not entirely. If the Darkslayers who were tracking her yesterday had managed to tell anyone else that she worked at Mordred and Penelope's Mortar and Pestle... Well, she didn't let herself think about that. If she did, she just might have a heart attack.

"And how will I know when the magic runs out?" she asked.

"Easy: the talisman will disappear." He offered it to her, and after another moment of deliberation, she closed her fingers around the chain. But he wouldn't let go, and his gaze bore into hers as he said firmly, "These are not only rare but they're also expensive, so don't take it off and don't lose it." Only after she'd nodded did he release his hold on it.

Loren undid the delicate clasp and hooked it around her neck, feeling queasy as the magic shivered over her skin. It felt like putting on an invisible coat.

She crossed her arms and stared straight ahead, out the rain-streaked windshield, refusing to say thank you just yet. With reluctance, she mumbled, "How expensive is *expensive?*"

He shifted into reverse and spun the car around to face the gate. "Three hundred thousand."

She whipped her head around to face him so quickly, she swore she gave herself whiplash. *"Gold* mynet?" she bit out. Darien wouldn't look at her. "I hope you don't expect me to pay you back, because you'll be waiting a really long freaking time if you do." Correction: she would be in the grave long before he ever saw so much as half of that money.

"Don't worry about it," he muttered. He flicked on the windshield wipers and sped through the gate.

He became quiet after that, concentrating on nothing but the road before him. Loren began to feel like an idiot as she realized

Darien had left that morning to go and get this talisman. And she'd planned on ditching him, entirely unaware that he was off forking out three hundred thousand gold mynet solely for her benefit.

Loren cleared her throat. "Thank you," she said quietly. "You didn't need to do that."

"No, I didn't," he said, his voice cold and clipped. She didn't blame him for this, especially after how rudely she'd just treated him. Shame colored her cheeks.

"May I ask where we're going?"

"Dusk Hollow," he said. He picked up speed, and fresh air swept into the cab and blew through Loren's hair. "If there's anyone who might have a clue where your ancestor's bone powder came from, it's graverobbers."

"Are we going alone?"

"Max, Jack, and Tanner are meeting us there." Another fact that added to her nerves. Not only would she have to be around Maximus again, but another two Devils she hadn't met yet.

As he drove, Darien's tattooed hands wouldn't relax on the wheel, his knuckles showing white through his skin. Every action he performed—flicking on the turn signal, braking at a stop sign, adjusting the temperature dials—was rougher than what was necessary.

Loren took a deep breath. "I'm sorry," she said in a small voice.

But his hands still wouldn't relax, and neither would his jaw; a muscle ticked in his cheek. He looked like he wanted to hit something.

"It wasn't right for me to leave without at least telling you first," she continued tightly. "I just..." She pressed her fingers to her temples. Cripes, her head hurt.

Darien glanced at her for the first time in minutes.

"I'm overwhelmed," she admitted pathetically. "And as I'm sure you know, I'm terrified. Terrified of *you*, too. Even though you've done nothing but help me."

It took him so long to answer her that she wondered if he even would. But then his hands visibly relaxed, and he said, "Don't worry about it." His voice held no trace of the sharp tone it had before.

"Just don't do that again. If I hadn't made it in time to stop you from leaving my property, we probably would've had to move Hell's Gate. We've lived in that house for a long time, and the others are pretty attached to it, so it wouldn't have sat well for anyone." He slowed to a stop at a red light that was nothing more than a smear under the rain pelting the windshield. "And that's the best-case scenario. The worst would've involved a lot of blood."

He didn't need to add that the blood he was referring to might've belonged to some of his Devils, not just their enemies.

"I'm sorry." She hadn't realized how selfish she was being.

"Like I said: don't do that again and we won't have a problem."

Loren remembered back to the photos she'd seen last night. She was beginning to understand that the Devils were a family, and Hell's Gate was as much a home as anybody's.

She was silent for the rest of the ride to Dusk Hollow, the weight of the talisman around her neck nothing compared to the guilt now burdening her heart.

DUSK HOLLOW WAS Angelthene's oldest graveyard.

While date palms lined either side of a dirt road that swept uphill, the rest of the grounds were shaded with the heavy canopies of laurel figs. The area was lush, fenced in by cast iron so old, only pieces of it remained.

Aside from the pattering of the rain that was softening to a drizzle, the snarl of the engine and the crunch of dirt and gravel beneath the tires were the only sounds. There were no cars lining the road where visitors were meant to park, and not a single person could be seen carrying flowers to the time- and weather-worn headstones dotting the grounds.

The only vehicle that was here aside from Darien's was an SUV that looked like it belonged on battlefields with armed forces. The same SUV she'd seen outside Hell's Gate last night—Maximus Reacher's vehicle.

As Darien pulled up beside it, the driver's door of the SUV

swung open, and Maximus leapt out, tan overcoat swaying. In one hand he carried a rifle; in the other a cigar he threw to the ground and crushed beneath the sole of his cracking leather boot. The other men that came around to stand beside Max were Jack and Tanner, who Darien introduced to Loren as soon as she found the courage to get out of the car.

Jack was the one with deeply suntanned skin, curly brown hair that matched his eyes, and the smile of a flirt and a jokester. He was known in the city and well beyond for his gambling addiction—and ability to win absurd amounts of money.

Tanner was taller and wiry, with sharp facial features, light-brown hair clipped close to his head, and a serious expression that gave Darien's resting-asshole-face a run for its money. Tanner was the one Devil who spent more of his time at Hell's Gate than he did collecting; he was incredibly smart, his hacking skills unmatched. He could break through nearly any grid of protection spells within minutes, allowing the Devils access to buildings where their targets might be hiding. He was a large part of the reason why they were so lethal—so unstoppable.

"You got a plan you'd like us to follow," Jack said to Darien with that contagious smile as they wove around the mossy headstones, "or are we just winging it?"

"The last time I saw Benjamin, he made it very clear to me that he didn't like surprises," Darien said as he loaded up a pistol. He flashed them a smile as he slapped the magazine back in. "So, in traditional Darkslayer fashion, I thought we would surprise him today by showing up uninvited."

The boys laughed. Maximus said, "At least he'll know for next time that slayers don't follow any rules but their own. And we also don't listen nearly as well as we should."

Darien chuckled. "The more you know." He came to a stop several feet from a massive, weathered tomb in the center of the graveyard. The pale stone of the broad, sealed door was inscribed with an array of runes.

Holstering his pistol at the front of jeans that were as faded as they were tattered, Darien gave a sharp whistle.

Loren nearly had a heart attack as Darien's Familiar hurtled out of his shadow and bounded for the tomb. Black as a silhouette, it was a large, short-hair dog with cropped ears, a docked tail, and a long muzzle, its face like a dog's skull with red eyes. Its movements were graceful yet powerful as it leapt into the slip of shadow outlining the sealed door and disappeared into the tomb. Like all Familiars, Darien's was able to communicate with him through his thoughts — in a voice no one could hear but him.

Loren felt a dull stab of jealousy. She'd always wanted a Familiar of her own, ever since she was a little girl. She wanted a lot of magical things that were denied to humans like her.

But she had Singer, and for that she was grateful. The dog was as much a friend to her as Dallas and Sabrine, and sometimes she felt like Singer could understand her — could comprehend the secrets she told no one but him. The secrets she guarded with her life, even from Dallas.

As they waited for Darien's Familiar to return, a cold wind swept through the graveyard. The temperature was unnaturally cold for Angelthene, and Loren knew she wasn't the first or only person who noticed it, as they all turned around to find a dozen cloaked and hungry spirits descending upon them.

13

Darien yanked Loren behind him so quickly, she almost fell.

The wights—ghostly skeletons cloaked in dark, tattered robes—encircled their group, the swiftness of their movements creating a vortex of wind so cold the rain froze to hail.

Three whistles cut through the air. Snarling as they were called forth from within their shadows, sprang Tanner, Max, and Jack's Familiars—a wolf, a mountain lion, and a jaguar respectively. The spirits took up their places equidistant apart, standing between the Darkslayers—and Loren—and the wights.

Covering her ears against the withered voices slithering into her mind, Loren shouted at the Devils to *shoot*. None of them had taken aim with the weapons in their hands; they were merely crouched in defensive positions in a circle, their backs to each other with Loren in the center, refusing to take their eyes off the wights.

It took everything Loren had not to demand to know when they'd all lost their minds.

"Bullets don't do shit against barrow wights, sweetheart!" Jack's shout was nearly drowned out by the vortex. Even with the danger they were in, he seemed to be enjoying this, a hint of that cocky smile in his voice.

Dead leaves, soft overturned earth, and bits of frozen rain spun around them so rapidly, Loren swore her feet would lift off the ground. The vortex began to pull at their bodies. At...at their *auras*, she realized. The wights were *tasting* them.

The Familiars gave snarls of warning and leapt forward. The wights reared back, the swift pace of the vortex stumbling, though only slightly.

On the opposite side of their circle, Tanner called, "Benjamin's really taking his sweet-ass time, Dare."

As if someone heard him, the door to the tomb groaned open. The slayers barely took their eyes off the wights as a tall, thin figure appeared in the doorway. Before him stood Darien's Familiar; at the sight of the wights, the dog sprinted forward and came to a stop just before Darien's boots, joining rank with the other Familiars who immediately adjusted their positions, working as a single unit to accommodate their fellow soldier—their *leader*. Just as Darien led the Seven Devils.

"Benjamin," Darien shouted over the wind, dipping his chin in the direction of the shaggy-haired man who was watching them with mild amusement.

"Darien Cassel," Benjamin drawled. "It's been a long time. I was beginning to think you'd forgotten about me." He appraised the wights. "Though I think it's safe to assume that what you *did* forgot was my request not to drop in uninvited."

Darien smirked, entirely unconcerned by the wights licking at the wisps of his aura. "I have some questions for you. Call off your pets—we've had enough of your games for today."

From this distance, Benjamin's smile was hard to see beneath his pale, unshaven face, though his eyes danced with amusement as he surveyed the cloaked skeletons floating around them. "But my dears were having so much fun," he murmured, almost to himself.

Benjamin clapped his hands once.

The vortex ceased, the hair that was spiralling around Loren's face falling to her shoulders in tangles. The slayers relaxed their defensive positions, their Familiars doing the same.

Benjamin inclined his head in a gesture for them to follow him into the tomb. "Come, come." His gaze became curious as it slid to where Loren stood behind Darien. His smile widened into a grin, nostrils flaring. "It seems we have a great deal to catch up on."

"THE GIRL WILL COME WITH ME," Darien told Benjamin. "The others will wait outside."

"Always so careful," Benjamin crooned. "You wound me, Darien." But he merely smiled and strode into the fire-lit mouth of the tomb, footfall slapping against the walls.

The other three slayers didn't question Darien as he stalked into the tomb. With a deep breath, Loren stamped out her fear and followed behind him. It was somewhat of a reassurance when his Familiar kept pace beside her, the muscles in its powerful side mere inches from her leg.

The air inside the tomb was humid and smelled of wet earth. As the door slowly groaned shut behind them, Max made a clicking sound with his tongue. A mere second before the door slammed shut to seal them in the tomb, Max's lion bounded to Darien's side. Darien's Familiar nipped playfully at the cat's whiskered cheek, and the two led the way to the tunnel where Benjamin had vanished.

"No matter what he asks you," Darien said quietly to Loren as they walked, the torchlight gilding his strong jaw, "let *me* do the talking."

"Scarlet Star forbid I say something wrong," she muttered.

Darien's voice became a harsh whisper. "Scarlet Star forbid you say something that will lead to you lying dead on the floor."

Loren bristled. "You don't have to be so blunt."

"And you don't have to question everything that I say or do. Since you seem to have already forgotten, allow me to remind you that I'm trying to *help* you."

"I still don't understand why. You don't seem to like me much."
Correction: he didn't seem to like her at all.

"I wouldn't say I don't like you. But you can be a thorn in my
side sometimes."

Loren bared her teeth at him. "And you're a thorn in mine."

"At least that's one thing we have in common."

Loren's heart pounded faster as they walked deeper into the
tomb. The sound of the rain striking the earth above became muffled
the farther they walked.

The tunnel eventually branched out into three separate ones.
Darien took the middle without hesitation, as if he were shopping in
his grocery store of choice. Loren stuck close to his side, the sleeve of
her jacket nearly touching his, as they walked into shadows black as
pitch. When the slayer's tattooed knuckles brushed against the back
of her hand, they looked at each other as if they'd been electrocuted
by the touch.

Loren crossed her arms and made a point to keep her distance
from him for the rest of the walk, Darien doing the same beside her.

Not a moment too soon, light glowed around a corner up ahead.
They rounded it and found themselves in a room lined with shelves
of potion bottles and other magical paraphernalia. A table was in the
middle of the room, weapons strewn across the wooden surface, and
hanging from the ceiling by wire were string lights.

Benjamin was waiting for them by the table. He smiled at Loren
as she and Darien came to a stop several feet away.

The graverobber's Familiar was perched on his shoulder, the
great owl assessing the dog and the lion with wise gold eyes. Loren
wondered if the three were talking.

Benjamin was still smiling at Loren. She dropped her gaze to the
floor, and only when the graverobber spoke did she look up to find
that he was now — finally — looking at Darien. "How long has it been,
Cassel? Two, three years?"

"Something like that." Darien's tone was casual and amicable.

"Things must've changed a lot in that time, for you to come here
with a human girl in tow." Amusement shone in his eyes as they
flicked to Loren.

"Actually, she is the reason I'm here." Benjamin cocked his head. "A number of Darkslayers are tracking her with bone powder that belongs to one of her ancestors. We were hoping you might have insight as to which graves have been dug up recently." Graves that were dug up without his people having arranged for it. Loren gleaned enough to conclude that if anyone would know a grave had been dug up in the city or the surrounding areas, it was Benjamin.

Benjamin crossed his arms and leaned his hip against the table. "I seem to be missing something here. Why would a Darkslayer want to track a human?"

"Your guess is as good as ours. The fastest way to find answers is by figuring out whose bone powder was taken."

"Were you given this bone powder as well, my friend?"

Darien gave a smug smile. "Of course."

Curiosity shone in the graverobber's eyes. "How much were you offered?"

Loren swore she saw a muscle tic in Darien's jaw. "Does it matter?"

Benjamin shrugged, though his interest in the amount was clear. Instead of prodding, he diverted to another question. "Why not track the bone powder to the grave?"

"It doesn't work that way. When I track someone with bone powder, finding them isn't possible unless they have a visible aura." Only living people had auras; once a person died, their aura left their body and journeyed through the river to the Lower World.

Loren had asked Darien that same question before she'd gone to bed last night—about the people he'd killed on the Avenue of the Scarlet Star. She'd hoped the trails they'd left in the city might lead them to Sabrine.

She had been more than a little disappointed by his answer.

Darien continued, "And even if I could, I needed to use all of it to simply find her. There's none left."

Benjamin canted his head. "And when you found her, you decided to protect her instead. How very curious."

A phone pinged, and Loren nearly jumped out of her skin.

Benjamin retrieved his cell from his pocket. "Excuse me for one moment," he told them with a smile that didn't touch his eyes.

After reading the text message, the graverobber slipped his phone into his pocket and disappeared into an earthen doorway partially hidden behind a tattered yellow curtain in a corner of the room.

"I don't know if I have a good feeling about this," Loren whispered to Darien. But he ignored her. There was tension in his jaw, but whatever he was thinking as he scanned the cluttered shelves, he didn't reveal it to her.

While Darien's back was turned, Loren stepped up to the table and scanned the items scattered across it, studying them as Darien was now doing with the shelves behind her. After several minutes of searching, she found a crumpled sheet of paper—folded several times —beneath a filthy shovel. She tugged the paper out from beneath the shovel, unfolded it, and read the words scrawled across its surface.

Four million gold mynet. Underlined.

Devil's Advocate.

Female. Eighteen/nineteen y/o.

Find her. Underlined three times.

At the very bottom of the page was a phone number, along with the title of another Darkslaying circle and a name.

Reapers... Geller???

It took Loren three painful, erratic heartbeats to realize she'd stopped breathing. The paper rustled in her shaky hands.

The graverobber had been looking for her, too. Going after the reward he was sure to receive, should he find Loren before anyone else did. But as a warlock, he didn't have the Sight necessary to track her, so she figured he was looking to hire someone to split the reward with him. And judging from the words scrawled on this paper, that someone was a person who worked for the Reapers.

It seemed Benjamin's curiosity over the sum of cash Darien had been offered was more of a concern than she'd thought.

"Darien," she called weakly, the paper crinkling in her hands. "What's the Devil's Advocate?"

Darien came to her side, snatched the paper right out of her fingers, and scanned it. He scrunched it into a ball, nearly pulverizing it as his eyes turned black. "That *cocksucker.*"

Footsteps sounded behind them. The two Familiar Spirits, immediately aware of the change in atmosphere, now stood at full attention on either side of Darien and Loren.

Before Benjamin could fully raise his hands in surrender, Darien had his pistol aimed at the space between his eyes.

"I can explain," Benjamin ground out. The owl on his shoulder gave a low hoot and rustled its wings.

The click of the safety releasing was loud in the otherwise silent room as Darien snarled, *"Start talking, asshole."*

14

Darien knew he had two problems to deal with, and he had to deal with them fast.

One of those problems involved the graverobber standing before him, his dirty hands trembling above his head. The second involved the mortal girl at his back, each breath she took shallow and erratic.

If Benjamin didn't provide Darien with enough of a reason not to shoot, he *would* kill him. And if anyone else had been informed of Loren's whereabouts during the time that Benjamin was absent, he would need to get her the hell out of here before they showed up—or this place would turn into a bloodbath.

"I can explain," Benjamin repeated. Sweat beaded on his forehead.

"I sure hope you can," Darien threatened.

Two dusky faces appeared from behind the tattered curtain, but before Darien could pull the trigger on the other robbers, they raised their hands in unison, stumbling back into the dirt wall so hard that a couple pebbles shook free from the ceiling.

Benjamin bellowed, "DON'T SHOOT! Do *not* shoot, for the love of the gods! Please, Darien—*we're on your side.*"

Darien's index finger teased the trigger, and the eyes of the three graverobbers tracked the movement. "Judging from what I just read —about your intentions for my friend here," Darien said with a baring of teeth, "I would say that's a lie."

"It's true, alright?" Benjamin's throat bobbed. "It's true, I *was* looking to track her—I won't deny that. But until you came here today, I had no idea that she was human. I thought the target might've been a High Demon or a mobster—someone I wouldn't feel guilty for offing. But now I see that I was dead wrong."

Darien's lethal expression thawed, though only just. "Why do you give a shit about a human life?" he barked, the volume of his voice causing Loren to suck in a breath.

"I could ask you the same thing." Benjamin's voice dipped to a fierce whisper as he added, "We all know we would be fools to cross you, Darien. And I don't intend on dying a fool."

Three full minutes passed as Darien deliberated. He had the sense that everyone in the room was holding their breath. And the robbers all knew damn well that, should he decide to kill them, they would be dead before they even realized what was happening.

The hard line of Benjamin's mouth wobbled. His eyes were glazed with a fear that for once in his life he couldn't hide. Darien had known this man for years—and in those years he'd learned that he was shit at lying. Even without the aid of the Sight, he could easily discern when Benjamin was being honest.

But he called upon his sixth sense anyway—just in case—and saw that his gray aura was a steady glow. No flicker or blur that might indicate that he was deceiving them.

"How did you hear about her?" Darien said, blinking the Sight away. "And don't even consider lying to me, or this bullet is going to find itself a new home in your brain."

Benjamin wasted no time before he started explaining. "About a week ago, I was hired to find the bone powder necessary for tracking her—that's the only reason I know about her at all." His throat shifted as he swallowed, and sweat ran down his temples in tracks, clearing the dirt on his skin. "Before you ask, I'll have you know that I haven't succeeded in finding it. And the men who hired me only heard of her bounty through hearsay on the streets—from a conversation at the Devil's Advocate, to be more precise—and decided they wanted the reward for themselves. They'd assumed it was fine to take the job because the rumors suggested it hadn't been claimed by any of Randal's circles."

How very interesting, Darien thought.

The Devil's Advocate was the hardest, filthiest nightclub in the whole city. Darien and the others—mainly Maximus, Jack, Lace, and Travis—had witnessed some pretty fucked-up things in that building. Things they had never been willing to talk about.

Darien did not release his grip on the pistol. "Why are so many people looking for her? What do they want her for?"

"Beats me," Benjamin said. "I know as little as you—maybe even less. I've been told the bare minimum, and I know nothing of the conversation that went on at the Devil's Advocate. And from the sounds of it, no one knows who or what she is, at least not the people who hired me—only that she is a nameless and faceless target who's worth one hell of a lot of mynet. As high as four mil, my eyes in the city tell me." He paused to swallow. "Which is why, before you arrived, I was tempted to find her myself—to claim the reward. I think it goes without saying that four million would make a hell of a difference in my life. And it's not very often that a bounty comes available that hasn't been claimed by Randal Slade's circles."

Darien blinked. "Four million?" How interesting, that someone other than himself or the other Devils would be offered that much. He'd noticed the amount scribbled on the piece of paper, but he hadn't thought much of it until now. "You wouldn't happen to know which Darkslayer was offered four million, would you?" Loren's heartrate had skyrocketed, her fear permeating the room.

"I'm afraid I haven't a clue."

After a long and heavy moment of silence, Darien lowered his pistol, clicked on the safety, and holstered it. Everyone in the room released a collective sigh of relief, including Loren. "What's the deal with Geller?"

Benjamin slowly lowered his hands that were still vibrating in the air. "His name is Tyson. He's a Darkslayer who works—"

"For the Reapers—I know him," Darien finished, waving a hand in dismissal.

Benjamin smiled a little. "Right. I forgot that you know pretty much everyone in this city."

"How far did you get with Geller in this little plan of yours?" Tyson had been one of Darien's best friends for several months— back when Darien had ended his first serious relationship and turned to drugs, alcohol, and women to numb the pain. They would frequent the raunchiest bars and nightclubs in the city every weekend and do the kind of things he had no interest in admitting to or even remembering now. Their friendship had ended when Tyson decided to take it personally the day Darien made it his goal to clean up his act—to ditch the drugs and save the partying for once in a while instead of every weekend.

"I ran the idea past him to partner up with me. To use his Sight to find the girl as soon as I located the bone powder and share the four million once the job was done."

"And who hired you to find the grave?"

"Dresden. One of Cain's men." Hired for a mere fraction of the amount that Darien would've received if he'd found Loren and handed her over to the people who were looking for her.

Darien hooked his thumbs in the pockets of his jeans. "Cain is after her?"

"I wouldn't worry yourselves over Cain."

Darien smirked. "Cain isn't a threat to me. Only his mouth is."

"All I'm saying is he likely knows as little as us. He only chases the same shiny toys as everyone else in his hood."

"Yeah, well, I'll be paying him a visit." Darien appraised the robber. "You don't have any intention of finding the bone powder for Cain now," he began, his tone threatening as his eyes turned black with the Sight, "or working with Tyson and chasing the reward for yourselves. Do you?"

Benjamin was already shaking his head. "None." There was no hint that he was lying; his aura was a steady, gray glow that told Darien he could be trusted.

"Good." Darien blinked the Sight away. "We could use your eyes in the city if you're willing to provide them. Whatever Cain and his men were planning on paying you, I will match it."

Benjamin was shaking his head, his dusty hair swaying. "You don't need to pay me—"

"I said I'll match it." He stepped forward and extended a hand. "Do we have a deal?"

Benjamin closed the last of the distance between them without hesitation, and they shook on it. "We have a deal," the robber said. He gave a small smile that illustrated exactly how relieved he felt at this turn of events.

Darien turned to Loren and inclined his head toward the exit in a gesture that it was time to leave. She made for the tunnel without delay, her eyes on her sneakers.

They had a lead, at least. Two leads, to be precise.

Step one, pay a visit to Cain in Stone's End and get an answer as to which Darkslayer was offered four million.

Step two, track down the other scum who were after Loren— before they found her first.

———

THE RAIN HAD CEASED by the time they made it back up to the graveyard.

Loren wrapped her arms around herself as she walked beside Darien, to where the other Devils were waiting for them.

Loren's teeth chattered as she said to Darien, "I suppose it's a good thing we have allies in them instead of enemies." Her sentence held the tone of a question she knew he heard.

"I consider any outcome that doesn't end in bloodshed a good thing, Calla. And since Benjamin and his men are the best graverobbers to walk this city, I'd say you're right: it *is* better to have them as allies and not enemies."

"Judging from what I saw of you in the alley yesterday, I thought you were going to kill him before he could talk."

Darien flashed her a smile that showed off his shallow dimples.

Although she didn't care to admit it, that smile made her weaker in the knees than she already was. "I certainly debated it."

Darien quickly filled the others in on what had taken place inside the tomb. When he was finished, their Familiars disappeared into their shadows, and everyone made their way to the vehicles. As soon as Loren and Darien were back inside the car, Darien started the engine and turned the heat on.

"Thanks," Loren said in earnest, holding her hands in front of the vents. Even though most of her shaking was the aftermath of shock and fear, the heat would help calm her down.

"I'm going to need to be able to contact you after today," Darien said. He took his phone out of his jacket pocket and tried passing it to her. "The passcode is 9974421." Bewildered, she kept her hands over the vents and glanced between him and his phone in confusion —long enough to cause him to shake the phone with impatience. "Why are you staring at me like I'm speaking Ancient Reunerian?"

"I don't understand —"

"I can't contact you if I don't have your phone number, can I?"

Feeling very stupid for not having figured out what he'd meant, she finally took the phone from him and entered the passcode he'd given her—the one he repeated a second time because she'd already forgotten it. He spun the car around, gravel crunching and popping under the tires, as Loren pulled up a ridiculously long list of contacts.

"You must be used to having girls practically claw each other's faces off to get their numbers into your phone," she said, at last catching onto how he'd simply *assumed* she would want to give him her number—in that arrogant-asshole-who-knows-he's-hot-as-hell kind of way. She resisted the urge to scowl as she added herself into his contacts—and resisted the urge to scroll through the endless list of names, many of which were female—and then handed his phone back to him.

He took it from her only long enough to throw it onto the console, where it slid against the base of the windshield. "And you must be used to spineless boys fumbling through the process of asking you for your number." He paused, and then said, "Why didn't you scream?"

Loren returned to staring at him in bewilderment. "What do you mean?"

"When I found you in that alley," he clarified. "Most people would've been screaming for help. You basically ran right into a dead end, yet you stood there in silence."

She blinked, taken aback by the intensity in his gaze. "I didn't want to involve anyone. I wouldn't have been able to live with myself if innocent bystanders had died trying to help me."

The car crawled down the road, the shadows of trees flitting over the sunroof. Loren waited for Darien to say something more, but it seemed that he was done with this topic. Though there was something in his eyes that suggested it was still on his mind.

"So," she began. "When do we go and see Cain?"

Darien gave a derogatory snort. "*I* will be paying Cain a visit as soon as I have the time, which I'm hoping will be next weekend. And *you* will not be coming."

Her mouth popped open. "And why the heck not?"

"Trust me when I say you don't want to be anywhere near Cain and his turf wars." Loren made to argue, but Darien cut her off, holding a hand up between them to silence her. "It's not up for debate. It'll be enough of a challenge to keep *myself* alive there. I don't need you complicating things by tagging along."

Loren was too stunned by his blatant honesty to argue the situation further. "What are we doing now?"

"We're going back to Hell's Gate. You'll be staying at my place again and I'll drop you off at the academy in the morning."

Loren had half a second to feel grateful for this before she realized how she would feel when Monday morning came, and she would have to part ways with Darien. After everything that had taken place in less than forty-eight hours, she was beginning to understand that the safest place for her was wherever Darien was.

Only one thing was certain: when Monday arrived, it would be a long, long day.

15

Loren was sitting across from Darien in the dining room at Hell's Gate. It was almost Witching Hour, which meant she should be sleeping. Monday was coming faster than she thought possible, but she wouldn't miss this for anything.

Grains of Stygian salt dotted the surface of the oak table—the remnants of the rail Darien had inhaled into his system through a rolled-up banknote of fifty gold mynet. His eyes were closed, his elbows were propped up on the table, and his laced fingers were pressed against his chin as though he were praying.

Between his elbows sat Loren's phone, the cracked screen alit with a photo of Sabrine. Loren had snapped the photo at Her Infernal Majesty the night she was abducted. Sabrine was wearing a glowstick halo, her eyes squinted shut as she beamed at the camera with a smile brighter than the strobe lights behind her. The photograph would help Darien track Sabrine; it was the route most Dark-slayers took if the target they were assigned had a name they could search up in the Angelthene citizen database. When photographs failed, or a target's name or appearance was unknown, that was when something like bone powder came into play.

"How does it work?" Loren asked of remotely tracking. She

crossed her arms on the worn tabletop. The ceiling fan that hung above the adjoined sitting room was on low, the current of air raising her skin to gooseflesh. She wished she'd changed into sweats, instead of the avocado-print pajamas that were far from warm. "I've never seen it done before. Can you explain it to me?"

The sigh Darien blew through his nose sent a few grains of salt gliding across the burned table. The eerie devil face seemed to track her, no matter where she sat or stood. Kind of like Darien's stare, in a slightly-less-unsettling way. "The first step is very important," Darien said, enunciating every word. His eyes were still closed.

"Which is?"

"Are you sure you're ready?" he murmured. "I won't tell you unless you're listening very, *very* carefully." Despite that his eyes were shut, Loren nodded, leaning closer. Bits of salt dug into her elbows. Finally, he said, "Step one: annoying little girls named Loren must stop talking."

The eager expression she was wearing instantly crumpled into a frown, and she recoiled as if he'd flicked her nose.

Darien opened his eyes to shoot her a withering look. She nearly flinched at the sight of them—gleaming like depthless sockets. So black, they seemed to suck the light out of the room.

But Loren stamped down her fright and found the courage to glare back at him. "I would've thought *you* of all people would know how to focus through distraction." Holy crap, those eyes really *were* terrifying. Even when they were blue, they had a way of scaring a person out of their skin—which was exactly why she had nearly peed her pants at the Avenue of the Scarlet Star.

"My line of work doesn't usually involve someone prattling on and staring me in the face the whole time." Clearly finished with entertaining *and* arguing with her, he closed his eyes again, and this time Loren buttoned her lips as he focused.

As the seconds wore on, his eyes began to shift below the lids, as if he were dreaming. And aside from the odd muscle in his impressive biceps flexing beneath the sleeves of his black shirt, there was no further indication of what he was seeing with his sixth sense, or whether it was even working. Loren's foot was itching to tap out a beat; she had to curl her bare toes against the hardwood floor to keep them still.

Despite the complaint he'd made about being stared at, Loren didn't look away from him once. And beyond his eyes flickering below his lids, she found herself noticing other things about him — and found herself biting her bottom lip as she noticed these things, especially now that he was in no position to catch her.

Things like the curve of his broad mouth, the shapes of his inky brows, the way the longest strands of his undercut — still damp from the shower he'd taken — fell to the tip of his nose. The shirt he was wearing fit him like a glove, drawing attention to every hollow and curve in his strong arms and chest. She caught herself imagining what those tattooed hands would feel like gripping her waist, that perfect face of his between her thighs, and that mouth...

That mouth —

She pinched the inside of her thigh really hard. Hard enough to make her eyes water. Hard enough to almost —*almost*— erase the thoughts that had invaded her mind. The thoughts that involved him spreading her out on this table and showing her just how good he was with his tongue.

The dining room lights flickered. Where Darien's hands were laced below his chin, his fingers twitched, as if he wanted to reach for something that only he could see. The space between his brows knotted, and beads of sweat formed below his lower lip. That look of intense concentration had Loren imagining even filthier things that made her want to slap herself, made her squirm in her seat. Her heart was pounding, fast and hard, and her palms were slick with sweat where they rested on her knees, her sharp nails making indentations in her skin.

Her palms weren't the only things that were suddenly slick.

The dining room grew several degrees warmer as the lights flared so brightly, Loren swore the bulbs would burst.

When Darien's eyes flashed open to look at her, there was something feral in them — something carnal. It sent a thrill up Loren's spine and had her pressing her thighs together under the table. Heat pooled below her navel, making her head spin.

After a moment, the black faded out of his eyes, his irises melting back into that remarkable, steely shade of blue.

Loren dropped her gaze to a freckle on the inside of her left wrist. Regardless that mind-reading was an ability no one in existence was known to possess, she had the horrifying feeling that Darien knew exactly why her face was turning tomato-red.

And when she peeked up at him, watching as black swallowed the whole of his eyes again with a blink, she realized that she hadn't put the talisman back on after having a shower. Because of her absentmindedness, his hellseher senses were picking up on how her body was responding to him—identifying her aura and the telltale colors it was betraying. Colors that would tell him all he needed to know about the lust tearing like a force of nature through her traitorous body—and the filthy thoughts she simply couldn't control, even with him staring right at her.

She tried to swallow, but it was more of a gulp. And that throbbing warmth at the apex of her thighs—

When Darien spoke, his voice was low and slightly husky, the sound so enticing that her bones turned to liquid. "Would you do me the extreme honor of telling me why you suddenly want to drop your panties?" Those eyes were feral in a way that had nothing to do with the Sight, feral in a way that set her whole body on fire. Feral in a way that made the throbbing between her thighs more intense—if that were even possible.

She tried to reply, but her tongue was a deadweight in her mouth.

And she swore she felt something—his magic, she realized—reach out and caress her mind. With his heated gaze fixed on her, the invitation in his eyes clear as day, that warm ache in her core continued to build, and in response to it, the stroke of his magic grew deeper. Harder. As if he could use his sixth sense alone to undo her—to give her release.

"You like that, don't you?" Darien's voice was deep and dark and sexy as hell.

"No," she lied. She swallowed the whimper that bubbled up her throat. Her stomach fluttered, her lips parting, and when he zeroed in on her mouth with a predator's focus, she found that she couldn't draw air, couldn't so much as move without the risk of combusting.

Was it possible? Could his magic really do such a thing to her without him ever having to physically touch her?

His magic pulled back a little. "Would you like me to stop?"

"No." The word was out before she could still her tongue.

No, she didn't want him to stop. But she was torn—torn between the red-hot desire to invite him to test his magic on her to its limits and the knowledge that it would complicate this whole mess even further.

The most wicked smile she'd ever seen on a man's face ghosted across Darien's lips. "I didn't think so."

Loren didn't say anything, her breathing becoming rapid with his building magic. The need for release was so intense, her vision shimmered. But—

Knowing that what they were doing was wrong on so many levels, she crossed her legs, the muscles twitching slightly with the promise of ecstasy, and squeezed her thighs together. Harder than she had before.

Sensing her resolution—her silent answer to the question he'd asked her—Darien's eyes immediately became blue again, his magic fading away like fog in sunlight. But although he was no longer reading her aura, she knew he had seen enough, and could *still* see enough to know what she was thinking—the filthy show she was playing in her mind.

The show in which he was the main star.

"I had no idea you were such a dirty girl, Loren Calla." His teasing voice was practically a purr.

Scarlet Star help her. "I don't know what you're talking about," she stammered.

It was a lie. A big, fat lie, because that throbbing wouldn't stop, and her nipples were hard peaks against her shirt.

And…she wanted him to do it again, wanted him to stroke her with his magic and not stop this time until she climaxed.

"I think you know exactly what I'm talking about."

"You're being very inappropriate," she spluttered.

"So are your thoughts, apparently." A sinful smile colored his tone. And she could barely look at him, couldn't separate her legs.

Couldn't stop her tongue from stumbling as she said, "I'm sorry to squash your inflated ego, but I have zero desire to make love to you."

The corners of his mouth—that damned, distracting mouth—twitched with amusement, the dimple in his cheek making an appearance.

Loren blinked, her spine stiffening. "What's so funny?"

"Your word choice...amuses me."

"Well, if you wouldn't call it making love, then what *would* you call it?" she huffed.

"Fucking." The hint of a smile that was flirting with his lips had turned positively wicked. "I would call it fucking, Miss Loren."

She wasn't sure how it was possible, but she blushed even harder. The heat spread right down to her toes, as if she had been sitting out in the sun for too long.

Why did she have to be so naive? *Why?*

He was full-on grinning now. "You walked right into that one, sweetheart."

Loren cleared her throat and set about fiddling with her shorts string. "Can we talk about something else, please?"

"Like how you're such a little prude that you flinch every time I say *fucking?*" Indeed, she *did* flinch. Though she wasn't sure that being inexperienced was the same as being a prude—but she didn't want him knowing about that part of her.

When she dared to look at him again, his eyes were dark—not with the Sight, but with something else. Something that made her melt all over again as that piercing gaze swept over her mouth and her breasts, lingering on the latter in a way that suggested he was undressing her in his mind.

What she wouldn't give to know exactly what he was thinking.

"You're not being nice," she huffed, that heavy stare of his too much for her to bear. If he kept looking at her like that, she just might throw herself across the table and end up... What was the word he'd used again?

Oh yeah: *fucking*. She might end up fucking him.

"Because I'm not a nice person," he said, his voice rich and silky. He seemed to note her fidgeting and, evidently not being certain of the reason why she was doing it, he said, his voice incredibly gentle, "Relax, Loren. I'm only teasing you. I promise I won't bite—unless, of course, you want me to."

"That doesn't seem like it would be enjoyable, yet you make it sound like it is." Gods—what was she even *saying?*

"Anything is enjoyable if I'm the one doing it."

"That's a very cocky thing to say."

Darien laughed. It was a rich sound, low and deep, and she found that she liked it. She liked it a little too much.

"Call it cocky, but I know the things that I'm good at. And I am very, *very* generous, Loren Calla." The way he said her name had desire dripping like hot honey down her spine.

"You say that as if I'm going to find out."

"That would make you lucky," he crooned. He tipped up an eyebrow. "But you haven't had much luck lately, have you?"

"That's enough," she said, dropping her shorts string and deadpanning him. "You're being mean now."

He wouldn't stop smiling. "If I'm being mean, then why do you seem to be enjoying yourself so much?"

"I'm going to take a rain cheque on this conversation." He had been right when he'd called her out for enjoying this; having someone like him talk to her like that... Well, the heat pulsing between her thighs was evidence enough that she was enjoying herself very much, even though she *was* feeling a bit testy after the last comment he'd made. Luck hadn't been on her side at all lately.

Darien's grin only widened, deepening that cursed dimple. "If you say so."

She scrambled to change the subject while she had this window of opportunity, but she found herself deviating back to what he'd said a moment ago. "I don't think that what you said is true."

The dining room light gilded his damp hair as he cocked his head to the side. "Are we talking about the part where I said I was generous or the part where I know what I'm good at?"

What a ridiculous question. She had no doubt that he was very, *very* good behind closed doors; a face like that had likely gained him plenty of practice with women who were all too willing to take a tumble with him.

"The part where you're not a nice person," Loren replied, crushing her maddening thoughts into nothing. "I think that's only what you want people to believe."

That arrogant smile faded a little. Hah! Now it was *her* turn to drive this conversation. "Then you think incorrectly," he said.

"You wear a mask to keep people out but that's all it is: it's a mask."

The arrogant smile was gone now; there wasn't a trace of it left behind. "I seem to be missing how this conversation took a turn from fucking to talking about my hang-ups."

Loren blinked. Did he just admit to having hang-ups?

There were conflicting emotions in his eyes that suggested she was correct, but she didn't push him. Part of why she didn't push him was because she was afraid of him; the other part was because she hadn't exactly intended to crack through his carefully painted exterior so easily. The arms that were crossed over his chest were rigid, the hard muscles standing out beneath his tattooed skin.

Clearly, she'd struck a chord. The frown on his face said everything he was thinking: so much for the fun conversation they were having.

Loren cleared her throat. "So," she said, scrambling for the quickest exit out of this chat that had become all kinds of awkward. "What did you see?"

Darien mercifully said nothing more about the turn of their conversation and instead said, "Not a Star-damned thing."

"What does that mean?" His response brought her back to the here and now—to the things that were most important. The heat left her body like a window had been opened to the night.

"It means her captors are as good as I am. They're cloaking her aura somehow, maybe the same way I'm cloaking yours." He slumped against the backrest of his seat and pushed his hair back from his face with both of his hands. "I guess I shouldn't be surprised that more people are finding out about the talismans. The best things can't stay hidden forever."

"How *does* tracking work? Maybe you'll tell me now that you're not needing to concentrate." She gave him a cheeky smile.

One side of his mouth pulled up into a smirk. "It's hard to explain. The best comparison I can make is to a thermal camera. A lot of colors are involved, and I need to not only *see* them but know how to distinguish between different auras and the people they each belong to."

"Was it a challenge to learn?"

"I had trouble at first," he admitted. "A lot of my training involved learning what colors looked like with my eyes closed instead of open. Freezing temperatures, warm temperatures—even burns. It was a form of torture, at least in my case. I had to learn how to open my mind and see things without visually discerning them. *The third eye,* some people call it. My father...he had a horrible way of teaching me. His methods usually involved ice baths and saunas far hotter than any human body can handle." He gave a dark smile, his straight white teeth flashing in the light of the chandelier. "Good thing I heal quickly."

Loren's throat bobbed as she swallowed. "Clearly, his methods did what they were intended to." Her sentence held the tone of a question she knew he heard.

That smile turned into a frown. "Not quite. It was my mother who explained it to me in a way that finally made sense." Seeing the curiosity piquing on her face, he explained, "When I was a child, I went to her in times of distress, telling her the world was too big. When the Surges happened, and the Sight took over my mind, I would become overwhelmed and lock myself in my bedroom for hours, where I could do nothing but rock back and forth on the floor, squeezing my head in my hands. The person I was becoming frightened me, and my mind sometimes felt like it wasn't my own. I thought there was something wrong with me. But she told me it was the rest of the world that was wrong."

Loren tried not to look at the tattoo on his forearm: the beautiful face of a woman she realized must be his mother. Hair blew around her and blended seamlessly with the clouds edging the black and gray piece. She had angel's wings, and at the base of the portrait were roses. The detail was so extraordinary, it looked like a photograph. Both of his muscular arms were covered with full sleeves of ink that extended all the way to the backs of his hands, the left seeming to be reserved only for symbols he clearly associated with his mother.

"How did she explain it to you?" Loren asked.

It took Darien a moment to speak. And when he finally did, although his eyes were on Loren, she could tell that he wasn't really here, in this dining room. No—he was reliving a memory.

"My mother's methods were gentle," he began. "She had the kind of inexhaustible patience I strive for every day. Although she lacked the Sight my father possessed, that didn't make her any less capable of teaching me how to use it. It took me several months before I finally had a firm grasp on reading auras, but it was all because of her—because she refused to give up on me. And because she refused to surrender me to my father's cruel ways. Instead of ice baths and saunas, she helped me to see the colors with snow and sunlight; with the cool waters of a pool and the sound of the wind and the rain blowing through a forest."

Loren found her eyelids slipping shut as she envisioned what Darien went on to illustrate.

"She taught me that green was life. Green was wet grass; moss; birds chirping in trees. Pink was pleasure in the most innocent sense of the word. It was the texture of rose petals and the heat of when you blush; it was strawberries, bubble-gum, lollipops. Yellow was cheery and invigorating, like the taste of lemon. It was sunflowers and the soft down of a newly hatched chick. Orange was exactly as the fruit tastes; it was the glow of firelight and the feel of the desert sun warming your back. Red was complicated; it was seduction, violence, danger, anger—even love. It was the heat of a steak fresh off the barbecue, the taste of chili peppers." He paused, and Loren wondered if he was there, too—in his mind. In his heart. "The sound of the ocean...," he went on. "The sound of the ocean was blue. Blue was calm. Blue was relaxation. Blue was...blue was peace."

After a moment of silence long enough to confirm that he had said everything he wanted to say, Loren opened her eyes.

Darien was staring at her with an unfathomable expression on his face; no matter how hard Loren tried, she couldn't read it. And the longer she waited for him to break her gaze, the less likely it seemed that he would.

Blue was peace, he'd said. She didn't flatter herself by thinking that he was staring at her so intently because of the color of her eyes. Blue like the ocean, the color he associated with peace.

Loren cleared her throat. "That sounds much more enjoyable," she said. "So, it worked?"

Shaking his head slightly—not in answer to her question, but as if waking from a trance—Darien slid a box of smokes from the pocket of his sweats. "It worked."

Loren whispered, "What happened to her?"

A heavy pause. "She died of depression when I was fifteen." He wouldn't look at her, and his face had clouded over with emotions Loren knew she could never understand. Seeing such vulnerability in his expression did something to her heart—something that hurt more than a little bit. When Darien spoke again, the words were rough, expressed in such a way that suggested he was struggling to say them at all. "Some days I can still hear her voice…in my dreams and in my memories. And some days, that voice is the only thing still keeping me here."

He shook his head again, as if to rid himself of the unwelcome thought, and then took out a cigarette, placed it between his lips, and lit it. The lid of the metal lighter clinked as he snapped it shut.

Instead of the smell of tobacco Loren expected, she caught a whiff of birthday candles. And when she squinted hard enough, she spotted a shimmer of magic confining the smoke to one area— keeping it away from her and around himself instead. It might've simply been a force of habit for him, but this act of consideration, no matter how small, made her feel a little fuzzy inside.

"Aren't you worried about the Tricking?" With how much magic he was using on a daily basis, the highly deadly disease was bound to cross his mind from time to time.

"There's not a lot I'm worried about, Rookie." She was starting to see that. As he took another long drag on the cigarette, Loren was careful to look anywhere but at his mouth.

She fiddled with her shorts string. "What do we do now?"

"We go in blind." They would have to look for answers another way. And Loren had a feeling it would involve one heck of a lot of investigating.

"Soooooo, is Darien Cassel as hot as all the rumors say?"

From where she sat across from Dallas in the crowded dining hall of the academy, Loren reached across the table and swatted Dallas's freckled arm. *"Seriously, Dal?"* she fumed, though a smile tugged at her mouth. "After everything I just told you, *this* is the question you ask me?"

Dallas flicked a braid over her shoulder. "I'm just asking," she tsked. Her eyes danced as she prodded, "Well, *is* he?"

Loren rolled her eyes. "I guess so." She knew Dallas saw the color she could feel blooming across her cheeks.

She still couldn't believe how blatantly Darien had called her out last night! When she'd gone to bed, she hadn't been able to stop thinking about it—about how his eyes had practically devoured her upon realizing how dirty her thoughts had become. Needless to say, she'd had more trouble falling asleep than she cared to admit—especially knowing that his suite was right down the hall from hers. And *especially* after he'd practically invited her to discover just how generous he could be. She may be inexperienced, but that didn't mean she lacked imagination. Plus, she'd heard plenty from Dallas over the years that told her exactly what a guy had to offer, if they knew how to handle a woman. And it didn't take a genius to figure out that Darien certainly knew how.

"Can we get back to the more important things, like, I don't know…how many people want to *kill* me?"

"Sorry. You know humor is just my way of dealing with stress."

"It's okay." Loren extended a hand to her.

Dallas took it, lacing her fingers with hers. "Do you think the Devils could track Sabrine and find out where she's being kept?"

Loren fiddled with a lock of golden hair. "Darien tried to remotely track her last night, but he said whoever abducted her is somehow cloaking her location. Maybe the same way Darien is cloaking mine." She fingered the talisman around her neck, the pendant glinting in the light of the chandeliers. Her throat became tight. "It scares me how long she's been missing, Dal. They say the first three days are the most crucial in finding a missing person alive." Perhaps their only upper hand was knowing the Darkslayer had wanted Loren instead.

Dallas's throat bobbed. "I hate to think law enforcement might not be doing everything they can." Tears lined her catlike eyes.

Loren threw a glance around the crowded room before whispering, "I think we need to get into that restricted hall."

Dallas frowned. "It has a forcefield over it, Lor. It'll probably burn us alive."

"I'm willing to risk it." For Sabrine. She would do anything to get her back, even if the spellwork roasted her bones. "I can't do it without you though."

"And what if we find nothing?"

"Then at least we'll know we tried." She paused. "What are you afraid of, Dal? Don't you think it's at least worth looking into?"

Dallas's spine stiffened. "I'm not afraid of anything."

"Then help me."

"I'll think about it." High above, the school bell chimed. Seeing the defeat on Loren's face, Dallas added, "We'll find Sabrine alive. I know we will."

THIRD PERIOD INVOLVED a rare talk from Angelthene Academy's headmaster.

Ivador Langdon was one of the most powerful warlocks in the city. He'd lived alone for two centuries before he fell in love with a mortal woman. Six months after they were married, she gave birth to his half-witch baby girl.

That baby girl was now sixteen and had suffered a terrible car accident this past summer that had left her paralyzed. And although Loren could see the shadows plaguing his ashen middle-aged face, he taught her class that day with the same kind of passion that had made him a favorite among so many.

However, today's talk was different. Loren wasn't sure how to feel as the headmaster went on that afternoon to illustrate exactly how he viewed a human lifespan.

"A human lifespan," Headmaster Langdon was saying, his academy robes flowing as he paced the floor in the center of the tiers of benches, "is only a speck in the vastness of the universe. A single grain of sand on a beach." In other words, insignificant. Unworthy. Nothing but a blip in the grand scheme of things.

The class snickered. Loren sank in her seat, wondering why the headmaster seemed to be talking down on humans when he was not only married to one but had sired one as well. Beside her, Dal threw warning glances at the few cocky warlocks and witches who looked Loren's way.

But the headmaster's voice grew softer as he went on to say, "And yet they are the most extraordinary beings to walk the face of Terra."

The snickering stopped. Murmurs of confusion and disgust rippled through the classroom.

Loren lifted her chin.

"How can you say all that," came a voice from the back of the room, "and then go on to claim they're the most extraordinary?"

"Because their lives are fleeting," the headmaster said. He stood in a dusty beam of light that brought out the silver in his hair, bright as the reflective ring around each of his pupils. "And in knowing this, they succeed in doing what no immortal ever could: they live with the knowledge that every day could be their last. And because of this, they live fiercely. With more intent and purpose in the span of no more than a hundred years than any immortal would in a thousand."

The classroom was silent enough to hear the lights humming overhead.

"With all due respect, Headmaster," Loren began, hand half-raised. His eyes zeroed in on her, and soon all the students were turning to stare at her as well. "But as a human myself, I'd have to disagree. *Immortals* are the fiercest people I've ever known. I believe there's courage in knowing that it'll take a lot to kill you. There's confidence in this that no human could possess."

"But is it confidence, Loren?" he said in a kind voice. "Or is it arrogance?" He paused, waiting for his words to sink in. "I would sooner call it a false sense of security. Most immortals *are* courageous and confident, yes. But it's because none of them have ever known the immediate threat of being able to die so easily."

Loren had nothing to say after that, and neither did the other students.

The rest of the day passed by in a blur, and Loren couldn't stop mulling over the headmaster's words.

As she walked to the House of Salt at the end of final period, she wondered if it was possible that humans succeeded at living more beautifully because their days were numbered. And because they knew that, once those days were spent, they would never be here again.

16

The weekend arrived quicker than Loren thought possible.

She hadn't seen Darien since he'd dropped her off at the academy Monday morning, but he'd given her strict instructions not to leave the schoolgrounds until Saturday, when she would have to go to her shift at Mordred and Penelope's. Her Avertera talisman twinkled in the sunlight as she made her way to the apothecary by taxi and began her opening duties.

Dallas came to see her at noon. Loren was tacking her sign to the door, announcing that she was closed for lunch, while Dallas rolled around on the floor of the apothecary with Singer.

"Who's a good puppy?" Dallas crooned, scratching the dog's floppy ears. Singer's tail swished back and forth as he gave a yelp of satisfaction. *"Who's a good puppy?"*

Loren strode to one of the tables and flipped open the lid on the pizza box that was hidden among sentient plants, potions, bags of dragon scales, and vials of unicorn hair. "You'd better come get some or I'm going to eat the whole pie," she threatened as she took a slice, her mouth salivating at the sight of a gooey string of piping-hot cheese stretching until it snapped.

One of the potted plants on the table trembled as if stirring awake and snaked a leafy branch toward the box.

Loren snapped the lid shut. "Don't even try it," she told the plant as she bit off a mouthful of pizza. Clearly vexed by Loren's tone, the plant rustled its leaves and recoiled into its pot. It was to Dallas that Loren said, "We'd better eat upstairs, or we're going to have all-out war with the plants." She cocked an eyebrow at the plant, and it sank a little further into its pot.

Dallas and Singer leapt to their feet and were bounding up the stairs before Loren could reach the bottom step.

They ate in silence in the office that doubled as a staffroom, Dallas spinning herself around in the swivel chair while Loren perched on the edge of the desk. Singer got his very own slice, which he happily devoured at Loren's feet.

There were no plants in the office aside from one: a small wilting thing Loren was determined to revive. She kept it on the windowsill behind the desk, exactly where it would get the best amount of sunlight for its species. Dallas always made fun of her for trying to keep it alive when its small leaves were thoroughly crisped, its body drooping toward the sill as if someone had gravely insulted it.

Dallas finished off her fourth slice and propped her feet up on the desk. "So, when do I get to meet this mysterious Darien Cassel?"

Loren shrugged. "I don't know. Maybe never." She licked tomato sauce off her thumb. "He hasn't contacted me all week, so I don't know what's happening." If the magic of the talisman ran out before Darien contacted her, she would be screwed. She hoped she hadn't given him such a hard time lately that he'd decided he was done with her.

Dallas said nothing as she began picking at her red stiletto nails. Loren snapped the empty pizza box shut and tossed it into the waste-basket. "What's the matter, Dal?"

The redhead wouldn't meet her gaze. "You told me no boys would ever get in the way of us. Of our friendship."

Loren's eyebrows shot up, an incredulous grin spreading across her face. "Are you seriously being jealous right now? Of a *slayer*, of all people?"

Dallas crossed her arms and glowered at her. Loren couldn't help but laugh. "I don't see what's so funny," Dallas grumbled.

"What's funny is that you're bothered by Darien Cassel. I mean, he's smoking hot, I admit. But the last person he would ever be interested in is *me.*" Loren and Dallas had established from a young age that they would make life decisions based on each other, always taking care of their friendship first. No stupid boys would ever get in the way of the plans they'd made for the future.

Dallas ignored her as she spun the tip of a braid between her index finger and thumb. She used the ankle that was still propped up on the desk to swivel the chair back and forth as she mulled over Loren's words.

"Dallas," Loren prodded. Dal peeked up at her from under her eyelashes. "Are we cool?"

Dallas smiled. "Yeah, we're cool." She hopped to her feet and dragged a finger over the wilting plant as she passed by the window. "Bye, Mr. Crispy," she said to it as she made her way to the stairs. "Let me know if you end up going back to Hell's Gate, Lor. I have my first day of training with the Fleet tomorrow."

Loren's mouth popped open. "Star in heaven, Dallas! I totally forgot about that."

It was a big step for Dallas. Becoming a soldier in the Aerial Fleet was not only her birthright but her dream. She'd longed to join the winged forces her parents commanded ever since she was a little girl. Dallas had a fascination with birds; by receiving the magical wings the soldiers were given via surgery, she would be soaring with them through the skies in no time.

Dallas smiled. "It's okay. You've had a lot on your plate." She sighed, lingering in the doorway. "We both have."

Loren nodded her agreement.

Taking note of whatever expression was on Loren's face, Dallas said, "Things will go back to normal—I promise. If you're worried about anything, call me. I'm always here."

"Likewise."

"And let me know if Darien's ever being a prick. I'll happily beat him up for you."

Loren tipped her head back and laughed. Dallas picking a fight with Darien was the kind of entertainment she would pay good money to see.

"I'll see you at the vigil tomorrow night," Dallas said. And then she blew Loren a kiss before skipping down the stairs and out the front door.

17

D arien was a lethal wall of muscle at Loren's side as she made her way through the crowds of people at Sabrine's candlelight vigil. Loren's eyes stung with tears as she scanned the faces of the people they passed, the flame of the candle she carried warming her hands. In the crook of her elbow, she held the stuffed elephant Sabrine had given her when they were children.

Sabrine had been missing for over two weeks. Loren couldn't erase the feeling that too much time had passed; that they were too late. With a steadying breath, she stared at the amber stripe of sunlight hugging the dark desert mountains in the distance, begging the eight deities of the Scarlet Star that Sabrine would return home safely—and soon.

These past few days, she'd learned that Sabrine was not the only person who'd gone missing. A week before Sabrine disappeared, nineteen-year-old werewolf Chrysantha Sands had been reported missing to the police. Loren didn't think the cases were linked in any way, considering Sabrine had only been abducted because the Dark-slayer and the warlock hadn't been able to reach the target they were really after. But tonight's vigil was for them both.

"Any idea where we might find your friend?" Darien asked as

they maneuvered the crowd. He wore a black button-up shirt with the sleeves pinned at the forearms, dark blue jeans, and wingtip boots. Yet despite the more casual look, Loren didn't doubt there was at least one weapon on him. If she hadn't been so distracted by thoughts of Sabrine, she might've gawked at him like an idiot. He was ridiculously gorgeous. It was hardly fair.

"Not really. Somewhere near the front, I guess."

She *did* end up finding Dallas right near the front of the crowd, where people were leaving candles and other items of sentimental value around two framed photographs, one of Sabrine and one of Chrysantha Sands.

Dallas's sheet of red hair was loose today, the slightly curled ends falling several inches past the hem of her black leather jacket, the back of which was embroidered with a witch's symbol of protection. She was crouching down to set her own candle on the sidewalk, along with a bouquet of lilies, Sabrine's favorite flower.

Dal's keen witch senses alerted her to Loren's approach, and she lifted herself to her feet, dashing away tears. Beneath the jacket, she wore a white crop top that read *Witch Bitch* in glittery scrawl. Her jeans rode low on her hips, and the six-inch leather pumps on her feet were redder than her hair.

Dallas faced Loren and forced a smile. "Hey." She took in Loren's white shirt with the plunging V-neck and bell sleeves, the hip-hugging blue jeans, and wedge heels. "You look nice." As if remembering something, she scanned the crowds behind Loren. "I thought you said Darien was coming."

Loren turned around to see that he was gone. Sometimes that man moved as silently as a ghost. "He must've run into someone."

Dallas's eyes zeroed in on the tattered elephant that was squished between Loren's arm and ribs. "I see you found Stumpy." She laughed sadly. The stuffed animal was missing one of its button eyes and had fluff sticking out of its seams.

Loren shrugged, her throat tightening at the memory of her fifth birthday party, when she'd torn the wrapping paper off a box to find a brand-new Stumpy inside. "I thought Sabrine would like it if I brought him out into the world again. I stopped at the penthouse when Taega was gone and found him in the old toy chest."

Dallas's brows flicked up. "You're lucky she hasn't caught you sneaking about," she tsked. Before Loren could say anything, Dallas spoke again. "Did Darien say if he's followed that lead the graver-obber gave him?"

"Not yet," Loren sighed. "But I overheard him talking with the others, and it sounded like they're going to see Cain tonight—"

Dallas's attention was snagged by something—or someone—behind Loren. Loren let her sentence trail off as the witch's mouth literally popped open.

"Oh. My. *Gods.*" Judging from the smile on Dallas's glossy lips, Loren knew exactly who she was looking at. "That's them, isn't it?"

At Dallas's use of the word *them,* Loren turned around and followed her gaze.

Darien was heading this way, but he wasn't alone. At his side was Maximus. The two wore identical, deadly gazes that picked apart the sea of bodies, regardless of the fact that every person at the vigil moved aside as much as possible to give them a wider berth.

As soon as the two Devils were within acceptable hearing range, Dallas put her hands on her hips and looked them over, one at a time. "It seems Loren didn't do you two quite enough justice when she told me how hot you guys are."

Loren's mouth popped open in horror. She dropped her gaze to the sidewalk, blushing hard.

She wanted to kick Dallas in the head for saying that. Kick her and pull her hair.

It was Darien who spoke first, since the infamous Maximus Reacher was at a loss for words, gaping at Dallas like a fish washed up on land. It was sort of adorable, Loren had to admit. "You must be Dallas," Darien said, extending a hand toward the witch.

Dallas shook it, Darien's hand dwarfing hers. "I've been looking forward to meeting you, Darien Cassel," she said with the quirk of a copper eyebrow. The appreciation in her eyes sharpened as her gaze flicked to Darien's best friend. "And you must be—hold on, let me guess…Maximus Reacher." Several people within hearing range sidled away from the mentioning of these two names.

Maximus still couldn't find words. Darien clapped him on the back so hard it looked like it hurt, and said, "Max seems to have forgotten how to talk to women."

Max shook his head, as if waking from a daze, and extended a hand to Dallas. "Pleasure to meet you, Dallas."

Dallas beamed at him as she shook his hand for longer than what was necessary. "Believe me, the pleasure is all mine."

Across their tight circle, Darien caught Loren's eye and gave her a little smile she found difficult to return.

Her face instantly reddened from the attention, and she broke their eye contact by focusing on the fine silver chains he always wore around his neck. Avoiding him made her a coward, she knew. But she wasn't feeling up to their usual staring contests, especially not when it involved something other than glaring at each other in annoyance. She wasn't certain what, exactly, had been written in his expression a moment ago, but it seemed to carry a weight she felt she couldn't bear tonight.

Darien was still staring at her. She could feel it, but she refused to look up.

A moment later, he cleared his throat. "Does Sabrine have family here?"

Dallas locked eyes with Loren, her frown mirroring the one she now wore. "I doubt it," Dallas said.

"Sabrine's father is an alcoholic with a tendency to be abusive," Loren explained to Darien and Max in a hushed tone. "Her mother passed away when she was a baby."

"Is her father here?" Maximus asked. Loren wondered if he realized that he was cracking his knuckles. "I wouldn't mind having a word with the prick."

Dallas sighed. "As much as we would totally enjoy watching you beat that asshole to a pulp, he's not coming. Trust me: he's probably drinking his sorrows away in front of the telly like he does every day of his worthless life."

"We're not here to whale on deadbeat dads anyway," Darien cut in. "No matter how much we'd enjoy it." Taking note of the candle melting in Loren's hands, he said, "We'll give you girls a few minutes to yourselves. There's someone we need to speak with."

As soon as they were gone, Dallas turned to Loren and gave her a wicked grin, excitement sparking in her eyes. "I'm going to jump Maximus Reacher's bones the first chance I get."

"Shh!" Loren hissed. "Say it a little louder, why don't you?"

Dallas clicked her tongue. "Relax, Lor. No one's listening." She paused, and a curious glint entered her eyes. "So... Are you and Darien...?"

Loren stared wide-eyed at her, waiting for her to finish her question. When it became apparent that Dallas wouldn't say anything more, she demanded, "Are we *what?*"

Dallas grew visibly frustrated by Loren's puzzled expression. "You know...?" She made an obscene gesture with her hands.

"What?" Loren shrieked, finally catching onto what Dallas meant. "Eww! *No!* Of course not."

Dallas snorted a laugh. "What do you mean, 'eww'? The man's a walking sex god."

"That's not what I meant," she stammered. She wasn't really sure what she meant anymore, and Dallas's description of Darien was... well, it was spot-on.

"Can you blame me for asking?" Dallas said. "You've been staying at his house —"

"We are *not* sleeping together," Loren hissed. "Besides, even if I wanted to, he's not interested in me like that."

Dallas's brow tilted, her painted lips twitching. "Want to bet?"

The confusion that washed over Loren's face wasn't faked.

Dal's smile grew. "He looks at you like he wants to find out what you taste like."

It felt like someone had taken a match to Loren's face and lit it on fire. "Oh my god, Dal. No, he doesn't. I don't know what planet you're on, but it's not mine." Dallas grinned, and Loren gave a huff of frustration. "I thought you were worried about stupid boys coming between us. What changed?"

"I *met* them."

Loren rolled her eyes. "Can we focus on Sabrine, please? There will be plenty of time for you to obsess over boys, but it's not right now." She felt bad as soon as she said it, especially when Dallas's face instantly clouded over with guilt.

But the moment passed swiftly as the witch declared, "I'm coming over tonight."

Loren rolled her eyes. "Screwing Maximus so soon?"

"You know I won't deny the opportunity if it presents itself."

Loren gave a snort, but her amusement at Dallas's comment abruptly faded as the witch turned serious.

"You mentioned the Devils are going to see Cain," Dallas said.

Loren arched a brow. *"And?"*

"And I think we should tag along."

"Fat chance," Loren muttered. "Darien would never agree to that. Trust me — I already tried asking him."

"Who said anything about *asking?*" Dallas scoffed with a wave of her hand. "If he won't let us go with him, we'll go on our own. I'll follow his car on a freaking bicycle if I have to. I refuse to sit around while they get to play detective." Dallas crossed her arms and appraised her. "Are you with me?"

If Darien were to catch them trying to follow him into Stone's End, they would be in such crap. A deep, unending pile of crap. But Dallas was right: why should they sit around and do nothing while the Devils looked for their friend?

Loren sighed. "Let's hope they own some bicycles."

Dallas grinned, a mischievous glint in her silver-green eyes. "That's my girl!"

Dallas stayed at Loren's side as she knelt before Sabrine's photo and said a prayer to the gods and goddesses of the Star. She placed Stumpy on the sidewalk, next to the smiling face of their missing friend, hoping her prayer would help Sabrine find her way home.

"You DIDN'T TELL me Loren had a smoking-hot redhead for a friend," Maximus said to Darien as he walked at his side.

"And you didn't tell me the cat's got your tongue as soon as a pretty girl hits on you before you can hit on her." He might've laughed, had he not felt as tongue-tied as Max when he'd laid eyes on Loren earlier that evening. Luckily, he'd snapped the hell out of it before she could notice him gawking at the shape of her ass in the jeans she was wearing. Although she drove him up the wall more times than he could count, he had to admit she had an incredible body. Absolutely incredible.

Never mind that he'd sensed her arousal last week when she'd watched him remotely track her friend. He'd spent too many hours afterward wondering about the thoughts that had crossed her filthy little mind—and how it would've felt if he'd touched her between those glorious legs she'd pressed together under the table.

Fuck, he needed to get laid. This whole *protection duty* thing wasn't helping him think straight. He was already beginning to forget what life had been like before this human girl had come along.

Despite the crowd he was navigating, and despite that Max was at his side, remembering that night instantly put him in a state of semi-arousal. He had been so tempted to stroke her mind a little harder—just enough to see the look on her gorgeous face when release found her at his touch. It was a hellseher ability that was difficult to master, and not a lot of people knew about it, even other hellsehers. But no matter how much he would've thoroughly enjoyed watching her squirm, he wouldn't have done it. Not without her permission.

But…even if she had invited him to do so—or, rather, accepted *his* invitation, even if it had mostly been for teasing purposes—he likely would've declined. It would…complicate things. And besides, she was too good for that. Too good for *him*. The near-constant color of her aura was evidence enough to back that up. After all, white sheets were the easiest to stain.

Darien's Familiar Spirit spoke from within his shadow, his misty voice slicing into Darien's thoughts. *You could simply be nicer to her and see where it gets you. Maybe then I wouldn't have to listen to your filthy internal brooding.*

Mind your own, Bandit, Darien replied, though he found himself shooting a backward glance at Loren, who was barely visible through the crowds of people.

You're fond of her, Bandit said. *You don't need to deny it.*

Now's not the time.

The spirit countered, *Now's never the time.* But he stopped arguing after that.

"I think that's a moot point," Max mumbled, snapping Darien's attention away from his nosy Familiar. Darien gave his head a shake to clear his thoughts. "But maybe you shouldn't send me on any undercover jobs; I do better with blood than words."

Darien smirked. "Clearly."

They found Logan Sands near the edge of the crowd. The pure-blooded werewolf was by himself today; no pack members in sight, and the breeze that swept through the street carried no hints that any of them were lurking nearby.

Logan was a brawny brute with shoulder-length dark hair, brown skin that was windburned to a warmer shade, and eyes the color of the sun—upturned at the outer corners. The sun-colored eyes were a characteristic all werewolves shared; because of them, they were easy to pick out in a crowd, just as it was easy to pick out a venefica due to the silver cast to their irises. Easy even for humans, who had no enhanced senses to alert them to their presence.

Although it was against the law for a werewolf to hunt human flesh, there was the odd one who rebelled and did so in secret, unable to resist the taste of mortal blood for long. The law enforcement hardly gave enough of a shit to catch the offenders, since humans contributed so little to society that they usually weren't missed once they were gone. And then there was the issue of the Meatpacking District, its operators giving even less of a shit than the law enforcement.

This city was a mess, he had to admit. It was dark and dirty and riddled with sinners, but it was his city, the only land he'd ever known. On some sleepless nights, the horns of the sinners became halos, and the streets felt like paradise.

The werewolf's keen senses alerted him to their arrival seconds before Darien and Max reached his side. Logan turned to face them, concealing the surprise he felt upon seeing them here. Several months had passed since they'd done so much as talk.

Darien supposed that was his fault.

"Darien." Logan's chin dipped in greeting. "Maximus. What brings you two here?"

"We'd like to give our condolences for your sister," Darien replied. Chrysantha had gone missing one week before Sabrine.

"I appreciate that," Logan said, though his voice was strained.

Darien had a feeling Logan was holding his tongue against the words he really wanted to say—about what had taken place roughly ten months ago, when a tragedy had led to Logan rising in rank to leader of all wolf packs in the Silverwood District, Werewolf Territory of Angelthene. A tragedy that involved the death of Logan's father. Darien had been too...*busy* to help Logan and the other wolves. Truth be told, he and the other Devils were at a house party hosted by the Angels of Death, and Darien had spent the night locked in a closet with Christa Copenspire, a girl he was sort-of-dating-but-not. It wasn't a good enough excuse to miss a call for help from a friend, and Logan clearly hadn't forgotten about that yet.

Logan said, "Are you here just to give your condolences for my sister, or did you know the Van Arsdell girl as well?"

"We came here with Sabrine's two best friends," Darien explained.

A curious glint entered Logan's eyes, his nostrils flaring as he scented the girls on Darien and Max. "Has so much changed in the last few months that Darkslayers now run with witches and humans?"

Max said, "I wouldn't say we run with them, but enough has changed in the past little while that we've been...," his eyes flicked to Darien, "stepping in for a good cause."

Logan smiled, his canine teeth glinting in the candlelight. "Good cause or no, you and your Devils sure know how to keep things interesting, Cassel."

"Indeed," Darien drawled. "I want to ask you something while we're here. Where was Chrysantha last seen before she went missing?" It was a thought he'd had; while Angelthene suffered from a

CITY OF GODS AND MONSTERS

high level of crime, he wondered if there was a chance that the abductions—both the abductees and the initial target all university students, which didn't happen often—were linked. It might be a stretch, but he wasn't about to rule it out.

Logan's eyes were guarded. "You boys joining the law enforcement in their detective work or something?"

Darien hooked his thumb in his pocket. "I'm just asking."

There was a pause as Logan assessed them. "Last I heard from Chrysantha, she was serving drinks at a dive bar on the southern end of the downtown core. A shithole called Puerta de la Muerta, down on Red Water and Crystal Teeth." Puerta de la Muerta—literally *Death's Door.*

Darien's eyes flicked skyward as he mapped out the two streets in his head; he knew this city like the back of his hand. "Dennis Boyd's rat-infested hovel."

Logan nodded. "What about this Sabrine girl? Where did she go missing?"

"Canopus Street," Darien said. "Near the Avenue of the Scarlet Star." On their way to the vigil, Loren had given him every detail she could remember from that night. Darien added, "But the Darkslayer and his henchman weren't after Sabrine—they were after her friend."

Logan narrowed his eyes. "She was taken by a Darkslayer? Which circle?"

"None we know of. Ever seen a hellseher with a tattoo of a phoenix head?"

Logan looked as confused as Darien felt. "Never." He seemed to think of something, and then he smirked, his sharp teeth glinting in the moonlight. "Randal must be just loving this."

Darien didn't say anything. As far as he knew, Randal had no clue about the wannabe Darkslayers working his soil, and he wanted to keep it that way for as long as possible. The last thing he needed was the king of Angelthene's Darkslayers poking his nose into this fucking mess.

Logan said, "Why'd they take Sabrine if it was her friend they were after?"

"According to Loren, they caught up to Sabrine first—before they could get to Loren. They held Sabrine at gunpoint as a last-ditch effort to get Loren in their car. Peace officers showed up, so they took Sabrine instead." Darien had been listening carefully to the goings-on of the underworld for any indication that whoever had Sabrine in their clutches was looking to trade her for Loren. He suspected it would happen eventually, likely sooner rather than later. They wouldn't have taken Sabrine unless they'd had a plan to use her to get what they really wanted. The problem with that possibility was breaking the news to Loren. And it didn't take a genius to conclude she wouldn't take the news well.

"I'm guessing they've cloaked Chrysantha's scent?" Max asked the wolf.

"Of course." Logan's lip curled. "But I won't stop looking for her. I *can't* stop." Darien understood how he felt. Had it been Ivyana who'd gone missing, Darien would've refused to rest until he brought her back home.

"I keep waiting for something to occur to me," Logan murmured. "I've gone over that night again and again, but I can't figure it out. Nothing unusual happened; it was just another normal night. And by morning, Chrys was gone."

"We'll figure it out," Darien said. "Until then, we'll let you know if we hear anything."

Logan gave a stiff nod. "Likewise." He rubbed at his nose and stared out at the dark horizon. "I'll see you boys around."

They now had another lead. But first on the list was Cain—and Cain was exactly who Darien would be going after tonight.

As soon as they dropped Loren off at Hell's Gate and devised a plan, they would head into Stone's End to start crossing suspects off their list, and possibly—hopefully—adding new ones. He could sense that they were getting warmer, though it wasn't warm enough.

Darien disappeared into the crowd, Max on his heels. Leaving behind the werewolf that continued to stare at that empty horizon, as if it held the answer he was seeking, for a long, long while.

18

The sky had opened with rain by the time Darien reached the exit that led into Stone's End.

It was almost Witching Hour, but he didn't feel the least bit tired. He could thank adrenaline for that. Adrenaline and the red and blue lights oscillating at the roadblock up ahead.

Roadblocks were the norm at a place like Stone's End. The city's crime level was so high, there was a heavy presence of law enforcement everywhere a person went. But it peaked here in Cain's neighborhood, where turf wars were a nightly affair, and there were locks on things that didn't normally have locks on them—mailboxes, air conditioning units, vending machines.

Which was exactly why Darien didn't bat an eye as he drove up to the peace officers who waited by their squad cars. The other Devils in the vehicle weren't fazed either, though where she sat in the passenger's seat beside him, Lace shifted with what Darien knew was annoyance.

"Say one word," Darien warned her in a lethally quiet voice as he slowed the car to a crawl, "and you'll be walking home." Max and Jack snickered in the back seat.

But everyone grew quiet and serious as Darien lowered his window.

The officer lumbered up to Darien's door. The beam of his flashlight stung Darien's eyes as he lifted it, pointing it right at his face. Darien briefly held up a hand to block the glare; those who were gifted with the Sight and used it on a regular basis were prone to having sensitive eyes.

"I'm sorry, folks," the officer began, "but I'm afraid you're going to have to turn—" He choked on the rest of his sentence as he beheld the Devils in the car. And upon registering the tattoos marking each of their necks, he lowered the flashlight, the beam wobbling from his shaking hand. It took him a moment to speak, and when he did, his voice was a rasp. "What brings you to Stone's End?" The rain nearly drowned out his question.

"We have business with Cain Nash," Darien stated.

The officer—E. Baxter, the gleaming nametag pinned to his pristine uniform read—glanced over his shoulder, at the peace commissioner stationed by the squad cars up ahead. The commissioner—no more than a silhouette in the rain—looked to Baxter in question but made no move to come any closer.

When Baxter faced Darien again, he looked as if he'd seen a ghost. "Are you here to collect?" There was a curious undertone to his question—one that made Darien certain the law enforcement had become desperate for any sort of help, even if it wasn't done by the book. Even if it came in the form of one criminal cleaning up another's mistakes.

"Depends on why you're asking."

Baxter studied the Devils one by one, though it was Darien he spent the most time sizing up. Finally, after making his decision, Baxter spoke. "One of Cain's feuds crossed a line tonight. We don't have the evidence needed to make an arrest, but we have reason to believe it was his men who blew up the Starlight Mall. There was a Blood Potions dealer operating on the premises, using an ice cream parlor for a front." He paused, lines of grief deepening his expression. "Innocent lives were lost in the explosion."

"Burning Ignis," Darien swore.

It was no secret that Cain was a walking, talking piece of shit, but to blow up a mall... *Burning Ignis* was right, kids went to malls, families—especially ice cream parlors. If killing Cain wouldn't start a war they couldn't afford to deal with right now, Darien would personally bag his head tonight and leave it as a gift on the front steps of the holding center.

Darien drew a breath. "If you're making a request—"

"I'm not making any request," Baxter said, lifting his hands. "I just want you to know that I can talk to the commissioner. If he gives me the okay to let you guys through, we'll look the other way. No matter what you do to him."

Darien assessed the officer for a long minute. "Something tells me this tragedy is personal for you."

Baxter didn't say anything, but his expression told Darien enough: this man had lost someone tonight. In his years working as a Darkslayer, Darien had been approached several times by the kinds of people he never expected to see. Peace officers, lawyers, people who worked for the Magical Protections Unit. Men and women who'd lost someone close to them and had become desperate for retaliation. So desperate, in fact, that they were willing to hire a Devil to do their dirty work, so they could sleep at night without the hand of guilt squeezing their airways shut.

"Let your boss know we'd like to get through," Darien said. "But we make no promises, and our business is our own."

Baxter gave one sharp nod before jogging over to the huddle of squad cars, the beam of his flashlight bouncing with every step. When he reached the cars, he conversed quietly with the peace commissioner for several minutes, the rain drowning out every trace of their conversation.

In the back seat, Max murmured, "Sounds like Cain's become a problem even the commissioner can't handle."

"I'm banking on that," Darien replied. He didn't allow himself to feel sorry for the fact that he and his Devils had no plans to fix the problems Baxter was hoping they'd fix. They weren't here tonight to make right the deaths of those innocent people, but to get answers to help Sabrine and Loren. Cain would be dealt with eventually—of that, he had no doubt. But it wouldn't be tonight.

The hand of guilt would have to suffocate this officer a little while longer.

Baxter returned to the vehicle a moment later. "You're free to go in," he told them. "Once you get through the exit, take the eastern backroads to Cain's residence. Keep away from Crescent Street."

Darien gave a sharp nod. The officer backed away from the car, and Darien was about to push the gearshift into drive when something in the rear-view mirror caught his eye.

Two young women—a blonde and a redhead, roughly two dozen feet behind his car. Grappling with each other over what to do with the lone electric scooter they were both standing on. The scooter that appeared to have run out of battery life.

The other Devils turned around in their seats to follow his line of sight as Darien snarled, "You've *got* to be kidding me."

LOREN STOPPED PULLING on the handlebars of the electric scooter the moment she heard a car door swinging open. And Dallas fell silent beside her, her own hands stilling as she took in the Devil striding toward them, the promise of death in his eyes. The peace officers merely watched with vigilance from where they were turning away vehicles at the roadblock as Darien closed in on them.

The Devil did not stop until he was a terrifying force of nature looming over Loren and Dallas.

"What do you think you're doing here?" he snarled in Loren's face, raindrops flying from his lips.

Before Dallas could make the situation worse by saying the wrong thing, Loren stepped off the scooter. "It was my idea," she said. Her legs felt like jelly, and her fingers ached from grasping the handlebars. "And I'm sorry. We should've listened to you, but we wanted to help—"

"You're not helping by following us into a goddamn warzone on a scooter that hasn't been turned on since Ivyana was twelve fucking years old."

"I said I'm sorry," Loren bit out, teeth chattering. She was soaked to the bone. Dallas mumbled her own apology as she stepped off the scooter.

Darien shot them both a look of daggers before ripping the handlebars out of Dallas's grip and carrying the scooter toward his car. "Get in the back seat," he called over his shoulder. *"Now."*

Loren hurried after him, Dallas at her side, their sneakers splashing in puddles. Darien was throwing the scooter into the trunk as Loren swung open the back door—

She froze as she beheld Maximus and Jack in the back seat and Lace in the front. All of them were gaping at her and Dallas with expressions ranging from shock to fury.

The sleeve of Darien's jacket brushed against Loren's back as he approached the open driver's door. "Switch with Max," he barked to Lace. The platinum-blonde didn't argue as she unbuckled her seatbelt and did as she was told.

As Loren squished into the back, Dallas right on her heels, she realized why Darien had made Lace switch seats with Max: they wouldn't have fit otherwise. Even with Lace now sandwiched between Loren and Jack, with Dallas on the other side of Loren, everyone was practically sitting in each other's laps.

No one said anything as Darien rolled up his window, shoved the gearshift into drive, and sped past the roadblock, past the officers that waved them on...and into Stone's End.

———

LOREN'S BREATHING grew shallow as they drove deeper into Stone's End. The ride was entirely silent, save for the barking of dogs on front lawns and the chopping of helicopter rotors as the law enforcement flew over the neglected district. The roads here were dirty and riddled with potholes, and skeletons of cars that had long since been burned to a crisp sat in parking lots.

Darien pulled to a stop in front of a shabby house with a tattered green couch on the front lawn. A doghouse was bolted to a cement slab in the center of that lawn, but the thing that was chained to the kennel was not a dog at all. It was a storm-drain breed of demon, a hairless thing with curved horns, mottled skin, and a long, rat-like tail that was pointed like an arrowhead. It yapped and howled at the vehicle as Darien cut the engine.

Darien swivelled in his seat to face Loren, who was crushing Dallas's thigh beneath her own and squeezing her hand with a death grip. "You've had a bad habit of being deaf to my advice lately," he began, looking between her and the witch with as much patience as he could muster. "But if you two want to live to see another day, you will stay in this car. Are you going to listen to me this time?"

Loren's throat squeaked when she swallowed. She gave a faint nod, Dallas doing the same beside her.

Max snapped open the glovebox and passed a pistol to Darien, who promptly slid it into the holster at the front of his black cargo pants. Darien appraised Loren and Dallas again as the others prepared to exit the vehicle.

"Do not unlock these doors," he said. "Mortifer has control over the car tonight; he will make sure no one will be able to see or hear you, even if they come right up to the windows, but that doesn't mean you should move too much or talk too loudly. Do you understand me?"

"Yes," Loren whispered.

When he looked at Dallas for a reply, she bit out in a hoarse voice, "I get it."

"Good." Darien cracked open the door, and then turned to give the others a sharp nod. They dipped their heads in return, and they all exited the vehicle and approached Cain's turf, leaving Loren and Dallas alone in the now-silent car, the demon in Cain's yard their only company.

IT CAME as no surprise to Darien that Cain was already aware of their arrival. If the roaring of the car engine ripping through the night hadn't startled every sensitive immortal ear in this shitty neigh-borhood, then the yapping pest chained to a cement slab on the front lawn had certainly got the job done.

Cain was waiting on the rotting porch, his cruel, scarred face aglow in the yellow porch-light, as Darien and the others walked the decrepit stone path.

The half-warlock, half-human wasn't alone; six of his men stood on either side of the open front door, magic staves and automatic weapons at the ready. Despite that Cain's men all stood nearly seven feet in height, it was the one waiting in the open doorway—leaning heavily on a cane, the entire left side of his body perforated with burn wounds, according to the Daystar article Darien had read several weeks ago—who was the real obstacle tonight.

The house fire had certainly done a number on Cain's appear-ance. His left eye was hooded and scarred, and the side of his thin mouth was set in a permanent scowl. The details of that fire hadn't been revealed to the public, for obvious reasons, but Darien knew it was an explosion caused by cooking up illegal Blood Potions with cheap equipment that couldn't handle the spells necessary for fusing the ingredients. Law enforcement had been looking to eliminate the threat of Blood Potions for years; they were dangerous and addic-tive, and they had the tendency to make a person violent, and their magic unchained. Blood Potions allowed a person to perform dark spells that operated on Blood Magic, a type of power that had been banned a very long time ago. Cain's men had likely managed to cover up just enough of the evidence to avoid being locked behind bars, much to the disappointment of the MPU.

Cain waited until the Devils came to a stop at the base of the rotting stairs before he spoke.

"Cassel," Cain said, his voice gravelly and deep, and just loud enough to be heard over the sharp drumming of the rain on the tin roof. "What brings you here on such a fine evening?"

"We have a few questions only a man of your intelligence can answer for us." Darien's eyes flicked skyward as a helicopter flew over the house, rotors creating a wind that shifted strands of his hair out of place. Officers likely heading to the wreckage of the Starlight

Mall to see about rescuing anyone who'd survived the blast. Darien zeroed his gaze in on Cain. "This a bad time?"

Cain gave a greasy smile. "It's as good a time as any, as long as no whirlybirds bother you."

Darien's answering grin was cold. "Not at all."

"Then come on in." He turned and lumbered into the house, every step he took a little easier than what a person might expect from someone using a cane, even someone with warlock blood that allowed for the swift healing of most injuries.

So *this* was the game they'd be playing tonight. It was obvious that Cain had recently suffered injuries at the hands of fire, but he clearly preferred that any unsolicited visitors who came knocking at his door were kept under the impression that those injuries were worse than they really were. Likely so that any visitors who were up to no good might pity him too much to try anything...*unsavory.*

Too bad *pity* was seldom a part of Darien's vocabulary.

The Devils followed Cain into the house. It didn't escape Darien that not one of Cain's men asked the Devils to leave their weapons outside; Cain was smart enough to know that Darkslayers were weapons all on their own.

The inside of the house was cold, damp, and musty. The mismatched furniture was stained and moth-eaten, the kitchen counters littered with Blood Potions and the paraphernalia necessary for making them. The cheap floors were peeling at the corners and were covered in a tacky substance that stuck to the Devils' boots.

"How's Randal these days?" Cain asked as he slid a chair out at the lopsided kitchen table and lowered himself into it. "Go ahead and have a seat." He propped his cane up against a table leg.

"We'll stand, thanks," Darien replied.

"Suit yourselves," Cain mumbled. Returning to his former topic of conversation, he said of Randal, "I never see him at the Advocate anymore."

"He's the same as he's always been," Darien said, his eyes sweeping the house—the cluttered countertops, the scummy dishes piled up in the sink, the staticky television that was balanced precariously on a cardboard box in the living room. "He'd rather milk the benefits from the sidelines of his cash cows than get his hands dirty —whether that be nightclubs or collecting, it makes no difference to him as long as his pockets are full."

Tension rippled through the room, and for a long time, no one said anything. Cain appraised Darien closely, as if trying to decide whether he was making a joke.

And then Cain, drawing the wrong conclusion, gave a long, wheezing laugh. "I guess I shouldn't be surprised that you can get away with saying shit like that." He could barely get the sentence out between bouts of laughter. "You always were his favorite."

Darien didn't smile. "I doubt that."

The smirk on Cain's face faded just a little, but he didn't know Darien well enough to really figure out the hostility simmering beneath every word he uttered about Randal. "You said you have questions," Cain said. "Any friend of Randal's is a friend of mine. Go on and ask them, boy, and I'll do my best to answer."

"Word on the street says you're looking for a girl," Darien began. The frown on Cain's face deepened. Clearly, he hadn't expected this when he'd invited them into his house. "A girl worth four million gold mynet."

Cain shifted in his seat. "I seem to be missing what the question is, son —"

"Don't call me *son*," Darien cut in. Cain lifted his chin, a muscle in his bony jaw twitching. His silvery eyes flicked toward the door — his escape route, if there came a need for one. "Last time I checked, you and your men were very aware that there are only six Dark-slaying circles in this city. Since you claim to be a friend of Randal's, I think it's also safe to assume that you are *very* aware of the fact that no one may take a Darkslaying job in this city unless they are a member of an Angelthene circle. So, my question, *boy*, is why you think it's okay to not only steal this job from under my nose but also get paid more than me."

Cain, wisely, took a moment to consider his answer. "I had no idea that you were on this job —"

"Doesn't make what you're doing right. I was offered three mil for that target—money Randal Slade gets a cut of. Do you really think he'll be so forgiving when he finds out you're practically trying to rob him?"

Cain folded his hands in his lap. "Did he send you here to threaten me?"

"I'm not threatening you."

"It feels like you are."

"Trust me," Darien said with a sly smile. "If I was making a threat, you wouldn't have to ask me for clarification."

Cain merely watched him, his expression betraying nothing.

The room had grown tense. Darien decided the situation needed a minute to deescalate; he needed Cain to talk, and now that he'd planted the seed of fear in Cain's mind, he would allow him a moment to process it, a moment for that seed to bud, and for Cain to decide to give Darien the information he was looking for.

Regardless that Darien was bluffing, what he'd told Cain was the truth: no one was allowed to act as a Darkslayer on Angelthene soil unless they were a Darkslayer themselves, belonging to one of the six circles and answering to—and paying—Randal Slade. The fact that Tyson Geller had been willing to partner up with a graverobber to find Loren was enough of a betrayal that he could be stripped of his title as a Reaper. Or, worse, killed.

He was next on Darien's list.

Darien's gaze slid to the massive mosaic glittering on the wall behind Cain—the only thing in this nasty place that was worthy of a second glance. Made of shards of glass that were every shade of red and blue, the piece of art told the story of a hunted phoenix that rose from the ashes of its destruction, becoming more magnificent than it was before.

He'd certainly seen a lot of this extinct bird recently.

"Where did you find this piece?" Darien asked, jerking his chin at the mosaic.

"Won it at an auction." Cain turned in his chair to take in the image. "Beautiful, isn't it?" he murmured, almost to himself. "It's a shame the phoenix no longer exists. If it did, I would bottle its powers and use them to fix...well, *this.*" He gestured to the left side of his face. "And to make love to my old lady again." *Old lady.* What a disrespectful term. Darien wondered if Cain's wife minded being called such a thing.

The implication behind Cain's statement did not escape Darien; clearly, this man had suffered injuries that ran deeper than surface level when he'd got caught in that fire.

Cain went on, his voice a grumble, "Instead, all we've got is those pesky Firebirds. They do nothing but pose a fire hazard and wake me up every day at the ass-crack of dawn with their bloody squawking." He turned back around to face Darien, his scarred lip curling into a cruel half-smile. "I shoot them down in the yard when I see them. Feed 'em to the demon."

Darien shifted his hands into his jacket pockets. "I find it slightly odd that you're so critical of an animal descended from the one you worship."

Cain's expression sank into a frown. "I worship no one and nothing but yours truly. If the phoenix was alive today, I would snap its neck and suck the blood out of its veins if it meant I'd be healed of my scars. I would kill every last one of them and take them for everything they've got." He paused, and he looked right out of his mind as he leaned forward in his chair and repeated, the veins in his neck bulging, "I worship *nothing*, Cassel."

"Yeah," Darien clipped, "you said that already."

Cain visibly bristled. "Remind me again why you barged through my door."

Darien sensed his Devils' focus sharpening.

"I didn't barge through, you invited me in. And I'm here because you have answers concerning who else is trying to steal this job from me. And you're going to give them to me."

Cain gave a gruff laugh. "If Randal didn't send you, then I really don't give two shits about what you want. Besides, maybe the real reason you're here is because you're scared someone else will make it to that girl first. Maybe...maybe you're scared that if you don't deliver that three mil to the boss whose dick you suck, he'll kill you and every last one of your dicksucking Devils—"

One second, Darien was three feet away from Cain. The next, he was slamming Cain's scarred face down on the table. Bone crunched as Cain's nose flattened against the wood.

Cain's men made to move, but Darien's Devils were faster. They all had their guns cocked and aimed, their eyes black with the Sight, before Cain's men could so much as lift their weapons.

"Don't even think about it," Max crooned, holding two of them at gunpoint. Cain's men—wisely—held very still.

Darien splayed Cain's right hand out flat on the table. He removed a pair of pliers from his jacket pocket and slid Cain's middle finger between the pincers.

"Now tell me who was offered four mil," Darien said, his lethal voice hushed, "or I'll teach you a lesson you won't forget."

"You wouldn't," Cain ground out, spittle flying from his lips.

Darien gave a low chuckle. "Oh, I wouldn't, would I?" He looked up at the room full of people, giving Cain's men the invitation to try him.

None of them did. They merely watched with wide eyes, clearly having no idea what to do.

Sick delight washed through Darien.

"You seem to underestimate me just a tad," Darien crooned, applying pressure to the pliers. He squeezed a little harder, causing Cain to slap his free hand onto the table, the force rattling the over-flowing ashtray. Darien merely laughed. "We're not on a wrestling mat, bud. Speak." He waited, but Cain said nothing. The man was grinding his teeth, the sound audible. *"Speak."*

He squeezed harder—just enough to draw blood.

A half-sob burst through Cain's lips, followed by a string of curse words and a couple names.

Now they were getting somewhere. And at the cost of nothing but a little blood from a man who'd harmed his fair share of innocent people.

Darien leaned in closer. "Could you repeat that, please?"

Cain was trembling, his breathing ragged. Spit pooled beneath his cheek. "Koray and Xander," he gasped. The Demon Twins. "Koray and Xander were offered four mil. I don't know who employed them. It's just a rumor. I don't even know if it's true—"

"You heard this at the Devil's Advocate, correct?"

"Yes."

Koray and Xander, half-vampire half-hellseher, had belonged to the Vipers back when Darien had become leader of the Devils, but had gone rogue in the years since. They worked for no one except themselves now, only taking jobs when it suited them.

The sting of jealousy hit Darien deep. How nice. How fucking nice it must be to pocket every single copper that came out of a job, to not have to hand anything to the man standing behind the curtain.

"What else do you know?" Darien's eyes turned black with the Sight as he studied Cain's aura, checking for signs that told him the next words to leave his mouth would be a lie. His aura was dark as ink and warped at the edges, tinged here and there with the murky, purplish-green hue of fear.

"I heard they want her for something called 'The Initiation'," Cain said. Sweat beaded on his temples. "Sounded like a sacrifice or some shit, but I was only after the cash, Cassel. I swear."

The dull flicker at the edges of Cain's aura told him everything he needed to know. "Your aura tells me you had some interest in whatever this Initiation is." He would've used his magic to tunnel into Cain's mind, to mentally torture him until he revealed the truth he was hiding, if he hadn't been trained to keep such magic out.

"Having interest doesn't mean I was going to act on it."

"Right," Darien drawled.

Cain held his breath, every muscle in his body tight. "It's not a crime if I didn't commit it."

"That's some peace officer shit you're spewing. You're talking to a Devil." Darien tightened his hold on the back of Cain's neck. "Anything else?"

"That's all I know, Cassel —"

Darien twisted the pliers. "Oh, I highly doubt that." More blood dripped to the table, the salty tang of it flooding Darien's airways.

Cain bellowed, "All right, all right, ALL RIGHT." Sweat ran down Cain's face in streams. "I heard something else. There are people looking for the target — for the girl. The same people who have her friend. They put a message out that they're willing to make a trade—a ransom. If whoever is hiding the girl turns her in—or if the girl turns *herself* in—they will set the Van Arsdell girl free."

The blood drained from Darien's face.

Fucking hell. He'd suspected this would happen eventually, but for it to be so soon…

If Loren heard about this… If she even had an inkling that turning herself in would save Sabrine, she would rip that talisman off in an instant.

And then she'd walk right into their trap the moment Darien wasn't looking.

"Let go of me," Cain bit out, flexing the fingers of his shaking, bleeding hand. "I've told you everything. Now let me go, dammit."

Darien crushed Cain's face into the table. "When I'm good and ready."

"Fuck you," Cain bit out, spittle flying from his lips. "Fuck your daddy. And *fuck* your dead mommy."

A weightless feeling shook through Darien—one that had nothing to do with fear and everything to do with rage.

Maximus murmured, "You shouldn't have said that."

No. No, he really shouldn't have.

Where he crouched within Darien's shadow, Bandit growled and said to Darien, *Do you think if I bit him in the ass, he'd be a bit more respectful?*

Cain seemed to realize his mistake, but it was too late. "Wait," he panted. "Wait, I didn't mean that, man. You know I'm only playing—"

Darien tightened his hold on the pliers. And everyone in the room, including his Devils, held their breath as they waited for him to act.

But he removed the pliers and straightened, shoving Cain's face into the table. "It's alright, Max," Darien said, a smile in his voice. He put the pliers into his pocket. "I'll tell you boys what," he began, speaking to Cain's men now, who watched him with vigilance. "How about we all put the weapons away and settle this the smart way? No killing—just fists." He held his arms out in a what-do-you-say gesture.

Cain slowly sat up in his chair and looked up at Darien. A bruise was already forming on his face; there would be more where that came from tonight.

"Stand up," Darien ordered. "I'll even let you get the first hit in."

Cain paled. "You can't be serious." His eyes flicked about the room.

"Do I look like I'm joking?" When no one moved, Darien gestured for his Devils to lower their weapons. "Come on, everyone. Put the weapons down. Let's have some fun."

The Devils did as he'd instructed, and soon Cain's men were following suit. Lace would square off with a man bigger than Max, but she didn't look daunted by it. In fact, she was smiling. She could hold her own in any fight.

There was only one of Cain's men who wouldn't lower his weapon, and who Jack addressed with a grin. "What are you afraid of? Don't you enjoy a good, old-fashioned brawl?" A manic glint entered Jack's eyes. "Or are you too chicken-shit?"

After another moment, the warlock lowered his magic stave.

Cain lifted himself to his feet with a grunt and faced Darien.

Darien gestured to his own chin. "Go on," he crooned. "You get one hit in, and then I'm going to punch your teeth down your throat. Maybe that'll teach you not to blow up malls."

Cain had turned paler, and he reeked of fear. "Is that what all this is about?"

"Having your ass beat is clearly long overdue. Now hit me."

No one moved. No one breathed.

Until Jack shouted, "Let's dance, boys!" and nailed his opponent right in the jaw.

The brawl broke out, and Cain *did* hit Darien.

But that one punch was the only strike Cain got in, and then Darien stomped his face into the floor, letting himself think of nothing but all those innocent people—children included, he knew— who'd died because of this waste of skin.

19

Bloodcurdling screams and the sound of glass smashing tore from inside the house.

Loren jolted in the back seat of Darien's car, strands of her hair catching in her mouth as her head spun to face the closed front door of Cain's abode.

The key in the ignition suddenly turned without anyone's command—and it took Loren far longer than it should have to realize it was the Hob starting the electrical system without starting the motor. Hardcore metal punched through the speakers, causing Loren to jump again, Dallas doing the same beside her.

"I guess this is the kind of music Darien relaxes to," Loren joked over the noise.

"Guess so," Dallas muttered, sounding as rattled as Loren.

As if to prove her wrong, the Hob lowered the volume and began flicking through the music. The screen that was set in the dash flashed brightly in the dark car as Mortifer found the Favorites Playlist. To Loren's surprise, the next song that drifted through the speakers wasn't heavy metal at all—it was a classical piece.

She let her eyelids slip shut as she listened to it, and soon the elegant sound of the flutes and the harpsichord and the other instruments she couldn't place eased the tension in her muscles and drowned out the sound of the screaming going on in the house. It elevated her, carrying her away as if she were a soap bubble floating astride the world.

The song that came on after the first was a soft rock track about a found family with a bond stronger than blood. She found herself humming to it, even when the Devils came out of the house a moment later and she caught sight of the rag Darien was using to clean the blood off his rings.

Loren's stomach dipped and rose.

The Devils didn't say anything as they got in the car, Lace and Jack squishing into the back seat with Loren and Dallas again. And Loren and Dallas didn't ask questions as Darien spun the car around, tires screeching, and sped out of Stone's End.

The music kept playing. No one turned it down, and as the road flew under the tires, the tension in the vehicle melted away, like the final words of a song that faded into the next.

As THEY SPED through the city, back to the Victoria Amazonica District, Loren began to feel nauseous. Her tattoo was pulsing in warning—a sure sign that she needed to eat something. Sweat glistened on her skin, and she squirmed in the back seat, choking down the urge to throw up, until she couldn't take it anymore.

"Darien," she blurted.

He cut off whatever he was saying to Maximus, his eyes locking with hers in the rear-view mirror. "Yeah, Loren."

"I think I need to get something to eat. I'm not feeling well."

Where he was squished against the back door like a pretzel on the left side of the vehicle, Jack said, "I'd be pissed right off if no doctors could figure out what was wrong with me."

"Nothing's wrong with her, Jack," Darien said. The glow of streetlights passed over the car, shining in through the sunroof and gilding his night-dark hair. "Don't be rude." Having Darien defend her like that when he himself teased her on a regular basis... It made her feel flattered, she supposed, for lack of a better word. And it made her wonder if she really was right about the mask he wore.

"I wasn't being rude, you dickbag." Jack placed his boot on the back of Darien's seat.

"Get your foot off my seat or I'll throw you out the window," Darien threatened mildly. "And I won't open it first."

Maximus chuckled.

"Besides," Jack continued, as if Darien hadn't said anything. Though he did—wisely—remove his boot from the back of Darien's seat. "There's something wrong with all of us. I like to gamble. You like to throw punches at the Pit—"

"Jack," Darien warned, eyes flashing in the mirror.

That got Loren's attention, distracting her for a moment from the need to vomit. "You like to fight?" Darien was avoiding her gaze in the mirror as he took the exit into Jubilee Square. "Like, in fighting rings?"

Darien pushed up the turn signal as he approached a stop sign. "Sometimes," he admitted with a mumble.

"More like every weekend and most weeknights," Jack said, grinning. Lace swallowed a snort, fueling Jack's amusement, and their laughter soon became deafening. Dallas snickered, and Max merely pressed a hand to his temple and shook his head.

Darien shot Jack a glare. "Are you familiar with what cement tastes like? Because you're going to eat it in exactly three seconds if you don't stick a cork in it." Jack held up his hands in surrender, though he continued to snort under his breath over Darien's murderous expression.

The light turned green, and Darien accelerated into the heart of Jubilee Square, where Loren and Dallas shared a meal with four deadly killers at the Date Palm Café, one of the few restaurants that stayed open this late into the night. HID lamps lit up all of Jubilee Square, keeping the demons at bay.

It was an out-of-body experience to sit with the Devils in that café; to watch as the employees and customers who dared to be out at this hour gave them a wide berth. A few people even got up and left, taking their half-eaten food with them, upon seeing them enter.

It gave Loren a sense of power she'd never felt before—something she'd never receive on her own. As she sat with the slayers, Loren found herself pretending she was not only immortal like them, but strong and feared. It was nice, even if she was only pretending.

For one wild moment, she knew how it felt to be important.

———

DARIEN STEPPED out of the café and into the damp night. He'd told the others, who were still finishing their food, that he was going for a smoke. He supposed it wasn't a total lie, since he was currently retrieving a pack of cigarettes from the inside pocket of his leather jacket as he leaned against the exterior brick wall of the building.

He placed a cigarette in his mouth, lit it, and slid the lighter and half-empty pack into his pocket, never once taking his eyes off the *real* reason he'd stepped outside: the phone in his left hand, an unknown number flashing across the screen with an incoming call.

The call had almost gone to voicemail when he swiped right to answer and lifted the phone to his ear.

"Riddle me this," drawled a familiar, gravelly voice. Darien's stomach dropped like a stone in water, his fingers tightening around the phone. "A slayer and a gangster meet in the gangster's hood. The gangster arrives with one side of his fucking ugly face unmarked but leaves with the good side worse than the bad. What pissed off the slayer badly enough for him to decide the gangster needed a makeover?"

When Darien spoke, his tone was scathing, despite the feeling of his soul leaving his body. "Was it really such a big deal that Cain had to come crying to you about it?" He took a drag on the cigarette, willing the smoke filling his lungs to ground him.

"It's a big deal when my Devils are making decisions that I didn't instruct them to make," Randal said coldly. Randal Slade, godfather of Angelthene's underworld. Crime boss extraordinaire and leader of not only the Seven Devils, but *all* Darkslaying circles in the city. "Are you going to answer my question, or do I need to rely on a scumbag like Cain to get some truth around here?"

Darien thought fast. "He was getting in the way of a target I'm hunting. Someone had to put him in his place or he's going to start thinking he runs these streets the same way he runs his army of thugs and petty thieves."

"Sounds to me like he's not the only one who thinks he runs these streets." The prick paused long enough for the meaning behind his words to sink in. "If you step out of line again, it won't be Cain getting a makeover—it'll be you. And you can count your baby sister in on that promise, too." The threat erased every trace of fear from Darien's body, and his blood boiled in his veins.

He would kill Randal if he touched Ivy. He would *kill him,* and he would take his precious time doing it.

"Do you understand me?" Randal's voice sounded far, far away.

"I hear you," Darien gritted out. "Loud and fucking clear."

"Good," he drawled. "I'll be in touch."

Randal hung up, and Darien stood there for a long time in the mist and the rain, breathing hard and fast. He tried to stop the Surge from coming, but his efforts were futile. His eyes turned black with the Sight, and the need to hit—to *kill*—swept through his veins.

He took one last drag on the cigarette before flicking it to the wet sidewalk.

He had to make it back to the house. Had to get the others back home—and then he could find a way to deal with the rage that was swiftly turning his blood to acid.

Fighting helped. Killing always helped more. But he knew there was no chance in hell of the Surges ending for good, unless he were to kill Randal Slade himself.

One day. One day, he would.

He kept telling himself this as he managed to blink the Sight from his eyes and strode back into the café. Managed to somehow convince the others that nothing was wrong as he suggested they head home.

The minutes felt like years as he sped back to Hell's Gate, promising himself that the day would come when he would be more than…than *this*—more than Randal's personal attack dog.

He wanted to believe his own lie so badly.

He *almost* believed it.

DARIEN WAS silent the whole drive home. And for that whole time, Loren watched him in the rear-view mirror. His eyes never once met hers in the reflection; in fact, it was likely that he was hardly seeing the dark road in front of him.

And when he parked the car at Hell's Gate, he was the first to get out, the first to reach the front steps, the first through the set of arched doors.

As soon as Jack had exited the car, freeing up a path for her, Loren hurried to catch up to Darien, tangling her arm in her seatbelt and pinching Dallas's thigh in the process. She ignored the witch's cries of frustration as she launched herself out of the car and hurried across the gravel driveway.

Warmth wrapped around her chilled limbs as she rushed into the entrance hall, and she had just reached the bottom step of the broad, carpeted staircase that led to the upper levels as Darien was clearing the first landing.

"Darien!" she called, already out of breath as she followed him up the stairs. She was vaguely aware of the others entering the house behind her, vaguely aware of Dallas attempting to deter her, demanding to know when she'd become suicidal. She paid her no mind and kept following the dark-haired Devil. "Darien, wait—"

He whirled on a heel to face her, and she almost fell backward down the stairs when she saw how black his eyes were.

But...he wasn't tracking anything.

So why were his eyes black?

When she spoke, her voice was small, and she had to grip the handrail for support. "Are you okay?"

"What do you want?" he bit out. His hands were curling and uncurling at his sides, as if he was trying not to hit something. His nostrils were flared, and his jaw was clenched so tight, it looked like it was causing him pain.

"I wanted to apologize," she whispered. "For following you into Stone's End. I know it was stupid and reckless and—"

"It *was* stupid and reckless," he cut in. He turned and began clearing the stairs, two at a time. "Just forget about it." He waved a hand in dismissal and disappeared down the hall. A moment later, his door slammed shut hard enough for the chandelier hanging above the entrance hall to tremble, the crystals spitting white fire onto the spotless walls.

It took Loren a long moment to calm down, to convince herself that what she and Dallas had done really *was* stupid and reckless and Darien had every right to be angry with her.

By the time she'd gathered her thoughts and began ascending the last of the stairs, Darien's door swung open again. He emerged wearing torn and faded blue jeans, a gray long-sleeved henley, and combat boots that were caked in what could only be old blood. A duffel bag was slung over his shoulder, and his eyes were still black as onyx. He was so tense, the tendons in his neck were showing, his broad chest rising and falling with each rapid breath as he hurried down the hallway toward her.

Squashing down the voice of reason that demanded she leave him alone, she tried to step in his path...but her efforts were futile, the hallway wide enough for him to merely breeze past her like she was invisible, which was exactly what he did.

She knew she really shouldn't follow him, should give him some space. But, as usual, she didn't heed her own advice.

"Would you tell me what's going on?" she called, hurrying down the stairs. "Did something happen in Cain's house?" Cripes, he moved fast. He was already at the glass table, where he paused to retrieve a couple ancient coins from the curved wooden bowl. He stuffed them into the front pocket of his jeans and made for the door. "You can't possibly be that angry with me—"

But he was already out of the house, the door shutting behind him on a phantom wind Loren suspected was courtesy of the Hob.

For a long time, Loren stood there. Staring at the closed door. Listening to Darien's car engine rumble to life. There was the click of the emergency brake being lowered, the accompanying groan suggesting he'd nearly ripped it clean off. And then the car was snarling as he accelerated backward, spun it around, and sped off into the night, tires squealing loudly enough to wake the whole neighborhood.

The silence that followed was somehow worse than the noise. Heavy and suffocating, pressing on her eardrums as if her head was underwater.

Loren kept standing there, staring at the door. Trembling, despite the warmth of the house. Despite the food she'd eaten.

"When Darien needs his space, he *really* needs his space." Max's voice made her jump.

She whirled to face him, and it took her a second to realize why his face was so blurry.

She was… Was she *crying?*

When had she started crying? She couldn't remember, could barely breathe.

Someone was stepping on her lungs.

"I didn't mean to piss him off that badly," Loren choked out. Her face heated with an awful mixture of anger and shame and embarrassment. "I said I was sorry." It sounded like someone was strangling her. It felt like it, too. "Is he really that incapable of accepting an apology?"

"His anger is not meant for you, Loren," Max said softly. "But he's not in the right mindset to explain that to you tonight."

Her lungs just kept getting smaller, but she managed to squeeze out, "What's the matter with him?"

"It isn't my place to answer that question."

"Is there something I should know? Did something happen in Cain's house that he's not wanting to tell me?"

"It isn't my place to answer that question either." He kicked off his boots, opened the closet door, and hung up his jacket. Loren had a feeling he was performing every action slower than what was necessary, evidently giving her a chance to compose herself. He closed the closet door and studied her for a moment, and then motioned toward the staircase. "Get some sleep. It's late."

She wiped fiercely at the corners of her eyes but made for the staircase, exhaustion settling over her like a heavy morning fog. Her whole body ached, and her teeth were suddenly chattering. She felt like she might never be warm again.

"Do me a favour," Max called from the base of the staircase.

Loren slowly turned. Looked down at him.

"Don't hold his behaviour tonight against him," Max said, his bass voice gentle. "He *is* trying his best to help you. Don't forget that."

Loren managed a slight nod before retreating to her suite. It wasn't until she was half-asleep, with Dallas already snoring softly beside her, that she recognized the undertone to Max's words, the tone that suggested she possibly wasn't the only one in this house who was in need of some help.

20

Loren breezed into the kitchen at Hell's Gate the following morning, where she found Darien sitting at the island. He was sipping coffee from a mug, today's issue of the Daystar spread before him.

He glanced up at the sound of her polished academy shoes tapping on the floor, but Loren made a point not to look at him as she yanked open the fridge door and rummaged through the contents in search of milk.

He had kept her up all night screwing some chick he'd brought home from wherever he'd gone at two in the morning. She hadn't been able to sleep as the girl had moaned and cried out in pleasure; as the mattress had squeaked, the bedframe banging against the wall. Loren had been so desperate to drown them out that she'd stuffed earbuds into her ears, but the music had created barely enough of a distraction to muffle the sound of the girl's pleasure.

It was absurd, the amount of noise she was making. Absolutely absurd, and to be completely frank, Loren was disgusted by it.

Darien seemed to sense her frustration as she pushed aside cans of beer and takeout containers in search of the milk carton. Her head was right inside the fridge, the temperature chilling her skin.

"What are you looking for?" he asked.

She made to answer him, but then her hand finally closed around the carton. "Found it," she muttered as she yanked it out, kicked the fridge door shut behind her, and peeled open the seal.

"Help yourself to some coffee," Darien said, his tone so much softer than it had been last night. The Daystar rustled in his hands as he returned to perusing it. "You sound like you need it."

Loren peeked over her shoulder at him. The white muscle shirt he was wearing hugged his upper body like a second skin, drawing attention to his biceps and sculpted chest. Loren tried not to think about where those hands of his had been last night as she watched them turn the newspaper to the next page.

Loren bristled at the unwelcome thought. Why did she even *care?* "You're right, I *do* need caffeine," she snapped. She stood on her tiptoes and yanked a box of puffed rice cereal from the top of the fridge, ignoring the Hob crouching behind the box. She set about pouring herself a bowl, her motions so hasty that several grains of cereal bounced to the floor. "Especially after you kept me up until five a.m. with all that squealing."

Darien was silent for so many minutes that she eventually turned to face him. He was watching her with a hint of amusement in his eyes, the corners of his lips slightly upturned.

"As much as I would've thoroughly enjoyed making a girl squeal last night, that wasn't me." He took another sip of coffee, assessing her over the rim. Loren blinked, the question that was at the tip of her tongue evident in her gaze. "That was Travis," he clarified.

Loren felt her icy expression thaw as blush flooded her cheeks, spreading all the way down her neck and to her collarbone. "Oh," she said, feeling very stupid. She had assumed it was Darien—but she hadn't stopped to think about where, exactly, the squeaking and moaning were coming from. Come to think of it...the sounds had been drifting from the opposite side of the house—the side where Darien's room was...*not*. His was down the same corridor as hers. Only two doors down, in fact, which meant the conclusions she'd drawn made absolutely zero sense.

The blush flooding her cheeks grew hotter.

A smile played on the curve of his mouth. "If I didn't know any better, I'd think you were jealous."

"Hardly," she grumbled. The look on Darien's face had her glaring at him. "Oh, don't flatter yourself. It's not like I cared. I care about being kept awake, but you can do whatever you want. It's none of my business." She shoved the milk carton back into the crowded fridge, grabbed a spoon from the drawer, and took the bowl of cereal into her hands. She shovelled a heaping spoonful into her mouth, savouring the cold temperature of the milk on her tongue, willing it to calm her reddened skin.

Darien turned to the next page of the Daystar. "Whatever you say," he muttered, that hint of a smile still clear as day.

The irritation—and the sheer embarrassment of having borne such emotion to him, coupled with their argument last night and how she'd allowed herself to cry over this stupid, brooding boy—simmering in her veins overflowed like a volcano erupting, the last of her flimsy self-control snapping in two.

"You know what, Darien?" she said in a cheeky tone. "You're nothing but a cocky, narcissistic male who's managed to convince yourself that every woman in the world wants to screw you."

His eyes snapped up from the paper. His expression darkened—a darkness that had nothing to do with the Sight, and yet was somehow just as terrifying.

Loren bit her tongue. A metallic warmth flooded her mouth, and her tongue turned numb from the pain.

"You want to take that back?" Darien said, his lethal voice sharp as glass.

Every trace of the blood that had reddened her skin a moment ago vanished, her head turning weightless on her shoulders. "I'm sorry," she sputtered. "That came out wrong."

"I'll fucking say."

Pathetic—she was *pathetic* for saying that, especially after what Max had implied about Darien last night, that he didn't quite have it all figured out, at least not as much as he pretended to. She wasn't sure what had gotten into her, but she was mortified at the realization that she was doing a thorough job of pissing off the one person who could help her. The one and *only* person who was willing to help her. "I'm under a lot of stress—"

"And I'm not?" he countered. She had nothing to say to that. He looked her over with visible contempt—the school uniform skirt and white button-up blouse. She saw his words coming half a second before he spoke. "Maybe you should take care of yourself a little more often and release some of that tension."

The filthy comment had her bristling—and had her forgetting all about the apology she had been trying desperately to make. "I'm not in the mood for your obscene jokes—"

"And I'm not in the mood for your whining," he snapped. He set the paper aside, pushed out from the island, and stood. Loren found herself pressing back into the counter so hard, the edge of the quartz dug into the small of her back. Darien made a point of walking menacingly close to her as he rounded the island, heading for the sink. In a voice so quiet she barely heard him, he muttered, "I should spare myself this headache and let you turn yourself in."

Loren's head felt like it toppled off her shoulders. "What did you just say?" she sputtered, swaying on her feet.

Darien set his mug down in the sink so hard, it almost cracked. Something about the set of his jaw told her he was regretting his words. "Nothing," he snapped, waving her away. He turned the hot tap on full and grabbed the dish sponge.

"That's what you heard at Cain's house, isn't it? That's why you were so angry." Silence. *Tell me.* A heavy, dreadful pause. The bowl in her hands wobbled, milk dribbling over the sides and splashing on the hardwood floor. "Darien—"

The mug he was washing shattered in his hands as he literally *pulverized* it in his grip. Loren jumped out of her skin as shards of glass flew through the kitchen and slid across the floor.

"Sabrine's captors have offered a ransom," he said, his words lashing out like the crack of a whip. "They'll release her if the target they are really after turns herself in." He looked her over with a gaze that could cut. "If *you* turn yourself in."

Loren was slamming the bowl down on the counter and sprinting for the entrance hall before she fully realized what she was doing.

Her fingers had gone to her neck and snapped the gold chain that held the Avertera talisman before she could stop herself.

The front door. All she needed was to get to the door —

Darien was upon her in an instant. He tackled her into the wall so hard, it should've bruised her to the bone — but he put his body between her and the wall right in the nick of time, taking the brunt of the impact as he closed his arms around her waist, spinning her around before her face could smash right through the drywall.

They crashed to the floor, their limbs tangling together. Framed photographs came free of their hooks and shattered on the hardwood.

Loren was screaming. Kicking and thrashing and sobbing and swearing, but his hold on her would not relent. He was trying to talk to her — to console her. But not a word reached her ears.

He did not let go of her — not once during the whole time she fought him, not even when she threw her elbows into his ribs and practically clawed off his face and neck. Not even when she tore the collar of his shirt and scratched at the backs of the hands that would not loosen from around her waist.

Not even as she passed out right there in the foyer, the world slipping out from under her as she sagged in his arms.

LOREN CRACKED OPEN her eyelids sometime later to find that she was lying on her back on the leather couch in the sitting room. Darien was seated across from her in the armchair, elbows on his knees as he waited for her to come to. Staring at her with that piercing gaze, his expression somber. The Avertera talisman was dangling from his fist, the chain already repaired. The pendant winked in the morning light streaming in through the slats in the blinds.

Loren sat up so fast, the room gyrated. "What time is it?" she gasped. She looked over her shoulder — at the antique clock above the gas stove in the kitchen. Her eyes widened at the position of the hands. Cripes, how long had she been out? "I'm going to be late for school —"

"You're not going anywhere," Darien said, his deep voice quiet but firm. "I called the academy and told them you would be absent today."

"What —"

Oh.

It all came back to her then: her fight with Darien, Sabrine's abductors demanding Loren turn herself in, the wall her head had nearly smashed through as Darien had tackled her to stop her from exposing her location.

She took in the Devil sitting before her: the dark brows that were pulled together in what appeared to be concern instead of annoyance for once.

"I'm going to school," she declared.

"Not today, you're not. Tomorrow, you can go — if you manage to convince me that you won't do something so foolish as turn yourself in."

Loren curled her fingers into fists. "I won't," she fibbed.

Seeing right through her lie, Darien merely raised his brows.

"Fine," she huffed. *"I'll* stay here. You can go ahead and continue on with your day." She waved a hand in dismissal.

The Devil smirked. "Nice try." He grabbed the remote from the coffee table and flicked on the television. "I'm staying here with you."

She looked him over. "And what are we going to do all day, aside from claw each other's faces off?"

"I'm not the one doing the clawing," Darien said quietly as he began flipping through the menu of newly released movies.

Indeed, his neck, face, and arms were covered with faded pink lines from where her nails had torn into his skin. The sight of them sent pain stabbing through her chest; he hadn't tried to pull away from her that whole time — but had merely held her and took the blows like a punching bag, refusing to allow her to put herself in danger.

Without looking at her, he said in the softest voice she'd ever heard him use, "Pick a show with me."

Pick a show with me. It was perhaps the most ordinary sentence she'd ever heard this Devil say. It was a sharp contrast to what she'd seen of him in Stone's End, when he'd come out of Cain's house with a bloody rag.

She was starting to see that there were two very different sides to his coin.

Loren cleared her throat. "Go to Chick Flicks."

He snorted a laugh but finally turned to look at her. "Must you always make it your daily goal to be a thorn in my side?" Now that she was becoming more aware, the fog from passing out dissipating, she saw that she'd really done a number on him. He was lucky he was a hellseher and would heal without so much as a scar on that stunning face, but...

She was an awful person for doing that to him. Awful.

Loren drew in a deep, rattling breath. "More like every minute of every day." She tried to make her tone light, but the joke came out strangled.

Darien turned to look at her. "Hey," he said, dipping his head to catch her eye. When she met his gaze, she wondered if he saw them —the tears that were threatening to spill. Whether he saw them or not, his expression visibly softened. "Don't worry about it. I deserve every mark that's on me for speaking to you the way that I did." The apology—and the sincerity in his gaze—brought a strange fluttering to her stomach. Butterflies, she realized. She couldn't remember the last time she'd felt such a thing.

Loren felt her face heat up. "Hardly."

"I said don't worry about it, Rookie. You hear me? Besides, I like pain."

At that, she had to laugh, though it was a broken sound. "What kind of a person likes pain?"

Amusement danced in his steel eyes. "The fucked-up kind." He made to hand her the talisman. "Put this on." A pause, and then he added, "Please."

She leaned over far enough to take the talisman from him, her fingers grazing the tattoos on his knuckles. The skin-on-skin contact made her heart lurch into an unsteady rhythm, and her stomach fluttered again. The look of innocent curiosity that washed over Darien's face suggested his hearing had picked up on the change in her heartrate.

Desperate for a distraction—*any* distraction—she gave a pointed glance at the remote in his hand.

Darien sighed softly. "Alright." He kicked off his boots and propped his feet up on the coffee table. "Chick flicks, it is."

FIVE HOURS of chick flicks later, and Darien was more than ready to hand over watch duty to Maximus. The fact that he was somewhat…*enjoying*…a few of those chick flicks wasn't a good sign. Not a good sign at all. It was time to resharpen his edge and make some cold, hard cash.

But as he finished tying his combat boots in the entrance hall and made for the doors, he realized he didn't have his car keys.

He patted the pockets of his black cargo pants, his leather jacket… They weren't there. He checked the glass table, the curved wooden bowl that was starting to get low on ancient coins…

They were nowhere to be found. Which usually only meant one thing.

Slowly, Darien turned toward the stairs, looked up at the second-floor landing—and found his Familiar standing there with a look of expectance on his face, Darien's keys in his slobbery mouth.

"Bandit," Darien reprimanded, a touch of humor in his voice. The dog's cropped tail twitched. Darien held out a hand. "Give them here, boy."

Over my incorporeal body, the spirit replied.

"Bandit—"

One step in the direction of the staircase and the Familiar bolted, leaving a trail of black mist in his wake.

Darien took off after Bandit, taking the stairs three at a time, but the dog was fast. Bandit bounded up to the third-floor landing, nails tearing into the carpet, pictures rattling on the walls.

Darien thundered up to the third floor and hurtled down the

hallway after the Familiar, not realizing whose suite Bandit was leading him into until he caught himself against the doorframe, boots skidding across the carpet...

It was Loren's suite.

Loren shot to her feet from where she had been sitting on the edge of her bed, cradling her phone in her hands. Bandit now stood before her, facing Darien, and upon seeing Darien note the look of agony on Loren's face, the Familiar opened his mouth just wide enough for the keys to plunk to the floor in a puddle of drool.

Darien raised an eyebrow at Bandit. *Really?*

The dog merely smacked his chops, looking rather pleased with himself.

"You devil, you," Darien mumbled.

I learn from the best, the spirit replied.

You certainly do, don't you? Darien shot back.

And then he faced Loren, who was shifting from foot to foot and twisting her phone in her hands. She had changed out of her school uniform and was now wearing a leopard-print tank and denim shorts. "Tell me what's going on. Why are you upset?" He took note of the purse that was sitting on her bed, along with a thin stack of papers. "And why does it look like you're going somewhere?"

She wouldn't make eye contact with him, and her face began to redden as the seconds ticked by.

Darien leaned against the doorjamb. "Don't tell me you're still grieving over that last flick. The guy married the girl, and they got their happily-ever-after. What more can we expect?"

She shot him an irritated look. "I need to go to the hospital." Before Darien could speak, she added, "Don't worry, I planned on telling your watchdog before I left." Max, who was supposed to watch her the moment Darien left the house.

Darien frowned. "Why do you need to go to the hospital?"

"I need to get bloodwork done," she replied thickly. "Several times a year, and the appointment is nonnegotiable. When they call, I have to go—no questions asked. I also need this," she gestured to the medical tattoo on her forearm, "touched up. The ink is fading." That explained why she was in such distress. Tattoos created from magical ink were incredibly painful. Even Darien had never had any interest in getting one done, and that was coming from someone who welcomed pain—and often found himself seeking it out, for it made him feel like he was alive instead of just existing.

"When do you have to be there?" he asked.

"In an hour," she mumbled, unlocking her phone with her fingerprint. "I need to call a cab—"

"No cab," Darien cut in. "I'll take you."

A startled look crossed her face. "You don't have to—"

"Would you let me do this for you?" He shrugged away from the doorframe and backed into the hallway. "Please."

Loren was shaking her head. "But—" She struggled for words, and he waited until she finally managed to stammer, "You already do too much for me."

"Do I look like I'm complaining?" He disappeared down the hallway without another word. A moment later, he heard Loren zip her purse shut and hurry to catch up with him.

Regardless of how fast Darien was walking down the stairs, Bandit beat him to the door.

"You really are a sly devil, aren't you?" Darien said to his Familiar as Bandit disappeared into his shadow. The spirit merely ignored him. "I guess you have a thing for the pretty ones, too."

21

L oren sat in the back seat of Darien's car, sandwiched between Jack and Tanner. Maximus was in the passenger's seat, conversing quietly with Darien as he wove through traffic so swiftly, they were almost clipping other vehicles.

They were taking her to Angelthene General. When Darien had offered to accompany her to the hospital, she hadn't expected anyone else to want to tag along, for obvious reasons. Bloodwork wasn't exactly a party to anyone—well, except maybe vampires. But when Tanner had suggested Loren see his mother for the tests, Darien had extended the offer to Tanner to come with, and soon Jack and Max were expressing their extreme boredom of sitting around at home and wanted to come along for the ride.

Loren was starting to feel lightheaded. She hadn't eaten since breakfast—the bowl of cereal she hadn't finished—and the anxiety sweeping through her veins wasn't helping any.

She fumbled around in her purse until she found a half-empty paper bag of Tongue Twisters, Skull Splitters, and partially melted Witch Wafers crumpled at the bottom. She ate what was left of the candy she'd purchased from the sweets shop on campus before they made it to the hospital and met up with Tanner's mom, Doctor Atlas.

"Alright, Loren," the doctor said as she led the way to the examination table in a private room. The room felt even smaller with Darien, Jack, Tanner, and Max all crammed inside it. But Loren couldn't find it in her to ask them to leave. She appreciated the company, even if it did unnerve her to have four extra pairs of eyes on her. *Male* eyes, no less. Male, *bounty hunter* eyes. "Let's get these blood tests out of the way, shall we?"

Loren took a seat on the examination table, paper crinkling beneath her. She was wearing denim shorts, so there was nothing to stop her sweaty legs from clinging to the crepe. It was strange to be in a private room for these tests; she'd never experienced such... dare she call it *luxury?*

Doctor Atlas took a seat on a rolling chair and slid herself over to the examination table. "You seem to have a long medical history but no official diagnosis. How have you been feeling since your last tests?"

"A little worse," Loren admitted with a mumble. "But I would guess my stress levels have a lot to do with it."

Doctor Atlas gave a kind smile as she set about preparing a syringe. "That's an accurate guess. Stress can really take a toll on a person's health." Loren looked away as the needle plunged into a vein at the crease of her elbow. "How have you been managing with your fainting spells?"

"I've had a few." Her voice was little more than a croak. Sweat beaded on her forehead as the needle pinched, and a burning sensation spread up her arm.

"You didn't tell me it was that bad," Darien accused. He was leaning against the counter by the sink, watching her intently with that dreamy-but-intimidating gaze.

Loren shot him a glare. "You didn't ask."

The doctor hummed thoughtfully as she finished up with the blood tests and began preparing the items needed to touch up Loren's tattoo. "I get the feeling that it's not so much the blood tests that bother you as it is the tattoo."

Loren nodded, nerves fluttering in her stomach as the doctor set up the tattoo machine. The crepe paper crinkled as Loren began to squirm, instantly sick to her stomach at the sight of that magical ink. Its iridescence—the glow and colors like a jellyfish—should've made it beautiful, but to someone who'd experienced its sting before, it only made it look deadly.

"I certainly don't blame you," the doctor said, reddish hair gleaming in the rows of fluorescents. She had the same straight, angular features as Tanner, the same gray eyes. "Lay back and get comfortable. It'll be over before you know it." Loren did as the doctor said. "Though it might help if one of these fine men held your hand through the process."

Slowly, Loren turned her head to assess the group of Darkslayers.

Not one of them met her gaze. Jack coughed, Maximus idly scratched the back of his neck, and Tanner took a sudden interest in the ceiling texture as he rocked back and forth on the balls of his feet. Loren might've laughed, had she not been so nervous.

And Darien...Darien just stared at her. His expression was unreadable, as it often was.

She cocked an eyebrow at him, and he cocked one of his in answer, but made no move to come any closer.

She almost rolled her eyes. Did they think she had cooties or something?

The doctor spun around to face them, the wheels of her chair squealing on the linoleum. "What's the matter with you all? You have no problem hunting down demons and criminals, but you're scared to hold a pretty girl's hand?"

Maximus and Tanner looked like they might've stepped forward after another few seconds, but Darien moved first.

"Pussies," he muttered. He dragged up a stool and took a seat at Loren's other side, where he promptly gathered her right hand into both of his. The feeling of his warm, callused fingers wrapping firmly around hers made her stomach do a backflip.

Darien met her gaze, and she wondered if he picked up on the unsteady pulsations of her heart. Sitting this close to him, she could see every black eyelash, every fleck of silver in his irises.

As if aware of how nervous he was making her, his thumb began drawing circles on the back of her hand; the feeling caused a skip in her heartrate. And when his eyes found hers, and tightened a little with amusement, she scowled at him.

"Do I make you nervous?" He was horribly failing at stifling that smile. That charming, infuriating smile she liked more than she cared to admit. The dimple in his left cheek was showing again.

"Of course not," she lied. And it *was* a lie. A big, fat lie, just like the one she'd told him that night in the dining room.

His thumb was doing that lazy circling again, and she found the nerves in her stomach rustling faster. Everywhere he touched stimulated her skin like nothing she'd ever felt, and she didn't want him to stop. It was so distracting that she almost forgot about the pain that would begin at any second.

Darien was watching her with an expression she couldn't pin down, as if he was trying to figure her out.

"Don't flatter yourself," she muttered. "I'm only nervous about the pain." He looked like he wanted to laugh.

The doctor turned on the machine, and a familiar loud buzzing filled the room.

The pain was instantaneous, as usual. The first touch of the tattoo gun to her skin had pain zipping up her arm like bolts of lightning, and it took everything she had not to bite her tongue off as Doctor Atlas began to darken her tattoo. That stupid, awful tattoo she'd had to live nearly her entire life with.

Loren didn't want to admit it...but having Darien beside her made the whole process a little more bearable.

She wasn't sure what to make of that.

DARIEN HAD to admit he was impressed by how well Loren handled the whole situation.

For the first few minutes, she endured the tattoo in silence, her free hand gripping the hem of the leopard-print tank she wore. The fingers that were tucked beneath his own barely tightened, as if she was afraid to reveal to him just how much this was hurting her.

As Doctor Atlas neared the halfway point, sweat began to bead on Loren's forehead. Her hand squeezed his so hard, her painted nails dug into his skin like little knives.

He tried to think of something that might distract her from the pain. "What's your favorite color?"

She was breathing heavily now, and her eyes were gleaming with agony as they snapped to his. "My favorite color?" she repeated, every word tense. "You're asking me what my favorite color is."

Darien couldn't suppress the defensive tone that entered his words. "I'm trying to distract you."

Loren drew in a slow, deep breath that shook her whole upper body. "Blue," she bit out. Her eyelids slipped shut, her glossy lips pursing as another wave of pain cascaded over her.

The doctor cut in. "The pain is going to increase as the magic begins to bind to her bloodstream. I'll let you know when we reach the final minutes." A pause, and then she added, "Keep talking to her, Darien."

"What kind of blue?" he said to Loren.

The fingers of Loren's left hand crumpled the paper, and she made a visible effort to hold still. "I don't know," she hissed. She looked at him, her eyes exploring his features. "A gray-blue. Like your eyes, I guess."

Behind him, Jack gave a snort of amusement. Darien shot his sister's husband a glare that had him holding up his hands in surrender.

Loren bit her lip so hard, it looked like she might break the skin. Darien could tell she was quarreling with the desire to flinch from the pain and the determination to keep still so no part of the tattoo would need redoing.

"What made you want to attend Angelthene Academy?"

"Um." Loren could barely get out the words, her breath coming in shallow gasps. "I'm majoring in Botany and General Biology."

"Was it your decision to attend that academy, or is it something you're doing because of your friends?"

The question worked at distracting her from the pain she was feeling. Confusion and something like irritation flashed in her gaze.

Under the fluorescents, her eyes were cobalt blue. "What's that supposed to mean?"

"It's an honest question," he replied. "Were you *personally* hoping AA would accept your application, or was it because you didn't want to take a separate path from the one your friends were walking?"

There it was: the flicker of hurt that spoke a thousand words. "I can make my own decisions, thank you very much." *Bull's-eye.*

"What type of occupation are you going for?"

"Herbal magic." Interesting. While spellcasting wasn't something a human could physically do, he figured her career would involve the preparation and administration of potions. An assistant of sorts, but never the real thing. "In case you couldn't tell from my current place of employment, I like plants. I also like helping people —" She broke off with a hiss.

"You're okay," Darien murmured. Tears shone in her eyes as she looked at him, her lower lip caught between her teeth. "It'll be over soon." He tightened his hold on her hand, his thumb tracing her knuckles. She seemed to take comfort in the feeling; perhaps it was the repetition.

So, he kept doing it. And he tried not to read into it too much as his hearing picked up on the sound of her heart skipping beats. No matter how bad the pain she was feeling, it was only his touch that made her react that way.

The doctor said, "Sixty seconds and the ink will be fully bonded." Sixty seconds and he would have to let go of her.

Loren looked at Darien and sighed; her breath smelled of the candy she'd eaten in the back seat of his car. "Promise you'll hold my hand every time I need this done." Her eyes never wavered from his. But as soon as the words left her mouth, blush dusted her cheeks, and she looked like she would've kicked herself in the head if it were physically possible.

"Deal," Darien said quickly, before the embarrassment she was feeling could get any worse. "But only if you promise me something in return."

"Thirty seconds," Doctor Atlas announced. She wiped the tattoo with a damp cloth.

Darien said, "Look at all your options in life before you blindly follow your friends. You don't need to do everything they do simply out fear."

"I'm not afraid." She practically barked the words, and he had a feeling her hand tightened around his at that precise moment, not from the pain, but because she was angry at him for calling her out.

He lightly squeezed her hand in answer—in challenge. And when her heart kicked inside her chest from the gentle pressure, he realized he might never know what had caused that specific skip in her pulse.

"All I'm saying," he went on, "is there's a great school in Upper West Glen that teaches the field you're wanting to get into. If you find AA isn't everything you thought it would be, give this one a try. I know the hedgewitch who runs it. I could put in a good word for you."

"What's it called?" Her fingers squeezed his harder; they were so small beneath his own.

"Agatha's Post-Secondary Education for Botany. Agatha's for short." Loren was staring at him with unfathomable emotions on her face. "You haven't promised," he prodded.

Her full lips formed the words, "I promise."

Doctor Atlas completed the tattoo, and the machine vibrated as it shut down.

Darien and Loren pulled away from each other at the same time. The heat from Loren's touch still lingered on Darien's skin long after they broke the contact, like the kiss of sunlight on a cold day.

He wasn't sure what to make of that.

LOREN WANTED to laugh as she walked through the spotless white halls of the hospital. She was in the very middle of the group of Devils, Darien at the head, and not only was Loren the lone female among them, but she was the only one wearing any color, the only one who looked like she was more likely to blow a kiss at someone than kill them.

She blamed her near-uncontrollable amusement on the relief she was feeling at having her tattoo procedure over and done with. But her amusement abruptly faded as she glanced into several rooms they passed in the hospital, noticing that nearly every one of those rooms had an occupant—some more than one.

Where he was walking at her left, Tanner took note of where her attention had gone. "They're Tricking patients, most of them," he explained quietly, his words nearly drowned out by the pounding of boots on the floors. She tipped her head up to look at him, and she saw that he was frowning. "Mom said she's never seen it so bad."

The Tricking was the reason why immortals did not live for as long as they should. It was the leading cause of death in the world of Terra; nearly everyone contracted it at some point in their life. Because of it, no one had lived longer than six centuries.

One room they passed had a woman crouching on the floor at the feet of a patient, who was sitting on the edge of the crisp white bed. The woman was dressed in a white lab coat, and she was holding the patient's hands in her own. They both had their eyes closed, and what looked like a silver chain was wound around their hands in a pattern that seemed intentional.

Loren slowed as she passed the room, resisting the urge to completely stop walking—to gawk and demand to know what they were doing.

Instead, she asked Tanner. "What was that woman doing?" She picked up her pace again.

"She's an Aura Healer," Tanner replied. He nodded hello at a nurse bustling down the hall, who looked startled by the gesture—startled by *all* of them. "They're medical professionals with white or rainbow auras who've received the proper training to heal the sick or traumatized by pouring a part of their own aura into them."

Interesting, Loren thought. She wished such a thing could heal *her* from her own mysterious illness. It certainly would be nice to not have so many fainting spells. But she figured aura healing must have its limits.

"What was that chain thing?"

"A conduit," he said. Like magic staves but different, Loren realized. "Even aura healing has its risks and requires an object to act as safe passage for magic between the giver and the recipient. It helps the giver to not come down with the Tricking or any other side effects that come with using magic."

She gave a thoughtful hum. "Are the healers hellsehers?"

"Hellsehers, warlocks, and witches." They were nearing the front desk now. The low ringing of phones and the beep of machinery drifted down the hall. "They've also been known to help some people who suffer from Surges—"

Darien suddenly broke off from the rest of the group without a word and sped-walked through the automatic glass doors that barely slid open for him on time. Patients checking in at the desk and the receptionists that were helping them turned to stare.

And Loren stared, too, as he disappeared around a corner of the building outside.

"Speaking of Surges," Max sighed. He shared a look with Jack.

Not bothering to ask any of them what a Surge was, she took off after Darien before the others could stop her, sneakers slapping on the polished floors. The automatic doors reflected the image of her running toward them as they slid open, squealing on the tracks.

The sun was setting, and a warm breeze rippled through the parking lot, scattering palm tree fronds and tumbleweeds across the ground. The air smelled of creosote and sun-warmed pavement cooling after a hot day. A few people were heading to their cars, and headlights swept across the lot.

Loren found Darien at the side of the building. His open palms were braced on the wall, and his fingers were trembling—albeit very faintly, but Loren saw. His head was bowed, and his eyes were closed, his breathing ragged and laboured.

"Hey," Loren whispered. "Are you okay?"

His shoulders tensed up, as if he was startled by her presence, despite that he possessed immortal senses that should've made it nearly impossible for someone like her to sneak up on him.

"Stay away from me, Loren. Please." He pushed away from the wall, fingers curling into fists at his sides, and began pacing the same three feet of sidewalk, again and again, never once opening his eyes.

"What can I do to help?" Loren was vaguely aware of the other Devils watching from some distance away. Giving him space, she realized. Which was exactly what she was...not doing. She regretted her question the moment she voiced it, especially when Darien's eyes opened, and she saw how utterly black they were.

Blacker than his hair. Blacker than the night that was quickly sweeping into the parking lot. HID lamps buzzed as they flicked awake, spreading pools of eerie light across the pavement.

Loren couldn't stop staring at Darien. A look of...of *shame* flickered across his face. As if this—this...*thing* that was causing him distress—was somehow his fault.

That look of shame reminded her of herself. She wasn't sure what he was feeling exactly, but in her best moments her anxiety attacks made her feel weak and unworthy, and in her worst, they made her feel crazy.

That was how he looked right now: out of control. Ashamed. Defeated. Anxious.

Shaking his head as if the motion could somehow clear it, Darien patted his pockets until he found his car keys. He threw them to Loren, and she barely brought her hands up in time to catch them—to stop them from smacking her in the nose.

"The others will take you home," was his only explanation.

Loren's back stiffened. "And where will *you* go? No offense, but you don't exactly seem in any position to take care of yourself right now. You can probably see nothing except shadows and auras—"

"Just go home, Loren." It was obvious that he was trying very, very hard to keep his tone civil.

Loren swallowed, not quite understanding why she felt so wounded—why she was trying this desperately to stay beside him. He was under no obligation to watch her every second of every day, and the other Devils were more than capable of relieving him of watch duty once in a while.

So why didn't she want them to?

"I have to go to the academy," she said tightly. "I have school tomorrow, and I can't miss another day."

"One of the others will take you," he repeated. Every word was strained. "I just need some space, alright?" He turned then and walked away, hands in his pockets, before she had a chance to react.

She stared after him until she couldn't see him anymore—until the night had swallowed him up.

Until Max came up behind her. Loren was hit with déjà vu; this whole scenario felt like what happened at Hell's Gate last night—after their visit in Stone's End.

Had Darien been experiencing a Surge then as well?

"Let's go, Loren," Max said.

She turned around to face him, pulling her attention from the path Darien had walked. He wasn't coming back, not right now, and she had to accept that.

Max held his hand out in request for the keys. The cigar he was smoking burned a bright red in the murky darkness. "The demons are starting to wake up." As if to back up his statement, a dreadful baying ripped through the night, causing the hair on the back of Loren's scalp to prickle.

She crossed her arms, suddenly chilled to the bone. "I need to go to the academy."

He blew out a breath of rippling smoke. "I'll take you to Hell's Gate to get your things and then I'll take you to the academy." He inclined his head in the direction of the parking lot.

With a sigh, she nodded stiffly and rejoined their group. The Devils adjusted their positions so all sides of her were protected as they walked to the car. Despite Max's statement about the demons waking up, she didn't feel fear, not with the Devils surrounding her. And she knew Darien had little concern for the creatures, though she did worry about him while he was in this state. How could he possibly take care of himself if he hadn't been able to sense *her*—a clumsy human—when she'd walked around the corner?

As they neared Darien's car, she blurted, "What exactly is a Surge?"

The car chirped as Max disengaged the alarm system, and the locks clicked open. "A Surge is something that only people with the Sight suffer from. It's a nervous disorder that causes a person's magic to surge, hence the name, causing a type of panic attack that often can't be stopped until some of their magic is released. Aura Healers have tried to help him, but none of them have succeeded."

"And what do they do to release their magic?" Loren asked as she got into the car through the door Tanner opened for her. She waited until everyone else was inside before she amended, "What does *Darien* do to release it?"

Max seemed reluctant to give her an answer. The car rumbled to life, and he didn't speak until they'd left the parking lot. "He usually seeks out a fight." A pause. "Or goes out on a job."

Killing, then. She wasn't surprised, though she found herself shuddering. It seemed the concern she felt for Darien while he was suffering a Surge—and was out by himself at this late hour—was not warranted.

Max added, "I've had Surges before, and they're a real pain in the ass, I'll tell you that. Darien's probably going to a fighting ring right now, and I don't blame him for it."

"So, the only thing that helps is hitting things?" She found that she didn't want to say the word *killing*.

"Or fucking the first hot girl who gives him a double-take," Jack interjected with a laugh. He was typing on his phone, only seeming partially interested by this conversation.

Max sighed, shaking his head. "You're an inconsiderate dickbag, you know that, Jack?"

Jack was grinning, though his eyes were still on his phone. "And all you fuckers are mean to me, but I'm pretty used to it by now."

It was Tanner who said, "Well, how many times do you need to be told not to talk about other people's business? Especially your boss's. I'm surprised Dare gave you his blessing to marry Ivy, considering how often you get under his skin."

Jack shrugged. "I'm only speaking the truth. And I'm pretty sure Ivy would've had his balls if he'd tried saying no. I'm the whole package: looks *and* charm."

Max's voice was barely audible as he mumbled, "Whatever you say, Mr. Pretentious."

The tires screeched as Max picked up speed, merging onto the freeway toward the Victoria Amazonica District.

Loren had a peculiar feeling—a compulsion to turn around in her seat and stare out the back window. The more distance that was put between her and Darien, the less secure she felt.

As if she had lost something important or was leaving a part of herself behind.

22

Maximus was the only person in the vehicle this time—his SUV instead of Darien's car—as he took Loren to Angelthene Academy for Magic.

Loren had overheard the Devils talking while she'd packed her things, and it sounded like Travis and Tanner had taken Darien's car to wherever he'd ended up in the past little while. Loren had to resist the urge to demand to know where he was, to know if he was okay. It wasn't her business, and it certainly wasn't her place to ask. No matter how badly she wanted to.

The ride was entirely silent, but not because Loren didn't feel comfortable being alone with him. In fact, she dared to admit that she *liked* Maximus Reacher. She liked all the Devils.

Well…*most* of them.

The ride was silent because she couldn't stop thinking about Darien. Thinking, worrying—and wondering what he was doing at this very moment, how he had chosen to deal with his Surge. Was he out on a job, taking care of some creep on someone's hitlist? Was he in one of those underground fighting rings Maximus had mentioned, beating the living daylights out of the first poor soul who walked into the ring with him? Or was he…

She didn't want to finish her last thought.

She decided she was thinking too much, starting to *care* too much, which wasn't a good thing. There had to be distance between them; she couldn't allow herself to get so invested in Darien. They were hardly friends; he was simply doing her a favor by looking out for her for a while. He didn't owe her anything, least of all an explanation about his whereabouts. And the moment Sabrine was found, and Loren's safety became certain, he wouldn't even be in her life anymore.

With that thought, she began rebuilding the wall in front of her heart, envisioning it taking form, brick by brick by brick. She put her thoughts and feelings behind that wall, tucking them away and sealing them behind the brick. They wouldn't come out again — not if she could help it.

Max's SUV growled as they drove up the hill to the gates of Angelthene Academy. A crescent moon hung in the velvet sky, and far off in the distance, vampire silhouettes floated across it.

Max took one last puff on his cigar before flicking it out the window. "You'll be back next weekend?" He rolled up the automatic window with the flick of a button.

"Friday."

"Watch out for yourself until then." He slowed to a stop in front of the gates. And Maximus Reacher seemed a little shy as he added, "And say hello to Dallas for me, would you?"

Loren smiled. "I will."

She grabbed her bags and got out of the SUV. Maximus waited until the gates of the academy had swung shut behind her before driving away.

And those gates had barely shut before Loren spotted Dallas running toward her across the dark campus. She was shouting hysterically, but Loren couldn't make out a word.

"Dallas," Loren bit out as the witch drew closer. Dallas's footfall echoed far and wide. "What's the matter?"

"Another student has gone missing," Dallas panted, slowing to an unsteady halt before her. "A *human.*" The look in her eyes finished her sentence for her: a human, just like you.

Holy Star.

Loren found her head turning—found herself looking across the dark lawn of the academy.

The Old Hall was barely distinguishable from here, but Loren saw, clear as day, what had to be done.

Tomorrow, consequences be damned. She would wait no longer. And if Darien didn't want to help her, she'd do it alone.

THE HOUSE OF SOULS was right across the street from Angelthene City Cemetery. The sprawling mansion was a work of art straight out of a dead world, complete with large stained-glass windows, flying buttresses, pointed arches, and gargoyles so old only parts of their ornately carved faces remained, suffused here and there with the silver moonlight trickling through the clouds.

Darien parked to the right of the wrought-iron gates, beneath the cover of a jacaranda tree. Purple-blue, trumpet-shaped petals dusted the hood of his car as he cut the engine and retrieved a plastic bag of Stygian salts from the center console. He set about shaking a line of salts onto the dash and quickly arranged them into a line with the edge of a bank card. When he was finished, he leaned forward in his seat, shut one nostril with a finger, and snorted the line.

Thanks to the target he'd managed to track down before coming here, the edge had already softened off his Surge. It was what he'd wanted when he'd left the hospital, only now he would need the salts to aid him in finding a weak spot in the forcefield that protected the House of Souls. Years ago, he would have simply walked right through the gates, through the front doors without so much as knocking. But that was a different life, back when the Reapers were considered friends and Malakai Delaney wasn't out for his blood.

Darien closed his eyes and leaned back in the seat, breathing deeply. His airways burned with the salts as the drug burrowed into his bloodstream, opening the floodgates of his magic. His body turned weightless as the salts took hold of him, carrying his soul over the city.

But one moment later, everything about the world sharpened into crystal clarity, and he dropped back into himself like a soul rejected at the gates of heaven.

It was hardly fair that the salts were classified as a drug; they made him feel more awake and alert, like coffee but far more potent, and without the nasty side effects like the ones that came with using Crystalladum or Boneweed or the endless variety of Blood Potions available through illegal trade.

When he opened his eyes, he had the Sight in place, exposing the layers of spellwork rippling over the wrought-iron gates. Layers upon layers of colors that writhed like the inside of a kaleidoscope. Lucky for Darien, it had clearly been a while since Malakai had sent any of his Reapers to the Umbra Forum to purchase the latest protection spells; there was a weak spot to the right of the gates, just wide and tall enough for Darien to fit through.

He almost laughed. This was just too easy. No wonder the Reapers were no longer at the top of the pyramid; they'd become indolent and cocky.

Darien got out of the car and made his way to the gate, where he scaled the wrought-iron and launched himself through the weak spot in the forcefield. The magic burned a little as it rippled over his skin, causing him to grit his teeth. But by the time he landed on his feet on the other side, the effects of the magic snapped back to the gate like a rubber band, leaving no trace of itself behind but a phantom kiss on his skin. That burning sensation would've knocked a lesser person on their ass.

A warm gust of wind blew across the yard, rattling the peeling shutters on the windows. Darien rolled his shoulders and made his way up the path that cut through the lawn, cracked flagstones rattling hollowly beneath his boots.

Darien still felt sick to his stomach for how he'd treated Loren outside of Angelthene General. He knew she had only wanted to help him, but when a Surge took over his mind, there was very little room in his brain for rational thought. The only thing he could focus on was getting away from the people he cared about—and closer to ones he could hurt. Closer to the fighting rings that helped him calm the rage that coursed through his veins every time he suffered an attack.

Aside from that, he'd felt...weak when she'd found him like that outside. When she'd seen him shaking, his hands against the building, his head bowed. He'd always lived by one simple rule: never get caught with your head down unless you're praying. His strength was the only trait he'd ever allowed anyone to see, aside from the few times when his Devils had witnessed him breaking, and he preferred to keep it that way.

When he reached the arched front doors, he blinked the Sight away and sent a quick prayer up to the eight deities of the Scarlet Star that anyone except Malakai Delaney or Tyson Geller would greet him. And then he grabbed the brass skull knocker and rapped it against the door three times.

The protection spells encasing the house itself were thicker and more complicated; Malakai had taken care to keep these up to date more so than he had the fence. If Darien really wanted to, he could find a weak spot in one of the windows or doorways. But knocking was faster. And the longer he lingered out here, the more likely it was that someone would spot him. The sooner he got into the house and found the person he was looking for, the better.

A moment later, the door swung open with a groan, and the music thumping inside the house drifted out into the night.

A tall, lithe figure stood in the doorway. The black leather dress she wore was low-cut, the razor-sharp hem ending at her moon-pale ankles. Her deep mahogany hair was longer than the last time Darien had seen her; it ended in a blunt, angled bob that fell just shy of her shoulders.

Perfect. Just the girl he was hoping to see.

She stared at him for a long time, blinking her green, catlike eyes slowly, as if she couldn't believe what she was seeing. Darien merely waited. Finally, the Reaper seemed to surrender to the fact that she was not dreaming and muttered, "Shit."

Darien's mouth tugged up at one corner. "Nice to see you too, Aspen."

Aspen Van Halen crossed her lightly freckled arms. "What in the bloody hell are you doing here? Do you have a *death* wish?" she snarled. She thought better of her last question and amended with a wave of a hand, "Don't answer that last one. But seriously, what *are* you doing here?"

"I need to see Malakai," Darien said. When she cocked an eyebrow, he added, "I have a peace offering."

She looked him over, her sharp eyes lingering on the hands he had in his jacket pockets. "Do I even want to know what it is?"

"If you're feeling squeamish, then probably not."

Aspen grimaced. "I feel sorry for the bastard, and I don't even know what you did. Tell me: who was the victim of one of your Surge rampages this time?"

Darien allowed for a beat of silence. "Ian Gray." Aspen's face, already ghostly pale on a good day, became paler. Ian Gray was a former Reaper, recently excommunicated by Malakai for betraying Reaper intel to the peace officers in exchange for some extra cash. Malakai had been looking for him these past few weeks to do what every Darkslaying circle did to those who broke their trust, but the man was good at hiding.

Not good enough to hide from a Devil though.

Darien said, "Still think Mal isn't interested in talking?"

Aspen studied him for several minutes, the thumping of the music inside the house the only sound. Finally, she sighed, her shoulders slumping. "I'll take you to him. Hold my hand." She reached for Darien, but he kept his hands in his pockets, brows knitting together. Aspen beseeched, *"Trust me.* If the others see a Devil lurking at my back, they might get confused as to who is escorting whom. Especially *you* — no offense."

Darien smirked. "None taken." He took his right hand out of his pocket and laced his fingers with Aspen's. She was about to tow him into the house when she froze.

"Give me your guns."

Darien canted his head. "Do you really not trust me?"

"It doesn't have anything to do with trust. I'm putting my neck on the line by simply letting you walk into Malakai's house, so you'd better do as I ask so that any repercussions I face are as minimal as possible." Her voice wobbled a little at the end.

Darien felt his jaw tighten. "Does he hurt you?"

"I've never given him any reason to," Aspen said. "And if you don't mind, I'd like to keep it that way."

Darien removed the gun from the holster at the front of his pants and passed it into her waiting hand. "I only have the one."

"Of course you do." She tightened her grip on his hand and pulled him into the House of Souls. The door was coaxed shut behind them by Aspen's magic.

Even though the Reapers clearly had visitors, they somehow managed not to run into anyone except Pawns—men and women who did anything the Reapers asked of them out of the sheer, pathetic hope they'd one day be welcomed into the circle—as Aspen led the way through the narrow, dimly lit corridors. Malakai Delaney's office was on the third floor, down a long corridor that had no windows and held no other rooms. The few torches lining the black walls were the only source of light in this wing of the mansion.

"How's Lace?" Aspen asked. She tried to keep every trace of emotion out of her question, but Darien knew her well enough to detect the sorrow beneath her words. Aspen had been Lace's best friend, back before Malakai had declared that no Devils were to mingle with his Reapers again unless he said so.

He gave her a sidelong glance, taking note of how her shoulders had stiffened. Her hair swayed just enough to betray glimpses of the mark of the Reapers below her ear: the cloaked and hooded God of Death, complete with a scythe and a horned, long-snouted mask that bore a smile that was anything but friendly. "Why don't you ask her yourself?" Darien said.

Her cold fingers tightened around his, but she kept staring straight ahead. "You know I can't do that."

"Can't," Darien said, squeezing back lightly, "or *won't?*"

"Don't be an ass," she muttered. "The Reapers are my family, and if I were to lose Mal's favour, I would literally have nothing."

"You wouldn't have a circle anymore, but maybe that wouldn't be so bad. You would get to start over. Choose a new life for yourself, anywhere you want. Angelthene would be nothing but a distant dream if you only dared it to be."

Aspen gave a soft snort, though humored was clearly the last thing she felt. "Wouldn't that be nice?" she muttered. "How are you and her, anyway? Are you still getting along?"

"As well as any exes can, I suppose." When Aspen gave him a concerned, sidelong glance, he added, "We're still friends, Asp. No need to be so tense."

They were nearing the end of the hallway now. "I only ask because I care. I never thought it was a good idea for you two to date in the first place. You and the other Devils are all she's got."

"You don't need to worry, Aspen. Besides, that was a long time ago, and Lace and I have gotten along just fine since."

She sighed. "You're right. Clearly, it's been too long since I checked in on her." When Darien opened his mouth to speak, she said, "Don't you dare give me another lecture. I won't ever go against Mal, just as Lace would never go against you."

"She *does* test me at times, but I get what you're saying."

Aspen released Darien's hand as they reached the closed double doors of the office. "Wait here a minute."

Darien stepped out of view of the doors as Aspen knocked three times. A gravelly male voice Darien hadn't heard in months called for her to enter, and she slipped inside. Darien didn't have to strain to hear what the voices were saying, since Aspen had left one door open just wide enough for sound to drift through, the words unhindered by the spellwork rippling over the wood.

"Someone is here to see you," Aspen was saying. Darien knew her well enough to detect the edge of nerves in her voice.

"I'm a little busy at the moment."

"With all due respect, I think you're going to want to listen to what he has to say."

Silence stretched for several seconds before Malakai gave a low sigh. "Very well. Bring him in."

Darien didn't wait for Aspen to retrieve him. He stepped right into Malakai's office, and as soon as the leader of the Reapers caught sight of him, he shot to his feet from where he was seated at the curved mahogany desk, his massive leather chair nearly tipping onto the ground behind him. The men that were stationed at either side of the desk had their weapons drawn before Darien could say *Ignis*.

It was to Aspen that Malakai growled, "What is it about 'No Devils are allowed in here' did you not understand?" One side of the Reaper's face was marked up with blue tattoos, making him look like a mean prick even in the rare times when he smiled. His copper hair was cut into a mohawk he'd braided away from his face, and his beard was full and wiry, disguising the scars on his chin.

Darien had liked Malakai years ago, had even considered him a friend. But the moment the Seven Devils had overthrown the Reapers, taking their place at the top of Angelthene's pyramid of Darkslayers, Malakai had decided he could no longer call Darien and the others his friends.

Sucks to suck, Darien thought, biting the inside of his cheek to keep from smiling.

"That tone is a little hostile to use on a lady," Darien began, "wouldn't you agree?"

Malakai was practically vibrating with rage. "You did *not* come in here to belittle me in my own house."

"No, I didn't," Darien said coolly. "Like Aspen said, I bring a peace offering."

Malakai's upper lip pulled back over his teeth, exposing the metal coating on his canines that were filed into wicked points. "Lose the weapons and get on your knees, and maybe then I'll consider listening to you."

"I get on my knees for no one," Darien said, zero emotion in his voice. "And I already gave my weapons to Aspen." Out of the corner of his eye, Darien saw Aspen hold up the gun she'd taken from him to illustrate that what he'd said was the truth.

Malakai didn't spare her more than half a glance. "One gun?" he scoffed. "You expect me to believe that?"

"I travel light," Darien crooned. "I thought you knew that, Malakai." He paused. "Now, are you going to accept the gift I've brought you or are you going to keep shooting daggers at me with your eyes?"

Malakai's bright green eyes were swallowed by black. He, like Darien, struggled with Surges on a regular basis. There was a lot he had in common with this man, which had made them such good friends in the beginning. It was such a shame that everything they'd built together had fallen through, and at the cost of something so little as jealousy.

"Like I said," Malakai gritted out. "When you get on your knees." The men standing at attention nearby snickered.

"Alright." Darien shrugged with one shoulder. "I always thought you were partial to women, but if you'd really like me to suck your dick—"

"It's about respect, not sucking dick, you arrogant ass—"

Darien talked over him. "It's not my fault that the grudge you hold against my circle has nothing to do with me as a person and everything to do with the fact that you're a sore loser."

Malakai made to lunge over the desk, but Aspen stepped between him and Darien, shrieking to the latter, "Just show him the peace offering and quit baiting him, you suicidal maniac!"

Darien paused. So did Malakai.

"It's not suicidal if I know I'd win," Darien said, but he reached into his pocket, the action causing Malakai's men to tense. He gave them a cold smile as he retrieved the three objects that made up his peace offering and tossed them onto Malakai's desk.

Darien heard Aspen gulp as she took in the three bloody teeth clattering on the mahogany. Everyone else in the room was looking at them, too.

"I made sure your rat won't be talking again," Darien said. "All I ask for in return is your word. You must promise me that Tyson won't be running his mouth about the prize he planned on stealing from me." Before Malakai could ask him what he was talking about, he explained, "I was recently offered a job to track a target worth three million gold mynet. During my search for this target, a little bird told me Tyson made a deal with a graverobber to find the target before anyone else does. I don't think I need to explain what kind of fate this could spell for Tyson—and the Reapers—if Randal were to find out he was in danger of losing a cut of that three mil."

Malakai had gone still as stone. He studied Darien for a long time, clearly gleaning whether he was telling the truth.

"It was the next best thing to cutting out his tongue," Darien added, nodding at the teeth. He never really did like Ian. And causing him a little bit of pain tonight had certainly helped with the Surge. Hell, he should've thanked him, though it might've helped if Ian had been conscious after Darien had taken the liberty of extracting a few of his teeth in a back alley. "Take it or leave it."

Malakai took a moment to process Darien's words. He studied the teeth during this time, his hands braced on the desk. And then he slowly, *slowly* lifted his gaze to Darien's face. "Tyson should know that stealing from another circle is stealing from Randal."

"Apparently, he didn't think of that," Darien said. "Maybe he only heard of this job from the outsiders who are after the money. Maybe he honestly wasn't aware that one of Randal's circles had already been offered the job. I don't really care whether there was a misunderstanding or not, I need him called off this trail. I have enough competition as it is without other Angelthene circles interfering."

Mal licked his lips. "Who else is looking for the target?"

"I'll deal with the names," Darien said. "You deal with Tyson."

"I've already heard about the Phoenix Head trash working our streets," Malakai said in a hard voice. "I'm only asking in case there's anyone else I should know about—anyone I should be taking care of before Randal has to be bothered with this shit."

"Just Tyson," Darien repeated. "I'm sure word will get around soon that my Devils have their claim on this target, and the rest should fall into place."

Malakai appraised him for a moment, and then he gave a slow nod. "Alright." He looked at the peace offering on the table, a hint of amusement showing in his features. "You ripped out his teeth?" He looked up at Darien, who shrugged.

"He's going to have a very expensive dental bill."

Malakai's mouth tilted into the hint of a smile. This night had turned out better than Darien thought it would.

"If you want proof," Darien began, "you can either run a test or track Ian down and tell him to open wide."

A low, rumbling laugh slipped through Malakai's lips. "I have to admit, I missed you a little."

Darien grinned like the devil he was. The tension lingering in the room melted away, and he swore Aspen breathed a quiet sigh of relief. "Are we okay, then?" Darien asked Malakai.

The Head of the House of Souls straightened from where he was still leaning on the desk. "I think so."

Darien held out a hand in offer to shake on it. Malakai rounded the table, and they clasped hands. Both of them might've squeezed a little harder than what was really necessary, but they were smiling, and that was all that mattered right now.

"Welcome back, old friend," Darien said.

Malakai was still smiling as he said, "You're a fucking fiend, you know that?"

"Takes a fiend to know a fiend."

"Isn't that the bloody truth."

THE FOLLOWING DAY, while the rest of the students at Angelthene Academy were stuffing their faces with supper in the dining hall, Loren and Dallas made their way across the vast lawn.

A fourth person had been reported missing that morning. Eighteen-year-old Zoe Brown, a freshman at Angelthene City University. A human—the second human missing in less than two days. When Loren had texted Darien, he had told her he'd do some digging, but she hadn't heard from him since. Checking her phone every two minutes was a dangerous habit she'd fallen into.

And she had to admit she had her doubts that he was following through. For someone who'd offered to help her with this mess, he certainly was preoccupied with other things most of the time. Unless he was keeping what he was doing a secret from her, the same way he hadn't told her when he'd gone out and bought the Avertera talisman, hadn't told her everything Cain had revealed. And if that was the case, she would be more than a little irritated. Sabrine was *her* friend; she deserved to be in on the plans Darien was making.

Which was part of the reason why her and Dallas were out here tonight, attempting to do something Darien was simply too busy to help them with. Or perhaps he didn't think Loren was right about there being something worth finding in the Old Hall. Maybe if they found a lead and brought it to the Devils, Darien would be more inclined to include her in his decision making.

Loren looked over her shoulder as they reached the chain-link fence bordering the Old Hall. A few students milled about the lawn, poring over the grimoires spread before them. Magic sparked from staves as they practiced spells, entirely oblivious to what Loren and Dallas were doing—or so she hoped. The rosy light of the setting sun threw the loops of barbed wire at the top of the fence into stark relief.

Although the powerful spellwork encasing the dilapidated building wasn't visible to the naked eye, Loren could feel it humming through the air, real as the warm, dry wind that snaked across the lawn and sent the pleated skirt of her uniform flapping against her thighs.

"Let's go around back," Dallas said. She fumbled around in her bookbag until she found her Focus, then began picking her way through the brambles choking the fence.

At the back of the building, where they were hidden from the students dotting the grounds, Dallas tried for an hour to find a weak spot in the magic rippling over the hall. She tried for so long that by the time the hour was up, her face was slick with sweat. Her concentration was so wholly spent on testing the magic for apertures that she could no longer hang onto the glamor she used in place of makeup. If only Dallas was a hellseher; the Sight would certainly make this endeavor a whole lot easier.

"You can't let anyone see me like this," Dallas grumbled as they made their way back across the now-deserted grounds. She snapped open a pocket mirror and applied a coat of mascara to her copper lashes. Loren was impressed that she managed to not poke out her eye while walking.

"I'm sorry, Dal," Loren said, knowing full well that it was more than just her lack of beauty glamor that was bothering her. "You gave it your best shot."

Dallas tucked the mirror and tube of mascara into the side-pouch of her bag. "Why do you think they'd bother to protect the Old Hall anyway? Why not just tear the thing down?"

"Beats me," Loren said as she tipped back her head, holding her arms out at her sides to let the warm wind blow through her blouse and feather through her fingers. "That breeze is a godsend."

They were a hundred yards from the west entrance when Dallas suddenly froze. Her nostrils flared, picking up on a scent Loren couldn't make out.

"What's the matter?" Loren asked.

But Dallas didn't say anything as she slowly turned around, away from the school. She began making her way toward the empty bleachers flashing a bright silver in the sun.

Loren followed her, grass crunching beneath her shoes. "Dal, you're scaring me. What are you smelling?"

Dallas whispered one word that was nearly lost in the whistling of the wind. "Blood."

Every thought in Loren's head went dead silent. "Blood?" she stammered. "Maybe we should get inside, Dallas. We should tell one of the professors."

Dallas ignored her, instead turning the corner to the backside of the bleachers, her sneakers inaudible on the springy grass. It wasn't until Loren had caught up to her that her human sense of smell picked up on it: the sharp reek of urine and the salty tang of blood.

Wind gusted them in the face, carrying more rancid smells, just as they both saw it.

There was a dead body at the far end of the bleachers. The grass around it was soaked with blood, and looming overtop the torso, teeth ripping into the chest cavity, was a demon.

It was hairless and vaguely humanoid in appearance, the bare skin a mottled gray. The knobs of its spine were horribly sharp and pronounced, the fingers so elongated they looked more like claws. Beastlike feet were braced behind it in the grass.

There was the wet crunch of bone snapping and muscle tearing as the…the *thing* ate its way to the heart. A professor who taught the second-year students, Loren realized with sickening clarity. His mouth was stuck open in a silent scream.

"My gods," Dallas whispered.

Loren pressed her hands to her mouth, forcing back the acid that rose to coat her tongue. They had to run before that thing noticed they were here, but she couldn't move her feet.

The wind changed directions. A gust of it blew against their backs, tossing their ponytails over their shoulders, as it swept toward the corpse of the professor and the creature feasting on it.

That creature froze. Slowly lifted its hairless head.

Dallas's fingers closed around Loren's wrist. "Run." They began moving backward as the demon's head swiveled around, the triangular nostrils on its flattened face widening. *"Run!"*

They broke into a sprint, their fingers laced together as they ran like hell across the field, toward the academy that was somehow farther away than before. Claws ripped into the earth as the creature hurtled after them.

"Faster, Loren!" Dallas barked. "Faster! *FASTER.*" She released her hand, the smell of birthday candles knifing through Loren's airways as Dallas waved her Focus.

Loren didn't turn around at the sound of the creature releasing a wet snarl of anger. It stumbled under whatever spell Dallas had cast, buying them a measly two seconds at best. Loren's leg muscles burned as she barreled for the nearest set of doors.

"Help!" Loren rasped. "HELP. We need *help!"*

They were almost at the entrance, but they wouldn't make it in time to close the doors behind them. Not with the demon right at their backs, snapping at their heels with bated breath.

As if reading her mind, Dallas stooped mid-sprint to grab a rock that was larger than a man's fist and hurl it behind her. It nailed the demon in the head hard enough that it grunted and tripped, buying them just enough time to crash through the doors.

Those doors swung open under their weight and slammed into the walls of the corridor.

"Shut them!" Dallas screamed. "SHUT THE DOORS!" She grabbed one of them and began pushing it closed. Two other students who were gaping in the hallway dropped their binders and hurried to help.

The doors had barely sealed when the creature crashed into them full force. Loren stumbled back, jaw rattling as she fell to the floor hard enough to bruise her tailbone. Blood rushed in her veins, turning her head a thousand pounds heavier.

The dining hall emptied as students rushed out to see what was happening. Screams and frantic voices rippled among the crowd. Dallas pushed past two students and helped Loren to her feet.

A male voice boomed, "Out of the way." It was Headmaster Langdon. On his heels were three other professors, one of which was Phipps.

Students parted to let them through. Teeth and claws collided with the doors, cracking the magic-enforced glass on the window.

Headmaster Langdon held up his stave. Blood ran from his left nostril as he concentrated, the scent of magic once again filling Loren's lungs.

The chunk of onyx at the point of the headmaster's Focus blazed with red light. The demon's head slowly turned all the way around until it faced the other direction. There was a *crack* as its neck snapped, and it collapsed to the ground with one last snarl of defiance.

The silence that followed lasted barely five seconds before the sobbing and screaming began.

As she stood there in Dallas's arms, Loren couldn't stop wondering how in the hell that demon had made it through the spells protecting campus.

And from the look on Headmaster Langdon's face, Loren knew he was wondering the very same thing.

DARIEN'S BOOTS pounded on the floors as he ascended the stairs from the basement at Hell's Gate, making sure to close the door

215

behind him. The last thing he needed was Loren wandering down there and seeing something he wasn't ready for her to see. There wasn't much down there, at least not at the moment, but he was certain the assortment of weapons the Devils kept in those rooms would be enough to frighten her to the bone.

It was the last thing she needed after the scare she and Dallas had encountered on the academy grounds. He and the Devils had tried to figure out how the demon had made it through the academy's intricate spellwork that was designed specifically to keep creatures like it out, but they'd found no answers.

It was Friday, so Loren was here now for the weekend, which meant Darien could allow his mind to take a rest from this new mystery for a while. She was safe here. Dallas was here for the night too, after expressing that she was still feeling too rattled to want to stay at the academy by herself. Darien had a feeling Max had something to do with her request, but he didn't prod.

Darien strode to the fridge and swung open the door to find the Hob crouched inside it, partially hidden behind the beer cases on the bottom shelf.

"What did I tell you about hiding out in the fridge?" Darien said as he reached for a beer.

Mortifer ducked under his arm and clamoured up the fridge to duck behind the boxes of cereal at the top. He peered around one of those boxes to bare his sharp little teeth at Darien, his eyes glowing like red stars.

Darien cracked open the can of beer. "Don't give me that attitude," he said, though a smile tugged at his mouth.

Bandit, who was sprawled across the couch in the sitting room, lifted his head, eyed Mortifer, and said, *Can I play?*

No, Darien replied.

The spirit gave a low whine. *Why not?*

Because your definition of playing usually involves eating something you're not supposed to. And I quite like Mortifer, thanks.

Bandit sighed through his nose and lowered his head onto a couch cushion.

Darien turned around to the sound of heavy footsteps to find Max entering the kitchen.

"Evening," Darien said, nodding once in greeting.

"Hey." Max rubbed at his eyes and stifled a yawn. He'd clearly just got in a few minutes ago; he was still wearing his jacket, and the laces on his boots were still tied. His mouth curled into a frown as he looked Darien over. "Are you okay?"

Darien's frown mirrored Max's. "Why wouldn't I be?"

Max stepped up to the island and leaned back against it, hands in his pockets. "Where did you go last weekend? After we left Angelthene General."

Darien slumped back against the fridge; the stainless-steel door was cold through his shirt. To be honest, he was surprised it had taken Max so long to ask this question. He'd anticipated this conversation happening a lot sooner. "Just to deal with some shit."

Max's brows pulled together. "Yeah? Is that why I keep hearing about Tyson Geller's jaw having been broken?"

Darien grimaced. "That wasn't me. I brought a peace offering to Malakai Delaney."

"What peace offering could you possibly—" But he froze, understanding washing across his face. "Oh. His excommunicated Reaper."

"I didn't kill him," Darien said quickly. "I just made sure he wouldn't talk about Mal's dealings anymore in exchange for cooperation from Tyson. We need as few people looking for Loren as possible, and if I can at least make sure the other Angelthene circles are aware that the job belongs to *us*—and Randal—we'll only have to deal with the wannabes. Plus, it'll create rumors that will remove us from the list of suspects that could be hiding her." The list of suspects that those marked with the phoenix head had likely drawn up in their searching.

"You think this is a good idea?" Max said.

Darien shrugged. "It's our only option."

"And what about Malakai? If word gets out to Randal about this, he's going to want in on what's happening. Which means he might eventually find out about Loren."

KAYLA EDWARDS

"Then I'll tell whatever lie I need to tell to keep people from thinking our relationship is worth telling Randal. I'll say she's my latest…" He trailed off with a grimace, unable to finish his sentence.

"What?" Max prompted, humor tipping the corner of his mouth up. "Fuckbuddy?"

Darien sighed through his nose. "If that's the lie I have to tell to keep her safe, then I will tell it." He paused, measuring Max's expression. "You still with me on this?"

Max's mouth curled down, brows pulling together. "Through everything, man. You don't even have to ask me that."

"Good." He took another swig of beer. "Love you, bud."

Max tsked. "Quit trying to suck my dick already."

Darien smiled. "I don't have to. You have a redhead to do that for you now."

Max's eyes widened. "How'd you know about that?"

Darien barked a laugh. "We live in the same fucking house, you dumb shit." The witch didn't exactly hold anything back either; Darien could usually hear her when he was in his suite, and that was from quite some distance away. Sometimes immortal hearing was a real pain in the ass. He might have to talk to Mortifer about placing some audio-blocking spells around his room.

Max shushed him, glancing over his shoulder toward the staircase. "Don't tell Loren, alright? In case Dallas hasn't confessed yet."

"Those girls are joined at the hip. I bet there's not a thing they don't know about each other."

Max merely shrugged, looking a little worried that the cat was already out of the bag.

Darien pushed away from the fridge and clapped Max on the back. "Relax, my friend. Your secret's safe with me." He made for the stairs. "See you in the morning."

23

Seven days later—seven wholly and painfully uneventful days, aside from the disappearance of yet another girl—Loren marched into the dining room at Hell's Gate shortly before Witching Hour and slapped a stack of papers onto the oak table.

Darien was sitting—alone and perfectly still—at the head, eyes closed, hands resting palms-up on the oak. The song of cicadas drifted in through the screen of the open window at his back. A bag of Stygian salts sat before him, along with his phone, a handful of photographs, and a can of beer dripping with condensation.

"I decided to do some investigating into the Phoenix Head Society," Loren began sharply, "after you were too *busy* to help Dallas and I get into the Old Hall."

Darien's mouth became a thin line. His eyes opened, and Loren had to try not to flinch at the sight of the black shining there. Dark as the night sky at his back, it seemed to swallow the light in the room. "And what did you find?" he said flatly.

Loren fidgeted, shifting her weight from one fuzzy slipper to the other fuzzy slipper. "Well, nothing at first," she admitted. "Nothing on the worldwide web that regular folk like me use, anyway. I had to get onto the restricted side of it—something called the *Schades*. But when the system finally let me in, there was more information on the society than I thought there'd be." She paused, feeling quite proud of herself. But he didn't say anything. "Do you want to know what I found?" she prodded.

He took a swig of beer, then smacked the can back onto the table so hard, the aluminum crumpled at the bottom, liquid sloshing over the sides. "Now that you've interrupted me." He waved a prompting hand. "Shoot."

It was easier to speak to him when his eyes were closed—and when he wasn't so pissed off at her. And now that he was watching her, she found that her tongue was leaden in her mouth. "It was mostly speculations of what the society was and what its members did," she began. The longer her explanation went on, the more her voice began to fade, uncertainty creeping in. "A lot of it was kinda weird and spooky, but I think I could be onto something. I mean, as long as at least one of the message boards I found has somebody on it who knows what they're talking about—"

"Caligo spare me, and spit it out, Loren."

Loren stiffened, and then pulled out a chair and sat down across from him. The black faded out of his eyes as he lost concentration on the target he was tracking and crossed his arms.

"The Phoenix Head Society was a group of mortal outcasts who created a now-ancient artifact that could defeat Death. No one knows what it was or what material it was made from, but apparently this group that eventually called themselves *alchemists* found a way to keep themselves from aging. Overtime, they recruited new members into the society. But only if they passed all necessary tests would they undergo an experiment called the Initiation. An experiment that would give them immortal life."

There was a beat of silence, and Darien's expression—the way his face sank almost imperceptibly, his eyes hardening into cold glass —told her everything.

"Star," she breathed. "You knew about this, didn't you?"

"Not all of it," Darien said. "Cain mentioned the Initiation. He thought it was a sacrifice—"

"And you didn't think to *tell* me?" she bit out, nostrils flaring.

"It's better if you don't know everything, Loren," he cut in, speaking over her.

"Says *you.*"

"Tell me something." Darien's voice was calm and deadly. "You believe this society is connected to your friend's disappearance, and the people that are after you, *how* exactly? What's your theory?"

She traced a finger over a burned line that formed the edge of the devil's left wing in the pyrographic table, stamping down the urge to throw herself across the wood and throttle him. "I'm not sure," she admitted. "But I think if we get into the Old Hall, we could find some answers. Maybe something that will draw a connection between the tattoo of those bounty hunters and this group of outcasts." Darien studied her for such a long time that she squirmed in her seat.

"You didn't need to go through all the trouble of creating usernames and passwords, Rookie," he said with restrained impatience. "I have the best hacker in the city, and he's right over there." He inclined his head in the direction of the sitting room.

Loren stiffened. She looked over her shoulder, to where Tanner was lounging in an armchair, laptop propped open on his knees.

He lifted a hand in greeting, black-framed glasses sliding down his straight nose.

Cripes, she hadn't even noticed he was there.

Her cheeks burned as she realized she might've wasted the past five hours of her life—and she wasn't about to tell Darien that it was five whole hours. "You didn't seem inclined to listen to me, so I thought I'd find something to convince you that the Old Hall is worth our time."

"I never thought it wasn't worth our time, Loren. I was the one who offered to help you with this whole shitshow, remember? I just have a lot on my plate right now and a target whose head needs to be delivered *tonight.*"

Loren merely waited. The longer she sat there, the more frustrated Darien became.

Darien gave a heavy sigh. "In case you weren't aware, my time is not always something I can do with as I please. I have a boss who has an even worse temper than I do, and if I don't collect at a rate that is satisfying to him, he will have *my* head."

Loren didn't know what to say to that. She felt her expression soften, but his words weren't enough to totally put her mind at rest.

Darien's dark brows lowered, throwing his steel-blue eyes into deep shadow. "You don't think I'm doing anything to help you," he said. "Do you?"

She fidgeted. "Well, it would help if you actually told me what you were doing instead of always making me wonder."

"Part of the deal we made was that I would keep you safe," he said. "This is me making good on that promise." Seeing the defeat on her face, he added softly, "You just have to trust me, Loren."

Loren's expression hardened. "I don't do well with secrets. And for this to work, *you* have to trust me as well." She crossed her arms and lifted her chin. "I want all-in. I want to know everything you're doing to help me, or I'm taking this thing off." She fingered the talisman glimmering in the hollow of her throat.

Darien's stare could cut through stone. "You wouldn't be able to handle being *all-in*, Rookie."

"Try me."

He laced his fingers over his muscular chest, the dimple in his cheek showing at the challenge she'd presented him with. "A few nights ago, when you tried to stop me from leaving the hospital, I went to see an old friend named Malakai Delaney. You might've heard of him: he leads the Reapers."

Loren gave a nod as something twisted in her gut. Suddenly, she wasn't so sure she could handle where this was going.

"I brought a peace offering to stop Tyson Geller from looking for you, and to start some rumors that the job that involves finding you belongs to *me*. We need as much space between you and danger as possible, so I had to take some…precautions." The corner of his mouth quirked with humor. "I brought him a few teeth from the mouth of someone who betrayed him."

Loren paled, the hand in her gut twisting tight.

"He seemed to like my gift," Darien continued. "We're friends again, and the cost was only a few teeth and Tyson's jaw broken by

Mal to seal the deal." He allowed for his story to sink in, driving fear into her core. A wicked glint entered his eyes. "You look a little woozy, Rookie. Everything okay?"

She swallowed. "If you're trying to intimidate me, it's not going to work. I meant what I said: the deal is off if you don't share everything with me going forward."

The cocky tilt of his lips lessened. "I didn't realize you were in charge of whether or not I protect you."

"I've ran for that door before," she threatened mildly, hoping her words wouldn't push him too far. "I can do it again." She was bluffing, but he didn't need to know that.

Darien's frown deepened. "If the things you see or hear end up breaking you, that's on you, not me."

"Understood," she said, tossing her hair over a shoulder. She flicked her gaze between him and the papers she'd slapped onto the table, a look of expectance on her face.

Darien sighed. "Tomorrow night, I'll take you." He sat forward and shook another pile of salts from the bag. "Now give me a few hours of peace. *Please.*"

Loren smiled smugly before pushing her chair out from the table. Five hours of research hadn't been such a waste after all.

She glanced at Tanner again, who was clicking away on his keyboard. As Darien prepared to inhale another line of salts, she whispered to him, "I thought all hellsehers had perfect vision."

"We do," Darien said as he shut one nostril with a tattooed finger and snorted the line. His voice was slightly thick from the salts as he added, "He just wears them to look the part." He waved the hand that held the rolled-up banknote at her, as if to say *shoo*.

Loren rolled her eyes.

But as she lifted herself to her feet, the three photographs lying partially atop one another at the edge of the table made her pause.

They were photographs of the newly missing girls. Zoe Brown, Penny Thomson, and Eobha Doyle. Seeing them together like that brought a sick feeling to Loren's stomach.

Blonde hair. Blue eyes. Roughly nineteen, twenty years old. All of them university students.

"You're tracking the missing girls?" Her voice was hollow.

"I *tried* tracking them," he corrected. He dropped the curled-up banknote, sat back in his chair, and closed his eyes. He added with a murmur, "I couldn't find them."

Darien was too focused on the target he was trying to relocate to be bothered by her reaching across the table to grab the photos.

That sick feeling in her stomach became more intense.

"Darien," she whispered hoarsely. The images of the three girls rustled in her unsteady hands.

Darien's eyes flashed open to meet hers—black again. And very, *very* unimpressed.

Loren turned the photographs around so that they were facing Darien and held them up on either side of her face. "Notice anything?" Her voice wobbled.

"Yeah," he said in a frighteningly calm tone. "A little girl who's getting on my last feeble nerve."

She merely looked at him, waiting, her hands trembling harder as the seconds ticked by. Gradually, the black faded out of his eyes, and understanding—and empathy—washed across his face.

"They look like you," he said softly.

Loren nodded. "They look like me," she whispered.

Which meant *she* was responsible for the abduction of these girls; responsible for whatever fate they would meet at the hands of their captors. Responsible for the lives of their families being turned upside down. If any of them got hurt… If any of them *died*—

Star. She felt like she was going to faint.

"Tanner." Darien's voice cut into her bubble of panic. "Pull up the forcefield projections for Angelthene Academy." The rapid clicking of keys filled the silence. "There's an abandoned building on that property called the Old Hall." Darien met her terrified gaze, and she wasn't sure if he was still talking to Tanner or to her as he said, "We're getting in there tomorrow night."

LOREN COULDN'T STOP TAPPING her foot. Couldn't stop looking over her shoulder.

The latter didn't do her any good. The grounds surrounding the academy were so dark that her mortal vision couldn't tell the difference between a tree and a person. But it made her feel like she was doing something useful as Darien paced in the shrubs by the chain-link fence surrounding the Old Hall, cell phone glued to his ear as he listened to what Tanner was saying on the other end.

All power in the city came from the Control Tower. Located in the heart of the North End, it was a sleek pillar of glass called *cristala*. The tower acted as a conduit for the magic that stemmed from the energy grid of the earth—from the anima mundi itself, the world soul and the source of all magic that bound the universe together. It powered their cars, made spellcasting possible, lit their homes—it even created the forcefield, an invisible dome over Angelthene that kept its registered citizens safe from outside forces.

It wasn't perfect by any means, since the odd demon still managed to slip through—which was how the city had gotten its pest problem to begin with—but no matter how trained a person was in magic, no one could cause a power outage great enough to take down the entire grid. It was impossible; even Darien had said as much when Loren had asked him if he could do it to locate Sab. She'd had little hope of him saying yes, though she'd asked anyway.

And perhaps the only person in this whole city who was skilled enough in hacking to cause even a blip in the advanced spellwork shielding *just* Angelthene Academy was Tanner Atlas.

Tanner was the reason Darien was here tonight in the first place. From where he was currently stationed at Hell's Gate, Tanner was busy hacking the academy's spell network; earlier that evening, he'd bought Darien two seconds to jump the wrought iron surrounding campus, through the softest spot Darien could pinpoint in the forcefield around the school with his Sight. And now, Tanner would do the same to allow them into the Old Hall.

At least, if everything went according to plan. But the longer Darien spent on that phone, the faster Loren's foot tapped in the grass, and the more times she looked over her shoulder.

The Devil shot her a glare. His eyes were so black, they gobbled up the moonlight filtering through the palm trees rustling overhead.

"What?" she demanded, though her foot stilled at the sight of those all-black eyes.

"Your annoying little foot is distracting me." The phone speaker crackled as Tanner laughed on the other end.

She stuck her tongue out at him—and Tanner.

"Caligo spare me…," Darien muttered. Although she couldn't quite tell, she swore he was rolling his eyes. He made to say something else, but Tanner was speaking on the other end.

A hand grabbed Loren's arm.

A muffled scream clawed its way up her throat. She spun around, heart kicking in her chest at the sight of the shadow looming before her.

It was Dallas.

"Gods-damnit, Dal," she hissed, pressing a hand to the fluttering in her chest. Behind her, Darien was unfazed. "You almost gave me a heart attack!"

The witch was grinning, teeth gleaming in the moonlight. "You soft-hearted mortal."

"You're supposed to be keeping watch!"

"And miss out on all the fun?" At the sight of whatever expression Loren was wearing, she clicked her tongue. "Relax. No one's going to catch us."

Darien shushed them. He concluded his call with Tanner, hung up, and shoved the cell phone into his pocket. "Starting at two minutes past Witching Hour, Tanner will buy us sixty seconds to get through the forcefield."

"Sixty seconds each?" Loren asked.

"Sixty seconds *total*," he clarified. Loren tried to swallow, but her mouth was too dry.

Grass crunched beneath Dallas's heels as she stepped up to the fence, tipping back her head to survey the height of it. Her hair brushed the waistband of her low-rise jeans. "Where exactly are we getting in? You don't really expect us to climb."

"If you want to get inside, you'll do whatever I tell you to." His eyes narrowed as he appraised the witch. "Might I remind you that I specifically told you to keep watch over *there?*" He pointed a gloved finger at the academy.

"You clearly don't know me well enough, Slayer," Dallas said, matching his tone, "to understand that I never sit out on the fun parts."

But Darien's attention went back to the forcefield. Although invisible to the naked eye, his Sight allowed him to see the barrier clear as day. "Thirty seconds."

Loren didn't think Dallas was breathing either as they waited for Darien's signal. She tried to tell herself that it wasn't a big deal—it was just a silly fence. But if she didn't make it to the ground on the other side before those sixty seconds were up, she would be singed into nothing.

It would be a horrible way to die. Not even her bones would survive.

When two minutes past Witching Hour arrived, Darien gave Dallas a boost over the fence, where she scaled the chain-link, hefted herself over the barbed wire, and landed on other side with the nimble balance of a cat. As soon as she was clear of the fence, Darien gestured for Loren to hurry. She didn't let herself think about how she would manage to maneuver her body over the barbed wire without impaling herself on it as she stepped forward.

Darien offered her a hand, but she shooed him away. "I can climb just fine by myself, thanks."

Darien shot her a glare as she scuttled up the chain-link. "Accepting help from someone doesn't mean you're weak, Calla."

"Thanks, Tips. I'll keep that in mind." She swore she could feel his death stare burning a hole in the back of her sweater.

When she reached the loops of spikes at the top of the fence, she froze. She was shaking so hard, the chain-link was rattling. Darien ascended to her side so quietly she didn't hear him move, didn't even feel the fence shift under his weight. He swung himself over the barbed wire at a near-invisible speed.

"You need to get over here, Loren," he told her, his face level with hers as he held onto the fence on the other side. He made a show of glancing at his watch. "Unless you'd like to become a pile of ashes in T-minus ten seconds."

"You're not helping," she seethed. Her limbs had turned to jelly.

"Get the fuck over here!" he snapped. *"Now."*

"You don't have to swear." But she started moving, wishing she'd put on pants instead of shorts, as she reached the very top and swung a leg over the barbed wire.

"And you don't have to whine," Darien countered. "I can think of far better things for you to do with that mouth."

That mouth he was referring to popped open in a gasp, and she winced as a metal spike snagged the flesh of her thigh. "Don't talk to me like that," she hissed, wobbling at the top of the fence.

But her cheeks were burning. And despite that she felt no sturdier than a leaf rattling in the wind, warmth pooled somewhere deep inside her as she considered the filthy details of what he had in mind for her mouth.

Was it wrong of her to want him to not only tell her what he had in mind, but to *show* her?

She shoved the thought aside as Darien offered her a hand again. "I know you like it." He practically purred the words. "If I didn't think you did, I wouldn't tease you so much."

"Don't read my aura," she snapped, but she placed her hand in his—and then remembered the talisman that hung around her neck, which meant her tells had nothing to do with him reading her aura.

Damn it. He was good.

As if knowing exactly what she was thinking, Darien said, "I don't have to read your aura to figure you out, sweetheart."

Another spike bit into her palm, eliciting a hiss through her teeth as she lifted the other leg over, putting more of her weight on Darien's arm than anywhere else. That arm didn't so much as tremble under her weight. Cripes—how strong *was* he? "I'll have you know I'm not up to date with my tetanus shots." Blood dribbled down her wrist and calf.

Once she made it to the other side and eased down to Darien's level, he gathered her into the crook of an arm, holding her tightly against his chest. She was too surprised to say anything—or to ask him what in hell he thought he was doing—as he literally jumped, pulling her off the fence with him. Her fingers nearly came free of their joints as her grip was torn off the steel wire.

She landed right on top of him in the grass. The slayer gave a grunt like the wind had been knocked out of him, his legs tangling with hers. The forcefield snapped into place not a second later, and magic pulsed through the air so loudly, her arm hairs stood on end.

She pulled away from Darien, ignoring how the heat from his body affected her more than the fall from the fence, more than the magical barrier that had nearly singed her bones.

"*Caligo's tits*, girl," he swore, lifting himself to his feet. "The least you could do is try not to belt me in the face the next time I save your life." He swept a hand over his hair, smoothing it out of his face.

Loren lurched to her feet, dusting dirt and bits of grass off her legs. "Don't be such an ass and maybe I'll consider it next time," she said sweetly. She thought she'd felt a cheekbone under her elbow when he'd pulled her off the fence. Or was it his forehead? *Serves you right*, she thought, pressing her lips together to stop herself from laughing.

Although Darien was still glaring at her, she was starting to recognize when his teasing ways were creeping back into his carefully painted façade. A mischievous glint entered his eyes, and when he spoke again, his voice was so deep and smooth, it could almost pass for a purr. "Maybe I should teach you a lesson for talking back to me and spank your little ass."

Loren blinked, her whole face heating up. "I dare you to try." The words were nothing but near-unintelligible stammers.

Dallas was laughing so hard, she was snorting.

Darien quirked a brow, a smile teasing his mouth. "Sweetheart, you *do* not want to make that dare."

Loren cleared her throat, her eyelashes fluttering. "I didn't mean to hit you on purpose—it was an accident. And a warning before you pulled me off the fence would've been nice."

There was a slight quirk in his mouth that suggested he was enjoying himself more than he wanted to let on. "I could say the same about your bony elbows."

Dallas squawked a laugh, but all Darien did was get back on his phone to let Tanner know they'd made it to the other side. It was the quickest phone call in the history of phone calls.

And then he was stomping up the stone steps, toward the door that hung lopsided on the hinges. He mumbled something she couldn't make out and swept inside.

Loren supposed she shouldn't be surprised that he was literally ditching them out here in favour of the shadows in that building. Before coming here, she'd argued with him for a full thirty minutes about whether she should sit this mission out or go with him.

Needless to say, she'd won that particular argument.

"Is he always this charming?" Dallas said, wiping the tears of amusement from the corners of her eyes.

Loren hugged herself and surveyed the building, with its shattered windows and busted chimney. "Usually."

A gust of wind swept through the area, ruffling her hair and drying the blood on her wrist and leg. While most old and abandoned places gave a feeling of emptiness to the person looking upon them, this one only gave her the creeps.

She'd prayed long and hard to Caligo that they would find something tonight that would give them a lead. Something that might explain the meaning of the phoenix tattoo that had plagued her dreams since Sabrine's disappearance.

The fact that the schoolboard had gone out of their way to give this building an extra layer of protection... There *had* to be something valuable inside it. A secret worth keeping.

"Let's go," Dallas said.

As Loren crept after her, into the impenetrable darkness of the Old Hall, she wondered if it wasn't so much about the people they wanted to keep out.

But something they wanted to keep in.

PART THREE

WISH UPON THE LIAR

24

Loren was disappointed to find that there was nothing of interest in the Old Hall. Nothing except desks pushed up against the walls, cobwebs drooping in opaque curtains from a patchy ceiling, and dust. *Lots* of cobwebs and dust.

Loren kept close to Darien and the flashlight he swept about the room. The amber glow bounced off spider's nests and sent mice scurrying for holes in the walls.

"There's no way we came all this way for nothing." Loren's words echoed softly, evoking a hiss from a tarantula squatting somewhere in the shadows nearby.

"If there's something here that's worth protecting," Darien said as he led the way through the room, "no one with half a brain would hide it in plain sight, Rookie."

"Thanks for pointing that out, Mister Obvious," she grumbled. She knew she was pushing him tonight, but…after how wounded she'd felt at the hospital, she'd planned to distance herself from him. To force herself not to care what he was doing or who he did it with. It was easier said than done but…she had to try. Even if she made him hate her in the process. She cleared her throat and stepped in front of him, edging around the scattered desks, being careful to remain in the beam of his flashlight. "Where do you propose we look? All I see is four walls and a roof that's barely there."

Behind them, Dallas was muttering something about spiders and mice and how she should've listened to Darien—the *bossy slayer*, as she liked to call him—and stayed behind.

Darien was taking too long to answer Loren's question, so she turned around to face him, only to see him quickly looking away from her, as if he had been staring at...at—

"What were you staring at?" Loren demanded, her spine stiffening.

"I beg your pardon?" The words were coated with innocence.

Loren repeated, "What were you staring at?"

A smile flirted with the slayer's mouth. If he kept looking at her like that, she might just fall in love with him. "You have beautiful hair," he said, his voice a croon.

Loren tightened her jaw. "You were *not* just staring at my hair."

"What was I staring at then?"

She crossed her arms. "Why don't *you* tell *me?* Your smile suggests you were having inappropriate thoughts." Her face was warming up, regardless of how cool it was in the building.

And because she certainly wouldn't mind if someone like Darien had taken appreciation in the way her ass looked. Especially when he'd just been talking about spanking it.

Darien tsked. "Says the girl who was ready to drop her panties for me the other day."

Dallas choked on a laugh. "You guys *really* need to break that tension."

Loren looked at Darien, and he looked back at her. He tipped up an eyebrow, that smile on his face broadening. It wasn't long before she was scowling at him upon realizing just how they would break that tension.

"Don't say a word," she threatened.

Darien merely laughed. It was a rich, throaty sound that caused an inviting warmth to spread below her navel. Her body certainly had a mind of its own lately, its reactions traitorous and foreign.

Sure, she'd been attracted to plenty of males before, had even wanted to familiarize herself with the shape of their mouths.

But nothing she'd ever experienced had been as intense as what she felt when she was around Darien Cassel.

The slayer's eyes plunged into darkness again as he became all business. He scanned the interior of the hall, flashlight forgotten, the Sight giving him a far clearer line of vision than any glass bulb could provide.

As he searched, Loren stepped up to the floor-to-ceiling chalkboard on the north wall. Dust and the passing of time made the words scrawled across its surface mostly illegible, but after a moment of squinting she was able to read them.

Ad vitum aeternum.

"To everlasting life." Loren jumped at the sound of Darien's voice at her back.

She turned to look at him, her ponytail snagging on her sweater. "You can read Ancient Reunerian?"

"Bits and pieces of it." He moved toward one end of the chalkboard, taking the light with him. As Loren followed close on his heels, she couldn't decide if it was the light she was drawn to or the surety of his movements. Perhaps it was the weapons she knew he had on him.

The Darkslayer took the end of the flashlight between his teeth and felt around the brass frame of the chalkboard.

It shifted under his fingers. Dust shook free and fell to the floor in streams as the chalkboard folded in half, the rusted hinges squealing as one side of it swung open, like a page of a great book.

Behind it appeared to be nothing but a stone wall. But when Darien took the flashlight out of his mouth and shone the light upon it, Loren saw that the stones were covered in ancient runes.

Precisely enough stones to form the height and width of a standard door.

A single stone in the very center had no runes on it; instead, it had the simple mark of the Scarlet Star—a circle with seven rays. It would've meant nothing to Loren, were it not for the fact that she wore that same solar symbol around her neck—the pendant she'd had on since she was a baby. The universe's only hint that she'd ever had parents.

Darien turned to look at her, but she was already yanking the necklace out from where it was tucked beneath her sweater, the chain so long it nearly brushed her navel. She swallowed and stepped up to the wall, Darien backing up to give her room.

Holding the amulet in one hand, she used her other to trace the symbol in the wall, hoping her sense of touch would be more reliable than her depth perception.

The sun had been carved deep into the stone, as if something was meant to fit inside it.

Loren lifted the amulet, inserting it into the impression. It lined up perfectly, like a key sliding into a lock. She wiggled it, and the stone made a faint clicking sound.

The walls of the Old Hall gave a deep, rolling groan, like a beast stirring awake. Dirt hissed as it fell from the ceiling in streams.

Loren pulled her hand away, taking the amulet with her. She retreated so many paces that she stepped on Darien's boot. Her other heel caught on the leather toe of it, and her stomach plummeted through the floor as gravity yanked her backward.

Darien grabbed onto her, steadying her before she could fall, and although her sweater and his leather gloves formed a thick barrier between her skin and his, her heart picked up speed—and she found that she hated herself for it.

The rune-covered doorway hissed as it slid open. The air that wafted through the cracks around the door was so cold, Loren gave a violent shiver.

Darien pushed the door open all the way. The flashlight's glow spread across a steep staircase that spiralled deep into the earth.

He quirked an eyebrow at Loren. "Still think there's only four walls and a roof?"

It was Dallas, hovering behind them, who said, "Don't tell me we're going down there."

"You're welcome to stay here and keep watch, Dallas," Darien said as he began trekking down the steps. "Maybe this time you'll listen to me." It wasn't long before they couldn't see him anymore, and the earth soon swallowed up his pounding footfall.

Loren tried not to trip as she hurried after him, Dallas right on her heels.

"WHAT DOES IT MEAN?" Loren asked.

She was leaning on a wooden counter in the dark and otherwise empty basement of the Old Hall, studying Darien's expression as he looked over the three-foot-long scroll they'd dug out from underneath a flagstone. Two of Darien's pocketknives served as paperweights at the curled top of it. The glow of the flashlight slid steadily down the parchment as Darien deciphered the mystical and obscure symbolism and imagery decorating every inch of its yellowed surface.

Dominus Volumen was scrawled across the top of the parchment. The literal translation of the two words was *Master Scroll.*

Darien's face lined with frustration as he reached the end of the parchment. At least, the half of the parchment that was here. The other half was missing; there was a tear at the end, where it cut abruptly through an image of the eight points of the Scarlet Star.

"It means," Darien began, taking a deep breath. He blew it out in a sigh and admitted, "I have no idea what the hell it means." He gestured to the faded manuscript. "It's mostly riddles and metaphors. Little of it makes any sense."

"Can you not read *any* of it?" Dallas asked.

"I can read *some* of it. It talks of chemical baths, and something called an Arcanum Well. If I had to guess, I'd say this is a manual of sorts. Instructions for how to create this thing called the Arcanum Well. Look here." He read a line in fluent Reunerian. When he was finished, Darien pursed his lips in concentration. "In other words, it cannot be undone or replicated—only remade."

"The Arcanum Well?" Dallas asked.

"That's my best guess."

"What I found on the Schades was correct, then," Loren

concluded. Those five hours she'd spent trying to get into the stupid shadow web had been worth her time after all. "The Phoenix Head Society created an artifact that could grant mortals an immortal life."

Dallas cut in. "That still doesn't explain how any of this is connected to you. And what about that Initiation thing that Cain Nash mentioned? How does that tie into this?"

"According to what I found online, the Initiation was the name they gave to the act of turning a mortal into an immortal," Loren said. Her eyes flicked to Darien. "But Cain said it sounded more like a sacrifice. Didn't he?"

"Cain could've been wrong," Darien said. "His source of information is mostly rumors."

They considered it in silence for a time. Loren had hoped there would be more down here—a solid explanation for what was happening, left behind by the members of the Phoenix Head Society. But little remained. And aside from the Dominus Volumen, there was nothing that caught her eye—nothing but a line of demarcation on the floor that indicated that some piece of furniture used to sit there.

"It clearly has something to do with your bloodline," Darien said, the ghostly beam of the flashlight outlining his features in deep shadow. "Whoever is after you is using your ancestor's bone powder to track you. Which means you are related to someone who was perhaps incredibly powerful," he paused to jab the scroll with a finger, "or incredibly smart. Maybe it's something as simple as the abductors believing you have access to this scroll."

"And I *do*," Loren said. "Now that I have it, maybe we can trade it for Sabrine."

"Not so fast," Darien said. Loren blinked. "You don't just go handing over the one thing that might give us the upper hand, Rookie. First, we need to find out what they want. If it's the scroll, then fine. Problem solved. But if it's you they're after—you *specifically* —then our troubles are far from over."

Loren sighed. She blinked her tired eyes at the faded ink on the parchment, head spinning with exhaustion. The weight of all these sleepless nights was dragging her down.

"Do you remember anything at all from your past?" Darien asked. He straightened and crossed his arms, the scroll crackling as it curled back into a loose cylinder.

"I don't have any memories from before my fifth birthday. What I know about my past is only what I was told: that I was found by a priest at the temple and eventually adopted by Roark and his wife. The priest passed away several years ago, so there's no chance of us asking him anything."

Darien turned to Dallas. "And you? What do you remember from when your parents brought Loren home?"

Dallas shook her head. "Nothing. I have a terrible memory as it is; I can't even recall the first time I met Loren. To me, she was always just *there.*"

Darien pursed his lips in thought. "Do you think you could talk to Roark and see if he has any information that might help us?"

Sadness crept into Dallas's eyes. "He's too busy," she mumbled, dropping her focus to the floor. "Trust me. If I'm lucky, I hear from him twice a year."

As the Red Baron, Roark was hardly home. He was always training Fleets throughout the continent, the winged army that helped protect the world of Terra from unpredictable threats. They also dealt with demons if they became too powerful or great in number for cities—or Darkslayers—to handle on their own.

"And what about Taega?" Darien asked.

Loren grimaced, and Dallas gave a snort.

The slayer's brows pulled together. "What's funny?"

"Oh, Taega doesn't talk to us," Dallas said, her tone one that suggested this should be obvious to every person in the world, even if they didn't know Taega. "Like, ever."

Silence swept in again.

Loren was fiddling with her amulet when she remembered the engravings on the back of it—and how Darien seemed to know how to speak some Ancient Reunerian.

"Darien," Loren began, and he looked to her in question. She held up the amulet, the cold chain tugging against the back of her neck. "Can you try reading what this says?"

He stepped up to her and took the amulet into his hands. Loren found herself holding her breath from how close he was standing to her. He studied the engravings for a while, and as he studied it, Loren caught herself looking at him a little too closely. Worried the same thing as what happened that night in the dining room would happen again, especially as she found her focus drifting to his sculpted mouth, she forced herself to look away from him.

But her attention zeroed in on him again as he read his translation aloud.

"To the sweetest lily in all the valley...

Hold me close when the hour is dire

And wish upon the Liar."

Loren glanced between Dallas and Darien. No one seemed to have anything to say.

"What does that mean?" Loren said at last.

Darien shook his head. "No clue." He let go of the amulet, and it jingled softly as it swung against Loren's chest.

After several minutes, Loren said, "What do we do?"

Darien swiped up the manuscript and rerolled it tightly. "We take the scroll and bide our time until Benjamin and his robbers can get us some answers regarding who your ancestors are. If we can find out who your parents were—or find a connection to any living relatives you might have—we might be able to get some answers."

They didn't exactly have any more knowledge of the situation than they did before. If anything, they had more questions. But as they made their way out of the Old Hall, Loren felt something inside her she hadn't felt since before Sabrine went missing.

She dared to call it hope.

25

Darien was crouching before a massive cage in a back corner of Mordred and Penelope's Mortar and Pestle, his hands braced on his knees. The hexagonal mesh of the cage was designed to keep the carnivorous plant inside it from snaking its deadly branches through. But this didn't stop it from snapping tirelessly at the mesh, its razor-sharp teeth closing around the wire.

"Feisty little thing," Darien said with a smile, "aren't you?" Flytrapper plants hunted a wide assortment of insects; among their favorites were arachnids and myriapods, though they'd eat any type of flesh if they could sink their teeth into it.

Feeling morbidly curious, Darien lifted a hand to the wire…

But he froze mid-reach when Loren cleared her throat from where she stood at the top of the staircase that led up to the second floor. Her dog was at her side, ears standing vertical with curiosity.

Darien dropped his hand and straightened from his crouch.

Loren quirked an eyebrow and crossed her arms, a smile playing on her mouth. "I certainly hope you're not stressing out my plants, Darien Cassel."

"Of course not," he lied. But she wasn't buying it, and the longer she glared at him—with a look on her face that he had to admit was quite adorable—the faster the smile he was suppressing turned into a full-on grin.

She tucked a strand of straightened hair behind an ear, her face reddening like a little tomato. "I'm almost ready," she said without looking at him. "Five more minutes." She paused briefly before adding, "And you might want to give Prickles some attention."

She clomped back up the stairs and disappeared into the office, her dog following on her heels. The Mortar and Pestle was closed for the evening, so Loren was completing end-of-day paperwork.

Darien was about to ask her who Prickles was when he felt something brush against the sleeve of his jacket. He looked down at the table he was standing beside to see that a small potted plant had made its way over to the very edge of the table, leaving a trail of soil in its wake. It seemed ordinary at first glance, but when he looked closer, there were designs on its vibrant green leaves.

"Aren't you worried it'll fall off the table?" he called to Loren.

"*She*," Loren shouted back. "It's *Miss* Prickles, and she's female." Darien gave a snort of amusement.

Another few seconds passed before Loren came back down the stairs, the strap of her crossbody bag slung over a shoulder, the handle of a suitcase clutched in her hands. Loren added about the plant, "She gets jealous easily, as I'm sure you've already noticed. Sometimes she purposely tips herself over if I spend too much time doing paperwork. The Star forbid she be ignored for two seconds."

Darien chuckled.

Loren hadn't changed out of the clothes she'd worn to work today: a black shirt that showed a sliver of her flat stomach, and a plaid skirt. The latter was so short, Darien caught a glimpse of the hot-pink underwear she had on underneath as she maneuvered the steps. He somehow managed not to stare—though he had to admit, that flash of color turned him on like a light.

Darien forced himself to look away from Loren so he wouldn't do anything that would make her uncomfortable—like pant over her like a dog with a bone, which he was borderline doing.

The plant—Miss Prickles—was still vying for his attention.

"Aren't you pretty?" he said in a low voice. If a plant could blush, Miss Prickles certainly would've been blushing. She shrank a little in her pot, leaves curling inward.

Darien became aware of Loren's full attention falling upon him. He wondered what it was that he said, but by the time he faced her again she was making a point to look away from him, her expression impassive, though he swore he saw a peculiar spark in her eyes.

When Loren reached the last stair, Darien stepped forward to take the suitcase from her.

Her grip tightened on the handle, her shoulders stiffening. "I can carry it just fine on my own."

"I'm perfectly capable as well," Darien countered, matching her defensive tone.

Loren gave him a tight, closed-lip smile. "How about no?"

Darien felt his features harden into stone. "Your favorite word is *no,* isn't it?"

Loren hummed and pursed her glossy lips. "No," she said cheekily, and scrunched her nose up at him.

He scrunched his back.

Something about what he did made her lift her chin, made her blink rapidly, color pooling in her cheeks. "You're infuriating," she stated. Her voice was breathy.

"If I infuriate you so much, then why are your little dimples telling me you're trying not to smile?"

That inviting color in her cheeks deepened. "They have a mind of their own."

Darien smirked. "Oh, I'm sure."

They stared each other down for a full minute before Loren sighed and finally offered up the suitcase. He waited until he had it in his hand before speaking again. "Just so we're clear, when I offer to do something for you, you don't need to take it as an insult." Loren Calla was the very definition of the word *stubborn.*

"It's kind of a knee-jerk reaction," she said as she led the way to the door. "Growing up a human in Angelthene has made my abilities quite clear over the years. Or lack thereof."

"Fair enough."

A gust of scorching-hot air blasted them in the face as they stepped out onto the street. The light was changing in subtle ways, the hills in the distance shifting to a golden-brown with the arrival of fall. People milled about the avenue, poking in and out of the few shops, salons, and restaurants that kept their doors open until just after sunset.

Darien had given Loren the option to stay at Hell's Gate this weekend while he and the others investigated the new breed of demon that had been seen on the Angelthene Academy grounds. He had to admit he hadn't really expected her to say yes, what with the Avertera talisman still around her neck. But to his surprise, she had agreed to his offer instantly. She was beginning to spend more time at his house than anywhere else, her dog included most days.

As she yanked the door shut behind her, the sun fell upon her in slanted beams, turning her thick hair white-gold, and when she peeked up at him, he found that her eyes were the deep blue of the ocean, edged with a vivid shade of turquoise unlike anything he'd ever seen.

Loren dropped her gaze from his, color blooming across her soft cheekbones.

Shit. He was staring again, wasn't he?

Loren fumbled in her bag for her keys. "Did you figure anything out about the scroll?" Her hands started to tremble, and the longer he took to answer her, the more she fumbled. She made to swear, but instead she bit her bottom lip—that pouty, fuck-me mouth he just couldn't look away from, painted the gleaming pink of the inside of a seashell. Her habit of talking back to him only made him want to fuck that lush mouth of hers so badly, it sometimes kept him awake at night. It certainly didn't help that she was at his house every weekend, sleeping just down the hallway from him.

He wanted to fuck her so hard that every man she'd tasted before him would be erased from her memory.

She locked the deadbolt, plunked the keys into her bag, and looked up at him. Her expression was unreadable, but she tilted an eyebrow. "Something on your mind, Darien?" The question brought him back to that night in the dining room—when he'd called her out for wanting to drop her panties. "I had no idea locking doors got you so hot and bothered."

Fuck, this girl. She was giving him a run for his money.

He felt his gaze darken with irritation—and a deep frustration he had no intention of admitting to her. "Start walking."

She tossed her hair over a shoulder and breezed past him, so close that her arm brushed his with a heat more intense than the sun, despite that he was wearing his usual black leather jacket.

As they made their way to the car, his phone buzzed in his pocket. Upon seeing his sister's name on the screen, he swiped to answer and lifted the phone to his ear.

"Yeah," he said by way of greeting.

Loren was walking several feet ahead of him, and when two warlocks swaggering by catcalled her, fully turning their heads to leer at her perfect ass, Darien gave them a predatory smile that had them promptly averting their eyes and scuttling for the nearest storefront.

"I'm with the others at Queenswater Rapids." Ivyana's voice held a tension Darien instantly picked up on. Queenswater Rapids was an old park in the heart of the Silverwood District, otherwise known as Werewolf Territory. "We found something we think you should see."

LOREN COULDN'T BEAR to look at the body for long.

It was the corpse of one of those humanoid demons. The same type she and Dallas had run into on the academy grounds. It looked the exact same as the first one, with mottled and hairless skin, cracked and yellowed teeth, and bloodshot eyes.

The Seven Devils stood around her at Queenswater Rapids, a massive park overrun with old-growth trees in the Silverwood District. Darien's car, Lace's convertible, and Max's SUV were idling nearby. Three of the Devils had hunted down the demon after listening in on a law enforcement radio; a man who lived in an apartment not five blocks from here had called it in after sighting it in a nearby alley. And then those Devils had contacted the others to meet them here.

Ivyana Cassel was kneeling by the creature's head. Her shoulder-length hair, the same depthless black as Darien's, was damp with sweat from the dry heat.

"Its eyes are unsettlingly human," she noted. It was a challenge to hear her over the rushing of the twin waterfalls not ten feet away. "Look here, at the irises. No demon has ever had eyes this color."

Loren swallowed bile. The demon had hazel eyes; it was a very common color, but not for demons or any other type of monster. It was a very *human* color. Witches and warlocks could have hazel eyes as well, but it was commonly seen on mortals. She wasn't sure what that meant.

And judging from the looks on the slayers' faces, they didn't have a clue either.

Darien patted the pockets of his pants. "Anyone bring a syringe?"

Lace stepped forward, the stiletto heels of her thigh-boots clicking on slick rock. "Here." She produced one from the pocket of her red leather jacket and offered it to him.

Darien took it from her and bit off the cap. Ivyana shuffled aside to give him room as he knelt beside the creature and plunged the syringe into a vein near the elbow.

Loren looked away, nausea twisting her gut in a fist, as the barrel swiftly filled with blood.

He stuck the cap back on the syringe and slipped it into his pocket. "Who shot it?"

Tanner raised his hand.

"Atlas," Darien prompted. "What'd you use?"

"First of all, to be fair, it was extremely difficult to kill."

"I can see that." The head was riddled with bullet wounds.

"Second," Tanner continued, "I had to use a combination of chrysolite and silver bullets."

Darien drummed his fingers against his chin. "Interesting." He thought about it for another few minutes. And then he rose to his feet and tossed a lighter to Maximus.

"Burn it," he instructed. "It won't be long before someone sees us here, and I'd rather not cart the corpse all the way back to Hell's Gate. Arthur should be able to run tests to see if the blood has the presence of a disease. If we're lucky, we'll soon have some answers."

Loren had learned about this in school: there had been cases in history when animals had mutated from an unknown disease that could change them into demonic creatures crazed by the taste of flesh and blood.

Maximus sparked the metal lighter, the flame dancing in his eyes. "Gladly."

Lace picked up the jerrycan that sat on the ground near the front-left tire of her convertible. "Dusk brings ashes," she sang, dousing the demon's corpse with gasoline.

Max dropped the lighter onto the demon. The fire caught instantly, flames writhing as if to a song. "Smoke and flashes," he added, finishing Lace's rhyme in a low voice.

Loren looked away, the stink of gasoline and burning flesh stinging her nose.

Darien was patting his pockets, an unlit cigarette hanging from his mouth. "Shit," he muttered. Clearly, that lighter he'd tossed to Max had been his last.

He looked like he was about to ask the others for one when Lace took one out of her pocket and sparked it. "I got you." She stepped forward to light his cigarette for him.

Loren found herself looking away, putting her full attention on the damp ground at her feet, as if the simple action of Lace lighting his cigarette was incredibly intimate, despite that it didn't look that way for either of them.

At least...not for Darien.

But she forgot all about it when Darien took an incoming call that sounded important. When he hung up, he made an immediate beeline for his car, motioning for Loren to follow him.

"That was Kyle," Darien told the others, taking one last drag on his cigarette before flicking it to the ground. Loren hurried after him. "He got a lead on our wannabe Darkslayers."

Loren's mouth popped open. Was she finally getting some insight into what Darien was investigating in his spare time?

"I assume that means we're going to Diablo?" Travis asked.

Darien nodded once, and the others made for their vehicles.

"What's Diablo?" Loren asked Darien when she made it to the passenger's-side door.

"A tattoo parlor." It was to the others that he called, "We'll meet you out front. See you guys in a few."

DIABLO TATTOO WAS on Arcterus Boulevard, not far from the Temple of the Scarlet Star. Sandwiched between a laundromat and a store that sold handmade carpets, Diablo could easily be missed by anyone who was new to the area, for it was identifiable only by the horned gargoyle face that hung above the barred front door.

As Darien parallel parked in front of the parlor, the others pulling up in their vehicles behind him, Loren managed to locate the business name in window art that was designed to look like spray-paint. Surrounded by so many geometric designs, the word *Diablo* was hard to make out at all.

"Did this Kyle guy hide his business name on purpose or was it on accident?" she asked Darien.

Darien undid his seatbelt and slid a pistol into the holster at the front of his pants. It took an embarrassing amount of effort for Loren not to stare—and an even more embarrassing amount not to imagine him undoing a different type of buckle. "Maybe he did it accidentally on purpose," the slayer said as he opened his door.

Loren blinked. He merely winked at her before stepping out of the car. She hurried to follow him, wishing she wasn't wearing heels, wishing she wasn't wearing a skirt this short, as men who looked like they'd just got out of jail turned to stare at her as they walked by her on the street. Wearing an outfit like this to the Avenue of the Scarlet Star was one thing, but here...

Darien paused out front of the door to Diablo and turned the face of his watch until it made a near inaudible click. He held it up to

248

his mouth and said, "Wait here. I'll let you know if I need any assistance."

Loren looked over her shoulder, at the Devils that were waiting in their vehicles. She couldn't see them behind the window tint, but she knew it was them who Darien was communicating with.

And then he swung open the barred glass door of the tattoo parlor and strode inside, Loren right on his heels. Bells chimed, announcing their entrance.

The parlor was fairly crowded given the time of day. Nearly every one of the chairs had a person in it, most of them burly warlocks and werewolves getting full sleeves or detailed backpieces of extraordinary ink. The ceilings were low, the flooring made of cherry wood. It took Loren's eyes a few seconds to adjust to the dim lighting. Only a few sparse antique chandeliers of blown glass lit the parlor, their glow as warm as the floors. An L-shaped wooden desk was located at the back of the room, where a curly-haired hellseher with a full beard and a heavy build sat flipping through paperwork.

Loren was all too aware of the eyes that tracked her every movement as she followed Darien to the desk. Darien, on the other hand, seemed entirely at ease here. This must be where he got all his tattoos done.

The hellseher sitting at the desk glanced up at the sound of their approach. "Oh good, you're here."

"Oh good, you have news for me," Darien said with a teasing smile, keeping the volume of his voice low enough that nobody except this hellseher would hear him. That voice, so rich and low, reminded Loren of the way he'd spoken to Miss Prickles in the apothecary. The sound of it had stopped her dead in her tracks, made her stand up straighter…and made certain areas of her body tingle like never before.

The man gave a dramatic roll of his eyes as he pushed out from the desk and stood. "Even when it's something serious, you still need to imitate me."

"Imitation is a form of flattery," Darien said, leaning against the desk. "Besides, you know I love you, Kyle."

"Correction," Kyle said as he lumbered out from behind the desk.

"You love my *information.*" He made his way to a narrow corridor. "Wait here and I'll be back in two seconds."

As they waited, Loren began to sense that there were eyes stabbing into her. She slowly turned around to face the room of tattoo artists and their clients.

Every one of those clients was staring at her, looking her over from head to toe with slimy and appreciative expressions, as if she was something to eat. Their gazes lingered the longest on her ass and legs, on full display for them. She had the same feeling an animal might get from being gawked at in a zoo.

She turned back around to face the desk, trying as discreetly as possible to move her arms up and cover her chest. It was the least she could do, the only thing she was in control of right now.

Her uneasiness did not escape Darien. His focus zeroed in on her tightly crossed arms before he turned around to look at the room of warlocks and werewolves, his hands casually resting in the pockets of his unzipped leather jacket. A territorial look flickered across his face, and Loren found her heart skipping full beats at the sight of it. He looked like he would gladly get his knuckles bloody for her if it came down to that.

And he was addressing every single one of the gawking clients when he said, "If you don't stop staring, I'll beat you till you're sorry."

Most of the men lowered their heads or took a sudden interest in the pictures on the walls. But one of the wolves getting a sleeve done muttered, "She shouldn't dress like that then."

"I beg your pardon?" Darien replied in a low and lethal voice, black swallowing his irises and the whites of his eyes. The hairs on Loren's arms prickled. When the wolf didn't provide him with an answer, Darien smirked and said, "Yeah, I didn't think so."

Loren couldn't help but stare at Darien in shock as he turned back around to face her, a smug smile ghosting his lips.

Mistaking her surprise for confusion, he told her, "You can dress however you want to dress, and scum like them shouldn't think it means you're serving yourself to them on a silver platter."

Loren was speechless. And the fact that she was still staring at him as if he'd sprouted horns seemed to concern him a little.

He shifted his eyes from side to side in confusion. "What?" he asked quietly.

Loren was shaking her head. "I'm starting to think you're less of a devil than you paint yourself to be."

Darien gave her the kind of crooked smile that made the world tilt beneath her feet. "Sweetheart, I am not *a* devil. I am *the* devil. Don't start getting the wrong idea."

Despite the statement, she felt…warm and fuzzy inside, like there was a sun glowing inside her, melting a part of herself that she hadn't realized was frozen.

"Of course not," she said politely.

He didn't look like he believed her.

DARIEN DIDN'T LIKE the way the men inside the tattoo parlor had looked at Loren, didn't like the way their dark gray auras undulated like restless spirits, flickering here and there with the shade of red that spelled lust. It was enough to know what they were thinking without them ever having to say those thoughts aloud. The nasty sting of their arousal was a sharp and unwelcome odor that knifed through his airways and made him want to gag, made him want to do…bad things. Very bad things.

And although he himself had been caught staring too many times to count, the way he viewed Loren was so much different. If he'd ever thought for one second that he was making her genuinely uncomfortable with his flirting and teasing, he would've stopped. Wouldn't have ever done it again. But the men in here didn't care.

Kyle's return to the desk was a welcome distraction. He joined Darien and Loren on their side, set an open book of tattoo designs before them, and jabbed a finger on the illustration of a phoenix head. "Look familiar?"

Darien studied the side profile of the extinct bird. "Looks like the same one to me," he murmured. It was to Loren that he said, "What do you think, Rookie?"

She stepped closer to the desk, closer to Darien, and studied the tattoo. "Yes," she croaked. She cleared her throat. "It looks like the same one."

"How'd you get this?" Darien asked Kyle.

"Reggie had two clients in here a few hours ago who brought in this crafty design and asked to have it put..." He gave a pointed look at the tattoo on Darien's own neck. "Well, you get the picture. Lucky for you, not every one of our clients is aware that our magical little friend here," he poked the book, "makes a copy of every design my artists ink onto their clients."

"Who were they?" Darien asked, keeping his tone low—lower than what most immortals could pick up on. With the buzzing of the tattoo machines, his words would be no more than a hum to the other people in the room. "Reggie's clients—who were they?"

Kyle snapped the thick tome shut and tucked it under a beefy arm. "I don't think I need to explain to you why we don't take names. And we also don't have cameras for the same reasons, so don't bother asking, my friend." Right. Although Kyle ran a tattoo shop, he also occasionally dabbled in the contraband market. Nothing as dangerous as someone like the Butcher but could still land a person several years on the inside. "What I *can* tell you is that they were lamiae-hellseher halfies." Half-vampire, half-hellseher.

Darien felt the need to peel his skin off as thoughts began to race in his head, as he went through what Cain had told him, as he sorted through every half-vampire, half-hellseher in this city who was dangerous enough to be welcomed into some secret cult.

"Tell me what they looked like," Darien demanded.

"Twins," Kyle said. "A guy and a girl. Both had black hair, electric-green eyes—"

"Fuck," Darien snapped. Although he'd kept his tone muted, Loren jumped.

Kyle began to ask if Darien knew them, but his question was cut short as a hoarse male scream rippled through the parlor. More than one person was startled by the noise that abruptly broke off into a gurgle. Machines were shut off, and conversation ceased.

Darien pinned Kyle with a steely gaze. "Where's Reggie?" he demanded. "Did you actually *see* his clients leave the building before you called us?"

Kyle's mouth opened and closed like a fish. Darien didn't have time to wait for him to find words—besides, the shock on his face told him everything he needed to know.

He made for the corridor, heading in the direction the scream had come from, Loren right behind him.

He found Reggie with his throat slit from ear to ear in one of the private rooms in the parlor. The lone small window in the room was banging shut with someone's departure.

Darien felt the blood drain from his face as he realized they'd just walked right into a trap.

26

Letting the Demon Twins escape wasn't an option.

Darien felt sick to his stomach after realizing that he and the Devils had been baited; it was no accident that the twins had come to Diablo to get such a clandestine symbol tattooed on them. The people who were looking for Loren knew that someone powerful and wealthy was protecting her—knew her protectors would be seeking answers as to why she was wanted dead or in captivity. To get a lead on her whereabouts, all they had to do was set off a flare, luring Loren and her protectors right into the trap they'd set.

They were good, Darien had to admit. While he'd thought he was staying one step ahead by asking Kyle to keep an eye out for any recipients of the phoenix head tattoo, he had fallen two steps behind.

But even if he and the others caught the Demon Twins before they could get away, there was still that chance they might communicate with a third party, letting them know the girl they were after could be found simply by tracking down the Devils, by figuring out where Hell's Gate was located.

Which meant he couldn't just kill them; he had to torture them. Had to make them talk, follow the threads they'd strung between

Loren and any other dangerous people, and then snip those threads before rumor of her whereabouts could spread.

Darien booked it through the tattoo parlor, shoving people aside as he went. He communicated with the other Devils through his watch, telling them to block off the alley at the back of the building. Loren's heels clapped on the floor as she hurried after him, her human pace forcing Darien to slow down. His trust in the other Devils was the only thing that kept him from growing frustrated as he finally reached the door, throwing it open so hard the glass cracked.

Sorry, Kyle.

"Really, Dare?" Kyle protested, throwing his hands in the air.

"I'll wire you for the damage," Darien called over his shoulder. And then he was outside.

It seemed to take a lifetime to make it to the alley behind the building, and by the time they got there, Loren was panting. Jack, Ivy, and Max were standing in the alley, watching for any signs of movement behind the dumpsters and recycling bins. Their eyes were black with the Sight—but clearly, they were blind, the Demon Twins concealing their auras, likely with talismans of their own.

This shit was getting old real fast.

The others stood at attention as Darien approached the closest dumpster. Had the thick stench of rotting garbage not permeated the air, he might've been able to pick up on the twins' scents from farther away. But as he got closer, he caught a hint of the floral stink that coated every vampire's skin, like an embalmed corpse.

He gestured for the others to hold their fire as he slid his pistol out of its holster.

He took another step. Bits of glass crunched beneath his boot, and he swore.

The twins launched into the air, throwing the dumpster onto its side with a *crash* that startled several alley cats. The beating of their wings churned up gusts of wind in the alley. Darien and the others covered their faces as trash and shards of metal sliced through the air.

Darien swore and launched into motion, barking orders into his

255

watch for Travis, Lace, and Tanner, who were waiting nearby in Lace's convertible, to follow the twins.

They had no time to lose, no time to move at a mortal's pace. He scooped Loren into his arms and made for his car, running so fast he knew their surroundings would be nothing but a blur to Loren.

Far behind him, there was a rustling sound. Cats, probably. He threw a glance over his shoulder, blinking the Sight into place, but nothing was there.

They were in his car in no time, the others getting into Max's SUV. He pulled out into traffic and sped down Angelthene Boulevard after the Demon Twins, not letting them out of his sight once. The twins took off into the sunset, to opposite sides of the city, the sun shining red through their leathery, near-translucent wings.

Darien had Maximus on wireless interconnection. "Take the left!" Darien barked as he slammed the steering wheel to the right, merging with traffic on the freeway at one-hundred-and-sixty miles per hour. Tires screeched on asphalt and car horns blared from every angle.

In the passenger's seat, Ivy loaded up Darien's pistols, as well as her own, with silver stake bullets. Darien took a glance in the rearview mirror as he wove through traffic, making sure Loren was still in the back. She was so quiet, he almost forgot she was there.

"We should be back in time for dinner," he joked over the snarling engine. Loren didn't smile, her face pallid with fear.

They were gaining on the female twin—Koray—when she swooped right, diving at full tilt toward the Financial District. Darien had no choice but to go hell for leather across four lanes of traffic to stay on her tail. Horns blared as they shot through the closest exit and into the Financial District just as the streetlamps were winking awake. The car was going so fast, the undercarriage slammed against the road as they zoomed downhill.

"Pistol, Ivyana." Darien reached up and flicked the button to open the sunroof. Warm air rushed into the cab as his sister handed him a pistol. "I might need you to take the wheel."

Darien watched the cars he was passing out of the corner of his eye, steering partly with his knee, as he took aim over the lip of the sunroof. Ivyana kept one hand waiting in case she might have to steer, the other taking aim with her pistol should Darien's shot miss. But at this angle, he had the better view.

Koray began inching forward, barely out of the line of fire.

Darien flattened the gas pedal to the floor. Tires screeched, rubber burning up a black cloud as he fired.

Koray sensed the bullet and dodged it. He fired again, but she anticipated this one, too. The bullet he'd aimed to tear through her chest instead ripped through where wing connected with shoulder, and she cried out, though she didn't fall.

He watched her carefully, anticipating her next move, while becoming more certain of her goal as seconds ticked by.

She fell back again, as if the injury was too great to bear. Darien eased off the gas in case she was to disappear into an alley as Ivyana said, "She could fly over the buildings, Dare." He heard everything Ivy didn't say: Koray wasn't trying to escape. In fact, she didn't plan on leaving until she got what she wanted.

"You read my mind, sis," he said, just as Koray slammed onto the car.

Claws grabbing the sunroof, Koray shook the vehicle from side to side. Ivyana swore, struggling to steady her gun. In the back seat, Loren screamed. Koray's hair was like a dark flame spiralling in the warm wind.

"Can you get a clear shot?" Darien shouted over the sound of the car's body thumping from side to side. His teeth were rattling in his head. He might've slammed on the brake if he didn't think it would either prompt her to fly away or cause a multi-vehicle collision. If they didn't kill this bitch soon, she could flip over the car. Which wouldn't be a problem for Darien and his sister, who could survive a crash like that with barely a scratch on them. But Loren—

Loren began screaming as Koray pulled her up through the sunroof. Loren's legs thrashed as she fought to stay in the car, seatbelt tangling around her thigh.

Koray cackled with delight. "Would you like to *fly?!*"

"Darien!" Loren screamed, her voice breaking. *"DARIEN!"*

"I can't get a clear shot!" Ivy shouted. No—because Koray was making sure to hold Loren in front of her heart.

"For fuck's sake." Darien jumped to a crouch on the seat, still applying pressure to the gas pedal with his left boot. "You need to drive, Ivy." Ivyana took the wheel from him, already moving to take his place.

The car careened to the left as Darien launched himself between the front seats and into the back—just as Koray lifted a screaming Loren through the sunroof.

Darien dove through that sunroof, taking hold of Loren's bare legs before Koray could fly away with her.

But Koray wouldn't let go, and soon they were airborne. Wind filled Koray's wings like hot air balloons and carried them higher, turning the vehicles on the freeway the size of toys. Under their combined weight, Koray's wings beat faster.

Pistol in hand, Darien shimmied up Loren's body far enough to grab onto one of Koray's wings, his right arm wrapped firmly around Loren's waist. He pulled sharply on the wing, throwing Koray off balance. Her other flapped rapidly with a desperate attempt to stay airborne. The skyscrapers of the Financial District streaked by in a blur of spotless glass—glass that reflected the sight of Darien and Loren being towed through the air like goddamn rabbits caught by a hawk.

Their speed picked up again as Koray tried to free up her wing from his grip. She snarled in defiance—

And then gasped in horror as the window of a skyscraper neared. She tried in vain to backpedal, but it was too late.

Darien had half a second to shout for Loren to close her eyes before glass shattered and they were launched through the floor-to-ceiling window of an office halfway up a skyscraper.

27

L oren's head spun as she rolled across the flecked carpet. Glass was everywhere; it bit into her skin in more places than she thought possible. But she couldn't feel pain—not yet. Her ears were shrieking, blood rushing in her head as she finally stilled.

Three gunshots pealed through the air. Three gunshots from the pistol the slayer crouching before her held in a steady hand. Darien didn't seem fazed in the slightest by anything that had happened as he fired at the vampire with deadly precision.

The vampire's face was a mixture of rage and pain as the stakes tore into her bluish-white body. Two in the chest—directly where a heart should be—and one between her eyebrows. The silver burned her skin to ash as she fell backward, tumbling to the sidewalk below.

Darien leapt to his feet and strode to the sill, glass crunching beneath his combat boots. Wind whipped into the room, rustling his clothes and hair. From the way his features smoothed, and how he holstered the pistol near his belt buckle, Loren knew he'd succeeded at killing her.

From the street below, Ivyana called, "You got her."

He gave his sister one nod, then turned around to face Loren.

Where she sat, gasping in the middle of the destroyed office, Loren couldn't breathe. Fragments of the windowpane were spread around her in a mosaic, the red light of a deepening sunset reflecting in the hundreds of broken pieces. And among the glass, there was blood.

It was *her* blood. Every drop of it was hers. She almost threw up at the sight of it.

And then the pain began. It was everywhere, burning her shoulders, neck, and arms. Her bare legs were streaked with blood, the wounds glittering with shards of glass. Her breaths came faster, until it felt like her lungs were on fire, her tattoo flaring red.

Darien was suddenly crouching before her; she hadn't even seen him move. "You're okay," he said, his deep voice gentle. "You're going to be fine."

But Loren was hyperventilating, her vision spinning so rapidly she could barely concentrate on the handsome face that was lowered to her level. "It hurts," she bit out. Her cheeks were wet; whether it was with blood or tears, she wasn't certain.

"I know," he said softly. He opened his arms to her, but Loren couldn't move. She just gaped at him like an idiot, blinking fiercely against the spots of color floating across her vision. "I'm going to need to carry you out of here," he explained softly. "Is that okay?"

It took all her strength to nod. And then Darien was lifting her from the floor as if she were a toddler, hooking her shredded legs around his waist.

"I think you should close your eyes for this next part." He crossed the room to where the window had been, barely jostling her with each step. Loren buried her face against his chest and clasped her fingers around the back of his neck.

She was vaguely aware of wind spiralling around them and the sensation of their bodies moving in a freefall. Darien landed lightly on the glass-covered sidewalk—far below the shattered window— with perfect balance.

Loren cracked open her damp eyelids to see Ivyana waiting by Darien's car. Pedestrians wearing suits and holding briefcases were gawking from across the street, but they looked away and resumed walking as soon as Darien or his sister glanced in their direction.

"The others got Xander," Ivy said. In a voice so quiet Loren barely heard her, she added, "Alive."

Darien set Loren on her feet by the back door. She slid into the car, refusing to consider what the Devils intended to do to the Demon Twin, as she laid her head back against the cool leather seat and closed her eyes. She tried with all her might to will away the pain of the glass stuck in her wounds, but the burning of the fragments only grew worse with each passing second.

As Darien sped them toward Hell's Gate, Loren thought of Sabrine.

And she wished, for the entire drive, that she could have her back—that she could switch places with her and have Sabrine under the Devils' protection instead of herself. She would give all of this up for Sabrine—give up her *life*—if only she could see her one last time.

A NUMB FEELING was spreading through her arms and legs when the car slowed to a stop on the gravel drive before the red-brick manor house.

Darien parked and cut the engine. Loren squeezed her eyes shut again, only vaguely aware of Darien and Ivyana exiting the car.

A moment later, Darien opened Loren's door. A warm breeze that smelled of jasmine rushed into the car, the heady fragrance calming her, though only just. It took Loren a moment to open her eyes, and when she did, she found that Darien's gaze softened at the sight of her.

"Can you walk?" he asked.

Loren unbuckled her seatbelt with weak fingers. "I can try." He stepped back to allow her more room as she lifted herself out.

But her head spun, the gravel driveway rising to meet her as her legs folded under her.

Darien caught her before she could hit the ground and lifted her into his arms, being careful not to apply pressure to her wounds. He kicked the door shut and made his way up the front steps. Loren tried to force herself to take deep breaths, but it only made the salty tang of her blood even more noticeable.

When they reached the foyer, the house was so silent Loren figured the other Devils must not be back yet. She opened her eyes long enough to note that Darien was carrying her down a corridor that would eventually lead to the sunroom. He stopped halfway down that corridor and used his elbow to turn the handle of a closed door. He began descending a set of stairs to the basement, boots pounding loudly.

She closed her eyes again, and she did not reopen them until Darien set her down in a chair in a brightly lit room below ground.

Her watery eyes flicked about her surroundings. It looked like a kitchen turned into a makeshift emergency room.

"Still awake?" he asked. He was bending over so his head was level with hers, hands braced on his knees. There was concern in his eyes, she thought. Perhaps she was imagining it.

"Barely," Loren croaked.

"Deep breaths, Calla." He made his way to the sink and began washing his hands. She tried to do as he'd said, but every inhalation hurt.

There was the clop of heels on the floor behind her. Loren turned to see Ivyana approaching, her black bodysuit flecked with the blue-tinged blood of lamiae.

"Everything okay?" Ivyana asked.

Darien was sifting through a cupboard and setting various items onto the table beside Loren. "She has a lot of glass in her wounds." He shed his jacket and tossed it onto the counter. "I might need your help for the areas under her clothing." The areas that might require that she *remove* her clothing.

"Actually," Loren said thickly. They both stopped what they were doing and looked at her. She kept her eyes on the floor as she mumbled, "I think I'd prefer if Darien did it all. I mean... If—if he doesn't mind."

There was a pause. Out of the corner of her eye, she saw Darien give his sister a stiff nod.

Ivyana said, "If you need me, I'll be upstairs." She left then, heels clicking on the stairs.

Darien pushed the sleeves of his gray shirt up to his elbows, pulled up a stool before Loren, and took a seat, bracing his muscled legs on either side of hers. He went to work at once, taking the worst of her arms into a calloused hand. In his other, he held a pair of tweezers.

For several minutes there was nothing but the soft *plink, plink* of fragments of glass dropping to the table. Loren watched his face to distract herself from what his hands were doing.

"I'm sorry," she said. Darien kept working as if he hadn't heard her, but she knew he was listening. "I probably should've asked you how you felt before I insisted that you do this. It's just that—" She swallowed. "I guess I'd rather have as few people see me like this as possible."

Plink, plink. "She's not going to judge you." Darien pushed up her sleeve and gently twisted her arm far enough to see the wounds near her elbow. Loren tried not to wince as he picked more glass out with the tweezers. He looked up at her from under eyelashes that were so dark, they made his eyes look like they were lined with kohl. "And I don't mind, Loren. I was more concerned about whether it would bother *you.*"

She shook her head, unable to meet his gaze for a reason she couldn't quite place. When he was finished with her left arm, he moved onto the other. There were several cuts that were deep enough to need stitches; for this, Loren didn't bother trying to keep her eyes open. The prick of the needle and the pull of the thread was enough to make the ground rotate beneath her.

When he was finished with her arms and shoulders, it was time to move onto her legs. "Speaking of being bothered…," he said, as he reached down to hook a hand around her bare ankle. He paused and looked up at her. "Are you sure you're fine with this?"

She nodded, a whole different feeling than nausea in her stomach now. The ankle his hand was cupping felt like it had lit on fire—but a different fire than the fire of her wounds. Perhaps she should've taken Ivy up on her offer.

But Darien was already lifting her foot to rest it on his knee and set about extracting the glass from her shin and calf muscles. She knew it was her fault that he wasn't asking her to stand; he could probably tell that if she got out of this chair, she would faint. She tried not to think about how he could see right up her skirt as he took care of the wounds below the torn hem of it.

After that, he made her check underneath her shirt on her own. Luckily, the only glass beneath the fabric came free with a brushing of her own fingertips. There were no wounds that needed medical attention, so she pulled her shirt back down after a couple minutes in which Darien had busied himself with cleaning up the pile of bloody glass fragments.

It wasn't until she was completely covered by her shirt again that he turned to look at her. "All good?"

She nodded, and he rolled the stool back over to where she sat, bracing his legs on either side of her own again. He applied some sticky, amber-colored liquid to her wounds with an instrument that looked vaguely like a cotton swab.

"I apologize if I've been an ass lately," Darien said, taping gauze over the areas that needed the most attention. "It's no excuse, but I'm not used to being in the company of humans."

Loren blinked. "I thought *I* was the one giving *you* a hard time," she said. She closed her eyes again as he smoothed down another piece of gauze. It was easier to talk to him if she couldn't see him.

He gave a soft laugh. "Hardly. If you'd really like to know, I enjoy our little arguments. Having you test my patience is one of my favorite pastimes." As he leaned back to examine his work, Loren opened her eyes. Satisfied with whatever he saw there, he gave the hand she had resting on her knee a comforting pat. "All done." The heat from his hand lingered long after he'd let go.

He got up and strode to the counter, where he rummaged around in a drawer until he found a bottle of painkillers and a sleeve of plastic cups. After filling one with water from the sink, he passed her the cup and painkillers and ordered her to take two pills. She didn't hesitate, though her throat was so tight from emotion that it hurt to swallow them.

Darien cleaned up as swiftly as he did everything else, the smell of disinfectant sharp in Loren's nose. The events of the evening, coupled with everything that had happened since Sabrine was abducted, began to set in. Tears rolled down her face as she stared at a chip in the floor.

She wasn't sure how long Darien had been watching her for when he spoke. "I heard there's this thing called a hug." He threw aside the towel he was drying his hands with. "I'm not much of a hugger, but..." He shrugged. "It might help."

Despite the tears rolling down her face, she laughed. He gave her a smile, soft as his gaze, and held his arms out in invitation.

Loren got to her feet, her knees wobbling with a different kind of weakness. She stepped forward and into his strong arms, and he took her in gently, like flower petals closing at sunset. The warmth from his body spread through her and right to her heart, calming her instantly.

It took her longer than it should have to find a place for her own arms. But she finally closed them around his upper back and rested her face against his chest.

"You're good at this," she mumbled into his shirt with a breathy laugh. "I mean, for someone who never hugs."

"Mmm," he murmured in agreement, his smooth breathing ruffling her hair. "Your heartbeat is slowing."

She wasn't sure how long they stood there like that. It could've been seconds or minutes, but Loren found her eyelids slipping shut. With his arms around her, everything felt lighter. She felt safe in his grasp, like his strength was keeping the shattered pieces of herself together. The sound of Darien's steady heartbeat in her ear was the only thing that existed for those seconds or minutes, and she realized she didn't want to move. Never mind that he smelled so good, she could've breathed him in for ages and never grown tired of it. Her face reddened at the thought, the heat spreading all the way down to her chest, as reality began to set in.

The sound of the door opening at the top of the stairs broke her and Darien apart.

There was a commotion as the other Devils stomped down those stairs. Darien stepped away from Loren, taking with him the warmth of the quiet moment they'd shared.

Maximus, Tanner, and Travis appeared, carrying the screaming dark-haired Xander whose wings were riddled with silver-blackened wounds.

Maximus kept the twin's neck in a tight grip. "Where do you want him, Dare?"

Darien jerked his head in the direction of a narrow corridor to his left. "Last room."

Jack, Ivyana, and Lace came down the stairs a moment later as the other three towed Xander in the direction Darien had indicated.

Jack was grinning, a silver stake in one tattooed hand. "It's gonna be a great night, boys and girls." He disappeared down the corridor after the others, Ivyana following behind him.

Only Lace lingered, eyeing up Loren with a bitterness she didn't bother to conceal. "Are you coming?" she asked Darien.

"In a minute."

Lace disappeared to join the others, though she threw a curious glance over her shoulder.

Darien ran a hand through his hair and turned to face Loren, the rings on his fingers reflecting the lights. "You might want to go upstairs and get some rest." That familiar coolness entered in his gaze. "We could be down here for a while." She heard all the words he didn't say: they would be down here until the ex-Darkslayer started talking—and they would use whatever means necessary to *make* him talk.

Loren drifted toward the stairs. "Thanks." She gestured to her bandages. "For all of it."

He waved her gratitude away, as if what he'd done for her wasn't the biggest deal ever. It might not have been the biggest deal for him, but it was for her. "Don't mention it."

Loren was halfway up the stairs when she turned around to see him disappear down the corridor where the others had dragged the twin. Attached to his fist were Death's Head knuckles, an illegal weapon with four lethal spikes that were designed to rip apart a person's face with every blow.

Loren didn't turn around again after that. And she spent the rest of the night in her suite, music blasting through her earbuds at the highest volume for hours.

IT DIDN'T TAKE NEARLY AS LONG as Darien thought it would for Xander to start talking, though he had less information than what he and the other Devils had been hoping for.

What they ended up gleaning from the...*conversation*...only left them with more questions, but what Xander had revealed led Darien to make a new decision.

After having a shower so hot it burned his skin, he found Maximus and Travis seated at the island in the kitchen. Their hair was damp, too; the need to scrub themselves after a kill until every last trace of blood was gone was something the other Devils suffered from as well.

They looked up at the sound of his entry, pausing the conversation they were having.

"Already three beers deep?" Darien smirked. Travis slid a cold bottle his way, and he snatched it off the counter. "Looks like I've got some catching up to do."

"You think he was telling the truth?" Travis said.

"About Chrysantha?" Darien shrugged, popping the cap off his beer. "Guess we'll have to ask Dennis, won't we?"

The male Demon Twin had revealed some information about Chrysantha Sands during their little chat. Apparently, Chrysantha— known as Tundra in the Silverwood District—had gotten in deep with the wrong people just before she disappeared. She was doing jobs on the side for none other than Dennis Boyd, the owner of the dive bar called Puerta de la Muerta, where she worked. The twin didn't reveal who was willing to pay four million to find Loren, no matter how much pain the Devils inflicted on him. They'd got what little they could from him, checking his aura for any signs that he was lying as they worked on him, and then had put him out of his misery.

If what the twin had revealed about Chrysantha was true, Darien would need to confirm it before going to Logan, since he wasn't sure what the wolf would do if he found out Chrysantha was selling illegal goods. Specifically, Blood Potions.

The Blood Potions Syndicate of Angelthene was a clandestine operation the law enforcement had been looking to put an end to for years, and the person at the head of the operation was Casen Martel, a warlock otherwise known as the Butcher. He had been in the syndicate for so long that he had little competition, but every so often someone got it in their head to try and overthrow him and steal his clients. And it sounded like Dennis Boyd was the newest idiot to attempt such a thing.

Darien took another swig of his beer, blinking the Sight into place as he looked up at the ceiling—through the top floors of Hell's Gate and into Loren's suite. There wasn't a hint of her aura visible, not a single white or rainbow flicker, which meant she was sleeping with the talisman on.

Good. Even though he trusted the protection spells he regularly upgraded at the Umbra Forum, and even though he had complete faith in Mortifer's concealment work, it never hurt to have a little extra protection.

His worry for her was a tangible thing that sometimes shook him out of a dead sleep at night, sometimes had him using the Sight to check on her in her suite. It felt like an invasion of privacy at times, but he felt like he had to do it.

When he'd embraced her after tending to her wounds in the basement, he hadn't expected to not want to let go of her. He liked having her that close to him, liked being able to not only hear her heartbeat but to *feel* it. And when his family had come down the stairs, forcing him to break away from her, he'd found himself feeling irritated at the interruption. He hadn't been ready to let go of her; in fact, he could have stood there like that for hours, her aura flush with his.

Was this what crushing on someone felt like?

Call him crazy, but there was a part of him that felt like their fates were entwined now, and they were both in far too deep to ever turn back.

WHEN MONDAY NIGHT ARRIVED, Loren couldn't sleep.

She was getting used to sharing a roof with seven deadly killers, so tossing and turning was about as much as she could accomplish in her dorm room at the academy. Dallas had fallen asleep hours ago, her steady breathing from the bed beside hers the only sound.

Where it sat on the nightstand, Loren's phone gave a loud buzz. She leaned over to grab it and turned down the brightness.

DARIEN CASSEL appeared across the screen. Loren found her hands trembling, butterflies twitching their wings deep in her stomach, as she used her fingerprint to unlock the phone and read his message.

DARIEN

How are you feeling?

Loren typed up three different replies but ended up deleting each one before sending one word.

LOREN

Fine.

If she was being honest, her arms hurt like hell, and so did the few cuts on her legs. But she wasn't about to tell him that. He'd dropped her off at the gates of the academy that morning with a fresh roll of gauze and a full bottle of painkillers. She'd had to change her bandages herself that night, which wasn't nearly as enjoyable as when he did it for her.

Her face flushed at the memory.

DARIEN

Good. Let me know if you need anything.

Loren stared at the message. Realizing she didn't want to stop talking to him, she wrote:

> **LOREN**
> How are you?

A bubble popped up to indicate that he was typing. It disappeared and reappeared twice before he replied with just one word:

> **DARIEN**
> Fine.

Loren smiled into the dark.

> **LOREN**
> What are you doing?

It took him a minute to reply.

> **DARIEN**
> Just getting home.

> **LOREN**
> It's two in the morning.

> **DARIEN**
> So?

Nibbling on her pinkie nail, she typed up another reply.

> **LOREN**
> Sooo, shouldn't you be sleeping?

> **DARIEN**
> I could ask you the same thing.

Loren's smile turned into a grin.

> **LOREN**
> You woke me up.

> **DARIEN**
> You didn't need to answer me.

Darn, he made a good point. She could almost sense him smiling in triumph through the phone, and she found herself blushing.

LOREN

Have you had much luck deciphering the scroll?

DARIEN

Hardly. Any chance you could access the restricted section in your academy library for me?

LOREN

What do you need?

DARIEN

Any books on Ancient Reunerian would help. If I don't find some answers soon, I'm going to rip my hair out.

LOREN

I'll try.

And she was blushing again as she added,

LOREN

And you have great hair, so please don't rip it out.

DARIEN

Ha-ha, you're adorable.

Loren's smile grew so big, her cheeks hurt.
Circling back to their previous topic, he said,

DARIEN

Thanks, Rookie. I'll owe you one.

She typed up three different messages that didn't involve saying goodbye to each other just yet, before she settled on,

LOREN

I'm going to sleep now.

DARIEN

Same, I'm beat.

A moment later, after deleting whatever messages he'd typed up, he added,

DARIEN

Goodnight, Loren Calla.

LOREN

Goodnight, Darien Cassel.

She was still smiling like an idiot as she clicked off the screen and settled back into her pillows.

It didn't take her long to fall asleep after that, and when morning arrived, she found herself wondering why—and found herself shying away from the answer.

28

"*Hoc puella invisibilia.*" Dallas's soft voice echoed in the corridor outside the mirrored entrance of the House of Salt. Her Focus sparked in the shadows, throwing the smattering of freckles on her nose into stark relief. "Hide that which is visible, make this girl *invisible.*"

Loren closed her eyes tight and tried not to puke as the spell rippled over her. The chunk of amethyst at the point of Dallas's stave pulsed with purple waves. The color snaked over the tree trunks in the mirror's false reflection and wove around the stones of the corridor.

Dallas wore a grin as she appraised the empty air where Loren had been standing. "I can't believe I actually did it!"

Loren shushed her. "Do yourself now," she whispered. It took a couple tries for Dallas to make the spell work on herself, but soon neither of them was visible aside from their shadows, slanted in the torchlight as they began creeping toward the east wing.

If they were to get caught out of their House this late, they'd be in trouble. Worse: if they were to get caught in the restricted section of the library, they would be expelled. Loren tried not to dwell on this fact, instead reminding herself that Darien needed those books

—that *Sabrine* needed those books. If they couldn't figure out why the Darkslayers were after Loren, and what that scroll said about the Arcanum Well, they might never get Sabrine back.

When they reached the entrance to the restricted section, they remembered the poltergeist that guarded the rows of dusty bookshelves. The Staring Teenager, the students called the apparition—a student who'd died on campus hundreds of years ago. Some said he killed himself; others claimed he was murdered.

Dallas created a diversion by tossing an empty bottle of Morpheun tonic across the room. The glass pinged against the walls and shelves, and the phantom slipped through the aisles after it at lightning-speed.

"Pays to never clean out your purse," Dallas hissed into Loren's ear, her breath giving her chills. They crept into the restricted section, lit only by dripping candles suspended in the air by magic. They kept their footsteps light, because although they were invisible, there were some things they couldn't hide.

They scanned the book spines until they found the tomes on Ancient Reunerian, the section so small it was almost nonexistent. There was only one book worth their time—a tome bound in a type of leather Loren hoped wasn't as human as it felt. She knew enough Reunerian to tell it was a volume on the language itself—more specifically, a learner's guide.

"This is exactly what we need." She plucked the book off the shelf. "Darien's—"

"Entering the restricted section is an act punishable by expulsion, girls." Loren nearly screamed at the sound of the headmaster's voice cutting through the quiet. Beside her, Dallas whirled on a heel, hand flying to her throat.

Loren did a doubletake at Dallas, realizing the spell had worn off sometime these past few minutes. "Headmaster," Loren gritted out, heart thundering in her chest. "You scared us."

"If you wanted to look at the books," the headmaster said, his face grave, "all you needed to do was put your name down on the request form." His gaze became accusatory as he looked at the book

Loren was gripping to her chest. "You weren't really planning on stealing the book. Were you, girls?"

Dallas's voice tumbled over Loren's as they stammered, "No, Headmaster. Of course not." Loren added, "We were just...," she paused to gulp, "looking."

He didn't buy it. "These books are kept here by enchantment; not one of them may leave this section of the library without my authorization. Everything outlined in academy regulations says I should expel you." Behind the headmaster, the Staring Teenager floated by with a chuckle, eye-sockets like stones pushed into his transparent face.

Loren's gaze fell to the floor, but she didn't offer up the book. If Langdon wanted it, he would have to pry it from the fingers of her dead body.

The headmaster said, "I'm curious as to why you two have an interest in learning a dead language."

Loren struggled for an excuse that might be somewhat believable, but all her tongue could manage was an indecipherable stammer. Langdon knew every course and subject taught at this school, so lying about a project would do them no good.

But Dallas piped up. "We found an old diary that belonged to my grandfather," she said. "I'd love to be able to read what it says, Headmaster. I never had the chance to meet him."

The headmaster's eyes settled on Loren for so long, she began to squirm. But he said, "I'll allow you to check the book out of the library for two weeks. When those two weeks are up, there will be no need for you to physically return it; it will teleport itself back to the shelf."

"Thank you, Headmaster," Loren said. "That's very kind of you."

"Back to the House of Salt with you two." He turned on a heel and walked away. "I don't want to see you in this section of the library again, or you *will* be expelled."

Gripping the book to her chest, Loren smiled in triumph as they hurried back to the House of Salt.

THE REST of Loren's week dragged by horribly slowly, and there were three reasons for this.

The first reason, though certainly not the most important, was because each day was made worse by having to cover up her bandaged arms and legs with academy sweaters and the itchy uniform pants she detested.

The second reason was because she hated that another week had passed and Sabrine was still missing, the mystery of the Master Scroll no closer to being deciphered than before she and Dallas had found that book.

The third reason the week had dragged by was a slayer named Darien Cassel.

It was rare when Loren saw Darien on a weekday, so she found herself looking forward to the weekends now more than ever. She knew this wasn't a good thing—for too many reasons. But she still checked her phone every chance she got; still found herself texting him even when there was nothing to say except maybe a simple *How are you?* or *What are you up to?*

He always answered, even if it took him several hours, so she figured he must not dislike talking to her *that* much. She tried not to read into it, but like everything else that involved not thinking about, talking about, or talking *to* Darien, she failed horribly.

After what happened at Kyle's tattoo parlor, she wasn't the only one who was now constantly wearing a talisman around her neck. The other Devils wore them as well as a precaution—in case the twins had called in what they'd learned at Diablo to their elusive boss before the Devils had caught up with them. This mission was starting to get very, *very* expensive. But if Loren let herself think about it for too long, guilt would swallow her heart whole.

Another thing that was making her guilt extra heavy today was the fact that the Devils were now sharing watch duty outside the school. And starting this weekend they would alternate sitting in their vehicles in the alley behind Mordred and Penelope's while Loren worked. No one complained about it, at least not within earshot of Loren. Not even Lace, though she was rarely assigned watch duty. Still, Loren felt terrible for taking up so much of their valuable time.

This past Tuesday, watch duty had been assigned to Maximus, and Loren had met him outside the gates of the academy to give him the book on Ancient Reunerian so he could pass it along to Darien. Loren would be lying if she said she hadn't been hoping Darien would be on watch duty that day, but every day of the week had been assigned to every Devil except him. She knew it wasn't anything personal, and the gods knew he needed a break every now and then. But she couldn't help but wish she could see him on more than just weekends.

When Friday arrived, Loren had Phipps's class as her final period. Her vision was suddenly spinning, the wounds in her arms burning as the professor droned on and on. Thoughts of Sabrine knifed through her skull and right down to her heart, making the floor beneath her feet spin. She was a horrible friend for even letting her thoughts deviate from Sabrine for so much as a minute. Sab could be dead or dying right now, and Loren was sitting here crushing on a slayer.

It should've been her who was taken—not Sabrine. *It should've been her.*

Loren shot to her feet, startling several students in her vicinity. She gathered up her books, dumped them into her book bag, and made for the door.

"Loren!" Dallas called from behind her.

But Phipps said, "Have a seat, Miss Bright."

Dallas began to argue with him, but that was the last Loren heard as she hurried down the hallway. The gazes of the painted figures lining the walls tracked her every step. Class wouldn't finish for another fifteen minutes, but she couldn't bear to be stuck in one suffocating room for another second.

She made it through the gates and to the sunlit parking lot before collapsing onto a bench in the shade of a palm tree. Sobs tore out of her, her body shaking with the force of them. She felt like screaming, but there were vehicles idling in the lot. The last thing she needed was anyone else getting involved in this mess.

She hated this. Hated *everything*. She wanted Sabrine back—she didn't care if she had to give up her own life for it to happen. She *needed* it to happen.

Her breathing slowed, her fingers drifting to the talisman around her throat, twinkling in the bright sunlight.

All she had to do was remove it. All she had to do was unclasp it, and Sabrine could walk free. If Darkslayers came for her, then so be it. She would face them with what little courage she had.

The familiar rumble of Darien's car engine stilled her fingers. He parked along the curb closest to the bench and cut the engine. A moment later, his door opened and shut behind him.

How was it possible that the world suddenly felt lighter as soon as he was near? She could breathe again, and the shattered pieces of her heart felt like they were being knitted back together simply by being in the same vicinity as him.

He sat down on the bench beside her and settled his elbows onto his knees, but he didn't say anything as she continued to cry her eyes out into the sleeves of her academy sweatshirt, clutching the talisman in a tight fist.

One pull. Just one hard yank and the magic would be nullified.

Darien would never let her do it though, and if she was being honest with herself, she was too much of a coward to follow through.

Loren mumbled into her hands, "She's dead, isn't she? It's been too long. There's no way they're going to keep her alive forever."

"Switching places with her won't solve anything, Loren," Darien said softly. A sob rose in her throat, and she gripped the talisman tighter. "People like the men who took Sabrine have no interest in bargaining. The only sway they hold is hoping you'll be naïve enough to believe them when they say they'll let her go."

Loren had nothing to say to that. A hot breeze picked up, drying the tears on her cheeks.

"I don't mean to sound insensitive when I say this," Darien continued. "But I believe there's something larger at stake here than your friend's life."

Nothing was more important to Loren than Sabrine's life, but she knew Darien wasn't wrong in saying that. Which was exactly why the talisman was still clenched in her fist, the chain digging into the back of her neck. Until they figured out what the Arcanum Well was and how it was connected to Loren, they were stuck in place on the chessboard.

And she would be an idiot if she believed those men would let Sabrine walk free. Darien was right: whoever had taken Sab had no interest in negotiating a deal. They were only trying to lure her into a trap. If Sabrine was still alive, she was nothing more than bait. A bargaining chip.

The academy gates swung open, hinges squeaking. Loren knew it was Dallas approaching before she said to Darien, "Hey."

And then she was standing before Loren, her face lined with concern. "You okay, Lor?"

Loren swiped at the tears rolling down her cheeks. "I can't take it anymore, Dal. I can't *take* not knowing where Sab is."

Darien brushed a hand across Loren's back as he suddenly rose to his feet. "Let's take a drive." A strand of his undercut shifted out of place as he inclined his head toward the car. "Both of you."

Loren promptly stood and gathered up her things as Dallas said to him, "Where are we going?"

"City law enforcement only has so much sway over the scum of this city," Darien said as he made his way to the driver's side. "I think it's high time we paid a visit to a few places on my list. I was planning on going by myself, but..." He looked at Loren. "You wanted all in, Rookie. Now's your chance. Think you can handle it?" He lifted a brow in question.

Loren nodded. "Yes."

"Good. Then we're going to start with Puerta de la Muerta."

"Death's Door," Dallas mused as she slid into the back seat of the car. Loren hurried around to the passenger's side and got in. "A club or something?"

Darien turned the key in the ignition, the engine rumbling to life. "It's a bar where Chrysantha Sands was serving drinks the night she went missing." He pushed the gearshift into drive—but paused. He looked Loren over, and then turned in his seat to do the same to Dallas. "If you've got anything on underneath those sweaters, I'd take them off. Where we're going... Let's just say you don't want anyone to know what school you attend."

He didn't need to ask them twice. They pulled off their sweaters, leaving only the white nondescript tanks they had on underneath.

And then they made their way to Death's Door.

IN THE NINETEEN years she'd lived in Angelthene, Loren had never ventured anywhere near the Meatpacking District.

Unlike other Meatpacking Districts in distant cities, where plants and slaughterhouses only *used* to inhabit a large area of the metropolis, the one in Angelthene was still the same as when it was first built hundreds of years ago. All types of flesh were processed here, and it wasn't unlikely to find human among the flesh of swine and cattle. Which was exactly why, as a human, she'd kept far away from here. The smell alone was enough to make her gag.

North of this area of Downtown Angelthene were the Arts and Jewelry Districts, and three blocks away from the street they were driving down was the Historic Core. And it was just south of the Historic Core where one of the city's many dangerous places lurked. A place where no one who valued their life would dare wander, alone or otherwise. Even in broad daylight.

And daylight was fading fast as Darien parallel parked in front of the dive bar known as Puerta de la Muerta, right near the Meatpacking District. Every window of every building in this area was barred, and the few houses that remained were boarded up, fenced, and tagged. Garbage was all over every open lot and side street, stuffed into gutters and stuck on fences like glue after the wind had blown it there. Aside from bars and strip clubs, the only businesses around were pawn shops and liquor stores—all with bars on their windows.

Loren felt hot and cold and distant and alert all at once. Her heart raced as she watched Darien lean over and snap open the glovebox before her—and raced faster as the sleeve of his jacket brushed against her knees.

"Does your car have bullet-proof windows?" she stammered. He ignored her as he retrieved a pistol and slammed the glovebox shut.

Leather groaned as Dallas leaned forward to peer between the front seats. "They let you bring weapons in there?"

"The weapons are only a distraction," Darien said as he holstered the pistol and pocketed a pair of brass knuckles. He then slid a knife into the inside pocket of his black jacket.

Loren said, "A distraction from what?"

"The real threat." Darien gave her a demon's smile.

She swallowed. "And what's the real threat?"

That smile turned into a wicked grin that showed all his straight, white teeth. "Me, silly girl."

Of course, she almost said. But she found that she suddenly couldn't work her tongue to form words—for reasons other than the fear of her current location—as Darien leaned across the center console and took her Avertera talisman into his hands.

His knuckles brushed her collarbone as he studied the talisman, the familiar heat she'd felt the other day at Hell's Gate returning so quickly it made her head spin. He was close enough for her to smell the delicious, masculine cologne she'd noticed the first time she was in this car. She could see every fleck of silver in his eyes, made brighter by the contrast of his dark eyelashes.

In the back seat, Dallas was suppressing a smile. With Darien's attention otherwise occupied, Dallas took the opportunity to lift her hand to her mouth to form an obscene gesture.

Loren's face reddened as she tore her gaze away from the sight of Dallas's tongue pushing against the inside of her cheek—and found Darien grinding the pendant between his thumb and index finger. When he released it, the pendant jingling softly against her neck, there was a smear of gold on his hands.

"It's weakening." He unbuckled his seatbelt and opened his door. "It should last another day or two, but I'll have to find you a new one soon. I'll switch talismans with you tonight; mine is newer."

"You are *not* shelling out another copper on me, Darien Cassel," Loren warned. "And I'm not taking your talisman."

He smirked, setting one booted foot on the pavement. A gust of wind that smelled of the horrible deaths via butchering blocks swept into the cab, the stench turning her stomach. "Don't argue with me, Loren Calla. I'll do whatever I want."

Dallas was trying not to laugh as she and Loren stepped out of the car and followed Darien to the bar, where two bouncers stood outside a set of closed metal doors.

Pimps and sharks worked the street corners, and groups of witches and warlocks wearing filthy clothes sat at the base of a lamppost near the bar, smoking from water pipes and scribbling protection symbols and meaningless graffiti on the concrete. Just beyond the veneficae, a half-dressed werewolf was holding up a water-stained cardboard sign with a message.

F*CK THE IMPERATOR.

Another wolf some distance away had another opinion to share: WE WILL NOT BE EQUAL UNTIL WE MAY ALL LIVE IN PEACE.

Tearing her gaze away from the sign, Loren sidled closer to Darien as he came to a stop before the bouncers. The tallest of the full-blooded warlocks, with dark, shaggy hair and a goatee, took immediate note of the mark of the Devils below Darien's ear and squared his huge shoulders.

"What business do you have here, Slayer?"

"I need to speak to Dennis Boyd," Darien replied coolly, entirely unfazed by the fact that this bouncer stood a foot over his head. "I think he'll have no problem granting me an audience once he finds out why I'm here."

The bouncers shared a glance. It was the clean-shaven one who said, "Dennis is busy. We'll let him know you stopped by."

"You'll let him know *now*." Darien's voice was sharp. "I don't know Dennis as well as you boys, but something tells me he wouldn't be pleased to hear that you turned away a Devil at his door."

The cawing of magpies filled the sky. Loren didn't dare take her eyes off what was happening in front of her to count how many birds there were. Judging from the way the bouncers' mouths had become thin lines, it wasn't a promising number. And whether they were superstitious or not, only an idiot would ignore an omen.

Even the witches and warlocks nearby had stopped scribbling their chalk symbols. They still smoked from their pipes, but they now watched the scene unfolding before the bar, curiosity shining in their bleary eyes.

Darien smiled, fingers twitching at his sides, as the bouncers assessed him again. "Have I convinced you, or would you like to discuss this another time?"

The tallest bouncer got on his headset and let whoever answered on the other end know there was a Devil here to see Dennis Boyd.

Two minutes passed before the doors groaned open. Music with heavy bass drifted from inside as a stout balding man—part human, part warlock—pushed his way through the bouncers. He looked Darien over with eyes milky from substance abuse, and then took note of the girls standing on either side of him.

"Search them," Dennis ordered brusquely.

His bouncers set about checking Darien first, who was still smiling as he braced his feet apart and held up his hands on either side of his head.

Dennis jerked his stubbly chin at Dallas and Loren. "I'm not stupid enough to think these two are of drinking age, Cassel."

The bouncers retrieved Darien's pistol and brass knuckles, and Darien didn't bother to correct him as he went on to say, "I don't think you need me to tell you that we're not here to drink, Dennis."

The bouncers seemed satisfied with the weapons they'd found on Darien and moved onto the girls. It didn't take long to check them, and when the bouncers were finished, they stepped aside to permit them entrance. Darien led the way as they followed Dennis into the dark bar that reeked of vomit, watered-down booze, and stale cigarettes. The spongy orange carpet sank beneath Loren's feet as she passed the foggy-eyed drunkards gathered at the tables and the bar, sipping everything from beer to magical tonics. She stayed close to Darien's heels, Dallas at her back.

Dennis paused at the edge of the bar and scratched his bald head with his stubby fingers. "Before you get started with whatever game you're playing... Can I offer you a drink, Slayer?"

"No game, Dennis." Several people at the bar sidled away at the sight of Darien, while two witches who were heavily dolled up with makeup-glamors eyed him with interest as they fixed their hair. "No drink either. I'm simply here to ask you a few questions."

It was hard to tell beneath the few bulbs lighting the interior of the bar, but Loren swore Dennis's shiny face paled. "Alright then."

Dennis's eyes were wide and unblinking as he pushed away from the bar and gestured for them to follow him. He led them down a passage glowing with ultraviolet lightbars, to a dented door that hung lopsided on the hinges.

The office was roughly the size of a shoe closet, with barely enough space inside for one small desk and a peeling leather swivel chair. Dennis rummaged around behind a filing cabinet until he found three folding chairs and set them up on the opposite side of the desk, the legs squeaking against the linoleum. Darien claimed the chair between Loren and Dallas, while Dennis planted himself on the other side of the desk.

"Alright, Cassel." Dennis fished a cigarette butt from the over-flowing ashtray, lit it, and took a drag. "What can I do for you?"

"I'm here for Chrysantha Sands," Darien said, getting right down to business.

Dennis blew out a lungful of bitter smoke. "Did Logan send you?"

"I've sent myself. Word on the street says Chrysantha was bartending here the night she went missing. Care to go over the evening's events with me?"

Dennis settled his chapped elbows onto the desk. "Nothing happened. I've been over this with Logan—it was just another normal Saturday night. Chrysantha was serving my usual clientele: bikers and vampires and such." He waved the hand that held the cigarette through the air, as if it might help illustrate what he was saying. Darien tracked the movement with a deadly gaze. "Nothing beyond the ordinary happened." He flicked what remained of the butt into the ashtray. "She got off when the bar closed at two in the morning and went home."

"I didn't know you catered to vampires." Darien quirked an eyebrow. "What type of blood do you serve?"

"Animal." Dennis gave Loren a greasy smile. "Mostly."

She squirmed in her seat.

Darien's answering grin looked more like a baring of teeth. "So, you're telling me that nothing even vaguely interesting happened that night. No new faces to report, no odd behavior?"

"Correct," Dennis said. But the word was a choked whisper. And the pudgy fingers entwined atop the desk trembled faintly.

"That's it?" Darien prompted again. "That's all you have to say about Chrysantha?" Propping a boot up on the desk, he sank back in his chair and laced his tattooed fingers over his chest. "Sounds more like a rehearsed speech to me."

It took Dennis a long time before he nodded once. Moisture gleamed on his upper lip.

And Darien wasn't buying it. He cocked his head as he surveyed Dennis, no doubt noticing that his neck was throbbing in tune with his heartbeat. "How long have you owned this festering shithole now, Dennis?"

A drop of sweat rolled to Dennis's lower lip. "I don't see how that's relevant."

"Answer the question." Although Darien's voice was lethally quiet, Loren found that she jumped a little at the sound, as if he'd shouted, the legs of her chair screeching across the sticky floor.

Dennis bit out, "Almost twenty years."

"Almost twenty years," Darien repeated. "Almost twenty years of your measly quarter-human lifespan. You've poured your blood, sweat, and tears into this dump. And for what, Dennis? What do you make selling watered-down blood and ale to your clientele?"

Despite that his mouth wobbled with fear, Dennis leaned forward slightly and said, "Enough to feed my family." Sour breath wafted across the desk. "And that's all that really matters, isn't it?"

"I didn't take you for a family man. But being as you've stupidly offered up that information to me, I would be willing to guess you wouldn't like it if I shut down this lousy excuse for a business you're running."

Dennis's pimpled shoulders stiffened. "What would you get out of it?"

"I like watching people squirm, Dennis. It's part of the business *I'm* in. The one that puts food on *my* table. And even if shutting you down didn't bring me any more than that simple pleasure, maybe the threat alone will be enough to convince you to quit lying to me."

Loren was holding her breath. She had the sense that Dallas was holding hers as well as the clock that was shaped like a naked woman ticked loudly above the desk.

"What do you want?" Dennis ground out.

"I want you to tell me the truth."

"I just *told* you the truth—"

But Darien's eyes turned black. Dennis bolted upright in his chair, like a cow whose neck had been wrangled with a loop of rope. His filthy fingernails dug into the armrests, the cracking leather shredding apart beneath the force, as whatever Darien was doing to him began to work.

Darien watched Dennis in silence, slowly canting his head from side to side. His hair shone blue-black in the fluorescents.

"Get out of my head," Dennis whimpered, veins in his neck bulging. The smell of blown-out birthday candles choked the room as Darien's magic dove deeper.

Loren realized what he was doing. It was a power typically reserved for pureblood hellsehers: the ability to drag a mental claw down someone's thoughts until they revealed to them whatever information they were hiding. From what she'd heard of the ability, it couldn't be used on just anyone. Like all magic powers, it had its limits, and this particular one could not be used on other hellsehers, nor could it be used on anyone who'd trained their mind to resist such influence.

Suddenly, Loren remembered that night in the dining room — Darien's ability to make her...*feel* things without physically touching her. It must be similar to that, she realized.

Darien's chin was dipped toward his chest as he watched the bar owner with a gaze so terrifying it turned Loren's head weightless on her shoulders.

"As much as I would thoroughly enjoy seeing your brain leak out through your nose...," Darien began, spiralling into his magic, his

286

mental claws raking across Dennis's mind, "I have a feeling your bouncers wouldn't enjoy cleaning up the mess it would leave on your floors."

Blood dribbled from Dennis's nose as he struggled against the invisible hands that held him in place. The stink of urine cut into the smoke of magic as the owner of this dive literally pissed himself beneath the mental grip of Darien's magic. Moisture splashed on the floor, and Loren's stomach churned.

Dallas leaned forward in her seat, peering around Darien to share a *holy-shit* glance with Loren.

Darien didn't remove his gaze from Dennis for one second. "There's not much going on in your mind, is there," he murmured as red tears began to flow from Dennis's bulging eyes. "But you *are* keeping something from me. Are you going to tell me, or shall I turn the half a brain you've got into liquid?"

It seemed to take everything Dennis had to pant, "I'll tell you, you son of a bitch. Get your claws out of me." When Darien didn't relent, he barked, *"Gods-damnit, I said I'll tell you!"*

Darien released him, his face smoothing of its murderous expression as the black in his eyes faded away, like night shifting into morning.

Hacking and wheezing, Dennis grabbed a rag from the corner of the desk and proceeded to swipe at the blood streaming down his face and neck. And when he glanced at the floor—at the puddle at his feet—his pinched lips wobbled.

"I'm waiting, Dennis," Darien crooned. His voice took on a cold and peculiar note as he added, "And don't ever call my mother a bitch again."

Dennis shot him an irritated look, but went on to say, "I didn't want to tell Logan because I figured he'd blame me and have me killed. But the night Chrysantha disappeared, I kept her an hour late to clean up the broken glass from a bar fight that broke out between nomadic vampires and warlock bikers. She got out of here just after two thirty, and I didn't wait with her for her ride to show as I locked up and got in my car." To his credit, Dennis looked somewhat ashamed of himself for having done this.

"And?" Darien pressed.

"And…" His sweat-slick throat bobbed. "And as I was driving away, I saw Chrysantha get into a van she doesn't normally get picked up in."

"What did it look like?"

"Black and brand new. No windows except those in the front."

"Did you get the plate?"

Dennis shot Darien a glare that caused more red tears to dribble down his jowls. "Of course not," he said. "Like I said, she got into it willingly. I didn't think anything was amiss." Another of those heavy pauses. "Two of them had tattoos like yours. I thought they were Darkslayers, but I'd never seen the symbol before."

Loren sat up straighter, chair creaking beneath her. "What kind of tattoo?"

"Looked like a bird of some sort," Dennis said without looking at her.

"Look at her when she's speaking to you," Darien said coolly.

Dennis did as he was told, slowly turning his head toward Loren with reluctance. Loren forced herself not to shrink beneath his glare as he repeated between clenched teeth, "It looked like a bird."

"A phoenix?" Darien asked.

Dennis's attention returned to him. "Might've been."

Loren looked at Darien, but he was watching Dennis still.

"I recently got a tip that Chrysantha was doing jobs on the side," Darien began. "That she might've gone missing because she found out more information than she was meant to. And the side jobs she was doing were apparently for you."

The shock that crossed Dennis's face wasn't faked. "For me?" He gave a breathy laugh. "Why am I only just hearing of this? What sort of jobs are you talking about?"

"Blood Potion dealing."

Dennis paled. "Shit, Cassel. I barely have time to keep this bar alive. You think I have the spare hours to compete with someone like the Butcher?" When Darien didn't say anything, Dennis continued, "I'm flattered that anyone thinks I have the brains to do something like that, but I'm not dealing Blood Potions and I'm certainly not hiring young girls to sell them for me."

"Did Chrysantha ever give you any indication that she was pressed for cash?"

Dennis shrugged. "I mean, sometimes. Young girls like her—you know how they can be. I gave her an advance once in a while, but I never heard anything about her selling BP. I swear." When Darien didn't say anything, Dennis gave him a heavy look. "Do you really think someone like me could compete with the Butcher? I mean, honestly."

"No, I don't. But that doesn't mean I wouldn't put it past you try."

"You're reading my aura, Cassel. Do I look like I'm lying?"

After a moment, Darien blinked the Sight away. Loren hadn't even realized he was using it again.

"Look, if you want my advice—"

"I don't," Darien clipped.

Dennis stopped himself from rolling his eyes. "If you want my *opinion*, talk to Casen Martel. If Chrysantha was selling BP, I'm sure he'd be the first to know."

Darien was silent for so many minutes, Dennis began fidgeting in his seat. Loren started fidgeting, too, twisting her fingers together.

"If I find out Chrysantha resorted to selling BP to pay her bills," Darien began, "then perhaps you should consider paying your employees a living wage, Dennis."

Dennis didn't have anything to say to that.

The clock above the desk ticked and ticked. The crack of cue sticks against billiard balls floated down the hallway.

"Is that all the information you have?" Darien's voice could pass for a purr.

"Yes. Now get out of my office—*please.*"

Darien flashed him a grin that showed all his teeth. "So touchy," he tsked, but he lifted himself to his feet, and Loren and Dallas copied him.

Loren had to give the man credit for courage, considering he was still sitting in his own piss, as Dennis snarled, "You're lucky you're under Randal's protection, boy."

Darien paused, a dark look crossing his face. "Randal Slade has no sway over me, nor has he earned me my reputation," he replied calmly. "I think what you meant to say is that *you're* lucky, Dennis, that you had information valuable enough to convince me not to kill you tonight." Darien rapped a knuckle on the desk and then pointed a finger at the man that sat on the other side of it. The simple movement had Dennis recoiling into his chair so hard, he almost flipped it over, pants squishing beneath him. "But there's always another night. Isn't there?"

After that, Dennis wisely kept his mouth shut as they left his office.

Loren found that she couldn't breathe properly until they were back in the car. The sun was setting, the few mercury-vapor streetlamps throughout the district buzzing to life.

From where she sat again in the back seat, Dallas said with a grin, "I haven't had this much fun since Boris Sledgehorn's pants lit on fire in third year."

Loren pressed her lips together at the memory. It was a harmless —well...*almost* harmless—witch's act another student had played on Boris when they'd caught him lying. Loren could still hear the students chanting in her memory. *Liar, liar, pants on fire.*

What she could hear clearer than the chant was the smile in Darien's voice when he spoke. "That sounds like a story worth sharing one day."

"It is," Dallas cackled. "But maybe you could warn me the next time you do something like that again, Darien. For a moment there, I was afraid Dennis wasn't going to be the only one peeing his pants." Loren had to laugh at that as they peeled away from the curb and left the Meatpacking District and its rancid smells behind.

"There's more fun in surprises, Dallas," Darien said. He was laughing, too.

29

After paying a visit to the Meatpacking District, Loren didn't think any other place in this city could frighten her quite so thoroughly.

As it turned out, she was wrong.

She stayed closer to Darien than she had in Puerta de la Muerta as he strolled through the network of abandoned butcheries and warehouses that made up the Umbra Forum. A clandestine market where anything could be bought for the right price, the Umbra Forum was a lawless place inhabited by criminals and dealers. As with the Meatpacking District, all types of flesh were sold here; if a person knew what questions to ask, they could find contraband blood-infused brandy as easily as they could find human organs.

The warren of narrow gas-lit streets smelled of hookah and the musty reek of the Angelthene River flowing adjacent to the interconnected buildings. Loren peeked from beneath the brim of her sports hat at the stragglers gauging their trio like rodents sniffing out a meal, clearly gleaning whether the Devil—who was carving a path through food carts and ramshackle stalls—was here to sell Loren and Dallas or had purchased them himself.

Loren pulled down the brim of her hat as far as it would go.

Darien had found it in the trunk of his car and plunked it on her head in effort to conceal her human scent. When it hadn't sufficed to his liking, he'd not only told her to tuck up her hair beneath it, but also made her wear his jacket.

It was far too big for her, but it smelled like him, and it kept her warm. It was also heavy with the weapons that were hidden in the concealed pockets, which made her feel a little more at ease. Not that she would know how to use any of the blades or gadgets she could feel rubbing against her hips. She would be more likely to hurt herself than someone else.

In the pitch-black alleys between warehouses, the soft cries of children carried to her on a briny breeze. Loren slowed, peering into the shadows, as they passed one such alley. Darien and Dallas carried on, oblivious to Loren having stopped.

A thing was tucked behind a dumpster, its elongated, bony limbs barely visible from here. It was a slouching thing with great, floppy ears that might've been horns. The crying grew more frantic.

"I'm lost," the voice blubbered. Although it was childlike, something about it was wrong.

Yet Loren stepped toward it, as if pulled forward by invisible strings, her shoes dragging on the ground.

"Help," the voice said. "*P-p-please*. Help me."

Loren stepped out of the warehouse lights, the shadows wrapping like clammy hands around her limbs, urging her to keep walking, to not be afraid. The smell of sewer gas and decaying animals swept through the alley.

Terror froze her in place as the silhouette trembled and unfurled to clawed feet. There was the scrape of dead leaves on cobbles, and the sound of bones cracking.

And then the thing began to crabwalk up the wall, with arms and legs that bent the wrong way at the joints.

A hand closed around Loren's upper arm, and she nearly screamed as she was yanked out of the trance.

"We don't listen to the voices," Darien hissed in her ear, pulling her back into the light of the Umbra Forum. "Ever."

Once they were clear of the creature, he released her and

CITY OF GODS AND MONSTERS

resumed his position at the head of their trio. Loren blinked, shaking her head free of the spell-like feeling that had come over her in that alley.

"What are we doing here again?" she hissed. A crescent moon peeked through a gap in the tin roof. She shuffled closer to Darien as he edged around a metalworking vendor, and she stumbled a little when she stepped on his heel.

"We're here for Casen Martel."

"Remind me again who that is." But Darien didn't answer her, and soon they were slowing to a stop at a set of doors that led into a warehouse bedecked in spray paint. Music and cheering rattled the building.

Loren felt like she was having déjà vu as Darien said to the were-wolf bouncer guarding the doors, "I'm here for the Butcher."

The blood drained from Loren's face. No wonder Darien hadn't referred to Casen Martel by his underworld name; he must've known Loren would insist they immediately turn around and go back to the car.

The Butcher was the lead Blood Potions dealer in the state. The Magical Protections Unit had been itching to get the Butcher behind bars for years. According to the rumors, he'd earned his title after someone had tried to double-cross him. Needless to say, he hadn't just killed the man.

He'd chopped him into pieces.

Rumor also said the man wasn't entirely dead when Casen had started taking him apart. The violent nature of his killings hadn't stopped at just the one. No—from that day forth, every person who made the mistake of wronging the Butcher was met with the same gruesome fate.

The bouncer's fire-colored gaze dragged over Loren. "Those girls aren't coming in. Not unless you're looking to sell them." Loren stepped behind Darien. "A few clients came by looking for young meat. An hour, tops, and you can have them back." He inclined his head toward the doors. "They're in the front row."

"The girls are mine," Darien replied icily. "I've seen enough Fyxens here tonight to keep your kerb-crawlers occupied."

The bouncer's expression turned stony. "Casen is busy. You're welcome to come in and enjoy yourself, Devil. Or you can kindly fuck off."

Darien gave the wolf a nerve-wracking stare that had Loren rocking back and forth on the balls of her feet. But talking to the Butcher clearly wasn't an opportunity Darien was willing to pass up, even for a quick scrapping session she knew he'd enjoy, because he was soon turning to Dallas and Loren.

"Wait here." His eyes flashed to Loren's for a fraction of a second, but the message in them was clear: *don't move.*

Loren stepped toward him. "Darien —"

But he was already pushing past the bouncer and through the doors. Smoke that reeked of contraband Boneweed drifted from inside, coating Loren's skin like oil.

The bouncer stepped back to his post, barring their entrance. Seeing the terror on her face, the wolf gave her a smirk that showed his sharp, elongated canines.

Loren felt like her lungs were being stepped on. "Dal...I'm scared."

"Tuck up your hair, Lor," Dallas whispered. Loren scrambled to fix the strands that had slipped loose. "These people look like they will *eat* you." She dragged Loren by the elbow until they were standing below the mezzanine, upon which the vampire escorts Darien had been referring to—the Fyxens—were flaunting them-selves in dresses made from such sheer fabric that *everything* was on display.

With Darien no longer at their side, time slowed to a crawl. Dented trucks rolled through the market, one by one, carrying wooden crates of gods-knew-what. Men wearing heavy hoods unloaded the crates at warehouse storefronts, the steel doors rolling up to allow them in.

Loren tried to focus on breathing; tried not to dwell on the rumors of a human farm below the streets, the subterranean blood plant hidden from the law enforcement with magic. Any person abducted and taken into the tunnels were never rescued, and they never saw daylight again.

The market was turning splotchy, the medical tattoo on her forearm heating in warning. People watched her and Dallas with hungry and probing eyes, and creatures mimicking children's voices began to weep again.

As the seconds ticked by, three men that were staring from where they sat at an aluminum table by a raw-meat food cart rose to their feet, discarding red-stained paper plates in a garbage pail over-flowing with bones and napkins.

"Heeeeere, kitty, kitty," said the gaunt and pale one as the trio approached.

Loren stepped closer to Dallas as the witch's hand went for the Focus in her bag.

"Is that human blood I smell?" said another. The trio was strategic in the way they positioned themselves, the space between their bodies too narrow for even a child to slip through. The other people in the market turned a blind eye and hid behind the smoke of imported cigars as the men closed in on them.

Loren's eyes swiveled round the market, looking for an escape or help, whichever might come first, as she pressed her back against Dallas's. The bouncer did nothing but gaze blankly at the cesspool of a market, as if Loren and Dallas didn't exist.

The third man made a kissing sound with peeling lips. "Come here, my sweet half-life."

Loren jumped out of her skin as Dallas barked, "Beat it, shit-bags!" But the men only chuckled, their laughter hollow and raspy. They were no more than three feet away now.

The warehouse doors banged open then, and Darien appeared. Taking in the men blocking Loren and Dallas in below the mezza-nine, Darien's hand teased his pistol.

That was all it was: a tease. A silent threat. But the men got the message clearer than if he'd taken a warning shot, and wisely scur-ried away.

"Took you long enough," Dallas hissed. For once in her life, she was as pale as Loren, her freckled neck throbbing with her pulse.

"Relax, Bright," Darien crooned. "You're still breathing, aren't you?"

Dallas made to say something, but a booming male voice echoed from the shadows of a nearby alley.

"Well, if it isn't Darien fucking Cassel."

Loren turned toward the source of that voice, Darien and Dallas doing the same.

A tall, winged silhouette stepped into the buzz of the warehouse lights, the icy blue of his eyes contrasting sharply with the rich brown of his skin. A curtain of black waves brushed his broad shoulders, framing his defined jaw in shadowy wisps.

Dallas elbowed Loren in the ribs. "Holy shit."

Even without the wings, it would've been impossible to mistake him for anyone else. He was an Angel of Death, a member of a Darkslaying circle and former soldier for the Aerial Fleet. Dallas was practically glowing as she appraised the magical wings anchored to his muscled upper back, the feathers as black and shining as the Angel's hair. A bodysuit fit him like a glove, the material gleaming like a newly tarred road.

Darien was grinning like a fiend. "Dominic," he said in greeting.

"What brings you to shantytown on such a fine evening?" Dominic said, stepping forward to clasp hands with Darien. Two overlapping wings marked his neck in white ink. "Don't tell me you're into those fried pissers old Pat's been selling."

Darien barked a laugh. "Not a chance. I prefer my intestines intact and exactly where they are, thanks." The Angel chuckled. "I have some questions for Casen."

Dominic matched his grin. "Only you'd have the balls to come here and grill the Butcher with questions. I guess that explains why I always called you *Daredevil* when we were kids." His glacial eyes snapped to the warehouse doors. "Since when does Casen make you wait outside?"

Darien inclined his head toward the bouncer. "This fucker behind me won't let these two see the Chopping Block."

Loren didn't turn around to read the bouncer's reaction when Dominic Valencia threw a glance his way, though she had a feeling the wolf was beginning to realize his mistake.

"Wolves," Dominic muttered. "I hear you cleared your name from Delaney's blacklist. How'd you get him to forgive you?"

"Brought him a few teeth from the mouth of his recently excommunicated Reaper."

Dominic gave a husky laugh. "Shit." And then his focus flicked between Dallas and Loren. The corner of his mouth tipped up. "What do we have here anyway?"

Darien introduced Dallas and Loren to Dominic, and when they were finished greeting each other, Darien said, "These two are friends with one of the missing girls."

"I've been hearing all about that. Since when do college-age human girls go missing?"

"Beats me." Darien shrugged. "What brings you here, Dom?"

"The usual: a body to bag. The coin of the realm to rake in."

"Sounds like I've got some competition."

Dominic smirked. "We'll compare numbers at year-end and see who placed first."

"I'd say the winner takes a hundred gold mynet, but I feel sorry for your wallet already."

The Angel wheezed a laugh. "Douchebag." But he extended a hand. "You're on. I look forward to beating your conceited ass into the ground."

The Devil shook the Angel's hand. "Good luck with that, my feathered friend."

Loren fought a smile, while Dallas threw her head back and outright cackled.

Dominic was still smiling as he flipped Darien off and backed into the maze of food carts. "Gotta roll. I'm meeting Conrad in ten."

"Tell him we're overdue for a game of poker."

"Will do. Though I should warn you, he's been practicing. The guy's as much of a sore loser as you are."

Darien barked a laugh. "You're a cocksucker."

The Angel was grinning. "Catch you later." He'd barely finished speaking before he launched into the air, wings churning up dust as he disappeared through a gap in the roof.

As soon as he was gone, Loren whispered, "Are you sure you trust him?"

Darien merely said, "Dom's like a brother to me. He's one of the few people I would trust with my life, and that's saying a lot."

Darien's head suddenly whipped around, his eyes turning black as he swept the interior of the warehouse. He barely spared a glance for Loren as he stepped closer to her and tightened the folds of his jacket around her.

"The flesher's almost at the block," he warned.

Loren fixed her hair again; it kept coming loose from her stupid hat. She wished she couldn't be seen; that she could hide herself from the many curious onlookers. If only Dallas had performed the invisibility charm again.

Loren was about to ask Darien something, but the doors swung open then, and the Butcher emerged.

DARIEN KEPT an eye on the door the whole time, making sure no one shut and locked it as he sat in an office that was as much a dump as Dennis Boyd's.

Cardboard boxes were stacked from sticky floor to water-stained ceiling, and oil paintings from centuries past hung lopsided on molding walls, olive-green paint peeling off in strips. A statue of Okapi, God of Mercy, sat atop a filing cabinet, among a mess of grease-stained takeout bags and downright filthy magazines. Above the desk was a neon sign that read *Go fuck thyself,* the loopy scrawl burning a steady vermilion.

Unlike the knucklehead of a bouncer out front, the Butcher hadn't batted an eye when Darien had announced that he wasn't going anywhere without Loren and Dallas. Once he was finished retrieving the information he needed from this meeting, perhaps he would teach the wolf a lesson and punch his teeth down his throat.

"I know it's not the answer you were looking for," the Butcher was saying. He sat across from Darien at the metal desk, Boneweed smoke rippling from his mouth. "But it's the truth."

"Any chance she might've been hired from the outside?" Darien's gloved hands drummed the soiled armrests of his chair. "Even to fill in for someone for a one-night run?"

Casen was shaking his head, his stringy shoulder-length hair swaying. "I keep my circle small, and I know my dealers by name. It's how I root out the bad eggs; I get to know them personally, and I've learned to smell a rat long before they squeal." The seven-foot-tall warlock tapped the ash off the trip with a scarred hand nearly the size of a dinner plate. "If Shadowback's sister was selling for me, I would've been the first to know."

"Chrysantha's disappearance seems to be linked to a new circle of Darkslayers invading our turf," Darien said. "Have your eyes on the streets given any indication of this being true?"

"I didn't peg him as Darkslayer. But I had an anonymous client arrange to pick up a shipment of Blood Potions and chemicals last week. He was branded like you." Although his own was bare, he gestured to his unshaven neck, to where a tattoo would've been, if he'd had one. "A phoenix or some shit."

Where she was perched beside him on a stool of blistered leather, Loren straightened, her mouth parting as if she wanted to say something. But she didn't.

"Hellseher?" Darien said.

"Warlock." Interesting. Considering the Sight was a necessity when it came to tracking targets, the Darkslaying circles in Angelthene had only ever consisted of hellsehers, or at the very least hellseher halfies. This new 'circle' was starting to look a hell of a lot more like a cult than a band of copycats. "That's why I said he didn't peg me for a Darkslayer; he lacked the Sight."

"Any idea who this anonymous client was?"

"My clients usually have a middle-man do the picking up for them at the drop-off point." He butted out the last of the trip, the glass coffin-shaped ashtray near-invisible in the cloud of blue smoke. "I'd be surprised if it was the actual client who'd shown up for the trade."

"Any chance you could recontact them?"

"If he had half a brain, he'd have used a burner phone." A pause.

The warlock looked him over with eyes so brown, they were black. "What's your take on it, Cassel? Why would a warlock wear a symbol in the same place as a Darkslayer? Wannabes or some shit?"

"A cult," he suggested, half-shrugging. "How large was the purchase?"

"Unusually large. The difference in quantities seemed odd. The Blood Potions were purchased in individual vials, but the chemicals were ordered by the vat."

"Would you care to write down the compounds for me?"

The names scribbled on the back of a business card of the Doghouse Strip Club concluded the questions Darien wanted to ask, but as he was heading for the office door, the girls on his heels, Casen's voice stopped him dead in his tracks.

"If your sister didn't owe me so much cash, I might've considered giving you a call the next time I get a BP deal that raises red flags."

Darien frowned. "What cash?" he said, turning on a heel. The warlock was still lounging at his desk, half-invisible behind the cloud of sour smoke that burned Darien's eyes.

"She never told you?" The Butcher was wearing the closest thing to a smile, his teeth a stained white beneath a beard of wiry black hairs. "Ivyana owes me half a mil. She borrowed from me when that swindling husband of hers conned the wrong people out of their money. She became concerned they would retaliate, so she paid his dues for him." He looked Darien over. "That's one sweet sister you've got there."

Darien bit his tongue as a curse word bubbled to the tip of it. Jack and his fucking gambling addiction. Darien was always giving him shit for it, which was likely why Ivy had gone to someone like the Butcher to borrow money instead of asking her own brother.

"I'll cover what she owes you," Darien said. He dug his phone out of his pocket and stepped up to the desk to do the transfer.

But the Butcher said, "I don't want the money, Cassel." Darien paused. "I've thought of a far more entertaining way for your sister to pay me back." He heaved himself to his feet with a heavy grunt and beckoned with a wave of his hand. Dallas and Loren stepped aside to let him pass. "Come with me."

The Butcher led the way into the damp hallway, toward the Chopping Block, trench coat rippling against his ankles. Darien ignored Loren and Dallas's searching gazes as he followed behind him.

Vulgar neon signs were tacked to every inch of the walls of the hallway. Everything from middle fingers and naked vampire silhouettes to phrases like *Don't Be a Dick, It's Witching Hour Somewhere,* and *Down to Suck* flitted through the corners of his vision like fireflies.

When they reached the end of the hallway, one sign that was burning a bright white passed directly over their heads.

It was only a dream.

Darien drowned out the sound of Loren and Dallas conversing in near-frantic whispers behind him, always so close that they were nearly stepping on his boots. He followed the Butcher into the arena, where they were soon swallowed up by an audience that was slamming shoulder to shoulder with abandon.

A new match had started. The raised octagon platform below was blocked off from the screaming audience, not with ropes but with a cage. The canvas-covered platform was black with blood and guts. Seven people were brawling within the enclosure, wielding everything from wooden bats wrapped in barbed wire to knives and saws with curved and serrated edges.

Casen had to shout to be heard. "I hear you like to fight. The four in black are the best champions I've had on my Block all decade. Kill them and their opponents and I'll forget about the money."

Darien's fingers twitched, adrenaline sparking in his veins.

Dallas bit out, *"All of them?"*

As a last thought, the Butcher added to Darien, "Bare hands only."

A low chuckle rose in Darien's throat. "You're sick."

"So are you," the Butcher replied. "From what I've heard."

Loren stepped to Darien's side and made to say something to him. But Darien was already pulling his shirt off, leaving only the muscle shirt he had on underneath. White and practically brand new —for another few minutes.

"Hold this please," he said, offering the long-sleeved shirt to

Loren. She was staring at him, her eyes imploring. He had to force himself to look away from her, to not let her face distract him. It was to the Butcher that he said, "Get them out of here or it's no deal. And get some of your boys to watch them until I'm done. If anything happens—"

"Quit your fretting, Cassel," Casen said. "I'll make sure nothing happens to them."

"Good." Darien said. "And you'll tell me the next time you strike a BP deal."

Darien knew all about the kinds of potions and chemicals that were sold through the Terran Blood Potions Syndicate, and he believed once they deciphered more of the Dominus Volumen, they might be the same chemicals necessary for creating the Arcanum Well.

And if they could find out who was ordering them by the vat, they would be able to catch them. To turn them into the law enforcement and not only make Loren safe again but bring Sabrine back home. The next time the Butcher received a large order for Blood Potions and chemicals would be their chance to strike.

"Done." The Butcher signalled to two of his men.

"Darien." Loren's voice was a panicked whimper, but he made himself block it out. He had to focus.

And he was itching for a fight.

Loren's fingers had barely closed around the fabric of the shirt Darien had offered to her before he began jogging through the audience, shoving people out of his way.

It wasn't until he reached the cage and launched himself over the steel wire that he realized he was smiling.

"Did you seriously put your chewed-up gum in my pocket?"

When Darien had disposed of his bloodied-up muscle-shirt after slaughtering every contestant in the ring, he'd put the long-sleeve back on, along with the jacket Loren had offered him once they were clear of the Umbra Forum. Two of the Butcher's men had escorted her and Dallas back outside, where the warlocks remained with them until Darien was finished with the fight.

"I didn't see a trashcan," she mumbled. The gum had turned rock-hard and tasteless as clay from her frantic chewing; she had been desperate to get it out of her mouth.

Darien laughed. "That entire shithole is a trashcan, Rookie." He flicked the gum that was rolled up in foil to the sidewalk. The vast river snaking along the side of the road glimmered like liquid silver in the moonlight, the musty waters scenting the cool night air.

"So, if someone is dealing Blood Potions on their own agenda," Loren mused as they made their way back to the car, "where do we go from here? What's the plan?" Her mind had spun as she'd tried to keep up with the conversation in Casen's office, though she'd gleaned enough to know that dealing Blood Potions on the Butcher's turf was just as frowned upon in the world of illegal trade as Darkslayers who worked soil that didn't belong to them.

"We wait until the Butcher calls with information about a new deal," Darien replied. The mercury-vapor streetlamp they passed under gilded the sharp line of his jaw with eerie light. "And then we take whatever information we can get from the buyers and their middlemen and solve this case."

They were getting warmer. She could feel it.

They were almost at the car when Darien's phone buzzed.

He dug it out of the pocket of his pants that were now stained with blood, swiped to answer, and lifted it to his ear. "Cassel." The car chirped as he unlocked the doors.

The look that crossed Darien's face had Loren and Dallas stopping on the sidewalk. Loren tried with all her might to hear what the person on the other end was saying, but she could barely make out words.

Though she could've sworn the male voice said *Sabrine.*

Loren locked eyes with Dallas just as Darien snapped, "You *what?*"

30

It seemed to take a million years to reach the Silverwood District.

The entirety of Werewolf Territory was a mixture of houses of varying incomes; there was no obvious separation between the wealthy and the poor, as was the case in other parts of Angelthene. Families sat on their front lawns in folding chairs around bonfires, their heads turning as they watched the car flit by like a bat.

Loren couldn't sit still. Darien had warned her not to get her hopes up over what Logan Sands had said on the other end of that call. But Loren was bouncing in place as they drove through the neighborhoods at a speed that felt painfully slow.

The werewolf had told Darien that he'd found Sabrine. *Alive*. She only prayed Logan's definition of alive meant hanging on with more than an inch of her life.

The car slowed to a crawl. "This looks like the right house," Darien muttered as he turned onto a gravel driveway. A small house framed by towering palm trees sat at the end of it, the windows aglow with the lights that were on inside.

Darien cut the engine, unbuckled his seatbelt, and sat back, stretching out his legs.

The curtain hanging over the fogged-glass panel on the kitchen door parted to the side as someone peered through it. A moment later, that person stepped out onto the porch.

A man Loren assumed was Logan Sands jogged down the porch steps and across the driveway, gravel crunching beneath his running shoes. His dark, shoulder-length hair swayed with every step.

Darien opened the door and stepped out. "Let me get a few words in first," he told Loren and Dallas. Too eager to wait, they opened their doors and followed him out.

At the sight of Loren and Dallas, Logan froze, his knuckles turning white as his hands curled into fists. "You didn't tell me you were bringing company."

"You didn't ask," Darien said, hand hovering near his belt buckle—near the pistol Loren had watched him load with silver bullets before heading here. "These are Sabrine's closest friends. I wasn't about to deny them the right to see her."

Logan's square jaw was clenched. "She isn't well."

Dallas barked, "Like hell she isn't!" She made to move past Darien, but he held out an arm to stop her. She froze in place, but snarled at Logan, "Where is she? *What did you do?*"

"Cool it, matchstick," Logan retorted. "I only saved her *life.*"

Dallas bared her teeth. "Did you seriously just insult me by my hair color, you four-legged *freak?*"

Darien stepped between them. "Let's not start a brawl, shall we?" he advised. To Logan he said, "Where's Sabrine?"

"In the house."

Loren's knees weakened. "Can we see her?" Her voice was a hoarse whisper. *"Please.* We've been so worried about her."

Logan swallowed, though his eyes softened under Loren's pleading gaze. "It isn't safe."

Dallas's mouth popped open, but Darien spoke before she could get a word out. "What do you mean, Logan?"

"Is she hurt?" Loren cut in.

The werewolf looked at Loren. "She was. But she's okay now."

Dallas barked, "Then why can't we see her?"

Just then, the front door of the house cracked open. A moment passed before that door fully opened, and a lithe figure filled the frame. Loren's heartbeat stumbled at the sight of the angled planes of the girl's honey-brown face, softened beneath the glow of lamplight.

Loren sank to her knees as Sabrine stepped out onto the porch.

DARIEN STUDIED Logan as the werewolf took a seat across from him at the cluttered table in the cramped kitchen. The scarred brown hands that were wrapped around a mug of coffee seemed to have trouble staying still, his fingers constantly tapping the sides of the mug and rotating it back and forth. Printed across the mug in block letters was the phrase, *I don't do Moon-days.*

Logan's eyes flicked over the rim to assess Darien as he took a sip.

Darien assessed him back. He had half a mind to tell Logan what he really thought of the pigsty his house had become. The near-bursting trash bags piled up by the fridge, the animal heart in the sink, the dried-out banana peel that was literally stuck to the tile by his boot. The only thing keeping Darien from saying something rude was the thought that perhaps Logan hadn't bothered to clean because he was too busy tending to Sabrine.

But he found that he couldn't hold it back any longer as he said, "Does your neighborhood not have a garbage collection day?"

Logan looked over his shoulder at the leaning tower of trash. When he turned to face Darien again, he gave him a sheepish smile. "I've been busy," he said.

Darien smirked. "Yeah, busy hoarding trash."

Logan snorted, though neither of them were in the mood for humor. "Fuck you, Cassel." He took a sip of his coffee. "You sure I can't get you anything?"

Darien waved the offer away. "I take it you combed the buildings near the area where you found Sabrine?" The dark-haired half-witch was currently around the corner in the sitting room with Loren and Dallas. The three friends had embraced for a long time, crying tears of happiness, as they were reunited at last.

Logan nodded. "We checked everything. Whoever had her… They cleaned up quickly. Not a thing was left behind."

Darien drummed his gloved fingers on the coffee-stained table-top. "I'm assuming you checked for prints?"

"They had magic coating everything, in every building we searched. Not a single surface had one print or a trace of DNA. Whoever is doing this…" He pinched the bridge of his nose, the wolf-skull ring on his middle finger glinting in the kitchen light. "They've got money."

"A lot of people in Angelthene have money, so that doesn't exactly help us." Two flies were buzzing noisily around the heart in the kitchen sink. "Are you certain you found Sabrine close to the same place where they were keeping her?"

Logan's thick brows knitted together. "What's that supposed to mean?"

"It means her captors might've dumped her somewhere else in the city. To perhaps make sure no one could draw connections to the *real* location where they were keeping her."

The werewolf was shaking his head, his unwashed hair swishing across his shoulders. "Sabrine is certain she hadn't gotten far when I found her. And her captors didn't dump her—she *escaped*. She told me she jumped from halfway up a skyscraper and landed on a fire escape. I checked every building in the entire district, Darien. Every building with a fire escape *and* every building without one. Every abandoned business and every operating one."

Darien pursed his lips. "Which district?"

"Oldtown." Before Darien could ask for clarification on which part of Angelthene's former downtown core, Logan said, "Near the Iron Dock and the Bonefish Market."

"Does Sabrine remember anything from being held captive?"

"Not a thing," Logan said. "But I had a friend of mine in the medical field come to the house and examine Sabrine after I found her. There wasn't anything out of the ordinary. Except…"

"What?" Darien prompted.

"Except, when he swabbed her mouth, he found a trace of a plant substance not widely known. He said it was something like…

307

Essence of…bah, I can't remember. But apparently, it is an ingredient commonly used for concealment spells."

"That's likely how they were concealing her aura then," Darien said. No Avertera talismans for these guys. The fact that Sabrine's aura was now visible meant the plant substance had likely worn off sometime after she'd managed to escape her captors.

Logan was pursing his lips in thought. "Come to think of it, there were two substances. But my friend—Oren is his name—couldn't identify the second. The trace of it was far to miniscule."

"Any chance you could get a hold of your friend and see if he can give me the sample he took? I'd like to confirm which plant it was and see if I can figure out the second one."

Logan shifted in his seat. "I can try, but he did me a favor by coming to check on Sabrine without taking the situation to law enforcement. If he decided to dispose of any evidence to cover his ass, then you're on your own."

Darien would have to accept that. "Alright." He nodded. "Do whatever you can."

They sat in silence for several minutes, the hum of the refrigerator and the hushed voices of the girls in the sitting room the only sounds.

"I'm afraid Chrysantha's dead, Darien. She's been missing longer than Sabrine." Logan swallowed, a sheen of sweat coating his face. "And when I found Sabrine, she was so close to death that I…I had to change her."

Darien sat up straighter, a chill licking down his spine. "What are you talking about, Logan?" His mind backpedaled to the events that had taken place outside; how the only werewolf he'd smelled was Logan. There were no other wolves here.

Or so he'd thought.

Logan's voice dipped several octaves. "I need to find another place for Sabrine to stay. Someplace safe until all this blows over."

Realization swept across Darien's features as he glanced again in the direction of the heart—a *wolf* heart, he realized, one of the necessary elements for a successful transformation—in the sink, the pieces he'd been denying until now clicking into place. He recalled how Logan had said it wasn't safe for Dallas and Loren to see Sabrine.

But not safe for *who?*

"You *didn't*," Darien bit out. He felt his eyes turn black as rage flooded his body; he had to give Logan credit for not flinching at the sight.

"*I had to!*" Logan hissed. "The girl would've died. She was *seconds* from dying."

Darien tipped his head back to stare at the ceiling, fingers curling into fists as he forced the black out of his eyes. The reality of what Logan had done...

His fists tightened, leather gloves groaning as they threatened to tear from the force.

The son of a bitch had changed Sabrine into a werewolf to save her from the fatal injuries she'd sustained at the hands of her captors —as well as the ones she'd gained from apparently crashing down a fire escape. It was no secret that Logan didn't have a great deal of money, so Darien knew whatever spell he was using to temporarily cloak Sabrine's werewolf scent was hurling him deeper into the trench known as *debt.*

Logan had just buried himself in a giant pile of horseshit. While he was at it, he might as well dig his own grave. By changing Sabrine, he'd broken the pact the werewolves had with the vampires, who were far more powerful than the wolves.

Thousands of years ago, the werewolves rebelled against the vampires that had oppressed and slaughtered a great number of their kind. After centuries of bloodshed, they finally came to a truce, and a pact was made: no more vampires or werewolves could be created— only *born*—as both parties had been turning people against their will for millennia to fight in their selfish war.

It became the law from that day forward, backed by the Aerial Fleet, the winged soldiers who perched near the very top of the hierarchy on this western continent. If any new vampires or wolves were created through methods other than natural birth, both the person who was turned and their creator were to be imprisoned or executed —either by the law enforcement or by the opposing party of those who broke the pact. In this case, it was the vampires who now held the power to reignite an age-old war.

In other words, Logan was royally fucked.

Darien was shaking his head. "You just broke the law in an unforgiveable way—and that's coming from someone who's broken his fair share. Unless they decide to kill you, they'll throw you in prison, Logan. As soon as they find out what you've done, your life is *over.*" He was failing to keep his voice down; the conversation the girls were having in the other room had fallen silent. "And they *will* find out, Logan—because you need to tell them. Hiding the location of a girl who's been reported missing is possibly worse than having turned her into one of your own."

Logan's eyes were shuttered as he stared at the table, a hand cupping his mouth. "Perhaps saving her life will be reason enough for the law and the leeches to pardon me."

Darien smirked, though it wasn't with amusement. He couldn't believe the sheer idiocy of Logan's selfish decision. Because of this, every single werewolf in this city could be killed, every neighborhood in the Silverwood District razed to the ground.

"You'd better start praying to whatever gods you believe in, Logan," Darien said, shoving out from the table. "Because you know who else is coming for you now."

3I

Loren listened carefully to the conversation Darien and Logan were having in the kitchen. Although her human hearing was unreliable at best, she figured she'd caught the gist of what was causing Darien to raise his voice.

"Is it true?" Loren said to Sabrine, who sat cross-legged on the carpet between her and Dallas. She'd guessed as much after taking note of Sabrine's eyes; the near-black hue had already developed a warmer shade. By the sounds of things, they would soon be painted with the same fire as Logan's.

Loren felt a stab of sadness. Before all this happened, Sabrine was half-human. Loren had clung to that fact for years, constantly reminding herself of it. And as awful as it made her, when other students had called Sabrine *half-breed* throughout primary and secondary school, it made the word *half-life* a little easier for Loren to shoulder.

Sabrine's throat bobbed. "He said his options were to either change me or let me die."

Tears pricked Loren's eyes. "I'm glad he saved you." She gave Sabrine's hand, her fingers laced with her own, a comforting squeeze.

"Me too," Dallas said. "We were so worried about you, Sab. We're glad you're back."

Darien appeared in the doorway that led to the kitchen, looking more than a little pissed off. "Ready to go?"

"Do you think we might be able to sleep here?" Loren said. It was already almost one in the morning; she didn't think another few hours would matter.

"I think your friend will be able to tell you how bad an idea that is." The pact between vampires and werewolves was shot to hell, and it seemed Sabrine was not out of harm's way yet.

Sabrine gauged the slayer leaning in the doorway. "It's okay," she whispered. "You guys don't need to stay with me. I'll be fine." But neither Loren nor Dallas let go of her.

"We're staying, Darien," Dallas announced. She turned her head to look at him, her long red ponytail snagging on her academy sweater. "You can either come back in the morning or stay with us. But until tomorrow, we're not leaving Sabrine." Although her words were firm, she couldn't meet Darien's gaze for long. She added in a small voice, "Of course, we'd prefer if you stayed."

Loren wasn't sure why, but Darien looked her way again. She was pretty certain she was giving him what Dallas referred to as *puppy-dog eyes*, though she wasn't really meaning to.

As they looked at each other, Loren felt like they were caught in that same bubble they often got stuck in together, and suddenly it was just the two of them, the heat of Darien's gaze realer than the feel of Sabrine's hand grasping her own. Loren could've sworn the edge melted from Darien's face.

After a minute that felt more like ten, Darien held up a black-gloved finger. "One night. After that, we'll have to find other arrangements."

Logan appeared behind him, hardly more than a silhouette in the kitchen light. Darien stepped aside to let him into the room as the werewolf said to him, "I've got an extra guest bedroom. It's clean, unlike the rest of my house."

Darien smirked. "No, thanks. I don't sleep in wolves' dens." He settled into the sagging armchair in the corner and fiddled with the handle on the side of it until it reclined. A footrest sprang into place with a squeak. He rested his pistol atop his muscled thigh, clicked the safety free, and aimed it at Logan. "You're not leaving this house either, my friend. You're calling law enforcement at sunup."

Logan's mouth curled into a frown. "And what am I going to tell them?"

"You're going to tell them you found Sabrine. You're going to tell them you changed her into one of your own to save her life. They'll likely come here to ask her a few questions, and when they're finished, they'll decide if they want to wash their hands of you and let the vampires decide your fate or deal with you themselves."

Logan's face had turned pale.

Darien gave him a humorless smile, his eyes cold as ice. "My guess is it'll be the first one."

Sabrine's palm was slick with sweat. Loren gave her fingers another squeeze.

Picking up on the several rapid heartrates in the room, Darien said to Loren, "Don't worry. They'll be more interested in the set of teeth that changed your friend than your friend herself."

When Loren swallowed, the sound carried through the room.

"You think this is a good idea?" Logan bit out.

"It's your only option. Better to come clean than have someone else turn you in. Isn't it?"

Logan's nostrils flared, hands curling into fists at his sides. Regardless of the defensive stance he held, Loren saw the fear gleaming in his eyes. "I guess we'll see."

Darien settled into the cushions and crossed one ankle over the other. "Yeah," he agreed with a smile that was nothing short of threatening. "We will."

DARIEN DIDN'T GET a wink of rest that night. But as a Darkslayer, he was used to running on little to no sleep. His kind could function through exhaustion better than humans or wolves; sometimes he could go a full three days without feeling tired.

Loren and her friends, on the other hand, slept like babies on the couch. Darien spent most of the night conversing with his Devils via group text, warning them of the troubles that could befall not only the werewolves but anyone else involved in this screw-up—and that included Sabrine. The poor girl had escaped one evil in time to possibly meet a new one.

As the clock neared five a.m., the messages from the Devils became few and far between, most of their questions having been answered, their arguments addressed. Darien caught himself looking at Loren, where she slept sandwiched between Sabrine and Dallas. If he was being frank, he caught himself looking at her more often than he cared to admit.

There was an innocence about her that he found himself admiring. Perhaps it was the reckless devotion she felt for her friends, or the way she abandoned herself to the magical world she'd been thrust into. Loving it with her whole heart, even when it didn't always love her in return.

Or maybe it was the way her eyelids fluttered as she dreamed, completely at ease with her friends at either side of her. There was no trace of that guarded look she always gave him when they argued. But Loren wasn't the only one who was guarded, nor was she the only one who was stubborn. *Stubborn* was Darien's middle name, so it had taken him a while to admit it, even to himself…

But Loren Calla was gorgeous in a way that made his knees weak. He considered it an accomplishment; as someone who'd been cracking open the skulls of grown men and demons since he was fifteen, it took a lot for something to impact him. And it took even more for some-*one* to impact him. He'd had a couple almost-relationships, one real one, and his fair share of one-night stands, but this one… This girl was different for a reason he hadn't figured out yet. He couldn't get enough of her, of the way she tipped her head back when she laughed, of the way she scrunched up her nose when he was teasing her, of the way her eyes lit up every time he walked into the room. As if his presence made a difference to her.

He began to feel like a creep for watching her, so he pushed out of the chair, shoving the footrest down until it clicked shut, and made his way to the porch to have a smoke. He held his breath as he walked through the kitchen, waving away the flies that were still gathered around the wolf heart. He stepped outside, breathing deeply as the screen door banged shut behind him. The warm autumn air vibrated with the song of cicadas.

He'd just lit a cigarette beneath a sky that was gradually lightening to gray when the door creaked open. Loren's peaches-and-honeysuckle scent alerted him to her presence before he'd fully turned around.

"Hey," she croaked, rubbing at her eyes that were puffy with sleep. The hem of her academy sweater was rumpled. "Did you manage to get any rest?"

Darien resisted the urge to take another drag on the cigarette. "Like I said to Logan: I don't sleep in wolves' dens."

She crossed her arms against the balmy wind and gave him a saucy look. "You should get some rest once in a while. You're not a machine."

He braced his elbows on the porch rail at his back. "I'll rest when I'm dead."

Her eyes found the cigarette between his index and middle finger. "Are you going to smoke that or just let it burn out?"

Darien shifted on his feet. "It's a habit I'm not proud of," he admitted.

She pursed those perfect lips he had a hard time looking away from. He had imagined how that mouth would feel beneath his own —and what it would feel like on other parts of his body—more times than he could count. "Since when does the infamous Darien Cassel give a crap what anyone thinks?" It was true: he'd smoked in front of her before, but for some reason he'd always hesitated. Except for that one time in the dining room, when memories of his mother had become too heavy to bear.

The smile on his face faded as he looked her over, the answer he hadn't yet given her shaking through him like a tremor. "I usually don't." *But I care what you think.* He almost said it aloud, but the realization stilled his tongue. She was right: since when did he give a shit what anyone thought?

As if reading the conflict on his face and knowing fully what it meant, she smiled. "I wanted to thank you. For everything that you did tonight, as well as these past few weeks. Maybe the information we gathered will help us figure out what happened to Sab." Her delicate shoulders pulled up into a shrug. "She doesn't seem to remember much. Maybe we can use what we discovered tonight to stop this from happening to anyone else."

"Maybe." This girl was always more concerned with the wellbeing of others than the wellbeing of herself. Even when he'd found her in that alley, she hadn't screamed for help because she was afraid of causing harm to bystanders. He relit the cigarette, snapped the lighter shut, and took a drag. "But we've got another problem heading our way, if we want to keep your friend safe."

"Do you really think the vampires will be more interested in Logan than Sabrine?"

Darien shrugged, diving into his magic to keep her from smelling the smoke rippling from his lips. "Depends. The law states that both the newly created werewolf or vampire and the person who changed them will be held accountable." He paused at the fear that flitted across her face and caused the space between her eyebrows to scrunch up. "But again, that depends."

"On what?"

He took another drag before throwing the cigarette to the porch and grinding it beneath his boot. "I think," he began, crossing the distance between them, his footsteps echoing hollowly, "that you need to stop worrying about someone else for a minute."

Loren stiffened at his advance, her heartbeat becoming irregular. She held her breath as he stopped before her and took the Avertera talisman into his fingers. The edges of it were worn down worse than several hours ago, the ivory skin of her neck dusted with gold.

"I also think," he said, "that it's time I find you a new one of these."

"I already told you." She tilted her head back to meet his eyes. She took the talisman from his grip, her fingers closing around his gloved hand. For that split second, he found himself wishing he'd taken the stupid things off. The number of times she'd touched him were much too few and far between. "I don't want you shelling out any more money on me, Darien Cassel."

"And I don't want you dying," Darien replied. "How's that?"

Loren's eyes brimmed with curiosity as she canted her head, the hair she wore wavy tonight tumbling to one shoulder. "Why do you care?" Her voice was so quiet, it was nearly carried away by the breeze. There was nothing rude in the question; it was simply innocent curiosity. "I meant what I said that day at Rook and Redding's: what's in it for you?"

Darien wasn't sure he was ready to reveal to her the truth behind his motivations for helping her that day. And even if he wanted to, he lost his chance as the front door swung open with a low groan.

Logan stepped out, looking like he hadn't slept for one second. That made two of them. He stopped as he beheld them on his porch but made no move to leave.

Sensing that he had another argument on his hands, Darien sighed through his nose and said to Loren, "Why don't you go back inside? I need to talk to Logan."

She left without a word, giving Logan a wide berth. Before she disappeared inside, she threw a glance over her shoulder, her ocean eyes briefly locking with Darien's, as if it somehow helped her to look at him one last time, before she vanished inside.

And even though Darien had to argue with Logan for what seemed like the hundredth time over salvaging his peace with the vampires, he found that he didn't get as angry as he had before. Maybe it was the cigarette.

Then again, maybe it wasn't.

32

L oren swung her legs from side to side as she sat on the couch
in the sitting room at Hell's Gate. Sabrine was beside her,
flipping through channels on the television as they waited for
Dallas to finish rummaging through the drawers of the media center.

Shortly after Travis and Ivy had picked them up from Logan's
house, and Dallas had discovered that the drawers of the media
center were stuffed to the brim with videogames, she had insisted
they play. Other than Travis and Ivy, who were currently in the
basement, no other slayers were here; shortly after the peace officers
Logan had called had finished questioning Sabrine, Darien had practically thrown the girls out the door.

He hadn't needed to explain why. The law enforcement had
decided to do exactly what Darien had expected and wash their
hands of the situation. Which meant the vampires of the District of
Drakon would soon be showing up in Werewolf Territory to enact
whatever punishment they deemed necessary for Logan's breaking of
the pact. To protect not only Loren and Dallas, but also Sabrine,
Darien had called for Travis and Ivyana to bring them to Hell's Gate
while they dealt with whatever was about to go down with the
vampires.

CITY OF GODS AND MONSTERS

Loren couldn't stop staring at the front door. Couldn't slow her racing heart. Only an hour had passed, so she knew it was unrealistic to expect Darien to walk in at any second.

But she still stared.

And she still waited.

"Earth to Loren," Dallas sang from where she sat cross-legged on the rug, waving a game in her hand. "He's not going to be back anytime soon, so you'd might as well enjoy yourself."

"Sorry," she mumbled. She fiddled with the two still-damp braids that hung over her shoulders. "What game are we playing?"

But Sabrine had caught onto what Dallas had said and told Loren, "I never took you for someone who'd have the hots for a slayer."

Loren felt herself blushing. "I do *not* have the hots for him."

Dallas clicked her tongue. "Yes, she does. She's just in denial, Sab." Sabrine laughed, but then Dallas was assessing the witch-turned-wolf with a shrewd eye. "Tell us about Logan."

Sabrine stiffened. "What about him?"

"Ooh, *there* it is!" Dallas giggled, pointing a sharp, red-painted nail at her. "You liiiiike him."

Sabrine crossed her arms. "I do not!" she huffed.

Dallas tsked. "You're both screwed, and you know it."

"You're one to talk, Dallas," Loren cut in. "Miss I'm-going-to-jump-Maximus-Reacher's-bones-the-first-chance-I-get."

Sabrine gasped. "Did she *really* say that?"

Dallas popped the videogame out of its case. "The difference between me and you girls," she drawled, "is at least I *admit* when I like someone."

"I don't like Logan," Sabrine said again, her tone clipped. She slumped against the couch cushions. "Besides, I don't have time for boys. I need to catch up on my studies."

"Always the bookworm." Dallas gave a dramatic sigh as she plopped down on the couch between them and handed them each a controller. "I found *The Covenant*. Get ready to get your guts pumped full of lead, bitches."

Loren set her controller aside and got to her feet. "You guys can play first," she said. "I'm thirsty." It was a lie, but she didn't want to tell them what she was really doing.

Dallas merely shrugged and started the game.

When Loren got into the kitchen, she caught sight of Mortifer crouched behind the cereal boxes on top of the fridge. The *crunch, crunch* of ice chips shattering between his shadowy little teeth could barely be heard over the videogame blaring through the surround sound system.

Loren swung open the freezer door and flipped up the metal lever that determined whether ice would be made. Down for ice, up for no ice.

Mortifer immediately stopped chewing and peered around the cereal boxes, his tiny hand curling around the puffed rice box.

"I need a favor," Loren said in a low voice. Mortifer stared at her, clearly vexed by the fact that she'd shut off his precious ice machine. "I need you to tell me the next time Darien is having a Surge. I don't care what hour of the night it is…I need you to tell me." Her hand hovered on the lever, the cold metal biting into her fingers. "I know you listen to Darien, and I know you feel you should do everything he asks you to, but I *need* you to tell me, or this ice machine is not coming back on."

Mortifer glowered down at her, his eyes redder than Dallas's hair. For all Loren knew, the Hob might know how to turn on the ice machine on his own, but she was willing to try anything she could to find out when Darien was having a Surge again. She wasn't sure what she would do when that day—or night—came, but…she would cross that bridge when she got there.

"You care about him, too," Loren said gently. Mortifer merely looked at her, but the way his eyes softened said everything. Loren prompted, "Do we have a deal?"

The Hob finally nodded his shadowy head.

Loren flicked the lever back down, and the freezer rumbled as it prepared to fill the ice bin. "Thank you," she whispered.

The Hob merely shrank back behind the cereal boxes and resumed his crunching.

DARIEN STOOD at the head of the group alongside Logan as they watched the limousine pull onto the gravel driveway in the Silverwood District. A mist of rain started to fall, soaking them instantly.

Although Logan hadn't shifted for the occasion, several of his pack members who stood along the perimeter of the group insisted on being in their canine forms. They were nearly as large as horses, their coats varying shades of gray and brown. One glance in Max's direction, who stood at Darien's right, said he was just as bothered as Darien was by the stink of wet dog. Darien usually enjoyed the rain, but he could've gone without it today. And it wasn't just because of the smell.

It was because of the vampires who were inside that limousine. The vampires that hadn't exited the vehicle yet—and who were likely assessing the group that stood over a dozen strong in Logan's driveway. The vampires that hated sunlight, making today's stormy weather perfect for whatever they had planned.

Where he stood on the other side of Max, Jack murmured, "Are they going to just sit in there and stare at us all day?"

"Immortals have no sense of time, Jack," Darien said, hand tightening on his belt. Although Jack was immortal, he was physically— and literally—twenty-two years old. He hadn't lived long enough for time to become meaningless. None of the Devils had. The driver's door opened then. "Least of all four-hundred-year-old vampires."

And it *was* a four-hundred-year-old vampire who stepped out of the limousine, her door opened by her driver. At the sight of the tall, graceful woman with moon-pale skin and eyes redder than blood, Darien almost swore. He hadn't expected Calanthe Croft, leader of all vampire covens in Angelthene, to come here herself.

Apparently, Logan hadn't either. The muffled crunch of bone carried through the misty air as he fought the urge to shift at the sight of her.

"Easy," Darien muttered. "I'd be willing to bet she wants to talk first."

Calanthe's voice was strong yet feminine, old yet at the same time young. "But of course I want to talk, Darien Cassel." Damn. He'd nearly forgotten how keen a vampire's hearing was. It was even better than his own. "Especially now that I see the small battalion you've assembled for my arrival. I suppose I should feel flattered." Her short gray hair shone silver in the drumming rain.

Nobody said anything as one of the most powerful vampires to ever walk this continent strode up to their group, stopping a foot from where Logan and Darien waited at the head of it. Four bodyguards stood around her, two at each side.

And behind them, stepping out of the back seat with a fifth bodyguard, was Emilie, Calanthe's nineteen-year-old daughter and heir apparent.

At the sight of Emilie, Logan's shoulders visibly relaxed. He hadn't mentioned anything to Darien about Emilie during their many arguments these past few hours, but Darien sensed there was something going on between the two. Though Darien knew the way they looked at each other was strictly platonic; Emilie preferred the company of women to men.

To be more specific, she preferred the company of Chrysantha. Despite the centuries of hatred between werewolves and vampires, the two had been friends for years, but had become more than friends in recent months, according to rumor.

"Shall we get out of the rain, Mister Sands?" Calanthe said to Logan in a singsong voice. Emilie came up behind her, her white cherub-like face guarded, her spiky blonde hair sparkling with rain. "I'm not terribly fond of the wet and the cold."

Calanthe didn't wait for approval before strutting alongside her guards and heir apparent through the group of wolves and slayers, right up to Logan's peeling door, as if she owned the place.

Darien couldn't help but chuckle as he and the others followed them in.

DARIEN COULDN'T BELIEVE what he was hearing.

As they stood in Logan's kitchen — slightly cleaner now, thanks to

Logan having anticipated company—Calanthe waited for someone to speak. To either accept or deny the offer she'd made as she sat at the head of Logan's table. Beneath her, the chair looked more like a throne than the lopsided wooden seat it really was.

Calanthe had been notified by her people that several bounty hunters marked with a phoenix head were not only working Randal Slade's soil but were also searching for an ancient artifact called the Arcanum Well. Her eyes throughout the city—and the ongoing disappearances of mortal, college-age girls—had also alerted her to the fact that a human had something to do with it. Darien had offered up zero information about Loren, nor did he tell them about the half of the Dominus Volumen they'd found on the Angelthene Academy grounds. Neither had the other Devils—not even Lace, who Darien knew would gladly rip off Loren's face if given the chance. In fact, he and the other four Devils who were present had hardly said anything as Calanthe explained herself.

And seconds ago, Calanthe had offered to unite with the wolves and the Devils in catching those who were responsible for the missing girls and keeping the Well from falling into the wrong hands. Considering the power of Calanthe's covens, and the upper hand they would receive by having them for allies, it was almost too good to be true.

So, Darien kept his mouth shut, listening closely in case anything she said didn't add up.

It was Logan who spoke first. "Wait. You're telling me you want to *help* us." He gave the vampire an incredulous look, to which she did nothing but stare in stony silence at him. "I broke the pact. Why would you want to help us after that?"

Calanthe folded her gloved hands atop the table. "Because for the first time in what is possibly hundreds of years, we share a common enemy. And I have no interest in being ousted from my place in society to satisfy some lunatic's drive for more power."

Darien wasn't surprised Calanthe would find some way to make the situation about her. Scarlet Star forbid she be ousted by some unnamed force from her place near the very top of the corrupt hierarchy.

Where Darien was leaning against the counter by the sink, arms crossed, he said, "I have a few questions."

Calanthe cocked her head, somehow managing to look down her nose at him, despite that he was standing, and she was the only one in the room, aside from Logan, who was sitting. "I've been waiting for you to speak all afternoon, Mister Cassel. What can I do for you?"

"What do you know of this Arcanum Well? You say, 'some lunatic's drive for more power.' What do you know of this Well, and why does everyone want it?"

"According to legend, the Arcanum Well was a restorative body of water that had the ability to make a person into something Other via a process known as *transmutation*. Erasmus Sophronia and his best friend Elix Danik were two of several humans who were tired of being oppressed; tired of the bullying they were faced with throughout their years of education. I don't know how they did it, but over two thousand years ago, Erasmus Sophronia and Elix Danik created an object that turned themselves, and their friends, immortal. They called their little circle the Phoenix Head Society, named for the bird's regenerative abilities, for they, too, were regenerated by the Well. They were *reborn*. They named their act of rebirth the *Initiation*, and it was only granted to people Erasmus and Elix deemed worthy of receiving it."

Erasmus Sophronia and *Elix Danik*. Darien made a mental note of those two names so he could look into them later.

At Darien's side, Lace said, "You think someone is looking for it because they want to make themselves immortal?"

"The most obvious answer," Calanthe said patiently, "is that a mortal is behind this, Miss Rivera. Based on what little history remains of the Well and the Phoenix Head Society, one might assume that only a mortal would benefit from the creation of something like this Well. But so little information on the artifact exists that it's hard to say if granting immortal life is all the Well can do. Perhaps it can also give an immortal more power."

It was Tanner who said, "What if it has to do with the Tricking?" He drummed his fingers on the counter. "People have been looking for a cure to the Tricking for centuries; if this Well can grant immortal life or give a person more power, it might be able to heal the Tricking, too."

"Which means," Emilie continued his thought, her eyes widening with realization, "that a person would have unlimited access to their magic for the first time in history—and without the risk of getting sick."

Tanner was nodding his head. "Precisely."

"It's a highly plausible explanation," Calanthe said. "And one I commend you for making, Mister Atlas."

"And what does this have to do with a human girl?" Darien cut in. "Why look for her if it's just the Well they want?" Was it as simple as the Dominus Volumen? Would handing over the scroll make Loren safe again?

But Calanthe said, "From what I've heard, the girl is the only person in the world who has the ability to find the Well. To track it with a power she likely inherited from one of her parents."

Well, shit. This just complicated this whole mess even further.

"How is that even possible?" Lace interjected. "Humans are ordinary. They're...simple. They have never possessed magic."

Calanthe said, "That's a new mystery I don't know the answer to yet. But for a human to possess such an ability would mean their gift had to have come from a parent. If it were from a remote ancestor, the blood would be too diluted. It would've washed away through all the descendants that came before her. That is the conclusion I've drawn, at least." She gave a thoughtful hum. "If we can find out who her parents were, we might find some answers."

Little did Calanthe know that Darien was already trying to do this. He wouldn't tell her—not now, not ever.

The vampire allowed them a moment to process what she'd told them. And when she spoke again, her words were only for Logan. "If you refuse my offer to unite against this common enemy, I will need to re-evaluate the situation. Siding with me and catching those responsible for coveting this artifact would clear your name, Mister Sands. We would forgive and forget that the pact has been broken."

Before Logan could reply, Darien said, "I have another question." If Calanthe really expected him to side with her, he'd need proof that her intentions were genuine. Who was to say Calanthe wasn't wanting Loren and the Arcanum Well for herself?

Calanthe waited.

"This seems like a whole lot of legwork for you," Darien began. "Your fear of being ousted from your place in society can't be the only reason you're wanting to stop the Phoenix Head cult from finding the Well. Care to explain what your other motivations are?"

He blinked his Sight into place, and even though he knew Calanthe would be aware of what he was doing—checking her aura for any signs that she was lying—he did it anyway.

Calanthe assessed him for a long time. And then she reached into the inside pocket of her jacket, retrieved a handful of photographs, and spread them on the table before her.

Everyone in the room grew very silent. Darien didn't need to move from his place by the sink to see the horror displayed in the photos.

"Penny Thompson turned up dead last night in the District of Drakon, not far from the House of the Blood Rose," Calanthe said in a low voice. "I don't think I need to explain how bad this looks for my people." A human had turned up dead on vampire soil, not far from the mansion that housed Calanthe's Elite Coven. In all of Angelthene, there were only three places with the highest security and protection spells on the continent: Hell's Gate, the Avenue of the Scarlet Star, and the entirety of the District of Drakon—Vampire Territory. The fact that a girl had turned up dead in a place like this was...well, it was bad, to say the very least.

Tanner and Maximus had stepped closer to examine the photos. Penny Thompson had been the victim of a Blood Stave, an illegally altered Focus with blood magic at its core. Her body had been partially melted into an exterior brick wall of a building in the District of Drakon. The way her corpse hung on that wall reminded Darien of a hunting trophy. Blood was streaming from her closed eyes, and shimmering magic swept upward and out on the wall behind her in a pattern that seemed deliberate, her death every bit the symbol as the tattoo these wannabe Darkslayers wore below their ears.

Tanner said, "The way the magic is splattered on the wall looks like wings."

"Wings of flame," Max corrected, his gaze flicking to Darien.

"I want to catch the people responsible for the missing girls," Calanthe said. "And I want to make sure the Arcanum Well does not fall into the wrong hands. It must return to how it was before: a secret. Nothing but an old legend no one believes." She swept up the photographs and slid them back into her pocket. "If you still need convincing, I'll have you know that one of the vampires of Drakon went missing just last night. Lenora Aldonold."

Darien recognized the name. "She's one of your own." A member of the House of the Blood Rose.

Calanthe's aura displayed no signs that she was lying. In fact, it was drooping and tinged with shades that spelled grief. "She is not only one of my own, but she is my Second. The fact that she was taken is a great concern for me." There was a pause, and then the vampire said, "Are you satisfied with everything my aura tells you, Mister Cassel? I'm not enough of a fool as to think I can lie to someone as gifted in the Sight as yourself."

The black left his eyes with a blink, and Calanthe gave him a little smile that still echoed the grief her aura told him she was feeling.

And then she turned to Emilie, who stood at her side, and stroked her cheek with a gloved knuckle. "As if all that isn't reason enough, my daughter has decided to shed light on some recent events, and although I admit she is a bit of an idealist when it comes to her hopes for the future, as my heir apparent I am willing to give her a chance and try something different this time. Finding Chrysantha Sands will do us all some good, I would think."

Ah, yes. Emilie's hope for the future that most people thought laughable: a world where vampires and werewolves could live in harmony. A world where no pact would be necessary, and the two species could mingle without the bone-deep hatred that had divided them for so many centuries. A world where she and Chrysantha could be together without judgement.

And her mother was indeed willing to try something different this time. To side with wolves instead of fighting with them.

Calanthe looked about the room, at the werewolves and Dark-slayers crammed shoulder-to-shoulder with a small number of the vampires in her coven. "Will you accept my offer?"

"Consider it a yes from my Devils and me," Darien said. He would keep Calanthe and her coven at a distance, make sure they never found out he and the Devils had the key to the Arcanum Well currently living under their roof. He would take it step by step, being careful the whole way, and would use Calanthe's strength as a City Head to put a stop to the Phoenix Head cult that was looking for Loren.

Calanthe looked pleased with his decision. And then she looked at Logan and awaited his answer with an unblinking gaze.

Logan mulled it over. The other werewolves in the room made no noise as they waited for their Alpha to speak.

Logan sighed and dropped his hand to the table. "We're in."

Calanthe flashed a smile that showed her thin, elongated incisors. "Good." One of her bodyguards shifted her chair back, and she rose to her feet. "I think we'll get along just fine, given the situation."

"Vampires and wolves, working together," Logan mused. "Never thought I'd see the day."

"I wouldn't get too comfortable, Mister Sands. Might I remind you that the borders and the pact still stand? Regardless of you having recently broken it." Grace given life, Calanthe headed for the door, wrapping her trench coat tightly around her body. "My people will contact yours, should I receive any valuable information." She scanned the kitchen, making eye contact with every person—slayer and werewolf—present. "Until then."

Flanked by her bodyguards, she vanished into the rain, Emilie at her side. As the door closed behind them, leaving nothing behind that would indicate any vampires had been here but the scent of roses, Darien remembered an old proverb.

The enemy of my enemy is my friend.

"I THOUGHT you were fluent in Ancient Reunerian," Logan said to Darien as he took a swig of beer. The wolf was lounging across from him at the patio table at Hell's Gate, watching with amusement as he and Loren jotted down letters in the open notebook that sat between them. A full moon hung overhead, brightening the night. "Why's a little scroll like that taking you so long to decipher?"

Darien pulled his gaze from the lantern-lit Dominus Volumen and shot Logan a hard look. "Why don't you go play fetch with the Familiars? I'm sure they would love for a pup like you to join in on their fun."

In the center of the yard, not far from where Sabrine and Ivy were roasting coco-mallows over the firepit, Darien's Familiar sparred with Dallas's winged tiger for a murkball the witch had thrown into the shrubs.

Logan gave Darien a dirty look but got up and went to join Sabrine at the firepit. The wolf-witch looked more than a little happy to see Logan approaching her, and Darien was more than a little happy to be alone with Loren. The clock had ticked at a painfully slow pace all day until he was finally able to get back to Hell's Gate and see her again.

Paper fluttered as Loren flipped through the book on Ancient Reunerian. It was their last day before the old tome would teleport itself back to the library. Darien had deciphered enough of the scroll to conclude that the chemicals the Butcher's anonymous client had ordered were the very same ones necessary to create the Arcanum Well, written in the scroll under codenames that'd taken a million years to decipher. But it wasn't just the chemicals that were needed.

The scroll spoke of a material that formed the Well itself—the *tub*, for lack of a better word. But that part of the scroll involved words so ageless and elusive, even this old book insisted on keeping them secret. Darien hoped if they could find out what this Arcanum Well was made of, he might be able to track it with the Sight. Magical artifacts tended to exude their own color into the universe— a vibration he might be able to nail down and trace.

Loren had seemed just as surprised as Darien to hear of the information Calanthe had given them earlier that day—and just as doubtful as Darien that she had any magical tracking ability that might help them find the Well. There had to be a mistake; Loren was human, there was no doubt about that. Perhaps she *was* related to someone who had been able to track or use this Well, but the odds of her having inherited a magical ability like this... It was unheard of. And it was out of simple curiosity that he had asked Loren earlier that evening to reach within herself, to see if she could *feel* something in her soul, the same way he could feel the Sight—could feel his various magical gifts. She had come up empty, and more than a little frustrated.

If anyone would be able to track the Well, it would be a hellse-her, as long as they knew what material to look for. Darien wasn't certain what they would do with the Well if they *did* manage to find it; he would cross one bridge at a time and see where they ended up.

"I think I might've figured out what this part says," Loren said, her soft voice coaxing him out of the depths of his thoughts. She was sitting so close to him that her thigh was pressed against his, the warmth from her body spreading into his. Her dog was sprawled out at her feet, nose whistling as he slept.

A gust of wind threatened to tear the scroll out from under the chunks of crystal they were using as paper weights. Darien reached over and flattened the fluttering paper with a hand as she read aloud.

> "I am male and female,
> everything and nothing.
> I am heaven and earth,
> Body and spirit.
> The rainbow,
> the blood of the soul,
> the fiery and burning water.
> I am..."

When she glanced up at him, Darien found himself more at awe of the way her ocean eyes glinted in the moonlight than the fact that she seemed to have deciphered the most confusing part of the scroll.

"It's one giant riddle." She blew out a long sigh. "Every time we find an answer, there's always another question."

"This book is going back to the shelf soon," he said, "so let's look over what we've got."

She slid the notebook his way, and he read aloud from the middle section of the scroll.

> "Mortal is my father,
> Fire my mother.
> I shall tell you my secret,
> Oh, curious one.
> I am the Master,
> the one true god.
>
> The firewater be my child,
> my book of creation.
> It is a song in my heart,
> and it shall answer only one call
> The blood of my blood.
>
> Far and wide you may search,
> Long and hard you may build.
> But be recreated it cannot,
> nor replicated,
> nor destroyed.
> Only Remade.
>
> Death is only the beginning.
>
> From Stella I was born,
> from Luna,
> Sapientia,
> Ignis,
> And the Liar.

I am male and female,
everything and nothing.
I am heaven and earth
Body and spirit.

The rainbow,
the blood of the soul,
the fiery and burning water.

I am..."

For a long while, only the crackle of the fire filled the silence.

And then the book vanished from right under Loren's elbow, her arm clunking to the table.

"I guess that solves that," she grumbled.

Darien slid an arm around her shoulders and pulled her snug against his side. Her heart picked up speed at the contact; he could hear it as clearly as the cicadas humming in the palm trees. The feel of her aura flush against his made his skin tingle, made him want to have her closer still.

They sat in silence for a while, the scroll fluttering under the paperweights. With Sabrine safe, there was only Loren to worry about. And Darien wouldn't stop worrying, wouldn't stop trying to figure out what this scroll meant and how the Well was created.

If they could find the Well, they might be able to destroy it—to get rid of it once and for all and make Loren safe again.

But he couldn't stop thinking about that part of the scroll—the part that said it could not be replicated, nor destroyed. If that were true, would he ever be able to make her safe again?

Darien peered down at Loren to see that her eyelids had slipped shut. She was slumped against his side, her mouth parting as she drifted off.

He *would* make her safe again. Nothing bad would happen to her.

Not while he was still breathing.

LOREN WAS fast asleep in her suite at Hell's Gate when something cold and wet slapped her in the cheek.

Groggy, she sat up, untangling herself from the blankets that had ensnared her limbs. Utterly confused, she peered into the darkness of her bedroom.

A moment later, another cold, hard object hit her in the forehead. She hissed, pain blooming across her skin. "Hey!" she exclaimed, turning toward the unlit fireplace, where the object had come from.

Ice, she realized. Ice chips.

Mortifer had made good on his promise.

Loren made to say something, but the Hob threw another ice chip. "I'm awake, you pest!" she whispered.

She turned her attention toward the door then, watching the sliver of golden light beneath it for any sign of movement. If the Hob had woken her up, that meant Darien must be having a rough night.

Boots struck the floor as someone walked down the hallway. She watched as a shadow briefly blotted out the light under her door as that someone made for the staircase.

She had a pretty good idea who it was.

Loren swung her legs over the side of the bed, slipped her feet into her fuzzy slippers, and tiptoed into the hallway. Before she closed the door behind her, she whispered, "Thank you." She wasn't sure if Mortifer heard, but she had a feeling he did.

She had just made it down the stairs to the entrance hall as Darien was donning a dark gray jacket. His jeans were ripped and blackened with old blood, and his boots were the same bloodied-up pair he was wearing the first time she had tried to stop him from leaving the house at an ungodly hour.

His eyes were also as black as they had been that same night as they snapped to her face.

"What are you doing up?" he asked, his voice flat.

Loren stepped off the bottom stair she was lingering on, her fingers trailing off the polished handrail. "I heard you leaving, and I wanted to see if you were..." Her voice faded as it felt like someone punched her in the stomach. The grief that was etched into his features was so unbearable to look at, she almost couldn't squeeze out the words. But she managed to finish her sentence with a whispered, "I wanted to see if you were okay."

She wasn't sure how it was possible for his face to crumple when he already looked so broken, but it did.

"I haven't been okay since I was fifteen," he said in a hoarse whisper. The year his mother had died.

Loren felt her heart ice over and splinter.

And as Darien ducked his head and stalked toward the front door, one hand gripping the strap of the duffel that was slung over his shoulder, Loren hurried forward and blocked his path to the door. The wood of that door was cold as ice through her pyjama shirt as she pressed her back flat against it and looked up at him. He was mere inches away from her, looking more torn than ever, looking desperate to get out of here but more desperate not to disappoint her.

She held her hands out to him, palms up. He dipped his head slowly and studied her palms for a long time. And then, finally, he placed one of his hands in hers, his fingers shaking just slightly. His hand dwarfed hers, and a heat that was deep and inviting spread from his skin to hers.

"I want to try something," she whispered.

Darien's eyelids slid shut. "Loren."

"Humor me." She closed her fingers around his hand and gently tugged him toward the living room. "Please. If this doesn't work, you can go to your fighting ring. I promise."

The duffel on his shoulder slid to the floor with a thump as he let Loren tow him into the living room. She brought him to the couch, let go of his hand, and pushed down on his shoulders, forcing him to sit.

Loren sank to the carpet before him, and Darien spread his knees far enough apart for her to sit at his feet without the risk of bumping into the coffee table at her back. She took both of his hands into her own, lacing her fingers with his, and closed her eyes.

When she felt Darien's fingers tighten slightly around her own, she knew he'd put two and two together regarding what she was trying to do.

"Loren." His voice was gruff. "Sweetheart..."

"Don't laugh at me for trying," Loren pleaded, keeping her eyes closed. "Just…let me try." She paused, nerves curling in the pit of her stomach. "Close your eyes please."

She peeked at him for just a moment, only long enough to see that he'd done as she'd requested. There was such vulnerability on his handsome face, the sight of it so raw that Loren had the sense that she was witnessing something incredibly intimate. A secret he guarded with his life, ever since he was a child told by his abusive father that strong was all a man should be.

Loren began to feel shy as Darien waited for her to do whatever it was that she thought would help him. Suddenly, she wasn't sure, and as the seconds ticked by, she began to feel like a fool. She was human and possessed no magical powers, least of all aura healing. Regardless of what Calanthe seemed to think, Loren knew they were all mistaken. And if no real Aura Healers had been able to help Darien, there was no way she would make a difference.

But…she'd made it this far. And she wanted so badly to help him that she tried. Gods help her, she tried.

She focused every good and happy thought, every positive emotion in her body on him, envisioning them flowing from her heart and into his like a river of color, filling in the cracks and hollows in his like a river of color, filling in the cracks and hollows in his soul, making him a little more whole than he was before. She pictured color and light driving out the darkness, stitching together the damaged and murky bits of his psyche until all those old wounds were healed over, never to reopen again.

"I want you to picture a river," she whispered, her voice barely audible. "The waters of the river are crystal clear, and the sun refracts off the surface like a prism. The different colors are all so beautiful, they take your breath away. I want you to follow the river —follow it right down to where it bleeds into the ocean. I'll follow it with you. The ocean goes on as far as the eye can see, and it is every shade of blue you can dream up. There is no sound except the ocean waves. There is no one around but us. It is calm. It is relaxing. It is… peaceful." She swallowed. "It *is* peace."

She might've been imagining it, but she swore there was a soft heat spreading through her chest, like she was clutching a hot water bottle to her body. Not wanting to break the illusion that she was actually doing something to help Darien, she didn't open her eyes, focusing only on the image in her mind, willing for the camera in her thoughts to expand, encompassing Darien's and bringing them both into the same imaginary space.

As Loren watched the foamy ocean waves in her mind, the feeling of Darien's fingers lightly squeezing hers coaxed her back to reality. It wasn't until she'd opened her eyes that she realized her lashes were damp.

Darien gently extracted his left hand from hers and tilted her chin up, so she was looking at him.

His eyes were no longer black.

The Surge was gone.

Had *she* done that? Was she stupid for even thinking she had?

Those eyes tightened a little. "How did you—" He paused, and he used his thumb to gently wipe away a tear that slipped down her cheek. "Loren..." He opened his mouth to say something else—

But the front door suddenly opened, and Jack, Ivyana, and Travis returned from outside, where they had been drinking by the firepit. They were laughing drunkenly, their arms slung across each other's shoulders.

Darien only spared his family half a glance as they headed straight for the fridge before his focus returned to Loren. "You look exhausted," he said, his thumb brushing across her chin. Her breath caught in her lungs as that thumb swept over her lips, the contact causing her skin to tingle. His hand was rough and warm and inviting, and everywhere he touched, there was heat. A deep, rosy heat, and she didn't want him to stop. But he said gently, "Go on and get some rest."

When he released her face, a golden warmth lingered there. She instantly missed it, and she found that she had to close her own fingers into fists to keep from reaching for him.

"Are you okay?" she whispered.

It took him a moment to answer. "I'm okay," he said. "For now." Seeing the question in her eyes, he added, "I'm not leaving anymore. Not tonight." He took her hands into his, though only long enough to pull her to her feet with him. And he increased the volume of his voice as he said to his family with the hint of a smile, "But I *am* going to get the hell away from these chickens and their loud clucking."

Clucking was exactly what they started doing, and Jack even went so far as to flap his arms as if they were wings.

Darien rolled his eyes. "How'd I get so lucky?" he muttered, shaking his head. When he said it, he was looking at Loren, not in search of an answer, but as if he'd meant to say that she was a large part of the reason he felt lucky.

Loren yawned. She was suddenly so exhausted that she had no room in her body for more emotions.

"Don't make me carry you," Darien threatened mildly.

She waved him away. "Alright, I'm going. Big, bad Devil."

When she made it to the bottom of the staircase, she turned around to see that he hadn't moved, but was watching her with a kind of tender affection she'd never seen on his face before.

33

"I can't believe you just blew two hundred gold mynet on face jellies," Darien said.

Loren slid her wallet into her purse with one hand, the other grasping the ice-cream cone that was melting faster than she could lick it. *"Face jellies?"* She snorted a laugh.

Where he was walking at her side down the Avenue of the Scarlet Star, hair gobbling up the sunlight, Darien gave a wave of his hand, the devil rings on his index and middle fingers flashing a bright silver. "You know what I mean."

"I can't be sure," she teased, "but I *think* what you mean is *skin-care.*" Hoisting up the strap of her bag, she took a generous lick of her raspberry-flavored treat, the ice-cream inlaid with bits of bubble-gum. "We live in a semi-arid climate, Darien. My face needs hydration. I'm too young to start getting wrinkles."

"There has to be something you can use that doesn't cost half as much."

"Would you stop complaining?" She batted her eyelashes at him. "I can think of far better things for you to do with that mouth."

Darien blinked. And then he threw his head back and howled with laughter. "I can't believe you just said that to me." He was laughing so hard, his eyes were watering. He swiped at the corner of one with a knuckle. "You are just too much fun."

Loren herself was trying not to laugh, though she was doing a horrible job of it. "No one's ever given you a taste of your own filthy medicine, have they?"

"Not until you came along, Rookie." His phone buzzed, and he slid it out of his pocket and glanced at the screen. "Would you give me a minute, please?"

While he took the call, Loren stepped up to a jewelry kiosk near Ella and Prince. The vendor sold a variety of enchanted rings and anklets, magical symbols etched into each one. Little cardboard labels taped below the displays explained which piece of jewelry was enchanted with what spell. The possibilities were endless, most of them vain.

She was inquiring about a tongue stud that could change a person's eye color—a stud to replace the one currently hiding her freckles—when screaming barrelled down the avenue.

Loren barely had time to register what was happening before a blur slammed into her and she was thrown headfirst into the jewelry kiosk.

THE DEMON WAS FASTER than any Darien had hunted before, but he was faster.

He moved like shadow and wind, sprinting for the demon at a speed no mortal eye could track. As he ran, he fired two shots, bullets peeling through the sultry late-afternoon air. People screamed and fell as they scrambled out of his way, faces stricken with terror.

The bullets tore, one after the other, into the back of the creature's skull. But it didn't fall.

And as it whirled his way, triangular nostrils flaring, Darien rallied his magic.

As a hellseher, his perception of time was different. He could see things in slow motion, could smell and taste and feel every little thing that was happening in a millisecond, every miniscule detail that flew undetected under the noses of ordinary people.

The dark trickle of blood catching the sunlight as it seeped from the gash in the demon's temple; Loren gathering her bearings, ice-cream streaming down the front of her sundress; the people in the avenue scuttling for safety; shop doors slamming shut; stray napkins fluttering beneath silverware and werewolf-friendly cutlery on the outdoor food tables; fronds of palm trees scraping down the avenue.

His magic rent the air, and as the demon lunged for him, Darien mentally drove his power up in a slicing motion that only *he* could see and feel.

The demon's head broke off its shoulders. Blood sprayed from a severed artery, and it collapsed to the cobbles, the momentum behind its attack causing it to slide several feet before it stilled, two inches from his boots.

Time resumed its usual pace as Darien quieted the roaring power within him.

Loren was floundering about in the mess of wood and jewelry. Darien quickly holstered his pistol and made his way to her side. When he reached her, she was pressing a hand against her temple and staggering to her feet, barely able to stay upright in the destruction that was the jewelry kiosk. Behind her, the vendor cowered against the locked door of Ella and Prince.

"Did it bite you?" Darien's throat felt tight as he looked her over, his heart slamming in his chest. This was new to him; he was very good at staying calm.

What was he becoming?

Loren was in so much shock, she barely managed to shake her head in answer.

Afraid she might faint, he made to gather her into his arms, but she blinked and stepped away from his touch, staring down the avenue at the terrified people observing from a distance. Phones were glued to ears, and crying children clutched their mother's skirts.

"It doesn't make any sense," Loren mumbled.

"Loren." Darien gathered up the paper shopping bags of jellies—the *skincare* that she'd refused to let him purchase for her—and followed her as she drifted down the street. Her dress swished against her thighs. "Loren, sweetheart. I think you're in shock. You should sit down."

"The demon, Darien." She turned to face him, though her eyes were distant, and they wouldn't meet his own. "It shouldn't have made it onto the avenue. The spells here...they're even more powerful than those at the academy. Even *you* had trouble getting us into the Old Hall. And even then, it was only possible because Tanner had generated an outage."

"What are you saying?"

Her hair caught the sunlight as she shook her head. "The demons... What if they're not demons at all? What if they're connected to the missing students? What if..." She finally looked at him. "What if they *are* the missing students?"

Darien's mind reeled as he followed her train of thought. "And the spells here and on the schoolgrounds allowed them into the area because they still recognize their DNA," Darien concluded. "They still recognize them as citizens and students."

Holy burning Ignis.

The anima mundi—the world soul and the source of all magic in Terra, including forcefields—could not be fooled so easily. It was the same as glamors; witches or warlocks who used magic to glamor themselves might fool the naked eye, but they could never trick the forcefields, nor could they trick cameras. There were some things magic simply did not work on.

Darien spun around, surveying the avenue. There were too many people, too many prying eyes. Too many cell phones that could snap pictures or record video at any second, if he tried to take the demon or any part of it for testing. The blood he'd dropped off to Arthur, a weapons technician who worked for Lucent Enterprises... He should've taken more; shouldn't have been so quick to burn the body.

Sirens began to wail in the distance.

"We need to go," Loren said.

He was already at her side, a hand on her elbow, walking so quickly she could hardly keep up with him.

341

"That's why Tanner could only kill the other one with chrysolite and silver," Darien said, mostly to himself as they reached his car. "Whatever—*whoever*—that demon was... If you're right, Loren, then the demon at the Rapids must've been part-wolf, and part-witch." Silver for wolves; chrysolite for witches and warlocks.

Once they were in the car, Loren buckled her seatbelt, the *click* loud in the silence, and said, "What do we do now?"

Darien scrubbed his face with his hands. "I don't know," he admitted. "But if we're right, then we need to find a way to change them back. I'll have Tanner talk to Doctor Atlas and we'll see if she can figure anything out. Maybe she can look into making an anti-dote." He looked her over—the dress that was sticky with ice-cream and stained with blood, the tiny wood shavings stuck in her hair. "I think it's also high time you had a weapon so that you can protect yourself."

Loren slanted an eyebrow. "I thought *you* were my weapon, Darien Cassel."

But he didn't laugh. "I was distracted for *two* minutes, Loren." Blood was streaming down her leg, and bruises were already blooming on her sun-burned arms. "That could've ended really badly. Are you okay?"

"I'm fine." But she was still shaking, and she wouldn't look at him. He was starting to be able to read her tells without needing to see her aura.

She suddenly eyed him up, her features exceptionally soft. The sunlight slanting through the windshield turned her eyes a stunning shade of turquoise.

Darien stared back at her, longing to know the answers to her soul, wanting to learn every part of her, inside and out. The need to touch her, to comfort her and to know her on a deeper level, hit him like a fist to the stomach. He had no idea what emotions his face betrayed, but something flitted across Loren's own features. A look of worry, he thought. Or perhaps understanding.

"You're a good guy, Darien." Her voice was gentler than he'd ever heard it before. She was letting that stubborn wall of hers down, letting *him* in. "You know that, right?"

Darien had no words. And that wall she was slowly demolishing...it shouldn't come down. Not for someone like him. She deserved someone...better. Someone who couldn't hurt her by simply *existing*.

"Loren..." The way her name left his lips was raw and vulnerable, just like how his soul felt. How his heart felt.

"Oh, right. Sorry." She waved a scraped hand. "You're not *a* devil, you're *the* devil. I forgot."

She was getting too close to him, becoming too attached. And it was *his* fault. He had to put some distance between them to keep her safe, but the word *distance* made him literally want to die. He couldn't imagine being away from her—not after everything they'd been through.

But this wasn't about him.

He didn't allow himself to think about it any longer, especially when a slit in the side of her dress caught his attention.

"You ripped your pretty dress." *Pretty* was a massive fucking understatement.

Loren peered under her arm, at the tear that exposed her ribs. Darien's blood boiled at the sight of the wound—another scar on her perfect body. She would live, but he didn't like seeing her hurt.

If he was being completely honest with himself, he hated it.

"I just bought this," she muttered.

"Did it cost you two hundred gold mynet?"

"Don't be silly," she tsked. "It cost me two hundred and fifty."

Darien grinned. "You're a riot." He started the car and sped them to Hell's Gate.

34

The Devils had a shooting range in the basement at Hell's Gate, where they set up an assortment of targets for Loren, Dallas, and Sabrine to practice on, including clay pigeons that were fired into the vicinity by an auto-feed trap.

Darien worked with Loren, showing her how to shoot everything from a pistol to an automatic rifle. She found the whole thing interesting and even fun, though a few of the guns had enough kickback to bruise the muscles in her shoulder.

The basement air held a medley of sulphur, charcoal, and saltpeter. The smell reminded Loren of fireworks as she took aim at a target thirty yards away.

"Little higher," Darien murmured at her side.

But she brought up the gun a smidge too much. He placed his hands on hers and corrected its position, his calloused fingers brushing against hers. When she squeezed the trigger, the bullet tore a bull's eye through the chest of the paper target.

Darien wore a smug grin. "Beautiful," he said. "Do it again."

The hour continued like that. And perhaps she was imagining it, but Darien seemed to take any excuse to touch her, even to adjust the location of her fingers on the various guns.

And when her lessons brought her to another of the ten shooting stalls in the long room—all with varying ranges of distance—and she set up her rifle on the muzzle stanchion, he sat at her side, a hand braced on the back of her chair. Between shots, she caught him looking at her, and it wasn't always at her eyes. In fact, most of the time he was looking at her mouth.

Loren's body absorbed the kickback as she fired a shot at the last clay pigeon that spun through the air. It cracked and fell to the floor, where it shattered into smaller pieces.

A grin split across her face, and she clicked the safety into position and leaned back in the chair, where she found herself so close to Darien—whose legs were braced on either side of her, and whose hand was still on the back of the chair—that she could feel his body heat. Could smell the cool bite of the aftershave on his skin.

His eyes crinkled with a smile as he said something, but she couldn't hear a word.

"I'm sorry," she said with a laugh as she pulled her headphones off. Sound flooded her ears. "Can you repeat that?"

"I said you're an ace at this, Lola." The nickname made her blush, made her duck her head a little, hair falling in her face.

Several stalls over, Travis took aim at a target a sniper's length away. This one was generated by the house's spellwork—by the Hob himself. And it was Mortifer's grinning, black-flamed face that began zipping through the range. A ghostly giggle swept through the room as the Hob moved with blinding speed.

Six shots cracked through the room—six bull's eyes that tore right through the phantom projection of the Hob's face.

Travis whooped and threw a fist in the air. "Suck on that, dickbags!" The fist he was holding up switched to a middle finger that he threw in the direction of Jack and Tanner, who were standing nearly, looking unimpressed. "I hope you were watching, Max, because you and these sore losers each owe me fifty gold mynet."

Max was sorting through boxes of ammunition in the cupboards lining the wall. "I think the next bet I'll make you is which of us can go longer without cussing than the other." It was to Darien that he added, "Your phone's been going off nonstop, man." He snatched up

Darien's phone that was sitting atop a cupboard and held it out to him in offer.

Darien finished reloading Loren's rifle before he passed it into her waiting hands and strode over to take the phone from Max. His eyes scanned the screen as he read the messages.

"It's just Jessa," he mumbled, mostly to himself, and began typing.

Something in Loren's stomach tightened, her fingers doing the same on the gun.

"She still trying to date you, or what?" Travis said.

"The word *date* isn't in my vocabulary, Trav."

Maximus snorted as he began loading up a pistol. "I hope you didn't tell her that."

"I did." Darien chuckled, thumbs still tapping on the screen. "I also told her I don't know what *dinner* means unless it involves her kneeling stark naked before me, and she's the only one of us getting fed." The males in the room roared with laughter.

In the booth beside Loren's, Lace muttered, "Men."

Jack could barely contain his laughter long enough to bite out, "You're a savage."

Tanner said, "And she still wants to see you after that?"

Darien shrugged. "Apparently."

Loren's whole body was burning. The enjoyment of the evening suddenly vanished as sickness twisted deep in her gut.

Where was a hole to crawl into when she needed one?

Darien slipped his phone into the back pocket of his jeans. "Let's go for one more round, Lola." He didn't need to say that he was going to leave after that round—to go and see whoever *Jessa* was. To strip off her clothes until she was stark naked on her knees before him.

"Actually." Loren set down the rifle. "I'm good."

Darien stared at her in bewilderment as she pushed out from the stall and made a beeline to the staircase. She didn't care that everyone had stopped shooting and was now watching her. And she didn't care when Dallas and Sabrine called her name in concern.

She was halfway up the stairs when Darien voiced a question, the words floating to her above the quiet that had swept through the range. "What did I say?"

The crack of bullets resumed. Loren pushed open the door at the top of the stairs, the warmth of the ground floor wrapping around her limbs. Jack whooped in delight as he presumably hit a bull's-eye, the Hob cackling again.

Ivyana sighed. "You know, for someone so smart, you sure can be dumb, Darien."

Loren didn't hear anything else after that. She didn't exactly understand what she was feeling, nor what she'd expected to happen from crushing on someone like Darien.

But she supposed she'd simply hoped it wouldn't have been this.

"WHERE DO you think you're going?"

At the sound of his sister's voice, Darien froze near the base of the broad staircase in the entrance hall. He turned around to see Ivyana watching him—arms crossed, weight tipped to one leg. An eyebrow lifted as she looked him over.

He threw his hands up in a hell-if-I-know gesture. "I'm going to talk to Loren."

Ivyana's frown deepened. "You'd better not make it worse, Darien." He was far from clueless when it came to women, but for some time he'd been ignoring all signs that pointed to Loren having feelings for him beyond simple attraction. It couldn't happen; he wouldn't let it. Not because he didn't want it to, but because it wasn't safe—for *her*.

He wasn't safe for her.

As if reading his mind, Ivy said, "I always thought you knew what you were doing when it comes to women, but if you couldn't even tell that Loren is majorly crushing on you, then you truly are hopeless, Darien." When Darien didn't say anything, understanding washed across Ivy's face, and her slender shoulders slumped. "Gods. You *knew*, didn't you? You were trying to push her away."

Darien still wouldn't say anything.

"That is a new low for you, brother—"

"She can't fall for me, Ivy," Darien cut in. "She can't." It was part of the reason he'd been in touch with Jessa today; why he'd been the one to contact the copper-haired Viper for once, instead of the other way around. He'd hoped Loren would've been so turned off after hearing about his booty-call that she would stop looking at him the way she did. The only problem was that he *liked* the way she looked at him—as if he was worth something. He liked it a little too much.

Ivyana looked like she'd expected Darien to say as much and was more than a little disappointed by it. "And why is that?" She was always the rational one; the twin who knew how to handle problems that couldn't be solved by hitting things. Even in the days when their mother was alive, Darien was known by friends of the family as the *problem twin.*

He could still hear those whispers as if they'd been uttered only yesterday, things like, "That boy's going to be trouble one day," and, "Looks like Emberley's had herself a little devilish child." To be fair, their father had sunk his claws into Darien a lot faster than he had Ivyana.

Darien had made damn sure of that.

"Because…" His hands curled into fists. "You saw what happened with Mom and Dad. I won't do that to her. I refuse to ruin her the way Dad ruined Mom."

Ivy's gaze softened. With every day that passed, she looked more like the face tattooed on his forearm—like Elsie Cassel, the woman who'd raised them, the lost soul who'd given herself a new name when she'd run away with the man she loved. "You're not our father, Darien. You're *not* Dad." She looked him over. "You can't deny yourself happiness forever—"

"Yes, I can," he interrupted softly. "I can and I will. If my happiness involves the possibility of hurting someone like Loren, then I will *happily* be miserable forever."

Seeing the look on his face that brooked no contestation, she blew out a sigh. But her expression was soon hardening again. "Why Jessa?" she demanded. "What's going on with that? You haven't seen her in, like, a year."

He shrugged. Ran a hand through his undercut, smoothing the strands back. "I just wanted to forget," he whispered. "Even for one night." It was the truth: Loren made him feel things he'd never felt before. And truth be told, it scared him. And even though his plan involving Jessa was mostly to push Loren away, he was hoping that by meeting up with the Viper, it would smother the emotions out of him, even for a few hours. Would force him to remember why, until Loren had come along, all he'd needed was cold, hard no-strings-attached-sex.

Reading his mind, Ivy said, "You thought you could forget about Loren by making some meaningless booty call to one of your groupies?"

He snorted a humorless laugh at how filthy that sounded — and how filthy it made him feel. Another strange and foreign emotion for him. "I know — stupid, right? But it's what I do best." Fucking, killing, fighting — those were the things he was good at. "I'm not good with…" He waved a hand. "Whatever this is."

Ivy fought a smile. *"Feelings,* brother?"

"Yeah." He sighed through his nose. "I'm not good with them."

She jerked her chin toward the stairs. "Go talk to her." Turning on a heel, she drifted toward the shooting range. "And for the love of the Star, call that damn Viper and tell her you're not available anymore — *ever.* You can thank me later."

———

LOREN WAS HURLING her things into her suitcase when a knock came at her door.

She wasn't sure what she was doing, but she didn't want to stay here, at least not tonight. A little voice in her head told her she was being ridiculous. Childish, even. What Darien did in his spare time, and who he did it with, wasn't any of her business. But her heart was telling her to run, and it had no interest in behaving rationally. When she'd come to Hell's Gate that very first time, she'd only hoped to get Sabrine back. She hadn't planned for…well, *this.*

Falling for Darien had never been part of the plan.

"It's open," she mumbled.

The handle turned, and Darien stepped in. He looked her over before his gaze found the half-packed suitcase on her bed. She wasn't sure if she was imagining it, but she swore his features fell at the sight of the near-empty drawers. In the weeks that'd passed, she hadn't realized how many of her belongings had wound up here.

"What's going on, Lola?" Although he tried to make the question sound casual, his voice was low and gruff with emotions she couldn't nail down.

"Nothing." She grabbed another shirt from the drawer and refolded it. "Don't you have somewhere to be?"

Silence. And then, "I cancelled."

She grabbed another shirt and stuffed it into the suitcase. "That didn't seem like what you wanted a few minutes ago."

"I never wanted —," he broke off. She peeked at him to see that he was glaring at the oil painting on the wall. "I don't want Jessa."

Loren had nothing to say to that. Embarrassment had closed her vision in, making her feel like she should only look at the floor, at anything but Darien. Her face had flooded with heat, and her throat felt like a hand was squeezing it shut.

Heavy boots pounded on the floorboards as Darien strode over and took a seat at the foot of her bed, the wrought-iron creaking under his weight. She could feel him watching her for a time before he whispered, "I don't want you to leave, Loren."

Her eyes burned, but she forced back the tears. "I don't want to leave either."

He rubbed at the back of his neck. Another of her shirts hung limp in her hands, but she didn't fold it, nor did she stuff it into the suitcase. With every second that dragged by, she began to feel more ashamed by her own behaviour.

When Darien lifted his head, his eyes were more conflicted than she'd ever seen them as he scanned every part of her face. She didn't let herself imagine that he was looking the longest at her mouth again; she didn't need any more hurt. "What're we doing, Loren?"

She tried to swallow, but her heart was choking her. "I could ask you the same thing."

He simply shook his head, looking like he had about as much of an idea as she did. Neither of them had planned for this.

Loren glared at the zipper on her suitcase, hoping like hell that the tears burning at the backs of her eyes wouldn't betray her. With a sigh, she tossed the shirt she was still holding aside and scrubbed her hands over her face.

"Do you believe a person can change?" Darien said into the quiet room. "If they really want to?"

The breath Loren drew trembled. She wasn't sure where this question of his was coming from, but it sounded like her answer really meant something to him. "I believe, if a person has gotten so far as to ask that question, then they stand a fighting chance."

He nodded subtly, and this time it was Darien who seemed to have trouble looking at her. "Despite what you said about me earlier, I'm not a good person, Loren," Darien whispered, the words barely audible. "I kill, I lie, I…"

Loren forced herself to keep breathing. "But do you lie to me?"

His features softened. "No. Of course not. But that doesn't make who I am any better, Loren." He inhaled through his nose, chest rising with the movement, and then he blew the breath out in a sigh as he admitted, "I might've said all that stuff down there to see how you'd react."

Loren blinked. "You were trying to make me jealous?"

"Something like that," he mumbled. The look on his face suggested there was more to this story—a part he wasn't willing to explain to her.

Her mouth became a thin line. "That's an asshole move, you know."

Darien still wouldn't look at her. "I'm sorry."

Loren wasn't sure how to feel; whether she should feel flattered that he cared what she thought, or if she should be worried that he was playing games with her. And it cut her deeply to consider that she was perhaps no different than the other girls who fawned over him—no different than *Jessa*. Her childish behaviour was the only reason he'd come in here just now; the only reason he'd sought her out instead of leaving to go and meet up with that Darkslaying Viper.

To not come home until the morning, surely allowing him to forget about everything for the night, including her.

She couldn't believe herself. She should never have let her emotions rise to the surface like this. Her skin was burning all the way from her forehead to her collarbone.

"Forget about it, Darien." She forced a smile. "Honestly, I don't know what got into me. What you do is your business, not mine. Besides, we're just friends." That word hung like the crackle of a storm between them, and she swore something like pain entered his eyes. Loren's lungs suddenly felt like they were being stepped on, squished, pulverized. "Aren't we?"

Darien pushed to his feet. "Of course." He was so tall, Loren had to tip her head back to meet his eyes—and she saw that every trace of emotion in his features was gone, leaving behind nothing but a cold and careful mask. "Just friends, baby." The ticking of his watch was the only sound as silence dragged between them.

As that pet-name he'd called her clawed at her heart.

She was all too aware of how close he was standing to her, that nearness a storm that was realer than the crackle of that awful word.

Friends.

It made her feel sick inside. And the thought that she would eventually have to return to a life without him in it...a normal, *boring,* no-Darien-around life—

"You don't want to leave, and I don't want you to leave either," Darien said softly, his rich voice cutting through the panic enveloping her. "So why don't you come back downstairs and shoot some more bullets with me?" He held out a hand to her, his scarred palm facing up. "Okay?"

Her mind was screaming at her not to touch him, to walk away from what was sure to be a disaster, but her heart won the argument.

When she placed her hand in his, the warmth that spread through her from the skin-on-skin contact was excruciating. The feeling had her heart swelling with joy—her utterly foolish and hopelessly romantic heart. That heart of hers might as well draw a dotted line on itself where it was sure to be broken in half.

Stamping those thoughts into nothing, she whispered, "Okay."

Darien looked like there was something else he wanted to say, but his phone started buzzing. Loren stiffened as he dug it out of his pocket, keeping his other hand wrapped around hers. When he looked at the screen, his expression betrayed nothing.

Horrible thoughts sliced through Loren's head, most of them images of a phone screen with that name displayed across it: *Jessa*. The very worst of those images consisted of Darien's tattooed hand fisting in a girl's hair as she knelt before him.

"Are you going to answer that?" she whispered. It had rung so many times, it would probably go to voicemail soon.

Darien still didn't let go of her hand as he swiped to answer and lifted the phone to his ear. "Cassel."

The room was so silent, she could hear a familiar male voice say on the other end, "Get your asses down to the National. I'll meet you by the freeway." The line went dead as the graverobber disconnected the call.

Darien frowned. "Put a jacket on." He slipped the phone into his pocket. "Sounds like we've got a walk to take."

———

LOREN STOOD between Travis and Maximus in the very heart of the higher elevations of Angelthene National Forest as Darien sifted through the loose dirt of a grave, empty apart from the casket within —also empty.

The hole in the earth, nestled in a copse of oak woodland, reminded her of the mouth of a great beast. Night had fallen some time ago, the sprawling maze of old-growth trees awash in deep shades of blue.

"What do we have here?" Darien murmured as he retrieved something from the soil beneath the casket. Aside from Travis and Max, Benjamin was the only other person here, his owl Familiar perched on his shoulder. Loren squinted to better see the object Darien was holding up in the moonlight trickling through the trees, but she couldn't make out what it was.

Darien leapt out of the grave and came around to show her. In his gloved palm was a small, dirt-covered bone.

Not a bone, she realized. It was a single tooth.

"Is it enough?" she asked him. Enough to finally figure out who this mysterious ancestor of hers was. Benjamin and his robbers had located this grave upon looking into the ancient burial ground nearby, where a now-extinct species of High Demon was said to have been entombed in the earth below a Mournful Tree. High Demons were another term for the Nameless, sometimes used interchangeably to describe creatures like the Widow and the Pale Man who lived at the various Crossroads scattered throughout Angelthene. Those creatures had the ability to fulfill wishes if the person asking for them had something worthy enough to trade.

"Enough to run a post-mortem DNA test," Darien said. His eyes were alit with the same anticipation she could feel coursing through her own veins. But along with the anticipation she was feeling, she was also scared. Scared she wouldn't like whatever answer they found.

Maximus said, "Arthur will be pleased to have a new challenge."

Darien's answering smile glinted in the moonlight. "Oh, I know."

Benjamin crossed his rail-thin arms and said, "Nice to know a whole skeleton is being carted around the city." Darien had made sure to grill the robber with a series of questions to see if he had indeed found this grave exactly the way it was now.

"Demineralized bone powder doesn't last forever," Darien told him. "A lot of people are looking for Loren, which means most of that skeleton might already have been used up in their efforts to find her." It was to Loren that he added, "They can't hunt you forever, Loren."

A breeze picked up, rustling her hair. "Looks like I might finally get some answers about where I came from." She sounded as frightened as she felt. Her whole life had been spent not knowing where she came from or who her parents were. And although she'd always longed for answers, a part of her was scared to know.

Darien must've picked up on the unsteady pulsations of her heart, because his eyes noticeably softened in understanding. "Your past doesn't define you, sweetheart. Remember that."

Darien's phone buzzed in his pocket. Loren couldn't help but bristle, the tension from before they'd come to the National still lingering. It seemed he was getting a lot of phone calls tonight, or perhaps she was just imagining that it was more than usual. Her fear that he would leave at any moment was a tangible thing, and one she was worried he could sense.

He answered the incoming call with a muffled, "Cassel."

Loren was standing close enough to Darien that she could hear the deep voice on the other end—the voice of Casen Martel, the Butcher—say, "Devil's Advocate, Witching Hour. This is your only chance." A pause, and then he added before hanging up, "And bring the girl."

35

Darien stood in the kitchen at Hell's Gate with Max and Travis as they waited for the others to finish getting ready so they could head to the Devil's Advocate. Lace was standing in front of the gilt mirror in the entrance hall, perfecting her lipstick, and Tanner was lounging on the couch in the sitting room, looking like he'd much rather go to sleep than head to a nightclub.

Logan and Sabrine would be meeting them at the Advocate; the alpha had insisted on being kept in the know regarding anything that might lead to Chrysantha. Usually, Darien preferred to keep the dealings of his Devils on the downlow, but if anyone was owed a favor it was Logan. And if the tables were turned, and it was Ivy who'd gone missing, Darien would've wanted the same thing done for him. Plus, he supposed it wouldn't hurt to have an extra pair of eyes in a place like the Advocate. There was always shady shit going down in there, and he would need as little distractions from Loren and their goal of witnessing the BP deal as possible.

"You think this'll work?" Travis asked, spinning around a beer bottle by its neck on the kitchen island and nearly tipping it over in the process.

Darien shrugged. "Baylor has a thing for mortal women," he said, feeling sick to his stomach as the filthy words rolled off his tongue. Using Loren in this way... She'd agreed to every part of this plan, but just because she was willing to help them didn't make him feel any better about it. "It's our best chance at seeing who's buying all those chemicals and Blood Potions."

Max, picking up on Darien's tension, said, "Relax, Dare. She'll be fine."

Darien threw back the dregs of his beer. He'd hoped the drink would relax him, but it seemed to only make him more agitated. Hopefully there wasn't a Surge on his horizon any time soon. "I know," he said. "But just because I know she'll be fine doesn't mean I have to like it."

Max made to say something else, but the sound of heels clicking on the floor stilled his tongue.

Ivy, Dallas, and Loren were coming down the stairs, Jack trailing behind them. All three of the girls were dressed to the nines, in clothing that left very little to the imagination. But it was Loren that made Darien's heart stop in his chest. Stop and then start again, the rhythm erratic and borderline painful.

Her outfit—if you could even call it that—consisted of two pieces cut from sheer fabric that reminded him of a star-dusted night sky. The crop-top was held in place with ultra-thin straps, the top itself barely covering her breasts, and it tied up at the back in a criss-cross pattern. The skirt was ankle-length with a slit that exposed the sweep of her left leg, right up to the hip. Her eyes were lined in kohl, the lids dusted with a color so dark it was almost black. She wore her hair down, the slightly curled ends brushing the small of her back.

Forcing himself to tear his eyes off her, Darien leaned on the island, pinched the bridge of his nose between his thumb and index finger, and swore under his breath.

Travis chuckled.

"You're just loving this, aren't you?" Darien muttered without looking at his cousin. Still pinching the bridge of his nose, he glanced up, but he was looking at Max as he shook his head and said, "I don't think I can do this. I'm going to get into a fight with the first guy who looks at her."

"No, you're not," Max said. He drained the last of his beer and reached over to set the bottle in the sink. "Because that's exactly the kind of attention we don't need. If you go around breaking jaws, you'll clear the place out within minutes. What we need is for Baylor to notice her just enough to bring her into the back."

"Which he *will*," Travis cut in, an overconfident grin slashing across his face. "Hell, *I'd* like to take her into the back."

Darien let his hand drop from his face, rings clanging against the countertop, and straightened to full height. "You want to be the first guy I fuck up, get in line," he threatened.

Travis held up his hands in surrender, though he was still laughing under his breath.

Baylor ran the Devil's Advocate for Randal Slade. It was the filthiest, most dangerous nightclub in the whole city, and it was armed with such a powerful forcefield that not even Tanner could break through it—at least, not without some help. The Butcher had told Darien that the Blood Potions Syndicate often dealt in the back rooms of the Devil's Advocate. In order to witness the deal, and who was looking to purchase BP and chemicals in such ridiculously high numbers, they would need to get into those back rooms.

And Loren was their key. Their beautiful, mortal key.

Darien didn't like it. Not one bit. He would've preferred if the Butcher had simply known who was buying his shit from him, instead of doing all this extra legwork.

Max shoved away from the island and clapped Darien on the back. "Go talk to her or something and break the tension." He checked his watch. "We need to leave soon."

It took Darien longer to gain the courage to go over and talk to Loren than it would have if she were any other woman. But after a moment, he steeled himself and strode into the entrance hall, to where Loren was speaking quietly to Ivy and Dallas. Loren was likely receiving the downlow from Ivy, who Darien had asked to fill Loren in on exactly *what* they would need to do to get Baylor's attention.

Darien had to admit, it was a rather…unsavory plan. But it was their only choice. Now, he would find out if Loren would decide to back out of the plan after hearing about all those unsavory details or go forward with it.

Ivy caught sight of Darien approaching and pulled Dallas aside, leaving him alone in the entrance hall with Loren, Lace and Jack also having taken their leave a moment ago. As Ivy and Dallas passed him, Ivy gave Darien an encouraging smile he was too unsettled to return.

When Loren turned to face him, she was trembling delicately, her fingers interlocking before her. Darien had to resist the urge to reach for her; to stop her from teetering in those sky-high heels; to gather her into his arms and never let her go. Gods, she was even more breathtaking up close.

"Hey there, Ocean Eyes," Darien said in a low voice. The nickname had her ducking her head. "How are you feeling? Nervous?"

She gave a breathy laugh. "Very." She gestured to her outfit. "I mean, I feel…" She shrugged. "I don't know. Ridiculous, I guess."

"Far from it." Had she never looked in a mirror before? Had Ivy not shown her how utterly stunning she looked before bringing her down here? All his efforts at distancing himself from her were shot to hell as he told her, "You're the most beautiful thing I've ever seen." And she was. She really, really was.

Loren ducked her head again. Blush dusted her cheeks, still visible under the powder she'd swept over her face. "Doubtful."

"And why is that?" Darien stepped closer to her and tipped her chin up so that she was looking at him. "You could be wearing a hoodie and I would still think that of you."

The color in her cheeks deepened. "You're very kind, but…" She blinked rapidly, as if trying to clear herself of a daze. "Do you think it'll be enough to get his attention? I mean, I'm sure there will be tons of girls in there—"

"And none of them are you." No, they certainly weren't. "He'll have you in the back rooms so fast, your head will spin." The statement made him want to throw up, but he knew that getting into the back rooms was all that needed to happen for his Devils to witness the Blood Potions deal. Nothing else would go down between Loren and that vile vampire who managed the nightclub for it's even more vile owner. Darien continued, "And then you'll follow through with the plan. You remember what I told you?"

She nodded.

"Don't wait too long to knock him on his ass." He didn't let go of Loren's chin, and he held her gaze with his own as he said, "I *need* you to promise."

Loren gave another faint nod, and she trembled a little under Darien's touch as he brushed his thumb along the smooth line of her jaw. She let her eyelids slip shut as she leaned into his touch, a silent request for more — a request Darien longed to answer.

There would be more where that came from tonight. But Darien didn't allow himself to think about that. He had to focus, and Loren would need every part of his strength to follow through with what she had to do.

Loren opened her eyes and looked at him. She had a face that could crumble cities and bring conquerors to their knees. He would give her everything if he could. If he wasn't so...fucked up.

When she spoke, her voice was an airy whisper. "I promise."

"Good." He released her with some reluctance, spun around, and took in the people in the kitchen — his Devils and Dallas, who halted their conversations as his attention fell upon them. And then he gestured to the front door. "Let's roll out."

LOREN STUCK CLOSE to the others as Darien led the way through the towering, arched doors of the Devil's Advocate, past the battalion of bouncers checking identification cards, and through the crowded entrance. She was nearly stepping on Darien's heels as their group headed toward the steep staircase that swept down to the main floor.

The place was freezing cold, like they were standing inside a freezer. She supposed she should've expected as much from a night-club run by a vampire. The floors were slick with a coating of frost, and mist undulated through the room, making it difficult to see more

CITY OF GODS AND MONSTERS

than three feet in front of her. It was a good thing she was surrounded by people she trusted, otherwise she would've easily lost her way. Dallas stuck so close to her that their arms were nearly touching, and although the witch had always enjoyed club-hopping, she seemed as nervous as Loren to be at a place like the Devil's Advocate.

Heart slamming in her chest, Loren took in the club bit by bit. The mist swirled and parted around them as they neared the stairs.

The place was packed with vampires, wolves, witches, and warlocks, with the odd human halfie thrown into the mix. The red-lit balconies dotting the walls suggested this place had once been a theatre, though now those balconies had been transformed into private pleasure alcoves.

Loren didn't allow herself to look at what was happening inside those alcoves for very long. Needless to say, what her and Darien planned to do tonight would certainly not look out of place.

There was a giant statue built into the south wall, directly above the space where a stage had once been. It was an obscene piece of art depicting Tempus, the God of Time—also known as the God of Lies —and the goddess Ignis, Her Infernal Majesty of the Seven Circles. Loren imagined they were put here to symbolize how a person might lose track of two precious things at the Devil's Advocate: time and their soul.

Loren couldn't spot a single other pureblood human here, but she didn't allow herself to dwell on this. Besides, it should make tonight's task easier, if anything. Ivy had told her that Baylor's preference was mortal women, so Loren's job was to catch Baylor's interest—with Darien's help—just enough to get him to invite her into the back.

While they were getting ready at Hell's Gate, Loren had made the mistake of asking Ivy why Baylor preferred mortal women to his own kind, but as soon as Ivy had told her that he was a sadist who enjoyed feeding on his woman of choice while he had his way with her, she'd stopped asking questions.

Merely thinking about it made her heart slam furiously in her chest, and she had to dry her sweaty palms on her barely-there skirt.

Breathe. She had to breathe.

The crowd parted for the Devils as they walked through, but Loren's damned legs were trembling so badly she could barely keep up with them.

What made her more nervous, however, was thinking about just *how* she and Darien would have to attract Baylor's attention. The vampire was apparently the jealous type, and it was more likely that he would choose Loren instead of one of the many girls dancing in his metal cages that hung from the ceiling if he saw her being felt up by another man.

Especially Darien, who he apparently despised just as much as Darien despised him. Tricking Baylor into thinking the woman Darien had brought to the Devil's Advocate was more interested in him than Darien would make their plan a piece of cake.

Loren would just have to try to live through the next few hours, to not let her heart beat out of her chest the moment Darien started touching her.

Easier said than done.

They were approaching the top of the staircase when Ivy fell into step beside her. "Baylor is seated at one of the booths by the dance floor." She practically had to shout so Loren could hear her. "That's where we're headed."

Loren gave a shaky nod.

"Keep breathing, girl," Ivy said. "You're doing great."

Far below, the dance floor was studded with colorful lights and crowded with scantily clad patrons throwing back shots and grinding up against the laps of strangers. Over a dozen cages hung from the mirrored ceiling, where half-humans, vampires, and witches writhed provocatively behind the bars, stripping off their clothes bit by bit for an audience that just couldn't get enough.

At the head of their group, Darien turned midstride and held out a hand for Loren, and she hurried forward and grasped it. Butterflies twitched in her stomach at the contact, and her heart jumped into her throat, nearly choking off the uneven breaths she was drawing.

Could she do this? She was no longer sure, and her soul felt like it had snapped free of her body.

Every thought in Loren's head eddied into nothing as Travis

came to her left and took hold of her free hand just as they began descending the stairs.

Confused, she glanced between Travis, who winked down at her, and Darien, who was completely focused on the clubbers surrounding them. "Won't people think this is weird?" she asked.

"They'll just think we're sharing you," Travis said with a wolfish grin, his tattooed hand lightly squeezing hers.

Loren peeked up at Darien to see that he was stifling a smile, that adorable dimple in his cheek showing.

"The more the merrier in a place like this," Darien said, though the set of his mouth suggested the words tasted like ashes to him.

Needless to say, no one tried to bother her, not with Darien and Travis both holding onto her like she was their property, though there were a few men—most of them warlocks and wolves—who eyed her with interest and curiosity. The Devils led the way down to the dance floor, to a booth not far from the base of the staircase. Travis told her the location would give them the best view of the entire ground floor—and the best view of Baylor's booth, which was situated along the east wall, in exactly the right place for them to keep an eye on him all night. Logan and Sabrine were already here, reserving the booth for them. They must've arrived early to scope out Baylor and find the best seat, Loren realized. Sabrine flashed her a nervous smile as their group approached.

Travis let go of Loren's hand when they reached the booth, and their group took their seats at the bench that curved around a long table. Darien slid onto the bench beside Max, leaving Loren to sit on the very end. This decision made sense, she supposed, considering she would need to be in Baylor's line of sight for this to work properly. But she found that her stomach flipflopped as she lowered herself to the bench beside Darien, who wrapped his arm around her to pull her snug against his side. The bench was made of glittery plastic that was so cold, she shivered. She leaned into Darien for warmth and reassurance—well, that, and because she wanted to.

"That's him," Ivy said, leaning across the table so Loren could hear her. Ivy made a subtle gesture to where Baylor sat with another male vampire. Loren tried to look across the dance floor without making it obvious that she was staring, but she wasn't sure if she succeeded.

Baylor looked to be about thirty in physical age, with shoulder-length flaxen hair and eyes an eerily pale shade of teal. Under the strobe lights, his chalky skin and hair were tinged with a slight blue shade, the texture of the latter reminding her of cotton candy.

It wasn't a good look.

"He looks...charming," Loren said with a shudder. She tried not to look too closely at Baylor's elongated incisors as he tipped his head back and laughed at something the other man said.

Where he sat beside his wife, arm slung around her bare shoulders, Jack chuckled. "I hear he's even more charming when he sucks your blood."

Loren shuddered.

"Quit freaking her out," Darien cut in. "Maybe *you'd* like to take the task of getting Baylor's attention. I'm sure he'd enjoy a fine piece of ass like yourself."

Jack flipped him off. And Dallas, who was practically sitting in Max's lap, cackled so hard she was nearly in tears.

A venefica waitress, wearing little more than lingerie, approached their table with a bright smile. "Can I interest you folks in some of Ignis's Fire?" The shots that were balanced on the silver tray she carried were the deep red of blood, and a misty substance that reminded Loren of dry ice rippled out of the glasses.

"We'll take two each," Max said. The waitress used her magic to levitate the number of shots they'd requested to the table, where they floated to a rest before each person.

When Darien snatched one up, Loren copied him and grabbed one of her own, though her movements were far more hesitant than his. She sniffed at the mist rippling out of the glass, her nose crinkling. It smelled spicy and...green. Like a forest.

"What is it?" she whispered.

"Drink it." He was already throwing back his second. "It'll help with the cold. You're rattling like a little leaf."

Dallas shouted, "Bottoms up, biatch!" and tossed hers back.

Sabrine followed suit, though the encouraging smile she tried to give Loren when she was finished swallowing looked more like a grimace. Her eyes, now painted with the same fire as Logan's, were watering, and she looked like she was trying not to gag.

Loren muttered, "Here goes nothing," and threw back her first shot, wincing from the burning sensation that spread across her tongue and knifed down her throat. It tasted like pine needles and cinnamon. "Gross," she coughed, setting down the glass.

Darien pushed her second shot closer to her. "You'll need both, sweetheart. You won't be able to focus if you're too cold."

Although she hated to admit it, Loren knew he was right, so she braced herself before tossing back the second shot. Heat rippled from the crown of her head to the tips of her toes as the magic spread through her system. The warmth certainly helped, though she could have done without that awful taste. It lingered on her tongue, sharp and burning, and as the seconds wore on it spread into her stomach and settled there like a flame.

A squeal of excitement pierced the air, causing Loren to jolt and accidentally elbow Darien in the abs. She muttered an apology, but she was soon distracted by the person who had let out the squeal.

A hellseher with a blunt mahogany bob was sprinting to their table, where she was met by Lace, who practically knocked Tanner over in her attempts to scramble out of the booth. The hacker grumbled something about how he should've stayed home as he waved down another waitress to order a drink.

"That's Aspen Van Halen," Darien whispered to Loren. "She's a Reaper and Lace's best friend. Since I recently repaired our friendship with the Reapers, Aspen is finally able to talk to Lace again without the risk of being excommunicated."

"Malakai would've stripped her of her title for something so little?" Loren knew nearly all the names of the Darkslaying hellsehers in the city, and she certainly wasn't the only one. It was the kind of knowledge a person tended to gain simply by living in a place like this. The two most well-known and feared circles in the city belonged to Darien and Malakai.

"Yes," Darien said. "Mercy is a foreign word to most circles."

She turned slightly so she could eye him up. Maybe she was

biased, but he was the hottest man in this place. She knew she likely wasn't the only woman who would love to unbutton the black shirt that fit him like a glove. "Guess he liked your peace offering quite a bit, huh?"

Darien merely gave her a dark smile.

Aspen, who was now saying her greetings to the other Devils, took note of Loren sitting pressed up against Darien's side, put her hands on her hips, and looked her over from head to toe. "Well, well, well, what do we have here, Darien?" She was grinning from ear to ear. "I see you've plucked yourself a pretty little wallflower. What's your name, honey?"

Darien spoke before Loren could answer her. "Aspen, this is Loren," he said. "Loren, meet Aspen."

Loren pivoted in the booth and held out a hand to Aspen. "It's a pleasure to meet—"

But Aspen suddenly bounced forward, grabbed Loren around the back of the head, and bent down to kiss her. Loren turned her face just far enough to not get smacked right on the lips, taking the wet kiss on the corner of her mouth instead.

Blinking rapidly in shock, her face turning a deep shade of scarlet, Loren glanced at Darien—

Only to see that he was fighting a smile. And there was a glint in his eyes that suggested he wasn't exactly repulsed by what he'd just watched.

Words continued to escape Loren as she swung her head back around to face Aspen. Suddenly, she regretted having taken both shots of Ignis's Fire. She was certain she was turning as red as the drink.

The Reaper beamed at her. "You're just the hottest little thing I've ever seen," Aspen crooned. She took hold of Loren's hand that was still frozen in midair and shook it. And she kept Loren's hand pinned in her black-painted claws as she went on to say, "If you need anything—and I mean *anything* at all—I'm here for you." The implications were clear as daylight, and Loren felt the heat in her face spread all the way down to her toes. Sweat sprouted out of the parts of her body she hadn't known were possible to sweat out of.

The male Devils at the table howled with laughter. Even Darien couldn't seem to fully stifle the smile that crept to his lips.

Loren ducked her head, her hair falling over her shoulder like a curtain of light. "Thank you," she sputtered. "I mean...I guess."

Aspen only laughed, the sound like silver bells.

Loren was more than glad when Lace suggested that Aspen accompany her to the bar across the dance floor. The Reaper linked arms with the blonde Devil and disappeared with a wave of her fingertips and a backward glance in Loren's direction that assured her she'd soon be back for more.

"She's very pleasant," Loren said to Darien. She eyed him up— the dimple that was still betraying his amusement. "You enjoyed that quite a bit, didn't you?"

A full smile appeared. "Can you blame me?" But then his attention suddenly became fixed on something behind her. "Baylor's already taken notice of you. I suppose we have Aspen to thank for drawing his attention." He grabbed her around the middle, and Loren held her breath, her whole body electrifying as he pulled her into his lap. "Time to get this show on the road."

Loren stopped breathing as Darien angled her so that she was facing the roomful of people, her back pressed against his torso.

Suddenly, she was an object on display, a mortal puppet perched upon a Devil's knee. More than just Baylor was looking at her now, and Loren felt her body tense up at the realization of what had to be done. Even the man sitting across from Baylor had turned to look over his shoulder, clearly interested in what had drawn his companion's attention.

Darien slipped a hand through the slit in Loren's skirt and tucked it between her thighs—in a show of claim, she realized—while his other wrapped around her bare midsection.

Was it just her, or was it suddenly very hot in here? She wanted to blame it on Ignis's Fire, but she knew that couldn't be it. No—the heat she was feeling had everything to do with how close she was to Darien.

That and how many eyes were watching them, the immortals in this place clearly interested in Darien's new plaything. She wondered about the type of girls he usually brought here that had led to their extreme interest in his affairs. She thought it was safe to say he'd never brought anyone like her—a mortal—here before.

Loren found herself sinking down, wishing badly that she could hide, wondering what had possessed her to agree to this plan. Every part of her body was hyper-aware of how close she was to Darien—so close that she could feel his body heat, so close that she could smell the aftershave on his skin, the slight hint of that mouth-watering cologne he always wore.

Darien's arm tightened around her midsection, his thumb stroking a comforting pattern across her ribs. "Don't do that, sweetheart," he said softly. He pressed a kiss to her temple, making her heart skip a beat, and kept his mouth there as he said against her skin, "Don't duck your head, don't hide. We're roleplaying, remember? An hour, maybe two, and we can leave."

An hour, maybe two, and she wouldn't be this close to him again, wouldn't be sitting in his lap, wouldn't have his strong arms wrapped around her waist.

The thought made her vow to live in this moment, no matter how many eyes were watching from the dance floor and the red-lit alcoves lining the club. Made her sink into him, nuzzling against his chest.

She had denied this for so long, denied *him* for so long, and she couldn't do it anymore. She wanted him, wanted to feel his body against hers, wanted him to touch her. She wanted to *feel*, and she was tired of fighting it. Consequences be damned, even if she got hurt. But when she looked at him, there was a promise there, a promise in his eyes that seemed to say, *I will not hurt you, Lola.*

"I'm going to touch you now," Darien said. She felt her breasts turn heavy, her nipples peaking from the statement—from how rough and deep his voice was. "If I do anything you don't like, don't be afraid to tell me, okay?" There was a pause, and a tone Loren couldn't quite place colored his next words. "I don't ever want you to be afraid of me." His steel eyes bore into hers. "Promise me." The intensity in his voice, and the need for reassurance, made her heart ache.

Loren shook her head. "There's no way you could do anything I won't like."

"Promise me, Loren. Please."

She studied him for a long while. Time seemed to cease as they looked at each other. Perhaps it was just Loren's world that had stopped, but it felt more significant than that. She gave a slight nod, but because he seemed to need to hear the words leave her mouth, she whispered, "I promise."

"We'll start slow," Darien said, his words only loud enough for her to hear. His knuckles brushed back and forth along her ribcage, the feel of his hand on her bare skin igniting a heat that spread deep into her core. He was watching her intently, gauging her response, the look in his eyes asking a silent question that had her nodding in answer, desperate to erase that uncertainty from his gaze—the question of whether she actually *wanted* him to touch her.

"Slow is good," she breathed. Was it, though? Suddenly, she wasn't sure. And the more times he moved that hand across her ribs, the more eager she became to feel that hand on other parts of her body. Her breasts ached at the thought, and she was all too aware of how her nipples had pebbled under the sheer fabric of her top. Her whole body had sensitized from anticipation, and she became overly alert to the way her clothes felt on her skin, overly aware of every muscle in Darien's body pressing against her.

Darien seemed to pick up on the effect he was having on her. The hand that was between her thighs tightened while his other snaked along the seam of her top, right near the edge of her breast. A chill that had nothing to do with the temperature of the nightclub skittered down her spine, and she found her mouth parting of its own accord.

Darien focused on that mouth of hers, and Loren stopped breathing as he took her left arm into his hand, raised it to his sculptured mouth…

And pressed his lips against the tattoo on the inside of her forearm. The ink was barely visible tonight, since Darien had made sure she hadn't left the house on an empty stomach. He traced his mouth along the tattoo, kissing every scar she had sustained from crashing through the window of that skyscraper—every wound he'd so meticulously dressed for her.

Loren found her body bowing at the sight of his mouth moving against her skin, and when he was finished with her scars, he parted her hair to one shoulder and began doing the same to the side of her neck, to the area below her ear, to the skin just below her jaw.

The others at the table had begun conversations—to give them some privacy, she thought. To make her more comfortable, instead of feeling like even their closest friends had their full attention on her tonight.

Loren forced her body to relax as Darien's mouth brushed across the length of her jaw, forced herself to breathe in and breathe out, forced herself to partially listen to the conversations the others were having, if only to distract herself from her own jumbled thoughts. Darien participated in those conversations here and there, likely also to distract her, to make her feel like his focus wasn't entirely on her.

She knew better than to believe that. She could *feel* his attention on her like it was a tangible thing, and every time she shifted a little in his lap, he adjusted with her, as if they were dancers attuned with the way each other's bodies worked. She wished she could know every thought that lay buried beneath his mysterious front, could know why he was looking at her like that—like she was more than just Loren. Like he'd hit the jackpot on the lottery. It reminded her of how *she* probably looked when she was staring at him.

Loren wasn't certain if Darien knew the reason why she was fidgeting, why her back curved with every new kiss he pressed to her body. Wasn't sure if he was aware of just how much he affected her. The hand he had resting between her thighs was indeed gripping her in a way that felt very possessive—a symbol of claim she knew the immortal males in this place would catch onto soon, if they hadn't already. A claim Baylor had likely already noticed—and would take as a challenge.

That hand between her legs tightened a little, his rough thumb sweeping along the curve of her thigh the way his other swept across her ribs, edging beneath the fabric of her top. She wondered if he was too distracted to realize how close the hand between her thighs was to the most sensitive area on her body.

"Baylor's watching us like we're his favorite television show," Darien whispered in her ear, amusement lightening his words.

Loren shivered at the feel of his breath against her neck. Darien gripped her tighter, his fingers inching toward the apex of her thighs, and she arched her back into him. Desperate to have Darien not notice just how much his touch was affecting her, she joked, "Or his favorite porno." He gave a low laugh that had heat pooling below her navel. His breath sent tendrils of golden hair fluttering across her cheek.

Before she could check herself, she leaned into the hand that was teasing the curve of her breast and said, "Don't stop." The words were a breathy gasp, and she angled herself in a way that invited him to explore every curve of her body, placing his claim on it like his own personal map, leaving no part of her untouched.

He took the invitation, and when his thumb brushed over her breast—over her nipple that peaked under his touch—his focus on her became predatory, and his hand stilled.

"Loren." The way he said her name—the gravel in his voice—made the inside of her thighs damp with her desire.

"Darien," she answered, his name as tense as when hers had floated off his mouth.

His thumb brushed across her nipple again, hard enough to send a wave of pleasure rippling down her spine. She swallowed the moan that rose in her throat. "You're driving me crazy," he breathed. Her skin flushed at the declaration. "You're making me want to take you into the back rooms myself and forget about this whole thing."

"Why don't you?" she challenged. She tipped back her head to look at him. "Are you going to make me beg?"

"That's tempting," Darien murmured. "Why don't you start by telling me what you want?"

She dragged a hand up his thigh, feeling the hard muscle beneath her palm. "You. I want you." If she hadn't been drowning in her own lust, she might've felt embarrassed by how desperate she came across, how breathy her voice sounded.

Darien gave another of those low laughs that made the desire curling in her stomach more intense—a force she couldn't ignore. "You want me?" His voice could pass for a purr.

"Isn't it obvious?"

"Mmm." As he leaned in to press a kiss below her ear—in the spot where her own symbol of the Seven Devils would've been, if she'd had one—the hand gripping her thigh tightened to the point of bruising, but the feeling only turned her on more, made her wet and aching for him.

The Devil kept kissing her, though it was never on her mouth, no matter how she angled herself. She wanted to taste him, wanted to memorize the shape of his mouth beneath her own, wanted to become one with him. Every time he kissed her, every time he touched her, heat sparked between them and spread like molten gold. Her heart swelled with the longing to stay in his arms forever.

Their surroundings had bled so wholly away that when Aspen and Lace returned to the table, Loren felt like she was being pulled out of a dream. The most beautiful, delicious, *filthy* dream she'd ever had. And when she glanced up at Darien, their faces barely an inch apart, he looked as intoxicated by her as she was by him. He was so close to her that she could see every dark eyelash, every tone of blue in his eyes.

"Pardon me, lovebirds," Aspen said in a singsong voice as she stepped up to the bench, her heels clunking, "but I need to get through." She began to push by, wedging herself between Darien's knees and the edge of the table.

Darien lifted his knees up a little to give Aspen more room, the motion causing the hand he had resting between Loren's thighs to slip up—right into the space that would betray exactly how aroused she was by this whole situation.

Loren froze, every muscle in her body going stiff.

Darien's hand stilled at what he found there, though only briefly. And Loren's heart pounded hard and fast as Darien dragged his rough fingers, ever so slowly and lightly, up the hot and wet center of her.

The sensation caused her to tremble against him, her hips rocking into his touch. She didn't want him to stop, wanted him to touch her harder, faster.

"Fuck, Loren," he bit out.

She peeked up at him from under her eyelashes. "Guess I'm enjoying this whole pretending thing a little too much."

"Is that right?" He shifted her in his lap, centering her just enough for her to feel his erection pressing against her backside. Her heart stopped dead in her chest at the feel of him. She didn't have to be experienced to know that he had a lot to use and likely knew precisely how to use it.

"You're not the only one enjoying yourself," Darien said. He brushed a strand of her hair aside and leaned in close to whisper in her ear, "And you're not wearing any panties." Desire dripped hotly down her spine.

He slid his fingers up and down again, like he wanted to memorize the feel of her. He kept his gaze on her the whole time—watching the way her features changed as he touched her, she realized. Having his hands on her, with nothing in the way of her skin and his, made her grind her ass into his cock as if there weren't hundreds of people watching.

"I love those faces you make," Darien said. "I've never seen anyone so fucking beautiful." His thumb slipped a little higher, where it circled that sweet, sensitive spot, exploring her with expertise that had her moaning softly in a way she was certain should make her feel embarrassed. But she was too lost in him to care, and she was soon fisting his hair, pulling him closer to her.

"Don't stop." Her voice was breathless and nearly as rough as his. "Please." If he were to stop, she might cry. Cry and beg.

He gave a low, appreciative groan that she felt deep in her stomach. But he didn't stop—no. He kept going, working her harder, and it was bliss. Pure bliss.

The way he was touching her made her hips twitch, made her rock into his touch, moving in sync with him. The club and the people and the music melted away, leaving behind nothing but them—the two of them, lost in each other.

"Fuck, baby," Darien mumbled against the side of her neck, his breath sending a chill across her skin. "What are you doing to me?"

"I could ask you the same thing." Every word was strained and breathless as he coaxed her closer to that peak of pleasure.

"You're wrecking me is what you're doing. You're wrecking me for anyone else."

"I think you wrecked me the same way a long time ago." Her legs twitched as he played with her, her toes curling tightly in her heels. "Ever since that day at Rook and Redding's."

At Rook and Redding's, she'd asked him, 'What's in it for you?' Neither of them had known it back then, but at that precise moment, as they looked at each other beneath the blue strobe lights of the Devil's Advocate, lost in a world of their own making, she thought they had both realized what the answer was.

She shifted her hips, rocking into his touch, urging him to go harder, faster.

Darien obliged her, rubbing and pressing in all the right places, and with just the right amount of pressure. Every time she neared climax, he pulled her back from that shimmering edge, driving her mad with desire. He knew precisely what he was doing, and he seemed to take extreme pleasure in how her breath hitched in her chest with every stroke, how her thighs tightened around his hand when her pleasure soared.

"You're a greedy little thing," Darien breathed, "aren't you?"

Gods. The strength of what was building was staggering. She was worried she might pass out from the sensations coursing through her. It was never supposed to get this far, not even tonight, never supposed to progress to this stage, and although she had no regrets, she worried she would in the morning. Not because she didn't want this, but because she was baring her heart and soul to him, placing them in his hands. Where this went from here depended entirely on him. It made her feel powerless, yet wildly free.

"You asked me what I want," she said, every word breathless and strained. She was starting to see stars. "Why don't you tell me what *you* want?" When Darien didn't say anything, his hand slowing a little, she looked up at him and studied his face—the uncertainty there. The flickering lights of the club softened the sharp line of his jaw and reflected in his night-dark hair. "You're worried I can't handle it," she accused, "aren't you?" Her eyes narrowed, and she lifted her chin, her hand tightening into a fist in his hair. "I've been handling you for quite some time now."

He still wouldn't say anything, though he seemed to want to.

"Why don't you try me?" she urged.

Leaning forward slightly, she caught his lower lip between her teeth—before he could pull away, before he could realize what she was doing—and sucked on it. The taste of him—of that mouth she hadn't been able to look away from since that fateful day in Rook and Redding's—was enough to nearly undo her. She let go, pulling back just far enough to assess him.

He looked like he wanted to eat her alive.

She would let him. Gods, she would let him if she had the chance, and she didn't care if everyone in here watched as he laid her back on this table and fucked her with his tongue.

"Try me, Darien Cassel," she urged. He slid his hand lower as she pressed herself into his touch, and he cupped her, the heat from his body and hers fusing until they were one and the same. "See if I can handle it."

She wasn't prepared for his answer. Not prepared at all.

"I want to get down between your beautiful legs and wrap my mouth around your pussy," he began, every word rough and low, "so I can find out if you taste as sweet as you look. And when I'm finished eating my way to your heart, I want to fuck you, hard and deep. And then I want to fuck your pretty little mouth the same way." *Hard and deep.*

Oh, sweet Caligo. She knew he felt her body's response to his declaration, and he answered its request by working her again, harder this time, rolling that sweet, electric spot between his fingers until her legs were not her own—until her body was not her own.

"Think you can handle that?"

"Yes," she said, her stomach muscles fluttering. A whimper escaped her lips, and her words were wild gasps as she said, "I can, and I want to." More than anything, she wanted him to fuck her mouth until she was crying, until there was nothing that existed except the taste of him on her tongue. She wanted it more than she wanted to breathe—wanted *him* more than she'd wanted anything ever. Her need for him would be the death of her.

But Darien suddenly stopped, his hand stilling just as she was about to reach that brink of pleasure. The stars sprinkling her vision faded away, and she was left gasping, her body aching with the crippling need for him.

"Why did you stop?" Her voice was practically a whine.

"Because when I make you come, I want you all to myself. I'm not sharing you with anyone—least of all them." He inclined his head toward the crowded club—the people she'd forgotten all about. The people who were still watching them with sidelong glances that told her exactly how heated their performance had become. Darien's voice was a low growl as he went on to say, "When I make you come, you will be all mine. And no one, except me, will have the pleasure of hearing those little sounds you make."

Even though he was no longer stroking her, his words were enough to nearly push her to her climax.

Loren lifted her chin. "So, you're going to make me wait, are you?" She writhed in his lap, causing him to fist a hand in her hair. "Are you sure that's what you want?"

Darien made to either say something or lean in to kiss her, but he abruptly stopped, turning his head sharply to the left to look at someone. "Can I fucking help you?" he snapped.

Loren followed his line of sight, blinking the fog of lust from her vision to see a copper-haired warlock standing near their table with a drink in his hand, full-on gawking—

At *her*, she realized. He was gawking at *her*. The others at their table had halted their own affairs and were now at full attention. Something tugged at the edge of her mind, where it was buried deep beneath emotion and time. She wasn't sure what it was—

But Loren didn't care—cared about nothing except Darien as she writhed along his length again, loving how hard he was for her. Far too invested in the Devil to care about anything else, she barely noticed when the warlock dipped his head and scampered away.

Darien gave a dark laugh. "Easy," he mumbled against Loren's neck. He pressed his mouth against her skin, his tongue sweeping out to taste her. "If you keep rubbing up against my cock, I might have to lay you back on this table and give all these people the performance of a lifetime."

"Please do," Loren said, breathless.

But something caused her to look toward where the warlock had vanished, the puzzle pieces in her mind clicking together into recognition.

"Wait a minute..." Her mind sharpened into crystal clarity as her memory brought her back to that awful night when Sabrine had gone missing. "I know that guy. That's the warlock that was with the Darkslayer the night Sabrine was taken."

Darien's head snapped up, and he scanned the club, the area where the warlock had vanished to. The other Devils at the table became abruptly aware of the shift in atmosphere as they once again halted their conversations, their drinking, and—in Dallas and Max's case, as well as Jack and Ivy's—their making-out.

It was to Tanner and Travis that Darien said, "That warlock who was just standing by our table was one of the men who took Sabrine."

Sabrine, who was slumped against Logan's side, looking more than a little tipsy, was visibly surprised by Darien's statement. She sat up straighter, her bleary eyes finding Loren's. Loren saw that she was grappling for recognition, for the memories that had eluded her, and was coming up empty.

Darien added, "Do not let him leave this club."

Logan and Travis immediately stood and made their way toward wherever the warlock had vanished to, the people on the colorful dance floor stepping aside for them as they moved.

Darien settled back into the booth, his hand slipping under Loren's skirt again. She twisted, urging that hand back to where she wanted it, but Darien stilled when someone kicked him under the table.

He jolted, drawing a sharp hiss in through his teeth. The pain seemed to snap him out of his reverie, and he shot a hard look at Jack, who was laughing loudly with Ivy. Jack's amusement was abruptly cut off by Darien's question. "What the hell was that for, you cocksucker?"

Jack's smile faded as he glanced around, utterly confused. "It wasn't me—"

"I'm about to jump across this table and beat you senseless—"

"It was me," Tanner cut in. The sight of the tablet that was now resting on his knees seemed to alert Darien to how much time had passed. "I'm sorry but— Buddy's about to leave." He jerked his head in the direction of Baylor's table.

"Shit, she needs to go," Max added. He checked his watch. "Now, Dare. It's almost Witching Hour."

Loren gave Darien a nod to say that it was okay—that she was ready. That she could do this.

Darien helped her to her feet. Her legs felt like they might fold beneath her at any moment, but she managed to stay upright, Darien's hand clasping her own. He didn't let go of her.

"Remember what I told you," Darien said. "Don't hesitate." He didn't release her until she'd nodded.

And then she walked over to Baylor, where he was getting up from his table and saying his farewell to the other vampire. Baylor noticed her instantly, and Loren gave him an inviting smile that had him promptly excusing himself from his friend and pulling her aside. His large hand was clammy on her elbow as he guided her to a shadowed corner near the bar.

The invitation to go with him into the back rooms of the Advocate came quickly, and soon she was at Baylor's side as they headed for that metal, magic-enforced door she would need to get the Devils through. Where it was strapped to the inside of her thigh, the vial of sedative powder that Darien had given her felt heavy.

Don't wait too long to knock him on his ass, Darien had told her.

She only hoped she could follow through.

She *would* follow through.

Loren didn't have to turn around to know that Darien was tracking her every movement, his gaze was that intense.

But soon that metal door was slamming shut behind her, and she was alone with Baylor in the back rooms of the Devil's Advocate.

36

The Devil's Advocate was like a drug, and Darien had been addicted to it in years past. It was filthy and ripe with sin, a place that catered to broken hearts and lost souls. It had a way of welcoming you in like an old friend, tricking you into falling for its pleasures and making you beg for more—beg until you couldn't even breathe. By the time you figured out the floors weren't paved in gold but were coated in dollar-store paint, a part of your soul belonged to the devil, and nothing you did would ever get it back.

Months had passed since Darien had set foot in here. *Months.* But no matter how much time he spent away from this festering place, as soon as he'd stepped back in, it had felt as though he'd never left. It was the hand of the devil beckoning him back, as if he were saying, *I missed you. Care for a drink?*

"She'll be fine, Dare." Max's voice cut into the stupor Darien had fallen into. He blinked, tearing his attention away from the metal door that had shut behind Loren and Baylor several minutes ago. Max pushed a shot his way, liquid sloshing over the side of the glass. Beside him, Dallas looked as worried as Darien, the witch's eyes continuously flicking to the door. Max said, "Have a drink."

Darien didn't hesitate to toss the amber-colored liquid back, relishing in the weightless feeling that immediately washed through his body, lifting some of that fog of concern from his mind. That was some potent liquor.

"What if he hurts her?" The question slipped out before Darien could stop it. Hearing his concerns spoken aloud only made him feel like he was stuck in a nightmare. The evening had started out better than any of his wildest fantasies, but now...now that Loren wasn't with him—

"Then you'll kill him," Ivy cut in, where she sat slumped against Jack, who laughed and added, "And then Randal will finally have to find himself a new manager for this shithole."

Where he sat across the table from Darien, Tanner was busy clicking away on his tablet, waiting for the chance—the one Loren would provide for him—to hack into the spell system.

The club suddenly plunged into darkness as the power was cut. People screamed in surprise, but their fright soon turned into amusement, laughter rippling through the building as everyone waited for the power to be restored. The sudden absence of spellwork was like having a coat you didn't realize you were wearing removed.

The colorful auras in the building glowed as Darien blinked the Sight into his vision. So many gray and muddy distortions floating about the dance floor, most of them tinged with the color of lust.

"See?" Max said quietly, looking at Darien through his own Sight. "She did it."

Indeed, Loren had. Which meant she had listened to him and used the sedative powder to knock Baylor unconscious as soon as he'd gotten her into the back and started to feel her up. And then she'd made it to the breaker panel and turned off the club's security switch, the one that protected the spellwork from being tampered with, allowing Tanner to use his tablet to hack into the network and temporarily cut off the wards that were generated by the city's Control Tower.

It was some comfort, at least.

But she still hadn't returned.

Jack, Ivy, Lace, and Aspen had taken the darkness as their cue to leave. They only had seconds — minutes, if they were lucky — to get through the unguarded door and into the back. Darien found their auras across the dance floor and saw them slipping, one by one, through the metal door.

Five seconds later, the lights flickered back on with a shrill buzz. Music thumped through the building so loudly that several people jumped. The spellwork had returned, its sudden reappearance sending a piercing sound through Darien's eardrums and threatening a nosebleed. It made his brain swell inside his skull.

"Fuck," Max muttered, shaking his head to clear it of that high-pitched squeaking sound. "I'll never get used to that."

Darien turned his attention back to that metal door in time to see Loren slipping out of it. She was paler than before she'd gone in there, but other than that, she looked unharmed. There was no limp in her walk, no mark on what he could see of her body.

Darien released the breath he was holding.

Her eyes locked with his across the room, and she gestured to the bathrooms at the other side of the dance floor. He gave her a nod, but he kept watching her, making sure no one touched or followed her as she wove around the people who had returned to their drinking and dancing.

A few minutes later, she came back out the bathroom door, where she was intercepted by a strawberry-blonde girl wearing clear, sky-high heels. There was a tattoo below the girl's ear — a crescent moon of luminescent ink.

Darien felt the blood drain from his face. Felt his soul snap free of his body and drift up to the mirrored ceiling.

"Is that Valary?" Max said. It certainly was. Valary Sternberg, a Warg who answered to Channary Graves, Head of the House on the Pier. Darien's latest fuckbuddy — a clingy one to boot — who he'd met up with once in a while for nearly a year before he'd met Loren. Max added, "What do you think she wants?"

Darien's jaw was so tight, it felt like his teeth were breaking. "To get under my skin." He didn't blink as he watched Valary step toward Loren and pull her into a tight embrace, her hands brushing over her hair in a way that made Darien certain she was aware that he was watching their little exchange.

Darien's phone rang with an incoming call. He pulled it out of his pocket and didn't bother to check the caller identification before answering. "Yeah."

"They got away." Ivy's tense voice floated through the speaker, barely audible over the thumping music. "They were glamored and there are no cameras."

Darien swore. "Did they see you?"

"No, but—the cutting of the spellwork must've spooked them." He'd had a feeling that might've happened, but he'd hoped they still could've caught them on time.

"What about their auras?"

"We couldn't see them."

Shit. He scrubbed a hand over his face. "And the warlock?"

"Travis and Logan got him. They're taking him to Hell's Gate."

"Good." This night wasn't a total waste then, but the BP deal...

Fuck. This hadn't gone the way he'd intended. They'd lost what was possibly their only chance at intercepting a BP deal, and if Ivy was wrong and any of the buyers had spotted his Devils... "Get another drink if you want one and then we're going home." He ended the call and looked back across the dance floor to see that Valary was gone—and so was Loren.

Darien stopped breathing. He was immediately on his feet, ignoring whatever Max was saying to him as he left the table and prowled across the dance floor.

Whatever Valary had said to Loren, he knew it couldn't be good. Worse than that, Valary could've done something to Loren—something bad. He had to find her, had to make sure she was safe.

His head was suddenly pounding harder than his heart. There were too many faces on the dance floor, too much noise and color—

"Where are you going so fast, Devil?"

Darien froze at the sound of the high voice that floated above the music, that lilting Northern accent causing his shoulders to tense up. He slowly turned around to find Valary Sternberg standing behind him, a hand cupped over a glass of dark liquor.

The Warg's red-painted lips parted into a sinful smile. "You look like you've seen a ghost," she purred. Her ice-blue eyes raked over him from head to toe, lingering on certain areas he'd let her become all too familiar with, and for far too many months.

Yeah, the ghosts of my sexual past come back to haunt me, Darien longed to say. Instead, he told her, "If you don't tell me what you said to my friend, I'll be paying a visit to your Head and letting her know what you were really doing all those times you lied to her this past summer." Channary Graves would likely excommunicate Valary if she found out she had passed up countless Darkslaying jobs in favor of hooking up with him in places that were no more romantic that this raunchy, gods-awful club.

Valary's haughty smile faded a little. "I thought I would introduce myself after seeing how fond you are of her," she said, her voice saccharine. She tossed her head to one side, her thick, shoulder-length hair swaying. "She's a doll, isn't she? Too bad her pretty little face will soon be marked up with wrinkles." She gave an exaggerated pout. "Being mortal is such a drag."

Darien's hands curled into fists at his sides as he felt a Surge knocking at the back of his mind. "What did you do?" he ground out, willing the black to stay out of his eyes.

The Surge kept knocking. *Tap, tap, tap.*

"I already told you: I introduced myself because I knew you would never bother. Just like you never bother to answer my calls anymore." She eyed the fists that were hanging at his sides and arched an eyebrow. "What are you going to do, Darien? Hit me like you do all those scumbags at the Pit?" The joking undercurrent to her words suggested she knew he wouldn't take the bait.

No, he certainly wouldn't. It was a low he couldn't even imagine stooping to. He'd never hit a woman in his life, and he wasn't about to start, no matter how angry this Warg made him.

He stalked up to Valary. Every step he took made that smug look on her face falter a little more. A muscle fluttered in her jaw, but she stood her ground, even when he stopped not three inches from her — even as he towered over her like the shadow of a demon and said, "You're going to stay away from me and you're going to stay away from my friend." His voice was low and lethal. "Or I will make your life a living hell."

It seemed to be a challenge for her not to look away from him, but to her credit she didn't even blink. She had a backbone of steel, this one. It was why Darien had liked her at first, but now he only found her pigheadedness to be repulsive.

Valary gave a smirk. "You're a mean thing." She reached out, snaking a hand along his belt buckle, her sharp nails teasing the space between his pants and his pelvis. "It makes me want to bend over and let you fuck me on this dance fl—"

Darien grabbed hold of her wrist—firmly, but not enough to hurt. "Touch me again," he ground out, "and see where it gets you."

She yanked her wrist out of his grip, as if his touch was electric. "You can't be serious," she spluttered.

"Do I look like I'm joking?"

Valary stared at him as if he'd sprouted horns, her mouth hanging open. But her shock and fear barely lasted two seconds.

Stubborn was fucking right.

Valary huffed a laugh. "That's alright. I'm sure you'll get sick of that blonde tramp soon enough. And then you'll be crawling back to me to help you with your Surges when her perky little tits no longer get you off." It felt like Darien's teeth were cracking from how hard he was clenching his jaw. Valary reached into her bra and pulled out a small pendant attached to a gold chain. She held it up, where it glimmered softly under the strobe lights, the closed eye at the center of the pendant a cruel wink. "Though you might want to find her before someone else does."

A roaring sound swept into Darien's head, followed by a sharp ringing that made him feel like he was floating. Every rational thought in his head scattered to the wind.

He stalked into the crowd, slamming his shoulder into Valary's as he passed and ripping the talisman out of her grip. She shouted after him in anger, but he paid her no mind as he swept across the dance floor, looking for Loren. He tried using the Sight, but he couldn't find her, couldn't breathe—

He dug his phone out of his pocket and found her name in his

Favorites list. "Pick up, pick up," he muttered, pacing across the dance floor as he scanned the club. The look on his face must be lethal, as several people within his vicinity made for the wall like he was sick with something contagious. *"Pick up."*

The call reached the final ring before her soft voice drifted through the speaker. "Darien—"

"Where are you?" he bit out.

"I'm by the bar—"

"I need you to get to the car, Loren." He turned in the direction of the bar she'd mentioned. It was too far away—too fucking far. The fact that they were in a building protected by wards provided him with no relief. He knew the owner of this drinking den didn't give two shits about protecting his paying customers; the magic here wasn't meant to keep people safe, not like the wards that covered the Avenue of the Scarlet Star and Angelthene Academy. No—the ones shielding the Advocate were only there to keep the back rooms and the dealings that went on inside them inaccessible and hidden. *"Now!"* Darien barked. "Valary took your talisman—"

His sentence was cut short as he caught sight of three men who were practically running in the same direction he was headed, shoving people aside as they moved. Running straight for the bar.

Straight for Loren.

Darien hung up, shoved his phone into his pocket, and grabbed hold of two male dancers within arm's reach of him and banged their skulls together. They fell to the floor in a tangled heap.

He didn't have to punch many people before the whole club broke out into a brawl—before the men who were making a beeline for Loren were intercepted by right hooks and invisible walls of magic. Glasses shattered on the floor, and people screamed.

Darien spotted Loren heading for the staircase that would take her up to the top floor—to the doors of the club and outside. She was too far away for him to feel at ease.

Darien followed behind her, shoving through the crowds. People scrambled to get out of his way, the odd person throwing hooks that barely grazed him before he was knocking them out cold.

He caught the eyes of his Devils from across the room, who were all making for the exit in the sea of thrashing people, adding to the drunken brawl with uppercuts and boots thrust out to trip people.

His plan was working.

He only hoped it *kept* working.

THERE WAS something wrong with her. Something must've happened at the bar when she'd stopped for a drink after being accosted by that Warg, and now she felt like she was going to throw up. The music was louder than it had been before, every thump of it clawing at her eardrums, and her body was colder than the mist undulating through the room. People were fighting, slamming into her as she made for the staircase, nearly knocking her over. The floor beneath her feet surged and dipped like ocean waves.

Everything was a blur as she reached that first step and grasped onto the icy handrail. Cold metal bit into her palm, and her teeth chattered. She pulled herself up, bit by bit, swallowing the nausea roiling in her gut, blinking fiercely to stay awake — to stay alert. She had to keep going, had to get outside, had to get to the car.

She lurched up the last step, her vision as staticky as a television that was turned to the wrong channel. People felt her up as she stumbled through the crowds, grabbing onto parts of her where Darien's touch still lingered. She didn't want to feel any hands on her but his, no other hands *ever*.

Every thought in her head had jumbled together into a tangled mess she couldn't make sense of when three men closed her in between their bodies like she was a stray dog. A warlock and two werewolves who reeked of hard liquor and cheap drugs.

"Hey honey," the warlock said, his voice a low croon. He stooped so his head was at her level, and a big hand reached for her hair. "You lost?"

"I have to go home," she tried to say, but it was more of a gurgle, and they kept cutting her off, herding her farther away from the doors of the Advocate. The faces surrounding her were blurry, the club a whirlwind of color and light. She shouted for the Devils, but her words were swallowed up by the yelling and the thumping music. The features of the three men were so distorted, they looked like demons—like walking, talking nightmares. "Please—"

"She doesn't like that," one of the wolves laughed as he grabbed a fistful of her ass, his clumsy fingers hot and sweaty through the sheer fabric of her skirt. Loren nearly hurled. "But *I* do."

She tried to back away, to get away from them, but she only ended up pressing herself harder into his vile touch—

A shout ripped through the club, audible even over the clamor and the pounding music. It was a voice Loren recognized, a voice she longed to walk toward, but she couldn't move her feet to get to him. The words the voice had shouted had two of the men that were fencing her in dropping her immediately, though the third still hung onto her like she was his precious toy, one hand in her hair and the other squeezing her waist tight enough to bruise.

When she heard that deep, rich voice talking again, his name floated through the fog in her thoughts.

Darien.

His voice was so angry, so loud, that it made her jump out of her skin. The drug was blurring her vision, rendering her nearly blind, but from what she could see of Darien's features as he approached their group, pushing people aside so hard they crashed to the floor, he was livid. The other Devils were flanking him now, and under the pulsing blue lights sweeping about the room, Loren swore she saw sharp horns on their heads.

"She's *mine*," Darien growled, the two words ripping through the night.

The warlock gripping her waist said something else, but it sounded like static to Loren. Her tattoo was beginning to burn her arm, and she swayed on her feet, only held up the stranger's hold.

Loren blinked, willing her eyes to cooperate. She caught sight of the two other men in the trio—the wolves—heading for the club doors, the idea of challenging the Seven Devils clearly not something they were interested in entertaining.

But the warlock wouldn't let go of her.

Darien said to the wolves who were making for the doors, the warlock partially turning to glare at the backs of his friends' heads with fury, "You're lucky you're walking out and not crawling out."

The warlock spun around to face the Devil, his body pushing into Loren, though he did—wisely—let go of her waist. She teetered, grasping at the air, and barely stopped herself from faceplanting on the floor. "Who are you, her boyfriend?"

"I'm Darien fucking Cassel."

A beat of silence followed his words; it bled into the surrounding crowd until nothing could be heard but the thumping of the music and the distant sound of fighting continuing down on the bottom floor. Up here, movement had ceased, and all eyes were on them.

"Yeah, I'm his," Loren slurred, teetering in her heels. "And he's Darien fucking Cassel."

The warlock, at last realizing whose soil he stood on, fully stepped away from her, as if she'd suddenly burst into flames.

Loren staggered across the room, but before she could get to Darien, the warlock lunged for her in a dark blur—

And then Darien was there, grabbing the warlock by the windpipe, his grip so hard that the warlock's face instantly turned purple. "Touch her again and I'll cut your goddamn heart out." His words had Loren more sober than she was before, fear slicing so deep that whatever drug was in her system was nearly scared right out of it.

The warlock finally took that as his cue to leave, and the moment Darien let go of his throat, he practically ran for the exit, the doors banging open with his departure.

Loren gurgled a laugh. She didn't think they'd be back for a while. Her hands grazed one of Darien's arms, feeling the hard muscle beneath his skin. "I love these arms," she burbled. She was vaguely aware of him clipping a chain around her neck. *The Avertera talisman,* said a small voice in her head. "I *love* them—"

Suddenly top-heavy, she veered for the floor, propelled forward by her own weight. The ground got closer and closer...

And then she was floating.

No, someone was carrying her. His touch was gentle. Soft, yet very strong—stronger than the men who'd grabbed her. Her head felt light as a feather as this angel carried her out of the club and down the street, toward a black vehicle that was parked by the curb.

She was safe now. She *felt* safe. There was nowhere in the world that was safer than here.

Instead of trying to see, she listened.

The sound of a car door swinging open. Her gauzy dress tugging and sliding across cool leather. The door closing behind her, and other doors opening.

She peeked through her eyelashes to see that she was lying on the back seat of Darien's car. Darien had just got into the driver's seat and was starting the engine. Maximus was in the passenger's seat, and Dallas was sitting beside Loren, brushing Loren's hair back from her sweat-slick face. Dallas was speaking, but Loren couldn't hear a word, the sounds that were shaped by the witch's red lips nothing but unintelligible echoes. Loren's mouth was dry, and she felt like she had to vomit.

A strange, high-pitched music wailed through the night. Sirens, she realized. She felt like she was dreaming as the edges of her vision shimmered and sparked like fireworks.

Suddenly, people were shouting. Max and Dallas were screaming at Darien to start driving, to get away from here before the peace officers, who were screeching to a halt out front of the club, came up to the car. Loren had no idea what was happening, or why Darien was delaying, but then he was accelerating onto Angelthene Boulevard, the motion causing Loren to roll into the backrest of the seat. She nearly threw up, bile rising to coat her tongue.

Everything went black, and Loren didn't come to again until she was lying on the couch in the sitting room at Hell's Gate. Darien was leaning over her, hands braced on his knees, his face colorful and shimmery. The ceiling fan was on low, and she watched it like it was a mobile spinning above a crib.

"She's awake," Loren heard him say, his words echoing again and again and again. Her surroundings twisted and duplicated like the inside of a kaleidoscope. "I need you to sit up for me, Lola." His sentence was repeated by her own mind, again and again.

I need you to sit up for me, Lola.

389

I need you to sit up for me, Lola.

His fingers wrapped around her wrists, and then he was tugging her to a sitting position, shifting her so that her back was resting against the cushions.

Max stepped into view, but Loren couldn't keep her eyelids open long enough to notice if anyone else was here.

"We need to get that out of her," Darien was saying. Her head lolled against her chest, but a hand grabbed onto her chin, and another came down on her shoulder, holding her upright. "Open up, Loren."

Open up, Loren. The words echoed and echoed and echoed.

"Don't threaten me with a good time," Loren slurred. A laugh gurgled out of her, but it was abruptly cut off by Darien forcing her mouth open and placing something round and chalky under her tongue. She grimaced and made to pull away, but Darien didn't let go of her. She wanted *him* in her mouth, wanted to taste him, not some stupid pill.

He closed her mouth but kept her chin in his grasp, forcing her to let dissolve whatever he'd put under her tongue.

As soon as the pill had melted into her mouth, and Darien let go of her chin, her heart kicked into a sprint, and she broke down into hysterics, grasping at the empty air for him. But there were three of him, and she couldn't find him, couldn't get to the real Darien—

"Don't leave me," she blurted. "You can't leave me—"

"I'm not leaving you, Loren." Darien's voice was far, far away, fading with every word he spoke. His hands found hers and gripped them tightly. The squeezing in her chest eased, her heart slowing its erratic rhythm. "Do you hear me? Not now, not ever."

"Promise?" she croaked.

"I promise." His words calmed her, though only just. And soon darkness was ushering her away again, beckoning her into its claws.

She didn't want to go, but she had to. She wanted to take Darien with her, wanted him at her side, always—

Fog swallowed her whole, washing her wounded thoughts away like rain down gutters.

DARIEN WAS JUST HANGING up the phone when the front door to Hell's Gate swung open, and he turned around to see Logan and Sabrine rushing in, the other Devils with them. Travis and Jack were carrying the unconscious warlock between them, his limp arms draped across their shoulders.

Logan took note of the murderous look on Darien's face and hesitated in the entrance hall. Sabrine stilled beside him, her eyes flickering between Darien and Loren, who was passed out on the couch behind him, her head resting in Dallas's lap. Sabrine's mouth popped open as she made to say something, but Darien spoke before she had a chance.

"You called Calanthe?" Darien thundered to the alpha, gripping his phone so tightly the screen nearly cracked. Behind him, Loren stirred, muttering drowsily.

Logan's hands curled into fists at his sides. His whole body vibrated as he actively fought the urge to shift. The Devils who stood around him made for the sitting room; standing next to a werewolf when he shifted was never a good idea.

Logan bit out, "I made a deal with her —"

"And you made a promise to *me*," Darien retorted. "If you told her anything about Loren, I swear —"

"Don't threaten me, Devil," the wolf growled, his fiery eyes sparking. "I said nothing about Loren to the Head Leech. Forgive me for wanting to stay on Calanthe's good side so she doesn't change her mind about my breaking of the pact."

"Staying on her good side is pretty much shot to hell, now that she knows I'm keeping things from her." Calanthe wanted in on all their doings, and as soon as Logan had informed her of what went down at the Devil's Advocate tonight, she had called Darien, fuming about not being included in their plans.

Logan snarled and took two steps forward, hair swaying. "This isn't just about you. This is about every wolf in the Silverwood District, Darien. Innocent people could die if I don't follow through with the bargain I made —"

"If you're so worried about innocent lives, here's another one you should consider," Darien snapped, gesturing to Loren. "I don't care what I have to do to keep this girl safe, but you'd better learn to listen to me or we're going to have a fucking problem. If you get her killed, *I* will be the one to slaughter you and every one of the wolves in your Silverwood District so fast, you'll wish Calanthe had been the one to do it."

A growl ripped through Logan's bared teeth. The other Devils moved to stand at Darien's side, while Sabrine lunged forward and grabbed one of Logan's vibrating arms, stopping him from taking another step.

But she pulled back as soon as she touched him, drawing a hiss in through her teeth. The pending shift had caused his skin to heat up, burning her immediately upon contact.

Logan's fiery eyes cooled, the trembling from the shift ceasing. Darien saw his breathing calm as he faced Sabrine. "I'm sorry," he said to her, his voice rough and broken.

Darien bit his tongue to still the words that hovered at the tip of it. He turned around to face Loren, whose eyelashes were fluttering as she dreamed, and scooped her into his arms, being careful not to wake her. He concentrated on his breathing as he carried her out of the sitting room, toward the staircase in the entrance hall. The other Devils moved aside to let him through.

As he passed Logan, he slowed. "From now on, you will consult with me," Darien said, every word measured and low. "About *everything*. You do not go to Calanthe unless I tell you it's okay to do so. Can you handle that?"

Logan's nostrils were flared, his jaw tight. He glanced at Loren, lying limp in Darien's arms. "I guess I have to, don't I?" he hissed.

"Yeah," Darien said, "you really fucking do."

He strode past the wolf before he had a chance to say anything else and carried Loren up the stairs. He focused on Loren's beautiful face as he walked, being careful not to jostle her as he maneuvered the steps.

He didn't care how many enemies he made in his efforts to keep her safe. He would always protect her—no matter the cost.

37

Darien was trying desperately to calm the roaring in his head as he knelt behind Loren in the bathroom in his suite, holding her hair back as she threw up into the toilet, again and again and again. He knew this had to happen to purge the drug from her system, but he didn't like it, didn't like seeing her in discomfort. She'd tried to shoo him away when she'd first sprinted to the toilet, but he hadn't listened. She was still in no position to take care of herself, and until she got some rest and woke up with every trace of that drug gone, he refused to leave her side.

"Not bad for your first night at the Advocate," Darien joked. She tried to answer him, but she only retched again. Darien held her hair with one hand, his other rubbing comforting patterns over her back. She was shaking, and her skin was cold and covered in a sheen of sweat. All this discomfort he'd caused her—all of it was for *nothing*.

Well…hopefully not completely nothing. Even though they hadn't caught who was buying the Blood Potions, the warlock who'd helped abduct Sabrine was currently unconscious in the basement. As soon as he woke up, Darien planned on getting some answers out of him, no matter how much blood it took, no matter how wicked it made him feel. No matter how many burning-hot showers he would have to take afterward in order to feel clean. He sometimes hated this part of himself—the part that was a true Devil —but it was ingrained in his soul. Without it, he wouldn't know who he was.

One day... One day, things might finally be different.

Eventually, Loren stopped being sick, stopped shivering so hard that her teeth were chattering. She was slumped against Darien's chest, fighting to keep her eyes open, her hands gripping his shirt in tight little fists.

"Darien," she croaked. He loved the way she said his name, as if it was a light she walked toward through darkness.

"What is it, sweetheart?"

"Will you stay with me tonight?" Her eyes were fully closed now, her body limp. She had asked him that question nearly ten times since he'd brought her home from the club; it was why they were currently in his suite instead of hers.

"I'll stay with you, Loren," he said, his voice as sincere as the handful of other times he'd answered this same question in the past hour. He didn't care how many times she asked him; he would never grow tired of hearing those words float off her lips. "I promise."

He managed to get Loren from the floor and into his bed, where he covered her up with the puffy black duvet, tucking it up under her chin. When he'd brought her upstairs, Ivy and Dallas had stripped her outfit off and helped her into her pajamas. Darien had never been so grateful to have so many helpful women in his house.

He was just about to lie down on the bed beside her when a knock came at his door. Loren mumbled and stirred slightly, already half-asleep. Darien crossed the room quietly, walking heel to toe, and swung open the door.

Max stood in the hallway. His attention went briefly to the girl in Darien's bed. "He's awake," Max said of the warlock. "Dallas said she can watch Loren for a while."

Time to get this show on the road.

Max moved aside to allow Darien room to step into the hallway. He closed the door behind him and followed Max into the basement. Neither of them said a word as they walked, honing their focus, shoving every bit of emotion from their minds. It was their pre-kill ritual.

Darien paused at the table where he'd dressed Loren's glass wounds and grabbed a few of the weapons strewn across it, Max doing the same. The air down here was nearly as cold as the mist in the Devil's Advocate.

The warlock was tied to a chair in the farthest room from the stairs, where the Devils brought most of the people they had to question — the people they anticipated being difficult.

Where he was slumped in that same chair that countless people had been tied to in years past, the man looked up at the sound of Darien's entry. It looked like his head weighed a thousand pounds, and it was constantly dipping toward his chest. When his silver-brown eyes found the Death's Head Knuckles that were attached to Darien's right hand, there was — strangely enough — no fear in them.

"You're not going to need those," the warlock slurred.

"And why's that?" Darien said. Max stood, arms crossed, at his side, a crowbar in hand.

"Because I'm willing to talk," the warlock replied. His words tumbled into each other, nearly indistinguishable from the lingering effects of the drug the others had used to sedate him. "I'm willing to tell the truth."

Darien blinked the Sight into place. "I'm listening," he prompted.

There was a long beat of silence, and then the warlock finally spoke. "To be honest with you, I'm not sure where to start. Your boys sure did a number on me, and my brain is kind of jumbled. Why don't you ask me a question and I promise I'll answer it in full truth?" Promises meant nothing when they came from strangers, but that was why Darien had the Sight — the most reliable method of lie detection in all of Terra. It hadn't failed him, not once in his life.

Darien crossed his arms, the spikes on the Death's Head Knuckles glinting in the bright light. "You helped a Darkslayer abduct Sabrine Van Arsdell several weeks ago. Why?"

A slow, heavy blink. "Sabrine wasn't the one we wanted," he began. "It was that little human you had in your lap tonight. We were sent for her bounty shortly after we were recruited into a group that calls themselves the Phoenix Head Society. I was promised that if I helped find the human girl they were after, I would not only receive a reward in mynet, but I would be able to reap the benefits of an artifact called the Arcanum Well. An artifact the society could use only if they found the human girl they were looking for—they believe she is the key."

There was a pause. Darien said, "Keep talking."

"I was told that the Arcanum Well was a miracle machine. It could give mortals immortal life, could heal any disease, and could grant immortals more power and unlimited access to their magic without the threat of contracting the Tricking." As the warlock spoke, Darien listened very closely, every muscle in his body tense as the answers he'd sought for so many weeks floated through the room. It seemed everything Calanthe had told them in Logan's house was correct. She was right—about everything.

The warlock continued, "I wanted in on those benefits. I've had doctors tell me I'm maybe ten years, at best, from contracting the Tricking. I've been alive for too many centuries—been using my magic for too long. Helping the Phoenix Head Society find the Well would not only make me immune to the disease, but it would also make me more powerful." The corner of his mouth inched upward with a smile. "It wasn't exactly an offer I was about to pass up, and I certainly wasn't the only one who felt that way." He paused, throat bobbing as he swallowed. "They managed to create a replica of the Arcanum Well. But...but it isn't the same."

"What do you mean it isn't the same?" There hadn't been a single hint that the man was lying since the moment he'd started speaking. His aura was steady, not a single flicker to suggest that anything he'd said wasn't the whole truth.

"Their little machine doesn't work properly," the warlock said. "It's as if it was cursed. The Phoenix Head Society is still looking for the *real* Well—the original—because they can't make their replica work the same way. They've tried for a long time, and they keep trying—they keep purchasing the Blood Potions necessary for conducting the spells, along with the chemicals needed to fill the Well's chamber. But they keep failing. They can't seem to get the measurements right, perhaps, or maybe there are missing words in the spells they're using." He shrugged with one shoulder. "They need the *real* Well, is what I've been told. They need the real one, or their efforts will never work."

It cannot be replicated, only remade. That's what the Master Scroll had said. Darien wondered if the people who'd managed to build this Well replica perhaps had the other half of the scroll—the missing half that completed the piece Darien had in his possession. Or, rather, the piece he'd recently given to Arthur, a dear friend of his who was better at deciphering riddles than Darien.

"Their replica is causing mutations in the people they are experimenting on," the warlock continued. "It's turning them into monsters —into what the news channel has been referring to as a new breed of demon. The more their experiments failed, the less interest I had in reaping the benefits of it. Unless the Phoenix Head Society can locate the real Well, there are no benefits to be reaped. It is all risk and zero reward. But they refuse to give up. I didn't stick around long enough to find out anything else; I wanted out, wanted away from their experiments before I became their next guinea pig. Before they ran out of the missing girls they were shoving into the Well and decided to use some of their own people instead."

Darien's head was spinning. Beside him, Max was speechless.

Loren was right: the demons *were* the missing girls. Born from the waters of the cursed Well replica.

"Who's behind this?" Darien said. "Who's in charge of this fucking mess?"

The warlock shrugged. "I don't have the answer to that. I was considered so low in rank when I joined the society that I wasn't trusted with that information. I was never allowed to see the real face behind the Well replica. Everything I just told you about their experiments has been offered to me by lower members of the society. I'm merely taking their word for it. And after your human pet got away from me, I was trusted even less."

Max cut in. "And where do you stand on this situation now?"

"I already told you: I left the society. I wanted nothing to do with it after I saw what it was turning people into. I was promised immunity to the Tricking and an endless supply of magic; getting turned into some flesh-crazed creature wasn't something I was eager to step in line to receive."

Darien said, "If the society knows what the Well is and what it looks like, why can't the hellsehers who are working for them track it?" Remotely tracking a person or a magical object was usually a cinch if they had a photograph or a drawing of what they were looking for. To not be able to track something was new to him, just like so many people concealing their auras was new. He'd never been tested like this before, not once in his life.

"It's made from a material that cannot be tracked except by the girl. Even if you were to have a drawing of it right in front of you, you'd be blind. You would feel the Well's presence everywhere, as if it was right under your feet."

Shit. This just kept getting more complicated, didn't it?

"What is it made from?" Darien asked. Usually, magical objects exuded their own field of energy, so the fact that the Arcanum Well and its replica couldn't be tracked, didn't have distinct fields of energy that would point to their whereabouts...

It didn't make sense.

But—maybe this warlock was wrong. Maybe, if Darien could figure out the answer to this question, he would be able to narrow down its location, to learn how to feel its presence the same way all these people seemed to think Loren would be able to feel it. Understanding *what* he was tracking was at the very root of the Sight. If he could track the Well, he might be able to remove the target from Loren's back, erasing her as the only route to the miracles it could make. He would slap that target right onto his own back if he could. If it meant she would be safe.

The warlock shook his head. Clearly, he hadn't been trusted with that answer.

Darien pressed, "Where are they keeping the Well replica? Do you know where we can find it?"

The warlock shook his head again, and when Darien blinked the Sight back into his vision, he saw that his answer was not a lie. He really didn't know where to find it.

"The hellseher who helped you take Sabrine," Darien said. "Who is he?"

The warlock looked like he might pass out. "I was only given a first name: James." There were so many people in this city named James that it would take a million years to find out who he was and track him. "Nobody trusted each other enough to give any more info than that. If you want to find him, your best bet would be to try and catch a photo of him on one of the video cameras in the city." He seemed to think of something, and then he amended, "Though they're good at hiding their auras, so I doubt that even if you had an image of him, you'd be able to track him. They've been using Nacht Essentia—a plant that conceals a person's location. The veil it casts cannot be seen through, no matter how gifted someone is in the Sight." He gave Darien a little smile. "Even you, Devil."

Nacht Essentia. Essence of Night. It was what Logan had mentioned to Darien back when they'd found Sabrine, though the wolf hadn't been able to remember the name.

"Is there any way to heal the people who've been changed into demons?" Darien asked.

"I have no idea, Devil. If you find out, make sure to let me know." His eyes found the Death's Head Knuckles that were still attached to Darien's hand. "Are you going to rip my face apart now, or can you give me a clean death?"

Darien considered his question. The warlock merely watched him, an oddly empty cast to his eyes.

"I'm not going to kill you," Darien said at last. "But you won't remember any of this after tonight."

He sliced his magic into the warlock's mind, the force of it causing the man to pass out in the chair.

He would remember nothing after Darien was done with him. It was a hellseher ability that didn't work on other hellsehers or anyone whose mind had been trained to keep magic out. He would tunnel into this warlock's mind the same way he had Baylor's when they'd left the club, when Max and Dallas had been screaming at him to start driving. But instead of coloring his thoughts with false emotions the way he had Baylor—when he'd made sure that vile vampire would remember Loren differently and would never desire her again —he would wipe clean any trace of these last few hours from the warlock's mind. For once, there would be no blood on his hands— not tonight.

It was a step up from what he was used to, he had to admit. He had to start doing better.

For Loren, he *would* do better.

WHEN LOREN WOKE UP, dawn was pouring into the room, warming up the duvet that was piled on top of her. It took her a few minutes before she could remember anything—before her head and stomach stopped spinning in endless circles, round and round and round.

Groggy, she pushed the soft black duvet down and glanced about the spacious room, struggling to figure out where she was. She didn't recognize anything in here—not the bed she was sprawled on, not the floor-to-ceiling gilt mirror beside the bed, not the walk-in closet, not the impressive collection of music that spanned an entire wall.

Her lungs tightening, she started to panic—

Until she caught sight of the shirtless Devil sound asleep on the king-sized bed beside her.

Cripes. She was in Darien's suite. The events of last night flooded back to her then, and her body heated up just as it had when she'd sat in Darien's lap, when his hands had been all over her.

Darien was sleeping on his stomach, his head turned in her direction, his muscular arms stretched out above his head, inked hands loosely grasping his pillow. He looked so calm, so...vulnerable. His black eyelashes fluttered softly as he slept, his smooth breathing disrupting a strand of dark hair that hung to the tip of his nose.

He was absolutely exquisite, and she couldn't stop staring at him. She could've watched him forever and never grown tired of the way he looked. To think that those strong, tattooed hands had been touching her only last night, in places where no man had ever touched—

Loren gulped, clamping her legs together as that same heat she'd

CITY OF GODS AND MONSTERS

felt last night bloomed between her thighs, where it spread right up to her navel. She couldn't think about that now, and—

She still felt dizzy. Still felt like she might throw up, even with the drug now out of her system.

How had last night gone so horribly wrong?

Darien woke up a few minutes later, those eyelashes fluttering. Loren held her breath as that heavy, intimidating gaze of his settled on her, as real as a physical touch. Butterflies twitched in her stomach, the realization of exactly whose bed she was in setting those butterfly wings aflame.

From Rook and Redding's to this. So much had changed, and in so little time, that she sometimes wondered how they'd got here.

"Hi," Darien said, his voice rougher and deeper than usual.

Tucking the sheets up to her chin, Loren dipped her head and whispered, "Hi." With the weight of Darien's stare on her, the warmth between her legs spread throughout her entire body.

"How are you feeling?"

"I'm fine," she whispered. "How are you?"

Darien gave her a sleepy smile that made her toes curl beneath the sheets. "Fine."

Her heart was running a race in her chest, and she knew Darien could hear every thump it made. He was staring at her, those eyes darkening with something far more intense than the Sight. The way his eyes were slightly hooded as he looked her over made her body tingle. Her breasts turned heavy, and she pressed her thighs together below the duvet, desperate for physical contact—for a release she wanted only *him* to give her. Not herself, not anyone else—*him*. Wanted to give him full power over her body and her pleasure.

Her thoughts drifted back to last night, back to all they'd shared at that nightclub, everything they'd done. She couldn't remember much of what had happened after she'd been drugged, but the things that came before that moment were clear as day.

She remembered everything. Remembered every filthy thing Darien had said to her, word for word. Remembered the way the people in the club had devoured the sight of them touching each other, as if they were on a stage.

As if they were acting. The thought had Loren's shoulders curling inward, her breathing turning shallow. Heat spread through her forearm, warning her that she'd gone too long without eating. She ignored the signal, a sickness that had nothing to do with her mysterious disease twisting deep in her gut.

What did Darien remember from last night? Had their time at the Advocate felt as life-changing to him as it had to her? Or was she so pathetic that she was clinging to every word he'd uttered like it was a life raft for her pride? Had he said those same things to other girls before and meant them? It wasn't her business, but—

"Something's on your mind," Darien said, his voice exceptionally gentle as he propped his head up on a hand. His words snapped her out of the anxiety that had closed over her like a suffocating blanket. "Go on and ask me, sweetheart."

"How much..." The gray sheets rustled as she fidgeted. She cleared her throat, and then she forced her question out. "How much of last night was pretending for you?"

Concern deepened his features, the corner of his distracting mouth tilting downward. "None of it," he said. "None of it, Loren. All of that was real for me—every single thing." The space between his eyebrows crinkled with a new kind of worry, and suddenly it felt somewhat like looking in a mirror. "How much—"

"None of it," she whispered. His expression smoothed. "I meant everything I said and did."

An impish smile ghosted across his lips. "So you *do* want me."

Loren fought her own smile. "I meant everything I said," she repeated.

The heat in Darien's gaze had returned, and suddenly she was very aware of how alone they were. She was in this Devil's bed, and he was looking at her as if he wanted to lower himself between her legs, just as he'd told her last night. To eat his way to her heart and find out if she tasted as sweet as she looked.

"I should get ready for work," Loren spluttered. She disentangled herself from the sheets and duvet that were wrapped around her, and nearly toppled out of bed as she got to her feet. The floorboards were cold in the morning chill.

She swayed for a moment, the room gyrating. When was the last time she'd eaten anything?

Darien sat up, his full attention falling on her as she straightened her pajama shirt and tugged her fingers through the tangles in her hair. She was painfully aware of how awful she must look, and she became desperate to hide herself before he noticed she didn't look quite as sweet this morning as she had last night. She could feel the makeup still caked to her skin, could feel tightness at the corner of her mouth that suggested she'd drooled sometime during the night.

That smile on Darien's face grew. "Quit fussing, Rookie," he said. "You're beautiful."

"Says the perfect god with no shirt on," she joked, every word breathless. He really was a perfect god, and the way the light streaming in through the slats in the blinds illuminated his body...

She wanted to pounce on him. Wanted to call in sick to work and spend all day riding him instead.

Darien was full-on grinning now, and Loren became desperate for a need to take the focus off the tension building between them, desperate to draw his attention away from how hard her nipples were beneath her shirt. There was hardly any air in this room — hardly any air left in the world. If they ever progressed from feeling each other up to making love — or fucking, as Darien liked to call it — she might collapse from a death of her heart's own making.

Loren cleared her throat and said, "What happened last night? What happened with the warlock? Is he...?"

"We didn't kill him," Darien said, his smile fading as he became all business and no play. He leaned back against the cushioned head-board, propped up a knee, and balanced an arm on it. Gods, he was... He was stunning. She forced herself to focus on what he was saying, so she wouldn't have to ask him to repeat himself. Darien continued, "But I made sure that everything that happened last night will be nothing but a dream to him." He quickly filled her in on what the warlock had revealed — about the Arcanum Well replica, about Nacht Essentia, about the demons and the missing girls, about the Blood Potions deal going awry, about the phone call from Calanthe. When he was finished, she was speechless.

"What do we do now?"

"Don't worry about it for today," he said. "My main concern is keeping you safe and helping Doctor Atlas find an antidote for the girls who've been changed by the Well replica. I'll also be putting any purchases of Nacht Essentia on our radar; if we can't find who created the replica by intercepting Blood Potion deals, then maybe we can find them by tracking purchases of Nacht Essentia." He studied whatever her face was telling him. "You don't need to do anything, Loren. Do you understand me? We'll handle this."

She gave a faint nod. "I guess I should go get ready. I'm running out of time." She made for the closed bedroom door, all too aware of Darien's eyes tracking her every movement, all too aware that her pajama shorts barely covered her backside.

She was just about to open the door when the question he voiced gave her pause.

"Will you have dinner with me tonight?"

Loren turned to face him, and when their gazes locked, that adorable smile on his face grew. One hand resting on the door handle, she snickered, though her heart was skipping in her chest — with delight and nerves. "I thought dating wasn't in your vocabulary, Darien Cassel."

"It's not a date. It's just...dinner."

"Right. Dinner between two friends?" She had to bite the inside of her cheek to keep from laughing.

"Right. Friends." The dimple in Darien's cheek showed as he fought his own smile.

A grin broke like the sun across her face, and a rosy warmth spread through her chest. There was a tiny, rational voice in the back of her mind, screaming at her to be careful, to take it slow. But she ignored it, shoving it behind a door in her mind and locking it.

"Okay, Darien," she said. "I'll have dinner with you, but only as friends. We're not allowed to fall in love." She'd meant for the words to come out as a joke, but as soon as they were hovering in the air between them, she realized how painfully true they were.

They weren't allowed to fall in love — not really.

She was mortal; one day she would die. And sometimes she

wondered if it was better to accept the truth than to hold on so tightly to something that may never be.

She left Darien's room before he could reply, slipping out into the hallway with a sharp burning sensation behind her eyes. But she glimpsed his expression in her peripheral as she closed the door behind her—the one that told her the statement she'd made hurt him as badly as it hurt her.

Those awful, unfair words chased her all day.

She was mortal. One day she would die. And Darien...

Darien would live for a very long time. Maybe even forever.

LOREN'S SHIFT at Mordred and Penelope's felt far longer than the seven hours it really was, and she knew it wasn't just because of the lack of sleep she'd gotten last night.

It was because she was too excited—and nervous—for when Darien would pick her up, and they would go and have dinner together. As *friends*. Laughter threatened to bubble up her throat as she flitted about the apothecary, looking for the most minute tasks that would help the time pass faster. Friends didn't feel each other up the way they had last night; friends didn't call each other when there was nothing to say, just so they could listen to the sound of their voice.

Friends didn't think about each other every waking moment and count down the seconds until they could see each other again.

When four thirty rolled around at last, Loren's phone beeped where it sat on the desk upstairs, where she was completing paper-work for closing, and her heart skipped as his name flashed across the screen.

Sorry I'm late, Darien had written. She glanced at the clock; she wasn't sure two minutes counted as being late, but the message had her smiling. *I'm in the usual spot.*

She breezed through the rest of her closing duties, her legs wobbling the whole time. Before she left, she swiped on a fresh layer of lip-gloss, finger-combed her hair, and readjusted her white lace dress. She couldn't believe how nervous she was! She wanted to smack herself in the head for it.

When she got into Darien's car, he was on the phone, but as he listened to whatever the person on the other end of the call was saying, he gave her the kind of crooked smile that made her weak in the knees. It was a good thing she had just lowered herself onto the seat, otherwise she might've fallen on her face. She buckled her seat-belt, unable to take her eyes off him as he hurried through the conversation he was having.

When he ended the call, he tucked his phone away and pulled out onto the road. "Have you ever been to Blackbird 88 Above?" Located in the Financial District, Blackbird 88 Above was a ritzy restaurant only people like Taega and Calanthe Croft could afford to dine at.

Or a Devil.

Loren snorted a laugh. "Only in my wildest dreams. I'd have to sell my soul just for a glass of water."

"I'd like to learn all about those wild dreams of yours sometime, Loren Calla." He gave her a lustful glance that had her toes curling in her shoes. "All jokes aside, I'm taking you to Blackbird for dinner. And don't worry, I won't let them steal your soul—it's far too precious."

Her mouth popped open. "You are *not* taking me to Blackbird, Darien Cassel." Then she noticed what he was wearing: the white button-up shirt tucked into black suit-pants; the polished black shoes; the watch that probably cost a fortune. Damn, he looked amazing. And—

Damn, he really *was* taking her to Blackbird.

"Actually, you don't get a say in the matter."

Loren cocked an eyebrow. "Is that so? And did you make reservations, Mister Bossy?"

"I don't need them," he said with a sly grin as he stopped at a red light near the city's Control Tower. The panels of polished cristala that soared way, way up into the sky mirrored the rosy sunset.

Loren rolled her eyes. "Of course not."

Darien laughed. Trust a Devil to get into a place like Blackbird without a reservation.

The restaurant was on the eighty-eighth floor of a skyscraper in the Financial District. Every table in the place was sold out from open to close, no matter what day of the week.

Darien hadn't lied when he'd told Loren he didn't need reservations; after the hostess apologized for not having room to accommodate them, all he had to do was tell her what his name was and she'd found them the best seat in the house, right by a wall of windows with an incredible view of the glimmering district.

"What would you like to drink?" Darien asked as they looked over their menus. "Aside from the water that will cost you your soul." He winked.

Loren blushed. "I suppose I'll have wine," she said. "Sometimes it still strikes me as strange that I'm able to order alcohol." This was the first year she, Dallas, and Sabrine had been able to enter clubs and bars, and the novelty hadn't quite worn off yet.

"When's your birthday?"

"The first of Januarius."

"You're a Kalendae baby." Darien smiled.

"That's right. When were you born, Darien Cassel?" She realized she'd never asked how old he was, though she knew, from what she'd heard the other Devils saying, that none of them had peaked yet. The year at which an immortal stopped aging — their Peak Year, it was called — was different for every person, though it was usually somewhere between the age of twenty and forty. Hellsehers tended to stop aging earlier than other immortal beings, usually by the year thirty-five, though most lived their whole lives in their perpetual twenties.

It was hard for Loren not to feel the stab of jealousy in her heart, especially with Darien sitting across from her.

"On the fifth of Novem," Darien said, "twenty-four years ago."

She sat back, menu drooping in her hands. "The fifth was last Wednesday."

He must've seen the hurt on her face, because he said gently, "I don't celebrate my birthday, Lola. I prefer to have as few people know about it as possible."

Loren cocked her head, her curiosity outweighing the hurt she felt. "Why don't you celebrate it?"

"It has a lot to do with my mother. She died partly because Ivyana and I had been born, so I don't exactly see our date of birth as something worth acknowledging."

Loren left it at that. There was something about his expression — and the way he turned to look out the windows at the glimmering city, as if there was something he wanted to hide — that told her he didn't feel like discussing it further.

Darien asked her a lot of questions over their two-hour dinner. She'd never talked so much about herself, and because of this it took longer than usual to get through her duck confit and roasted vegetables. She didn't mind though, because the flavors were out of this world. She'd never had a meal like this before. For someone who'd grown up on the North End, she'd been to a lot of expensive restaurants over the years, so that was saying something.

Along with her past, Darien wanted to know the simpler things about her, like what her favorite flower was or why she'd named her dog *Singer.* She didn't understand how anyone could find these things about her interesting, but he didn't look bored by a single word she said.

At the end of the meal, as she savoured every bite of her rich chocolate mousse, he settled his elbows onto the table and said, "I have a confession to make."

Loren sucked on her spoon. Darien tracked the movement with a predatory gaze that sent a thrill down her spine. "Uh-oh," she crooned. "Don't tell me you can't afford the bill either and we're going to have to make a run for it."

Darien gave an attractive laugh, and it was the realest laugh she'd ever heard from his distracting mouth. "You're adorable, you know that?" The way he was looking at her — like she was something he wanted to eat — had her toes curling again. "I meant it when I said I don't need reservations for this place, but you thought it was because of *this.*" He gestured to the tattoo below his ear.

The spoon clinked as Loren set it in the empty dish. "Isn't it because of that?"

"Most of the time, yes. But for this place, it's actually because I own it."

She stared at him for a long time. As seconds turned into minutes, he began to look concerned by her silence. At last, she bit out, "You're kidding."

He shook his head slowly.

Loren propped her chin up on a hand. "How can you afford it? I mean, I know you make a lot of cash, but...*Blackbird?*"

He smiled. "When my mother was alive, this was her favorite restaurant. Three years ago, the owner decided they wanted to sell it. My father put a bid in, but not because he wanted to protect it—he wanted to have it destroyed."

Loren's forehead creased. "I don't understand. Why would he want to destroy something that meant so much to your mother?"

"Simply put, my father is a malicious man. When my mother passed away, he wanted no reminders of her left behind. To him, her children were enough of a reminder. Blackbird had to go." Every trace of humor in his expression had vanished. "So, I decided to outbid him. It cost me pretty much every copper I'd saved up, but I couldn't stand to see something my mother loved so dearly razed to the ground. I refused to let it happen."

"So, Blackbird became yours."

Darien nodded. "My bid was anonymous, of course. If he ever found out I'd outbid him...," he trailed off, his expression darkening. "Well, we won't get into that tonight."

Loren was still frowning. With a click of her tongue, she said, "I just can't believe—"

"What is that?" Darien interrupted, eyes gleaming with amusement as he lowered his head, as if trying to peer into her mouth—despite that she'd clamped her lips together upon realizing he'd spotted her tongue piercing. "Let me see," he commanded, his mouth twitching with the hint of a smile.

She stuck out her tongue only long enough for the stud

embedded in the center to catch the light of the chandeliers before snapping her mouth shut again.

Darien's smile turned wicked, his eyes crinkling at the outer corners. "When did you get that done?"

"This past summer."

The way he was looking at her suggested his thoughts were far from appropriate. "What's it for?"

She giggled at the absurdity of his question. "What do you mean, 'what's it for?'" She scrunched her nose. "Don't people get piercings only because they look good?"

"I can think of at least one other reason."

Her mouth popped open with a gasp. "You are a *shameless* flirt, you know that?"

Darien looked quite pleased with himself as he wheezed a chuckle. "I'm sorry. I just couldn't resist."

"How did you not notice it last night?" He'd opened her mouth to put that pill under her tongue, after all.

The memory had his teasing smile fading a touch. "I think it's safe to say I was distracted. I was very worried about you." The confession made her body turn hot. "It's a charm, isn't it?" Damn, she was hoping he wouldn't have noticed the rune carved into the side of the diamond. "What did you buy it for?"

"To hide my freckles," she admitted.

Disappointment lined his face. "To hide your freckles," he repeated. "Whereabouts would they be?"

"Just on my nose." She crinkled it, as if it might show the sprinkles of light brown that had cost her three hundred gold mynet to conceal.

"I don't want you to hide anything about yourself," Darien said. "Switch it out for another one. I'm sure your freckles are just as beautiful as the rest of you."

Her heart felt like it was exploding. "Darien..." she breathed. Gods, could he be any more perfect?

"Promise me," he urged.

Loren's heart was swelling with a rosy warmth as she whispered, "I promise."

When the waitress came by to gather up her dessert dish, and Darien signed the bill without a single copper leaving his pocket, they made their way to the sidewalk below. Nightfall had brought balmy winds that smelled faintly of the Angelthene River rushing beyond the freeway.

"I almost forgot." Darien stopped just down the sidewalk from the revolving doors to the restaurant. He reached into his pocket, a smile pulling at the corner of his mouth, as he produced a flat velvet box. "I got something for you."

"What is it?" Her voice was barely a whisper as he placed the box in her palm.

"Open it and find out, silly girl."

"You shouldn't be spending anything on me." Her stomach was leaden with guilt. "The talismans have cost you enough."

"Open it," he urged softly. "I promise it didn't cost three hundred thousand gold mynet."

She gave him a look that said she certainly hoped it hadn't. But he looked so eager for her to open the gift, that her heart squeezed, and she found herself lifting the lid off the box.

Inside was a charm bracelet of rose gold. Every charm was carved to perfection with the smallest details—and the charms, she realized with heart-stopping clarity, were miniature versions of the shops and restaurants on the Avenue of the Scarlet Star.

Of course, there was Mordred and Penelope's Mortar and Pestle, complete with a cauldron-shaped sign above the tiny door. Then there was Medea's Magic Tricks, Chico's Woodfired Pizza, the Cat's Meow, Bella's Beauty Bar, The Golden Onion, Ella and Prince...

Loren's jaw was hanging open. "It's the Avenue of the Scarlet Star." Darien was smiling at her. "You had this made for me?"

He shrugged, as if it wasn't the biggest deal in the world. "That avenue means a lot to you, so I thought you should bring it with you wherever you go."

She swallowed, entirely at a loss for words.

He held his hand out, palm up. "May I?" She handed over the box, and he removed the bracelet and hooked it around her wrist, where it glimmered softly beneath the streetlights.

Tears stung her eyes at the amount of thought behind this incredible gift. She closed the distance between them and threw her arms around his neck.

"Thank you," she said into his shirt. He wound his arms around her waist and pressed his face into her hair, holding her so close she could feel his heart beating against her own. It didn't escape her that this was the second time they'd hugged—and it was just as good as the first time. "No one has ever done anything this nice for me before."

He made to answer, but whatever he was about to say, he never had the chance.

Screams rippled through the night, causing them to pull apart from each other.

A crowd had gathered just down the street, and people were pointing in horror at something that was anchored to the wall of a jewelry store.

Every thought was wiped out of Loren's mind as she followed Darien down the street. As soon as her brain was able to make sense of what she was seeing, her heart stopped.

It was a dead body. Just like the one Darien had told her about that he'd seen in Calanthe's photographs.

Another of the missing girls was anchored into the wall like a hunting trophy, her flesh and blood—and the smattering of magic that was left behind by whatever spell had been used to end her life—were spread out around her in a way that looked like phoenix wings. Her eyes were closed, and blood was streaming from them, sparkling just like the magic that looked like fiery feathers on the white brick wall.

Two words had been drawn in blood below the girl's corpse.

WE'RE WAITING.

It was a message—for *her*. A threat of what she could expect from the days ahead, should she continue to hide.

Loren's blood turned to ice as three gunshots sliced through the night. The citizens milling about the sidewalks, and those who'd stopped to gawk at the dead body, screamed and scattered.

Darien pulled Loren behind him so quickly, her shoulder almost dislocated. He got her out of the way on time, firing his pistol at the two gunmen down the street. They fell instantly in sprays of blood, but it wasn't until Loren had gathered her bearings, where she now lay on the sidewalk behind Darien, that she realized that although he'd succeeding at getting *her* out of the way, he couldn't say the same for himself.

Loren stifled a scream as she lurched to her feet. As she saw the blood soaking his shirt.

One of the bullets had buried itself in Darien's shoulder.

LOREN WASN'T BREATHING.

"Darien." Bile coated her tongue as she stared at the blood spreading through his shirt. "We need to get you to a hospital." But Darien only began walking toward the men he'd shot.

As if he hadn't been shot himself. As if there wasn't a gods-damned bullet buried in his shoulder. She wanted to slap him for having such blatant disregard for his own life as he stalked toward the bodies. He was breathing heavily, but Loren knew it was from anger, not pain.

Loren hurried after him. "Darien—" Gray gathered at the edges of her vision, and her legs wobbled.

Sirens wailed through the night. Darien froze, hands curling into tight fists. Something like recognition washed over his face.

Lightning-fast, he scooped her into his arms. Emergency response vehicles and squad cars screeched to a halt by Blackbird, the lightbars on their roofs flashing bright red and blue.

"Darien, you shouldn't be carrying me right now." She was tempted to add that he also shouldn't be concerned with getting blood on her dress, because he was holding her in such a way that the white lace didn't touch his wound. If she wasn't so worried about him, she might've rolled her eyes. Stubborn Darkslayer.

They made it to the multilevel parking facility, where he loaded her into the passenger's seat of the car, ignoring her pleas to put her down and let her walk. He was in the driver's seat so quickly she would've missed it if she'd blinked. He started the car and peeled out of the garage, the rubber burning up a black cloud as he barreled through the exit and raced through the Financial District.

"Darien, slow down." A red light neared. The speedometer inched toward one hundred and forty miles per hour. "Please slow down." The intersection grew closer and closer. Loren sucked in a breath and shrieked, "It's a red light! *Darien, it's a red light!*"

He slammed on the brake with barely enough time to come to a screeching halt behind the row of cars waiting for the light to turn.

Darien banged his fist on the steering wheel more times than Loren could count, each strike making her jump. After that, the only sound in the cab was their frantic breathing.

The light turned green, and the cars rolled forward.

"Darien," she whispered. He wouldn't look at her as he started driving again. "What happened is no one's fault—"

"*No one's fault?*" he bellowed. "Look at your gods-damned neck, Loren." She gaped at him, not quite understanding. "Where's the talisman? *Where is it?*"

Her fingers closed around her neck. The talisman was gone; the only necklace she wore was the solar pendant.

Her fault, then. Darien had been shot because of *her.*

Loren tried to swallow, but her throat was too tight. "I'm sorry."

"That's not what I meant." He ran a hand through his hair, squeezing a fist in it. "It's not your fault. What I said—what I meant is that it's *my* fault. I should've already purchased another one for you, especially after last night." Darien pushed up the turn signal so hard, it almost broke.

"Where are we going? We need to get you to a hospital."

"No hospitals." Before she could argue with him, he explained, "A good friend of mine works in the weaponry at Lucent Enterprises. I was planning on going there anyway, before all this happened," he gestured to his bloody shoulder with irritation, "so I could try and find some answers about your lineage."

Loren swallowed, the smell of blood making her sick. "And this friend of yours will be able to remove that bullet for you?"

"Arthur used to be a doctor. And I trust him as much as I trust my Devils."

Loren nodded faintly. Her hands were shaking in her lap as she turned to stare out her window, at the buildings glowing with lights.

"Loren," Darien said softly. She turned her head to show she was listening, but she kept looking at the hands in her lap. "I believe those men were after me, not you."

"Why do you say that?" Her words were barely audible.

"One of them was Tyson Geller." As a Reaper, Tyson answered to Malakai Delaney, who Darien had paid a visit to several weeks ago. Loren remembered him telling her that he'd gone to the House of Souls with a peace offering—to make Tyson stay silent about the wannabe Darkslayers who were looking for a human girl. "Tyson never knew any details about you, and neither does Malakai. But Tyson has hated me for a very long time, and I suspect he didn't take it well when Malakai ordered Tyson's jaw broken because of me."

Loren gave a faint nod, still avoiding looking at Darien.

Darien reached across the center console and took her hand into his. "I'm mad at myself, Loren. Not you. And seeing your talisman gone only makes me angry that I haven't been watching closely enough. I should've taken more care."

It felt like she was choking, and she was still too rattled by what just happened to find her voice. So, she stared out the window, holding Darien's hand tightly in both of hers, concentrating on the feeling of his thumb tracing patterns across her palm.

Loren kept focusing on his touch, willing it to ground her the same way her essential oils did during her panic attacks, as she watched the bright letters of Lucent Enterprises pass over the car.

Along with its logo: three overlapping circles with a star at their center.

38

Arthur J. Kind was a weapons technician for Lucent Enterprises.

He was also seventy years old and as human as Loren.

But neither his age nor his mortality did anything to mar the deftness of his fingers as he extracted the bullet from Darien's shoulder. The slayer didn't flinch where he lay on the table in one of the hundreds of laboratories in the building as Arthur dug out the fragments.

Lucent Enterprises was not only a defense company that manufactured weapons and military technologies; it also dealt with experimental science and cross-species genetics. The weapons they manufactured were for the use of the country's Aerial Fleet. Taega and the Red Baron benefited greatly from the company's military research; Johnathon Kyle, founder and CEO of Lucent Enterprises, was the mastermind behind the magically enhanced mechanical wings that gave Fleet soldiers the ability to fly. The wings Dallas would eventually receive as a trainee at the Headquarters.

Loren winced at the sight of the blood bubbling up to the surface of Darien's skin as Arthur poked around inside the wound. Despite the blood, she found it difficult to look away—for two reasons.

One of those reasons was that Darien wasn't wearing a shirt again; the sight of his bare upper body had her blushing tomato-red. He had more tattoos than the numerals on his knuckles and the mark of the Devils below his ear; along with the full sleeves on both of his arms, he had a back-piece of detailed black flames that swept across his broad shoulders and down to his hips, the fire encasing a hauntingly beautiful masterpiece of the monstrous, three-headed watchdog of hell.

The other reason she couldn't look away was because of his scars. It made her angry to consider how much pain he'd endured because of those marks—bullet and knife wounds, with a handful of ridges that swept up and out on his back, as if he'd had angel's feathers etched or burned into his skin. Although he could clearly handle a fair deal of pain, the whole thing deeply upset her.

She looked away as Arthur dug out the remaining fragment and set about dressing the wound.

"They're from a belt," Darien said of the strange ridges on his back. When she looked at him, his face betrayed no emotion. "My father had a bad temper."

Loren swallowed the bile that rose in her throat, her stomach churning like a stormy sea.

His father was a monster.

When Arthur was finished dressing the wound, Darien sat up, slid his shirt back on, and rebuttoned it.

"Do try not to reopen the wound," Arthur said as he stripped the gloves off his pale, wrinkled hands and set about cleaning up the workspace, "like you did the last one."

Darien offered to help Arthur clean up, but the man refused with a cheeky remark that made Loren smile. She sensed the relationship they shared was like what a father might share with his son. A *proper* father, unlike the one Darien had spoken of tonight.

Arthur paused his cleaning and took something out of the pocket of his lab coat. "Open your hand," he said to Darien as he approached where the slayer sat. Darien did as Arthur had asked, and the weapons technician dropped an obsidian ring into Darien's palm. "Clearly, you need this more than I do. Put it on and turn it counter-clockwise."

Darien did as Arthur had said. The magic in the ring caused it to fit his finger perfectly, and it vibrated as he turned it counterclockwise. There was a faint click and a hiss, and gleaming black armor spread over his body, fitting him like a glove from his neck to his toes, complete with an invisible barrier Loren assumed protected a person's head. Loren could barely see the barrier, but when it spread to cover Darien's head, there was a faint golden glow that alerted her to its existence.

Darien looked impressed. "Where did you get this?" He examined the armor, flexing his hands before him.

Arthur held his arms out at his sides, gesturing to the room around him. "The Fleet Weaponry, of course. It's only just been created, and there aren't many of them yet, so make sure to keep it close. It might help you with all those bullets you keep walking into."

Darien snorted. He removed the ring, the armor vanishing back inside it, and slid it into the pocket of his pants. "Thank you," he said. "Any luck on Loren's post-mortem DNA test?"

"Still waiting for the results." The smell of bleach swirled through the air. "Though I looked into those names you gave me: Erasmus Sophronia and Elix Danik."

Loren sat up straighter.

"And?" Darien prompted.

"No records of them exist except death certificates," Arthur replied. "I photocopied them, so you can have a look. The dates of their deaths are too far back for either of them to be Loren's father, but maybe a distant ancestor. They both passed away nearly a thousand years ago." Which meant neither of them were the person whose bone powder had been taken to track Loren down, since it would've made the trail too diluted to find her. It had to have been a parent who'd given Loren this supposed magical ability Calanthe Croft and the warlock from last night had mentioned. If it were any person other than a parent, her gift would've been washed away in old blood. Arthur continued, "I also believe I might've figured out your little riddle." The riddle in the Dominus Volumen.

Loren shared a look with Darien.

After the book on the Ancient Reunerian language had teleported itself back to the academy library, Darien had entrusted Arthur with deciphering the riddle in their piece of the Dominus Volumen. He'd trusted the weapons technician would be able to figure out what the Well was made of, and it seemed Darien was right in assigning this task to him.

Darien said, "What answer did you find?"

"It is *chaos*," Arthur said. They both blinked and shared another look. "The Creature of the Gods."

"I don't understand," Loren muttered. "What does that mean?"

"Its proper name is *prima materia*," Arthur said. "It's the formless matter supposed to have existed before the creation of the universe. It is the base material for all creation."

"It…" Loren's mind was reeling. And then she sputtered, "It doesn't *exist?*"

Darien was staring at her, looking as confused as she felt.

"It *does* exist, Miss Calla," Arthur said. "Though it isn't a tangible thing. Some texts have described it as a fifth substance in addition to the four elements, thought to be latent in all things."

Darien said, "How would a person go about obtaining something like that?"

"The prima materia is primitive and mysterious; there is a reason it's called the *Creature of the Gods*. Some things are not for our realm to tamper with."

"But figuratively speaking…," Darien persisted, "if someone wanted it, how might they go about finding it?" If the Well was made of prima materia—a substance latent in all things—there was no way he would be able to pinpoint its presence, which was exactly what that warlock had told Darien last night. It seemed he hadn't been lying after all.

Because the prima materia had been used to create the universe —used to create *everything*. Which meant a hellseher gifted with the Sight would be able to feel it *everywhere*, not just where the Well was hidden. Tracking something like that would only make a person blind—because the prima materia was in the ground and the sky; in the buildings and the cars; in the river and the rolling desert beyond the forcefield.

They'd answered the riddle—yet they were no closer to solving this case. And this magical tracking ability everyone thought she had… There was no way. She'd never felt any hint of its existence, never experienced anything in her life to suggest she would be able to do such a thing. When she lay awake at night in her suite at Hell's Gate, she sometimes tried to call upon it, to reach deep into herself and see if she could find something that might explain all these rumors floating about the streets. But she was only ever met with vast emptiness, and the compulsion to simply give up and retreat into herself, even during the few times when she'd asked Darien if he could help her—if he could give her any pointers about tracking and see if they could find the Well on their own.

But nothing beyond the ordinary had ever happened. Nothing.

Darien answered his own question before Arthur had a chance to speak. "They would have to go to a higher power," he murmured. His eyes found Loren's.

Understanding settled in her gut like a heavy stone. A god—or one of the Nameless. Greater creatures of mystery and power that might've granted someone like Erasmus Sophronia and the Phoenix Head Society access to the formless matter. A creature of the Cross-roads that had the ability to grant wishes if the person on the asking end had enough to offer for the wish.

Arthur looked pleased with Darien's conclusion as he returned to cleaning up. "That is exactly right, Darien."

Darien jumped off the metal table and strode to where Loren was perched on the edge of a chair. For someone who'd just gotten shot, he didn't show a hint of pain as he placed two fingers beneath her chin and tilted up her head until she was looking at him.

His eyes were soft with what she thought was guilt as he mouthed, "I'm sorry."

Loren took the hand that was beneath her chin into one of her own, lacing her fingers with his. "We have to talk to one of them," she whispered. She knew Darien was aware of exactly who she was referring to as his eyes clouded over, his mouth pulling down at one corner. She didn't like this idea either, but it might be their only chance at getting to the bottom of this.

The creatures of the Crossroads were dangerous, wicked things. A person couldn't just stroll right into their dens without having set a plan beforehand—and without knowing exactly what information they were asking for and what they were willing to pay to get it. And if the creature considered your offer unworthy, you might never walk out of their lair again.

When Arthur was finished cleaning up, he looked Loren over, taking note of the hand that was entwined with Darien's, and said to the slayer, "Best be finding another talisman soon." Something about Loren sitting before Darien with her hand in his, and Darien gazing down at her the way that he was, had the old man smiling as he dried his hands with paper towel.

"That was my fault," Darien sighed.

"It isn't anybody's fault," Arthur corrected. "Just find another one." From the look on Darien's face, Loren knew she wasn't the only one who liked that answer.

It wasn't anybody's fault. The only thing that mattered now was stopping it from happening again.

———

LOREN HAD FALLEN asleep in her suite two hours ago at Hell's Gate, but something woke her at Witching Hour. She tossed and turned for several minutes before deciding to go downstairs for a glass of water.

When she swung around the corner and into the kitchen, she discovered everyone else in the house was awake, too. All seven Devils were either standing or sitting in a group around the kitchen island, engrossed in a conversation she was seconds from interrupting.

Darien was the one who looked at her first. The stress lining his face had her slowing.

"What's the matter?"

Jack, Travis, and Lace looked at her, but only for a moment, their expressions betraying nothing, while Ivyana, Tanner, and Maximus continued to either stare at nothing or share meaningful glances with one another.

Darien was also one of those people who was now staring at nothing.

"Darien," Loren prompted. She felt like puking, and the floor was spinning beneath her bare feet. "What's going on?"

He rubbed a hand over his face. "Randal Slade has been informed that a human has been staying at Hell's Gate."

Loren's blood ran cold at that name: Randal Slade. He was not only a Darkslayer but the city's most powerful crime boss. He'd been in and out of Blackwater Penitentiary so many times the law enforcement had lost count.

Loren's fingers flew to her neck—to the brand-new Avertera talisman resting in the hollow of her throat. "Does he know about..." She couldn't bring herself to finish the sentence.

It was Maximus who said, "We don't know, Loren. We're hoping not, but at this point we aren't sure what information he's managed to uncover."

"Randal has...*requested* that I bring you to him." From the rage sparking in Darien's eyes, Loren knew Randal hadn't requested it; he'd *demanded* it. "So that he can see for himself what all the *fuss*, as he likes to call it, is about."

"Who do you think told him?" Loren asked.

"Could've been anyone," Lace cut in. "The wolves know what's been going on with us. Calanthe, along with every vampire in her coven, has enough eyes in this city that someone might've simply spotted you with us at the club and put two-and-two together. Which means other covens might've found out as well. Aside from that, the wrong person simply might've taken note of you two at the Devil's Advocate and thought it was worth mentioning to Randal."

"You forgot about Benjamin and his graverobbers," Tanner said. "It could've been one of them who sold us out."

Darien shook his head. "Doesn't matter who it is right now. We'll deal with that after we've handled Randal."

Loren ventured closer to the island. Spread out on the counter was a map of the city.

"Which Darkslayer House is Randal in?" Of course, the circles of Darkslayers were not marked on the map the way Calanthe's five houses—the Blood Rose, the Silver Torch, the Corpse Flower, the Hammer Orchid, and the Blue Lily—were. As bounty hunters and frequent breakers of the law, Darkslayers operated far more secretively than the four-hundred-year-old vampire. And although this whole city and those beyond were aware of the existence of Hell's Gate, very few people knew where it was.

"He's not technically a *part* of any of them," Darien replied. "He *leads* all of them. And he's here." He smacked two fingers onto Angelthene Boulevard, a main artery that ran from the Meatpacking District to the Control Tower.

Loren's brow creased. "His residence is on Angelthene Boulevard?"

"Not *on* it," he corrected. *"Beneath* it. At least, that's where he spends most of his time."

She took a steadying breath. "I don't suppose we have any say in the matter. Do we?"

"We're afraid not," Tanner replied. The kitchen light shone off the black-framed glasses perched on his straight nose. "When Randal makes a request, no matter who is on the receiving end—whether it's Darien, me, Calanthe, or Johnathon Kyle—that request gets answered."

Ivyana smoothed the wrinkles in the map. "Which entrance into the godfather's lair will be taking this time?" Despite the teasing tone she used, her face was cold with rage.

Lace said, "We're not going *now.*" Even though it sounded like a statement, it was really a question, and she looked at Darien in search of the answer.

And Darien looked at Loren before saying, "Randal can wait a day. We'll go tomorrow." He tapped a finger on the north end of the downtown core, near the Flower District and Arcterus Boulevard. "We'll go in closest to the temple." He didn't need to explain that it was farthest from the Meatpacking District and the dregs of society, which meant a lesser possibility of running into other kinds of trouble on the way.

The tension in the room was a tangible thing; it made Loren sick to her stomach.

"I'm guessing no matter where we enter," she said, "paying a visit to Randal is going to have its risks."

It was Travis who spoke. "This is the first time anything like this has ever happened. The first time any of us have had a human in our company. I imagine Randal is going to have a few questions for us."

"And maybe a few bullets." Although Jack seemed like he was joking, his brown eyes gleamed with worry.

Darien said, "It'll be questions and nothing else."

The Devils had a few more things to discuss, and once their questions were addressed, they either shot off to bed or left to track down bounties. And although they hid the stress of the situation well, the fact remained that, come tomorrow night, they would all need to face the kingpin of the city's organized crime. And they would be facing him for Loren.

The thought didn't sit well. She barely slept the rest of the night, and she had the feeling she was now living on borrowed time—and might've been for a while already.

39

Randal's lair was a near-labyrinth of tunnels that intersected with the sewers below the city.

Darien brought Loren and his Devils to a manhole on Arcterus Boulevard at sundown the following day. It was the safest entrance into the crime lord's lair, if any could really be considered safe. He wouldn't have been so concerned any other day, but not only did this visit involve Loren, it was strictly *because* of Loren. For this reason, he would take zero chances.

He kept Loren at his side as he strode through the tunnels of the municipal water system with Travis, Maximus, and Jack. Waiting on the street above, near the manhole they'd slipped into, were Ivyana, Tanner, and Lace. Darien had been able to tell that Ivyana hadn't wanted to come here, and although she'd tried to refuse his offer to wait on the street, he hadn't allowed her to have any say in the matter. Not for this.

It was bad enough that Loren was down here. Having to listen to her heartrate triple in speed as they walked in complete darkness through the tunnels, sometimes for ten whole minutes before reaching a source of light again, was difficult enough.

He'd given her one of his pistols; it was strapped to the weapons belt Ivy had lent her. But regardless of the cargo pants, the combat boots, the weapons belt, and the leather jacket, she still looked like she didn't belong. Still stuck out like a sore thumb that Darien knew Randal would want to break off immediately.

They found the crime lord near the underground waterfalls. Moments ago, his cronies had converged on them from where they were stationed in the darkness of the labyrinth. Darien had a feeling his thugs had been aware of their presence in the tunnels long before they'd bothered to approach. But the closer anyone got to Randal, the more precautions his men tended to take; the faster they herded them toward Randal, like wolves nipping at sheep's legs.

His thugs were not your average brawlers. Yet despite the honed physiques and hellseher magic that could be considered weapons all on their own, they wore bullet-proof vests and carried automatic firearms in their hands instead of just on their bodies.

Randal was no different. As someone who'd been in and out of Blackwater Penitentiary more than anyone in history, he took no chances.

So, Darien wasn't surprised to see the vest strapped to his muscled and scarred upper body; the weapons belt that was heavier than Darien's own; the boots equipped with retractable blades at the toes. This was a man that wasn't just ready for a fight; he *welcomed* them—and he often was the one who started them, simply for something to do. Just *for shits,* as he often said.

It'd been several months since Darien had seen him last, but no amount of time—not years nor centuries—would ever be long enough. He hated seeing this man; hated that every time he looked in the mirror, he was reminded of this prick.

Randal shoved his chair away from the candlelit table that was pressed up against one graffitied wall and stood, straightening to full height as he turned to face their group.

And when he smiled, it was anything but kind.

———

LOREN'S BREATH caught in her throat at the sight of Randal Slade.

At those steel-blue eyes set in a face as brutal as it was handsome; at the short, night-dark hair and cold smile. The most obvious difference was the age: while Darien had just turned twenty-four, Randal was frozen in his mid-thirties. Loren's thoughts spun as she pieced the similarities together, and when he spoke, his deep voice only confirmed what she feared.

Randal Slade was Darien's father.

"It's been a long time since I saw any of my Devils," the crime lord said, as if they'd dropped in for tea. Eyes that were rimmed in red, as though he hadn't gotten a good night's rest in a long while, swept over their group. "And where's my daughter? Where is my precious Ivy?" His voice—slightly scratchy, as if he might cough at any second—boomed against the walls.

Loren stiffened.

Randal was dying of the Tricking.

When Darien didn't say anything, Randal looked at Jack for the answer.

Jack's voice held no trace of emotion as he said of his wife, "She couldn't make it."

A long, heavy pause. Randal said, "You sure about that?"

Everyone turned at the sound of footsteps. Everyone except Darien, who stared at his father with hatred as his sister was dragged into the room.

Walking on either side of the two men that pulled Ivyana in by her hair were Lace and Tanner, whose eyes held apologies for Darien. The men holding Ivyana did not release her until Randal gave them the okay to do so.

Ivy snarled as she pushed away from the men and came up to stand between Darien and Jack. Her eyes were glassy with fear, and the way she was holding herself suggested that she was in pain.

"I'd be careful about lying to me," Randal warned. And then he smiled, and it was a cold and deadly thing. "Now that we're all here." He clapped his hands once, and his eyes settled on Loren, curiosity gleaming in his cruel gaze. "I see the rumors are true."

Darien said, "I can explain that."

"I certainly hope you can." Randal's eyes turned black, and the

427

ground disappeared beneath Loren's feet as he formed a claw with his right hand and made an upward gesture.

It felt as though an invisible claw was wrapped around Loren's middle, pulling her up through the air, where she came to float several feet above Randal's head. She couldn't move a single limb, couldn't even scream. But in spite of the fact that she'd lost control of her body, her breaths came in terrified gasps as she hovered twelve feet in the air. Magic burned her airways, and her hair swirled around her face as though she were underwater.

Darien stepped forward, his own eyes turning black. Randal's men readied their weapons, but the other Devils moved to meet them, hands flying to their pistols, Familiars bursting forth from within their shadows.

"Put her down," Darien warned. At his side, Bandit snarled, red eyes flaring like fiery coals.

"I wouldn't do that if I were you," Randal crooned. "You have three minutes to convince me not to snap the neck of your new squeeze, Darien. And if I detect that you're lying to me, you'll walk out of here afterward as a group of seven—as it should and will always be. They call you the *Seven* Devils for a reason. And might I remind you that you all belong to *me?*"

Tension pulsed through the air as Randal looked between every one of the Devils. Not a single person breathed too loudly.

Sensing compliance, Randal smiled. "Countdown will begin in three, two, one… *Go.*"

"Loren has been under my protection since I was hired to track her down back in Septem," Darien began, every word strained. "The messenger who offered me the job gave me no information, but when I found her there were other Darkslayers tracking her." If Loren had been able to speak, she would've begged Darien not to reveal the information they'd hoped to keep from Randal tonight. But her tongue wouldn't move. "Their circle isn't any we recognized; their symbol is a phoenix head."

"Sounds like I've got some competition. Why are so many people after a human girl?"

"The truth is, I don't know. She has no magic, no obvious reason as to why anyone might want her. The bounty hunters and other people in this city that are after her... If they find her, they'll kill her."

"I seem to be missing the part where I should care," Randal said. Rage sparked in Darien's gaze. "I sense you're not telling the whole truth, my son. Do you need some persuasion?" He turned the hand he was still holding aloft counterclockwise. Pain wrapped around Loren's neck, as though that invisible hand was preparing to snap her head off her shoulders.

Holy Star, that hand... *That hand.*

A whimper slipped through her immobile lips.

The anguish in Darien's eyes made Loren's heart nearly crack.

"The people who are after her...," he trailed off, the conflict she could read on his face stilling his tongue for a moment. "I believe they could be in want of an ancient artifact called the Arcanum Well." Loren tried to shake her head, but she couldn't move. And that hand around her throat kept tightening and tightening—

"The Arcanum Well is nothing but an old legend," Randal said.

"I'm starting to wonder if the stories are true."

"And they believe she has a link to it?"

"I think they believe she can figure out where the Phoenix Head Society hid it." That hand around her neck squeezed, and blood slipped from her nostrils and ears, where it dripped to the filthy cement far below. Darien's chest heaved with heavy breaths. "If the rumors are true, the Well can reverse the effects of the Tricking. We wouldn't need to worry about contracting it, and you...you could rid yourself of it." The lie came so smoothly that Loren found herself falling for it, too.

The wicked glint in Randal's eyes faded, the hand around Loren's throat loosening just enough that she was able to draw in a ragged breath of precious air.

"You plan on finding the Well yourself," Randal said, "with the help of your little squeeze?"

Darien gave one slow nod.

Randal looked at Loren. "And is your girlfriend willing to help you find it?"

He loosened his hold on her just enough for her to nod. More blood dripped from her nose to her chest, sliding down her shirt.

Randal's cold smile came back. "I want this Well, Darien. You and your girl are going to find it for me. Understood?"

Darien only nodded. Seeming content with this answer, he lowered his hand.

Loren sank to the floor, regaining movement in her limbs as her boots touched the concrete. Darien came to her side, drawing her away from the crime lord who looked between them with amusement. Loren wiped the blood off her nose with her sleeve, her ears still ringing.

Randal folded his brawny arms. "For the trouble this has caused me, I expect more than just the Well as compensation." The slayers waited, and Loren gave them credit for not flinching as Randal said, "All of you will give me half of whatever earnings you receive for the next twelve months."

Before anyone could dare argue with Randal, Darien said, "Done." The other Devils echoed him; their voices held no emotion.

"And the Well, Darien," Randal said. "Would you be willing to swear on it?"

The Devils stiffened, and several of them shared glances with one another. Loren's heart thundered in her chest as she tried to understand.

And then Darien stepped forward and stripped the black glove off his right hand. When his father's hand shot out and gripped his, squeezing hard, a couple of the joints in Darien's fingers cracked from the force.

"Repeat after me," Randal said. With every word that followed, Darien echoed it. "I, Darien Cassel, solemnly swear on the Scarlet Star itself, that I will see Loren Calla's search for the Arcanum Well through to the end, and hereby allow my father by blood to use the Well for any and all purposes he may deem necessary. The Well will belong to only Randal Slade unless he himself states otherwise. This vow shall not be broken in any way, except by the death of either takers of the Blood Covenant."

A slow smile spread across Randal's face as the Blood Covenant snapped into place.

Their hands separated, and the mark of the covenant spread all the way up to Darien's elbow, turning his skin a splotchy, ashen gray, marked here and there with symbols from a forgotten language.

"We'll be in touch," Randal said, the same mark on his own arm. "And if you see any Phoenix Head scum, shoot them on sight."

Darien and Loren were the last ones out the door. Before they left the room, Randal said, "If I detect you're toying with me, you'll be in for a world of trouble, boy."

Darien smirked. "I'm sure I will."

"Wipe that arrogant look off your face," Randal snapped. "Or you can join your mother in City Cemetery."

Darien's smile faded. But not into grief—into red-hot rage.

Within two seconds, he had composed himself. Not a single hint of that grief remained, though there was a glint in his eyes that told Loren he wouldn't suffer the antics of this idiot for much longer, not if he had any say in it.

Randal Slade was the real devil of them all.

Darien gestured for Loren to head into the tunnel, and he followed behind her.

But Randal got one last comment in. "She really is a pretty little thing, isn't she?"

Loren looked over her shoulder to see Randal wearing the smile of a shark. She recognized his words for the threat it was, for he must've seen the way Darien looked at her.

And he must've decided, in that moment, that should he discover they were hiding the truth from him, Loren would be his first target.

The target that would make Darien talk.

———

NOBODY SAID a word as Randal's men escorted them through the murky tunnels. Loren stuck close to Darien, relying on the strong energy she could feel emanating from him as they plunged on through the tunnels.

She figured they were about halfway out when Darien slowed. His attention was fixed on a tunnel they were passing by—and whatever he'd seen—or sensed—in the alit room at the end of it.

He gestured for Loren to keep going. Maximus, having sensed that something was amiss, stepped in to take his place beside Loren as Darien slipped through the shadows.

It took a moment for Randal's cronies to notice Darien's absence. "Back in rank, Cassel," one of the brutes barked, his voice echoing. The group slowed.

A female voice as pleasant as windchimes called Darien's name from the tunnel he was heading toward. Everyone stopped at the sight of the lithe silhouette strutting toward them.

The beam of a tactical light mounted on the gun of one of Randal's cronies fell upon her, illuminating a face so lovely, it pained Loren to look at her.

Lips painted a stunning shade of ruby; eyes so big and dark, they seemed to swallow the light. Her porcelain skin was made whiter by the thick mane of dark hair that framed her delicate, heart-shaped face and tumbled over her generous breasts.

The way her name floated off Darien's lips made Loren's heart stop cold.

"Christa." The name was colored with surprise, along with a handful of other emotions Loren couldn't place.

The raven-haired beauty looked as surprised to see Darien as he was to see her. Her smile broadened as she drank him in, and then she gave a breathy laugh that managed to be sultry as hell as she batted her long, dark eyelashes and said, "What are you doing here?"

As if things couldn't get any worse, Darien told everyone to go and wait in the car. *Everyone*—and that included Loren. The worst part about it was how he didn't even look at her when he said it; his eyes were all for Christa.

So, Loren walked with the others to the dark street above. Once they were outside, and out of hearing range of Randal's cronies, the others began to discuss what had happened tonight. Loren barely heard a word they said as she followed them to the vehicles.

But she looked over her shoulder as she walked. And she

continued to stare down the street long after she'd climbed into the back of Darien's car with a couple of the others to wait for him. There were far worse things to worry about than the girl who was speaking to Darien in those tunnels, but Loren couldn't help how she felt.

She knew she should get a grip, but in that moment her own imagination was her worst enemy. And for those few minutes it took Darien to get to the car, something worse than what Randal had done to her in that room had taken hold of her heart.

40

Loren couldn't sleep. Considering it was Monday, she knew she should try to get some rest for school the next day. But try and stop them as she may, her thoughts continued to race.

Darien had said little about the black-haired beauty named Christa Copenspire after getting into the vehicle. Tanner had inquired as to why she was in Randal's lair, but Darien's only reply was that she'd moved to the city two months ago and worked for Randal now. No one pressed him for more information, clearly sensing that Darien didn't want to talk about it. It seemed Loren was the only person who was bothered by the lack of details—and clearly the only person who couldn't sleep because of that lack.

Though when she ventured downstairs, tiptoeing through the quiet house, she found Ivyana seated at the island in the kitchen, a book spread out on the quartz countertop before her.

The dark hair that brushed her collarbones caught the light as Ivyana glanced up from her book. "Can't sleep?"

Loren shook her head, ponytail swaying from the movement.

Ivy dog-eared the page and set the book aside. "Me neither. Then again, I usually can't sleep after I've been graced by my bastard of a father's presence."

Loren grimaced. "It was a hard night for all of us, I guess." She slid onto a stool beside Ivy. "I hope I don't sound insensitive for asking this, but what did your mom see in him? Has Randal always been this way?"

Ivy shrugged. "To an extent. And to answer your question, I suppose Randal was simply her *type*. She was young, easily influenced, and fell head over heels for him—his occupation aside." Her mouth curled into a frown, and she shrugged again. "Maybe it was the sex. Honestly, when I consider the man that I know him to be, I fail to understand what she saw in him. But she got pregnant with twins barely six months into their relationship."

Loren chewed on her lip. "Was she a hellseher, too?"

"No. My mother, Emberley—her real name was Elsie Cassel—was as human as they come."

Loren blinked. "But you and Darien... You're both full-bloods." Darien wouldn't be the person he was today if he had been born half—or even a quarter—human.

Ivy was nodding. "She was human, and he was a Darkslayer, but she gave birth to two full-blooded hellsehers Randal would raise to become deadly killers. It's possible, but extremely rare. And it only happens with hellsehers, not wolves, vampires, or witches." A peculiar look crossed her face. Loren thought it looked a bit like sadness.

"What happened?" she whispered.

Ivy appeared to be concentrating on her breathing. "She tried to run away from him and raise us without his influence. But he tracked her down and fed her the pretty lies he knew she wanted to hear. She wished for her children to have no part in the life Randal planned on giving us, but she stayed with him out of fear. And when we were fifteen, she became so overcome with depression that she threw herself off the roof of the apartment building where we were living at the time." Cold rage transformed Ivy's beautiful features into a brutal mask.

Loren whispered, "I don't think she killed herself."

When Ivy met Loren's gaze, there was nothing kind in it. "Neither do we," she whispered. A moment of silence stretched between them before she said, her words hollow and barely audible, "I keep begging Darien to kill him. He could do it—I know he could. If anyone in this city could kill that bastard, it's my brother."

A chill licked up Loren's spine. "Why doesn't he?"

She shrugged. "Plenty of reasons, I suppose. He's worried about the repercussions he could face from Randal's supporters, but his worry is not for himself; it's for me and the other Devils. Randal has a lot of very powerful men, which I think is part of the reason he's lasted so long as kingpin of Angelthene's underbelly. No one would dare overthrow him because of the thugs that might sniff them out afterward—that is, if someone were to succeed at killing him. You'd have to get past those thugs first, and they put up one hell of a fight when provoked."

They sat in silence for a few minutes, the humming of the refrigerator and the ticking of the clock the only sounds. Loren thought she finally understood why Darien had offered to help her that day in the alley.

Because she was human and fresh out of luck, just like his mother.

"Can I ask you something?" Loren said. "It's unrelatable, but I thought if anyone would tell me the truth, it would be you."

Ivy cocked her head, her dark hair tumbling to one shoulder. "Go ahead."

Loren wrang her hands in her lap, wondering what her question might cost her. Before she could change her mind, she blurted, "What sort of relationship does Darien have with Christa?"

Ivy blinked, and then gave a soft laugh. "I try not to get involved in my brother's personal affairs, but...from what I understand, their relationship has only ever been physical for Darien, which is usually what he prefers. They've been on and off again for a little over a year. Long story short, Christa wanted a relationship with him from the start, but he's never really wanted one with her."

Loren nodded. "I guess I can handle that."

Ivy trilled another musical laugh. "There have been a few girls who've asked me that same question."

Loren shifted. "That's not exactly comforting," she mumbled.

"Maybe not," Ivy said. "But if you want my opinion, you're the only girl who's ever had the *right* to ask me that question." Her lips curved with a smile. "He really likes you, Loren." The statement sent a rush of heat through her body.

Hearing the words said out loud like that...and by someone who wasn't directly involved... It made this whole thing between her and Darien—whatever it was—more real. And it made her...giddy. And nervous.

Ivy studied Loren's expression—whatever it was. She had no idea what her face looked like in that moment. If she had to guess, she would say raw and vulnerable.

When Ivy spoke again, her voice was soft. "Look. I know my brother is a bit of a jerk sometimes, but it's only to protect himself—because he's been hurt more times than he cares to admit. But the day he dares to fall in love, he will love forever."

The front door swung open, and Darien strolled in, tossing his keys into the wooden bowl that sat on the glass table. He was about to kick off his boots when he noticed Loren and Ivy watching him from the island.

"What are you two troublemakers doing still up?" He forgot about his boots and made his way into the kitchen, his footfall echoing against the walls.

"We could ask you the same thing," Ivy replied.

"I was running an errand." He winked at Loren as he retrieved a glass from the cupboard and filled it with water from the dispenser on the fridge door.

"What errand tickled your fancy this time?" Loren asked, twisting the end of her ponytail between her fingers. "Was it a demon, vampire, warlock...?"

"Demon," Darien said. "A belua. It slipped through a weak spot in the forcefield and decided to terrorize some old folks in the Narrow Hills." He downed half the water. "Though I wouldn't exactly say it tickled my fancy to hunt it down and gut it." He set down the glass, stepped up to Loren, and smiled down at her as he gave her ponytail a playful tug. "Not in the way *you* tickle my fancy."

The smile that broke across her face made her cheeks ache.

Ivy snickered. "You guys are adorable. You should get a room already."

Darien abruptly turned serious as he faced his sister. "You and I need to talk."

Ivy crossed her arms. "About the Blood Covenant on your arm?" she said. "You're damn right we need to talk. Exactly *how* do you plan on dealing with that, Darien?"

Darien waved her away. "Doesn't matter."

But Loren reached for his right hand and took it into both of her own. Beneath his tattoos, the skin was blackened and shimmery, as if dusted with soot. "Darien," she whispered. "Is there any way we can get this off of you?"

"It'll only go away when I fulfill the oath." Darien gave her fingers a light squeeze. "That, or it'll disappear when a taker of the Blood Covenant dies."

Loren sucked in a sharp breath.

Darien gave her fingers another squeeze as he slid his hand out of her grip. "Don't worry. I have zero intention of dying before Randal does."

He was looking at Ivyana again, who merely cocked an eyebrow at him.

Loren took that as her cue to leave. She bid them both goodnight and made her way back upstairs, suddenly more tired than she was before.

As she drifted off, she remembered what Ivy had told her—that Loren was the only girl who had the right to ask the question she'd voiced tonight.

It was a good thought.

A very, *very* good thought.

As soon as Loren was up the stairs, Darien faced his sister, who merely lounged in her chair, arms crossed.

"Really, Darien," Ivy said. "How *do* you plan on dealing with that? The longer you go without trying to fulfill that oath, the more pain you'll be in. And even *you* have your limits."

"I can handle it."

Ivy tsked and shook her head. "He says that now."

Darien waited to see if she was finished, to see if she was finally ready to talk about what had happened at Randal's.

She sighed. "Just say it, Darien."

Darien stepped closer to her, leaned on the kitchen island, and held her gaze with his. "Are you okay?"

"Why wouldn't I be?" Her voice was tight, and a muscle was working in her jaw.

"Gee, I don't know. Maybe because you've avoided me ever since we went to dad's humble abode."

"I haven't been avoiding you," she said cheekily. "You're the one who left to go monster-hunting."

Darien merely looked at her, waiting.

Ivy drew a deep breath. "I didn't enjoy being there, but that goes without saying. Besides, I'm fine now."

Darien's brows flicked up. "Are you sure?"

Ivy's eyelids slid shut as she drew another deep breath. "I mean, I would be better if he was buried in the cold ground, but until then..." When she opened her eyes, every trace of weakness—of fear and vulnerability—was gone. She was almost as good as Darien at masking her emotions. "I'm fine, Darien. You don't need to worry about me."

"I'll always worry about you. I wouldn't exactly be a good brother if I turned a blind eye to your feelings, would I?"

Ivy's lips twitched with a smile. "And you pretend you're heartless."

He smirked.

His phone buzzed in his pocket. With a sigh, he retrieved it and checked the caller identification.

CALANTHE CROFT was flashing across the screen.

The phone was at his ear instantly, and he knew his sister was listening as he said, "What is it?"

"Get down to the Blood Rose," the vampire replied. "I've found something I think you'll be interested in seeing."

AT THE HOUSE of the Blood Rose in the District of Drakon, Darien stood before the broad window that provided full view of the padded cell beyond the glass.

The demon was sedated. It was strapped to a table in the cell, its mottled chest rising and falling with frantic breaths, despite the sedative Calanthe's men had administered before the vampire had called Darien. The demon looked the exact same as the one Atlas and the others had hunted down at Queenswater Rapids—the same type of demon that had torn a path of destruction through the Avenue of the Scarlet Star.

Darien frowned at the sight of the creature's eyes, twitching beneath near-translucent lids as though it were dreaming. To think that this...*thing*...might be one of the missing girls...

"I take it you're planning on running tests?" Darien said to Calanthe without looking at her. The vampire stood just behind him with bodyguards at the flank, and around those bodyguards were several of Darien's own.

Shortly after Darien had talked to that warlock in the basement of Hell's Gate, he'd filled Calanthe and her henchmen in on what he'd learned about the Well replica and the monstrosities it was spitting out. Calanthe had seemed skeptical at first, but the more he explained to her, the more open she became to the idea.

Open enough to go out of her way to hunt down one of these creatures and sedate it in the basement of her sprawling mansion.

It was why Darien had decided to tell her; to share this part of their investigation with her. Being able to use Calanthe's many resources to their advantage wasn't something he was willing to pass up, since the blood Darien had dropped off to Arthur had been passed over to Doctor Atlas before the weapons technician could run tests on it to confirm their theory. They'd prioritized giving the only sample they had to Doctor Atlas, who could run the necessary tests faster than Arthur, who had to do so in secret at Lucent Enterprises to avoid getting caught. But more blood was needed; Doctor Atlas didn't have enough to confirm their theory. Darien had been waiting for another one of these things to turn up, but clearly Calanthe had found one first.

"We've already begun, Mister Cassel," Calanthe replied.

Darien ran a hand through his hair as he turned around to face the crowded room, his hellseher sense of smell overwhelmed by the different types of blood flowing in the confined space. With several of his Devils present, along with Logan and Sabrine, it was a heady mixture of hellseher, witch, wolf, and vampire blood that made him feel a little nauseated.

"In fact," Calanthe continued, "we're already completed the tests." Darien's thoughts snapped into order like a rubber band. Nobody uttered a word until Calanthe said with a smile, "It seems you were on the right track after all, and your little warlock wasn't lying. The demons *are* the missing people."

Murmurs rippled through the room. Darien had anticipated this, especially after the information he'd received from the warlock, but he was careful about who he'd shared that information with, only telling Loren, his Devils, and Calanthe.

He'd made the decision not to tell Logan, who stepped up to the window and spread his fingers on the glass. He was pale, eyes dazed and jaw slack. "That means Chrysantha might still be alive." Alive, maybe—but likely terrorizing the city and ripping into innocent civilians to sate her hunger. Darien wasn't sure if being turned into one of these creatures was any better than death.

"It's possible," Calanthe agreed. She turned to the red-haired vampire at her side and said, "Viktor, tell them about the DNA."

Viktor lifted his square chin, his blood-red eyes slightly milky with age. "The DNA is mutating at an unprecedented speed," he said. "We're hoping to create an antidote that can return the infected people to their former selves, but their behavior changes by the day. The transformation may be reversible, but only if we can catch it early."

Darien gestured to the window—and the demon lying motionless within. "Is this one beyond saving?"

"We believe it could be," Viktor replied.

It was Emilie, who stood next to Logan before the window, who spoke next. "But we'd still try to change them back, if we found an antidote." Her big eyes flicked to Logan.

Maximus cut in. "We have Doctor Atlas working on one already, but she's having trouble. No offense, but if someone *that* experienced can't do it, what makes you think *you* can?"

"It will certainly be a challenge, Mister Reacher," Calanthe said. "I'm not denying that. But my people have done it in the past when animals have fallen sick and transformed into similar creatures. We may need to perform tests on animal subjects by injecting into them the toxins we've found in the blood of these creatures. From there, we'll study the antibodies their immune systems produce in effort to fight the transformation."

Logan and Emilie shared a hopeful glance.

Calanthe said, "As you've already seen, there are countless cells in this house." The House of the Blood Rose used to be an asylum, but was transformed into a mansion when the borders of the District of Drakon were first created. "Round up more of the demons and we'll keep them here while we search for an antidote. By doing this, it'll keep them out of the line of fire—and *safe*—until we can change them back into the people they were before."

Jack grinned and clapped his hands together. "Sounds like we've got some hunting to do, boys and girls!"

ONE BY ONE, the Devils rounded up as many of the demons as they could find over the course of two weeks. The demons were getting smarter; they stuck to the shadows and preferred stormy weather over clear skies, when they were less likely to be spotted.

More people had gone missing. The front page of the Daystar had a new tally every day, along with reports on the new breed of demon the law enforcement was also trying to track down. But the cops and the MPU only killed them, believing these demons were the same mindless creatures who crept through weak spots in the city's forcefield. The Devils corralled as many of the demons as they could, in hopes of saving as many lives as possible.

Loren stayed with the slayers that were on watch the first night —stationed atop skyscrapers while the others in their group hunted below. They worked in rotations, though Darien tended to hunt more often than he kept watch. And it was on that first night that she was reminded of a peculiar ability he had.

Stationed on a skyscraper near City Park, directly across from the mall where Loren stood watch with a few of the Devils on the roof, Darien leapt off the edge of the building.

Loren's hand flew to her mouth. Floor upon floor upon floor spun past Darien as he plummeted to the parking lot below, his black jacket flapping like wings through the cool night air.

"Relax," Maximus murmured as Darien continued to fall. Loren could barely see Max's face beneath his heavy hood. Despite his reassurance, her heart continued to race, and she couldn't tear her wide-eyed gaze from the Devil falling through the air.

Darien landed softly on the sidewalk, his knees bending to absorb the impact—

And then, as though nothing unusual had happened, he continued walking, not missing a step. As if he'd merely descended the last step of a staircase. There was nothing in the way he walked to suggest that he was hurt, nothing to suggest that he was affected by what he just did.

"He's fine, Loren," Max said as Darien disappeared into the shadows, following the demon that had crept into the park a moment ago. "He does it all the time."

Jack gave a low laugh. "He likes to show off."

"How high can you guys jump from?" she asked.

"Heights *can* kill us," Max said, "but not as short a distance as humans. Jumping from the top of the Control Tower, though…" He turned around and craned his neck to look at the tower he'd mentioned, the panes of cristala gleaming pearlescent in the moonlight. It stretched up and up, disappearing into a sky stuffed full of stars. "A height like that would definitely kill us."

Perhaps it made her a coward, but Loren couldn't stomach going with them after that first night. She stayed at Hell's Gate with Singer —at the house that was quickly becoming her home.

By the end of the week, every cell in the House of the Blood Rose was full.

And testing to find an antidote began.

ON FRIDAY NIGHT, Loren stayed up late, scouring the internet on the spare laptop Tanner had lent her. She was looking for any information that might help them understand more about the prima materia—the creature of the gods. She'd learned plenty so far, but not enough to really help them with this case. The information she'd found was interesting, though, to say the very least. Especially the articles she'd dug up about the Law of Names—and how that law was connected to the creatures that lived at the different Crossroads throughout the world of Terra.

Her eyes were beginning to feel like they had sand in them when she heard Darien's door open down the hallway.

She stopped scrolling through the article she was reading and checked the time.

It was half past Witching Hour.

When she heard boots on the floor of the hallway, she snapped the laptop shut, stuffed her feet into her fuzzy slippers, and made for the door.

Darien had nearly made it to the top of the staircase that led down to the entrance hall when he stopped at the sound of Loren's door opening. He turned around to face her, his eyes turning black and back with every blink. He was wearing the same clothes he usually donned before heading to a fighting ring, that same tattered duffel slung over a shoulder.

Loren waited, standing there in the hallway, her heart snapping in half at how defeated he looked. His jaw was clenched so tightly, it looked like it was causing him pain, his shoulders so tense she could see the hard lines of every muscle through his long-sleeved henley. And although his eyes were now fully swallowed up by the black of the Sight, the set of his brows and mouth told her precisely how conquered he felt in that moment—how *worthless*.

She would not push him. If he felt he had to leave, she would let him leave. She should let *him* come to *her*.

Another minute passed before Darien lowered his head slightly, dropped the duffel from his shoulder, and walked down the hallway toward her. He kept his head tilted down the whole time, blinking fiercely, as if trying to rid himself of the Surge—of a nightmare he couldn't control.

When only three feet stood between them, he picked up his pace, as if he were running away—

Running away from *himself*.

And then he dropped to his knees before her, wrapped his arms around her waist, and buried his face in her shirt.

"Talk to me." He sounded so broken, so tortured, that Loren's already-cracked heart fell to pieces, and she, too became desperate— desperate to help him in any way that she could.

"What would you like me to say?" she whispered.

Gods, he was *shaking*. The arms around her waist were *shaking*.

"Anything," he bit out, his voice thick and wobbling. "Every-thing. I just need to hear your voice."

Loren settled a hand in his smooth hair, brushing it back from his face, hoping he might take comfort in the feeling. He drew in a deep breath, his upper body trembling harder. His hands tightened on her hips as he grabbed fistfuls of her shirt.

She had no idea what she should say, so she began to sing. It was a hum, really. An old nursery rhyme that she remembered from the dawn of her life but had never known where it came from. A part of her had always believed that perhaps her parents had sung it to her before they'd left her at the Temple of the Scarlet Star. She'd never shared it with anyone, not until tonight.

With every line she sang to him, her voice a whisper, the less his arms shook, the smoother his breathing became. She kept one hand in his hair, the other wrapped around his broad shoulders. Her own eyes were closed too—just like his. She found herself picturing that ocean again—the ocean she had envisioned the first night she helped calm the storm within him. She wondered if he saw it again, too. If he was there with her, standing on that white sand beach as the waves rolled in the distance.

By the time the song ended, Loren's head had turned featherlight. She swayed where she stood, her vision shimmering, and suddenly her legs crumpled from under her, and she fell backward.

Darien caught her before the back of her head could smack against the floor. He lifted her into his arms, calling her name softly, though urgently. She tried to walk toward that voice she loved so much, but it was like she was stuck in the in-between. It felt like she was floating, but she had the vague knowledge that he was carrying her away from here.

She would go with him anywhere. No matter how far, no matter how dark the road, she would go with him, if it meant they would be together.

Eventually, she came to. Only minutes had past, but it felt like a lifetime.

Darien had carried her to the couch downstairs, where he'd laid her down on the cool leather. He was sitting beside her, her legs slung over his lap, a glass of water in his hand.

"Loren," he breathed in relief. He leaned over to press the back of his hand against her forehead. "Sweetheart, you scared me." He helped her sit up, and she took a long drink of the water he offered her. Her fingers were so weak, they could barely grasp the glass. "Are you alright?"

"I think so," she said, her voice no more than a croak. The cold temperature of the water coursed through her body, making her more alert, though no less nauseous. "That happens to me some-times." She gestured to the tattoo on her forearm—at the symbol glowing a dull red. "This stupid thing is always making a fuss."

The look on Darien's face suggested he was worried it was worse than that, but he didn't voice his concerns.

Desperate to erase that look of worry from his handsome face, she said, "Would you like to watch a chick flick with me?"

A smile flirted with his mouth. "I'd love to watch a chick flick with you."

They stayed together on that couch until dawn. The night brought stillness—a sense that they were the only two people in the world. Loren reveled in the feeling—at the opportunity to be alone with this Devil, and so close to him that she could feel his strength that had returned, could feel his body heat. She couldn't get enough of him.

They eventually fell asleep side by side, their auras as tangled up in each other as their bodies. She slept with her head on Darien's chest, the sound of his heart beating steadily against her ear. Her arm was wrapped around his middle, gripping him tight to her, and she did not let go once, not even in rest.

Her anxiety could not touch her here. Her usual awful night-mares did not show their ugly faces. With Darien beside her, her own personal dreamcatcher, she slept better than she had in years. Whether he called himself a Devil or not, he had quickly turned into her angel.

Perhaps she was becoming his, too.

41

It was Singer's birthday on Sunday.

Well, as close to his birthday as Loren could get, considering she'd plucked him out of a cardboard box she found on the street, and therefore didn't know the true date of his birth. But she figured the day she adopted him was close enough, so she started whipping up a treat for him in the tiny kitchen above the apothecary shortly before closing.

Underestimating how long it would take to mix up the ingredients and pop them in the oven, she lost track of time. She was about to text Darien and let him know she would be a few more minutes when the door to Mordred and Penelope's swung open below.

"Loren?" Darien called. The door clicked shut behind him. "Everything alright?"

"Everything's fine, sorry," she shouted as she rinsed the soap off the last dish and set it on the rack to dry. "I was about to text you. I didn't realize how late it was." She turned at the pounding of his boots as he scaled the steps and strode into the office that doubled as a staff room.

Singer leapt up from where he was spread out on the floor and sought out Darien for ear-scratches. As the slayer crouched down to accommodate the pup, Loren took the opportunity to gawk at him without the risk of being caught—at the shapes of his muscles beneath the gray button-up long-sleeve and dark pants. Her body had ached with the absence of his touch ever since that night at the Devil's Advocate—when his hands had been all over her.

The memory alone caused her body to heat up, her heart skipping so loudly she knew it was only a matter of time before Darien's keen hearing picked up on the sound.

His gaze flicked to hers at that exact moment.

Speak of the devil.

"What are you thinking about?" His tone was casual, yet his stunning eyes were playful.

The oven pinged. Loren spun around, grateful for the interruption, and slid her hands into the oven mitts. "I was thinking it's time to celebrate Singer's birthday."

From where he now sat on the floor playing tug-of-war with the growling dog, a nylon tug-toy trapped in Singer's teeth, Darien glanced at the pan Loren slid onto the stove. "Is that a cupcake?"

"A *pupcake,*" she corrected. "It's mostly peanut butter, applesauce, and shredded carrots. And flour, of course." She licked peanut butter off her pinkie. "I'll have you know it's a big day for Singer. He turns one today."

Darien's eyes gleamed with amusement. "Aren't you a sweetheart." She blushed a deep scarlet as she plopped the pupcake onto a plate and fished the plain yogurt she was using in place of icing from the fridge. "You should win a gold medal for World's Best Dog Owner."

"That's kind of you, but I don't agree. Some days I feel like the worst owner in the universe, and I wonder if...if I maybe shouldn't have even rescued Singer."

"What makes you feel that way?" There was concern in his voice.

"Well, I don't exactly have a steady home for him." She spooned yogurt from the container and slathered it onto the pupcake. "Having him live at the apothecary doesn't seem fair, especially when I can't sleep here with him." She sighed. "It's been nice having him at Hell's Gate."

"He's more than welcome there any time, Loren. I think Bandit's grown fond of him." Hearing Singer snarling as the game of tug-of-war continued, Darien's Familiar released a low growl from within his shadow. Darien grinned as the snarl broke off into a pleading whimper—a request to join in on the fun. It was to his Familiar that he said, "You'll have your turn, Bandit. This is Singer's day." The spirit quieted after that.

Loren stuck a birthday candle in the pupcake and set the plate on the ground before Singer, who promptly dropped the toy and came over to investigate. Darien retrieved a lighter from his pocket and offered it to Loren. She lit the candle, and Singer sat patiently as she sang him a happy birthday tune. Something about what she was doing had Darien at a loss for words, and so he merely smiled at her as she sang the lyrics and blew out the single candle.

Singer devoured the pupcake in a far shorter amount of time than it had taken Loren to bake the darn thing, and when he was finished, he had the audacity to sit back on his haunches and beg for more with those huge brown eyes.

"That's the last of it," Loren declared, showing him her empty hands. She swiped up the plate that was licked clean of all crumbs and carried it to the sink.

"Why do you have a dead plant on the windowsill?" Darien blurted.

Loren laughed. "That's Mr. Crispy, and he's not dead." She turned to look at the wilted thing drooping on the sill. "Not yet, anyway. He was an investment that cost Mordred and Penny quite a bit of money, but none of us could keep him alive. They thought we should just get rid of him, but I think he has some fight in him still." His leaves—when they were healthy—were used to brew some teas and tonics.

"You're the most unselfish person I've ever met, Loren Calla."

Loren merely shrugged and squeezed a stream of soap onto the dish. She opened her mouth to reply—

A loud *smash* cracked through the silence. Loren jerked, splashing soapy water, and spun on a heel, Darien turning around as well where he sat on the floor.

Singer had knocked Mr. Crispy off the windowsill. Dirt and glass surrounded his paws. When he saw Loren take notice of the destruction, he shrank, his ears flattening to his head.

"Not Mr. Crispy!" Loren exclaimed. The tone of her voice prompted Singer to slink beneath the desk.

Loren dropped the dish she had just started washing into the soapy water, where it sank to the bottom. She hurried over to coax Singer out from under the desk, while Darien got to his feet and started picking up the pieces of broken pot.

"Does this mean it's finally time to say goodbye to Mr. Crispy?" Darien asked.

"No way," Loren huffed. She was on her knees partway under the desk, stroking Singer's soft head. "I'll find him a spare pot. I'm *determined* to bring that plant back to life. He cost Mordred and Penny way too much money to just throw away like that."

Darien drew in a hiss through his teeth. Loren turned to see that a piece of glass had bit into his thumb. Blood dripped into the clumps of soil at the plant's roots.

"Are you okay?"

He sucked on the wound. "Yeah, it's already clotting." With a grin, he showed her the wound that was already knitted together.

Loren rolled her eyes. Hellsehers and their insane healing abilities. "I don't know why I even waste my time worrying about you," she said.

She found another pot for Mr. Crispy in the storage room, and Darien helped her replant it. After they'd placed the plant back on the sill, Darien returned to playing tug-of-war with Singer while Loren breezed through the last of the dishes.

"Why are you dressed so handsomely tonight, Darien Cassel?" she said as she scrubbed the last dish in the sink. "Are you going to Blackbird again?"

"Not tonight." There was a smile in his voice. "But I thought you might need a night off from everything that's been going on lately, so I have a surprise for you."

"A surprise for *me?* I didn't know it was *my* birthday, too."

Darien snickered.

"What's the surprise?" She looked over her shoulder at him as she rinsed the last plate and set it onto the rack to dry.

The way Darien was looking at her turned her bones to jelly. It didn't seem like he'd expected her to turn around, since it took him a while to hide that delicious look in his eyes—and she swore he had been staring at the slope of her ass in her pleated mini skirt. It was plaid and pink, and she'd paired it with a white bodysuit that exposed nearly her entire back, right down to the waistband of the short skirt.

And she might've been guilty of having selected this outfit with the sole intent of seeing that precise look in his eyes.

Loren's body turned hot. It felt like the world stopped as they stared at each other. In reality, it probably hadn't been more than a few seconds before Darien spoke.

"It wouldn't be much of a surprise if I told you, would it?" She wasn't sure if she was imagining that his voice was lower and rougher than usual.

And when she spoke, her voice came out breathier than she meant it to. "Why are you being so good to me?"

His mouth sank, his brows knitting together. "Because you deserve it." He said it as if it were obvious, and she felt her heart swell with rosy warmth. "You deserve everything."

Until this moment, she hadn't thought it was possible to feel so happy and so terribly sad all at the same time.

"Better not keep me waiting, then." She stepped up to where he was sprawled on the floor, her wedge heels clicking on the wood panels, and offered him her hand. "I'd like to see what this surprise is, Darien Cassel."

NOT ONCE HAD Loren ventured beyond city limits.

There were plenty of good reasons for this, and she knew she wasn't the only one who'd stayed within the city's forcefield their entire life. Wicked and terrible things dwelled beyond it, worse even than the demons that prowled the sewers. The creatures that hunted outside of city limits and the barren landscape farther inland were so ancient and cruel, not a single text knew what to call them. They weren't demons, nor were they wights, though there were also a fair number of those.

They were the Nameless, the ageless beings a person could summon at a Crossroads. The same creatures Erasmus Sophronia and Elix Danik had likely sought out to obtain access to the prima materia. Considering the men were once mortal, Loren wondered how they'd managed to convince the Nameless to give them such a thing. The Nameless were rarely interested in talking, and rarely did they bother to make bargains with those who were foolish enough to seek them out. The Nameless were wise and unholy beasts that saw every sentient creature only for the blood, bone, and aura that would feed their unquenchable hunger.

So, as Darien sped down the six-lane twilit highway outside the forcefield, on search of the surprise he'd said he had for her tonight, Loren found that she couldn't relax.

They were in his truck this time—a vehicle she'd had no idea he owned. The truck was huge and as black as his car, with smoked tail-lights, tinted windows, and massive tires complete with flat-black rims. He held his arm out the window as he drove, feeling the rain falling on his skin from a cloudless sky.

It took her a moment as they barreled down the highway, the sun setting swiftly in the distance, to notice that Darien was watching her.

"I need you to relax," he said softly. "I promise nothing bad is going to happen to you."

Loren's breathing was shallow. "I didn't know being calmer would convince the Nameless not to eat me." It was supposed to be a joke, but the concern in her voice was clear as bells.

"It *does* help. Think about anything but them." He reached over and took her hand. For a moment, she thought he was simply going to peel her white-knuckled fingers off the seatbelt, but he laced them with his own instead.

And it worked. She stopped thinking about the Nameless, her thoughts consumed by the feel of his warm, rough hand clasping hers. With her skin against his, that energy she felt every time they touched coursed between them without restraint.

He looked at her then. Long and hard, as if her eyes held the answer to some silent question he was asking. And she found that she couldn't look away from him any more than he seemed able to look away from her.

In fact, he barely broke her gaze, except to maneuver traffic, until they reached the exit he was looking to take. Their vehicle was the only one out this far, the steep road before them dark aside from the glow of their headlights and the full moon.

No Blood Moon tonight, thank the gods. They were a rare occurrence, which was a great mercy in their world. Loren knew Darien wouldn't have brought her out of city limits tonight if he'd seen one in the forecast.

Darien parked the truck on a hill overlooking the highway below. The city was a speck in the distance, its usual light pollution unnoticeable from here. And yet it was still so bright.

She noticed them then—the stars—and she gasped aloud at the sight of them. They filled every inch of the sky, and they glowed in impossible shades of red, orange, green, and blue. There were so many of them—more than what was visible beneath the pollution of a city as large as Angelthene. They lit up the darkness like a beacon. And although Loren lived in a world where anything was possible, what she was seeing in that sky above her felt like magic.

"Darien." Her voice was a choked whisper. She unbuckled her seatbelt with her free hand and slid to the edge of her seat to get a better look. "Are you seeing this?"

He laughed softly, lifting their twined hands to brush a kiss against the back of hers. "The stars are why I brought you here." The feeling of his breath against her skin made her tremble all over. He cut the engine. "Considering you've never been outside the city before, I thought it was high time you got a look at what you've been missing." He seemed reluctant to let go of her hand for the time it would take him to get out of the vehicle, but he released her and swung open his door.

"Darien," she hissed. Fear coursed through her, but he'd already

walked around the truck and was opening her door. Cool air rushed into the cab. "I don't know if we should get out of the vehicle."

"What did I say about fear?" He offered her his hand, and he helped her step down onto the dry earth. It smelled sweetly of the rain that pattered softly from the cloudless sky; *serein*, Loren remembered it was called, when there was rain but no clouds. She'd learned that in class once. "And we won't technically be staying *out* of the vehicle." He tipped his head toward the truck bed.

She followed him as he led her to the tailgate. He lowered it and helped her step onto the bed, where she made her way to the side that was closest to the cab. As he went to retrieve a blanket from the back seat, she flattened her skirt under her thighs and sat down.

They talked for a long time as they watched the stars, the blanket thrown across their laps. Loren found herself so entranced by the galaxy wheeling above them that she didn't spare a thought for the Nameless. Darien sat so close to her that their arms were pressed together, and it wasn't long before he wrapped that arm around her shoulders. She rested her head against his chest, his steady heartbeat adding to the feeling of calm washing over her.

"This is amazing," Loren whispered as she marveled again at the colorful stars. "Isn't it the most beautiful thing you've ever seen?"

"At the risk of sounding corny as hell, I'd say it holds a firm second for me." There was a smile in his voice that confirmed exactly what Loren thought he meant by making that statement.

"Darien Cassel," Loren crooned, her tone teasing as she sat up and braced a hand on the truck bed behind her, "are you meaning to tell me that *I* hold first place in your mind? Over the *galaxy* of all things?"

Darien was fighting a smile. "That is exactly what I mean."

"Wait." She gave him a suspicious look, and then playfully scrunched up her nose. "Is this a *date?*"

"No." He huffed a laugh. He propped up a knee and braced an elbow on it. The action brought him out of his lounging position and closer to his true height, so she had to look up at him as he looked down at her, a warm smile on his face. "Definitely not."

Loren's throat bobbed as she felt it: the atmosphere that crackled between them from the close proximity. He seemed to notice it too, his eyes darkening with something akin to hunger. It was the same look she'd seen in his eyes that night at the Devil's Advocate.

When she spoke, her voice came out quiet and airy, as Darien reached up and trailed his knuckles along the edge of her jaw, just like he had that night at the club. And even though she'd felt this once before, the effect he had on her was no less intense. "First Blackbird, and now stargazing..." She drew in a breath that trembled with the rest of her as that hand continued to brush along the length of her jaw. "I'm beginning to think you're trying to date me, Darien Cassel."

That hand cupped her chin softly, the rough pad of his thumb tracing the shape of her lips, over and over again. Her skin tingled as blood rushed to the area, and her head turned weightless. She couldn't breathe.

"What would you say if I told you that you're right?" His voice was gruff as he hooked his thumb over her bottom lip, pulling it down slightly. The look in his eyes told her exactly what he was thinking about her mouth. "That I'd intended for tonight to be a date?" Her heart galloped in her chest at that word.

In the shadows, his face was so close to hers that the night could do nothing to mar the look in his eyes, the intensity that only grew the longer they drank each other in. She knew that once she kissed him, she would lose a part of herself, and in losing that part, she would gain another—something unfamiliar and brand new. She felt a rush of helplessness that left her limp.

Because there was something about Darien she simply couldn't resist, something that called out to a piece of her she hadn't known existed until he'd entered her life. And if she crossed this line with him, her heart would fully transform into something different. Something wild, unrecognizable, and perhaps untameable.

This fear of the unknown didn't stop her from wanting him; from desiring so badly to memorize that perfect mouth beneath her own.

She was *his*, she realized. Perhaps she had been since the moment she met him.

Her heart was beating hard and fast, and she knew Darien heard every pulsation. "I would tell you that I'm happy to be here with you," she whispered at last. "And there's no one I would rather share this moment with." It seemed to be the answer he was waiting for.

He closed the small distance between them, his fingers still grasping her chin, and pressed his lips firmly against her own.

The kiss was brief but sweet, and he pulled away after only a moment, but stayed close enough to breathe her air. She could smell the rain on his skin, the subtle hint of cologne and tobacco in his clothes. He was gauging her response, as if he didn't want to push her too far. But already, she missed it. Already, she wanted more.

She was the one who closed the distance between them this time, hooking her wrists around his neck. His arms wound around her waist, and they were as sure and hard as that night he'd held her after dressing her glass wounds, every trace of hesitancy vanishing as he drew her in. This kiss was unguarded, as pent-up desire unleashed itself at last. And Loren...

Loren was unraveling.

It was a thousand times better than she'd dreamed it would be, and she found her fists in his soft hair, pulling him closer and harder against her. That familiar, warm ache spread through her body, heating her core. She was fireworks, a billion stars, molten gold, and the sun itself.

The intensity of the kiss left her dizzy, and she clung to him as though he were an anchor in a storm. His tongue was in her mouth, and she breathed him in, her head spinning as she savored the taste of him. It was even better than that night at the Advocate — everything she'd dreamed it would be.

A sound that could only mean she wanted more slipped through her lips. He groaned in answer, low in his throat, and hooked her leg around his waist, lifting her up so that she was straddling him. His hand swept down the length of her spine, pressing into the small of her back, and then lower, past where the open back of her bodysuit met the waistband of her pleated skirt.

And still, she wanted more. More, more, more.

Her hand slipped under the hem of his shirt, and she felt the hard muscles of his abdomen, tracing the grooves with nervous fingers.

At her touch, the hand that was fisted in her hair tightened, and he mumbled a vulgar word against her mouth before kissing her deeper. With her chest pressed against his, she felt his thunderous heartbeat on her breast. That delicious ache inside her built and built, and she swore she would combust if the hand that was knotted in her skirt slipped any lower —

But Darien broke the kiss. "Wait," he bit out. He was as breathless as she was.

Loren pulled back, but before she could voice her confusion, he spoke again.

"This is wrong." Those three words cut like a knife.

And suddenly, the world around her turned quiet and cold.

"What's the matter?" Her words were nearly inaudible, but the worst part was how wounded she sounded. She hadn't kissed many boys, so it was because of this that for one awful moment she thought he wasn't enjoying himself. "Did I do something wrong?"

Darien gave a cold, hard laugh. "No." He ran a hand through his hair, frustration lining his face. "Hell no."

"Then what is it?"

He waved the hand he'd just had in his hair between them, as if this simple gesture would explain everything. "All of this. Me and you—*us*." His tone softened to a whisper as he said, "We shouldn't be doing this."

Loren reared back like he'd slapped her. Still straddling him, her skirt hiked up her thighs, she felt exposed and vulnerable and stupid. Her cheeks burned, and her eyes turned hot with tears that stung as badly as his words.

"I suppose this makes me the next Christa, doesn't it?" Seeing the incredulity on his face, she said, "What, you didn't think I'd notice how you looked at her? You didn't think I'd ask around and figure out what your deal is with her?" She swung her leg over him to stand.

"Loren —"

"Is this because of Valary?" she fumed, squeezing her hands into fists. "Is it because that stupid Warg almost caused me to be taken at the Advocate?"

"Loren—" he tried again.

She held up a hand. "You know what, never mind. I don't want to know how your mind works or I'm going to get whiplash. Just take me home, Darien." She fixed her rumpled skirt and backed away from him.

"Would you just hear me out?" He got to his feet and shoved the blanket aside with his boot. "You're not being fair—"

"*Fair?*" Her voice cracked. "Don't even get me started on what's fair, Darien—"

"What I feel for you is not the same as Christa—"

She held up a hand. "I've heard enough." He opened his mouth, but she bit out in a wavering voice, "I don't want to be around you anymore."

He had the audacity to look wounded, as if *she* was the one who'd given *him* mixed signals for weeks. For a moment, she wondered if she was being too harsh.

But then she remembered what he'd just done to her, and she didn't feel sorry at all.

It took everything she had not to burst into tears as she leapt off the tailgate and hurried to the passenger's-side door. She hated herself for crying. For *this.*

She hated herself for falling for him. She'd lost that part of herself she was so afraid to lose, and now she was left with nothing but a new weakness that had a name, and a heart that was so close to fracturing into pieces.

Darien got into the truck and started it. He didn't say anything as he sped down the rocky terrain, toward the highway.

The tears burning her eyes threatened to spill over as she stared out her window.

As she glared at all those stars and failed to stop it as her heart cracked and shattered.

DARIEN COULDN'T FIND words as he sped Loren back to the city, the dark expanse of the highway eaten up by the tires at a hundred miles an hour.

She didn't say anything either. In fact, she hardly moved the entire time, except for when they passed through the city's invisible forcefield, the dome of magic that rippled over the vehicle causing her to shiver in her seat. She didn't need to tell him to take her to Angelthene Academy; he knew she wouldn't settle for being brought to Hell's Gate. Not after this.

What they'd shared tonight was better than he'd dreamed it would be, yet she'd asked him if she'd done something wrong. How she made him feel was the farthest thing from wrong. He would've gladly kept his mouth on hers until sunrise, had his warring thoughts not caused him to pull away from her. It angered him that she didn't have a clue how extraordinary she was. He wished she could see herself the way he saw her.

They were still on the freeway, passing by the Miracle Plaza, when he finally found the right words. "If I explain myself, will you at least try to understand?"

She merely turned her head a fraction to show that she was listening. It was the most he would get—and the most he deserved.

"This whole thing that's been going on with us… We only met each other because of the cult that's after the Well, Loren. And because of the job I took to track you down. When this is over—when I find out who is behind this and can make you safe again—you can move on. You'll no longer be in danger. No one will hunt you anymore. Do you understand me?" He paused. But she only continued to stare out her window in silence.

"As for me," he continued, "I can never move on. Violence and danger are my *life*, Loren. And if you were with me… If you chose to have a life with me, that danger would follow you everywhere. There wouldn't be a single moment when you wouldn't have to watch your back. People would view you as a weakness of mine. They would target *you* to get to *me.*" He paused to draw a deep, shaking breath. "You were almost shot outside of Blackbird the other night. Tyson was after *me*, yes, but you almost got hurt. If I hadn't pulled you out of the way on time, you would've died. And your precious life would've ended because of *me.*"

She still didn't say anything. Still wouldn't look at him. They were minutes from the academy; minutes from the moment when she would slam the door in his face.

"You're into the kind of guys that are in your chick flicks, the guys who court the girl and give her the family life she deserves. I can't give you that, and I'm not going to pretend that I can. I'm sorry." His voice broke on the last word. "You deserve better than what I have to offer you, sweetheart. So much better."

Loren didn't say anything until the parking lot came into view. When she finally spoke, her tone was scathing and sarcastic, but he could hear the pain she was feeling beneath. "How very kind of you to think this through *before* you led me on like you did." She finally looked at him, and he hated himself when he saw the tears gleaming in her beautiful eyes. "I don't suppose I get any say in this, do I? You're the one making all the decisions about us, as if what *I* want doesn't matter—"

"This is your *life,* Loren!" His voice was so loud, she blinked in surprise, the motion sending a single tear sliding down her cheek. "Forgive me for trying to protect you. I will protect you from anything—even from myself. *Always.*" The truck had slowed to a crawl without Darien having realized he'd done it. He knew that as soon as he reached those gates, he might never see her again.

She didn't say anything as she glared at her painted toenails. The truck continued to inch horribly closer to those gates. He had half a mind to stop it entirely, but he had a feeling she would get out as soon as he did, not caring how far she'd have to walk.

Not wanting to find out if that were true, he pulled right up to them, and she didn't say anything as she slung the strap of her bag over her shoulder and unlocked the door.

"Loren, I'm sorry." He felt like he was choking. "Maybe we should discuss this further."

But her seatbelt was already off. She leapt from the cab and slammed the door in his face.

Darien stared after her as she made her way through the gates.

Unable to contain the rage and hatred he felt for himself, he struck the steering wheel three times, the force of each blow nearly cracking it in half. The breaths he drew in through his nose were fierce, his jaw clenched so tightly it felt like his teeth would crumble to dust. The Sight took over his mind as a Surge swept in, instantly turning the blood in his veins to acid.

This night had gone so horribly wrong.

Loren didn't turn around once, nor did she slow.

He peeled out of the parking lot, hating himself for this night.

Hating himself for everything.

42

Darien stood in the Pit, the bodies of five demons crowding the sand at his feet. His bare upper body was caked with black blood. Gore was jammed up under his nails, and his mouth held the rancid taste of demon skin from when he'd taken a chunk out of a caroeldua's neck. Limbs and entrails and gods-knew-what-else covered every inch of the enclosure.

This was a performance to end all performances, and he was only getting started. The crowd had never cheered so loudly, not in the eight years he'd fought in this ring.

And even though he'd gutted and ripped apart five demons, he still hadn't had enough.

He stalked up to the bouncers that stood on the other side of the latticed grille and said, "I need another one."

"We're running out of demons," the eldest replied, his face glistening with sweat. "We can't do this all night."

"Then bring me someone else!" Darien snarled. "A different opponent."

"No one wants to fight you," the other bouncer said. When Darien swung his head around to look at him, the bouncer stammered, "They know it would be suicide."

"Then bring me another demon!" he barked. "You can always catch more."

"We can't," he gritted out, his voice wobbling and pathetic.

Darien had to restrain himself from grabbing the pricks by their throats and hauling their asses into the ring. It would be so easy to make them bleed—to make them *beg*. His wrapped hands curled into fists as he spun around to face the crowd.

"You want more?" he bellowed.

The crowd roared and stamped their feet.

"Would you pay double?"

The screaming grew in intensity, the buzzing lights mounted high above trembling from the force.

"DO I HEAR TRIPLE?"

The building nearly came down from the barrage of noise the crowd made, the ground beneath his boots rumbling.

Darien stalked back up to the bouncers; they were seconds from wetting themselves at the mere sight of him. "Radio Perez and tell him Darien Cassel needs another demon. *Now.*"

IT TOOK Darien nearly twenty minutes of scrubbing to get all the demon blood and bits of flesh off his skin. He welcomed the icy temperature of the water spurting from the shower in the change rooms; it helped him not to think.

But as he made his way through the gates out front of the building that housed the Pit, to where he'd parallel parked on the dark street after speeding through the city to get here, he found that all his efforts not to think about Loren were shot to hell as he retrieved his cell phone from the pocket of his hoodie.

It was past three in the morning. He figured she would be sleeping, but he scrolled through his list of contacts anyway, searching for her name. Little did she know he'd put her into his Favorites category weeks ago; he also had her on speed dial, but for that moment in which he hesitated, his thumb hovering over the screen as he warred with himself about calling her, he took the slower route to finding her number instead.

But those extra seconds did nothing to change his mind—to stop his thumb from tapping the call button.

The phone rang several times. He'd almost made it to the car when the answering machine picked up, and her bubbly voice drifted through the speaker. "Hey! You've reached Loren—" He hung up, gripping his phone hard enough to nearly crack the screen.

A warm gust of wind blew down the street, carrying palm tree fronds and a scent.

Slowly, he turned.

A rabbit messenger stood several feet away, the dips and grooves in that horrible mask carved deeper by the shadows of the night. He recognized her build, the small scar on her jaw.

It seemed he had a fresh problem on his hands.

"Your boss isn't any more patient than the other people who are looking for this target," Darien observed. He slid a hand into the front pocket of his jeans and clicked the ON button on the side of his flash drive audio recorder. He would've scanned her aura, would've gotten a precise read on it so he could track it later, if he wouldn't have run the risk of having his eyes give him away.

"My boss," the messenger countered, "would like to know what he needs to do to convince you to close this mission."

"More mynet," Darien said. "Word on the street says another bounty hunter has been offered more than what you and I negotiated. Knowing someone else was promised four million when I was only promised three doesn't sit well with me, Long Ears."

"He figured you might say something like that," she replied. Darien waited. "He'll pay five million gold mynet, Slayer. And you'll get every last copper the moment you turn in what he wants." Those words made him want to throw up. If Loren wanted nothing to do with him after tonight, she would soon find herself in the middle of a gods-damned warzone of cash-hungry, coldblooded killers again. The magic of the latest talisman he'd bought for her would run dry sooner than later.

"Tell him this job comes with a few complications," he said. The rabbit cocked her head, the mercury vapor streetlamp turning those bulging eyes an eerie green. "I have a pretty solid idea where she is, but I need his patience. And I'm not interested in wasting my time explaining why. He needs to trust me."

For a moment, he wished he could rip himself apart the same way he had those demons in the Pit. The hatred he felt for himself for having pushed Loren away ran deep.

"Find her before anyone else does, and any of the days or weeks you'll need will be forgiven, bounty hunter."

Darien clicked off the recorder. "I'll find you."

He certainly would. In fact, he had plans to follow this messenger as soon as he got back in his car.

He kept his eye on her as they parted ways, walking opposite directions down the shadowed street. He hurried to his car and unlocked the doors, being careful not to look away from her for too long, though the night was threatening to swallow her up fast.

But Darien's plans to follow the rabbit were shot to hell when his phone starting ringing with unknown caller identification.

Darien swore as he debated what he should do. A part of him—the pathetic, broken part—hoped it was Loren on the other end of that call. But he wasn't so much of an idiot as to think she would be calling him from another phone, let alone calling him at all. For one wretched moment, he allowed himself to believe it might be her, and then he stamped out that flame of hope until not one spark was left.

He swiped right to answer the call as he got into the driver's seat, closing the door on a gust of wind that carried the stench of blood and the musk of the Angelthene River. Blinking the Sight into his vision, he glanced again at the messenger, and he was not surprised in the least to see that her aura was being concealed. He was getting used to this garbage. What was the point in having the Sight if it rendered him so painfully blind?

But he took relief in remembering that he'd thought to record her voice as a backup plan as he lifted the phone to his ear. "Yeah?"

"This Darien Cassel?" came a husky male voice.

"Who's this?"

"I'll take that as a yes," the voice replied. "This is Detective Finn Solace of the MPU. We met a while back under Delaney's roof."

Ah, yes. Darien recalled that night quite well. Malakai had thrown one hell of a party; it had turned into such a rowdy night that Darien and several of the other Reapers had spent a large chunk of that party in holding cells. And Detective Finn Solace was one of the officials who'd broken up the fun and hauled several Darkslayers away in handcuffs.

"I don't remember giving you my number," Darien said.

"No offense, but I don't think you remember much at all from that night."

Darien smirked. "What can I do for you?"

"I was hoping you might be able to help me with Cain Nash."

Darien blinked. "I'm listening."

"I heard a while back that you were allowed into Stone's End the night the Starlight Mall was blown up."

"And?" Darien prompted.

"And I'm wondering if you saw anything of interest when you stopped in for a visit at Cain's house." When Darien didn't say anything, the detective continued, "We need him behind bars, Cassel. And we have reason to believe he might be selling the Blood Staves that are being used to kill these missing girls. If these staves are used incorrectly, they can burn whoever is conducting the spells—"

"You and I both know that Cain's burns were caused by that house fire." Darien's jaw flexed.

Finn blew out a sigh that rattled the phone. "Look, I know that. But we need to get a handle on these killings, and getting Cain in for questioning should at least help our odds."

"Cain's not behind this, so how can it help your odds?" Cain wasn't smart enough to be behind something so complicated as the Phoenix Head Society and the Arcanum Well.

"I know he isn't. And we won't stop looking for who is, but impli-cating Cain will get rid of another problem we've been struggling with for some time."

"You want to frame him," Darien concluded.

"If you want to call it that," Finn said stiffly. "As I know you're very aware, we're having a hard time cleaning up the streets, and killing two birds with one stone by framing Cain and *then* going after whoever owns the Blood Stave that's killing these poor girls is our best option right now."

Darien considered his request. "We're a lot alike, aren't we?" he said. "Both of us striving to do good in this world and neither of us quite succeeding, but we lie to ourselves all the same because it's the only way we can get from today to the next sunrise." Finn didn't say anything, but there was a tension on the line that suggested he was hanging on every word. "What sets us apart? Your badge and my tattoo?" He smirked. "We're one and the same. Because the truth is, neither of us like looking at ourselves in the mirror." No, Darien certainly didn't like seeing his own reflection. He'd broken several mirrors in his life because of the darkness that lay in the eyes—a darkness that stared back at him from the cold glass.

His father's eyes.

There was a beat of silence before Finn said tightly, "I take it you don't want to help us."

"It's not that I don't want to help you," Darien began. "I just don't think you have your focus on the right threat."

He looked toward the street where the messenger had vanished. She was gone. No one was here but him.

Darien sighed. "Unblock your identification, and I'll reach out if anything jogs my memory." He hung up before the detective could reply.

He stared out at the dark street—where the rabbit had walked only moments ago. He would find her. With the help of the audio recording, he would find her.

More importantly, he would find her boss. Tanner would be able to run the recording through his voice recognition software, and as soon as this rabbit talked on her phone long enough to get a read on her whereabouts, Darien would trail her, digging up at least one of the psychos behind this mess.

He only hoped it would be soon.

43

Nearly two weeks had passed since that night in Darien's truck.

It was Sunday, and another shift crawled by. Loren worked hard, stopping only to eat a granola bar instead of a proper lunch, ignoring her tattoo that glowed blue all day. Foot traffic was steady, and for that she was grateful. It kept her from looking at her phone; from listening again and again to the messages Darien had left on her answering machine. There were only three, though he'd tried to call her over a dozen times since that night.

As her shift wound down, and foot traffic slowed, she found herself listening to all three messages again as she sat at the foot of the staircase, ignoring the sentient plants that were peeking at her with concern from where they squatted in cages and pots.

The first message was short and tense. "Loren, it's Darien," he began. "Look, I know you probably never want to hear from me again. But I wanted to say that I'm sorry for last night. I never meant…I didn't mean to hurt you." There was a pause, and then he said, "I'm sorry," before hanging up.

That message had made her cry the first time she'd heard it. *Hard.*

Because although it was an apology, it wasn't the words she wanted to hear.

The second message was left two days after the first. "Loren, it's me again. If you could call me back, or even shoot me a message... *Please*. I need to know you're safe."

The final message had come through Friday morning. "Lola." A sigh rattled the phone. "This is the last time I'll bother you—I promise. I realize I've already called too many times, and I should be giving you space... But I need you to know how sorry I am. I warred with myself for weeks about my feelings for you. It was never my intention to lead you on like I did. I should've realized how badly this would hurt you. I should've thought only of *you*, instead of acting so selfishly, but I...I found it impossible to stay away from you. I *still* do."

There was a long pause. The first time she'd heard it, she wondered if the answering machine had run out of room.

But then he spoke again. "I guess what I'm trying to say is that I'm sorry. I wish I could go back to that night and never pull away from you like I did. I wish...I wish you would come home." Another sigh. "But what's done is done, and all I can hope for now is that you'll forgive me. If you need anything, please, *please* don't hesitate to call. I'll always be here for you."

No calls or messages had come through since. And she'd cried after hearing that final message, harder than she had after the first.

When four thirty rolled around, Loren breezed through her closing duties and locked up shop. But she wasn't heading back to the academy; she had to pick up Singer from the groomers on West Rigel Road. The groomer had a habit of running late, so Loren decided to call and check in on how the appointment was going. It came as no surprise when the groomer told her she wouldn't be finished with Singer until five thirty, so Loren stopped at the Terra Caffe for supper.

It was quarter past five when she boarded a city bus. The vehicle was packed to full capacity as it meandered through Jubilee Square, past City Park, and finally to Yip n' Clip.

She thanked the groomer and gave her a generous tip before

hooking Singer's leash to his collar and making her way out the revolving doors. The streets were cast in the amber half-light of dusk. She might've marveled at the sheer beauty of the sunset, had it not been an omen of the things that would soon prowl the night.

She picked up her pace, urging Singer to a sprint as she made a beeline to the bus stop. As she walked, she dug her bus pass out of the pocket of her jeans and unfolded it.

The streetlamps were winking awake as the bus door squealed open. She skipped up the steps, her bus pass in hand.

But the driver blocked her path with a beefy arm. "No dogs allowed, Miss."

Loren blinked. "I've had him on the buses plenty of times before—"

"Not this one," he cut in, bubble-gum snapping in his small yellow teeth. "Not anymore. No dogs. New rules, I'm afraid."

Dread curled in her stomach. She hesitated, Singer waiting on the sidewalk behind where she stood on the bottom steps, as she scanned the interior of the bus that was crammed full of witches, warlocks, and humans.

Not one of them spared her a glance. Not one.

Loren turned to the driver. "It's getting dark. Please—"

"I'm sorry, Miss." He pulled the lever partway, the doors nearly shutting on Singer's leash that was stretched out in the space between where Loren stood on the bus steps and the sidewalk below. "I don't make the rules."

Her fist closed around her bus pass, crumpling the paper to a near pulp. She stepped down to the half-closed doors, and the driver opened them just wide enough for her to squish back through. They slid shut behind her, and the bus hissed and sputtered away down the street.

It was almost full dark, and she didn't know what to do. Singer whimpered and pawed at her sneaker. "It's okay." Loren's voice was a strained gasp. "We'll walk."

Mordred and Penelope's suddenly seemed so far away. If only she'd had enough money; she would've called for a taxi in a heartbeat, but she'd used up most of what was in her bank account to get to and from work these past two weeks.

They began making their way back to the Avenue of the Scarlet Star, staying beneath the protection of the streetlamps whenever possible. But the shadows were sweeping in quick. And aside from Loren, no other pedestrians were in sight.

They made it to Jubilee Square when she began cutting through back alleys, though only if they were lit. And it was in one of those alleys, not far from the Avenue of the Scarlet Star, that she began to hear them.

Movement rustled in the shadows, followed by hungry baying and yips.

The demons hunted in packs. They often dragged their prey below ground, where they could feast on them slowly. They savored every drop of blood, every last trace of the soft, fatty marrow in a person's bones.

A snarl carried down the alley she was cutting through, sending a chill from the crown of her head to the balls of her feet. The lone bulb fixed to one brick wall was the only source of light here, and it began to flicker, threatening to die out entirely, just as she caught sight of them.

There were two behind her. Claws scraped and hissing sounded before they slipped into the shadows of a dumpster, so quick they were no more than streaks of darkness.

Heart in her throat, Loren hurried toward the flickering glow of warm light halfway down the alley. Her breath tore apart her lungs in wild gasps. Singer's hackles were raised, his warm side pressed up against her leg.

If they made a run for it, they might make it to the other end of the alley, toward the brightly lit street beyond. She wrapped the leash around her hand several times to keep from tripping on it.

She was almost beneath the glow of the bulb halfway down the alley. Her heart thundered in her chest, her sweaty palm dampening the leash. She was about to pick up speed when two more shadows crept into the mouth of the alley, blocking the path to the safety of the street up ahead.

She froze. There were four of them now.

With deadly clarity, she realized that she and Singer were being herded, and possibly had been for some time now.

The demons moved like a pack of wolves, orienting themselves around the one that was clearly their leader. They were hairless and walked on half-bent hind legs, their postures so hunched, their bony knuckles dragged on the ground before them. The lack of horns on their heads suggested these ones were younger—weaker than some that hunted the streets. But it made no difference to someone like her —they would kill her. And Singer, too. Guttural snarls shook from deep in their fleshy throats, the sound reminding Loren of the laughter of hyenas.

From somewhere far away, Loren saw herself sprinting to the wall, to the warm glow of the light she'd nearly passed. She moved so quickly she slammed into the bricks, directly below the flickering bulb. Singer growled, hackles raised, as he sank into a protective stance before her.

Her fingers shook as she reached into her bag for the pistol Darien had given her before they'd gone to Randal's lair. There were too many demons for her to handle on her own, but she wouldn't go down without a fight. And they wouldn't get to Singer. They wouldn't touch him—not if she could help it.

The light mounted on the wall blinked rapidly, rendering her blind every time the glow waned as it threatened to go out entirely.

And the demons crept closer. Their throats made deep clicking sounds Loren understood was the pack's form of communication. They had smooth, near-translucent skin and wide maws lined with razor-sharp teeth. Their eyes were nothing but depthless sockets, like stones had been pushed into their misshapen skulls.

The pistol shook in Loren's hand as she pointed it at the two demons closest to her left. They were inching forward. Testing the ground where shadow ended and light began.

Loren used her free hand to dig her phone out of the pocket of her jeans, her fingers shaking so badly they barely cooperated.

The phone wobbled like jelly as she found his name under the

Favorites category. And for the first time in nearly two weeks, she hit CALL.

"How does he win even when he's distracted?" Jack muttered from where he sat across from Darien at the dining room table.

"The man's a god," Lace murmured sourly as she threw down her cards.

Ivyana threw hers down as well, where they nearly slid off the table. "How did he get all the brains in the family?"

Darien might've smiled, had he not been in such a foul mood. And he *was* distracted, it was true. He honestly had no clue how he'd won this last round of poker, but apparently, he had. Maximus suppressed a smile as he shoved the stacks of mynet his way, while Travis and Tanner, who sat on either side of Darien, grumbled under their breath.

Darien threw back the last of his whiskey. "I'm out." He set down the empty glass and shoved his chair back. Of the stacks of mynet, he told them, "Keep it." He was about to stand when his cell phone buzzed on the table.

Assuming it was someone he didn't feel like talking to, he began to swipe left to reject the call —

But then he saw LOREN CALLA flashing on the screen.

The phone was at his ear instantly. "Loren."

"I need help." The panic in those words turned his blood to ice.

Six pairs of eyes snapped to his face, the Devils' keen hearing picking up on that short, desperate sentence.

Darien was already heading for the door. "Where are you?"

"The Miracle Plaza." Her breath rattled the phone. "I'm not far from Canopus Street. I'm in an alley...I'm not really sure where —" She broke off with a muffled swear word as Darien snatched his keys out of the bowl in the entrance hall. "Darien, I'm sorry. I'm so sorry for not answering your calls —"

"Never mind that now. I need you to breathe, Loren." He thought he should take his own advice, since it felt like no air was entering his lungs. "I need you to focus. You're going to be fine; do you hear me? I'm going to find you, and you're going to be fine."

A whimper slipped through the phone as Darien shoved his feet into his boots and swung open the front door.

"Dare," Maximus called. "You need help?"

Darien waved his hand in dismissal and swept out the door. "I need you to turn on the location services on your phone, Loren." Gravel crunched under his boots as he sprinted to his car.

"There are demons, Darien," she whispered. "They're hunting us." He was about to ask who she meant by *us* — when he heard her dog bark in the background.

It was Darien's turn to swear as the baying of demons crackled through the phone. "Turn on your location. *Now,* Loren." He was already in the car, reversing at eighty miles an hour through the gates that barely swung open on time.

Loren sobbed, "Darien, I'm sorry — "

The phone cut out, as though she'd dropped it. But not before he heard the snarling.

Not before he heard her scream.

<hr />

THE LIGHTBULB BURNT OUT.

Everything happened so quickly, Loren could barely make sense of it all.

As soon as that bulb imploded with a noise like a paper bag popping — and the disc of light she and Singer were standing inside plunged into murky darkness — the demons snarled and lunged.

She fired the pistol into the shadows, the kickback reverberating through her wrists hard enough to bruise. Each bullet cracked through the night.

There was a spray of blood, and claws tore into the flesh at her collarbone as a demon slammed into her with the force of a truck. A sharp burning arrowed deep, the feeling so intense she almost passed out. Her thoughts were barely clear enough for her to realize she should shield her throat from those teeth and claws as she went down.

She hit the asphalt, bones barking, one hand gripping the pistol while the other took the brunt of the attack. Teeth like razors ripped into her hand.

A dark shape blurred in front of her. The claws were jerked out of her skin as the demon attacking her tumbled down the alley. The demon was yowling in pain, fighting to stay on its feet under the blows of the dark shape that had intercepted it.

Singer had tackled the demon to get it off her and was now pinning it beneath his paws. But his strength was waning as the thing thrashed and bit and swept with sharp and deadly hands. Four yellowed claws struck deep, sinking right into the soft flesh between two of Singer's ribs.

Singer arced his back and gave a pained yelp.

Loren was screaming as she fumbled to take aim. She wasn't sure what she was saying. It might've been *no*. It might've been *stop*.

She squeezed the trigger.

Another demon charged for her, knocking the gun out of her grasp. There was a bang and a crack as her bullet careened off-course and connected with brick, shattering it into red dust.

She had to get to Singer; had to save him.

Loren moved. Fast, like she'd seen the slayers move.

She wound up her leg and kicked the demon hard in the side of the head. It yelped and stumbled, allowing her just enough time to grab the gun again. She whipped back around, took aim, and shot a bullet right through its open mouth as it dove for her exposed neck. The bullet tore out the back of its head with an explosion of brains and black, sticky blood.

It collapsed onto her, dying with one last click of its jaws.

She drove its limp body aside with an upward push of her legs and whirled until she was kneeling, taking aim again for the demon that was now upon Singer. A *second* demon, for Singer had managed to kill the first.

Singer's body bowed in agony as those black teeth tore into his throat, easily digging through skin and muscle and tendon —

Loren fired.

And fired.

And fired.

There was no room in her head for thoughts. No room in her heart to feel anything as an icy, numbing rage washed over her. As she killed that abhorrent creature—as she *butchered* it.

And she was as much a demon as those creatures were as she growled, *"Don't. You. Touch. Him."*

Rising off the cold, blood-covered ground, she emptied the magazine of bullets, each shot cracking through the night. By the time she was finished, the creature's misshapen skull was riddled with them. Black, reeking blood dribbled in lines down its wrinkled skin, fizzling like acid as it moved.

Cold and hollow silence swept through the alley.

Blood was everywhere. *Everywhere.*

Darkness engulfed Loren's vision. She blinked rapidly, fighting to stay alert, the ground beneath her feet rising and falling, again and again.

She had to get to Singer. Had to make sure he was okay—

A low, keening whine slipped through Singer's teeth as he limped toward her, tail between his legs. His ears were flat to his head, and his eyes were glistening.

At the sight of him, bitten and battered, Loren couldn't hold herself up any longer. Her legs collapsed, her kneecaps popping on the cobbles.

She crawled toward him, through puddles of gore, where she gathered him into her lap, like she had that fateful night she had found him whimpering in a cardboard box on the street.

She wasn't sure how long they sat there in that dark alley— shaking and covered in blood that was their own and not. Tears rolled down her face as she held Singer tightly, his heart pounding beneath her palm. His muscles were contracting in pain, his nose whistling with uneven breaths.

Her arms shook under Singer's weight as she scooped him up and carried him out of the alley. Her body felt buoyant, like her soul was no longer attached to it. Sputtering gasps tore through her quivering lips, but she spoke to Singer through the hysteria, promising that everything was going to be fine. Everything was going to be okay.

She wanted to believe it. She wanted so badly to believe it.

They'd almost made it to the Avenue of the Scarlet Star when Darien found them.

44

Darien screeched to a halt on Canopus Street, where he caught sight of Loren limping down the sidewalk, her arms straining under the weight of the bloodied and battered lump she carried.

That bloodied and battered lump was her dog.

Loren was covered in so much blood, he barely recognized her. Her shirt and jeans were nearly black with it, and she herself was bleeding from a deep wound by her collarbone. Her filthy face was so pale, he wondered how she hadn't fainted yet.

Time ceased to pass for one agonizing moment before lurching forward again. He wasn't sure how he got out of the car, but the next thing he knew, he was walking toward her. The world rotated beneath his feet as he took in the sight of her up close. As he realized he hadn't made it in time.

He was too late.

Loren didn't speak as Darien opened the passenger's-side door and helped her inside.

He was already dialling the closest veterinarian office as he got into the driver's seat and gunned the engine into motion. His heart was pounding so fast, he swore he was going to throw up. When the first office didn't answer, he dialled another.

And another.

And another.

None of them picked up. It was late, but he'd thought at least *one* of these godsforsaken businesses would answer for an emergency —

Loren began sobbing, rocking back and forth as she sang to her dog in a breathy voice.

The phone rang and rang and fucking rang. Another answering machine picked up.

Shit. *Shit.*

Darien's hand tightened on the wheel, the dark road flying under the tires.

"Hush, little baby, don't say a word. Mama's gonna buy you a mockingbird." She sniffled through the lyrics, stroking the dog's head. "And if that mockingbird don't sing, Mama's gonna buy you a diamond ring." The dog didn't look away from her once as she sang to him, though his vacant brown eyes began to blink more slowly as the seconds ticked by. Darien could hear each pulsation of Singer's heart, every beat a tiring thump that got heavier and slower.

Darien cursed and threw his phone onto the dash as another of his calls went to voicemail. He kept driving, weaving through traffic, as he came to the decision to take the dog straight to the emergency ward at Angelthene General. Someone there would help. And if they weren't willing to, he'd *make* them help.

Loren kept singing, her voice thick and wobbling. "And if that diamond ring turns brass, Mama's gonna buy you a looking glass." She was crying so hard, she could barely form words. But she kept trying. Kept rocking her dying dog back and forth in her arms. "And if that looking glass gets... If it gets...broke..." Her voice trailed off. Darien heard the breath leave her lungs in a soft, panicked gasp.

Silence swept into the car. One heartbeat picked up to a sprint, while another faded to a weak flutter.

Gravel popped as Darien pulled to a stop at the side of the road.

Loren gave the dog a gentle shake. "Singer," she whispered. The single word was a plea. A prayer. She began rocking him again. "If that...looking glass...gets broke," she tried to sing, but the words were cut off by a muffled sob as she pressed one bloodied hand to her lips, her mouth opening with a silent scream.

Darien heard it the same time he felt it—the heart that went quiet and still. Those brown eyes that had so lovingly looked at Loren a moment ago went blank as the flame that was Singer's soul guttered...

And went out.

The dog had died.

Singer was dead.

Loren's words were barely discernable whimpers. "No. No—*please.*" She pressed her ear against the dog's chest and gave him another gentle shake, as if it might convince his heart to start again. One arm tightening around the dog's body, the other stroking his floppy ears, she gasped to no one, except maybe a god, "Wait... *please.* Don't do this. Don't take him from me. *Wait.*" She buried her face in his fur as sobs wracked her body.

Darien said nothing as he leaned over and held her as best as he could in the limited space in the vehicle. Words had no sway here; nothing could fix this. This was something beyond anything he could ever say or do.

She'd lost a friend. A dog, of all things—the one creature in the world that would never do anything to hurt the person they loved.

Except for when they died.

Loren leaned over far enough to rest her head against Darien's shoulder, her arms still squeezing her dog to her chest. Although she'd leaned into him, he wasn't sure if being held was what she wanted at this time.

But it was all he could think to do.

———

DARIEN PACED BEFORE HIS BED.

Hours had passed, and Loren hadn't come out of her suite. When they'd got back to Hell's Gate and he'd tried to help her out of the car, something in her had snapped. She'd screamed and thrashed and nearly clawed his face off. It'd taken her a long time to come back from that wild place where she'd lost herself, and when she finally did, he'd helped her bury Singer in the yard.

For a long time, she'd knelt before the dog's grave. Darien stood beside her, not saying anything, simply being there in case she needed him. When she'd finally allowed Darien to bring her inside, he'd dressed her wounds. She hadn't responded to anything he said, her eyes expressionless. It was an awful, empty contrast to the lovely, high-spirited girl he'd come to know.

Something inside her had died; had passed on with the animal she loved. The girl who'd disappeared into that suite hours ago was a shell of her former self, and Darien had the dreadful feeling that he was responsible for all of this.

As the clock neared five in the morning, he ended up sinking to the floor at the foot of his bed and falling asleep in a sitting position, head resting back against the bedframe.

When he jerked awake four hours later, he hardly felt rested. He took a shower and got ready for his next target.

On his way to the ground floor, he paused outside Loren's door. His hearing picked up on her heartbeat, the rhythm slow and steady enough to suggest that she was still sleeping.

He found Tanner downstairs, where he gave him the audio recorder and asked him to upload the clip and run it through the voice recognition software. The moment the messenger used her cell phone again, no matter how far away in the city, they would be able to trace the call and figure out who she was—and more importantly, who she worked for.

As he made his way to his car and pulled up a mugshot that would allow him to track his next asshat of a target, he found himself staring at the windows that were aglow with light on the third floor. He wanted nothing more than to stay here in case Loren decided she needed his company when she woke up, but he knew he shouldn't kid himself. After what happened last night—after her dog had died because of *him*—she would hate him now more than she had before.

And he deserved it. What he didn't deserve was *her.* He'd never deserved her, and he'd been stupid to think he did.

He supposed that made two of them.

For he now hated himself more than he ever had in his extremely long and painful life.

THE NOMADIC VAMPIRE begged long and hard for Darien not to kill him.

He didn't listen. Darkslayers didn't listen, and they sure as hell didn't deign to bargain with their targets.

Darien took his time breaking him, slowly and thoroughly, as per the request of the faceless person who'd hired him last week. Although that person would never know whether it'd been done quickly—whether he had simply slit the target's throat or had taken his sweet time pulling him apart over the course of several hours—he followed his orders. Because he was every bit a monster as those who hired him.

But even though he tried to pretend it didn't bother him, every scream, every word whimpered as his target begged him to stop, gnawed a little at what was left of his soul. The black scrap of it he was convinced would soon flutter away, leaving him every bit the diabolic shell rumor claimed him to be.

People like him didn't need souls; they were for good and honest people. And he wasn't a good person, nor was he an honest one.

He shouldn't give a shit. Shouldn't care in the slightest.

And he *didn't* care.

At least…that was what he tried to tell himself.

DARIEN FOUND himself at Lucent Enterprises shortly after eight p.m., after spotting Arthur's car in the near-empty parking lot.

The weapons technician must've sensed his approach, because he met him at the door to his private laboratory. Darien was preparing to use his stolen fingerprints on the keypad out front when the door swung open.

KAYLA EDWARDS

"Might I remind you that we can arrange to meet at the front entrance?" Arthur was frowning. "Stolen prints are not always necessary when we live in the days of cell phones, and you have a weapons technician for a friend." Arthur looked him over, as though he could see the blue vampire blood Darien had scrubbed off before coming here.

"Where's the fun in that, Arthur?" Darien teased.

But Arthur didn't laugh. "Where's Loren?" he inquired as he stepped aside to allow Darien into the laboratory. The hum of machinery was the only sound.

Darien frowned, hands in the pockets of his jeans as he followed Arthur inside. He paced on the floors that were so clean they reflected the rows of fluorescents like a mirror. "She hasn't been around lately."

"Shame," Arthur sighed. "You were quite fond of her. As was I. When you brought her here, I'd actually hoped you'd finally found someone and were settling down."

Darien stopped pacing. "She deserves better than me, Arthur." His voice was burdened with regret that cut deep. "She deserves someone normal. Someone who's not going to put her in danger by simply being in the same room as her. By *existing* around her." He shook his head in disgust and pushed back his still-damp hair.

Arthur gave a thoughtful hum. "What if she was already in danger all her life?" He folded his wrinkled hands before him. "What if simply being human is enough for her to need saving?"

Darien's brow creased. "What are you saying?"

"I'm saying, what if trying to spare Loren pain only ends up causing her more?" Darien started to shake his head, but Arthur continued. "I think that perhaps she needs someone like you. Someone who can protect her while she finds her place in the world. Someone who can face the pain of this unbalanced system and be able to take it."

"Nothing good can come of me being with her. I won't risk it." He sighed, and he couldn't look at Arthur as he went on to admit how he'd emotionally snapped two days after he'd kissed Loren. "At the same time, I don't know if I can stay away from her, Arthur. Last

CITY OF GODS AND MONSTERS

week, I...I broke the library doors off the hinges at Hell's Gate. I shattered a bunch of dishes. I literally cracked the coffee table in half. Scared the shit out of the other Devils."

He was always so careful about containing his rage, only setting it free in underground fighting rings and on his targets. Never had anything caused his temper to fly off the hook in his own household; around the people he called *family*. Not until Loren came around.

Not until he realized he couldn't have her.

"Have you tried asking Miss Calla how she feels about the situation?" Seeing the deliberation on Darien's face, Arthur gave him a little smile. "I think, Darien, that perhaps you should allow her to have her say. It might help with this internal conflict you're experiencing."

Darien strode to a table and leaned back against it. "I think I might've lost my chance. I've done a thorough job of pushing her away lately."

"So, let her come to you," Arthur suggested. "You might be surprised by what you find if you give something a little time and breathing space."

Darien sighed and scrubbed his hands over his face. "Speaking of time and breathing space, have you found anything of interest lately?"

"I did." He went over to where a silver briefcase sat on the counter. He snapped open the latches and retrieved a roll of paper from within. He spread it out on the table before Darien, though he didn't say anything. He didn't need to; the drawings said enough.

They were blueprints.

"The Arcanum Well." Darien felt like the wind had been knocked out of him.

"A replica of it," Arthur corrected.

"Where did you find these?"

"I did some snooping in our databases and found some restricted files. I'm not sure who created them, but I have every intention of finding out."

"How did you manage to access the restricted files?"

"Oh, it was quite easy. I used that little trick of yours and wore a set of stolen prints."

Darien cracked a smile. "I don't ever want to hear you belly-aching about me and my stolen prints again." Arthur chuckled. Darien looked over the drawings again. "It looks to me like you've got some digging to do, my friend."

Arthur looked quite pleased with himself. "I've already begun. I think we're going to be finding a lot of skeletons soon."

"Keep me posted."

The fact that someone here at Lucent Enterprises was behind the Arcanum Well replica...

It wasn't good. This person not only had money, but they were powerful—a person trusted by the law and the Aerial Fleet. They would need to tread carefully going forward.

The man who'd been one of his mother's dearest friends smiled, his blue eyes twinkling. "Oh, you know I will." As he rolled up the blueprints, Darien remembered something.

"What about the post-mortem DNA test I asked you to run? Have the results come back yet?"

"Oh yes, how forgetful of me," Arthur said, waving a hand. "I finished analyzing the results this afternoon." He placed the blueprints back into his suitcase.

"And? Did you find out who the ancestor is?"

"It was her father." Darien stiffened. Arthur turned to him, smiled softly, and said, "I know exactly who he was."

45

The stone lip of the wishing fountain bit into Loren's bare knees as she knelt on it, her folded legs braced far enough apart that the cold winds battering at her back couldn't shove her into the yawning pit below.

Where the bicycle lay in the grass behind her, near the edge of a dirt road that converged with another, the wheels still spun. The clicking of the spokes was the only sound that could be heard for miles. The usual noise of the city—the honking of car horns, the screech of tires on asphalt, the rushing of the river, the din of conversing pedestrians—could not be heard here. It was the silence of a darker world, as if a gate had peeled back to allow her in.

A bucket sat on the edge of the fountain. It was so rusted, the bottom of it was speckled with holes.

In one fist, Loren held a switchblade. In the other, she carried two pieces of silver she'd grabbed from the bowl in the entrance hall at Hell's Gate.

Despite that she was the same person she'd always been, and despite that the events of these past couple months had done nothing to change that fact, her hands somehow didn't shake as she clicked open the switchblade and sliced open her palm.

She held it over the rusted bucket, her blood plinking as it hit the bottom. Along with her blood, she dropped in the two pieces of silver — the wage necessary for entry here.

She grabbed the handle and threw the bucket into the depths of the fountain. There was no splash or clang to indicate when it had reached the bottom. No — there was only silence here.

It was the silence of Death.

Loren tipped back her head, breathing deeply.

A light had gone out inside her. Every day that had dragged by this past week was more painful than the previous. Most of those days had been spent alone in her suite at Hell's Gate, with nothing to mark the time but the food the slayers left outside her door. She watched each hour tick by as though she were a ghost, hollowed out and drifting, with little sense of the goings-on in the world around her.

It felt better that way. Better to separate herself from the pain than to be a part of it.

Fog began to ripple in from the outer reaches of the brown field, curving around the fountain. The silhouettes of distant skyscrapers vanished into the whirling, opaque mass, and soon that fog was swallowing her whole.

The temperature bit deep into her bones. It was the cold of distant starlight, of a world without a sun. A world without love.

Loren closed her eyes.

She'd heard plenty of stories about the Crossroads. There were three in this city alone: The Fig Tree, the Chalk Door, and the Wishing Fountain. She knew of the Widow that dwelled at this Crossroads, deep within the fountain; the arrangements she had the power to make.

When Loren opened her eyes, she was still kneeling on the lip of the fountain. But she was no longer in the field.

The windowless walls of a tall, dark room curved around her. The shadows on the other side of the fountain were so thick, her mortal vision couldn't penetrate them, but she knew which eternal being now watched her from within.

Loren lifted her chin. "I've come to make a bargain."

The shadow trembled. Hissing ricocheted off the walls. Moisture dripped into the sewage, the sound repeating itself again and again and again.

"Tell me the desires of your delicious human heart," came a lilting, childlike voice. "Tell me, Liliana Sophronia, what it is that you wish to bargain for."

PART FOUR

TEMPLE OF THE SCARLET STAR

46

"What did you say?" Loren whispered, her voice breaking. "What did you just call me?"

"I called you by your name," the spider said. "Is there another name you would like to be called by?"

It took a long time for Loren to find her voice, but the spider showed no signs of impatience. Loren imagined having all the time in the world, and having lived long enough to see several centuries, could do that to someone.

"I didn't know," Loren said, her voice hollow as a drum. As hollow as her heart. "I've never known my true name."

"Now you know," the Widow said. "I'd say a thank you is in order, wouldn't you?"

"I have questions." The Widow held so still it was unsettling, and the reek of its habitat was like oil in Loren's throat. So thick, she could taste it. "If I am Loren—*Liliana*—Sophronia, then that means I am a descendant of Erasmus Sophronia."

"You are no mere descendant with watered down blood," the spider said. "You are his daughter. The child of the creator of the Magnum Opus himself."

Loren was shaking her head. "That doesn't make any sense. We saw his death certificate." Arthur had provided Darien with photocopies of the documents for both Erasmus Sophronia and Elix Danik, and Darien had shown them to Loren. The math didn't make sense. The dates of their deaths were long before she had been born —nearly a thousand years ago.

"I'm afraid the knowledge I am able to give you has run out."

"Please—"

"What I can tell you is to dig deeper. If a person wants to hide badly enough, they will go to great lengths to do so. I'm sure you can relate to that."

Loren's mind was reeling. "He forged his death certificate?"

A beat of silence. "This is where the knowledge I am able to give you runs out," the spider repeated.

"What would be the point to him changing the date of his death?" Loren was asking herself these questions more than she was asking the spider. The spider seemed to understand this, because she did not bother to repeat herself a third time. "Why would he want to do that?" If the results of Arthur's DNA test came back to show that the bone powder belonged to Erasmus Sophronia, then that meant he *was* dead. It was the only way people could have his bone power; if he wasn't dead, there would've been no grave to dig up. Which brought her back to her question, and it made her wonder if someone else had changed the date on his death certificate.

Again, she was faced with that same question: why would someone want to do that?

"You've come to strike a bargain with me," the Widow said. "I am thirsting to know what you would like to offer. Speak, child. Tell me your wishes."

There was a sharp tug on Loren's heart as she recalled the reason why she was here. "I lost someone I love."

"You speak of your pet."

"He wasn't a pet," Loren said, her throat choking up. "He was my friend."

The Widow regarded her. "And you would like this friend of yours to come back from the dead."

"Yes," Loren croaked. "Yes, I would like that very much."

The spider weighed the request. Loren saw the creature's answer coming long before it was given. Still, it hit her like a punch to the stomach. "I'm afraid—"

"*Please,*" Loren whispered. "I'll give you anything you want. What is your asking price? There must be something."

The Widow considered. *Drip, drip, drip,* went the moisture. Finally, the Widow said, "Usually, there is something. But most of my visitors are in far more favorable circumstances than you."

"What would be your price," Loren bit out, "if I was in a more *favorable* circumstance?"

There was a clacking sound, like bones knocking together, as the spider adjusted its position slightly, as if she had grown uncomfortable from staying still for so long. "Usually, it is years off a person's life. Or perhaps knowledge if they possess a great deal of it. Sometimes, it's beauty. And your beauty is a rather enticing thing, I must admit. It makes me..." The spider made a smacking sound. "It makes me thirsty."

The space behind Loren's eyes burned. "I'll give it. I don't want it anymore—you can have it."

A pause, heavy and silent. "I'm afraid it isn't enough."

Loren wasn't sure what emotions her face betrayed, but a peculiar atmosphere entered the fountain. She thought it felt a little like pity.

"Seeing as you've come all this way for nothing, I will gift you with an answer to one question, as long as it is in my power to give it." *Drip, drip, drip.* "You may ask. And if it is a question that I cannot answer, you may ask another."

"Alright," Loren gritted out. "Who is out for my blood and how can we stop them?"

"Those are two questions, and I may answer neither. Choose another."

Loren's jaw tightened. "It's useless to have gorged on so much knowledge only to be unable to share it."

"Trust me, child," the spider said, "there are many truths that are begging to come out of me. It feels like my skin is stretched taut with the burden of holding them in, but I am sworn to secrecy by magic older than our world. Now, go on and ask another."

Loren thought fast, the questions she wanted to ask bouncing against each other in her head. "Where can we find the other half of the Master Scroll?"

"It has already been found and it is being hidden even from my sight. Someone bartered with the Pale Man to possess it." Another creature of another Crossroads. Another of the Nameless.

"Where is the Arcanum Well? The *original* Well?"

A slithering chuckle. "I'm afraid I cannot tell you that. Besides, you've already used up your one free question."

"And what if I called you by your true name?" The misty shadows that made up the spider stiffened. The thing didn't make a sound as Loren went on to say, "What if I called you *Araneae?*"

Loren had read up about the Nameless in secondary school, and she'd read up about them more in recent days at Hell's Gate—before Singer had died. She had checked ancient books out of the library that had no place on anyone's shelf. She knew that the Nameless were bound by the Law of Names; to know one of the creature's names was to give the person who knew it some level of power over it.

The spider's voice dipped low. "There are some things I am sworn not to reveal."

"Then tell me what you can." Loren lowered her chin, and in a voice like a purr she added, "Araneae." The spider was silent and still. "If I am Erasmus Sophronia's daughter, then why haven't I been able to figure out where the Well is?"

"Because you do not truly wish to find it, child," said the Widow. "When your father hid the Well, he gave the power only to himself. For many years it did not belong to a single living soul—not until the daughter he bore grew into a woman, and she inherited his gifts. But your father made certain his mistake could never be replicated; all attempts at recreating the Well would fail. And even if another person managed to Make it, the prima materia would only listen to its master—to the original Creator."

"That's what the scroll meant," Loren mused. "That's what it meant when it said, 'Blood of my blood.'" Her mind reeled, the yawning pit of the fountain before her churning like a dark potion. The coppery reek of all the blood that had been offered to this creature over the years knifed down her throat. "How did my father make it? How was a human able to access the prima materia?"

"He made a deal with one of us—a Nameless." The spider's voice slithered over the walls. "Upon finding out the true name of one of us infernal beings of Ignis, the Nameless granted him access to the creature of the gods, and Erasmus went on to use it to create the Arcanum Well."

"How can we destroy it?"

"It cannot be undone, Liliana Sophronia. And to try to destroy it would have deadly consequences for all involved."

"How can I find it?" She was breathing so hard, she was panting, the sound echoing against the slimy walls. "Where can I look?"

"Inside yourself," the Widow said.

"I don't know what that means," Loren snapped, "and to be frank, I am tired of your riddles."

The spider stirred. "Very well. Regardless, that is all I may share. And to be *frank* with you, I have shared plenty. It isn't my fault if you choose not to listen."

Loren stared into the churning fountain before her. Her reflection was murky and distorted, and her skin seemed to glow white. "I shouldn't have even come here," she muttered.

"A word of warning," the Widow cut in. Loren lifted her head. "Use your magic and you will die, Liliana Sophronia."

Loren stared into its shadows. "I don't have magic." She was starting to get frustrated that everyone thought she did.

"And I'm not thirsty." There was a strange pause. "Is what you wear around your neck not indicative enough that you are more than ordinary?"

Loren's fingers went to the talisman—the pendant with a closed eye at its center. "The Avertera talisman is only hiding my aura."

"I do not speak of that pendant, child. I speak of the conduit you've worn since you were a baby. *Hold me close when the hour is dire and wish upon the Liar.* Does that not ring a bell?"

497

Loren was shaking her head. "I don't understand."

"But you will. The wish was bought for you by your father for you to use in a time of need. And you *must* wish upon the Liar. It will be your only chance." The urgency in the spider's voice sent a chill down Loren's spine.

"I have to go," she whispered, suddenly lightheaded. Her tattoo was glowing, just like her skin in her odd reflection. The meaning behind the engraving on her solar pendant pulsed inside her skull, begging for her to understand it. She thought, perhaps, she did. "How do I get out of here?"

"The same way you came in, child. Blood."

Loren cut her clotting wound back open and dripped blood into the yawning pit at her knees. As the fog began to close in again, the spider's voice drifted through the murky darkness.

"I am curious," the creature said. "Why do you care so much for an animal that might only have lived for ten years at best?"

"He was my friend," Loren repeated.

The fog grew thicker.

"Most people have lots of friends." The spider's voice echoed faintly, repeating at Loren from all sides, as if there were twelve spiders instead of one.

When Loren opened her mouth to answer, the fog had already closed in, a thick and milky blanket folding over her. She wasn't sure if the spider would hear her, but she replied anyway, and if her heart had been made of glass it would've broken then, worse than before, filling the hollow space in her chest with shards.

"I don't."

DARIEN KEPT a close eye on his target as he tailed him on foot through the streets of Discovery Square. Not only was this target worth two hundred thousand gold mynet, but he was a member of an organized group of violent criminals that were known for their copycat killings.

Specifically, killings done by Randal Slade and his cronies.

It was a joke—this man was a joke. Copying a group of killers as though they were idols.

Darien would take his time with this one. He would make him pay for his sins over the course of several long and brutal hours, and he wouldn't feel sorry for it, not one bit. This scumbag was a wanted rapist and murderer. No matter how many times the law enforcement threw him behind bars, whether it was Blackwater Penitentiary or the Irongate Institute, the prick never stayed locked up for long, thanks to his many connections.

And today, Darien was going to snip those connections, one by one.

His phone buzzed in the pocket of his jacket. He dug it out, keeping an eye on the walking money sign a block ahead. Grinding his teeth at the inconvenient timing for a call, he swiped to answer and lifted the phone to his ear. "Lacey. Is this important?"

"I thought you might like to know she left the house." Lace's voice carried none of the sour tone she normally used when talking about Loren, but she also didn't sound excited to be the bearer of this bad news. Considering Lacey was Darien's ex and the one long-term relationship he'd ever had, he thought she might've hit a milestone in finally moving on from him.

Darien stopped walking. "Any idea where she went?"

"I have a pretty good guess." From the rattle of dishes and the thud of cupboard doors closing, it sounded like Lace was unloading the dishwater. "She took Ivy's bike out of the garage." There was a heavy pause. The background noise turned to silence as well.

Darien gripped the phone tighter. "What else?"

"I don't want to jump to conclusions, but two pieces of silver are missing from the bowl in the entrance hall."

He swore. Pedestrians passed by him in a blur as his thoughts whirled.

"Darien." Lace's voice was soft. "I wouldn't worry. You know nothing she offers them will get her what she wants." She was right; humans had nothing valuable enough to offer to a creature at a Crossroads. But that didn't stop him from worrying about her.

"Unless she offers them her soul," he sighed, running his fingers through his hair.

"You really think she'd do that?" The rattling of dishes began again. Darien knew it was solely out of curiosity that she asked, "Which one do you think she went to?"

"Judging from the bike, I'd say either the Fig Tree or the Wishing Fountain." She probably boarded a bus first, since biking to any of the locations would be a long and dangerous journey. Bus routes would take a person straight to the Chalk Door in Hooded Skullcap; a bike wasn't as necessary there as in Ebonfield or the National. And she would've been right out of her mind to go and see the Pale Man behind his chalk door, so it had to be one of the other two.

"I think you've found your answer," Lace concluded. "Neither the Widow nor the Faun will accept anything she offers them." But Darien couldn't shake his feeling of unease. "You need to let her do this on her own, Dare. She'll come back."

He set off down the street. "I've got a walking trash bag to beat to a pulp and two hundred thousand gold mynet to rake in. Call me if anything else comes up."

He'd wanted to talk to Loren about what Arthur had told him — about Erasmus Sophronia, the genius and creator of the Arcanum Well himself, who supposedly died nearly a thousand years ago, being her father. But with everything going on, no time felt like the right time.

Lace said, "Will do."

He hung up, and he tried not to think about Loren facing the Fawn or the Widow. Tried not to think of how frightened she would be when she spoke to them — nor how disappointed when they told her no.

DARIEN MADE it home before Loren, despite that he'd taken his sweet time with his target.

He was sitting at the island in the kitchen with Travis and Max when he heard bicycle wheels crunching through gravel, his sharp hearing picking up on the sound even through Mortifer's audio-blocking spells. A moment later, the front door swung open.

Loren didn't look at any of them as she breezed into the entrance hall and kicked off her low-top sneakers.

"Everything okay?" Darien called.

"Fine," she bit out. She still wouldn't look at him, and when that second sneaker sprang free of her foot, she sprinted up the stairs, ponytail bobbing with every step. Beneath the hem of her denim shorts, her bare legs were pink from the sun, her white long-sleeved shirt spotted with dust.

A minute later, the door to her suite slammed shut.

Darien had spent a good, long while thinking about the Cross-roads; how Loren had likely had her heart broken even further from the Fawn or the Widow declining whatever bargain she'd tried to strike with them. She had done nothing to deserve this. Nothing to deserve any of it.

He pushed out from the counter and stalked into the foyer.

"Darien," Travis called softly. He thought better of whatever he was about to say and didn't say it.

Beneath the initial whiff of her peaches-and-honeysuckle scent, and that faint hint of cedar smoke, Darien found decay and soil and rocks. He took another breath and picked up on the briny smell of the sea, along with the musty and slightly fishy hint of the Angelthene River.

The Fountain, then.

The Widow.

Darien pulled on his boots and stomped up to the bowl in the entrance hall. He picked out two pieces of silver and shoved them into the pocket of his gray hoodie.

Max came up behind him, his footfall echoing softly. "Dare," he said. His voice was gruff. "Don't do something you'll regret."

Darien was already pulling open the door. Cool air rushed into the entrance hall, rustling his hair and clothes. "I won't," he said. And then he left, closing the door behind him.

What he'd really meant was that he would do it — but he wouldn't regret it.

IT WENT without saying that humans were the weakest race in the world. They could barely tread water in the unjust society they were born into, and nothing they could possibly offer to creatures like the Widow would get them anywhere.

The only powers a human could possess had to be given to them by someone else; someone whose place was above theirs in the hierarchy. It was because of this that Darien knew the Widow had refused to strike a bargain with Loren. The eight-legged demon might've entertained the idea purely out of curiosity, but Loren had nothing to sate the Widow's greed, so she'd left the spider's den emptyhanded. And although he knew better than to think the Widow had taken anything from Loren during her visit, in a way she had, even without knowing it.

The Widow had taken from Loren the last of her hope. And in taking this, the remaining pieces of her shattered heart had likely been ground down to a fine dust.

Darien barely felt the bite of the blade in his palm as he leapt to a crouch on the edge of the fountain at Ebonfield. The salt of his blood filled his nostrils as he let it dribble into the bucket. He tossed in two pieces of silver and then punched the bucket into the fountain.

That field disappeared swiftly, and mist and shadows swept in as he was carried off to some faraway place of liminality that was neither here nor there; betwixt and between.

The Widow's habitat was dark and windowless. It consisted of nothing but curved walls and a cement floor that was covered by an inch of murky water that smelled of oil and sewage.

The thing watched in silence from the shadows across from the fountain he was crouched on. No matter how sharp his vision, he could barely see the silhouettes of those eight long and slender legs.

"A human girl came to see you today," he said to the spider, his voice echoing faintly.

"Liliana Sophronia." A chill skittered up his spine. *Liliana*. The Widow must've sensed his reaction, because she paused then, as if in thought. "Yes. I know who she is, Devil."

"Can you tell me what it is about her that everybody wants?" His lungs felt tight, and his heart was slamming in his chest. "Can she find the Arcanum Well? Is that what it is? Can she find it because she is Erasmus Sophronia's daughter?" Could this be it? Would he finally find out for certain why everybody wanted Loren, and more importantly, how he could keep her safe?

But the Widow said, "I'm afraid I can't tell you that."

Darien bristled. "What's your cost?" he barked.

"It's not a matter of cost, Devil."

"You're forbidden to say." When the Widow said nothing, he took her silence as affirmation.

As one of the Nameless, the Widow was a creature of immense knowledge, but that didn't mean she was free to do with it as she pleased. If a person could afford it, they could pay a creature like the Widow to withhold a secret for the rest of time — until the universe was nothing but dust.

"What did she offer you?" He had to make sure Loren hadn't done something so foolish as offering up any part of her precious soul to this gluttonous beast.

The Widow's voice reminded him of a little girl. "What is it that you'll offer for that information?"

"What is it that you want?" he countered.

Her voice was the hiss of water over hot stones. "A taste."

Darien didn't hesitate as he cut open the wound that'd already clotted in his palm. He squeezed his fingers into a fist, dripping more blood into the yawning pit before him. The first cut was to pay for the teleportation here; the second was by the Widow's request — and thirst.

A wet smacking drifted from the shadows.

"She offered plenty, Slayer," the Widow began. "Years, knowledge, beauty." What little value Loren had for her own life excruciated him. "As I'm sure you're already aware, I couldn't take those things from her. Not without leaving her either dead or in a coma. Though I admit her beauty was rather tempting."

His hair stood on end. "What is it that she wanted?" he bit out.

"I think you know the answer to that question, Darien Cassel."

He did. It just hurt too much to admit it.

"I'd like to bargain on Loren Calla's—Liliana Sophronia's —behalf."

The eight-legged shadow trembled with delight. "You know I cannot bring the dead back exactly the way they were before." Bringing something back from the dead was a tricky and highly dangerous task. It was somewhat easier where animals were concerned, but when it came to people, someone was required to take that person's place in the Lower World. A life for a life.

But Darien wasn't bargaining for the life of a person.

He could hear the smile in the Widow's voice as she said, "What are you willing to trade for the dog's life, Darien Cassel?"

47

Loren lingered in the entrance hall at Hell's Gate, one foot on the bottom stair. She couldn't believe what she was hearing, yet the words didn't lie.

Neither did Darien's voice as he conversed with a female in the recording Tanner was listening to on his laptop in the library.

"My boss," the female was saying, "would like to know what he needs to do to convince you to close this mission."

"More mynet," Darien said. Loren sucked in a breath. "Word on the street says another bounty hunter was offered double what you and I negotiated. Knowing someone else was promised four million when I was only promised three doesn't sit well with me, Long Ears."

"He figured you might say something like that." There was a short pause. "He'll pay five and a half million gold mynet, Slayer. And you'll get every last copper the moment you turn in what he wants."

"Tell him this job comes with a few complications. I have a pretty solid idea where she is, but I need his patience. And I'm not interested in wasting my time explaining why. He needs to trust me."

Nausea twisted in her stomach, and suddenly her legs were so unsteady it took all she had not to sink to the stairs.

Loren didn't stay to hear the rest. She sprinted up the stairs, wondering how it was possible that her heart could still be breaking after everything.

She reached the second-floor landing when the front door swung open below. Her hands curled into fists as she skidded to a stop—as she heard the familiar sound of his boots on the floor. Slowly, she turned and braced a fist on the polished handrail.

Darien was looking up at her, the door behind him wide open to the cold night. His boots were caked with mud, his gray, fitted hoodie and jeans streaked with dirt.

"Can we talk?" he asked her. She couldn't make sense of the expression she could feel on her face. He didn't bother to kick off his boots or close the door as he made his way up the stairs.

When he reached where she stood on the second-floor landing, something inside her snapped. "I can't *believe* you."

He froze, confusion plastering his face.

He took one tentative step forward. "Loren—"

"Don't," she snapped, stumbling back into the wall. She was breathing heavily, her head spinning on her shoulders. "You're an asshole! You're *such* an asshole, Darien." She tore off the stupid bracelet she was still wearing and threw it at his face.

He barely held up a hand in time to block it. Several of the charms came free of the metal chain and clattered like marbles against the walls.

In Darien's shadow, Bandit whined. "I don't understand," Darien said. He looked like he was going to drop dead from exhaustion. "Can you please tell me what's going on?"

She knew he heard it then: the tapping of Tanner's fingers on his keyboard in the library downstairs; the voices that were nothing but a hum to Loren's mortal ears from this distance.

Understanding washed across his face, and his jaw fell slack.

She didn't give him a chance to speak. "I suppose that what you said to Randal was true, too: that you were keeping me safe because you want to find the Well for yourself. You sure are a *player*, Darien. In every possible way!" Angry tears sprang to her eyes.

"Loren." He spoke softly, carefully, clearly able to see how out of control she was. She could feel it, too. She was going to break again. "I know this seems bad. But will you let me explain?" He stepped toward her.

She reached out and shoved him, but he didn't even budge. "I can't *believe* you," she sobbed. "I can't believe *any* of you! You're *all* awful—" She broke off into incomprehensible sobbing, and when he reached for her again, his gaze beseeching, she slapped his hand away.

Downstairs, the tapping of Tanner's keys fell silent. The voices stopped drifting through the speakers, and a moment later Tanner was jogging up the stairs, a look of concern on his face. Darien was trying to talk to her, to console her, but she heard nothing of what he said. And she could hardly make sense of what was coming out of her own mouth as she barked insults at him through her tears, her rage a living thing coiled to spring inside her.

And then Tanner was there. "Loren," he began gently. "Can I explain, please?" She swung her head around to look at him, strands of hair sticking to her damp cheeks.

Darien sank to his knees on the floor across from her, where she was now sitting, though she couldn't remember having lowered herself down. Perhaps she'd fallen.

Tanner spoke softly and slowly. "Darien recorded himself when the same messenger that hired him to find you reappeared the other night outside of the Pit. I've been running the clip through my voice recognition software because we want to find out who she works for. As soon as she talks on her cell phone, the software will recognize her voice and we should be able to trace the call and get some answers about her boss."

When Loren looked at Darien, she could barely see his face through all the tears in her eyes. "You were pretending?" Her throat hurt like she'd swallowed a blade.

He nodded, and she blinked enough tears from her eyes that she was able to see the hurt etched into his face.

And suddenly, her heart was breaking again. Because she was a goddamn idiot—and she'd hurt him by making assumptions, by not being able to see clearly through the fog of her grief.

She was the monster.

"I'm sorry," she stammered, first to Darien and then again to Tanner.

Tanner said, "It's okay. I just thought I should get up here before you clawed Darien's face off." He dusted his hands on his jeans absentmindedly. It was to Darien that he said, "I'll leave you to it," before disappearing back down the stairs.

Loren's face was hot with embarrassment as she sat on the floor with her scraped knees tucked up to her chin, unable to meet Darien's gaze. "I'm sorry," she whispered again. She ran a shaking hand through her unbrushed hair and finally looked at him.

Concern was written on his face, but he made no move to touch her as he sat slumped against the railing, an elbow on a propped-up knee. His clothes were as dusty as her own.

"I'm broken, Darien." Loren buried her face against her sunburned knees. "I can't take this anymore."

"I can't take it either," he sighed. "I can't handle seeing you like this, Loren. It's *pains* me to see you like this. Which is why—" He drew in a ragged breath. "I'm not sure how you're going to react, but I did something tonight. Something I thought might help you."

Loren lifted her head.

Darien was staring at her with an unfathomable expression on his face, as though he was pained. As though he was...as though he was scared. Of *her*.

"Darien." His name was a broken whisper on her lips. "What are you talking about?"

The rings on his fingers flashed in the light of the chandelier as he ran a hand through his hair. "I think it's best to simply show you, but I want you to be openminded about it. I did what I could, but you have to understand I couldn't bring him back the same way."

An uneasy feeling spread through her stomach. "Bring who back, Darien?" Her words were nearly inaudible.

Only then did his eyes meet hers, and she found that she couldn't read them. He gestured to his shadow that was spread on the floor, and a low whistle slipped through his teeth.

The silhouette of a shepherd dog crept out of Darien's shadow. It moved slowly and hesitantly, as if it was still getting a feel for its body.

When the dog caught sight of Loren, his floppy ears perked up. He came out of the shadow he was sharing with Bandit, edging out of the darkness bit by bit, his large, soft paws entirely silent on the floor.

Loren's face was wet with new tears as she gaped at the silhouette—the spirit.

A Familiar Spirit.

The dog crept closer, sniffing at the air, before placing one paw on Loren's socked foot.

"Singer?" The word was a strangled gasp.

The dog gave a long, low whine and rested his head on Loren's bent knees. He looked at her the same way he had the last time she'd seen him.

When he'd died in her arms, and she'd sang him a lullaby.

DARIEN SANK onto the bed in his suite and hung his head in his hands.

Loren's bracelet lay beside him on the duvet. It had taken barely a minute to repair it, but his hands had shaken the entire time. He wasn't sure what he was becoming. He wanted to blame it on the mark of the Blood Covenant spreading up his arm, but he knew that wasn't it.

The day had been taxing. The lack of sleep he'd suffered this past week was beginning to catch up with him, and he found himself nodding off as he sat on the side of his bed. His head seemed to get heavier in his hands by the second, until he could barely hold it up.

It had been worth it. The years off his life he'd offered to the

Widow were worth parting from, if only to see the look on Loren's face when she'd realized she would get to have her dog forever now. It was an act of selfless love that had convinced the Widow to do a deal with him, and although what Loren felt for her dog *was* selfless love, she didn't have an offer valuable enough to settle a bargain.

But Darien did.

Loren was possibly the first human in history to have a Familiar. Never again would she have to endure the death of her four-legged friend; the dog would go everywhere with her in her shadow, and he wouldn't die until she did.

Despite how her inescapable mortality was forever looming on the horizon, Darien hoped that would be never.

She'd cried for a long time after the dog had greeted her. Darien had slipped away sometime after, as dog and girl had wrestled with each other on the floor, the two of them so distracted by their own happiness that neither of them had noticed him leave.

A soft knock came at Darien's closed door, jolting him back to attention.

"It's open," he mumbled into his hands.

The door creaked open, and he caught her scent as she stepped inside. Darien lifted his head that suddenly weighed a metric tonne to see Loren lingering in the doorway, her hand resting on the handle. Something about the way he looked made the space between her eyebrows scrunch with worry.

"What did you offer the Widow?" Her words were flat, but there was new life in her eyes. A spark had been rekindled.

And Darien found that it was enough.

"Nothing," he lied. "Doesn't matter."

"It *does* matter," she whispered, her fingers slipping off the handle. She looked him over, and he looked her over, just like they had the night they'd kissed. "Can we talk?"

He was so exhausted that it took all his energy just to nod.

Loren crossed the distance that separated them, her socked feet silent on the hardwood, and although he gestured for her to sit beside him, she stayed standing. Her golden hair glowed brightly in the bedroom light, like a halo around her head.

She really was an angel. An angel in a house of devils.

"I wanted to apologize —," she began.

But he cut her off in a quiet voice. "I would like to go first if I may. So that I don't pass out before I get out the words. Not that I don't want to hear what you have to say, but I need to tell you something."

Loren waited, lacing her fingers together before her.

He looked up at her, elbows on his knees, as he spoke. "Loren, I'm crazy about you. Since the moment I pulled away from you — like an idiot, might I add — I haven't been able to get you out of my head. You're all I think about." He drew in a ragged breath. "You're all I want."

Loren's eyes shone with tears. Her lips parted as she made to speak, but Darien held up a hand to tell her he wasn't done yet.

"I need you to understand that what I did was only to keep you safe. I never *wanted* to be away from you." He shook his head at how ludicrous that sounded. What man in his right mind would want to be away from her? "That's the last thing I could ever want. Until you came along, my life never made sense. You are the kindest thing that has ever happened to me. You are…you are my home. And I think it's safe to say that my life would be a whole lot darker without you in it. You light up my life, Loren Calla."

She stepped closer, and he spread his knees to accommodate her advance. As she took one of his hands into her own, he slid his thumb beneath the sleeve of her shirt and over the inside of her wrist, feeling the flutter of her pulse.

"What about what *I* want?" she whispered.

He'd been waiting days for her to ask this question. The relief he felt from hearing those words almost made him pass out. "Arthur asked me the same thing. It seems I'm the only idiot who didn't think to include you in making a decision about this." He smirked, but the last thing he felt was amused.

Her pulse fluttered beneath his thumb, and even though he could hear every thump of her heart without the contact, he found reassurance in feeling it directly beneath his skin.

"And what are we deciding?" She bit that lower lip he'd had

trouble looking away from since that fateful day he'd met her in that alley; since she'd sat across from him at Rook and Redding's and sipped on the cherry cola she'd ordered.

Since she'd walked into his world and flipped it upside down. Or maybe it was finally right-side up, and he'd been upside down all his life. She'd fixed things he hadn't even realized were wrong, and he… he needed her.

"I decided," Darien breathed, hooking his free arm around her waist, and pulling her right snug between his legs, "to let *you* decide."

Her breathing hitched as she steadied herself with a hand on his chest. "And what happens if you change your mind? What happens when you decide again that this isn't what's best for me?" Concern shone in her eyes, and he hated himself for having put it there.

"You're the only person who can decide what's best for you, Loren Calla. No one else."

Loren took the hand she had resting against his chest and ran it through his hair. He groaned at her touch, his head tilting back, eyelids slipping shut.

"I think," she began in a breathy voice that had him looking up at her again, "that *you* are what's best for me, Darien Cassel. Where you are is where I belong. And I don't think you could ever convince me otherwise." He thought he'd never hear those words, and he'd worried for so many days that he'd smothered the precious spark between them.

"Then you're going to have a hell of a time keeping me away from you, sweetheart."

His hand slipped off her wrist, pressing into the dip at the small of her back. He drew her into his lap, so that she was straddling him, those glorious legs on either side of his thighs. And suddenly they were back in the truck bed, finishing what they'd started under a sky full of stars.

Their mouths came together with unguarded passion, his tongue claiming hers with savage and unrelenting strokes. The taste of her filled his mouth, and he groaned as he gathered a fistful of hair at the back of her head, pulling her body harder against his.

Loren was the one who broke the kiss first. "Darien," she gasped. "I'm sorry for everything. You didn't deserve to be yelled at—"

"Apology accepted," he said. "Now use that beautiful mouth for something better."

He tipped them both back onto the bed, where she stayed astride him, her fingers flying to his belt buckle.

"Wait," he managed to bite out when she came up for air.

"Don't you *dare* tell me to wait again, Darien Cassel," she snapped, though her fingers had stilled on the buckle.

It wasn't exactly what he meant, but he almost laughed at the irritation in her breathy voice. It was adorable. And...*fuck*. This gorgeous girl was trying to take off his pants and he'd just told her to *wait*. Had he finally lost his mind?

But he didn't want it to happen like this—not from some false sense that she owed him for the bargain he'd struck with the Widow. And as much as he would love to lay back and let her ride him for hours, it wasn't how this should happen. Not for someone as special as Loren—not this soon, after everything.

"That's not what I meant," he said, but she swallowed his words as she came in for another kiss. "As much as I'd love for you to tear off my pants, you don't owe me anything—"

But she told him to shut up by kissing him again. That kiss snapped his self-control, and this time it was *his* hand that went to the button on *her* shorts—but he stopped himself from springing it open, fingers instead snaking below the seam at the front, his knuckles brushing against the plane of her stomach.

"I want you," Loren said, the words wild gasps. "For better or for worse."

A cunning smile ghosted across his lips. "It'll probably be for worse."

She swatted him, though she couldn't help but smile. "You can never resist, can you?"

"You're too easy to tease." His hand slid lower, and Loren held her breath. "But maybe I'll just have to start teasing you another way."

A tremble coursed through her as his hand slipped even lower —

His phone started buzzing. Mouth still on hers, he lifted her up, so he could grab his cell phone and make it stop vibrating against his thigh.

But his eyes snagged on the name flashing across the screen.

For a moment, they both gasped for air in silence. Darien's hoodie was pushed halfway up his stomach, his belt partly undone. Loren's hair was a mess from his hands, her own shirt rumpled, her full mouth as rosy as her cheeks from all the kissing.

Darien sighed and snatched up the phone before the call could go to voicemail. "Cassel."

The Butcher's gravelly voice drifted through the speaker. "It took me a while, but I finally got a lead on your little substance buyers."

Darien sat up, and it was with regret that he took his hand out of Loren's shorts, wrapping his arm around her waist instead to keep her balanced in his lap. "Who was it?"

"Get down to Route 378 and see for yourself." There was a crackle, and the Butcher added, "You have fifteen minutes. Don't be late, or you'll miss it." The line went dead, and Darien looked at Loren, who stared back at him.

For a long while, they said nothing.

And then Loren whispered, "We have to go, don't we?"

Darien's eyelids felt like they weighed a thousand pounds, and although the thought alone of getting behind the wheel made him nauseous, he gave a faint nod.

"Rain check," she breathed as she swung her leg over him so she could stand; the motion gave him a striking view of her perfect ass.

But he caught her wrist before she could make for the door and clasped the bracelet around it in one swift movement.

Loren's eyelashes fanned over her cheeks as she looked at the charms, glimmering softly in the light. "You fixed it," she whispered.

"I plan on fixing a lot of things." He stood up and refastened his belt buckle. Loren's bowlike lips wobbled with emotion as she fixed her clothes and dragged her fingers through her tangled hair. Darien had to look away from her to get his thoughts under control; it was either that or he would have to take the world's coldest shower.

Once he'd contained himself enough to look at her again, he winked and said, "Now let's go see what this prick wants."

She laughed and squealed as he chased her out the door and into the hallway, where her new Familiar met them with a bark and a prance.

Well done, Bandit whispered in his shadow.

Darien's heart swelled with pride at the look that came over Loren's face upon meeting her dog near the landing.

He'd never seen her smile so hard, and the best part about it was that he'd put it there.

THEY MET the Butcher on an overpass at Route 378. They'd left the car parked on a side road a safe enough distance away that it wouldn't be spotted by any passers-by, and then they'd walked from there to the overpass, where the Butcher and several of his men were waiting for them. Their location was concealed by a copse of blue jacaranda trees that hung over the pass, the angle at which they stood providing them with an unobstructed view of the stretch of highway below.

When they were close enough to Casen that they wouldn't need to shout, Darien gave a nod. "Casen. What's the plan?"

"Cassel." The Butcher tipped his head down in greeting, his dark hair swaying. "The plan is to see whoever rolls up to that van down there in the next few minutes." He waved a large, scarred hand at the windowless black van parked a short distance away. "One of my connections gave me a tip that I might be able to witness a deal for Nacht Essentia here tonight."

Darien's mouth tilted down at the corners. "No leads on any more BP deals lately?"

Casen's smirk looked more like a baring of teeth. "I thought you might ask. I had a BP deal come in this morning—another unusually large order that also involved vats of chemicals. If you're willing to follow me back to the Block after this, I can show you the photographs I managed to get."

515

The frown on Darien's face altered into a smile. "I'm impressed," he crooned. "Nacht Essentia and BP in a single day?"

"Hey," the Butcher protested, holding up a thick finger. "I'm not dealing this Nacht Essentia shit. I don't dabble in sissy plants. This was all an outsider's tip."

Darien looked like he was trying not to laugh. "Right."

Both of them grew abruptly quiet as a vehicle zipped below the overpass, stirring up blue jacaranda petals that spun through the air. The car, as unremarkable as the van, carried on down the highway and gradually slowed to a halt on the dirt shoulder where the windowless van was parked.

"Get down," Casen said, gesturing to the cement barricade. They all lowered themselves to the pavement.

Casen passed a camera to Darien. "Here," he said. When he saw the confusion on Loren's face, the warlock explained, "In case the buyers are glamoring themselves, which I'm seeing a lot of lately."

Right. Cameras could not be fooled by glamors, just as the force-fields generated by the anima mundi could not be fooled by Nacht Essentia, nor could they be fooled by the monstrosities the Arcanum Well replica had turned the missing girls into.

The passenger's-side door of the black sedan swung open. Loren held her breath as she waited…

A tall, lean woman with a head of copper-bright hair stepped out of the sedan, the muscles in her golden legs flexing as she walked the short distance to the van, wings rustling behind her with every step.

Recognition twisted Loren's gut into a fist. Time seemed to still as every thought in her head eddied into nothing.

Casen said, "Is that Taega fucking Bright?" His voice sounded far away, the words echoing in Loren's dizzy mind, as if he'd shouted down a hallway.

Darien snapped a photo, and then clicked to enlarge the screen. Loren shuffled closer to him so she could see the photograph, her legs wobbling so hard that she nearly had to grab onto him to stay upright. He and Loren were both blinking heavily and quickly, unable to believe what they were seeing.

It was Taega, all right. There was no doubt about it.

Taega was purchasing Nacht Essentia.

No one who was innocent would buy such a thing, not unless they had something to hide.

"We can't tell her," Loren whispered. Her heart slammed in her chest, and bile rose to coat her tongue, the taste of it bitter and stinging. "We can't tell Dallas—"

"We'll keep it from her for now," Darien said. "Until we have more proof."

They needed more. Purchasing Nacht Essentia didn't tie her to anything more than the illegal substance trade. It didn't mean she had anything to do with the Arcanum Well or the missing girls.

Loren clung to these facts like they were an anchor in her storm.

"How are we going to get proof?" Loren asked. When she glanced back at the highway, she saw that the van was gone. And so was the sedan Taega had rolled up in.

"I have Arthur looking into the blueprints he found at Lucent Enterprises," Darien replied. He pushed to his feet and then helped Loren stand. "Maybe...maybe those will give us something concrete."

Loren nodded, her stomach roiling.

Darien turned to the Butcher. "You said you have something else for me."

Casen pushed away from the cement barricade and rose to his feet. "You sure are getting a lot of gifts today. Meet me at the Chopping Block." He waved a signal at several of his men who were waiting nearby, where they were parked behind another copse of jacaranda trees farther up the hill. The vehicle's headlights lit up as they started the car and drove down to pick up Casen.

Loren tried to collect her thoughts as she and Darien made their way back to his car. But the more she thought about what she'd just seen, the more her brain hurt.

She would leave it alone for now. She would wait until they had concrete evidence to tie Taega to a crime, just as Darien had suggested. She'd waited this long for answers; she could handle waiting a little longer.

Regardless, she still felt like gagging, like her legs were going to

KAYLA EDWARDS

crumple beneath her with every step she took toward the car. To think her guardian was behind this mess, and was possibly one of the people who were looking for Loren, completely unaware that the target she wanted had lived under her roof nearly her entire life…

Was this what betrayal felt like?

48

Loren didn't make a sound where she sat at Darien's side in the Butcher's office at the Umbra Forum.

Spread out on the desk before them were three photos—three grainy black-and-white shots of a blond hellseher half-breed.

The very same hellseher half-breed who'd abducted Sabrine so many months ago. Who'd caused Loren's life—and those of everyone she loved—to screech to a halt. The Butcher had said his boys had snapped the photos only that morning, and although the images were fuzzy due to the distance from which they were taken, Darien was still attempting to remotely track the half-breed. To find the replica of the Arcanum Well, once and for all. When he'd tapped into his Sight, he'd been able to spot the man's aura, however diluted it was, and now he was trying to nail down his location.

Darien was sitting—perfectly still and upright—as he focused, eyes closed, hands clasping the armrests of his chair. Where he was lounging across from Darien at the desk, the Butcher didn't make a sound either, apart from the exhalations of Boneweed smoke rippling from his lips. The plumes made Loren's eyes water. Every now and then, the Butcher would glance at Loren and give her a greasy little smile that reminded her she shouldn't be looking at him to begin with.

Seconds turned into minutes. Loren stared at the neon letters above Casen's desk until they'd seared themselves into her vision, until the words had become doubles—

Until Darien jumped, knees banging against the underside of the desk. The pornography magazines and takeout bags that reeked of molding deep-fried potatoes launched into the air and hit the cement floor with a series of slaps, the contents of the latter spilling.

The Butcher sat up, scrambling for the trip of Boneweed that had slipped out of his mouth and was now burning his lap. "Piss and tits, Cassel," he grumbled.

Darien was standing in the middle of the room, gasping through his teeth, chair lying on its side behind him. His expression was wild, nostrils flared and eyes black. It was to himself that he whispered hollowly, "They pushed me out."

Loren was sucking down startled breaths, gripping the armrests of her chair so hard, her nails were screaming. *"What?"*

The black was slowly fading out of his eyes when Darien's still-unfocused gaze finally rested on her. "I don't know how. But they—it was like he pushed me out. *Stopped* me from tracking him."

Casen said, "I take it that's never happened to you before."

Darien looked like he'd seen a ghost. "Never."

Grunting, the trip pinched between his lips again, the Butcher shuffled the photographs into a pile. "Take these with you. Maybe you're just having an off day."

But Darien was shaking his head again. "I don't have off days."

"Everyone has off days," the Butcher countered. The cracked cell phone on his desk beeped with an incoming message. He didn't look at them as he mumbled, "Take the photos and go. I've got another deal coming."

It took Darien a while to step forward; to grab the photographs and say a hasty thank-you to the Butcher.

Darien made for the door, and Loren hurried after him as he called over his shoulder, "Thanks, Casen."

The Butcher said, "Don't mention it."

A moment later, as Loren was walking at Darien's side down the damp hallway, the photos now tucked into the inside pocket of his black jacket, she wondered if this nightmare would ever end.

Though not all of it was a nightmare. The Devil walking at her side as the result of this strange and uncertain path was something she wouldn't trade — not for anything.

Loren's eyes flicked up as they passed under the white neon sign at the end of the hallway. The words that said: *It was only a dream.*

DARIEN WATCHED on the surveillance feed as Arthur's car rolled to a stop at Hell's Gate.

The weapons technician lowered his window. Even from this distance away, Darien could see him squinting in the pounding rain that had started drumming on the rooftop when he and Loren had returned from the Butcher's office at the Umbra Forum. The road beyond the wrought-iron gates was lit only by the amber glow of streetlamps.

Arthur was rarely up this late in the evening, but he had been working hard, looking for anything that might give them more of a concrete answer as to the role Taega Bright was playing in this mess.

Darien flicked on the intercom system, and he smiled as he said into the speaker, "Should I make you wait in the rain a while longer?"

The rain was so heavy, Arthur had to shout to be heard. "I'd appreciate if you wouldn't!"

Darien's smile broadened into a grin as he said to wherever Mortifer was hiding in the house, "Lower the spells, Mortifer. Let's put poor Arthur out of his misery."

Outside, the gates groaned open, and Arthur drove up to the front steps.

Once Arthur was settled at the dining room table, Darien handed him a mug of freshly brewed tea, pulled out a chair, and took a seat across from him.

The house was quiet tonight; only Loren and Dallas were here.

Loren had made Darien promise not to tell Dallas what they'd witnessed on Route 378—not until they had more details behind the story. Once Darien heard what Arthur had to say, only then would they decide what to do next.

Arthur took a sip of tea and hummed in approval. "You make tea like your mother, Darien."

But Darien didn't smile. He knew Arthur well enough to detect the undercurrent to his words.

Darien's brows pulled together. "Something's wrong."

Arthur kept his hands wrapped around the steaming mug, his wrinkled fingers tapping against the sides. "I was…fired today." His lip wobbled, and he wouldn't look at Darien. "By the CEO himself."

"Fired?" Darien's blood was hot in his veins, and his hands curled into fists atop the table. The movement caused the mark of the Blood Covenant to burn like a corrosive substance was poured over it. "Johnathon Kyle fired you. What the fuck for?"

"There's no need to curse, Darien."

"What for?" he repeated.

"For taking the Well blueprints and for accessing restricted files," Arthur replied. To get the proof Darien had asked him for. "I thought I was doing a decent enough job of keeping out of sight of the cameras but…they saw me. Johnathon saw me."

Darien made to swear again but stopped himself right in time. "Arthur, I'm so sorry."

Arthur's throat bobbed. He took another sip of the tea, hands trembling. Darien gave him a minute to compose himself.

And then Arthur said, "Her e-signature was on the files." His eyes flicked up to meet Darien's. "Taega Bright's."

Darien felt the blood drain from his face. "You're certain?" It was true, then. Dallas's mother was the person—or at least *one* of the people—responsible for the replica of the Arcanum Well and the missing girls. And by the sounds of it, Johnathon Kyle might have something to do with it as well.

"Unless someone managed to not only uncover her username and password but also lift her signature…," Arthur mused. And then he dipped his head in a sharp nod. "I'm certain."

"You have to be certain, Arthur. Because that is a fucking huge accusation to make if we're wrong." It was bad enough if the Red Baron's wife was behind this, but Johnathon Kyle? He was loved by so many people in this state; he was practically a celebrity.

"I don't know how I can be any more certain," Arthur said. Although they were finally starting to get answers, relieved was the last thing he looked. Fear shone in the watery eyes that flitted about the kitchen.

"You're scared," Darien said. "Aren't you?" He couldn't believe the mess he'd caused for Arthur. He should never have involved him. How many mistakes would he have to make before he finally learned?

Arthur shifted in his seat. "I'm thinking it wouldn't be a bad idea to stay here until all this blows over," he said. "If you'll have me. I brought some of my things with me, just in case." Arthur was afraid something worse than losing his job would happen to him now.

It was Darien's fault. He shouldn't have done this, should've looked into things himself instead of asking someone like Arthur to put his job and his life on the line.

"Of course, Arthur. You don't even have to ask."

The man gave a little smile but said nothing else. They sat in silence for a few minutes, not a sound to be heard but the plinking of the rain on the windows and the muffled voices of Dallas and Loren drifting down from the third-floor landing.

Seeing how intently Darien was watching him, Arthur gave him a smile that didn't touch his eyes. "It was high time I retired anyway," he said, taking another sip of tea.

The statement didn't make Darien feel any better. Arthur loved his job, and Darien couldn't suppress the sickening guilt he felt upon realizing *he* was the reason why Arthur no longer had that job.

———

LOREN SAT beside Dallas at the top of the staircase in the entrance hall at Hell's Gate. She'd joined the witch minutes ago, just in time to catch the gist of the conversation Darien was having with Arthur in the kitchen below. The conversation about Taega and the blueprints of the Arcanum Well the weapons technician had found in the restricted files at Lucent Enterprises. Darien had wanted Arthur to find proof about who had created the replica, and it seemed Taega was to blame for this whole mess after all. With her signature on the blueprints of the Well replica, they might finally have enough evidence to implicate her, to throw her behind bars for eternity. Of course, they would have to figure out what was going on with Johnathon Kyle but...

Loren's mouth tasted bitter from the betrayal, and she knew that what Dallas was feeling as Taega's daughter by blood was worse. Far, far worse.

"I just can't believe she would do something like this," Dallas said. "I know I've always said that I hate her, but...a part of me hopes it isn't true. At least for my dad's sake. It could ruin his name if she's going behind people's backs to create something so dangerous. And for what? She's never had a hint of the Tricking, and she's lived for a long time. Why would she worry about it now?"

"Maybe there was a mistake," Loren said softly, sliding closer to Dallas on the step, until her arm was pressed against hers. "Maybe she *did* have her signature lifted." It was something both Darien and Arthur had thought of. They had to tread carefully, had to take Taega down properly, no dirty work involved. Especially since it was obvious that she wasn't acting alone; she was only one of possibly several people who'd banded together to recreate the Arcanum Well.

Dallas sighed. "Regardless, it's time to get out of the nest, Lor." Loren stiffened as she saw where the conversation was heading. "Now that I'm bringing in a steady paycheque at the Fleet, we should be able to get a place this summer."

"Dal...," Loren struggled for words, shifting on the stair. "There's something I've been meaning to talk to you about."

Dallas visibly stiffened. "What," she bit out, the word less of a question and more of a go-on-I-dare-you.

Loren clasped her hands between her knees to keep them from shaking. "Well, I'm dating Darien now," she said. "Like, for real. And I...well, I kind of like it here. At Hell's Gate."

Dallas's lip curled over her teeth. "Are you seriously copping out on the plans we made together in *eighth grade?*"

"That was a long time ago, Dal," Loren said. "A few things have changed now, don't you think? I need to consider how Darien feels." Her shoulders pulled up into a shrug. "I'm...I'm happy, Dal. With him. Here." Hell's Gate was her home now, the only place she'd ever felt like she truly belonged. The only place she'd ever felt safe. She couldn't imagine leaving it behind.

Dallas's eyes glowed like green fire. "So you're just going to forget about your friends?" She was practically shouting, her words bouncing against the vaulted ceiling. "About your sister?"

"I'm not forgetting about you," Loren stammered, though she bristled at Dallas's words. How dare she make her feel bad for something like this! "I've followed your lead my entire life, Dallas. Maybe it's time I branched out a little bit."

"So now you have courage just because you're dating a big, bad bounty hunter?"

Loren's hands curled into fists atop her knees. "You're dating Maximus," she snapped. In an effort to soften the blow of this whole conversation, she added, "Maybe you can live here. With us. There's plenty of room —"

When Dallas's lip curled back over her teeth, Loren stopped talking. "I'm not dating Maximus, I'm *fucking* him," Dallas snapped. "There's a difference."

Loren bristled. "Maybe you should tell him that."

"Whatever." Dallas pulled away from her side, leaving her arm instantly cold. "Don't come crawling back to me when Mister Heartbreaker dumps your desperate ass again."

Loren reared back like Dallas had slapped her. "He never dumped me," she hissed. "We weren't even together yet, and he was just trying to protect me."

Dallas got up and made her way down the stairs. "Keep telling yourself that."

"Dallas, where are you going?" Loren shot to her feet and hurried down the stairs after her, her mortal legs moving as fast as she could make them.

"I have training at Fleet Headquarters," Dallas mumbled. "Just leave me alone, Lor."

"Someone can drive you, Dal." Loren nearly tripped down the stairs. She grabbed onto the handrail to steady herself. "It's getting dark."

But Dallas had already swept out the door, slamming it shut behind her, the chandelier tinkling up above.

Loren balled her hands into fists as she stared at the oak. Her vision was swimming, the blood in her veins hot as lava.

She couldn't believe her. It was true: Loren had spent her entire life following Dallas. She'd never once questioned her, never tried to walk her own path. And now that she was, now that she finally had the courage to make her own footprint, Dallas was making her feel guilty for it.

Could she really call her a friend?

Or was her judgment clouded, and *she* was the one to blame?

Out of the corner of her eye, she saw Darien come around the corner from the kitchen.

She had the feeling Darien had heard every word of their argument—Arthur included.

"Everything alright?" Darien asked.

"Dallas...," she swallowed. In case he'd been too busy with Arthur to listen in on their conversation, she scrambled for a likely explanation. "She overhead you guys talking. About Taega. I think she's taking it pretty hard."

"Loren." Darien's voice was soft, his tone suggesting he knew so much more than he was letting on. He stepped toward her. "Look at me."

She flattened her hands against her thighs as she turned to face him. A migraine was pulsing at the backs of her eyes, which meant she only had minutes to make it to her dark bedroom before it would feel like her skull was splitting open. It had been a while since she'd had a headache, which usually meant it would be extra awful this time.

Darien's gaze was filled with understanding. "She'll come back," he told her.

Loren gave one shaky nod and drifted toward the staircase. She only hoped that he was right.

———

LOREN FELL ASLEEP QUICKLY, the sharp pangs of her migraine chasing her into her dreams. The peppermint oil she'd dabbed onto her temples and the back of her neck was the only thing that ebbed the pain, making it just bearable enough to get some rest.

When she woke back up shortly after Witching Hour., she saw that Dallas had never replied to the messages she'd sent her before falling asleep. In fact, she'd never even *opened* Loren's messages.

The migraine had dimmed to a dull throbbing in her temples, but when she leaned over in bed to flick on the lamp on the nightstand, she found her eyes were still sensitive to the light. It took her a while before she could make sense of the letters on her screen as she typed her query into the search engine.

The rainbow cursor spun for an aggravatingly long time as the web browser pulled up the phone number for Fleet Headquarters. Once the page loaded, Loren dialled and hit call.

The phone rang for so long, Loren wondered if anyone would pick up, but then the receptionist answered in a tired voice.

"Fleet Headquarters," the woman greeted. "How may I be of service?"

"Hi," Loren croaked. She blinked rapidly, forcing herself to focus. "I was wondering if I might be able to talk to Dallas Bright."

"One moment." The clicking of a keyboard punched through the speaker. "I'm terribly sorry, but Miss Bright has gone home for the evening."

Loren's hand tightened on the phone. "When did class end?"

The receptionist hummed thoughtfully as she clicked another few keys. "Training was finished at eleven o'clock tonight."

Loren thanked the woman and hung up. It took her several minutes of thinking through the sharp pangs of the headache that was starting up again before she decided to call Dallas.

The line didn't ring once; it went straight to voicemail.

Loren felt oddly cold. Dread curled in her stomach, her phone shaking in her hand.

Throughout her life, she'd had plenty of arguments with Dallas. And while Dallas was certainly the type to storm out of whatever room or the building they were in, she always came back, and never after dark.

She always came back.

Loren tossed aside the quilts, stripped off her pajamas, and picked the first warm clothes she found out of the dresser.

It didn't take long to figure out she was the only person at Hell's Gate, aside from Arthur, who was sound asleep in the east wing. She'd hoped Dallas had come back while she was asleep and was in Max's room, but that wasn't the case. And the others had gone out, Darien included, so she had no one to ask for advice as she debated what to do.

The first thing she did was call Darien, but he didn't answer. Next, she called Maximus, followed by Ivyana; they didn't answer either. Neither did Travis, Tanner, or Jack. And then she took her chances with a person she'd never considered calling before; she had her number in her phone only because Darien had insisted on giving it to her in case of an emergency.

Lace picked up on the third ring. "What can I do for you, *Lauren?*" She sounded bored to tears, and Loren grinded her teeth as she mispronounced her name —*again.*

"I need you to tell me where Darien is."

A pause.

Loren pressed, "Did he go to a fighting ring?"

Another painstakingly long pause that told Loren that was exactly where he'd gone. "I don't think he would appreciate —"

"Cut the sanctimonious bullshit, and just tell me where he is!" Loren snapped. Darien must've been suffering from a Surge —and she'd been unable to help him due to feeling unwell, hadn't even woken up when he'd left the house. She'd just *had* to be slammed with a migraine on this night of all nights, didn't she?

The next pause was even heavier. But Lace relented with a heavy sigh. "He's at the Pit," she said. "Is there something I should know?"

Loren didn't want to tell her. This didn't concern her. And she knew Lace was only asking because she would get in a boatload of trouble from Darien if Loren ended up in danger.

So, she simply said, "No. I'll be okay as soon as I find Darien."

Lace told her, somewhat reluctantly, "When you get to the Pit, it might take him a while to realize you're there. He fights so that he can lose himself to his rage, so he sometimes blacks out from it. I'd advise you to take a cab as far as you can and don't engage with anyone until you get to the arena. Don't look at or talk to anyone." She hung up before Loren could say anything.

Loren's fingers shook as she typed a new query into the search engine.

It took her a while to find it. The Pit was a no-holds-barred underground fighting ring that didn't show up on any map. According to the limited information she found online, weapons were allowed, no protections were given to those who entered or watched, and if someone died on the premises, no one took responsibility. It was a place where spectators placed bets and could win a lot of money by doing so. To even set foot in the building was considered a crime.

The fights were held at an arena privately owned by one of the city's mob bosses, a man named Antonio Perez who'd purchased the building as a place to host his bloody brawls in an effort to skirt the law.

Loren typed the address into the worldwide navigational system on her phone. When the blue pin dropped on the map to mark its location, she swore.

It was in the Meatpacking District.

"Why am I not surprised?" she muttered. But she called for a taxi, and when the driver showed up at the gates, and she told him where she would like to go, he looked like he might shit his pants.

It wasn't an encouraging reaction, but Loren tried not to think as the cab rolled toward the city slums.

49

The taxi crawled to a stop in the heart of the Meatpacking District, not far from a nondescript warehouse with boarded-up windows. The mercury-vapor streetlamps in this area were either burnt out or shot out, and with the sun having set hours ago, the place was shrouded in darkness that was thick and eerie.

Loren glanced at the navigational system on her phone. This area of the city was crumbling and forsaken; it was a place where the streets didn't have names, and dealers ruled like kings from their restless thrones in opium dens.

Sensing the question poised on her tongue, the cab driver said, "You'll find the Pit two blocks from here." He pointed a thick finger at the rows of featureless buildings up ahead.

Vagrants milled about, and raw-boned prostitutes loitered in alleyways and beneath the torn awnings of deserted businesses, their silhouettes distinct in the flickering red light of the bulbs they were stationed beneath.

"You can't expect me to walk the next two blocks by myself."

The coward wouldn't look at her. "This is as far as I'll go."

"What is it with cab and bus drivers?" Loren muttered, but she handed him the thirty silver mynet that would cover the carfare and no more, unbuckled her seatbelt, and stepped out into the Meat-packing District.

Decem weather in Angelthene wasn't much different than any other time of the year, though the wind was cool enough that she wouldn't look out of place in her hoodie and leggings.

As she hurried down the sidewalk toward the Pit, she pulled up her hood and kept her face tilted downward. The air was heavy and fetid thanks to the slaughterhouses nearby, the malodor of flesh inside the brick facilities making her stomach dizzy.

In the alleys she passed, people rootled through dumpsters bursting with trash bags, and addicts shot up in doorways and on the benches near the green-lit bus stop. Prostitutes flaunting their assets eyed her with judgment from where they stood half-naked on street corners, the odd one pausing to taunt her, or to squawk out half-garbled insults. A couple were witches, a few of them werewolves. But most were human.

Loren had almost made it to the Pit when four men stepped out of the misty gloom of a passageway between buildings, the narrow stretch of cobbles separating an old factory from a one-woman cathouse alit with a single red light on a rotting porch.

They encircled her like wolves rounding up a lamb. Her heart skipped in her chest, her sweaty fingers tightening around the strap of her purse. She had half a second to wish she'd taken out the pistol that was still in the bottom of it.

Where he stood at attention in her shadow, Singer whined and pawed to be let out.

The heaviest of the four men rasped, "What do we have here?" Loren cringed away from the filthy hand that reached out and grazed her hair.

A reedy one with a beard clicked open a switchblade. "Let's have a taste of those lips."

"Which ones?" said an oily voice at her ear. Bile burned Loren's mouth.

She pivoted toward the small space that remained between two of the men, but they closed her in tighter, their bodies shoulder to shoulder. Their breath reeked of cheap drugs, a smell that reminded her of old tires and melted plastic.

"Fresh human meat at the market," another of the men jeered with a blackened smile.

"You selling, darlin'?" A palm slapped her ass, grabbing a fistful of it, grubby fingers digging in deep. "Or *for sale?*"

Loren's blood roared in her ears as she stumbled away from his touch, her attempt at fleeing only bringing her closer to the other three. One of them barked in her face like a dog, the noise startling her so badly she nearly jumped right out of her skin.

"I wouldn't touch me if I were you," she stammered.

"And why's that?" drawled the same man who'd grabbed her.

All four of them laughed. All four of them looked her over suggestively. The delight shining in their bleary eyes was enough to make her physically ill.

"There's a Devil in that building." Her words were louder now and clear as bells, and they did not tremble—not like the rest of her. "And when he finds out you pieces of scum were touching his woman, he'll tear you apart. Limb from limb, like he does those demons in the Pit."

As if in affirmation of her words, the arena that housed the Pit rumbled as the people inside it roared at the tops of their lungs.

The greasy smiles of the four men fencing her in faltered.

"She means Darien Cassel," the heavy one murmured.

"She's bluffing," hissed the one who'd grabbed her ass, the stubble on his face an oily smear of black in the red light.

"Only an idiot would wait to find out," Loren crooned. "Are you boys idiots?"

Their eyes no longer shone with sick anticipation. Now, they were glazed with fear.

For a long while, they assessed her, as though she were a threat.

As though they were beginning to understand that while they were busy cornering a mouse, they, too, had fallen prey—to an apex predator with far bigger claws.

"She's not worth it," the heavy one said, backing away a step.

A third one muttered something about having other fish to fry, and Loren couldn't stifle the smile that spread across her face. She lowered her head and slipped away, through the space they provided to let her pass.

Gravel crunched beneath her sneakers as she hurried through the gates to the nondescript building, and into the Pit.

EVERYTHING about the Pit screamed that she didn't belong here.

Faces leered at her, unwashed bodies jostled her, and clouds of smoke that reeked of cat urine burned her eyes. She tried her best to block out the noise and the stench as she shoved her way through the rowdy patrons that were crammed shoulder to shoulder around the fighting ring, the dense crowd a wall of flesh blocking her view of the Pit, the floor of which was roughly two-dozen feet below where the audience was gathered to watch.

The squalling of a bullhorn cut through the clamour of the crowd, the noise startling her as she pushed her way through the throng of writhing and jumping bodies. The closer she got to the Pit, the stronger the smell; it was a blend of smoke, sweat, and oil, all tangled up with the coppery stink of blood.

Before she made it even halfway through the crowd, an elbow swept up and nailed her square in the nose. The crunch and snap of bone from the Pit below scared her for a moment into thinking her nose had been broken. Blood was gushing down her face. Stars sprinkled her vision, and her eyes watered from the pain.

"Darien!" she called, her voice swallowed up by the yelling of the patrons and the stamping of feet. Elbows struck her in the ribs, and fists that were raised in excitement bumped her from behind.

There was another sharp *crack* from the pit, and the cheers of the audience turned into an ear-shattering roar. The telltale *thud* of a body hitting sand could barely be heard over the barrage of noise.

"Darien—" Someone shoved her from behind, and she barely caught herself before she fell, palms shredding on the sticky cement floor. Someone stepped on her hand before she could right herself, and she drew in a hiss at the twinge that knifed through her fingers.

Boots scraped against stone.

And then she heard his voice.

"Move aside!" Darien boomed, but the cheering barely dimmed as he approached the throng of adoring fans.

Through the spaces between the rows of heads, she caught sight of him as he scaled the last few feet of the steep wall he'd jumped up. As he stalked into the crowd, people began backing away, but not fast enough for his liking.

"Move!" he bellowed, voice like the crack of a whip.

The sound of heavy boots pounded above the rustling of the crowd, and she knew he'd spotted her then, where she was doubled up in pain between two sweaty males, blood pooling in the hands that were cupped to her face. The sound of his footsteps slowed only just, and then picked up again, to a faster pace.

"Back the fuck up!" Darien snapped to the people that were still cheering; still trying to get a word in to their champion. The few who had half a brain shrank from his gaze, and those who were sober enough to notice the murderous look on his face went so far as to step behind their companions.

Darien grabbed the closest person to him and broke the man's nose with one lash of his fist. The man yowled in pain as the bone flattened into his face.

Nobody made a sound after that.

And the sea of bodies parted, as though invisible hands had pushed them aside, their roars of enthusiasm quieting to whispers as they let Darien through.

The denim of his jeans was black with blood, his boots caked with it. The filthy white shirt he wore hung off his honed body in tattered ribbons. He found a clean end of it near the hem and ripped off a strip of fabric.

"Loren, baby," he whispered, pressing the fabric to her nose. "What's going on?"

"Darien, it's Dallas," she panted, forgetting about the crowd watching in silence. Blood slid down her throat as she tipped back her head. "She hasn't been answering my messages, and the receptionist at Fleet Headquarters said the students went home hours ago." The panic in her voice dropped to a croak as she told him, "I think she's in trouble."

Darien's eyes hardened with determination. Of her still-bleeding nose, he told her, "Keep pressure on it." He let go of the piece of shirt as soon as she'd gathered it in her hand.

Before Loren could figure out what was happening, he'd picked her up and hooked her legs around his waist. The crowd sidled farther away as he stalked back toward the fighting ring, Loren hanging from his neck like a chain. She ducked her head and rested her face against his shoulder. He leapt off the sheer edge of the ring and into the sandy pit.

They landed among the mutilated corpses of demons and vampires. Flesh squished beneath the soles of Darien's boots as he walked across the bodies as if they weren't there, toward where two bouncers stood watch at a corridor. The cement walls were cast in blue, the flickering bulbs that were mounted on the ceiling threatening to burn out.

The bouncers said nothing as they hauled up the latticed grille to let them into the corridor. When they reached the end of that corridor, Darien turned a corner and descended a staircase, into a change room that smelled of bleach and chlorine.

Once he was inside, the cement door banging shut behind them, he set Loren down on a peeling green bench and found a bag of Stygian salts in his duffel.

Barely two minutes passed before Darien located Dallas. She was across the freeway, just south of the Meatpacking District. Near the river.

THEY FOUND Dallas by the Iron Dock.

As soon as Darien had pinpointed her aura with the Sight, he'd ushered Loren through the doors of the Pit, not bothering to change out of his blood-soaked clothes.

And it was a good thing he didn't, because when they found Dallas, she was slumped at the base of a streetlamp, the greenish glow of mercury-vapor the only thing protecting her from nine fevered and ravenous demons. Passed out on the rain- and blood-damp asphalt before her was Ghost, the Familiar a flickering silhouette.

Darien set about killing the demons, shooting half of them with his pistol and tearing apart the other half with his bare hands. Not one got in a swipe or a bite.

Loren skidded to a stop below the streetlamp and fell to her knees before Dallas. "Dal," she whispered, taking Dallas's bruised and battered face into her hands.

Blood was everywhere. *Everywhere.*

The deep and broad river that was only feet away trembled, water sloshing from the fins of a great creature swimming through it.

A groan slipped through Dallas's split lips. "Loren," she gurgled. "Taega... My mom —"

"Deep breaths," Loren told her. She tried to take her own advice for her head spinning at the sight of all the blood.

Once Darien was finished with the demons, he eased into a crouch beside Dallas. "Step aside, baby," he said to Loren. "We need to get her to Hell's Gate."

Gods, if Taega had done this to her...

If Taega had done this, Loren would make her pay.

DALLAS DIDN'T WAKE up until the following evening.

Loren stood at her bedside and tried not to grimace at the sight of the witch's battered body. Even though she was finally awake, she barely looked like it, the skin around both of her eyes puffy, shiny, and bruised.

"How are you feeling?" Loren knew it was a stupid question, but she didn't know what else to say, how else to help.

"Fucking peachy, Lor," Dallas grumbled. Silence hung between them, heavy and cold. And then Dallas peeked up at her, the skin around her left eye so swollen the lids could barely stay open. "Thank you for finding me," she whispered. "I'm...sorry. I shouldn't have reacted the way I did about you and Darien. I was…out of line."

"I'm sorry, too," Loren whispered.

"Don't be." Dallas's cold fingers found Loren's, and they were stiff and trembling as they wrapped around hers. "I'm just scared, Lor. I'm scared of change." A tear slipped down her cheek, and she scrubbed it away. "You and Sabrine are all I have. And if you were suddenly gone, I…"

Loren squeezed her scraped fingers, being careful not to press too hard. "I'll never be gone, Dal." Tears pricked at her own eyes as she watched Dallas's lip tremble. It had been years—*years* since Dallas had cried in front of her. Since she'd opened herself up to feeling any emotion other than anger. "We'll always be sisters, and I'll always be your friend. No matter what."

Dallas's eyes were swimming as she looked up at her. "Promise?"

"I swear it on the eight deities of the Scarlet Star." A tear slid from the corner of her own eye. "I swear it on my life."

Dallas smiled back at her. "Good," she said thickly. "Because if Darien ever tries to keep you from me, I'll chop off his balls."

Laughter burst through Loren's lips. "You're hilarious, Dal."

A knock came at the open door. Loren turned to see Darien and Max strolling in.

"What was that I heard about chopping off my balls?" Darien wore a poker face, though the tone he used was colored with amusement.

"Oh, nothing," Dallas said sweetly.

"Took a million years to find this asshole," Darien said of Maximus, who strode up to Dallas's bedside and gave her a peck on the forehead. "Now that he's here, we're all ears, Dal."

Dallas pushed herself up higher on the pillows, her jaw clenching with pain. "I overheard what Arthur told you about my mother, Darien," she began. "About the blueprints with her signature of approval. When I went for training at Fleet Headquarters, I couldn't stop myself. I broke into her office after hours…and I did some snooping."

Loren swore everyone was holding their breath.

"I found evidence on who's responsible for receiving shipments of chemicals and potions." Dallas's voice was a hoarse whisper. "The same kind the Dominus...," she struggled to remember the full name but opted with, "the Master Scroll talks about." Dallas's throat bobbed as she swallowed. "It *was* her. Taega was the one who organized a receiving party for the latest shipment through the Blood Potions Syndicate. It wasn't the Butcher for this one—it was someone else who was dealing."

Darien and Max swore.

Taega hadn't just been purchasing Nacht Essentia, hadn't just had her name on the blueprints of the Well replica—she was purchasing chemicals and Blood Potions.

It was enough. It *had* to be enough.

But—

"You didn't happen to take that evidence, did you?" Max said, voicing the thought that sliced through Loren's mind.

Dallas shook her head. "I didn't see who attacked me in the office, but I know it was one of my mother's men. Who else would it have been? I found evidence that can lock her up for the rest of her immortal life; I needed to be done away with." Loren shuddered at those last words. They must've hoped the demons would've finished the job for them, would've dragged Dallas into their dens beneath the city.

"We need to get into the penthouse, Dallas," Darien said. "We need to find something the Magical Protections Unit can work with—something concrete, like what you saw at Fleet Headquarters."

While the signature Arthur had found on the Well blueprints had been enough to convince Loren and the others that she was behind the troubles that had befallen them, the MPU would need more—something to show that Taega's intentions had been anything but good when she'd set about to rebuild the Arcanum Well. Something to fully explain what was happening with the artifact and the missing people. "It's either that or we kill her."

"As much as I despise my mother at times," Dallas said with a wobbling sigh. "I'd rather see her behind bars."

"When is she usually at Headquarters?" Max asked.

Dallas glanced at the clock on the nightstand. "She's there now. For about another hour."

Darien pushed away from the bedframe and made for the door. "Let's go."

Sheets rustled as Dallas tried sitting up, kicking Loren in the hip in the process. "Like hell you're going without me!"

"Dal—" Loren tried, shuffling out of her way as she continued kicking the sheets off.

"You're not coming," Max said. He placed a restraining hand on her shoulder, but Dallas shook him off with a baring of teeth.

It was to Darien, who was lingering in the doorframe, that Dallas barked, "Drug me." Her chest was heaving with wild breaths, her eyes alit with a frenzy of determination. "I know you've got something for the pain."

Loren looked to Darien in confusion, but no one explained a damn thing to her. In fact, for a long time, no one said anything as Darien and Max stared each other down, the latter with an expression that could rival a stone statue.

And then Max began shaking his head.

"Max," Darien beseeched softly.

Max's jaw was set, eyes blazing. Whole minutes ticked by before he finally snapped, "Fine." He wouldn't look at anyone as he added, "I'm going to wait outside."

He swept out of the room, his overcoat rustling behind him. Darien left as well, and when he returned a moment later, he had a narcotic he said would ease Dallas's pain.

Darien wouldn't look at Loren as he offered the plastic bag to Dallas. She practically ripped it from his grasp. She opened the bag, shook a small pink star into her palm, and tucked it under her tongue.

Five minutes passed and she was able to move—to stand without flinching, as if her pain didn't exist; was able to leave the room with barely a limp in her step.

Darien still wouldn't look at Loren.

And when she followed him downstairs, where she hastily stuffed her feet into her shoes before trailing him out the front door, swinging it shut behind her, she blurted, "You used to be an abuser." The air was wet and cold tonight; it raised her skin to gooseflesh.

"A while ago," Darien admitted, the words a near-inaudible mumble. He unlocked the car doors; Max and Dallas were already in the former's SUV, where they were waiting for Darien and Loren to get in their own car before they would follow them to Bright Penthouse. "I couldn't deal with the shithole that is my life. They helped with the Surges for a time, but I...I wanted to do better. So I stopped."

Darien didn't say anything more as he got into the driver's seat and buckled his seatbelt, the click of the ends connecting loud in the silence.

Darien scrubbed a hand over his face, while he used his other to start the car. "I told you I'm a trainwreck." His words were filled with regret.

"You're not," she whispered. "You want to do good—*be* good. I can see it in you."

Darien was breathing so hard, his nostrils were flared wide.

Loren took his hand from the steering wheel and gave his fingers a light squeeze, being mindful of the mark of the Blood Covenant that had gone from a light gray to a deeper one, the symbols stark.

"You don't have to change anything about yourself, Darien," she said softly. "I know you, and I want you—*all* of you."

"I swear I'll never use them again," he said in earnest. He lifted her hand to his mouth and brushed his lips across the scrapes in her palm. She trembled under his touch, warmth pooling in her abdomen, despite all they'd learned tonight. Despite what they were about to do. When he spoke again, his voice was gruff, his gaze intent. "I'll stop the fighting, too. I will. I hardly need it when I have you anyway." He swallowed, the strong column of his throat bobbing. "I would do anything for you."

Loren's throat tightened, her vision fogging over. "I know."

"Kalendae is in two days," he said, the words now tinged with hope instead of regret. He offered up a little smile. "It'll be my New Year's resolution."

Loren's heart was squeezed so tight, it hurt. "You don't have to do anything you don't want to —"

"I want you," Darien said. The three words heated her body from her head to her toes. "If the fighting bothers you, I'll change it. I will."

"Darien." His name was a hoarse whisper, her heart that had been pinched with emotion a moment ago now swelling from the determination behind his statement — the promise he was making her.

He winked, kissed the back of her hand again, and said with a grin, "Let's go catch a witch."

50

The Bright Penthouse was dark and silent.

Taega was scheduled for training at Fleet Headquarters for roughly the next hour, making this the perfect opportunity to break in and reaffirm what they'd learned.

Loren let the others do most of the searching. It felt wrong to snoop, even in a place she'd once called home. Taega's office was the first place they looked for evidence to suggest that Dallas was right —in the safe hidden behind the oil painting of the Red Baron; in the curved mahogany desk that sat before a cushioned bay window; in the floorboards beneath the carpet spread before the hearth, the glowing of the dying fire the only light in the room.

They found what they needed in a false bottom of a desk drawer. In a brown manila folder were six sheets of text messages with date-and-time stamps. The messages Taega had received from a nameless middleman working for Casen Martel's competition.

It was enough to put her behind bars for many, many years. The conversation that was dated exactly one week ago consisted of Taega arranging to pick up a shipment of Blood Potions and chemicals at a drop-off point near the freeway just beyond the forcefield.

Dallas pressed her fingers to her lips as if she might throw up, as the four of them pored over the messages printed out on glossy paper. "Holy shit," Dallas breathed.

Loren said, "With the information Arthur found at Lucent Enterprises, this should be enough to implicate her. Shouldn't it?"

But Darien's face was lined with confusion. He gestured to the papers spread out on the desk. "Why would she print out these messages? It's almost like —"

"Find anything of interest?" From the multiple intakes of breath, Loren knew she wasn't the only one who nearly had a heart attack at the sound of the female voice slithering through the room.

Taega Bright stood in the doorway, her glossy hair burning a flame-bright copper in the light of the dying embers. The wings at her back were tucked in tight, white feathers gleaming.

Dallas stepped forward, baring her teeth. "Would you care to explain why you're buying from the BP Syndicate, mother dearest?"

A mirror of her daughter, Taega crossed her arms. "I wasn't buying from them, you foolish girl. I've been going undercover."

Loren stiffened. "Your name and signature are on the blueprints for the Arcanum Well," she said. "Someone we trust found them in the restricted files."

Taega gave her a hard smile. "We live in a world of magic, Loren. It doesn't take a genius to figure out how to lift a signature. Not where Johnathon Kyle is involved." Johnathon Kyle: CEO of Lucent Enterprises himself.

Darien's eyes were full black; he was reading Taega's aura, Loren realized. Checking to see if there was any indication in its glow that she was lying. But — Taega was likely disguising her aura with the Nacht Essentia they'd seen her purchasing on Route 378.

"If you've been going undercover," Darien said, "then I'm sure you wouldn't mind telling us who's really behind the chemical shipments and the recreation of the Arcanum Well."

"I wish I could," Taega said. "But whoever is responsible is very careful about hiding and letting their minions do their work for them. The only people we've managed to catch are the lesser of several evils. We'd hoped that by arranging to pick up illegal potions and chemicals from the traffickers, it would confirm the regular pickup spots for the clients, and we'd be able to watch for the next time an unusually large deal was made—for the *real* offenders."

Darien said, "You're working with the Magical Protections Unit?"

"I don't see why you're surprised," Taega crooned. "The Fleet holds a firm place in the law enforcement, Darien Cassel." Her green eyes shifted to Loren, the silver ring around the pupils reflecting the flames crackling in the fireplace. "I'm sure by now you've figured out who your father was. If you'd cared to trust me with everything that's been going on, I could've told you that weeks ago. Back when Darien Cassel first took you under his wing."

Loren bristled. "What do you know of my father?" The fact that she'd known this whole time that she'd been under Darien's protection did not escape her either.

"Everything," Taega said. "Roark was your father's best friend for years, which is why Erasmus trusted him to take care of his only child." Her eyes settled briefly on Dallas. "In those days, Roark—your father—was called by a different name: Elix Danik."

Loren wasn't breathing.

"The two were as mortal as can be," Taega went on. "And back then, mortals were treated with far more disdain than they are today. They had a hell of a time making friends; they were bullied all through their school years, and when they got to university, they formed their own club. In the beginning, it didn't have a name—they had only wanted to make friends. But when Erasmus made an arrangement with a Nameless creature for access to the prima materia, and created the Arcanum Well, they began calling themselves the Phoenix Head Society."

No one moved as the story of Erasmus Sophronia's past floated through the room, punctuated only by the spitting of the coals in the hearth.

Taega continued, eyes now on Loren, "I was in love with Erasmus. Roark was my second choice, which is why I've found it so hard to look at you. You only remind me of the woman your father chose over me." She gave a cold, bloodless smile. "That woman was infertile because of illness. But after hundreds of years spent alone, she and Erasmus had become lonely; they wanted a child so badly that Erasmus created you with the Arcanum Well. One last blessing —and they swore to never use the Well again."

Dallas barked, *"What?"*

The room tipped and lurched as Loren's whole body went numb. She had to grab onto the edge of the desk to keep from toppling to the floor.

Was this real?

Was *she* even real?

She was *nothing*. She had been created from *nothing*.

Darien's voice was like the crack of a whip. "He created life from a *machine?*"

"He used a piece of his own aura," Taega replied. "Drawing it out of himself and submerging it in the Arcanum Well gave it a life of its own, and a child was born. The first child in the world who did not come into being via natural birth."

Loren sank to the carpet, her medical tattoo red as the firelight; as Taega's hair.

"That's not the only thing he created," Taega went on. Her words became distant as Loren's eardrums vibrated. She blinked fog away, forcing herself to stay awake—to pay attention. But her body wasn't her own, and she swore her heart had stopped beating. "The procedures not only gave them immortality, but they enhanced their senses and healed whatever ailments they might've suffered from before. Their eyesight became clearer than 20/10, they could hear whispers that took place behind closed doors, and they could run faster than vampires could fly. Not only that, but they were gifted with the rare ability to see a person's aura—a gift that in the years to follow became known as the *Sight.*"

It was Darien's turn to look like he was going to fall over. His fingers went to the edge of the desk, gripping the wood so hard that his knuckles were showing white through his skin.

"Have you drawn the conclusion yet, Cassel?" Taega said with another of those knowing smiles. "He created *you,* too." Those upturned eyes flicked to where Max stood beside Dallas, face ashen and jaw slack. "And you, Reacher. The hellsehers exist solely because of the Arcanum Well. Without it, you never would've been born. Everything that you are, everything special about you, came from an *experiment.*"

"How?" Darien barked. "How is that possible? He...he was...he was *human.*"

"Through blood magic, anything can be possible," Taega said simply. "But it comes with a cost—a sacrifice. And it was blood magic that made the experiments of the Arcanum Well a success— that made humans immortal and healed a person of any disease. Not only that, but the Well could regenerate limbs—could heal a person from paralysation. It was a miracle worker—a wishing fountain of sorts. And the cost to Make a person into something Other was their old life—their mortal body died and became something new. Became *hellsehers.*"

Maximus said, "Wouldn't that just kill them?"

"Not if the aura was strong enough to hold on. It had to survive in the flames of the Arcanum Well while the body—the vessel— burned to nothing." That explained the name of the society: the Phoenix Head. A symbol of regeneration—of rebirth. "If the aura held on, and didn't fade into the Afterlife, it would be reborn and healed from everything."

"Everyone who's looking for Loren...," Darien began, every word taut. "We figured it was because they believe she can locate the real Well—the original one, so their experiments will no longer fail. Is this true?"

Taega nodded. "At least, that's what we believe. And what Loren's father believed. But Erasmus had a great deal of secrets; there were some things he didn't reveal to anyone, even his closest friends." Her gaze settled on Dallas. "Even your father."

Dallas was too stunned to say anything.

Taega went on, "Shortly after creating Loren and hiding the Well, they brought her to the city temple in an effort to protect her. There were people that had dug up the old history of the Arcanum Well—the secret Erasmus had so carefully buried nearly two thousand years prior—and they wanted to use Erasmus and his wife to find the Well and take it for themselves—and then kill them. They knew they couldn't hide forever, and they wouldn't risk their child's life, so they gave her up. A priest at the temple took her in under strict instruction that only Roark—then named *Elix Danik*—could adopt her. Little did Erasmus know that his precious human baby would eventually inherit his gift and be able to track the Well herself—and therefore be put in the same danger as him. To protect Loren, Roark and I changed our names, our jobs, and began using Nacht Essentia to hide our auras. We've been using it for years, and we were some of the first people to discover the plant's existence. It only hit the streets in recent months, which alerted me to the problem we now have on our hands."

Darien said, "Where is the Well now?"

"No one knows. It could not be destroyed. It could not be replicated without the experiments creating cursed creatures." A heavy, unusual pause. "It could only be remade. Legend says, before he died, Erasmus hid it where no one would ever find it."

Darien said to Loren, Maximus, and Dallas, "We need to find the other half of the scroll. There needs to be a way to find the Well replica and destroy it. I don't care what Erasmus said—if something can be created, it can also be destroyed."

"You can try," Taega said, and there was nothing unkind in the words. She was speaking only to Loren when she said, "Your mortal body has problems handling the gift you inherited from your father, which is why your blood sugar tends to drop so low and without warning. Human bodies simply aren't built to hold magical abilities." Loren pressed a hand to her mouth, her stomach churning. This was all too much.

Too much.

"Your real name is Lily," Taega went on. *"Liliana.* That's why I gave you the last name of Calla. It wasn't because I didn't want to acknowledge you as a part of my family; it was because I wanted at least one of the names you were called to have some truth to it. So that not everything in your life was such a blatant lie."

To the sweetest lily in all the valley, her amulet said. Not meaningless after all.

A sharp knock came at the front door. Loren jumped in place, knee bumping the desk.

Taega's hair glinted in the firelight as she turned to peer out the doorframe—at the foyer. Her wings rustled.

The door handle rattled. "Open up," barked a gruff male voice. *Bang. Bang. Bang.* "Taega Bright, we have a warrant for your arrest."

Darien's hand went to his holstered pistol. "Fuck."

Taega looked like she was going to throw up. "It was a setup," she whispered. "You need to get out of here."

"Wait," Darien said. "This whole thing is a *fucking* conspiracy?"

"We were getting too close to the heart of this case," Taega murmured, as if to herself. "I knew we were getting too close."

Maximus was shaking his head. "This'll never stand up in court."

"It can," Taega countered. "If a person has the right connections." The people who had attacked Dallas last night...they must've been at Fleet Headquarters to plant evidence against Taega, something big enough that even the MPU would need to investigate her—one of their *own*. And when they'd found Dallas snooping, they'd had to do away with her.

A fist banged on the door again. Taega ushered them to the window and pulled it open. Cool air swept into the room, drying the sweat on Loren's skin. One after the other, they slid over the sill and clung to the wall outside, Loren going last.

"Taega," she panted as she slid onto the sill. "Do you know who's doing this?"

But the lock on the penthouse shattered as the door was kicked open, slamming into the wall with a bang. Darien's arms wrapped around Loren's waist as he helped her sidle down the building.

Loren glanced up once last time, to see Taega shoving the window shut.

And although she forced a smile, her eyes were anything but happy.

WHEN THEY MADE it back to Hell's Gate, Darien cut the engine. For a long while, he and Loren sat in the car in silence, the song of the cicadas vibrating through the night.

Darien opened his mouth to speak, but Loren cut him off.

"I don't want to talk about it." Her face was so cold, her downcast eyes so empty, that Darien felt his heart crack in half.

"Don't you do that." His voice was thick, and he was shaking his head. "Don't you close yourself off from me, Loren. What Taega said... You are the same person you've always been. You are just as real and important as everybody else. The fact that you were born from the Arcanum Well doesn't mean anything." *He* was born from it, too. Descended from it. He wasn't sure how to feel. About *anything*.

And Loren still wouldn't look at him.

He leaned across the center console and took her face into his hands. "You are *beautiful*, Loren Calla," he told her. "And you are special." Tears pooled in her eyes, and her mouth wobbled. "Don't you ever doubt it—not for one second." He pressed his lips to hers, tasting the salt of the tears dripping off her nose. When he pulled away, his breathing was as ragged as hers. "You hear me? *Not for one second.*"

She gave a shaky nod, and he pulled her into his arms, burying his face in her hair. He held for a long time as she trembled against him, sobbing silently into his chest until his shirt was damp. The night was still and silent, and even though their world had just been flipped upside down, this right here—the two of them together—felt so right.

"What's it like?" she whispered, her voice cracking. "Not being afraid of anything?"

Darien stroked her hair. "What makes you think I'm not afraid of anything?"

Without pulling away from him, she waved a delicate hand at him, as if his appearance alone was enough of an explanation.

When she peeked up at him, a cheek still pressed against his shirt, he smiled a little, but he could feel that it didn't reach his eyes.

"I'm afraid of plenty. But my greatest fear is losing you. I've always been afraid of losing you."

Loren only hugged him tighter, like he was an anchor in her storm. He wished he was that important. Instead, he felt so...weak. So useless. It was a feeling he wasn't used to.

The distant buzzing of the cicadas was the only sound again as Loren's sniffling quieted at last, her tears running dry.

"What do we do?" she whispered in the heavy silence of the car. "We need to help her."

"We will," Darien promised. He kept holding her close. He couldn't bear to have a hint of space between them, but more than that, he didn't want her to see his face—to be able to read the utterly helpless look he could feel etched into his features.

For the first time in his life, Darien had no idea what to do.

"I NEED A FAVOR."

Darien was standing in the front yard—alone, now that Loren had gone to sleep. She hadn't said anything more to him after he'd held her in his car, and it killed him not to be with her now, not to be holding her, comforting her. But he'd needed to make this phone call. And regardless, he'd sensed that she needed some space, some time to consider everything she'd just learned.

A beat of silence followed Darien's words before Detective Finn Solace of the Magical Protections Unit recognized his voice. "I'm listening."

"If I give you the information you need to get a search warrant on Cain's house and put him behind bars, would you give me something in return?"

Finn didn't hesitate to answer. "Name your price."

Darien felt his shoulders relax, the breath he was holding leaving his lungs in a heavy rush. "I need you to get Taega Bright released of all charges. She was set up and wrongly taken into custody earlier tonight."

The line was silent for so long that Darien wondered if Finn had hung up. But then, finally, he spoke. "That'll take some time. Whoever set her up did a very thorough job of making sure she won't get out again." Darien supposed it was a good thing Finn seemed to be aware of this mess, and aware of the fact that Taega had nothing to do with the Arcanum Well, the missing girls, and the Blood Potions Syndicate.

"Explain," Darien said curtly. And then he added, "Please."

"The stave we found on the scene of Eobha Doyle's murder belongs to her. It belongs to Taega Bright."

Darien ran a hand through his hair. "Shit. You're sure?"

"We pulled the latest spells out of its memory; it *is* her stave—"

"That doesn't mean shit, and you know it. She was set up."

"I know," Finn said. "I know that. I'll do everything I can, Cassel. I swear it. But you have to realize how bad this looks. And the stave isn't the only evidence; without going into too much detail, we found more items of interest at her office at Fleet Headquarters." The planting of evidence Dallas had nearly intercepted on accident—had nearly *sabotaged* on accident. Finn continued, "The MPU can't just brush something like this aside—we have to get to the bottom of it before we can absolve her of all crimes. But something tells me as soon as Roark hears of his wife's arrest, he'll be all over this to clear her name."

"Alright," Darien sighed. He was starting to get a headache. "Alright." He stared out at the wrought-iron gates at the end of the gravel driveway, his eyes burning from exhaustion. "There's a mosaic in Cain's house—an image of a phoenix being reborn. He told me if he could bottle the phoenix's powers and use it to heal himself, he would do it. Take that to your boys and see if it's enough to get a search warrant." He knew the MPU was looking into anything that might have a connection to the phoenix wings the dead girls were marked with; the phoenix head tattoos on the necks of the wannabe Darkslayers. From the deep breath Finn drew on the other end, he knew he was correct in assuming so. "If you manage to get into his house, you'll find everything you need to jail him. The place is a breeding ground for Blood Potions."

"Alright," Finn said, satisfaction coating the word. "Thank you."

Darien ran a hand through his hair. "Don't thank me. Just...just call me when you have an update, would you?"

"Will do." Finn hung up, and Darien stood there for a long time in the front yard at Hell's Gate, staring into the dark sky. Begging the eight gods and goddesses of the Scarlet Star to give him some truth.

51

When morning came, Loren took a bus to Mordred and Penelope's.

Counting the cash float took her longer than it normally did, since her thoughts were consumed by everything they'd learned last night—by Taega having been arrested and thrown behind bars. The law enforcement had apprehended the wrong person, and not one of the Devils knew what to do about it. It seemed like this nightmare only kept getting worse.

As Loren pushed out from the desk and took the float into her hands, she backed up against the window and almost knocked Mr. Crispy over. Only—

Loren lowered the float to the desk as she stared slack-jawed at the plant on the sill.

Mr. Crispy had grown to three times his previous feeble size. He was three feet tall, his leaves no longer brown.

They were green and vibrant with life.

Her mind reeled as she considered what this could mean; as she remembered back to a couple weeks ago, when Darien had cut himself on the glass, and his blood had dripped into the soil at Mr. Crispy's roots. She found her breaths coming faster as she realized—

Was it possible that Darien's blood held a key ingredient to the antidote they needed? The antidote that might change the demons back into the people they were before?

If this were true, that meant she might've discovered what Doctor Atlas and Calanthe were missing in their antidotes. The missing ingredient was hellseher *blood*—more specifically, the missing ingredient was the healing properties in hellseher blood, gifted to them by the Arcanum Well.

Loren sank into a chair.

It took her a long time before she found it in her to call Darien, but she only received his voicemail. She left a message explaining what she'd discovered about Mr. Crispy and the antidote.

When she was finished, she called Mordred and Penelope and asked to take a sick day. As usual, the twins had plenty of prying questions for her, but they finally agreed to cover her shift and told her they'd be down at the apothecary in forty minutes.

And when those forty minutes were up, Loren took a soil sample and hopped on a city bus to Angelthene General.

AFTER BRINGING the soil sample to Tanner's mother, Doctor Atlas, at the hospital, and after explaining to her what she'd discovered about Darien's blood and the healing properties it seemed to possess, Loren made her way through the spotless white halls.

It felt like a weight had been lifted off her chest. They still hadn't reached the end of this dark road, but she was starting to feel like she could see the light. If they could heal the missing girls who had been turned into demons by the Well replica, it would take one less problem off their hands.

Loren was walking down a hallway on the second floor, only partially paying attention to what was going on in the rooms she passed, when one of those rooms made her skid to a stop. Made her approach the open door for a closer look at the person lying on the crisp white bed.

It was Headmaster Langdon's daughter. It appeared as though

she had received a surgery—likely one that would help her to regain the ability to walk after the accident that had left her paralyzed this past summer.

The thought gave Loren pause. She remembered back to what Taega had said at the penthouse last night—about the Well being able to not only heal diseases but also regenerate limbs.

If the Arcanum Well could work such extraordinary miracles, then it must make it possible for a person who'd lost mobility in their legs to walk again.

Loren's lungs felt like they were half their size as she stepped through the open door, being careful to keep her footsteps light. Aside from Ivador Langdon's daughter lying on the bed, the room was empty.

Minutes ticked by as she stood there beside the girl's bed, the hands on the clock that hung on the wall clacking loudly as the seconds were swallowed up. She tried to make sense of her jumbled thoughts and the conclusions she was slowly piecing together—

Heels clicked on the floor behind her.

Loren spun around to see a female vampire entering the small room. Her short, spiky hair glistened like liquid silver in the light slanting in through the arched window at Loren's back. A rose was tattooed on her collarbone with ink that looked like blood.

"Calanthe," Loren stammered.

The vampire was smiling at her. "It's a pleasure to finally meet you, Miss Calla."

Loren stiffened. How did she know her name?

Calanthe came to a stop at the end of the bed, where she gracefully folded her hands in front of her. The black velvet of her floor-length dress formed a stark contrast with her papery skin.

Loren's breath was coming fast as she tried to gather her thoughts. "What are you doing here?" she choked out.

She'd barely finished voicing her question before Headmaster Langdon strode into the room. His academy robes swished behind him as he swept up to Calanthe's side, the door snicking shut behind him on a phantom wind.

The floor was rotating beneath Loren's feet. "It was you," she whispered to Calanthe. "It was you all along." Her mind spun as she remembered back to the events of these past few months, the pieces of the puzzle falling into place at last.

How the Demon Twins had attacked Loren, and she swore she'd heard a sound in the back alley as she and the Devils had taken off after the twins—the only two people they'd believed were watching them. The only two they'd thought they would need to track down and kill. Little had they known there was a third person—a vampire who'd gone on to tell Calanthe of the human girl in the Devils' protection.

How Sabrine had conveniently appeared in that alley by the Bonefish Market, as if someone had dropped her off for a werewolf —who was searching the area for his missing sister—to find. To turn her into one of his own in the hopes of receiving information that would lead him to his sister, the biting of Sabrine initiating a call to action from Calanthe herself.

How Calanthe had then offered up an alliance to the Devils and the wolves to keep the Arcanum Well out of the wrong hands. In the weeks since, no one had attacked her—no one had shown up at the apothecary while she was most vulnerable, with only one Devil watching her from the street. And like an idiot, she'd believed it was the Avertera talisman keeping her safe and hidden.

The alliance had been a tool—a tool to weasel in close to Loren. To be the first to know if—or when—she found the Well.

"You knew the whole time that the demons were the missing students," Loren said, her words hollow. "You were only using that to trick us into trusting you. *You* were the one doing the experiments on them with the replica."

"I have to admit, it wasn't just me," Calanthe said. "I had some help." Calanthe smiled smugly as she waited for Loren to piece it together.

"Randal," she hissed. That night in the kitchen at Hell's Gate, when the Devils had been contacted by Randal to go to his lair— when they hadn't been able to pin down who'd sold them out. *"You* told him about us. You made him take the Blood Covenant with Darien so it would make me want to look for the Arcanum Well."

And she *had* wanted to get the mark off Darien—the *mark*. Her want had had nothing to do with finding the Well.

"Yes," Calanthe said. "Yet you still couldn't find it. The Dominus Volumen says the Well can only be found by will. There was no way we could force you to find it. No—you had to do that all on your own." And so they'd stood by, having one foot in the door with the alliance they'd set, and possibly stalking them the whole time from afar.

Loren bared her teeth, fingers balling into fists. "You were the one who set Taega up. Weren't you? And then your people attacked Dallas when she was sifting through the evidence you planted at Fleet Headquarters."

"Taega and the Magical Protections Unit were hitting too close to home. And when she started to nail down our regular pickup locations from the Syndicate, I knew I had to do away with her. A little signature lifting on Johnathon Kyle's part, turned in to the law enforcement, and I knew they'd be more than happy to wash their hands of the situation—and that goes for the MPU as well. What more devastating end to an investigation than to discover it was one of your own people—the respected Commander of Angelthene's Fleet herself—who was responsible?"

Loren's fists were shaking. "That'll never stand up in court."

"It will," Calanthe said patiently. "If a person has the right connections."

They'd all been played. It had all been one grand, manipulative plan to set people up; to cover their own asses and get their hands on what they wanted.

"We know you've found the other half of the scroll, Calla," Calanthe said. "And you're going to give it to me."

Loren looked at the headmaster with wide eyes. "That's why you didn't expel Dallas and I for trespassing in the restricted library." Her lungs felt like they were being stepped on, and her surroundings shimmered. "You were hoping we would uncover information from the scroll that you could use."

Langdon wouldn't even look at her.

"I'm tired of waiting, Calla," Calanthe said. "And while you've been taking your sweet time deciphering your half of the scroll, and no doubt withholding information from us, we've managed to translate ours. As it turns out, it isn't just *finding* the Well that the blood of Erasmus Sophronia can do—you can operate it. You can turn our little prototype into the real thing, Calla. You can make it as real as the original."

Loren was shaking her head. "I won't."

Calanthe's smile broadened, fangs glinting in the sunlight. "Oh, but you will."

Loren hadn't realized she was backing away until she bumped into the heartrate monitor, causing it to rock back and forth. "Why are you doing this?" she whispered.

"For the greater good," Calanthe said. "For a world of equality—one without half-breeds and humans."

"You can't call it equality if you're exterminating entire groups of people to create your vision of a perfect world."

"The imperator is always looking to the future," Calanthe said. The imperator—the Head of all of Terra and the criminal mastermind who must've employed all those Darkslayers and warlocks; employed Calanthe herself and the House of the Blood Rose and marked them with the Phoenix Head. "The Tricking could kill a great many people, Miss Calla—and the Arcanum Well will stop that from happening. Not only that, but it will also turn people like you into something better. Something that will add to society for far longer than the measly century—at best—that your kind is known to live for."

"What about the people who don't want that?" Loren's voice was shaking. "What if an immortal life isn't what they want for themselves?" Contrary to the haughty belief of immortals, there were people who liked being human, who had no craving for an unchanging and permanent life.

Calanthe pretended to consider, her red eyes flicking to the ceiling. "They will be done away with," she said plainly, those eyes settling again on Loren.

"Whatever happened to freedom of choice?" Loren sidled along the wall by the window behind the bed. She was buying herself time.

Maybe Darien would figure out what was happening; maybe he could help her. "And what of *your* people? You need human blood to survive. Are the blood donor clinics not good enough for you?"

"The imperator has made arrangements for our survival needs."

"You mean blood farms," Loren seethed. She shuffled another foot to the right; the vampire tracked the movement with mirth. "You're sick."

"They'll be kept in a state of coma. They won't even know what's happening."

"Again," Loren gritted out, "you're sick."

"No," Calanthe purred. "But I *am* tired of talking, Miss Calla. You can either come quietly by will or by spell. The choice is yours."

Some choice.

Loren felt like she was going to throw up. She was trapped, and Calanthe was going to take her away from here—to the Well replica. Darien and the others...they would never even know what happened to her.

She had to remove the talisman—had to break the chain. Maybe Darien would think to track her.

But then she remembered how Sabrine's location had been cloaked by her captors, and she realized it would likely make no difference if Calanthe decided to do the same thing to her. Her breath was coming fast, her eyes swiveling round the room as she looked for a way out.

The window at her back. If she could break it with something—

The door clicked open, and the blood drained from Loren's head, her bones turning to water, as she watched Randal Slade stride into the room. The buckles on his boots jingled, his eyes so alight with excitement that he looked deranged.

The headmaster cast his heavy gaze to the floor as Randal took up position between him and Calanthe.

"Loren," Randal crooned, those crazed eyes of his raking like coals over Loren's body. The smile he was wearing was more like a baring of teeth. "What a pleasant surprise."

Loren was shaking.

She had to move. Had to get out of here, had to find help—

Loren pushed off the wall at her back and bolted for the door, shoving aside a gurney as she moved.

But the invisible claw of Randal's power slammed into her, and she was hurled across the room, into the window behind the bed.

Glass shattered as she was thrown nearly right through it.

Hot air swirled into the room as Loren slammed to the floor with a cry. Shards of glass showered down on her, tinkling softly like frozen rain.

Loren's arms threatened to give out on her as she tried to push herself up. Through the damp strands of hair in her face, she saw Randal's eyes turn black as his magic pieced the window back together, glass clinking as the fragments slid into place and melded together.

"When we're finished with you," Darien's father said, "there will be no trace of you left behind." He reached for her with a scarred hand, the skin blackened with the other half of the Blood Covenant.

Loren screamed for help, but magic slammed into her, and the world faded away.

52

Darien stuffed his change into his wallet as he strode out the doors of the convenience store in Devil's Cross.

The bounty he'd raked in that morning would bump up his bank account by sixty thousand gold mynet. Thirty thousand if he factored in Randal's recent stipulation, but he didn't allow himself to think about that. And there was another job he would head to as soon as he got back in his car—a gangster whose head was worth fifty thousand.

A gangster who'd bought out several shipments of Blood Potions from Casen these past few weeks. He and the other Devils who were stationed throughout the city were searching for answers—for anything that might free Taega and shed light upon the *real* people behind this shitshow.

What a gods-damned mess this had all become. His brain was still grappling with the information Taega had unveiled to them last night.

Who knew his kind had been descended from a machine? From an *experiment?*

Who fucking knew?

As he got in the car and turned the key in the ignition, he paused to check his phone. There were several messages from the other Devils and a couple from the Vipers. But the name he was looking for was Loren Calla, and he saw that she'd sent him a heart and a winking emoji, along with a voicemail.

He made to click on the mailbox icon when his phone rang, and a photo of Loren popped up on the screen.

A grin split across his face at the sight of her. He'd snapped the photo in his truck bed, minutes before he'd kissed her that first time. The wind was blowing her golden hair as she gave him the peace sign, her tongue sticking out the side of her mouth, as she beamed at him as radiantly as the colorful stars behind her.

Darien could hear the smile in his own voice when he answered. "Hey there, sweetheart."

"Are you busy?" Her voice was raspy and serious. "I need to talk to you."

He sat up straighter. "I'm never too busy for you, Loren. What's going on?"

A heavy pause. And then, "It isn't working between us."

The blood in his veins ran ice-cold. "Baby—" He tried to swallow, but his tongue was a deadweight in his mouth. "I don't understand—"

"It's not working, Darien." Her voice was a harsh whisper. "Me and you—*us*. We shouldn't be doing this."

The hand Darien ran through his hair trembled. "Loren. Sweetheart." There was a fucking lump in his throat—a hand squeezing his vocal cords. "Can we please—"

A sob rattled the phone. "It's not *working*, Darien! Why can't you just accept that? Even you said you can't keep me safe—you weren't able to keep me safe from this—" There was a muffled thud in the background.

Darien's breaths were rapid and shallow. "Can we talk about this in person?"

"I'm sorry, Darien."

"Baby, *please*—"

The phone beeped as she disconnected the call. The phone felt heavy in his hand as he kept it glued to his ear, his lungs tightening as he forced himself to keep breathing; to not pulverize the phone in his grip.

He needed to hit something. Badly.

The next target—the gangster worth fifty thousand gold mynet… Darien was going to break that piece of shit apart, bone by fucking bone.

The phone began ringing in his hand, and he answered with a flat, "What."

"This a bad time?" came the gravelly voice of the Butcher.

"Not unless you have a set of teeth that I can punch down someone's fucking throat."

"You're a grouchy son of a bitch." The Butcher chuckled. "Meet me at the Iron Dock at half-past—and don't be late." The Butcher hung up.

Throwing his phone onto the dash, Darien nearly ripped the emergency brake off as he lowered it and sped out onto the street, gripping the steering wheel so tightly that it groaned. He flew through stop signs and red lights, tires screeching, horns blaring from every direction, as something inside him he hadn't known existed snapped and splintered.

———

Try as he may, Darien couldn't uncurl his hands from tight fists as he strode across the Iron Dock. The rotting wood groaned and sank beneath his every step. Gulls perched on buoys, squawking out tuneless songs.

The Butcher was waiting at the end of the wharf, the hem of his ankle-length trench-coat flapping in the wind. Ramshackle boats were tied to wooden posts, where they bobbed and dipped in the choppy waves. Although the wind was warm for late-Decem, Darien felt cold, his heart a chunk of ice in his chest.

He should've known better than to let this happen. Loren deserved someone who would give her the kind of life a good girl like her was born for—a safe and happy life. It was only a matter of time —it had *always* been only a matter of time before she realized how wrong he was for her. He'd only hoped it might've lasted longer than this—longer than the pathetic few days he'd had with her in which he'd been able to call her his own.

The Butcher turned to face him, cigar hanging from his lips. He made a show of glancing at his bare wrist. "You're late."

"Get to the point," Darien said. "Unless you'd like to become that set of teeth I was talking about."

Wind swept the ashes off the end of the cigar as Casen smiled, yellowed teeth digging into the moist end. "You're a sick son of a bitch, you know that? I've never seen anyone fight like you. You should come to the Block more often; people will pay good money to watch the slaughters if they know you're playing."

"Maybe I'll take you up on that offer," Darien crooned, "if you get to the point and stop wasting my time."

The Butcher waved a giant hand. "Alright, alright." He flicked the cigar to the dock and squished it flat beneath his peeling boot. "Thought you might like to know that little tip you got from Boyd a while back was off just a tad. Chrysantha wasn't selling for me or any competition I have; she was *buying*. From *me.*"

Darien stiffened. "And none of your people recognized Shadowback's sister, *how?*"

"Some witch or warlock must've glamored her. I only figured it out after I realized the deal was done in sight of a highway cam. When my boys were trashing the evidence, I saw the *real* her—it was Shadowback's sister, no doubt about that."

"Any idea who she was buying for?"

"That's where it starts to get really messed up. One of my boys tells me a black limousine was spotted waiting for her near the river drop-off point. Exactly like the ones Calanthe's rich ass is chauffeured around in."

Darien's head became weightless, the squawking of the gulls and the lapping of the water against the dock fading away. "Calanthe," he muttered. His vision fogged over as he lost himself to his thoughts. "That's impossible."

"Is it?" Casen lifted a bushy brow. "Apparently, the Sands girl needed some extra cash. My guess is that when she found out what she was buying—what the people employing her planned on doing with those chemicals and potions—she wanted an out."

"And they didn't give her one." Instead, they'd used the Well to change her into a demon—or rather, experiment on her until she became of no use to them—and set her loose with the others to terrorize the city, to distract the peace officers from what was really happening. "The Blood Potions—what were those for exactly? Do you know?" He hadn't thought to ask. He'd been so caught up in simply trying to find suspects and trap anyone who was remotely guilty that it never crossed his mind to ask the Butcher exactly *what* they were buying. The warlock they'd captured at the Devil's Advocate had mentioned that they were necessary for conducting spells with the Arcanum Well, but—

"They make a person compliant. They keep them from remembering anything, reacting to anything." That explained why Sabrine could remember nothing from her capture. The Butcher went on, "Not only that, but I found out if you mix them with Nacht Essentia, you can not only hide your aura, but you can also use it to hide your tells—even to completely change your aura into something different, so if someone with the Sight is looking at you, they'll *think* they're seeing your real aura." He gave a dark laugh. "Shit's messed up. Ever heard of something like that before?"

Darien's mind was spinning too hard for his tongue to form words. He certainly hadn't heard of anything like that before. No— he'd become too reliant on his magic, too cocky.

The Butcher said, "Oh, and there's another thing. Nacht Essentia has an opposite called Dies Essentia—Essence of Day."

Darien snapped back to attention. He was breathing so fast, it felt like he was going to faint. "What does it do?"

"While Nacht Essentia hides a person's aura, Dies Essentia will expose it."

"What's the point in that?"

"Maybe when a person gets tired of hiding, or no longer has a reason to hide, they'll use Dies Essentia."

The Butcher said something else, but Darien was no longer

hearing him as he pieced together the events that'd happened since that day Calanthe had offered an alliance with them.

He'd scanned her aura to make sure she wasn't lying but—

But that wasn't to say someone couldn't learn how to disguise the tells of their aura when they were lying. Or to completely change it, like Casen had just said.

And it seemed Calanthe had done exactly that, with the aid of Nacht Essentia.

Logan had told him he had a friend in the medical field who'd swabbed Sabrine's mouth when they'd found her in Oldtown. They'd discovered Nacht Essentia on the inside of her cheek, along with trace elements of another plant they couldn't identify.

Sabrine's captors had revealed her location on purpose. They'd dumped her, half-alive, where Logan would find her—again, on *purpose*. The Blood Potions had probably made her hallucinate so badly that she'd believed she had escaped her captors—crashing down a fire escape just before Logan found her.

Another thought floated through Darien's mind—a realization.

No matter how big and bad you think you are, there's always someone who can play the cards better than you.

"Cassel," the Butcher was saying. *"Cassel."*

Darien couldn't look at him, couldn't tear his gaze from the sopping dock at his feet—from the hints in his memories that he'd overlooked for all these weeks. Amid his preoccupation with chasing Loren's heart, a part of him hadn't wanted to solve the mystery of why everyone was after her—because solving the mystery would've meant they would have to say goodbye. He was being selfish—and he might've just cost them their lives.

"I have to go." He made for the shore. "Thanks, Casen."

"Whatever it is that you're going to do," Casen called, his booming voice nearly swallowed up by the wind, "make sure you really want to do it." It was the closest to a *be careful* someone like the Butcher would ever give.

When he got back in his car, Darien sat there at the side of the road for several minutes, mind spinning as he tried to calm down, as

CITY OF GODS AND MONSTERS

he reminded himself that Loren wanted nothing to do with him anymore —

Or *did* she?

Shit.

Feeling sick to his stomach, he dialled Tanner and watched the palm trees lining the sidewalks sway in the choppy wind.

The line connected on the fourth ring. "I was just about to call and see if you wanted pizza for dinner — "

"Atlas," Darien bit out. "I need you to pull up Loren's cell phone location."

Keys clicked in the background. "Everything okay?"

"I don't know. But I need you to tell me if she turned on her location services." The software on Atlas's computer was faster at bringing up locations than a cell phone — and Darien didn't have time to piss away right now.

"It was toggled on approximately…," *click, click,* "ten minutes ago."

"What location?"

Tanner bit out a curse word but didn't hesitate to give him the location.

Darien uttered a thank-you and a warning that he might need assistance before he hung up and gunned it to Randal's lair.

———

IVADOR LANGDON PACED BACK and forth beside the stormwater runoff in one of the many rooms in Randal's underground lair. Aside from the rushing of water at Loren's back, the only sound was his polished shoes clapping against cement.

Where she knelt on the ground with her hands tied before her, Loren tracked his movements. "Headmaster." She kept her voice low, so the rushing water might stop her words from being heard by the guards stationed at theirs post outside the room.

The wave of Randal's magic that'd slammed into her at the hospital was so intense, she was still seeing stars. Not only that, but he'd also given her a drug to make her compliant and rendered Singer unable to respond in her shadow.

Loren swallowed. "Headmaster, please don't do this. We can't use the Well. What they want to do with it... Nothing good can come of it—"

"You don't understand!" The words were thrown against the cement walls and back at her several times, his silvery eyes sparking with rage. "It was never supposed to get this far! I only wanted the antidote so that my daughter might walk again, but Calanthe—" Realizing he'd said too much, he stopped, his hands shaking at his sides.

"Is Calanthe making you do this, Headmaster?" Loren spoke softly. "You don't need—"

"You know nothing, Miss Calla," he seethed. "You don't even know the beginning of it."

"Then tell me." She was trembling so hard, it was a miracle she wasn't lying face-down on the floor. "Tell me, so that I might understand. So that I can help you—"

"You can't help me." He began pacing again. "You can't help anybody. This city...it's doomed. The people—we're all doomed."

"Headmaster—"

Footfall sounded from the tunnels. Loren held her breath as Randal and Calanthe strode into the room, along with two of Calanthe's bodyguards and several of Randal's cronies.

More footfall echoed—lighter footfall.

And then Emilie Croft and Christa Copenspire swept in, where they came to a standstill on either side of Calanthe. Neither of them said a word, nor did they look at where Loren was kneeling on the ground. Trailing behind them was Lenora Aldonold, the vampire Calanthe had claimed was missing, back when she'd offered up an alliance to the Devils and the wolves.

Randal was assessing Loren as though she were a piece of meat. "It took us a while to figure it out. But it seems you were exactly what we needed all along."

The water behind her rumbled as some manner of creature swam through it. She might've considered throwing herself into the water, so that it might carry her away from here, if it weren't for the flesh-hungry serpents that swam upstream from the ocean.

When Darien's father spoke, it was to Langdon. "Did Darien buy the lie you made her tell him?" That lie had snapped Loren's soul in half. Darien had sounded utterly broken on the other end of the call. She hated herself for saying it—for saying those words. And it pained her that he honestly believed she would want to leave him, would simply want nothing to do with him after everything he'd done for her, everything he'd sacrificed.

While she was calling him, she'd managed to toggle on her cell phone location, in case Darien realized what was happening and might be able to come and help her—though the thought alone terrified her and had her wishing she hadn't done something so selfish.

He couldn't come here. He *couldn't*. She had been stupid to turn it on—

"Sounded like it," Langdon replied.

"Good. We don't need any distractions." Randal crouched before her, bringing his head down to her level. When she refused to meet his steely eyes, he snatched her chin into a hand, fingers digging into her flesh. "I'm dying, Loren Calla." His eyes shone with a strange medley of anticipation and agony; he truly looked like a man who'd lost his mind. "A slow and painful death, to which there is no known cure—except the Arcanum Well."

"Let go of me," she bit out.

He shoved her face aside and pushed up from his crouch. A smile spread across Calanthe's face as Randal strode to a plastic tarp that covered a massive object at the very back of the room, near the bend of the river that snaked toward the outdoors.

He grabbed a corner of the tarp, and with one flick of his arm he pulled off the tarp to reveal—

The Arcanum Well.

Holy gods. Loren was trembling so badly, it felt like the earth was shaking beneath her.

The Well replica was a six-feet-deep tank made of material so black, it sucked up the light. A scent rippled from the contents splashing within, like that of violets. The few bulbs illuminating the room buzzed and flickered, and time seemed to slow, as if cowering under the presence of the prima materia.

The floor tipped beneath Loren knees, speeding up and then dragging. Veins of energy zipped from the earth's core far below — from the anima mundi — and into the Well's molten chamber.

Food for the Creature of the Gods.

Randal said, "Let's get started, shall we?" His eyes turned black, and he picked her up as if she were a doll and threw her into the Arcanum Well.

Water and chemicals splashed as Loren was sucked under, pulled into the Well as if by a magnetic current. Loren held her breath, kicking for the surface that seemed so, so far away. Pain barrelled into her as someone's magic — Randal's — was poured into the Well.

The obsidian-like chamber of the Well replica electrified with bolts of blue and white as Loren broke the surface of the chemicals at last, gasping for breath. The Well glowed with power, and it felt like lightning was zipping into Loren's body.

She arced her back, her spine nearly snapping from the force of how hard her body moved against her will.

The pain grew, and she threw her head back and screamed.

RANDAL'S MAGIC wouldn't let up.

For what seemed like an eternity, he poured his magic into Loren, driving her aura out of her body. Streams of white and rainbow light poured from every inch of her in tiring bursts, snapping back into the human body that was her aura's vessel again and again, like a rubber band. Her body convulsed with each blow, limbs jerking as she lay buoyant in the contents of the Well, the scent of violets sharp in her nose.

Another wave of magic had her back arcing until it felt like her spine had split in two; had her fingers digging into the curved inner wall of the Well, her nails cracking from the force. Tears streamed down her face, mixing with the blood that was pouring from her nose.

She'd never felt anything like it. Never felt pain quite like Randal's raw hellseher magic barreling into her, where it set her blood on fire — set her aura to screaming.

Until the magic stopped.

And a different, far worse sort of pain swept through her as she lifted her head to see Darien, with only his Familiar Spirit at his side, walking into the room.

53

"Darien." His name was a broken whimper on Loren's breath.

Darien almost lost it at the sight of her, soaking wet in the contents of the Well replica, blood leaking from her ears and nose. The delicate skin of her throat was splashed with bruises Darien knew would match up perfectly to someone's fingers—to his *father's* fingers, he'd be willing to bet.

Darien's eyes turned black. "Let her go."

Ears erect and teeth bared, Bandit stepped forward, awaiting his signal to attack.

"Not until we have what we want," Randal crooned.

From the look of terror on Loren's face, and the sheer agony gleaming in her eyes, Darien knew his father was using his own magic as a claw to grasp either her mind or her heart with his piercing grip. It was just as effective as holding a gun to a person's head, and Darien knew that if he made one move—if he even attempted to dispatch this area full of fuckheads—Randal would kill her. It was a powerful type of magic Darien himself sometimes used on his own targets; he could lacerate a person's heart into a pulp without laying a finger on them. Though it came with a risk not many hellsehers were willing to take, including himself; it used so much magic that it increased a person's chances of contracting the Tricking tenfold.

But his father, having already fallen sick with the Tricking, had little concern for the things that could harm him. The damage was already done. And Randal, having honed his crafts for over a hundred years, was faster than Darien when it came to using this gift.

Which was exactly why Darien let the black dissolve from his eyes. He relaxed his hands that were trembling with rage at his sides and forced himself to concentrate on breathing. They *had* to survive this.

Loren had to survive this.

"Whatever you want," Darien gritted out, "I will give it to you. Just let her go."

"Make her use the Well," Calanthe said, where she stood like a statue by the river. On either side of her were Emilie and Christa; neither of them would look at him. They were cowards—they were both cowards. Also among the group was Lenora Aldonold, a member of the House of the Blood Rose—the person Calanthe claimed had gone missing. He couldn't believe how much of an idiot he'd been these past few months. Calanthe continued, "We know she can do it, Darien Slade. And you're going to tell us how."

Darien's mind spun, and his heart raced as he looked about the room, searching for something—*anything*—that might even their odds. But he came up empty, his usually sharp mind nothing but useless putty.

"We're waiting, Darien," Randal warned. Loren's eyes were becoming bloodshot, every breath she took drawn through clenched teeth.

"You're making a mistake," Darien began in a strangled voice. "Loren can't operate the Well—she doesn't have that power you think she has." He tried to say more, to come up with an explanation they might believe.

But Randal interrupted. "Wrong thing to say, my son." He tightened his mental hold on Loren, squeezing so hard that blood slipped from her nose and dribbled down her lips. She gasped in pain, curling over her middle where she knelt in the Well, as though she'd been punched. Violet-scented waters splashed around her, the stench as cloying as the floral reek of vampire skin.

Darien stepped forward, hands curling into fists again, but Randal's men converged on him. One of them offered him a plastic bag filled with chalky pills.

Darien bit out, "What the hell is that?"

"Take one," Randal said. "Take one and perhaps I'll stop squishing your girlfriend's brain."

His breaths were coming heavy and fast, and grey was closing around the edges of his vision. He'd never fainted before in his life, had never known how it felt to have the threat of falling unconscious looming like a shadow before him.

He would kill these fuckers—

"Next is her heart, Darien," Randal said. "You and I both know human hearts are not as resilient as ours."

Loren was shaking her head, blood gushing from her nose and dripping into the waters of the Well replica. When she blinked, red tears leaked from her eyes.

Darien didn't hesitate any longer. He retrieved one pill from the bag one of Randal's men was still holding before him and placed it under his tongue.

The effects were instantaneous. The drug short-circuited his thought process and had his Familiar Spirit flopping to the ground and disappearing into his shadow with a low whine. The ceiling began rippling as though it were an ocean, the shades of gray changing to bloodred. The faces of every person around him shifted into those of grotesque demons, with horns and pits for eyes. Even Loren—

Loren—

Darien blinked.

And blinked again.

"Fantastic, aren't they?" Randal smiled. "I bought them at the Umbra Forum. They're very addictive; that first high is so extraordinary, you'll find yourself aching so badly for another that you'd gladly kill yourself to get one more pill." Randal's tone turned mocking as he said, "I thought if anyone would enjoy that, it would be you."

He stepped up to Darien's side and slapped either cheek, seeing how he'd respond, if at all. Darien's body did not comply with the instructions his brain was screaming at him.

Unable to hold himself up under the crippling nausea that was suddenly gripping his gut, Darien fell to his knees, bone popping. He was only vaguely aware of someone tying his now-compliant hands behind his back, while another person removed every weapon that was on him.

As soon as his hands were tied, Darien grazed one wrist against his watch, turning the face of it with an inaudible click. Everything that was said from this moment on would be broadcast through a radio system to the other Devils, who he'd called on his way here. If they could somehow get to Loren and take her away from here…

The thought trailed off as the drug dug its claws into his brain, forcing the faces of demons into his vision. Maniacal faces with sharp teeth and curved horns.

"I'm going to ask you one more time," Randal said. "How do we operate the Well?"

When Darien didn't speak, Randal stepped up to the Well, reached over the curved edge of it, and grabbed hold of Loren's hair, pulling so hard that she gasped aloud.

Darien barked, *"Don't you fucking touch her!"*

Randal clicked his tongue. "The Well, Darien," he pressed. "Or I'll feed your useless girlfriend to the river scum." As if in affirmation, the water of the river flowing below ground trembled as the ridged back of a great serpent rose out of its depths.

Darien wracked his brain for an idea, but the drug was making it hard to think. Every sound in the room—the rushing of the river, the rhythms of multiple hearts, the thrum of the Well sitting there like some giant cauldron—was ten times as loud.

Randal was pulling on Loren's hair again.

A sob burst out of her. *"Darien,"* she gasped.

"Alright," Darien snapped with a shake of his head, as though it

might rid him of the hallucinations. His brain was liquid. "Alright, I'll tell you!"

Randal waited, a cold smile on his face.

"There's a house near Dusk Hollow," Darien gasped out, blinking against the hallucinations. He let his eyelids slip shut as he forced himself to concentrate. "On the corner of Bernard and Tulsen." He saw that house in his mind, clear as a photograph. He'd never forgotten it.

Not for a second.

He opened his eyes again and looked at Calanthe, whose chalky face was alit with anticipation. Her lips pulled into a triumphant smile, her elongated incisors gleaming in the eerie lights.

When Darien spoke again, his words were meant for Calanthe. "You'll find the other half of the Dominus Volumen there. The spell words necessary for operating the Well are in our half." His eyes burned as he looked at Loren, his vision flashing between the face of a demon and her beautiful, tear-stained features. "Now let her go." He swallowed bile, his eyelids slipping shut again, so they wouldn't be able to see. *"Please."*

Darien heard Randal release Loren with a shove, water splashing around her. And then he strode up to Darien's side, where he leaned in close to his ear.

"Lead the way," Randal hissed, the stink of booze wafting Darien's face, *"Devil."*

As Darien pushed himself to his feet, he kept his eyes closed. He didn't open them again until the last second, so the black of them wouldn't give him away.

Calanthe and Randal shouted in unison as Darien threw out his one remaining burst of power, launching Loren out of the Well—and into the river current.

PART FIVE

THE GARDEN OF REMEMBRANCE

54

The current sucked her under, propelling her toward the floor of the pipe as the rushing water carried her away from Randal's lair, to one of the dozens of stormwater outlets that bled into the Angelthene River.

She kicked fiercely against the current, fighting to stay upright as she spiraled through the muddy water. It was no use — the water was too fast, too strong. Against its pull, she was limp as a ragdoll. Her lungs were tight and burning, and her heartbeat was gradually slowing, every thump heavy and painful. There was pressure on her skull, so heavy she knew it was only a matter of time before she lost consciousness.

The drugs made her see things that may or may not be real; made her scream and thrash as the scaly hides of creatures rubbed up against her sides.

The water was cold as ice, and so dark, she could scarcely see a thing. Her lungs were burnt to a crisp as the last of the air in them was sucked dry.

Light filtered weakly through the water, falling upon rows of sharp teeth.

Bubbles exploded from her mouth in a scream as she kicked and kicked against the current. The teeth kept coming at her, closer and closer.

Something hard struck her in the back of the head, and everything went black.

LOREN JERKED awake in the mud, beneath a sky that was a deep and churning gray. Someone turned her onto her side as she retched up a lungful of stormwater.

It took her a while to gather her bearings; to see that she was lying on the riverbank below an overpass. Cars were crossing it, the sound of their tires unbearably loud. The edge was softening off the drug, but her vision still shimmered as she tried to make sense of the faces above her.

Four people were crouched around her, murmuring to one another as they waited for her to come to. And as she blinked her burning eyes, Loren finally recognized them.

Maximus, Sabrine, Tanner, and Dallas.

Loren blinked one more time, praying like hell that she wasn't dreaming.

Dallas's face became crystal-clear as she threw her arms around Loren and fell to the ground beside her, knees squelching in the mud. "Loren, I'm so sorry," Dallas sobbed, squeezing her tight.

"Thank gods you're alive, Lor," Sabrine said, crouching down beside her. "When we heard what happened through the audio on Darien's watch, we came as fast as we could." She smoothed a strand of wet hair from her face.

"You had us going for a second there, Calla," Maximus said. "It would be nice if you stopped trying to die once in a while."

Loren gave a gurgled laugh, her teeth chattering.

"Holy Caligo," Dallas breathed, still holding onto Loren with a death-grip. "You're shaking like a leaf. Let's get you in the truck."

Loren tried to stand, but her legs were too weak, and the drugs made her sink into the slippery mud again. It felt like her lips were turning blue.

The riverbank disappeared beneath her as Maximus lifted her into his arms. "Stay with me, Calla," he said. She wrapped her arms around her middle, trying to warm herself. "None of us will want to see the mess Darien turns into if you don't pull through."

Her body swayed with every step as Max carried her to the SUV. After loading her into the back seat between Sabrine and Dallas, he found her a zip-up hoodie in the back and draped it around her shoulders.

Shivers wracked her every limb as she watched Maximus start the engine. She clung to the hoodie, burying her white fingers in the soft fabric.

"Where is he?" Loren's teeth clacked together as Maximus pulled the SUV onto the road. "Where's Darien?"

"Randal and the others are taking him to Bernard and Tulsen," Tanner said from the passenger's seat. He had his laptop open on his knees, clicking through maps and windows displaying tracking software so rapidly that Loren couldn't make sense of what he was doing. He tapped the screen and said to Maximus, "It's up here — by Dusk Hollow."

"Where're the others?" Maximus asked as he merged with traffic on the freeway. "Pull them up on their communication lines."

Tanner found a headset in the glovebox, which he proceeded to put on. He flicked a switch on the side, wincing as the audio connected with a screech.

"Where are you guys?" he said into the mouthpiece. "Does anyone copy?"

"Pull up any street cameras, Atlas," Max instructed.

Tanner clicked a few keys and found a lone street camera on the corner of Bernard and Tulsen. "Lace says they're at an abandoned house. Randal and his men took Darien inside a minute ago."

Bile rose to coat Loren's tongue, her heart bursting into a sprint.

Maximus leaned across the middle seat and shifted the laptop two inches to the left, so he could see the screen better.

"What is that?" he murmured, taking care to keep an eye on the cars cruising along the freeway. "Zoom in."

Tanner enlarged the feed with a few clicks.

581

The house was old and decrepit. It was on a corner lot where the streets labelled Bernard and Tulsen converged. The black-and-white feed was so ancient, it was full of static.

There was a sign in front of that house. Loren leaned forward in her seat, blinking against the drugs as she tried to read it...

"Blackgate Manor," Tanner said quietly, taking the words right out of Loren's head. He looked at Maximus, his mouth turning down at the corners. "What is that?"

Max shook his head. "I don't know." The SUV accelerated as Max flattened the gas pedal to the floor. Horns blared as he wove through the lanes of vehicles. Loren fought to stay upright as the acceleration pulled her against the backrest of her seat.

And then Loren stiffened, gripping the hoodie tighter around her shoulders, as she watched Lace, Travis, Jack, and Ivyana appear on the blurry screen, pistols in hand as they strode across the lawn, to the doorway that was nothing but a yawning black pit. Even with the bursts of static disrupting the image, Loren could see that they were approaching with hesitancy, every step slow and careful.

Tanner flicked up the audio to the highest volume.

That was when they heard it: the noise drifting from the bowels of the house. It was like...like screaming.

No—like *roaring*.

Loren whispered, "Do you guys hear that?"

"Static charge?" Tanner's voice was hopeful.

Max shook his head as he passed Dusk Hollow, the shadows of trees flitting over the sunroof. "I don't think so."

The Devils disappeared through the doorway. There was no motion on the screen; nothing showed in the grimy, shattered windows.

But the noises started again. There was no mistaking it this time: guttural roars were coming from inside that house.

"Fuck me," Maximus ground out.

The roaring grew in volume. The sound was so loud, it nearly blew out the speakers on the laptop. An awful screeching carried through them as the audio threatened to cut out.

Maximus held his hand out to Tanner in request for the headset, who promptly placed it in his waiting hand.

"Stand down!" Max said into the mouthpiece, gripping it in a tight fist. His hand was *shaking*. "Can any of you hear me? I need you to *stand down*."

"Max." Loren's voice was a croak.

"He led them into a trap," he bit out.

Randal and his men... That meant Darien had given them the location of Blackgate Manor because he knew something about this house that no one else did.

Something lived inside it. Something evil.

Something hungry.

With the headset in Max's hand, Loren could just make out Lace's voice through the earpiece. "We can barely hear you, Max," she said. "What's going on?"

"*Stand down!*" Max's voice broke. "Lace, do you copy? You need to get out of there. You hear me?" He was breathing hard, eyes alit with terror. "Darien didn't intend for you guys to follow him. It's a trap, you hear me?! *Darien led them into a trap!*"

DARIEN BLOCKED OUT EVERY THOUGHT, every emotion, as he led Randal and his men deeper into Blackgate Manor, through corridors that were black as pitch. The rotted wood floors beneath their feet groaned and flexed with every step.

It had been a long time since he'd set foot in this house. He used to come here as a teenager, back when he had grown so desperate to learn how to use the Sight that he was willing to risk his own life to get his father off his case. To stop Randal from beating his mother into oblivion in the dead of night because of the failures she'd given birth to.

Back before his mother had taken Darien's training into her own hands and shown him another way. A path of light, not darkness.

Calanthe and her bodyguards had parted ways with them in the

Angelthene Underbelly to search for Loren, so only Randal and six of his men were present.

It would be enough. It *had* to be enough.

The shadows were as thick as he remembered them. The darkness wasn't normal; it was something tangible — something *other*. The shadows belonged to the ancient creature that lived here; the evil spirit that took its time feasting on a person's fear before it devoured the body from the inside out. It was not a creature of a Crossroads.

It was something worse. It wasn't a wish-granter.

It was a death-dealer.

It started with the blood, then the bone. And it finished with the muscle and the tendons and the skin. It was meticulous in the way it ate, for meals were everything to it — the one thing it looked forward to. It was very thorough — and it left nothing behind.

The first guttural roar had Randal's men slowing to a shuffle.

"What was that?" Randal snapped. Darien could smell his fear; it permeated the air and set his aura to a flickering and muddied glow.

Perfect.

Darien's voice betrayed nothing as he said simply, "Just a little further now." His words rippled far and wide down the empty hallways.

They started walking again, the men herding him forward, the muzzles of their guns constantly nudging his back. The deeper they walked, the less those guns prodded him. And as the seconds passed, and the shadows beckoned them deeper into the heart of the house, the scuff of their boots on the floor became hesitant.

A hollow clatter sounded.

The tactical lights mounted on the guns of Randal and his men swiveled. One of them swore as the light fell on the floor at their feet, illuminating the horror spread across it.

Every inch of it was filthy, but not with the blood and bone a person might expect upon stumbling into the lair of a beast.

Instead, the floorboards were littered with clothes and personal belongings — watches and wallets; wedding rings; staves. And hair — lots of hair. The one taste the demon didn't like.

The shadows wolfed down the glow of the tactical lights, and the room plunged into a darkness that was petrifying and impenetrable. The air was so cold, Darien knew that if he could see his breath, it would be fogging before him.

The first snap of bone cleaved the silence, and the men began to scream.

Darien stood completely still as he stared and stared into that darkness. He did not balk; he did not blink. And he did not flinch — not once.

Not even as his father began begging. Not even as the wet crunch of teeth ripping into flesh swept through the house, and droplets misted the side of his face.

Not even as the towering, horned creature materialized out of the gloom.

Darien lifted his chin as the creature looked him over — as it clinked the claws that were dripping blood. It stared at him for a long time, that gaping mouth lined with stumped teeth.

Darien stared back.

And then he smiled at the demon — at the death god of the Ancient World, eternally starved and bound to this house for the rest of time — as though he were greeting an old friend.

LOREN'S LUNGS felt like they were half their size as someone's breath rattled the earpiece on the headset. There was a muffled curse word, followed by shouting and screaming. Hungry roars and screams of terror vibrated the speakers on the laptop.

A moment later, the four Devils appeared on the camera. They were literally *running* out the front door of the house, a phantom wind carrying leaves at their heels.

Ivyana tripped over her boots and fell to the ground out front, while the others lurched to unsteady halts and braced their hands on their knees.

Lace's voice came through the headset, loud and clear now that they were out of that house. "Shit, Maximus," she wheezed. "What the hell was that?"

"I don't know," he said. "But do *not* go back in there, you hear me? That's an order."

Ivyana flicked on her headset with a wobbling hand. "What about Darien?"

Maximus had nothing to say to that. His expression was torn as he pushed the SUV faster. The engine groaned.

Loren spared a glance out the window. The street sign marking Tulsen flitted by.

They were almost there.

Maximus pulled to a jarring stop behind Lace's car that was parked a block from the manor. From this distance, Loren could barely see the spires on the house poking above the canopy of the laurel trees dotting the yard. She held her breath as she stared at the camera feed. As she waited with the others to see whether Darien would emerge.

Another two minutes passed before he limped through the front door—alone.

Loren sat up, a choked whimper slipping through her lips at the sight of him, alive and still in one piece. Her fingers loosened on the hem of the hoodie she was grasping in her fists as relief flooded her body.

He was alive. He was *alive*.

But the relief that weakened her knees disappeared as she realized Darien's clothes were soaked with blood, his face and hair spattered with it.

Ivyana's voice drifted through the camera feed on the laptop as she approached her brother, her every step slow and cautious.

"Darien," she croaked. "Are you okay?"

"Where is she?" Darien bit out. "Where's Loren?"

It was Jack who answered. "She's alive, Dare. She's safe."

It took him nearly a full minute to find words. His shoulders were trembling and heaving. "Go on and wait for me in the car."

Lace's voice was so quiet, it was nearly inaudible. "Are you okay?"

"I'm fine, I just…" He gave a wave of his hand, the skin of it unmarred.

The mark of the Blood Covenant was gone.

Darien added in a thick voice, "I need a minute."

The others left at his request and came to wait at the SUV. Max and Tanner lowered their windows to speak to them, the lingering fear they'd felt a tangible thing. Dallas opened her door and scooted toward Loren, so that a breathless and trembling Ivyana could squish onto the seat beside them.

Loren couldn't tear her eyes off the laptop—off the grainy image of Blackgate Manor. After a moment, everybody else was watching it too.

On the camera feed, Darien slowly sank to his knees on the front lawn. For a moment, he swayed in place, staring at nothing. And then he pressed the heels of his hands to his eyes and began rocking back and forth. Dead leaves spun around him as he drew up a wall of magic—as he created a sound barrier that would stop anyone from hearing him, Loren realized.

As he threw his head back and screamed.

Tears welled in Loren's eyes as she watched him break. There wasn't a hint of the man she'd come to know these past few months. There was no strength left in the way he held himself in that moment, none of the cocky and cool-headed killer she'd gotten so used to. Whatever had happened in that house had reduced him to a shell of his former self; had stripped him down to this raw and vulnerable being.

Had the camera not been there, no one would've seen it. No one would've had a clue of the emotion that broke him in that moment. The rippling barrier of magic he'd dredged up blocked out every sound that came from his mouth.

Not a single person said a word as they watched the leader of the Seven Devils, who'd just led his own father into a death trap, break down on that lawn.

Tanner snapped the laptop shut.

Nobody said anything. For a long time, there was nothing to fill the silence but the sound of everyone's breathing.

And then Darien came into view. He was striding toward the

vehicles with his head high, shoulders back. Not a trace of emotion showed on his face. He wasn't even limping anymore.

Loren scrambled over Sabrine's legs and fumbled with the door handle, nearly falling out onto the pavement as it swung open under her weight. She pushed off the cold pavement and sprinted for Darien, the road beneath her shoes eaten up as she ran and ran.

As soon as she was close enough, she leapt into his arms and hooked her legs around his waist. He caught her, crushing her body to his as he embraced her. His arms shook as he buried his face in her hair, breathing her in.

"Darien, I'm sorry," she sobbed against his chest. "I'm so, *so* sorry. I didn't mean anything that I said. I swear I didn't mean a word of it." He tipped up her chin and slammed his lips into hers, as though he'd thought he would never get to kiss her again.

"Lola," he sighed, kissing her cheeks, her brow, her nose. "Are you hurt?"

Loren was vaguely aware of the others exiting the SUV.

"I'm fine," she panted. Darien had pulled back far enough to survey her. She said again, "I'm fine."

"How did you do it?" Max said. "How'd you manage not to be killed by that...thing?"

Darien set Loren on her feet but kept an arm wrapped snugly around her waist. "I'm not afraid of it," he said simply. "Monsters are only what you make of them."

Loren remembered back to that night Darien had taken her stargazing; how he'd told her not to fear the Nameless creatures roaming the landscape—how he'd claimed it really *would* help if she betrayed no hints that she was afraid. She hadn't known then how literally he'd meant it.

Sabrine said, "What do we do?"

Everyone looked to Darien for the answer. Loren leaned into his side, tipping her head back to drink in his handsome face as she waited for him to speak.

"We take down Calanthe," he said at last. "And we fix this mess once and for all."

55

"If what Calanthe told Loren is the truth, and the imperator is behind all this," Darien began, stroking a comforting hand across Loren's back as he spoke to the roomful of people gathered in the kitchen at Hell's Gate, "we need to tread carefully."

Where she sat at the island, Loren sipped on her juice. Surrounding her were the Seven Devils, the Vipers, and the Angels of Death, along with Dallas, Sabrine, and Logan. Arthur sat on a stool at Loren's side, looking as troubled as she felt.

She wasn't sure how it was possible that Dominic Valencia looked more intimidating in the kitchen light than he had in the shadows of the Umbra Forum. Perhaps it was the impressive sword strapped to his muscled back.

Or maybe it was the other two Angels on either side of him. Conrad Valencia and Hanli Shadid had the same gleaming black wings as Dominic, the same magic-enforced bodysuits. Conrad looked very much like his brother: brown skin and black hair, though his hair was cropped short. Hanli's curtain of midnight tresses fell to her waist, her upturned eyes—black against her smooth, amber skin—sharp as an eagle's.

The three Vipers that were present were Jude Monson, a blond and tan middle-aged man with a kind smile; Race Hunter, ivory-skinned and brawny, one side of his long, red hair shaved; and Jessa Gilchrist.

Loren tried her best not to stare at Jessa, but it didn't help that the copper-haired, blue-eyed Darkslayer kept looking at *her*.

It didn't matter. Now certainly wasn't the time to care about something so trivial.

The Darkslayers were going over their options on how to handle this situation with the least likelihood of being killed, when the doorbell rang, echoing throughout the sprawling house. Mortifer, who was munching on ice chips in his usual spot behind the cereal boxes, fell silent.

On the surveillance feed mounted on one side of the island, there stood a raven-haired young woman. And when she turned to look directly into the lens, her stunning face becoming clear, Darien's hand stilled on Loren's back.

"Mortifer," Darien said to the Hob, who peered around the boxes of cereal to look at his rescuer. "Lower the audio-blocking spells." A pause, and then he added, "After tonight, she's not allowed through those gates unless I say so."

For a long time, no one said anything.

And then Christa Copenspire stood on her tiptoes and said into the camera, "I know you guys have little reason to trust me right now, but there's something I think you should know—about the Arcanum Well." Her breath was coming fast, showing pale in the air that was unseasonably cold for a place like Angelthene, even on the last day of Decem. *"Please.* Darien, if you guys don't listen to me, the entire city will be destroyed. I'm *begging* you... Just give me a few minutes of your time."

Darien stepped up to the screen and jammed a finger onto the intercom button. "You can tell me from there," he said in a hard voice. "And then you can get the hell off my property."

Christa's porcelain throat visibly bobbed. "The Well has become a weapon. A bomb—and if it blows, this entire city and everyone in it will burn."

DARIEN STARED at the surveillance screen—at the girl standing on his doorstep. The girl he'd once stupidly believed gave two shits about him.

Everyone in the kitchen waited in silence.

Loren was the first to speak. "Randal tried to force my aura into the Well. He tried to make me operate it. The Widow said when my father hid the original Well, he made sure no one could ever recreate it. That all replicas would be cursed."

Another minute passed as Darien thought about it in silence. He looked at Loren the whole time, and she looked back at him.

And then he pushed away from the counter and strode to the front door, boots pounding loudly on the floors. He unlocked it and swung it open.

Christa was halfway down the steps, her back to him. The fall of coal-dark hair that skimmed her waist caught the moonlight as she looked over her shoulder at him. She froze, blinking several times, though she made no move to come any closer.

Darien's face betrayed nothing as he opened the door wider and stepped aside to allow her in. She ducked her head as she clomped back up the stairs and entered the house, the tip of her nose pink from the bite in the air. Darien slammed the door and strode into the kitchen. Christa trailed behind him, the stiletto heels of her leather boots clicking on the floor.

Darien crossed his arms over his chest and turned around to face her. "Explain."

Christa's eyes flicked about the room, lingering the longest on Loren, who stiffened a little under the brunette's gaze. Whatever Christa was thinking, she—wisely—didn't say it. And when she spoke, there was only a slight tremor in her voice.

"When Randal tried to force Loren's aura into the Well, it must've activated a new magic—a self-destructive kind. Shortly after you guys left, the power waves that started coming off it activated the grenades he had in the tunnels. The protection spells he has underground managed to shield the blast from hitting the streets, but it blew up the tunnel walls. He had other demons—other failed experiments there." She drew a long, shaky breath. "They got loose."

"Fuck." Darien started pacing.

"The Kalendae celebrations begin in an hour," Ivyana said. Which meant those demons would soon be enjoying a blood-and-flesh buffet.

"The antidote," Loren said. She was perched on the edge of her barstool, her hands clasped between her knees. Her eyes fogged over as she thought through whatever idea had just crossed her mind. When she spoke again, her eyes found Darien's. "We need to get it as soon as we can from Doctor Atlas."

"We would have to catch all the demons," Lace cut in, clicking her long, sharp nails on the quartz countertop. "And we'd need a shit-tonne of antidote for them all."

"It would take too long," Logan said. He was right. There were eight million people in the city—far too many to handle in so little time.

"They're also mutating," Christa added. "The venom in their saliva has become more potent. It's changing bitten people instantly. Literally within *seconds.*"

"Which means," Darien said, "there will soon be a hundred times the amount once they start attacking people in the streets."

"Do we call for a citywide evacuation?" Tanner proposed.

"It would cause panic," Arthur chimed in. It was the first thing he'd said all night. "Better to figure out how to quickly administer that antidote."

Loren's eyes lit up. "What about the Control Tower?"

Darien snapped his fingers. "You're a genius, Lola." He dug his phone out of his back pocket and scrolled through the contacts until he found the name he was looking for.

It was Dominic, massive black wings draped on the floor, who said, "Who are you calling?"

"Doctor Atlas," Darien replied. "If she can cook up a large enough amount of the antidote in a granular substance, we should be able to get it up the Control Tower and plug it into the forcefield projection."

"And it would heal everyone in the city," Jude concluded, eyes glinting with admiration as he looked Loren over.

Darien nodded. "Exactly."

"And what of Calanthe?" Jessa chimed in at the same time that Christa said, "What happened to Randal?"

Reading whatever expression was on Darien's face, Maximus said, "We took care of him." Darien threw him a grateful look.

"As for Calanthe," Darien said. "Let's just say she'd better stay the fuck out of our way."

Jessa tossed her hair over a shoulder. "And the bomb? How do we plan on dealing with that? There's no use in projecting the antidote if the Well's going to blow the city sky-high."

Where she stood beside Max, Dallas chimed in. "What of the protection spells on some of the streets and buildings? Is there any hope of surviving the blast?"

Christa explained, "The Arcanum Well draws its power from the energy grid below the earth—from the anima mundi itself. That type of raw magic would rip through any and all protection spells. Nothing will survive it."

"The blueprints might come in handy," Arthur said. "I won't be able to do it alone, but if we were to make it to the Well on time, we might be able to remove the reactor chamber." The suggestion made Darien stiffen.

"I can't ask you to do that, Arthur," he said. "I can't ask you to risk your life like that."

"So you'd risk the lives of eight million people before you'd risk mine?" Arthur replied. He waited for Darien to argue with him, but he didn't have the words. "Regardless, you don't get a say in the matter. I'm dismantling that Well, and you're going to take me to it."

Darien stared at him, his mouth a thin line. The weapons technician stared back, resolute in his decision. Erasmus had said in the Master Scroll that the Well couldn't be destroyed, but perhaps its blast could be stopped if they took it apart.

Some days it was easier for Darien to see why his mother had gotten along with this man so well. They were both stubborn as hell

—Darien supposed that was where he got his own dogged determination.

"Alright," Darien sighed. He ran his hand through his hair, and then he surveyed the room of people—hellsehers, wolves, witches, humans. His *friends*. "If anyone wishes to have no part in this, feel free to walk out now. I won't ask you to do this against your will."

No one said anything.

Even when Darien tried to prompt a response with an upward flick of his brows, everyone stayed silent and rooted in place.

Maximus said softly, "No one's leaving, Darien."

"We're with you," Travis added. Several others echoed it.

Jack said, "Tell us what you want us to do."

"We're going to need more firepower," Darien said. And then he smiled a little, and it was the smile of a true devil, as he added, "And maybe some more teeth."

THIRTY MINUTES, and everyone was ready to go. Darien hoped the plan would work—and that Calanthe and her henchmen would stay out of their way until they secured the safety of this city.

Darien paced in the empty kitchen, where Christa had finished apologizing to him a minute ago. He'd accepted her offer to help tranquilize the demons, but he'd stationed her with Maximus and Travis—the best eyes he could have on her. After his magic had proved unreliable in detecting Calanthe's lies, and had almost got Loren killed, he would take no chances. He felt blind for the first time in his life, going off instinct alone, though he felt more at ease knowing Christa would be under the careful watch of his cousin and his Second.

Darien was wearing the obsidian band Arthur had given him from the Fleet Weaponry, the armor that might be the only thing that could withstand a magical explosion like what the Arcanum Well might generate. Arthur had insisted he wear it, considering he was the one who would have to get closest to the Well. He didn't bother telling him that it wouldn't matter either way; if the bomb went off, and he was right beside it when it did, he would never survive the blast.

Besides that, if he was the only person in the city who survived — if he was the only one left standing after every building had been razed to the ground — the last thing he would be was happy. This life meant nothing if he didn't have the people he loved — if this city no longer existed.

The click of shoes on the floor interrupted his brooding, and he lifted his head to see Loren walking into the kitchen.

The breath left his lungs at the sight of her, wearing one of the black bodysuits belonging to the Devils. Designed to withstand most attacks, such as bullet or knife wounds, he supposed he should feel more at peace over seeing her wearing it.

But he didn't feel at peace. Not one bit. His heart was heavy and breaking, and every breath he drew was painful, as if there were shards of glass in his lungs.

Darien stepped up to her, their bodies so close that her peaches-and-honeysuckle scent wrapped around him like a hug. He could feel her aura — felt it glowing so brightly with his presence that it warmed him, lifting some of the weight off his heart that suddenly felt like such a burden. Her hair hung in two thick golden braids over her slender shoulders.

"Are you sure about this?" His voice was a hoarse whisper.

"I need to feel like I'm helping, Darien. And hiding here while you all risk your lives..." She drew a shaky breath. "I can't do it. I *can't.*" And then she amended, "I *won't.*"

Darien's heart was bleeding out in his chest. "Baby, you don't need to prove anything —"

"I'm not," she said. "I don't want to prove anything, Darien — not anymore. That's not why I'm doing this." She gave him a sad smile. "I want to help my family." Her throat bobbed, her eyes flicking to the floor at her feet. "I just wish...I wish we would've had forever."

Forever. They'd come such a long way to consider that it may not be an option anymore — that this could be the end of everything they'd built.

All this way...only for nothing.

The space behind Darien's eyes burned. "Lola," he rasped. He drew in a steadying breath as he reached out and trailed the curve of her jaw with his thumb. She shuddered under the contact, leaning into him like she had that night at the Devil's Advocate. "Even if we don't have forever, we do have today. And I believe that alone is worth celebrating."

Tears pooled in her eyes as she looked him over. Slowly and thoroughly, as if she feared it might be her last chance to do so. A tear slipped free, sliding down her cheek. He swiped it away with the pad of his thumb, a burning sensation pushing at the backs of his own eyes. The last time he'd felt raw emotion so deep, he was no more than fifteen. A boy whose heart had been broken by the passing of the first woman he'd ever loved.

"Loren, I…," Darien pushed his hair out of his face. His hand was shaking so badly that the weapons hidden within the arm of his bodysuit gave a metallic rattle. "There's something I wanted to say. In case I might not get the chance."

The space between her eyebrows scrunched with concern. "Don't talk like that, Darien."

"It's important."

"Okay," she whispered. "Then what is it?"

Darien stepped toward her, taking her hands into his own. He willed his grip to be steady. He needed to be strong—for her.

He opened his mouth to say it—to say those three words, the three he'd never said to anyone before, except to his mother, sister, and occasionally his Devils.

But footfall echoed in the entrance hall as Maximus and Dallas, followed by Conrad and Dominic, clomped down the stairs.

They were ready. All of them were ready. To fight for this city— and to possibly die trying to save it.

"Kalendae festivities have begun," Max said as he strode into the kitchen, tranquilizer rifle in hand. "When are we heading out?"

"As soon as the others are ready," Darien said. He looked down at Loren, who was still gazing up at him, her ocean eyes beseeching. Squeezing her small hands gently, he whispered, "I'll tell you. When we come back home, I'll tell you."

Her eyes shone with agony, but she smiled, her mouth wobbling. "Okay."

Cupping her face with his hands, he bent down and kissed her, long and deep.

He only hoped it wouldn't be the last time he would get to do it.

56

The network of tunnels below the city smelled like death, like Ignis's hellish realm.

Corpses torn to bloody ribbons littered the floor—Randal's cronies, thank fuck. One less problem to have to deal with. The tunnel walls had been gouged by brutal claws—what was left of them, anyway. It seemed Christa had been telling the truth about the Well having set off Randal's grenades. Crumbled and charred stone covered every inch of the floor, the acrid smell of smoke permeating the damp air.

Darien kept his feet light, his finger poised on the trigger of the tranquilizer rifle, as he and the others crept through the sewers. Conrad was at his left, Jack his right. Lace and Ivyana brought up the rear, while Arthur shuffled along in the middle of their tight group. At their left, the wide channel of the stormwater runoff was red with blood.

The Kalendae festivities were underway. On the streets above, people had gathered in the square to watch the floats and performers parade down Angelthene Boulevard, protected by the city's law enforcement and the HID lamps that fended off the demons—

entirely unaware of a new danger lurking just below the soles of their shoes.

By now, Loren would be stationed with the others on one of the many skyscrapers near the Control Tower. It had taken a lot of convincing on Loren's part to make Darien agree to her role in this. He understood what it meant for her to help them, to not have to stay at Hell's Gate alone while she waited for their return. But that didn't mean he liked it—not one bit.

The sooner they either moved the bomb to another location or dismantled it—and the sooner Doctor Atlas finished cooking up the antidote, allowing Dominic to fly it up to the peak of the cristala tower and plug it into the forcefield projection—the better.

The sooner Loren was safe in his arms, the better.

They passed by the underground series of cascades that marked the entrance to the heart of Randal's lair, the rushing of water deafening in the otherwise silent tunnels. Considering the number of grenades that had detonated, it was a miracle the HID lamps mounted on the walls were still functioning. A few buzzed and flickered, barely hanging on, but the handful that maintained a steady, glaring glow were a godsend. The demons that had escaped...

Darien could smell them.

The distant pop and sizzle of fireworks floated to his immortal ears. Cheers and whoops of joy set the street above their heads rumbling as the clock struck Witching Hour.

This night was a first for Darien: spending Kalendae below the city, instead of at a rowdy Darkslayer house party, counting down the minutes with drunk and bleary-eyed revelers, fucking the hottest chick he could find in a closet or some stranger's bedroom.

Those days were behind him now, and he didn't miss them, not even a little. Though he'd hoped to celebrate the start of a new year with her —with Loren. The only girl, aside from his mother and sister, who'd ever truly mattered to him. He would have kissed her when the clock struck twelve—signifying the start of a new and better life with her by his side.

There was nothing he wanted more.

They plunged on, into the final pocket of shadow that remained before they would reach where Randal kept the Well—the tunnel where Darien had seen Christa that night. He remembered back to how he'd tried to walk down this very tunnel, sensing something at the end of it, when she'd called his name, appearing out of the gloom. The perfect distraction.

And a damn good one, he had to admit. He felt like such an idiot.

Shadow stretched on, and so did the silence—until a siren on the streets above began wailing. Darien itched to move faster, but Arthur was having trouble making the long walk.

Something wet trickled down his cheek. *Drip, drip.*

Darien smelled it then—the metallic reek of blood.

He barely had time to shout in warning before the creature that was hanging upside-down from the ceiling slammed onto his head.

LOREN'S TEETH rattled so hard, she nearly bit her tongue clean off as she fired another shot.

Fireworks were still exploding in the starry sky as the civil defense siren began wailing, the high-pitched noise slicing through the night. Down below, in the crowded square around the Control Tower, people screamed and ran. Demons slammed into the revelers, teeth ripping into flesh, bowling over person after person at lightning speed, as if grazing the dishes at a buffet in search of that perfect taste.

As the demons sank their teeth into the revelers, the victims were changed instantly. No longer was the transformation gradual; the hunger for flesh took over their bodies immediately and had them hurtling for the nearest person to quench their appetite.

Blood sprayed buildings and parked vehicles. It streaked the roads in smears of red and dyed the water of the babbling fountain in the center of the square a deep scarlet. The sizzle and pop of fireworks punctuated the night, forming an awful and mocking contrast with the horror befalling the city.

At either side of her, lying on their stomachs on the roof of the skyscraper, rifles propped against the building's ledge, were Dallas,

Sabrine, and Hanli. They fired dart after dart, never once missing their targets. The tranquilizer was so strong, the demons dropped like flies and somersaulted into buildings, the momentum of their attacks propelling their bodies onward seconds after their minds had fallen into slumber. But the demons were infecting more people than Loren and the others could shoot, and soon the entire Kalendae festival was a bloodbath.

"There has to be a faster way to do this," Loren said, firing another shot at a demon that dove for a stroller. The rifle's recoil shoved her shoulder back, deepening the bruise forming in the muscle. While the bodysuit had helped in the beginning, the continuous jerking motion was quickly wearing her shoulder thin.

"Just keep firing, Lor," Dallas said.

One more shot, and she had to reload. She was reaching for another box of ketamine darts when her surroundings plunged into darkness, the lone bulb atop the roof of the skyscraper flicking off with a *pop* and a *hiss*.

Loren's blood ran cold at the sight of it.

At the darkness that swept into the square, rendering the screaming and crying people utterly blind. There wasn't a light in sight — not the glow of a single pair of headlights nor one streetlamp. There was nothing to see by but the moon and the stars.

One last firework popped into a smattering of red and blue sparks. And when its glow faded, they were left in a darkness that was somehow worse than before.

Loren never thought she would see the day, but it had come at last. And she knew it was the Well that was responsible; nothing else in existence had been known to do it — for the Control Tower gave electricity to the city via anima mundi itself. The force binding the universe together. A force believed to be unstoppable.

Not anymore.

For the power grid of the entire city had just gone out.

57

The tunnels plunged into darkness as the lights mounted on the walls flicked off with a *pop*.

Utterly blind, Darien drew upon his Sight as another demon divebombed for his throat.

Through his sixth sense, the black flame of its aura burned like a dark star.

He parried the attack with an uppercut to the chin. Bone crunched as the demon slammed into the wall with a snarl of defiance, cement crumbling under the force of the blow.

In the shadows to his left, Lace shouted, *"Darien!"*

He caught the tranquilizer rifle she tossed his way, and as the demon scrabbled back to its feet, he shot for the jugular.

It fell instantly, ketamine turning its aura into a muted and compliant glow.

They had two seconds to catch their breath. Two seconds before they heard baying and yips snaking through the tunnels beyond.

"Shit." Darien's Sight picked up on them, crawling on the walls and ceiling, hurtling along on the floor toward them, like spiders scuttling for prey.

There were dozens of them.

Darien flicked on his headset. "Tanner." He blinked against the darkness, willing his Sight not to fail him. He had no salts on him — nothing that could open the floodgates of his sixth sense, should his mind tire. It was sheer power of will alone that would keep him from falling blind. "Tanner, do you copy?"

The line crackled. "I'm here."

"You need to get the power back on." He and the others began moving backward, rifles at the ready, toward the Well he could feel vibrating just around the corner.

If Tanner hurried, he might be able to get the backup power system on, the one that would give the magic system of the Control Tower a kick in the ass hard enough to light the city back up — and hopefully allow the antidote to rain upon the streets from the force-field projection.

An awful screech deafened him, rifle nearly slipping through the fingers that suddenly wouldn't work for him —

"Tanner," he gritted out.

"I'm here," Atlas repeated. "Did you not hear what I said?"

The screeching grew. It was so loud his eardrums were bleeding. "I can hardly hear a fucking thing. Get the power back on! We can't use our Sight forever."

Tanner said something else, but Darien hadn't a clue what.

They reached the Arcanum Well at last. And he understood exactly where that sound was coming from as he beheld the monstrosity looming before them.

The Well had fused with the earth. Currents of magic were running directly from the energy grid and into the chamber — from the anima mundi itself.

They couldn't move it. They wouldn't be able to move it — it was rooted in place.

They would have to dismantle the reactor chamber.

Darien felt like his skin was peeling off his bones. The waves of magic were so loud, so *awful*, he had to grit his teeth against the sound. Beside him, Arthur seemed unfazed, though his white hair blew like cotton in the ripples of magic.

"We need to find the reactor chamber," Arthur shouted as he

unrolled the tube of blueprints. He turned to look over his shoulder, watery eyes peering into the shadows at their backs. "We've got another problem."

"Yeah, fucking dozens of them!" Darien readied the rifle. "Get moving, I'll cover you." Darien tried to hide it—tried to hide how badly the screeching and pealing and rumbling of that god-awful Well was affecting him.

He gritted his teeth against it, blood dribbling from his ears and nose. It ran over his lip and spread across his tongue.

And he fired. And fired and fired.

There was a crackle in his ear. A muffled voice uttering words he couldn't quite decipher, as the last demon hit the floor with a thud.

Darien shoved the earpiece further in, holding it there as hard as he could with his index finger as he listened.

"Someone lose a headset?" he gritted out.

Bloody and panting all around him, bodysuits gouged with claws and streaked with ash, everyone shook their heads.

Darien tipped his head down as he listened, concentrating on that muffled voice.

It was Loren's headmaster. He was down here—in the tunnels. Darien could hear the rushing of some distant waterfall in the background. Darien wasn't sure how he was hearing him; maybe it was the Well. Maybe it was bending the world as they knew it.

Conrad said, "What're they saying?"

"It's Loren's headmaster," Darien whispered.

"What's he saying?" Jack repeated.

"Shit," Darien muttered. *Shit.*

"Darien—," Ivyana tried.

"He's praying," Darien choked out. Begging for forgiveness for his sins, repenting for his wrong doings to the deities of the Scarlet Star. "He's *praying.*" Darien took off for the next set of waterfalls— but he didn't make it in time to help him.

Not before a single shot cracked through the tunnels.

Not before Headmaster Langdon put a bullet in his own skull.

58

The city was in hysterics.

The waves of magic pulsing through the air grew stronger. Faster. The call of the Well was ten times as horrific as when Randal had poured his power into Loren, the awful and ancient language of the universe blown out over the city like a horn.

Loren's knees threatened to buckle as she lurched to her feet, looking out over the destruction that was Angelthene—that was *home*. She could barely see anything in the blinding darkness.

But then the streetlamps buzzed back to the life, the city twinkling with light.

Tanner had managed to get the power back on.

And down below, she saw it.

Saw Dominic, glass vial in hand, swooping up the base of the cristala tower.

The antidote. Doctor Atlas had completed the antidote on time.

But something was wrong.

As Dominic swept up the length of the tower, he barely made it a quarter of the way up before the powerful pumping of his wings faltered, as if forced back by a phantom wind. Even from this distance, even in the half-dark, the pain gleaming in his eyes could not be mistaken.

He crashed into the side of the tower so hard Loren could hear it from way over here—could hear the crunch and snap of wing and bone over the bloodcurdling screams and roars of the citizens and demons.

The antidote slipped out of his hand, plummeting to the ground below.

Followed by the Angel of Death, who hit the asphalt hard enough that his wings snapped again, twisting at horribly wrong angles.

"Dallas—," Loren gasped out.

But the witch beside her had her hands cupped over her ears, sniper forgotten. She was writhing on the balcony, mouth open in a silent scream, as if some sound unheard by mortal ears was clawing its way into her brain. At Loren's other side, Sabrine was doing the very same thing.

And Hanli—

Not a single one of them could move. Could unclasp their hands from their ears.

Across the square, where they were stationed on another skyscraper, Travis, Maximus, and Christa were doing the very same thing. And Jude and Jessa and Race—

None of them could move, could unpin their hands from their ears, could open their eyes.

Heart galloping, Loren looked out at the sea of people—all stumbling, all screaming, fingers plugging their ears, no longer able to run from the demons that continued to rip into their bodies with teeth and claws. No longer able to do anything but writhe in pain over the sound.

It was the Arcanum Well. The waves of power coming off it was incapacitating magic-born people worse than it was mortals, rendering them blind—rendering their brains liquid.

At the base of the tower, the glass vial containing the antidote glimmered in the light of a streetlamp.

Beside her, Dallas drew in a ragged breath. "Loren," she panted.

Tears of agony gleamed in her eyes. "What the hell is going on?"

But Loren was already on her feet, sprinting for the steps of the fire escape.

"Loren!"

Her name was swallowed up by the clanging of the metal steps beneath her boots as Loren reached them, sprinting down them as fast as her legs could take her, to the ground below.

To the antidote.

IT WAS pure luck that kept her alive.

Luck and adrenaline, as she barreled through the sea of people and demons, firing tranquilizer darts at the latter as she ran, her body twisting in ways it'd never moved before.

She kept a corner of her eye on that tower as the crowd pushed her, jostled her. She had to make it. Waves of power continued to ripple from the Well, shaking the ground below her feet and cascading over the square like a tidal wave of death.

Buildings trembled. Signs clattered to the asphalt, and awnings were torn to ribbons as demons scrabbled up alley walls and businesses. Streetlights burst, and car alarms were set off left and right, horns blaring, security systems chirping.

People screamed under the effects of each wave, their legs collapsing beneath its call, as though bowing to it.

And Loren kept running.

A demon divebombed for her, and she fired a shot straight for its jugular—

The trigger gave a faint click.

She barely realized she'd ran out of darts before the demon slammed into her, throwing her into the cristala tower.

THE WELL WAS GOING to explode.

Removing the reactor chamber had been a fool's errand. The

Well had fused with the chamber, binding to it, just like it had attached itself to the ground beneath their feet and the anima mundi in the earth's core. There was nothing they could do —*nothing*. It had planted itself here, rooting itself in place, and when it went down it would take everything and everyone with it. Not a single person would survive.

The tunnels shook as the final seconds wound down.

Darien kept his arm around Arthur, supporting most of his weight as they hurried through the tunnels, the others before them carving a path of destruction through the demons that were still coming. Bodies covered the tunnel floor, piling atop one another like fallen trees.

"We need to move faster," Darien panted, sweat running in rivulets down his temples, as Jack and Conrad cut down the last two demons like stalks of wheat. *"Faster—"*

Lace whirled to face him, a strand of platinum hair catching in her mouth. *"It's no use!"* she shrieked. "When that Well blows up, it doesn't matter how far we've made it. This entire city will be nothing but ash—"

"You think I don't know that!" Darien shouted in her face. His voice was so loud, she flinched. "They have nothing without hope! *The* world *has* nothing *if it doesn't have hope."*

Tears slipped down Lace's face, the thin line of her mouth wobbling. All around them, the others didn't say a word. Fear turned the air thick —tightened his lungs.

He couldn't breathe.

His earpiece crackled, and Dallas's voice drifted through the speaker. He could barely make out the words through the shrieking in his head, could barely focus enough to keep limping through the tunnel, after the others who were carrying on toward a certain and terrifying end. Arthur's arm was trembling where it was slung across Darien's shoulder, every heavy, pained breath the man drew as ragged as Darien's soul.

Dallas's broken words fell into place, forming a sentence at last.

And Darien froze, his blood turning glacial.

Loren had gone up the tower.

The others stopped walking and were now staring at him. Covered in blood and dust, they looked every bit as mortal and helpless as he knew they felt in that very second.

"Darien," Ivyana pleaded softly, her eyes swimming. "We need to keep going."

"Loren—" He tried to swallow, but it felt like someone was stepping on his throat. "She's on the tower."

Understanding flashed in her gaze. It was possible that Ivyana might've realized what he was going to do before he even realized it himself.

She gave one faint nod. "It's okay," she whispered, words wobbling. "It's okay."

Jack's eyes shone with agony as he stepped forward, shifting Arthur's weight from Darien's shoulders to his own.

Ivyana closed the distance that stood between them and cupped Darien's cheek with a gloved hand. "I love you, Darien." Her voice was quavering. "Through everything we've been through, I've never stopped loving you. I couldn't have asked for a better person to call my brother."

He gathered his sister to his chest, squeezing her to him with arms that trembled as hard as the breaths he drew. "I'm sorry," he whispered into her ear. There was so much more he wanted to say, but he didn't have the time. They'd run out of something they'd stupidly believed they would have forever.

Immortality was nothing but an illusion—a false promise that had kept him from living out his days as if they *meant* something. It wasn't the guarantee of the years ahead that mattered.

It was what a person did today that truly counted.

If only he'd known this through all those years in which he'd buried his feelings, running from them like a coward; avoiding the anniversary of his mother's death, unable to endure emotional pain the same way he could physical.

He'd thought he was strong. He'd believed he was so much stronger than this.

When Ivyana pulled away from him, her face was wet with tears. Darien held his free arm out to the others. They stepped close, arms thrown around each other's shoulders, heads down and eyes closed as they embraced.

One last time.

These people—they were his family. Realer than blood. Growing up he'd always hoped for a better father; for someone more than just his sister to call his own.

Too bad it had taken twenty-four years and the end of his world to figure it out. To realize that what he'd needed had been right in front of him the whole time.

When they broke away from each other, Darien's own face was wet. "We'll see each other again," he said. "I believe it." He *had* to believe it.

He broke away from them, his hands trailing off their shoulders, leaving nothing behind of his family but a phantom touch.

And then he sprinted down the tunnel without another word, leaping over bodies and rubble as he ran.

He knew that when the Well exploded, there would be no surviving the blast. It would incinerate everything within five thousand miles of the city, turning everything they'd ever known into a wasteland. It would be as though the city had never existed.

But there was a chance Loren might live. If Darien could make it to her on time, she would survive.

He wouldn't be able to live out her years with her the way he'd wanted to; wouldn't be able to love her the way he'd planned.

But he would get to kiss her one last time. The thought was enough to make him run faster, the ground eaten up beneath the soles of his boots; enough to erase every trace of the regret coursing through his veins at the realization that this would be the last time he would get to see her face.

He focused only on that last kiss—on holding her for his final minutes.

She would survive. *She* would live.

And Darien found that it was enough.

THE STEPS inside the cristala tower were unending. They wound up and up, the staircase snaking around and around until she was dizzy.

She had to make it. She *had* to. Because even if Darien and the others managed to dismantle the Well, these demons would destroy everything—could be in the tunnels with Darien at this very second, delaying Arthur from removing the reactor chamber.

She had to do her part.

Had to try.

When she reached the last of the steps, she hurtled through the door at the top, to the narrow ledge of cristala jutting out over the city.

Dozens of feet above where she stood, the top of the Control Tower tapered into a sheer, blade-like finial. And at its very top, hovering between two spokes of cristala, was the magic that created the forcefield—burning like a red star. Like the Scarlet Star.

Loren was just considering how she was going to get to the top when a white blur smashed into her, and she went flying into open air.

59

Calanthe slammed into her with the force of a truck.

Loren dug her nails into the cristala as she skidded across the ledge, the leather-like material of her bodysuit squealing on the glass.

She slid to a halt just in time not to topple off the tower—though her legs kicked as she scrambled back onto the overhang, the sight of all those cars and people, no larger than pinholes, sending her stomach plummeting out her ass and through her feet.

Calanthe alighted on the finial of the Control Tower, her vampiric form more horrific than Loren had imagined it.

Skin white as bone, with talon-like hands and feet. Her leathery wings were so vast, they blotted out the rising sun spreading its light across the desert hills in the distance. Blood-red eyes were set in deep sockets, the papery, near-translucent skin beneath stained the bluish-purple of bruises.

The vampire gave her a cold smile, her elongated canines glinting. "Give me the antidote, Calla."

Loren tightened her hold on the glass vial as she pushed herself to her feet. "Never."

"That our replica failed means nothing," Calanthe said matter-offactly. "You can still find the real Arcanum Well. And as long as that is true, my people and I will always be looking for you. There's nowhere you'll be able to hide."

"Correction," Loren said in a hard voice. "As long as *you* are still alive, there may be nowhere I can hide."

Calanthe's grin exposed all her teeth. "Do you mean to say that you're going to kill me, Miss Calla?"

Loren smiled back. "That is *exactly* what I mean to say."

Calanthe's wings snapped open, and she dove for her with an ear-shattering screech.

Loren bided her time, planting her feet in place as Calanthe neared and neared. Her heart was pounding in her chest, but she forced it to quiet, to steady its thundering.

Just as the vampire swept for her, clawed hands and feet aimed to punch through her throat, Loren called Singer out of his shadow.

———

THE FAMILIAR WAS a streak of darkness as he leapt for the vampire with a guttural snarl, the surprise of his attack—and existence—catching Calanthe off-guard and sending her careening into the tower, where he began tearing viciously into her wings with teeth and nails.

As soon as Calanthe collided with the cristala, the force of the blow cracking the panel, Loren ran for her, pressing the latch mechanism on the inside of her left wrist as she moved.

A silver stake shot out of where it was concealed against her forearm and into her waiting hand, the wicked point at the one end flashing like the stars that'd faded away into a dawning sky. She moved as fast as she could, arms pumping at her sides, as she hurtled for the vampire of the Blood Rose, eyes zeroing in with deadly intent on her silent heart.

The Well gave another awful call that rolled over the city, shaking the tower and rendering Calanthe immobile and deaf for one precious second. A second that meant everything.

But as Loren dove for her with a battle-cry, silver stake raised in hand, the vampire parried the attack with a sharp kick to Singer's ribs.

Singer's body soared through the air, where he slammed into Loren, knocking the breath out of her lungs in a *whoosh*. He hit Loren so hard, she crashed to the ground, pain crackling up her tailbone and into her spine. Gritting her teeth against the ache, she sat up—barely in time to see Calanthe swooping full-tilt for her neck, her mouth a horrible gaping pit.

Loren counted the seconds—the measly three that she had—mustering every ounce of energy that remained in her tired and aching body.

And when the vampire reached her, Loren's hold on the stake tightened. She jumped to her feet and struck.

The stake tore through Calanthe's chest, the force of the blow through bone and muscle reverberating up Loren's arm and into her shoulder.

The silver burned Calanthe's skin black, her features twisting as she howled in pain, the wings that were riddled with bite-wounds and claw-marks flapping as she tried to right herself—as she tried dislodging the stake from her shoulder.

Loren dove out of the way before one of those wings could slam into her, and she watched as Calanthe tumbled off the edge of the tower, gravity yanking her and her flightless wings toward the asphalt far below.

The city rumbled; Loren nearly fell off the tower from the force of it. She crouched down to keep from losing her balance, closing her eyes and bracing her hands on the ground as she rode out the tremor, counting the seconds.

It would stop. It *had* to stop.

But the city kept shaking.

Pushing the sweat-damp hair that had come loose out of her face, she lurched to her feet, crossing the short distance to the tower.

Singer disappeared into her shadow as she began climbing, clinging to the grooves in the panels of cristala with weakening fingers.

As she climbed, the tower shuddered and cracked. The fissures in the glass spiderwebbed beneath her palms, but she kept going, moving as fast as her legs could take her. Her muscles were shrieking in pain—in defiance. But she pushed on, gritting her teeth against every throb.

When she reached the very top, she wrapped her arms around one of the finials to keep from falling while she used the other to remove the forcefield projection. The magic burning there was so hot she had no choice but to drop it to the ledge below, the movement sucking her stomach through her ass.

Hundreds of feet of open air loomed below her feet, the sight of the city sprawled all around her—the businesses so small, it was as though they were toys—churning her gut.

And then, trembling with exhaustion, sweat streaming down her temples, she plugged the antidote into the forcefield's place.

DARIEN FELT it when the antidote washed over the city.

The screaming of the people he was pushing past, and the howling of the demons he was parrying out of the way with fists and ketamine darts, immediately ceased. It was as though the whole city fell asleep, as the demons began a reverse transformation, dropping in place like flies, the stupors they'd fallen into clearing an easier path to the Control Tower.

She'd done it. Loren had done it.

The medicinal stink of the antidote swept through the air, smothering the reek of blood and flesh and dust. It covered everything in golden granular too fine for mortal eyes to see.

And Darien kept moving. Toward the tower—toward Loren. Stepping over bodies as he went, he kept his eyes trained on that shimmering tower, praying she was okay. Praying she was alive.

The ground beneath his feet kept groaning and rumbling, the call of the Well growing to a blood-curdling shriek as the final seconds wound down.

And the end came at last.

THE ANTIDOTE WAS MAKING her drowsy.

It felt like her legs weren't her own, every step she took slow and clumsy as a doll bopped up and down by strings. Loren kept a hand braced on the glistering wall as she stumbled along the circumference of the tower, toward the door and the stairs waiting just beyond.

But making the short journey to that open door felt like an impossible task, and she found her legs crumpling beneath her. Her kneecaps slammed to the ground, bone popping on the cristala. She barely registered the pain, the antidote numbing everything, even her thoughts. The panic barking in her head quieted to the faintest whisper.

On the streets far below, the screams had fallen silent. Loren knew if she were to look, she would see hundreds upon hundreds of Angelthene citizens blinking away the nightmare of what had happened, only to find themselves surrounded by corpses and blood, the taste of their mouth rancid.

And it *was* a nightmare. This was a Star-damned nightmare.

A little voice crackled in her ear. Calling her name.

Slowly, Loren turned her head to look over her shoulder, trying to find the source of the voice. It took longer than it should have for her to realize it was coming from her earpiece—from the headset perched atop her head like a lopsided crown.

Her fingers fluttered as she slid the earpiece that'd popped partway out back into place.

"Darien?" The word was a breathy whisper.

"Loren, I need you to get off the tower," Darien was saying, every word a strained gasp. "You—" *Crackle.* "The Well is—" *Crackle.*

"Darien." Her vision swam, and she closed her eyes tight as nausea ebbed and flowed in her gut, the tower rotating like the gears of a great clock. "I can't hear you." Her heartbeat was an unsteady thump in her skull.

It took a long time to piece together the gaps in his sentences. From some faraway place in her mind, she finally understood was he was saying.

She had to get off the tower. The Well was going to blow—the others hadn't succeeded at stopping it. This whole city was going to crumble.

And everyone in it was going to die.

Loren tried to move. But she only sank further onto the roof, legs spreading wider as she tipped face-first onto the ground. She was so tired.

So very tired.

DARIEN MADE it to Loren with two minutes to spare. He could feel it —the pressure increasing in the air. The Well was seconds from exploding. His head was going to pop like a balloon, the shrieking in his ears so sharp it felt like his brain was leaking out of his nose.

By the time he found her, Loren had made it halfway down the tower. She was barely on her feet on the outdoor landing—the strip of cristala that curved like a sheer blade around the perimeter. Blue blood was spattered across her bodysuit, and her sun-bright hair was dusty, most of the strands having shook loose from her braids.

"Darien," Loren croaked. She limped the last few feet toward him, and he caught her around her middle, where she collapsed in his arms, as shaking and utterly spent as he felt.

He breathed her in, breathed in the scent of her. He couldn't slow his racing heart, couldn't smother the sickness twisting in his gut, but holding her eased the tension in his mind and brought him some peace at last. Regret cut his heart in half as he realized that he would never get to do this again—never get to hold her, touch her.

"Loren," he sighed, burying his face in her soft hair. "Thank heavens you're safe."

"Can you jump?" The words held a tinge of hope, and he felt like screaming—because it was no use. No use at all. Even if he could survive the fall, they wouldn't have enough time to even make it to the pavement.

"We're too high." He drew her to him, gathering her into his arms and kissing her soundly—desperately. His thoughts were a nonsensical roar, but she was here with him now.

They were together.

A feeling of calm washed over him as he took her hands into his own and kissed her again.

"Darien," she mumbled against his lips. Tears were streaming down her face. He could taste the salt of them, the dampness wetting his own cheeks. "We're going to die. Aren't we?" The sound of her broken, pained words ripped his soul apart.

"Not you, Loren." He kissed her again, holding tightly to her hands. "You're going to live, you hear me? *You are going to live.*" Something like panic shone in her eyes, but before she could register the message behind his words, he bent down to kiss her again—one last time.

And in her distraction, he slipped the onyx band onto her finger.

LOREN SHOOK her head mechanically as she tried to dislodge the ring. But she didn't know how, and the stupid thing just kept spinning around her finger.

The black armor of Fleet Headquarters had vanished off Darien, leaving him in a white t-shirt and blue jeans, the shining, magic-enforced leather of the bodysuit instead covering *her* from head to toe.

"Darien." Her voice was a wild, panicked gasp.

The tower rumbled beneath their feet as their final seconds were swallowed up. They were out of time.

She couldn't breathe. *She couldn't breathe.* "No—"

Stilling the hand that was fumbling with the ring, Darien leaned down and covered her mouth with his own, swallowing her protest. He wouldn't release his grip from her hand, wouldn't let her take off the ring.

A sob burst through her lips, barely audible against his mouth.

This couldn't be happening. It couldn't be.

His lips left hers, only for a moment. Long enough for her to say what she'd been so afraid of admitting, even to herself.

"I love you." The words—the only three that mattered—were a strangled gasp.

Those steel-blue eyes welled with tears. The sight of them broke what was left of her—had her heart splintering into pieces inside her chest. How was it possible that she was still breathing, after all this hurt?

"I love you," she repeated against his mouth, every word a croak. "I don't want to live without you, Darien. Please—" He slammed his lips against hers again. She could feel his thunderous heartbeat against her chest, could feel him shaking. A sob bubbled up her throat. "Darien—"

The world was swallowed by bright light as the Well exploded and the tower collapsed.

60

Time seemed to slow as they fell.

Down, and down, and down.

Darien did not let go of her. One of his arms was wrapped tightly around her waist, the other cupping the back of her head, holding her face against his chest. Planes of cristala and chunks of stone and cement plummeted through the air with them, and a blast of smoke and fire swept up to gather them in infernal hands.

People were incinerated in the blast. Buildings were razed to the ground. Asphalt rippled and crumbled as seismic waves crashed over the streets.

Powerlines snapped.

The bridges over the river burst into dust.

The vast ocean trembled in the distance, the waves that were generated from the Well undulating far and wide.

Still, Darien held onto her, and she closed her eyes, her fingers squeezing his shoulders.

Until the glass and stone and cement were a torrent of destruction all around them, and she was ripped out of his grasp.

A wave of black swallowed her whole, ushering her off to some quiet and faraway place, where all of this was no more significant than a dream.

Sometime later, Loren came to, jerking to attention with a horrified gasp among what remained of the Control Tower—what remained of her city.

That single gasp echoed far and wide. There was no other sound in the world. There was nothing but silence.

Skeletons of cars continued to burn, and plumes of acrid smoke twisted into the rosy sky of a new day—a new year no one but herself was around to see.

She should've died. By all rights, she should've died. But the ring Darien had slipped onto her finger had kept her alive. The leather-like armor was tattered and warped, hot against her skin from the force of the city's incineration.

And Darien…

Where was Darien?

Loren's leg was pinned beneath a twist of metal and cement. She shoved it aside with a scream of frustration and pushed herself up from the rubble.

But her legs refused to carry her. They collapsed from underneath her, bruises splitting through her kneecaps.

Throwing back her head, she sucked in a breath and screamed out his name. *"DAAARRIIEENNN!"*

An awful, heavy silence stretched all around her, and she realized she was alone. Not one person remained, not one demon. Not one building or home was standing.

Corpses were strewn about the square. Hundreds of them.

Thousands of them.

Through the twisting smoke, she spotted him several feet away, buried beneath the debris of the tower, the horrible, battered lump of him reflecting in the sharp planes of cristala standing vertical around him like a mirrored fence.

She blinked her eyes as she tried to make sense of what she was seeing.

His body was a bloody pulp. That handsome face was charred and peeling, blackened by the hands of fire and raw magic. His clothes had been torn, hardly more than tattered ribbons, blowing in the smouldering wind that swept through the square.

A strangled sound clawed out of her throat. Loren crawled to his side through the wreckage, shoving aside glass and metal and rock from where they were piled on top of him, not caring when the bits of piping and jagged windowpanes chewed through what was left of her armor and into her palms, as she carefully gathered his head into her lap.

"Darien." The word was a soft gasp. *"Darien."* She shook him, but he wouldn't move. "Wait," she stammered, her voice thick. "Don't go. Don't go. Walk with me, Darien. I want you to follow the river. *Please*. Go to the ocean with me—*please.*" A sob ripped out of her, cutting through what was left of her heart. "Stay with me! *Please.*"

He was so lifeless, so still.

He was gone.

The silence of the city pressed on her eardrums as every thought eddied from her head.

And in that silence, she began screaming.

Screaming and screaming and screaming.

From some faraway place, she saw herself. Kneeling in the rubble, shaking Darien—shaking what was left of him. Willing him to come back to life, *begging* anyone who might be listening to give him back. *To take this back.* Take it *all* back—

Her head swiveled left and right as she looked for something or someone—*anything*—that might fix this. That might make things right again.

"Help!" The single word broke in several places, like the crackle of the warning Darien had given her about the tower—as he'd ran for her with the sole intention of keeping her alive. Of making sure she would live—that *she* would live. Not him. *Never him.*

She couldn't breathe. *She couldn't breathe.* Her heart was drowning in the blood of all this hurt.

"HELLLLLPPP! Somebody!" The crackle of words drifted far and wide across the wreckage that was her city—her home. The place she'd always loved but had never quite belonged—the place she would love forever, until her mortal heart stopped beating.

Now, that city was nothing but a graveyard. A garden of remembrance.

A whimper tore out of her. "Anybody," she whispered into the silence.

But no one answered. She was alone.

And Darien was dead.

LOREN BENT over to press a kiss to Darien's mouth. The tears streaming down her face blinded her, lips wobbling against his.

"I'm sorry." The apology crackled out of her, and she kissed his lifeless mouth again, hating her heart for still beating when his had ceased. "I'm so sorry."

One magpie flew over the destruction of the city.

One for sorrow.

Setting Darien's head down as gently as she could, she lurched to her feet. And in the silence, it was no longer the help of the living she called for, but something beyond.

"Please," she tried. But her voice was a croak. She sucked in a deep breath. *"PLEEEEAAAASE!"* She stumbled through the rubble, head tipped back as she shouted at the sky, in a voice as shattered as her heart, "Take me. *PLEASE, I BEG YOU. TAKE ME INSTEAD."* Her words turned into hoarse screams, with nothing but her own echo to answer her. *"TAKE ME INSTEAD!* I offer my life in his place, *please! JUST LET HIM LIVE."*

No one answered. An eerie silence fell as the last rolling echo of her own voice rippled away. Even the replica of the Well was gone, the awful calls of the prima materia silenced.

Loren lifted her head, more tears falling down her cheeks as she blinked. As she remembered.

As she *realized*.

"I can do it," she whispered. Her heart was slamming in her chest, her shaking hands balling into fists at her sides. "I believe that I can find it—I believe in *myself*. I can find the Well. *I can find the*

Well." The *real* Arcanum Well—the one she'd never had any desire to find.

Until now.

Closing her eyes tight, she called upon it. Throwing out every ounce of hope she had in her to find her father's invention, to be able to use it to fix this—to bring Darien back. She wasn't sure how she would do it, but she would die trying, would submerge herself into the Well if it meant she could make him live again.

"I can do it," she whispered again, her mouth trembling. "I can find the Well. Where are you? *Where are you?"*

Eyelids flying open, she pivoted in the rubble, looking.

"Whereareyouwhereareyouwhereareyou."

A warm glow emanated from within her.

She spun around, looking for the source—for a beam of light or an indication that might tell her where to walk, where to look for the Well.

A broken panel from the mirrored Control Tower snagged her attention.

In the filthy and spiderwebbed reflection, she beheld herself standing there. Bruises were blooming across her neck and forehead, and her hair was covered in dust and soot and blood and ash. She looked as human and pathetic as she felt—

Aside from the white flames rippling out from above her heart. From inside her.

Her aura.

Loren's eyelids slipped shut as her mind traveled back to that day —to the words the Widow had said to her, deep in the reeking shadows of her habitat.

In the ruin of her beloved city, Loren remembered.

"If I am Erasmus Sophronia's daughter, then why haven't I been able to figure out where the Well is?"

"Because you do not truly wish to find it, child," said the Widow. "When your father hid the Well, he gave the power only to himself. For many years it did not belong to a single living soul—not until the daughter he bore grew into

a woman, and she inherited his gifts. But your father made certain his mistake could never be replicated; all attempts at recreating the Well would fail. And even if another person managed to Make it, the prima materia would only listen to its master—to the original Creator."

"That's what the scroll meant. That's what it meant when it said, 'Blood of my blood.'" Her mind reeled, the yawning pit of the fountain before her churning like a dark potion. The coppery reek of all the blood that had been offered to this creature over the years knifed down her throat. *"How did my father make it? How was a human able to access the prima materia?"*

"He made a deal with one of us—a Nameless." The spider's voice slithered over the walls. *"Upon finding out the true name of one of us infernal beings of Ignis, the Nameless granted him access to the creature of the gods, and Erasmus went on to use it to create the Arcanum Well."*

"How can we destroy it?"

"It cannot be undone, Liliana Sophronia. And to try to destroy it would have deadly consequences for all involved."

"How can I find it?" She was breathing so hard, she was panting, the sound echoing against the walls. *"Where can I look?"*

"Inside yourself," the Widow said.

"I don't know what that means," Loren snapped, *"and to be frank, I am tired of your riddles."*

The spider stirred. *"Very well. Regardless, that is all I may share. And to be frank with you, I have shared plenty. It isn't my fault if you choose not to listen."*

Loren stared into the churning fountain before her. Her reflection was murky and distorted, and her skin seemed to glow white. *"I shouldn't have even come here,"* she muttered.

"A word of warning," the Widow cut in. Loren lifted her head. *"Use your magic and you will die, Liliana Sophronia."*

Loren stared into its shadows. *"I don't have magic."* She was starting to get frustrated that everyone thought she did.

"And I'm not thirsty." There was a strange pause. *"Is what you wear around your neck not indicative enough that you are more than ordinary?"*

Loren's fingers went to the talisman—the pendant with a closed eye at its center. *"The Avertera talisman is only hiding my aura."*

"I do not speak of that pendant, child. I speak of the conduit you've worn

since you were a baby. Hold me close when the hour is dire and wish upon the Liar. *Does that not ring a bell?"*

Loren was shaking her head. "I don't understand."

"But you will. The wish was bought for you by your father for you to use in a time of need. And you must *wish upon the Liar. It will be your only chance."* The urgency in the spider's voice sent a chill down Loren's spine.

"I have to go," she whispered, suddenly lightheaded. Her tattoo was glowing, just like her skin in her odd reflection. The meaning behind the engraving on her solar pendant pulsed inside her skull, begging for her to understand it. She thought, perhaps, she did.

LOREN OPENED HER EYES.

That was when she'd realized it. She'd figured as much from her visit with the Widow, but she'd hid the truth from everyone—even from herself.

Because she was terrified. And because she didn't think finding the Well was going to do them any good, wouldn't make her safe again—would only put her in greater danger.

Because there wasn't a Well to find. When her father had hidden his invention, he'd put it where no one would ever find it.

The Well couldn't be recreated, nor destroyed. And all replicas were cursed to never function the same way.

The only way to get rid of the Well was to remake it. And Erasmus Sophronia had done exactly that. He'd transmuted it and bound it to his aura, putting the Well into *himself.*

Little had he known his daughter would go on to inherit the ability from him, years after he'd used the Well one last time to create life—to create *her.*

The Well was a part of her. It was inside of her, as vital to her existence as her beating heart.

Rubble crunched beneath her boots as she stumbled to where Darien lay immobile in the wreckage. She gathered his head into her lap, cradling his face with her hands.

"Please work," she whimpered, smoothing his hair back from his face. *"Please."* She tried to remember what she had learned in school

—how a person's magic was entangled with their aura—and she wondered if her power worked the same way. As a human unable to perform magic, those were the lessons she'd always had to sit out on.

But she'd always observed. And she'd learned.

During the times when Loren had tried to help Darien with his Surges, perhaps there had been more going on. Perhaps the power of the Well that lay dormant inside her had been helping him, and that warmth she'd always swore she could feel against her chest was the conduit she unknowingly wore around her neck. She'd always felt lightheaded after attempting to help him, but she'd brushed it off as another of the many side effects that came with her medical condition.

There seemed to be a lot of things she'd brushed off over the years.

It was time she finally started believing in herself. Time she stopped allowing herself to drown in the ashes of her lack of faith.

She would be like a phoenix and rise.

In the dead silence, Loren spoke. "I am male and female, everything and nothing. I am heaven and earth, body and spirit. The rainbow, the blood of the soul, the fiery and burning water. I am the prima materia. I am the Arcanum Well." A deep breath rocked through her. "I am...Liliana Sophronia."

She concentrated on pouring her aura onto Darien, *willing* it out of her and into him—to heal him, to bring him back.

White flames appeared, like tired arms stretching from within her. They glowed brighter than the sun spreading its light over the city, brighter than the stars and the moon—brighter than anything her eyes had ever beheld. The conduit around her neck began floating as it channeled the energy of her aura, driving it from her body and into Darien's.

The flame disappeared into his chest, directly above his heart, swallowed up like a sponge soaking up water.

Loren waited, holding her breath.

She began to count. *One, two, three, four, five...*

But nothing happened.

More tears, tinged with white light, slipped down her cheeks and dripped onto his neck and face. The light sank into his skin without a trace. "Don't leave me," she croaked. "Please."

Gently, she gathered up Darien's limp hand and pressed it against her filthy cheek. That hand was so heavy; so lifeless. Her eyelids slipped shut as she forced herself to breathe deeply.

This couldn't be it. This couldn't be the end.

This couldn't be happening.

The shadows of seven birds flew overhead, darkening the inside of her burning eyelids as they flitted past.

More tears fell, slipping through the space between Darien's palm and her skin.

All of it had been for nothing. A part of her had believed, from that very moment he'd saved her life on the Avenue of the Scarlet Star, that they'd met for a reason. That fate had forced them together, giving them exactly what neither of them were aware they needed.

But she was wrong. And Darien had left her—*alone*.

Loren began sobbing in silence, holding Darien's hand to her cheek. Slouching in the sharp rubble, her body shook with every breath, the world around her quiet and cold.

There was a flutter against her cheek. A flutter of fingertips.

Was she imagining it?

"Lola," came Darien's voice. Rough, as if he'd just woken up from a deep sleep. "Why are you crying?"

Loren's eyelids flew open. "Darien?" The word was a startled sob.

Although he was still covered in blood and the debris of the cristala tower, his face was no longer the bloody pulp it'd been a minute ago. No—his features were exactly as she remembered them from before the tower collapsed, exactly as she remembered them when she'd seen him for the first time in that alley.

Exactly the same as when she'd told him she loved him.

A laugh croaked through her wobbling lips as she threw herself on top of him, holding him so tightly that she could hear his heart beating in her ear.

He was breathing. He was *breathing*. She clung to the sound, savoring every beat and every breath, as she held onto him, her anchor in her storm, and sobbed into his shirt.

Darien's arms wrapped around her, pressing her harder against him. "I feel like I got hit by a truck." The rumble of his voice in her ear was a sound she would never forget.

"You were dead!" she gasped against his tear-damp neck. "You *died*."

"Dead?" he repeated. His voice was thick. "I'm not dead, baby girl. Just a little sore is all." A hand stroked her back, igniting the fire within her that had very nearly gone out. "You saved my life."

Loren pulled back to look at him, to touch him. "You left me," she said, every word a strangled gasp. *"You left me."*

Darien's expression lined with concern. "I'll never leave you, Loren," he said, brushing aside a strand of hair clinging to her cheek. "I'm yours to keep." It was his turn to gather her face into his hands as he repeated, *"I am yours to keep."*

He noticed it, then: the hollow silence. Slowly, still cupping her face, he looked out at the wreckage of the city, finally seeing it for the first time.

Darien's hand didn't feel like his own as he reached up to read-just his earpiece, flicking it on.

When he spoke, the words were nearly inaudible. "Does anyone copy?"

Loren pushed up from the ground. Sickness spread through her as she realized that, although she'd managed to bring Darien back, she couldn't say the same for anyone else.

The city was destroyed, the population obliterated.

And they were horribly, and utterly, alone.

DARIEN FELT like puking as he said, again and again into the speaker, "Is anybody there?" The words were tense, his every breath coming so fast he swore he was going to pass out. *"Is anybody there?"* Bile burned his tongue.

But he choked it down, repeating those same words, again and again and again.

"Do you copy?" Nothing.

"*Do you copy?*" Silence.

And then Loren took off through the city, hurtling over the rubble at a speed Darien had never seen her move before.

He pushed himself up off the ground, nearly tripping in the wreckage strewn about what was left of the streets he'd walked a thousand times.

"Loren!" he called, grunting as he stumbled over chunks of stone and fallen streetlamps. Over dismembered bodies and burning car bumpers and tires. Clumps of ash floated on the wind, settling on his shoulders and in his hair. *"Loren!"*

She didn't slow until she got to the Avenue of the Scarlet Star.

To what remained of it.

The entire road had been razed to the ground. The Mortar and Pestle was nothing but a husk, the buildings lining it and the other side of the avenue nothing but piles of broken bricks. All those plants had been singed into nothing. Every trace of the job she'd loved with her whole heart—gone. Mordred and Penny—

Gone.

There was nothing left now for them to remember the avenue by, nothing except the bracelet Loren still wore around her wrist, the charm of the apothecary peeking out from beneath a scrap of magic-enhanced leather. The real thing was no more than an echo of the mind, a footprint on the heart, both of which would fade too quickly with the passing of time.

Loren sank to her knees on the ground before the giant sundial that spanned the width of the avenue. The marble that was struck through with veins of gold was cracked and crumbling now, like everything else in Angelthene. Broken. Never to be the same again.

Darien didn't say anything as he came up behind where she knelt. Charred remnants of everyday life—the Daystar paper, coffee mugs, shattered potion bottles, appliances, pots and utensils—were strewn about. He didn't have the words; there was nothing he could say that would help. Nothing that would change this.

Entire minutes passed. And then Loren whispered onto the ashy breeze, "I can fix it."

"Loren," Darien croaked. "Sweetheart—"

"I can fix it," she said again, the words so quiet they were a challenge even for him to make out. "I can take it back."

He made to say something else, but Loren took the solar pendant into her hands. When she looked up at him, her eyes were bright and wild with determination, her nostrils flaring with the frantic breaths she drew.

"Hold me close when the hour is dire, wish upon the Liar," she said. "It's talking about the God of Time, Darien. It's talking about Tempus the Liar." Her chest heaved. "The Widow told me my father bought me a wish." She shook the amulet, and it jingled softly in her white-knuckled grasp. *"This* is my wish. My gift."

Loren reached up to grab him by the wrist, and she pulled him down, so he was kneeling on the sundial beside her. She shuffled closer to Darien and lifted the long chain so that it was around both of their necks. When she saw the uncertainty in his eyes, she whispered, "You're just going to have to trust me." She took his hands into hers and splayed his fingers on the sundial, as she did with her own.

Tempus's sundial.

Clumps of ash had settled on her hair and lashes. When she spoke again, every word was a quavering whisper.

"Tempus the Liar, hear me now." Her throat bobbed as she swallowed. "Hear my plea. In this dire hour, I wish—I *pray*—upon the Liar. I, Liliana Sophronia, daughter of the Magnum Opus, ask that you take it back. Let me have the wish my father bought me—and let this city be healed."

Several minutes passed. Darien barely breathed the whole time Loren sat there, hands cupped before her, eyes squeezed shut.

A white flame slipped through her chest—from her heart. It filled up the solar pendant she wore around her neck—not a simple piece of jewelry but a conduit, Darien realized. And then it spread to every inch of the sundial, lighting the marble up like a beacon. The gold pointer gleamed so brightly that Darien could barely see.

As soon as that glow dimmed enough for him to look, Darien glanced around at the rubble strewn about the Avenue of the Scarlet Star, and his jaw fell slack as he felt the wind shift directions, saw the ash that was falling from the sky suddenly floating back up. Palm tree fronds that had scraped by a moment ago now returned in the opposite direction, and the sun began to shift, moving toward a past sunrise.

Time was moving backwards. Darien and Loren were frozen where they were, kneeling on the sundial, but everything around them was moving. Loren was glowing as brightly as the sundial, her features awash in every shade of the rainbow, her skin luminescent with color.

Their surroundings shifted until they found themselves in Randal's lair.

Darien saw himself—saw himself and the other Devils—standing before the replica of the Arcanum Well in the moments when they'd realized it couldn't be destroyed. In the moments when they'd realized they had failed.

Darien had no words as Loren rose to her feet, unhooking the necklace from over his head. He remained kneeling as she walked up to the Well replica, past the frozen figures of his family and himself, stuck in the past, in a moment that was lasting a lifetime.

As Loren stood before the Well replica, she began to speak in a low, metallic tone—in a language he'd never heard before. She seemed to be speaking to…to someone.

Tempus the Liar, perhaps.

Loren's eyes turned full white, like when Darien's shifted to black with the Sight, and her aura shot out of her and up, forming a wall of light around the Well.

A shield, Darien realized. A shield for when the Well exploded. Stopping it from exploding wasn't possible, but Loren seemed to have discovered how to save this city, how to save all of them.

With Tempus's help, she had not only reversed time, but was giving this city a second chance. Giving the people in it the chance to live again.

Darien had no words as Loren opened her arms as though they were wings — like a rainbow phoenix.

Darien threw up a hand to shield his eyes as the wall her aura had built shone like a molten rainbow, bright as the Scarlet Star itself, encircling the Well and towering far and wide.

He still felt it when the Arcanum Well exploded — when time began to move again. It lurched forward, picking up where it had left off, leading them straight to their destruction again. Only this time, there was no destruction — no blast that would destroy the city they loved so dearly.

By the time Darien was able to see again, he blinked. And blinked again, his face draining of color.

He couldn't believe his eyes.

For the first time in his life, he couldn't believe what he was seeing.

THE ENTIRE CITY had been rebuilt with the reversal of time. Put back together again, as though it had never crumbled to begin with. The Avenue of the Scarlet Star was the same as he remembered it, the cars lining the curb no longer burning skeletons, the streetlights at the end of it glowing a steady green, eagerly awaiting traffic to direct. They'd been teleported back to the avenue — back to the sundial of Tempus the Liar.

And all around the avenue, there were people. Living, *breathing* people. Picking themselves up off the ground that was no longer strewn with debris, shaking their heads as if in a daze; poking their unmarked faces out of repaired shop windows and doors; staggering down the avenue as though sleepwalking, clearly trying to remember what had happened.

And there was Mordred and Penelope's Mortar Pestle, every brick back where it belonged. There was the cauldron-shaped sign, the front door where Darien had watched Loren fumble for her keys so many months ago.

There was the alley where they'd met, when fate had brought

them together, changing their lives in ways neither of them had ever imagined.

There was Rook and Redding's Restaurant and Bar, where Darien had first learned Loren's name. When she'd sat down across from him at that booth in the back corner, trusting him and the offer he'd made to help her, even when she wasn't certain if she should.

The last of the missing people were found at last, covering themselves up with whatever scrap of clothing they could find.

Darien didn't quite understand it—didn't know how it was possible that these people had been healed of the antidote when time had been reversed, the future changed. It seemed Tempus the Liar had worked a fair bit of magic in his wish, had perhaps answered requests Loren had made of him when she'd spoken in that strange tongue. It made Darien wonder what else now remained from before the shift—and what had been forgotten about.

But although Loren hadn't saved everyone—only those who'd died in the blast, not the people who'd fallen before it, the smaller number of them still lying on the sidewalks and the road—the streets were teeming with people.

Still kneeling before him, wholly spent and no longer glowing, the medical tattoo on her forearm a glaring red, Loren swayed in place—and collapsed on the sundial, the marble of which had been repaired.

"Loren." Darien shuffled closer to her, drawing her limp body into his arms. Heart hammering, palms slick with sweat, he bent down, pressing his ear against her chest.

Relief weakened his knees at the sound her heart beating there, as present as the ground beneath him.

"Oh, thank the gods," he breathed, swallowing hard. Clutching her to him, he tipped back his head and stared at the brightening sky as he whispered into the heavens far beyond, "Thank you. Thank you."

There was a crackle in his ear.

And it was his sister's voice that said thickly, "Darien." She sounded like she'd woken up from a deep sleep. "Where are you? What happened?"

A sob burst out of him. "You're alive," he said into the speaker. In his arms, Loren stirred at the sound, her eyelashes fluttering. *"We're alive."*

Loren peeked up at him, her irises ocean-bright in the light of dawn. The light of a day that was theirs for the taking.

Darien whispered, "Happy Kalendae, Lola." It was a new year.

And they had survived.

61

L oren slept for a long time.
When she finally woke up, the windows were dark, the
sky a star-flecked canvas. She was in her bed at Hell's Gate,
tangled up in the teal and ivory quilts.

It took her several minutes to remember, to make sense of everything that'd happened.

Was it only a dream?

Sheets rustled as she rolled onto her side, wincing as her back
spasmed.

Every bone hurt, every muscle. Instead of the bodysuit that had
kept her alive during the blast, she wore her pajamas, nearly every
inch of the skin that showed beneath her shirt sleeves and the hem of
her shorts marked up with deep purple bruises and scrapes.

The only light in the room filtered through the gap between the
bottom of the door and the threshold. Voices drifted through that
door, distance muffling them to a hum. As she listened to the sound
of those voices — the voices of her family — she closed her eyes and
breathed, focusing also on smell of freshly ground coffee and fabric
softener and what she thought was pizza. The voices and scents
calmed her heart and grounded her.

She was safe.

She was *home*.

Loren leaned over to grab her cell phone from where it sat, plugged into a charger, on the end table. Squinting against the bright glare of the screen, she checked the date.

It was still Kalendae—still her birthday—for two more hours.

When she had unleashed her magic on the Arcanum Well replica, forcing it to self-destruct, she had seen down every alley, into every home and building, as though she were omnipresent. As though she were a god.

As though she were seeing through the eyes of Tempus the Liar, whose mouth she had spoken through with the wish her father had bought for her.

Every person who'd died in the blast had been brought back to life, every wound they'd suffered from healed with the miraculous reversal of time—healed, even, from the disease that had turned so many of them into hungry demons. As for those who'd died before the Well exploded—people like Randal and his men—they remained dead. A part of her felt terrible for even thinking it, but the world was a far better place without people like Randal in it.

She didn't allow herself to think about Calanthe, though. How there was a chance the vampire was still alive—her life spared by the clock that had ticked backward, erasing everything that'd happened on the Control Tower.

She wouldn't think about it. Not tonight.

Kicking off the covers, she swung her legs over the side of the bed and crossed the room. She grabbed a clean pair of underwear from her dresser and tiptoed to the bathroom in her suite. She flicked on the lights and turned on the shower, cranking the faucet as hot as it would go. By the time she'd stripped off her clothes and slipped into the shower, the bathroom was clouded with steam.

Once she was scrubbed clean, her muscles no longer taut, her hair blow-dried, she put her pajamas back on and swung open the door to the hallway.

She didn't even make it to the staircase before Darien came up the steps and around the corner. Loren froze as something like a sob clawed its way up her throat.

For a long while, they stared at each other. Standing several feet apart, feet frozen in place, as if not believing what their eyes were telling them.

And then they were moving.

Loren crossed the distance to him in a sprint, her eyes stinging with tears. He met her halfway, and she launched herself at him. He bent to catch her behind the thighs, lifting her up so her legs were wrapped around his waist, and crushed his lips to hers. Her hands fisted his hair, and she pulled him close, unable to get enough of this — of *him*. She would never get enough.

Only when they had no choice but to come up for air did he speak. "I think you and I need to have a little talk." Their faces were so close, Loren could see every fleck of silver in his eyes, every black eyelash. Still clutching her thighs and supporting her weight, he drank her in, his gaze soft. Every part of her body tingled at the look that darkened his eyes.

"Oh?" Loren breathed, smoothing a strand of hair from his face. His handsome, unmarked face. "And what do we have to talk about?"

"You said something to me." Every gasped word was gruff with emotion. "Three words, if I'm remembering correctly."

Loren arched a brow. "I have no idea what you're talking about, Darien Cassel."

"Don't play with me," he growled, coming in for another deep and delicious kiss. That kiss quickly turned to tongue and teeth, the hands that were wrapped around her thighs gripping her tighter, as he pinned her against the wall so hard the painting hanging on it rattled.

When he finally broke the kiss to speak again, the words were thick and raspy with emotion. "You love me?"

Loren's mouth wobbled. "Yes, Darien Cassel," she said, cupping his face. "I *do* love you. I'm so in love with you, it's crazy."

A smile flirted with his mouth. "Good. Because I love you more than anything in this world, Loren Calla."

Tears rolled down her face, her heart swelling with such joy that it felt like she was glowing.

Darien kissed those tears away, one by one. "I believe everything happens for a reason," he said, his mouth moving against her cheeks, the rumble of his voice reverberating deep into her bones. "And I believe that all the years that I spent killing and fighting—if all of it was just to lead me to you, then I am grateful for it. I'm grateful for *this*." His lips brushed tenderly over her closed eyelids. "And I'm grateful for you, Loren Calla." He kissed her mouth, long and deep, until she lost her breath. "I'm so grateful for you."

"I want you," she whispered hoarsely, her cheeks still wet with the tears that wouldn't stop. "I want *all* of you. Right now." His eyes darkened with such carnal desire that she instantly knew she was in trouble. The *best* sort of trouble.

His voice was a mirror of her own as he said, "Are you sure you're ready?"

"You're not going to make me beg," Loren said with an upward flick of her brows, "are you?"

Darien gave her a devilish grin that stole her breath right out of her lungs. "Whose suite?"

"Mine." And when she nipped at his bottom lip, a groan rose in his throat.

Her room—because it was closest.

Darien carried her to the door, where he turned the handle with his elbow and swung it open. Even when he set her on her feet, she wouldn't let go of him, couldn't get enough of him. Skin to skin and mouth to mouth, Darien nudged her toward the lamplit bed. As they moved, he pulled his shirt over his head and threw it aside.

When her thighs hit the foot of the bed, he lay her back gently among the rumpled covers. Her heart was slamming in her chest, and she found that the muscles in her legs were rigid.

The tension didn't escape him, and he froze in place where he knelt on the bed between her thighs, his hands gripping the stretchy band of her pajama shorts. "Loren." It was a question.

Loren's words were pathetically small when she whispered, "I guess this might be a good time to tell you I've never done this before."

Darien took so long to speak that Loren began to worry. Finally, he blurted, "You can't be serious. All that flirting we did, everything I said to you—"

"Was because I wanted you to say it," she interrupted gently. "I wanted everything you gave me, and I want more. I want all of you, Darien." She slanted an eyebrow. "Are you going to give it to me, or do I have to beg you for it?"

Darien smiled and dragged a thumb across her bottom lip, his touch igniting a fire deep inside her. "Hearing you beg is tempting, I have to admit."

"I want you." Those three words were the softest breath. And then, just because she wanted to, she added, "Please."

When he kissed her this time, his touch was gentle—as soft as her breath. She slipped her arms around his shoulders and opened her mouth to him. His tongue swept in to claim hers with savage strokes. A sound that could only mean she wanted more floated from her lips as the taste of him filled her mouth, as she felt his hand slip under the hem of her shirt, where it traveled over her breasts, cupping and circling. Her breasts turned heavy and tight under his touch, her nipples peaking under his palm.

The sensation of his skin on hers had her knees inching farther apart in invitation. She'd longed for him to touch her like this again, ever since that night at the Devil's Advocate. Had longed to go the whole way with him.

As if he could read her mind, Darien said, "You have no idea how long I've wanted you. You light up my life, Loren Calla." He lifted her up so he could pull her shirt over her head. When he eased her back down, he lightly swept his fingers between her breasts and down to her navel, tracing the shape of her body as if she were a work of art he was admiring—a sculpture he needed to touch for the full experience. Her stomach fluttered as that hand traveled lower and lower—

Until it slipped under the elastic band of her shorts. Beneath the lacey trim of her underwear.

Heat spread through her core. She arched her back, slowly rotating her hips—urging that hand of his to go exactly where she wanted it.

But he suddenly slid his hand back out, grabbed her behind the knees, and dragged her down the bed. She squeaked in surprise as he spread her out below him, opening her legs wide. He snaked both hands under her, cupping her ass, and with one sharp tug he removed her shorts and underwear and tossed them aside.

There was nothing covering her now, and the look on Darien's face as he drank her in, admiring every part of her... That look was heavy and heated, and every part of her body ached with the need for him to touch her, to fill her with himself until there wasn't a hint of space between them.

"Now it's my chance to see if you taste as sweet as you look," Darien said, every word deep and rough. He kept his eyes on her as he lowered himself down—until that stunning face of his was right between her legs. Pressing a kiss to the inside of her left thigh, he said, "Should I find out, Miss Calla?"

"Please do," she gasped.

"I like it when you say please." And then he lowered his mouth, lower and lower, holding her stare as he moved...and licked up the slick center of her. The first touch of his tongue lit her whole body on fire. Desire curled low in her belly as he let out an appreciative groan that seemed to say he was quite pleased with how she tasted.

"Good?" Her breath was a wild gasp.

"You're fucking delicious." The words left her dripping.

And then he set about doing exactly what he'd promised at the Devil's Advocate, eating his way straight to the heart that was already his, the only man it would ever belong to.

His tongue circled and pressed on her clit with such precision that her legs twitched, each stroke making her want to buck her hips. Darien kept one hand flat on her stomach, pinning her to the bed beneath him, while he used his other to alternate with his tongue. The feeling became more intense—almost unbearable—as he stroked her harder, and she tipped her head back into the sheets, arching under his touch.

"I love those little sounds you make." His thumb was working magic. "I want you to come for me, Loren. And then I'm going to fuck you." He coaxed her clit into his mouth, sucking on it and rolling his tongue against her.

Oh, gods. The pleasure rippling from her head to her toes made her body feel like it wasn't her own, like she was drifting into some distant dream. The things that he was doing to her, with only his tongue and his hands...

They almost made her black out.

And when she lifted her head from the sheets slightly, and she saw just how intently he was watching her writhe beneath him, she reached her climax. Hard and fast, the sight of his stunning face between her thighs—and the sight of his eyes gleaming black as he read her aura, a sight she'd once been afraid of but now found incredibly sexy—too much for her to bear. Her hands found his soft hair, and she cried out his name, pulling him harder against her as his tongue flicked across her clit, carrying her from one orgasm to the next.

Only once she was wholly spent and limp beneath him, her breathing no more than ragged gasps, did he slow.

He gave her a wicked, triumphant grin. *"That* is exactly why I've never had any intention of sharing you."

Somehow, even with her lying naked before him, he still managed to make her blush.

And then he was sitting up, settling himself between her legs. She felt a strange mixture of nerves and excitement as Darien looked her over, admiring the sight of her lying naked before him.

"Ready, sweetheart?" His voice was husky as he let the black fade out of his eyes.

She nodded faintly, her stomach flip-flopping.

Darien seemed to remember something, because he froze. When he cursed under his breath, his head turning toward the door, Loren realized where his attention had gone.

That was an easy fix.

She reached up to undo his belt buckle. "I've been taking a contraceptive tonic," she told him. Their heated encounter at the

Devil's Advocate had prompted her to make an appointment at the clinic. It was mostly a precaution—she'd had no idea where their relationship would go after that night. She had only known that she didn't want it to end.

His expression smoothed, though only just. "Are you sure?"

"I've never been more certain of anything," Loren said. "And besides, I don't want anything between us. I want to be able to feel you—*all* of you." Her hand closed around him through his pants, feeling how hard he was for her.

She'd never wanted anything the way she wanted this Devil.

The look that came over his face suggested just how badly he'd wanted her to touch him, how impatiently he'd waited for this moment. It made her even wetter than she had been before, made her hands tremble less as she undid his belt buckle. But Darien took note of her shaking, no matter how subtle, and the way her fingers fumbled on the metal, so he helped her through the rest of the movement, kicking off his jeans and boxers.

When there was nothing left to conceal him, she found herself not only gulping, but in awe of him. Not just because of the way he looked, the curves and hollows of every muscle in his impressive body gilded with gold from the lamplight, but because of how special she felt to be sharing her first time with someone she loved so deeply. Someone who had sacrificed so much, not just for her but for this city. The city they both loved.

Slipping a hand under her back, he slid her up farther on the bed, until her head was resting on the pillows. When he looked down at her, she nodded once, signalling that she was ready. She was nervous, it was true, but she'd never been more ready for anything.

He gripped the wrought-iron headboard with one hand, the other clenching her waist firmly yet gently, and pushed himself inside of her in one long, slow movement. In, and in, and in. She bit her lip and clenched her eyes shut. There was a sharp pinch, followed by a dull, tight ache that arrowed deep.

He paused, allowing her to adjust to the feel of him.

"Look at me," Darien said. She peeked up at him to find that he was looking down at her, his eyes as intense as they were soft. "If you need me to slow down or stop, you tell me. I'll do whatever you need me to. Okay?"

He rocked into her again. And despite how slow and heartbreakingly careful the movement, she almost cried out from the sting. But she swallowed the sound, focusing only on him. Her hands fisted the sheets, her thighs tightening around his hips with every stroke.

"Okay?" he repeated. She tried to speak, but all she could manage was a nod.

As he continued to move inside her, she began to relax, to get used to the feeling. The motion of his body against hers became more rhythmic as he sensed her comfort increasing. One hand on the iron and the other gripping her waist, he rocked into her again and again and again.

Loren began to dissolve, every part of her body tingling with desire, at the realization that they were finally doing this—that he was hers, and she was his, and they were together at last.

She arched beneath him, the movement slipping the brutal length of him in deeper, making her gasp aloud. The feeling set her whole body on fire. He gently caught her wrists, pinning them above her head as he leaned down to brush a kiss across her collarbone.

And she couldn't get enough of him—of the scent and feel and taste of him.

There was nothing in the world but this—nothing in the world but him. Them. Their bodies moving as one, yearning crackling between them like a firework.

"You are mine," Darien said as he pumped inside her, both hands now braced on the wrought iron above her head. Every stroke verged on the point of pain, but she wanted it, wanted more, wanted *all* of him. She loved how his tattooed arms flexed with every deep thrust, loved the way he looked at her, as if he was seeing her for the very first time. *"Mine."*

Her legs quivered with every movement, the headboard banging into the wall. His name floated from her lips as he hit that golden spot. Release barrelled down her spine, the feeling so intense it felt like she was floating.

"Look at you," Darien breathed, pumping harder. Faster.

Drawing out her pleasure until she couldn't remember her own name. "Look how beautiful you are."

The way he was devouring her with his eyes undid her again, and her stomach fluttered, the soles of her feet tingling, toes curling tightly, as another wave of pleasure cascaded over her, so soon after the first that the two blended together. A groan floated from her lips.

"Say it again, baby." He was as breathless as she was. "I want to hear you say it again." She immediately knew what he meant— because she was thinking those three words at that very moment, as he looked her over with admiration, the hard muscles in his arms flexing as he thrust into her. Again, and again. And again.

"I love you, Darien," she said. "I'll love you forever."

His movements grew more urgent. He bent down to kiss her deeply, swallowing the sound of her cry as he thrust into her one last time, and he trembled as he found his own release, the warmth of his pleasure filling her as he cried out her name.

Their heavy breathing filled the silence. Loren's legs were quivering on either side of his waist, her body aching deliciously.

Darien bent to brush a kiss to her forehead. "Happy birthday, sweetheart."

She ducked her chin. "You remembered."

"Of course." His voice was rough, and his throat bobbed with emotion. "I love you, Loren."

They lay there for a long time afterward, tangled together with nothing but their own beating hearts and the sound of their gradually slowing breaths filling the silence.

Darien fell asleep before she did. And although she'd never felt happier in her life, a part of her didn't want to slip away just yet.

She'd almost lost him today. The memory brought a rush of fresh tears to her eyes.

But he was here. Beside her. He was hers, and she had saved him.

They'd saved each other.

"I love you," Loren whispered, nestling into the crook of his shoulder. Darien was so tired, he didn't so much as stir at the sound. "I'll love you forever."

645

She stayed awake as long as she could, until the night felt like a dream. Until she fell asleep in his strong arms, his heart beating against her own.

WHEN LOREN WOKE up in the morning, she found that she had slept better than she had in years. Perhaps even forever.

She cracked open her eyelids to see sunlight pouring into the room through the slats in the blinds. It washed the suite in gold, giving everything a hazy glow that reminded her of late-summer magic and desert sunsets.

The events of the previous night rushed into her mind, flooding her body with a warmth more intense than the sun streaming in through the windows.

Her body felt...different. Like it was hers but not. It was a strange feeling, but not a bad one. She welcomed the difference, because it came with bonding with the person she loved in the closest way possible. There was a dull ache between her legs, but aside from that she felt good. Better than ever, in fact.

Darien was sprawled on his stomach beside her, his head turned the other way. The duvet and sheets were tucked down around his waist, leaving the ink on his muscled back visible for Loren to admire in all its glory.

And she did.

Slowly, Loren turned toward him, being careful not to shift the sheets and wake him. She reached up and traced her fingertips over the scars on his back, the ridges barely visible beneath the ink. She tried not to picture a beautiful black-haired boy with steel-blue eyes, struck repeatedly with a belt, those eyes going dark—not with the Sight, but with the art of blocking out the pain.

Still, try as she may, Loren found that her breathing hitched at the thought, her hatred for Randal grabbing her heart in a fist and squeezing tight.

Darien deserved a better hand of cards than the ones he'd been dealt. So much better.

She focused instead on the tattoo, brushing her fingers across the teeth of the hound of hell, over the ignited chains that bound it, over the flames encasing its muscled body. The fine details were so extraordinary, it looked like a photograph.

"That feels amazing." Darien's voice made her jump, made her hand still on his back.

She pulled away as he rolled over to face her. He was exquisite, and it had very little to do with what he looked like. She sank into the pillow, a sudden bout of shyness sweeping through her.

"I didn't mean to wake you," she said.

The corner of his lips tipped up into a smile, showing off that dimple she loved so much. "And I didn't mean to make you stop." He took her hand and flattened his palm against hers. For a moment, he admired the sight of her hand flat against his, the two of them so different in size. And she admired him—before his eyes locked on hers, and he caught her staring. "Hi," he whispered.

"Hi," she whispered back.

He laced his fingers with hers and rested their joined hands in the soft sheets. "How are you feeling?"

"I'm good," she said. "I'm really good."

Darien tilted a brow. "Sore?" When she hesitated, he said, "It's normal, Loren. You're not going to make me feel bad for telling the truth." When she still didn't answer, concern flitted across his features, that little smile curling into a frown. "What's the matter?"

Loren fiddled with one of the rings he wore. "I didn't want to say I'm sore in case I caused you to not want to do it again," she admitted. Nerves clenched in her stomach, and her face heated up.

When she peeked up at Darien, she spotted a wicked glint in his eyes. "Even if you told me that you could barely walk, I still wouldn't be able to leave you alone."

Letting go of her hand, he rolled, and suddenly he was on top of her. Loren gasped in surprise, but he was hooking her legs around his waist before she could say anything.

He braced his hands on the wrought iron above her head. The space between her legs pulsed at the sight of him above her again so soon. "Tell me you want me," Darien said.

"I want you." Her voice was colored with urgency.

He was pushing himself inside her before she was finished saying the last word, and they moaned in unison.

He wasted no time before he began to move, but Loren winced a little, causing him to pause.

"Keep going," she said, her voice breathy.

He did, but three thrusts later, he stopped.

It was her fault, wasn't it? She'd hinted that she was feeling pain, and he'd stopped.

"Darien—" Loren objected.

But he only said, "I want to try something different." And then he flipped them again, the silken sheets rustling around them.

And then *Loren* was on top of *him.*

She let out a gasp as she sank down his length, the angle filling her deep and snug.

Darien let out a low, appreciative groan. "Show me what you've got, sweetheart."

Loren froze, her whole body tensing up. "What if I..." Her tongue became clumsy and dry. "What if—I mean, I don't really know what I'm doing. What if I'm not...?"

Darien surprised her by looking angry, not at her, but at how she'd found it necessary to voice such a question. "What if you're not what?" he prompted softly. "Not good enough?"

She merely looked at him, embarrassment spreading hotly through her face.

Holding her gaze, Darien took her left hand into his and pressed the tips of her fingers to his lips. "You are better than enough, Loren Calla," he said against her skin. "You are perfect." He kissed her palm before letting go, instead grabbing hold of her hips. The heat from his rough hands was inviting as it spread into her—

And then he started bobbing her up and down...up and down.

Loren's breath caught in her throat.

Oh. *Oh.*

"Like this." His voice was husky and sexy as hell. "All you have to do is move, and I promise I'll love it." He let go to allow her to take the reins, but when she still hesitated, he reached for her and tipped up her chin. His gaze was beseeching as he attempted to read her expression. After a moment, he said, "I love you, Loren."

Loren's heart swelled at the statement; the way he said it was like a shout out into the universe. "I love you, too." She grew concerned by the look on his face, and she grazed her fingers across the crease between his brows. "What's the matter?"

His mouth pulled down at the corners. "I might die if you don't start moving."

Loren recoiled like he'd slapped her. "Don't say that word!" she nearly shouted. She didn't *ever* want to hear any jokes about him dying. Not now, not ever.

"Then fuck me," he said, grabbing hold of her hips again and rolling them against his. Loren nearly swore; it felt so good. "Fuck me like my life depends on it."

A breathless laugh slipped out of her, but it was soon silenced by the feel of him moving inside her, teasing that golden spot he'd hit so precisely last night. It was unfair, how good he was. Unfair, because she would want him every day of her too-short life.

"Tilt your hips a bit, baby." He angled her. "Like this. It'll feel good, I promise." He moved her body up and down to illustrate, grinding her into his pelvis. He did it again.

And again.

"*Oh,*" she gasped. It *did* feel good. And she found herself picking up where he'd left off, melting into the rhythm he'd set, and forgetting all about the embarrassment she'd felt a moment ago. His gaze felt like a caress as he drank in her body moving above him. It gave her a sense of power she'd never known before, and would likely never get from anything else.

"That's it, baby." The words were slightly husky and dripping with sin. "Just like that. Keep going." He braced his hands above his head, holding onto the headboard as she rode him. The muscles in his arms flexed every time she did something he liked, which was often enough that she quickly learned what his favorite moves were, desperate to please him as much as she could. He watched her intently the whole time, his stare nearly as potent as what was going on between her legs. She kept her eyes on him too, loving the way he watched her, loving the carnal look that transformed his stunning face into something truly mouth-watering.

"Come for me, baby." His voice was rich and so deep, she felt it in her belly. Something she did brought a groan of approval to his lips, and his grip tightened on the wrought iron, causing it to bend just a little, the iron roses shuddering from the tension.

Loren's mouth popped open in surprise.

She did that. *She* made him do that. The realization almost undid her, but she fought the wave of ecstasy rising within, not wanting this to be over just yet.

Darien's jaw hardened, the muscles in his arms standing out beneath his tattooed skin. Sweat took form in tiny beads below his lower lip as he ground out, "Come for me, Lola."

She did—hard. Bliss rolled over her like an ocean wave, causing the muscles in her legs to grow taut. She tipped her head back slightly, gasping as ecstasy rippled across her skin. She felt her insides tightening around him, her thighs becoming damp with more than just sweat.

He removed his hands from the headboard, instead using them to hold her by the hips, setting a faster rhythm that would take him over the edge. She knew she would go over that edge again too, but this time it would be *with* him. She wanted it, wanted to give him the world.

He moved her up and down, faster and faster, each deepening thrust verging on the point of pain, but she only wanted more, wanted to take everything he gave her, wanted to see the look on his face when he let off inside her.

And he did a few minutes later, shuddering beneath her, her name rolling off his tongue in a low oath. The feel of him pulsing inside her with his release made her climax again, and their bodies moved as one in the throes of their pleasure, dragging their orgasm out like the final note of music in a song that only they could hear.

When they stilled at last, both of them trembling and damp, only the sound of their rapid breathing remained. They stared at each other for a long time without saying anything; or perhaps they were speaking without words. It certainly felt like it.

Gently, Darien cupped Loren's face, and he pulled her down to his level so he could kiss her soundly. "Good morning," he mumbled against her mouth. Her bare chest was pressed against his, the closeness allowing her to feel his words reverberate through her, touching her heart like the sweetest kiss.

"The *best* morning," she corrected.

The corner of his lips tilted up. "There will be plenty more where that came from. I'm afraid you'll grow sick of me."

"I highly doubt that." She couldn't catch her breath. He was still hard as granite inside her; the realization turned her to liquid all over again, and she knew her body's reaction did not escape Darien. Her heart was slamming in her chest, and she could feel Darien's heart crashing too, felt it in different parts of her.

"Is that right?" he crooned.

He suddenly flipped her onto her back, pinning her beneath him, and she gasped. The room spun, but parts of her body tingled with a silent request that dizzied her more than the movement. She hadn't known it was possible to want someone so much, and all the time. She just couldn't get enough of him.

"Again so soon?" she breathed. It was a ridiculous question, she knew; he was a hellseher, and hellsehers could go at things like sex at a far different pace than humans. Hell, they hardly needed sleep.

He tsked, bopping her nose with a finger. "You say that like you're surprised."

He took hold of her left foot, brought her leg up, and hooked her ankle over his shoulder. His humor vanished then, sharpening into primal focus as he fully sank into her, the angle deep and oh...*oh*, so good. He began moving inside her, and a groan slipped through her lips at the sensation. The tenderness she felt between her legs somehow made the pleasure more intense.

"Is this alright with you, Miss Calla?"

"Yes."

He bowed over her, brushing her hair aside as he whispered, "I can't hear you, baby."

"Yes," she gasped, the air squeezed out of her lungs as he rocked into her deeply.

He looked down at her as he moved inside her, his gaze feral. He seemed to like the sound of that word, so she said it again.

"Yes."

The next thrust was even deeper than the previous, causing her to claw at the sheets and dig her heel into his shoulder.

"Yes."

Another thrust to reward her, so deep she *did* swear this time.

She was convinced she would never get tired of this, never get tired of him, would never feel like any thrust was deep enough to fully satisfy her craving for him. Their souls were one and the same, begging to be joined the same way as their bodies. The closest they could get was this act of love, and it would have to do—it *would* do, until they were nothing but memories. Until the *world* was nothing but a memory.

The morning continued like that. And even though she was late for school because of it, she didn't have any regrets.

Not one.

62

"Watch where you're going, *half-life*."

If it weren't for the events of these past four months, Loren Calla might've run out the front doors of Angelthene Academy for Magic right then and there.

Instead, she shouldered her book bag and spun around to face the werewolf who'd slammed into her in the crowded hallway.

She pinned him with a cold stare, smiled sweetly, and said in a voice as sweet as her smile, "You have all of eternity to be a jerk. Why don't you take the day off?"

The wolf was too surprised to say anything. He gaped at Loren, his mouth hanging open like a fish, those fiery eyes bugging out of his head.

Loren tipped up an eyebrow, loving how every student in their vicinity was watching.

Where she stood at Loren's right, Dallas cackled as the wolf spun and took off into the crowd as if he'd seen a ghost, his bookbag thumping against his back. Whispers of amusement nipped at his heels, and several students gave Loren a smile that suggested they were impressed.

Sabrine sniggered, a honey-brown hand pressed to her lips.

"Maybe you should smite him with the power of the Well," Sabrine whispered as they continued making their way to the entrance hall, weaving their way through the students.

"There's always next time," Loren joked.

But Loren wasn't sure there would be a next time. Her wish from Tempus the Liar was all used up, and not once had she felt her powers since Kalendae—since the moment she had used her aura to bring Darien back to life and shield the city from the blast. Not that she'd felt her power often in the years leading up to the Well's explosion.

But several times these past couple days, she had tried reaching out to that mysterious part of herself when she couldn't sleep at night, only to be met with nothing but a strange and heavy emptiness she had never felt before. It felt like someone had stripped her of something vital, leaving her hollow and brittle inside.

When the Red Baron had caught wind of the absolute garbage that had gone down with his wife, Taega had been released from the holding center immediately. Pardoned by the imperator himself, who'd apologized for the...*mistake* the law enforcement had made in apprehending her. Loren had a feeling that although the imperator had opened the gate to Taega's cell, he'd put her in a far different— and potentially far worse—sort of cage, if what Calanthe had told Loren of his plans that day in Angelthene General was anything to be believed.

Loren only hoped it was over—well and truly over. That she could finally move on from all of this and return to some level of normalcy. That one day she might be able to leave home without the weight of an Avertera talisman around her throat; without the urge to look over her shoulder.

And it was home where she was heading now, as soon as she finished packing her things.

They reached the mirrored entrance to the Salt dormitory, where they passed through the rippling glass and made their way to their bunks.

Once Loren was finished packing, suitcase in hand, she tossed her hair over a shoulder and faced Dallas and Sabrine, who were gathering up their own things. "Are you guys coming to Hell's Gate?"

"Not until later," Dallas said. "I've got a date with the boyfriend."

Loren's brows flicked up. *"Boyfriend?"*

Dallas snapped her bubble-gum in her teeth. "Turns out I enjoy Max's company more than just his dick."

Loren choked on a laugh.

It was to Sabrine, who was zipping her suitcase shut, that Loren said, "What about you?" She eyed up the stack of books on Sab's nightstand. "Do you have to study?"

"Studying can wait," the half-wolf said as they made their way out of the House of Salt. "But I *am* busy."

Dallas grinned. "Did Logan finally convince you to go steady with him?"

"For the last time, Dal," Sabrine huffed. "We're just friends." But her cheeks were blazing, and Loren knew Dallas could see through the lie just as well as she could.

Dallas waved a dismissive hand. "Sure, sure."

Chrysantha was finally home, her body healed. She had reunited with Logan not long after the city was rebuilt with time's reversal.

Loren wondered about Emilie, Calanthe's daughter and heir to the Blood Rose. How did she feel about everything that'd happened? Had she moved forward with her mother's vile plans because she felt she had to, or did she believe in them, too?

Loren wondered about Calanthe herself, and whether she was somewhere out there. Waiting for her chance to strike again, if the reversal of time had gone back far enough to spare her. Wondered if the imperator would decide to enact revenge on Loren and the Devils for wrecking his plans for his vision of a perfect world.

She forced herself to breathe. Those were problems for another day. They were still alive, and that was a gift.

Every day was a gift.

Before they could make it to the staircase that swept down to the entrance hall, Dallas paused to skim over her text messages. She slipped the phone into her bag, bounced forward, and gave them each a wet peck on the cheek.

"Max is telling me to hurry up or we're going to miss the premiere of Fang-ciful. Tootles, losers." She skipped down the corridor and disappeared down the forked staircase at the end of it.

Sabrine's arched brows flicked up. "Walk with me?" she asked Loren.

Loren linked her arm through hers. "Always."

Outside, a Januarius sun peeked through the clouds. Although it was no longer raining, the air was misty with it, the damp sidewalk beneath her uniform shoes covered with blue jacaranda petals.

Loren's stomach flipflopped the moment she caught sight of Darien's car parked by the curb that looped around the lot. Blue petals were scattered across it, reflecting in the glossy black paint. The car she had once run from. The Devil who was now her angel. They had barely been able to keep their hands off each other these past couple days—since finally breaking the tension between them, as Dallas had once called it—and the novelty still hadn't worn off. She would never get tired of him—of this, she was certain.

A smile pulled at her mouth as she said goodbye to Sabrine, and as she made her way to where Darien waited for her in his car, heavy bass rattling the frame, a limousine glided up to the curb at her side.

The windows were so dark, she couldn't glimpse anything within. But she knew why they were here—who they were here for.

And she knew, even without being able to see him through the spells and tinted windows, that Darien was watching in the rear-view mirror as she swung open the back door of the limousine and slid onto the cold leather seat.

A pane of tinted glass separated the empty back seat from the one in the front, betraying no more than a silhouette of the person sitting before her.

But the moment the deep voice snaked through the cab, slightly muffled by the glass barrier, she realized her problems were far from over.

Their world was changing. And this city of gods and monsters was only the beginning.

Death was only the beginning.

EPILOGUE

Darien watched from where he was parked at the side of the road as Loren strode onto the dock at Jade Beach. The salty wind blew her hair over her shoulders and set her pleated skirt flapping against the backs of her thighs.

Tanner had called him an hour ago, filling him in on how the rabbit messenger who'd hired him to track down Loren all those months ago had finally used her cell phone long enough for him to get a firm read on her whereabouts.

When the pin displaying her location had first appeared on the map, Darien had almost thrown up. He might not have cared so much—were it not for the fact that the pin had fallen directly atop the Mortar and Pestle.

Darien had hoped their problems would've stopped nipping at their heels, at least for a while. Long enough for them to catch their breath for more than the measly three days that had passed since the city was decimated by the Well.

But it seemed that whoever this rabbit's boss was had found Loren at last.

Darien stayed in the car, cracking open his window to allow the brisk air to slip through—and any screaming that might otherwise be swallowed by the wind, should Loren end up in trouble—as he watched her trail the masked messenger to the end of the dock. He'd followed the sedan Loren had gotten into from a distance, never once letting it out of his sight, praying to every god and goddess that had ever existed that she knew what she was doing.

Waiting at the end of the ocean-slick dock was a man.

As Darien watched that man slowly turn around to face Loren, he wondered how it was possible that everything he thought he knew about the world could suddenly be proven wrong in the span of so little time.

Darien swallowed a surge of nausea that rolled through his gut like the waves caressing the shore as he leaned forward in his seat, blinking his Sight into place. As Loren shuffled across the dock toward the man.

Although Darien's sixth sense told him that the man's aura was a far different glow than Loren's, his regular field of vision somehow gave him a far clearer truth as he took in the ocean-blue of the man's eyes, the golden hue of his silver-streaked hair.

For several minutes, Darien watched them. They conversed in voices too quiet for him to hear from this far away, but after a moment, Loren took three steps across the dock, closing the distance that separated herself from the man.

And then daughter and father embraced for the very first time in years.

The messenger watching nearby turned her head, and even though she wore that same awful rabbit mask as the night she'd hired him, Darien could tell precisely when her eyes landed on his vehicle.

Slowly, she raised a gloved hand in greeting—in thanks.

The job she'd offered him four months ago had all been for this. For the man who had defeated Death but had somehow welcomed it back into his life with open arms—by becoming mortal again—to be reunited with his daughter. The man who'd spent months—years, maybe—looking for Loren, but no longer had the Sight needed to track her down himself, who didn't know that his former best friend

Elix Danik and his wife—who'd hidden their auras with Nacht Essentia—were now called by different names.

Every thought in Darien's head was a nonsensical roar as those waves rose and fell in the distance, eerily in tune with the ticking of the watch on his wrist.

Water moving in rhythm with the passing of time.

TO BE CONTINUED...

BONUS SCENE

Continue reading for an exclusive behind-the-scenes sneak peek at what Darien and Loren were up to shortly after the events of *City of Gods and Monsters*…

A SECOND FIRST DATE

S aturday was the Mortar and Pestle's busiest day of the week. Loren Calla was exhausted. She bustled around the apothecary, flitting between customers as she packaged up potions, poultices, tinctures, and bouquets. Mordred and Penelope were working today too, thank gods. It was far too busy for Loren to handle all these people on her own.

She finished wrapping up a beautiful bouquet of white roses, pink dragon snaps, and fuchsia daisies, and passed it to the witch standing across from her at the cash register.

"Thank you so much for your patience, Greta."

Greta fluttered a weathered hand. "Oh, any time, dear. You make sure you rest your poor feet soon."

"Oh, I will." She wore sneakers today, but her feet were aching like mad. She couldn't wait to sit down. "See you next week."

Greta winked. "You got it."

"Next person," Loren called, the words weighed with exhaustion.

Mordred and Penelope glided over. "Take a break, darling," Mordred said. Penny added, "You look like you're darn near ready to wither away on us." She clucked her tongue.

Loren forced a smile and said, "I'm fine."

But they didn't buy it. They waved their hands at her. "Shoo. Upstairs—go rest your little mortal feet."

She sighed in relief. "Thank you." They switched places, and Loren disappeared into the staff room upstairs. She shut the door, grateful for the quiet and the space.

Now that it was safe to come out, Singer trotted out of her shadow and stretched his hind legs, his mouth opening with a big yawn that made his throat squeak.

"Long day," Loren whispered.

Singer wagged his bushy tail.

Loren grabbed her purse from the floor, threw it on the desk, and collapsed in the swivel chair.

Gods—she needed a massage. And water.

Her phone buzzed. She took it out and checked the message.

> **DARIEN**
> Is your day as crazy as mine?

> **LOREN**
> Crazier.

> **DARIEN**
> Want to trade jobs?

> **LOREN**
> I'm not sure you'd be able to handle all the bouquets.

> **DARIEN**
> You're right—too much sneezing.

> **LOREN**
> What are you doing?

> **DARIEN**
> You don't want to know.
>
> You up for taking a drive tonight?

> **LOREN**
> I'd love to <3

DARIEN

I'll pick you up.

Loren got off right at four thirty, thanks to Mordred and Penny insisting on handling the closing duties tonight.

Feet and back still aching like crazy, she walked out into the Avenue of the Scarlet Star, pulling the door shut behind her. The weather today was mild for early Januarius—no rain for the first time in days. The sun warmed her head as she made her way down the avenue, weaving around the last of the customers and the other employees who were locking up for the evening.

Darien's truck was parked on the street just ahead—right where she could see it, like always. He had yet to fail at snagging a spot closest to the entrance; sometimes she wondered if he bullied other drivers into leaving with no more than a hard glance. She wouldn't be surprised; it seemed like something he'd do.

The moment Loren caught sight of that big black truck, she walked faster, new energy in her step.

The Devil got out and came around to open her door. "What happened, baby?" Concern creased his brow as he eyed the limp in her step. "You slay a demon or something?"

"Worse—I slayed like five thousand customers, I swear." She climbed into the truck, and Darien shut the door behind her.

Loren watched the sun play in his black hair as he rounded the truck and got in the driver's side. He'd asked if she was up for taking a drive tonight, but his white button-up shirt and black suit pants told her a drive wasn't the only thing he had planned.

Darien eyed her again as he buckled up. "Are you eye-fucking me?" A smile teased his mouth.

She tucked a strand of hair behind an ear. "You look nice," she told him, her face heating up. 'Nice' didn't even begin to cover it.

"There's a bag in the back—go on and grab it."

"You're *welcome*," she snickered.

"I don't like compliments, baby. You know that."

Loren rolled her eyes, but she was smiling, and so was he. "Fine," she huffed. She turned to see a big white gift bag sitting on the floor of the truck, pink tissue paper stuffed in the top of it. Another three presents sat on the back seat. "You said *a* bag!" she exclaimed with a gasp. "What is all this?"

Darien was fighting a grin. "Birthday gifts."

"But it's not my birthday anymore."

"True. But none of us got to celebrate it."

"I don't know about that..." She knew she shouldn't say it, but she did anyway. "I thought it was quite the *bang.*"

Darien deadpanned. "Ha-ha." He put the truck in drive and merged into traffic.

"Tasteless?"

"I'll tolerate it. But only because it's you."

She reached into the back seat, grabbed the big white bag, and set it in her lap.

"That one's from Ivy," he said. "She thought you might want to wear it tonight."

"You just spoiled what it is."

"Open it."

She pulled the puffs of tissue paper out and let them drift to the floor. Inside the bag was the cutest white romper that tied at the back. She held it up, turning it to study the tiny pearls embedded in the lacy back. "This is beautiful. She has great taste."

"She knows what you like," Darien said. "Open the others."

She had to practically dive into the back seat to grab them. She piled them in her lap, and opened the second present—also from Ivy. Jack had scribbled his name underneath hers on the tag, and Loren laughed when she realized Ivy had crossed it out. The second present was part of the first—a pair of pearlescent wedge heels that went perfectly with the romper.

"She *really* knows what I like," Loren said, setting the shoes on the floor.

Lace gave her a pair of diamond earrings that had to be worth a small fortune, and Tanner gave her a camera.

"How did Tanner know I wanted a camera?" she asked, holding it up. It was heavy and expensive—no surprise there. The Devils didn't shop for bargains.

"I might've given him a clue." They were in the Financial District now, pulling to a stop not far from Blackbird 88 Above.

She picked up the last present—a small white box tied with a rose ribbon—and opened it. There was no tag saying who it was from, so she assumed it was from Darien. Judging from the way he peeked at her out of the corner of his eye as he finished parking, her assumption was correct.

Inside the box, nestled in a bed of black velvet, was a charm of a calla lily—rose gold to match the others on her bracelet.

"Darien," she whispered. She pouted, shoulders slumping. "I said no more spending money on me!"

"I can't hear you, baby, you're mumbling." He shut off the truck, and beckoned with a hand. "Give me your wrist. I'll help you put it on."

She rested her wrist in his hand—the one with the bracelet he'd purchased for her, the little charms glinting against her skin. He attached the calla lily to the chain with ease.

Darien smiled, that adorable dimple showing off. "There— another for your collection." He gently turned her wrist to see the other charms. That smile grew. "Beautiful."

"This is the *last* one," Loren told him, the words firm. "You've already spent...*how* much on me?" She squinted at him, her wrist still in his grip.

He lifted her hand to his mouth, his breath warming her skin, and brushed a kiss to the back of it. "No one's keeping track."

"I hope not, or I'd be millions in debt. I'm going to have to claim bankruptcy."

He let her go, and undid his seatbelt. "Let's make a deal. A million kisses, and we'll call it even."

"A million kisses?" she gasped, smiling. "That'll take a lifetime."

The corner of this mouth twitched. "I plan on it." He grabbed the romper off her lap. "Arms up."

She blinked at him. "I'm changing *now?*" She glanced out at the cars breezing down the street. "Right here?" She pointed.

"No one can see you through the spells, sweetheart." He bit the tags off the romper. "I'll help you. We'll be done in no time." He set the plastic tag fasteners aside. "Come on, baby, we're going to be late."

She held up her arms, and Darien tugged her shirt over her head. The minute her breasts were exposed, the tiny sparkles in her white bra catching the light, he lost focus and came in for a kiss.

Several. He wouldn't let go of her, and soon her hands were fisting his hair. Desire kindled within her, and suddenly she didn't care about dinner—she just wanted him. This Devil—her everything.

"Done in no time, hey?" she said against his mouth. He silenced her with another kiss, his tongue parting her lips.

They managed to control themselves—with difficulty—long enough for Loren to get changed, though they barely made it inside in time for their reservation.

Not that it would've mattered. Darien owned the place.

The hostess led them to a candlelit table—draped with a white cloth—by a wall of windows. The lighting was soft and romantic, and there was live music, just like last time. Darien pulled out Loren's chair for her, and she sat down. The waitress placed a menu before each of them, and after briefing them on the specials, she left.

Loren opened her menu. As she turned her head to gaze out at the magnificent spread of Angelthene, she realized—

"This is the same table as last time," she said, looking across the table at Darien.

He merely smiled.

She had the daily soup to start, and for her entrée she chose the chicken. Everything was as incredible as last time, and the chocolate mousse she selected from the dessert menu was just as good as she remembered it.

After dinner, Darien held her hand as they returned to the truck. He allowed her to lead, watching her back like always, as they walked through the revolving glass doors. Night had fallen, and the air was cool. Stars winked above the city, the greenish tint of the forcefield more visible than it was during the day.

"What are we doing now?" she asked him.

"Taking that drive I mentioned."

"Wait." She peeked up at him, sucking on one of the mints the waitress had left with their bill. "You're recreating our first date, aren't you?"

"Technically, I'm recreating our first *and* second dates."

She beamed up at him. "Stars?"

"Shh, you'll spoil it." He fought his own smile as they crossed the road. He opened her door for her again, and she got in, the warmth of the truck raising a chill on her spine.

It was a clear night, just like the first time Darien had brought her out of the city, to his secret spot under the stars. He held her hand the whole time as they sped down the highway, music drifting quietly through the truck speakers.

"Nervous?" Darien asked. He was watching her closely.

She pursed her lips as she considered his question, and shook her head. "Not like last time." Coming out to a place where demons roamed freely after dark used to scare her, and while it still did, to a certain extent, she trusted Darien with her life. If he told her she didn't need to be afraid, she listened.

The truck bounced as he drove off-road, parking in what looked like the same place as last time.

Yup, he was definitely redoing this.

"Did you remember the blanket?" she asked him as he shut off the truck. She remembered everything about that night—even something as simple as the feel of the blanket. Every detail was etched into her mind.

"Of course." He reached down to grab a bottle of wine off the floor by his seat. "And wine."

Loren's brows flicked up. "Did you have that by your feet this whole time?"

"I had to hide it from you somehow." Gods, that was dangerous. What if it had rolled under the pedal?

"We didn't have wine the first time we came out here," she pointed out, just to tease him.

"I'm allowed to make adjustments."

He got out, and she followed him to the back of the truck, where he helped her up into the bed.

They talked for a long time—just like they had on their first date. Loren had a feeling the wine was limbering up her tongue; she did most of the talking, but Darien didn't seem to mind. He listened the whole time, even when she was convinced she must be boring him.

She took another sip, and offered him the bottle. "Have you even had any?"

"I bought it for you. I'm not really into wine."

"Try it."

He took the bottle from her, and she watched his mouth as he took a swig. Was it ridiculous of her to feel jealous of the bottle? "It tastes like...strawberry," he said.

"Do you like it?"

He set the bottle aside, and leaned in for a kiss; she could taste the wine on his lips. "I like you," he breathed against her mouth. When he kissed her again, she decided she had every right to be jealous of that bottle. "I fucking love you."

And just like that, they were right back in the same spot as last time—hands in each other's hair, teeth and tongues clashing. Loren pushed to her knees and straddled him, drunk off his kisses more than she was the wine.

She came up for air, and Darien dipped his head, trailing kisses along her collarbone and the swell of her breasts. "I was so nervous," she confessed in a whisper, "the first time we kissed."

He smiled against her breast. "I know."

"Were you?" She knew it was a silly question; nothing scared this man.

When he answered, he raised his head to look at her. "I felt more lucky than anything." He cupped her face, his thumb tracing the shape of her mouth. "Every day I get to spend with you makes me the luckiest man alive."

She tucked her hair behind an ear. "You're just saying that."

"I'm not. Now get on your knees—over here." He gestured to the floor of the truck bed a couple feet away. "I want to act out a fantasy of mine." Gods—a fantasy of his? She was already soaking.

And she was more than willing to obey, swinging her leg over him and shuffling on her knees to the side of the truck.

He took up position behind her, his presence like the crackle of a storm. "Put your hands up here, baby," Darien said, tapping the side rails on the truck bed.

She did as she was told, holding on tight. Her heart was slamming in her chest, but the desire pooling inside her was stronger.

Darien's fingers went to the ties at the back of the romper. He undid the bow, and then moved onto the little zipper at the small of her back, his knuckles grazing her skin.

He slipped the romper down to her knees, exposing her body to the cool night air. "Fuck." He dragged a warm, callused hand down her back, his touch leaving trails of fire everywhere. "Will you be too cold like this?"

She turned her head to look at him. Under the fall of night, his eyes were a deep gray-blue, and his hair shone like ink. "I'm sure I'll be fine once we get started."

"Get what started?" he teased.

She snickered, and he winked, his smile growing.

He undid the buttons on his shirt, and then he tugged his arms out of the sleeves and dropped the shirt to the truck bed. No matter how many times she saw him like this, it always felt like the first time. The novelty of getting to call this man hers would never wear off; the way her heart reacted was evidence of that.

And when he undid his belt and pants, and shifted the latter down, her mouth dried out at the sight of his length springing free.

Gods—she would never get tired of *that* either.

Darien came in for a kiss, his warm, rough fingers diving between her legs. She was already dripping for him, his fingers slipping around the area easily.

But he must have noticed how quickly her heart was moving, because he murmured against her mouth, "You're nervous."

"A little," she admitted.

He pulled back to look her in the eyes. "It's just you and I out here, sweetheart." That rough hand kept moving, his fingers rubbing her clit, each movement sending little bolts of pleasure through her body. Her legs twitched, her thighs trapping his hand.

"Yeah—you," she breathed. He continued to coax her toward

climax with those deft fingers, his potent stare heating the areas of her body where the night had cooled. "Darien Cassel."

His brow creased. "I'm nothing special, baby. You, though…" He dipped his head, his lips brushing her shoulder. "You're fucking perfect."

"No—you," she argued, but the words were breathy, and she knew he wouldn't let her win.

His hand dipped lower, and he slipped his middle finger inside her. Deeper…and deeper. He kept his mouth close to hers, hovering but not kissing. She could feel his breath—as ragged as her own—on her lips, and she knew he could feel hers when a soft whimper slipped out of her, that hand working magic.

As he slid his finger in and out, his thumb rubbing her clit, he watched her closely; he loved seeing her reactions just as much as she loved seeing his.

"You're so beautiful," he said, his lips grazing hers. "I couldn't stop staring at you the first time I brought you out here." He finger-fucked her harder, carrying her closer to the edge, but not close enough to finish. "If I've done one thing right in my life, it was falling for you." His kiss stole the last of the breath from her lungs, and as his tongue flicked against hers, he groaned, deep into her mouth.

He pulled his fingers out of her, and she felt the crown of his cock rub against her entrance.

Finally, he slid inside her—a couple inches at first. And then he pulled back out and started anew, moving with patience as her body adjusted, accepting him inch by inch.

He came in close again, and kissed her softly. "How's that?" His words fanned her mouth.

"Good."

"How good?" He pushed deeper, stretching her enough to make her groan.

"Really good," she panted.

"Can I go harder?"

"Please."

He didn't hold back. He gripped her by the waist, going deeper this time but not faster as he slid out and back in… Out and back in.

Faster came a few minutes later, when they were both running out of air and desperate for release.

He pounded into her, fucking her so hard her breasts were crushed against the truck, and she had to hold onto the night-cooled side rails so tightly it felt like her fingers might break.

But she begged him, "Don't stop." She was almost there. Whenever he lost himself in her like this, she couldn't get enough of him, never wanted him to stop.

And he didn't stop. He pounded into her harder, driving himself in at an angle that made her legs and stomach quiver.

"Gods, sweetheart, you're fucking soaking. That little pussy wants to come—"

It was his filthy mouth that undid her. She shattered around his cock with a high cry, her inner walls fluttering around his pulsing length. Darien came a few minutes later, driving into her so hard that he had to wind an arm around her middle to stop her from slipping face-first into the side rails.

When they were done, his release dripping down the inside of her thighs, he brushed his lips against the top of her shoulder.

"How's that for a second first date?" His voice was a low rumble, and she could still feel him throbbing inside her with the aftermath of his release.

She turned her head to kiss him—a soft press of her mouth against his. "Perfect," she whispered. *He* was perfect, this night was perfect, and they were perfect together.

He nodded, and then he kissed her again—harder this time. "Perfect," he agreed.

ACKNOWLEDGMENTS

It's a strange feeling to have finally reached the end of this book. I first began writing this story when I was in high school, so the characters have been with me for a huge chunk of my life. And although I set this book aside over the years in favor of writing other ones, the characters never left my mind. They're a part of me, and I'll always be grateful for having dreamt them up back when I was only eighteen. A lifetime ago.

I never know where to begin with acknowledgments, and for a book that has been in my heart and mind for over twelve years, that is especially true. I know there will be some people I forget to mention — some people I've lost contact with over the years, but who might've encouraged me in days past to get this book published. If you ever knew about this book, or told me to pursue publication for it, I want to thank you. You are part of the reason I've made it this far — part of the reason why this book is finally finished and in your hands.

As far as specifics go, I'd like to start by thanking my husband, Jeff. You really are my rock, my best friend, my safe harbor, the Mandalorian to my Baby Yoda, the Darien to my Loren (but with far less problems than Darien) ...The list goes on and on. When I met you, you changed my life for the better and showed me what true love is. Being able to share my life with you is a gift, and I am always in awe of the sacrifices you make for me; whether they are big or small, they never go unnoticed. I guess this is just a longer way of saying thank you, Jeff, for always being there for me. I love you. I'll love you forever.

To Jordan, for being one of my greatest friends and the best brother in the universe. The support you give me in everything in my life is unmatched and I will always be grateful for having you in my corner. Thank you for all the memories (especially the ones in the 90's, when life was so much different), for sharing my enthusiasm for The Legend of Zelda, and for tagging me in LotR memes about Denethor. Never stop being you.

To Mom and Dad. I am a firm believer that I have the best family in the world—extended family included—and you guys are at the very heart of it. Thank you for everything you do for me. These past few years have held some challenges that I don't think I could've survived without you, so thank you for helping me through them.

To Rachel, for reading the very first (very sucky) drafts of this book, back when I was still learning how to find my voice, and for reading the new version that is *hopefully* far less painful than the old. Thank you for encouraging me for so many years, and for showing such enthusiasm for Darien, even back when he was half the character he is today. Love you!

Again, to Louise Fury, for being such a supportive friend, and for being one of my very first fans. Thank you for always answering my questions and for encouraging me for so many years. I'll never forget the kindness you've shown me.

To Sarah Hansen, for the absolutely kick-ass cover. This one literally took my breath away when I saw it. Thank you for taking the random mess of ideas I throw at you and turning them into something beautiful. I am in awe of your talent, and I'm so glad I found you!

Again, to my fluffball Rio. You still haven't learned to read, but I'm including you here anyway (and because dogs feature quite prominently in this book). Thank you for bringing life into a house that was simply too quiet without you. Dogs are a gift, and a home isn't quite the same without one. I'm using Loren's words when I say they aren't pets, they're friends. Love you, little guy.

And finally, to the wonderful members of my Street Team. You guys have helped me to reach new readers at a rate I simply couldn't have accomplished on my own, and your ongoing support for my books is absolutely incredible. I don't know where I would be without you all, but I want you to know how grateful I am every time I see your posts or comments on my social media, or the reviews you leave on Goodreads and Amazon. Your efforts do not go unnoticed. Thank you, thank you, thank youuuu.

ABOUT THE AUTHOR

Kayla is the author of the *House of Devils* series—*City of Gods and Monsters, City of Souls and Sinners,* and *City of Lies and Legends.* She is also the author of the upper-YA romantasy novel, *Dreams of Ice and Iron.* She started writing *City of Gods and Monsters* when she was in high school, so the characters and the world they live in are very close to her heart. When she isn't writing, she enjoys traveling, spending time in nature, and binge-watching her favorite television shows with her husband.

For access to bonus content, join her Facebook group at www.facebook.com/groups/kaylaedwardsstreetteam.

instagram.com/kaylaedwardsauthor

amazon.com/author/kaylaedwards

pinterest.com/kaylaedwardsauthor

bookbub.com/authors/kayla-edwards

tiktok.com/@kaylaedwardsauthor

Milton Keynes UK
Ingram Content Group UK Ltd.
UKHW040135130324
439347UK00018B/194/J